# MANIFEST EMPIRE

## BOOK ONE: THE HIGH MAGE OF HELL

BY

CAMERON TRINDALL

ISBN: 978-0-6484040-0-2 (pbk)
ISBN: 978-0-6484040-1-9 (ebook)

*For Dad, for believing*

# PART ONE:

# THREADS

# Prologue

The arcane chanting resonated within the incongruous confines of the abandoned cement factory. Words unspoken since the world was flat were intoned relentlessly by the dark figures cloaked in mission brown, but the faded ads on the wall of Fatty's Cement Works—complete with a gaudy caricature of Fatty himself—proved too distracting for the summoning of dark forces.

'This is fucked,' declared one of the figures, shattering any hope of the group's success.

'Gavin's right, it just hasn't been the same since Anton left,' said another figure as the group stopped their chanting completely and started milling about.

'Quit your whinging, the both of you,' said Matt, the biggest and ugliest of the group. 'The High Priestess…'

'Her name is Karen, for fuck's sake.'

'The High Priestess knows what she's doing,' Matt continued, ignoring Gavin. 'If she says there's a ley-line running through this dump, then there is.'

'Then why can't we summon anything more sinister than moths and Christmas beetles?' asked a skinny fourth figure who had wandered over to join the conversation.

'Our time will come,' Matt said. 'We just need to have faith in the High Priestess and our fellow children of Lucifer's Coven. But for now, we'll call it a day and return to the Grand Satanic Headquarters for further instructions.'

'One other thing,' said the skinny man. 'Why do we have such pompous fucking names for everything?'

'Didn't you hear, mate?' Gavin shouted over his shoulder as he packed his robe into his backpack and headed for the exit. 'It's the fucking goddam apocalypse—it's about as pompous as it gets!'

# January

Darkness: 34 BZ

*Clawing ever upward, ever clawing, always upwards. Slick and suffocating, sucking and smothering, climb, climb, climb. Escape. Must escape. Find it. Find a hole. Find…a dream.*

\* \* \*

### Canberra City, Australian Capital Territory: 9 January 34 BZ

Bentaz Mullberry smiled as he was punched through the foundation wall of the historic Sydney Building in the heart of the city's grotty bus interchange. *I never did like this place,* he thought as he was smashed through one of its pillars and into the street outside.

Before he could regain his senses, his giant, naked opponent hammered him from above with a hefty fist that drove his face into the asphalt. Stärke Mensch repeated his blows in quick succession into the back of Bentaz's head until the ground cratered from the relentless pile-driving. A powerful stomp followed, which ruptured the street's integrity, collapsing it into the sewers below.

It was Stärke Mensch's turn to smile as he admired the scene before him: panicked civilians either fleeing or staring back dumbfounded, shattered buildings crumbling on all sides, his fellow team members beside him, and the so-called most powerful man on the planet lying in a heap at his feet. It was almost like a comic book.

'Look at mighty Ballistic,' the grey behemoth bellowed, his face level with the gawking onlookers staring through the second-storey windows. 'Broken and humiliated in his home town by *das Super Sechs*! Not laughing now, are you, *fotze*?'

The laughter from beneath his immense foot took Stärke Mensch by surprise.

'The problem with going into battle naked,' Bentaz said, quickly springing out from under the foot, 'is that it lets me do this.'

Bentaz grabbed Stärke Mensch by his weighty scrotum and squeezed hard, causing the Nazi supervillain to double over in agony, and bringing him down to the perfect height for Bentaz to ram an energised fist into the base of his jaw. He used the momentum from the uppercut to swing the giant around by his titanic testicles and hammer him down, making the crater in the street even bigger. Stärke Mensch stirred once and then fell into unconsciousness.

Bentaz took a moment to adjust his helmet and pauldrons, which were a vibrant red that matched his gloves, boots and cape. The rest of his leather outfit was obsidian black and looked completely out of place in a city renowned for its public servants and politicians.

'You can never look too good,' Bentaz said to himself. 'I am sporting new colours after all.' He turned to face the rest of the Super Six: once a scourge of World War Two, but now just a bunch of archaic Nazi supervillains that looked out of place pretty much anywhere. 'So, are you racist pricks going to stop this ludicrous display of penis envy—which "starkers" here obviously took literally—and come along quietly?'

'*Nein*,' was the muffled reply from the leader of the group, a stoic individual by the name of Baron Von Ritzer. 'You refused our offer.'

'Nein? Did you just say nein? Seriously, can you get any more cliché?' Bentaz asked incredulously. 'I mean, you're standing here dressed like B-movie rejects—you've even got a swastika face, for fuck's sake,' he said pointing at the Baron. 'Not only that, but you generate fucking energy swastikas from your hands! How does it feel to be a walking stereotype?'

'Enough talk,' the Baron said, unleashing the aforementioned swastikas upon Bentaz while the other four Nazis tried to outflank him.

Lichtschein Geschwind was first due to his ability to move at supersonic speed, but Bentaz anticipated this and stretched out his arm to coat-hanger his attacker. He followed this up with a blast of energy from his other hand, which stunned the floating oddity, Unterbewusst Botschaft.

Bentaz allowed the swastikas to dissipate harmlessly on his chest—being invulnerable had its merits after all—and incapacitated the Baron by crushing his swastika-faced helmet into a mould around his head. That only left Laser Mensch: a comparative lightweight in the superhuman game, and Squido: a genuine alien from another world that had fallen in with the Nazis for reasons unknown.

'I never understood why you threw in with this lot,' Bentaz said as he tussled with the rubbery squid-man and used him to swat Laser Mensch into the gutter.

'The Kaiser willed it,' Squido gurgled before passing out and going limp in Bentaz's hands.

*The Kaiser?* Bentaz wondered, and quickly dismissed it. He removed one of the fallen girders from the piles of debris that decorated the now-abandoned bus interchange and used it to bind his opponents. No time for that now. He had to get these clowns back to the Powder Keg.

\* \* \*

### Parramatta: 9 January 34 BZ

The dark enchantress gibbered and frenzied to an unheard tune that would never have made it to CD, even if it could be heard. Sweat beaded on her pale forehead as her blank eyes struck fear into the vermin that accompanied her in the outdoor industrial complex. Summoning sentient beings was exhausting.

*I bet that weirdo, Summon, doesn't get worked up getting people to come to him,* she thought. *But I suppose if your name's a verb, you get shit done.*

'And that's why I call myself the Manipulator,' she said out loud, addressing her worm-like undead lackey as it glided up to her. 'This is my most ambitious project yet, and you, my ugly little thing, have provided the ethereal strings to weave the destiny of the living embodiment of destruction.'

The worm creature merely stared blankly in response.

'I have waited a thousand years for a chance to weave the destinies of the world,' she soliloquised, as all beings over a thousand years of age tended to do. 'My plans continuously fail because someone always tricks me with lies. But not this time! This time I will finally get what I deserve.'

Dooming herself with those words and proving that immortality and stupidity were not mutually exclusive, the Manipulator smugly continued:

'The only thing standing in my way is that accursed Heroes Squadron! I can't believe a bunch of kids could be so much trouble. If they didn't have that Ballistic on their team they wouldn't be so tough.

'But I'm smarter than them,' she lied, without seeming to draw breath. 'I will create my own team. Yes, a team of villains to match their team of heroes. And at its black heart, will stand an entity of such evil that we will be unstoppable. He will strike terror into Ballistic and then the rest of Australia will follow. That's it! I will call this team of villains Terror Australis!'

'I ain't bein' part a dat!' said a sudden, fresh voice, slicing through the stale monologue on the back of an excessively long descriptive sentence.

'How long have you two been standing there?' Manipulator squealed, being taken completely by surprise.

'Only about ten minutes, boss,' said a skinny man in a stylised power suit. 'We didn't want to interrupt your big speech.'

'I wish ya had,' said his chunky companion, who was wearing a triple XL version of the same suit. 'An' I still don't unnerstand why we naming ourselves "southern land"—dat's a dumb name for a gang.'

'It's spelt different, you dumb fuck,' said the skinny man. 'It's terror—you know, like fear. I think it's a good name, boss,' he added.

'Of course it is,' the Manipulator said, having regained her pretentious composure. 'I thought of it.'

'Where'd you learn all that "southern land" shit anyway?' the skinny man said, addressing his husky companion. 'You're as dumb as a fucking shit-stained butt plug.'

'I dunno,' the big man said defensively. 'Maybe I ain't as dumb as you think I am, Gunther. An' butt plugs don't even have brains, so look who's dumb now.'

'You're right, Brund, you ain't as dumb as I think, you're even fucking dumber,' Gunther said. 'And call me Beam when we're on a job. We're professionals after all.'

'You are my thralls and don't forget it,' the Manipulator said, trying desperately to dominate this scene.

'Yes boss,' they both said.

'Good. Now get ready because the psychic tendrils I have attached to my puppets are growing taut, which means our guests will soon arrive. And after that no force on Earth can stop us!' she cried, adding to the list of things that shouldn't be said aloud.

* * *

### Barton Correctional Facility, Great Victoria Desert, Australia: 9 January 34 BZ

Walter Screw reclined in his chair and basked in the dirty pleasure he got from smoking his fat Cuban and openly defying the state's policy on smoking indoors. He was also openly defying the state's policy on torturing inmates, but that was different. That was his day job.

Sure, the government officials he 'answered' to would be publicly outraged by his rehabilitation methods, but Walter had been in this business a long time and knew that results were all they really cared about. *Results, and keeping their names out of the media, of course.*

He drew back on his stogie, savouring the rich smoke and admiring the general ambiance. It was really hard to get a moment's reflection and Walter was soaking in every drop.

*Well the powers that be don't pay me to sit on my arse all day. Smoko's over.* He uncrossed his legs and rose from the chair.

'Such a guilty pleasure,' he said, taking a final puff of his cigar. 'But they're also a fire hazard so I better butt it out.'

Walter quickly paced across the room and shoved his cigar in the genitals of the naked and beaten man before him. The black-haired man screamed in pain.

'Better make sure this is completely extinguished, don't you think?' Walter asked his captive as he ground his boot down on the cigar—and the genitals it was stuck to.

The man blubbered something about revenge and then passed out.

'Typical,' Walter said. 'Take away his giant robot and all of his powers and he's just a fucking pussy.'

A knock on the metal door behind him brought Walter back to the moment.

'What is it?' he snapped.

'Sorry for the intrusion, Warden,' said one of the guards as he entered the room. 'That kid Ballistic is here and wants to see you in the usual spot. He's got that Nazi super team all wrapped up in metal girders and wants to drop them off.'

'The Super Six, eh? I can't wait to welcome them back. Get their cells ready and put together a team to manhandle them,' Walter said. 'Get some of the new recruits on the job—got to learn somehow.'

'Yes sir,' the guard said before leaving the room.

Walter straightened his uniform and donned his helmet. Turning to his semiconscious prisoner, he said, 'I've got to pop out for a bit, but you just sit there and contemplate what an arsehole you are while I'm gone.'

Walter closed the door behind him and walked up the stairs to the elevator. *Why do these superhero types always want to meet on the bloody roof? What's wrong with a nice air-conditioned office? Some of us can still get sunburnt,* he thought, getting into the lift.

He exited the elevator and walked straight out onto the roof of the panopticon-style prison and into the harsh desert sun.

'Hey kid, you wanted to see me?' he asked of the being hovering nearby.

'Call me Ballistic, Warden,' Bentaz replied, floating down to stand in front of him. 'Besides, I'm not a kid anymore.'

*Fucking teenagers. How old was he? Fucking seventeen or something?* He hated pandering to this self-righteous child and all his fucking super friends. Problem was, this child was most likely the most powerful individual on the planet.

'Force of habit, no offence meant,' Walter said with a perfect smile that belied his inner thoughts. 'I almost didn't recognise you in these new colours. Where's all the yellow, blue and white, my young friend?'

'I thought red and black looked cooler,' Bentaz said honestly. 'Time for a more mature me.'

*Mature indeed.*

'Surely you aren't here for a fashion parade? What can I do for you?'

'Well, on the way over from Canberra, I heard a few disturbing things about this place,' Bentaz said. 'You're not mistreating the prisoners here, are you Warden?'

Walter could have won an Oscar with his portrayal of shocked disbelief.

'You believe Nazi filth over a duly appointed representative of Australia to the United Nations?'

'That isn't a denial,' Bentaz said, 'and don't overstate your importance. You're a prison warden.'

'True—warden to the most dangerous fucking prison in the universe,' Walter exaggerated. 'There's a reason that this place is nicknamed the fucking Powder Keg—it's because it's a fucking bomb waiting to fucking explode!'

'There's no need to get excited...'

'As you very well know, this place holds Manifest psychopaths, killer fucking robots and honest-to-God space fucking aliens,' Walter said, calming down. 'Sometimes things get rough, and we puny earthlings have to fight hard just to survive among you fucking super-beings. So before you come off all judgemental, drawing from your deep well of life experience, just remember that not all of us are fucking invulnerable.'

'Well, you just remember that some of us are,' Bentaz said as he started to fly away. 'So play nice or we might accidentally step on you one day.'

'Fucking teenagers.' Walter sighed under his breath.

* * *

## Undisclosed location: 16 January 34 BZ

The two efficacious doctors whispered in front of Courtney like she wasn't even there. Didn't they know she could hear them clearly just by the reverberations travelling down their legs and into the floor? The floor heard every little thing.

'This is Patient 1432, once known as Courtney Yeht,' whispered the silver-haired senior doctor.

'Courtney Yeht? Her parents must've hated her,' said his officious assistant, stepping away from the small rectangular window in the door. 'Why are you whispering? She's been sedated and couldn't hear you even if we weren't on the other side of this door.'

'I'm not risking it with this one,' the older doctor replied. 'She's the next big weapon of mass destruction. Word has it she can control the earth with her mind.'

'So it's like telekinesis then?'

'Not quite—she can only control soil, dust and rock, but she controls it with surgical precision,' the old doctor said, almost in awe.

*You know nothing.*

'But she's only fourteen,' the assistant said. 'At what level will her power be when she's an adult?'

'That's what we're here to find out, Amy.'

'Well, Phil, there's nothing like making a career out of human experimentation.'

'Don't fall for the trap of thinking she's human,' Phil said. 'She and her kind are a threat to our very way of life, and don't ever forget it.'

*We will end your way of life,* Courtney thought, shivering alone in the dark.

# February

## Darkness: 34 BZ

*Upwards, ever upwards. There. There it is. A gap. A hole. Unconscious, subconscious, don't lose momentum. Upwards, ever upwards. Out of the subconscious and into the dream. Escape.*

\* \* \*

## Paris: 9 February 34 BZ

Lorraine Freeman smiled at the cameras as dozens of flashes hit her simultaneously. The paparazzi continued their barrage of snapshots (including a few attempted up-skirt shots for trashy magazines) as she emerged elegantly from the back of the hot-pink limousine.

Lorraine waved at the throng and then turned and walked down the red carpet and into the winter fashion show, her light brown hair flowing over her shoulders like a shampoo commercial. Tonight she was going to be the star model, after her meteoric rise to fame over the last month.

*It's all happening so fast,* she thought as she was surrounded by her ubiquitous entourage of random agents and sycophants. It was hard enough growing accustomed to becoming a Manifest in the last month, let alone it granting her the ability to be loved by all who laid eyes upon her. She was fast becoming a global phenomenon, and yet the public was so far completely unsuspecting as to why—although a few commentators did say it was uncanny.

Lorraine was herded through her dressing room door—number 7 of course—only to be confronted by a sleazy looking Frenchman, replete with pencil moustache and sweaty countenance.

'Oh Lorraine, darling, I am delighted to meet you,' bleated the balding chubster. 'I am Pepe Larouche, and you will be modelling my fabulous new winter collection. I took the liberty of asking everyone to give us a little privacy,' he said, proceeding to pick up some leopard-print lingerie and wave it about.

'You should really put these on to match the dress and coat. I can stay to measure you up and ensure they got your size right,' Pepe said while subconsciously licking his lips and putting his left hand in his pocket.

'You do realise I'm fifteen, don't you? You filthy pervert!' Lorraine snapped.

Pepe suddenly produced a dirty handkerchief from his pocket and began mopping his glistening bald patch.

'I…I only meant that…' he stammered, turning a deep purple colour. 'I will leave you to get changed,' he muttered and hurried out of the room without looking Lorraine in the eyes once.

'Gross,' Lorraine said as Pepe closed the door behind him, leaving her alone for the first time in days. The welcome quiet finally allowed her a moment to reflect on her crazy life.

'Okay Lorraine, recap,' she said aloud, her mind racing, playing over the last month at frenetic speed. 'Superhero mum: check. Hermaphrodite other-mum: check. Two annoying little sisters: check, check,' she said, counting on her fingers.

'Screwed up childhood, extreme parental expectations, followed by rebellious teen angst…' She continued on her other hand. 'Always told that one day I would have my special "seed" spontaneously Manifest, but I never would have thought it would happen by smoking from a homemade bong. Never thought it would turn everyone around me into pervy stalkers either.'

*Get a grip, Lorraine, you're talking to yourself.*

Lorraine quietly changed into the winter collection by Pepe 'sleazebag' Larouche, which was about as wintery as the set of some crappy Tarzan movie. However, she liked leopard print and decided to wear the lingerie despite Pepe Fiddle-Fingers' creepy way of showing it to her.

'Mum's got a lot to answer for, making me do these stupid modelling gigs,' Lorraine said changing into the age-inappropriate outfit. 'But I suppose it's better than going to school.'

A brief knock from behind was suddenly followed by the all too familiar entourage bursting through the door and into her personal space.

*Then again...*

* * *

## South Western Sydney: 14 February 34 BZ

Mark Adams raced into the florist without heed of innocent bystanders. The clerk, who was just closing up for the night, jumped away from the door in fright.

'Gak,' was all she managed to say.

'Whoa, sorry, didn't mean to startle you,' Mark said, raising his hands in a non-threatening gesture.

'It's okay, for a second there I thought you had red eyes,' the florist replied. 'It's been a really long day and I guess my mind's playing tricks on me. I was just packing up, actually.'

'I, um...came here for some roses,' Mark said, feeling slightly awkward.

'I'm afraid you're out of luck,' the florist said, slightly rudely. 'It's Valentine's Day, after all. We've completely sold out.'

'Okay, well if not roses, then how about some tulips?'

'You misunderstand me,' she said. 'We've sold out of everything!'

'But you're a florist, surely you have something,' Mark said with frustration. 'Who's ever heard of a florist with no flowers?'

'I admit it's strange,' the florist said. 'It's like everyone thought it was the last Valentine's Day on Earth.'

Mark left the shop and the frazzled florist with a defeated thank you and started walking home. It was getting dark, and for the first time he had no flowers for Desci on Valentine's Day. Married for eighteen years and he hadn't failed to deliver yet. *It's funny how the smallest things could carry so much importance if repeated long enough.*

Working on the construction site ate up all his daylight hours, but he had to do as much time as possible to make ends meet. Raising their son, Obie, had been difficult on his wage, especially as Desci couldn't return to modelling after giving birth all those years ago. That was shortly followed by the car accident that claimed Desci's sister, forcing them to adopt her young children, Samara and Sebastian.

Mark strolled up the road towards their rented apartment as twilight finished and the true darkness of the night crept from the shadows to blanket the land. The poorly maintained street lamps provided little illumination at the best of times, but the ones in this part of the road hadn't even been turned on yet.

'Heh. The work experience guy must be on tonight,' he said under his breath.

Mark's thoughts wandered and he became almost hypnotised by the rhythmic beams of light from the constant traffic passing him by. It was then that one of the beams danced across the irregular pattern of an oleander tree. He followed the light trail with his eyes and they fell upon a bunch of roses lying unattended on the footpath.

He picked up the roses and looked around to see if they belonged to anyone. There was no one around except a large cat silently watching him from a window in the house across the street.

Mark looked into the wrapped cellophane. *Thirteen roses. Score! Looks like it's my lucky night after all.* He picked up his pace in case his luck didn't last.

He noticed a card inside, tucked away deep among the stems. He reached for the card instinctively and pricked his finger as he pulled it out. *Ouch!* A single droplet of blood dripped onto the reflective face of the small card.

Mark examined the card while he sucked his finger. It had a tiny mirror on the front and inside it simply said in type font:

Thanks for the kiss.
You will see yourself soon.

*Weird,* he thought, turning the card over in his hand. *Nothing on the back. This is turning out to be one strange day.* He tossed the card and continued up the driveway.

Mark trudged up the three flights of stairs to his apartment, untying his black hair and letting it fall freely around his shoulders. *Should look my best for my better half.*

His enchanting wife was waiting for him and opened the door just as he arrived on the doorstep. Her beautiful Eurasian features radiated warmth.

'These are for you,' he said, giving her a slow kiss on the lips. 'Happy Valentine's Day, beautiful.'

'Oh Mark,' Desci said, accepting both the flowers and the kiss. 'Eighteen years and you haven't failed once to get me flowers. You're always there for me.'

'And I always will be,' he promised, putting his arm around her and shuffling her back inside the apartment. 'Didn't you say this morning that the kids were going out tonight?' he asked, squeezing her butt cheek.

The return grope signalled the affirmative.

\* \* \*

### Grand Satanic Headquarters, Kings Cross: 15 February 34 BZ

Tuesday mornings tended to be a time where bugger-all happened as far as Gavin was concerned. But not today. Today he had to get up at the crack of dawn and catch the fucking bus into town to attend some 'emergency' coven meeting. *Karen probably had a fucking nightmare and wet the bed or something.*

*That woman was getting seriously crazy lately,* he thought as he lounged in the couch at the back of the meeting room. She was always on the weird side—decorating their office like a genie threw up in it for starters—but insisting she be called High Priestess and ranting about dreams featuring Merlin the wizened cunt of a magician, for fuck's sake? That's the type of crazy featuring monkeys on bongo drums.

*At least the couch is comfortable.* He had to admit he'd nothing else to do except watch daytime television. Being unemployed brought with it all the thrills of shows that were as exciting as a fresh rash.

The door opened and Matt, the walking sinew-fest, marched into the incense-filled meeting room. Usually a frothing-at-the-mouth devotee, on this normally mundane Tuesday he was behaving like a constipated ostrich.

'This better be good,' he said, pacing around the room. 'I had to call in sick from work to make this meeting, and I'm already in their bad books. If this is another dream about mouldy wizards prophesising the End of Days, I think I'll spontaneously combust!'

'Actually, that was some random guy only last week,' Gavin said from within a cloud of sandalwood smoke from the burning joss sticks. 'People are saying he was some loser Manifest. Like a one-time super-guy or something.'

'Trust you to joke around. Some of us actually work for a living,' Matt said.

'Well, it's true. But what's even more amazing than a man who suddenly bursts into flames is that you actually have a fucking job!' Gavin said. 'What do you do, strangle puppies for supervillains?'

'I'll strangle someone,' Matt muttered. 'If you must know, I'm a junior accountant.'

'Seriously?'

'Why do you think I'm in this inner clique? It's because I'm the only one of us who knows how to balance the books,' Matt said. 'Satanic propaganda isn't cheap, and neither is maintaining such a grandiose presence in this part of town.'

'That I can believe—it's the "junior" part that I don't understand. You look about fifty,' Gavin said.

'I'm thirty-five...'

'Close enough,' Gavin said, stroking his downy beard to further emphasise his youth.

'How can you even be in the inner circle?' Matt complained. 'You are almost blasphemous in your endless commentary on the faults of the coven.'

'I'm really only on the council because I always show up, as I have nothing better to do,' Gavin said. 'Yeah, plus I get out of my job search requirements by claiming this is voluntary work for a religious organisation. Besides, it's a Tuesday morning and here I am. That shows unwavering loyalty.'

'That shows what now?' Matt asked.

Before Gavin could answer, the meeting room door opened and the rest of the council filed in. There was Floyd, a creepy bald guy who may have been inbred; Navid, a quietly spoken man who was on another level of creepy; Tom Higginbottom, yet another weirdo who insisted on saying his full name in the third person; and finally Karen, self-proclaimed High Priestess and recent drooling lunatic.

'Now that you, my faithful disciples, have gathered at the appointed hour, I can enlighten you with the unholy scripture about the apocalypse that was revealed to me in a dream by great Merlin,' she pontificated.

A collective groan went up among the group.

'Despite what many of you think, I really have been in contact with an actual demon from Hell,' Karen said, ignoring her disciples. 'And yes, he was once known as the magus Merlin, but now he should be known throughout the land as the High Mage of Hell!' Her eyes grew wide with religious fervour as she said the apparent demon's name.

'Tom Higginbottom believes you,' said none other than Tom Higginbottom.

'I am glad that at least one of you remembers why we were founded,' Karen said.

'I seem to remember that Anton set the whole thing up to compete with the Church of Satan and to pick up women,' said Floyd, who was one of the few founding members who didn't leave with Anton.

'That was the old way,' Karen said. 'Lucifer's Coven now only has room for true believers. Now, do you believe, Floyd?'

'Sure, I believe,' Floyd said cautiously.

'What about you, Matt?' Karen asked.

'Of course I do,' Matt declared. He'd since stopped his pacing and sunk next to Gavin on the couch.

'Navid?'

The quiet Persian merely nodded.

'And finally, Gavin,' Karen said, staring at him with eyes like twin vortices of madness. 'Are you a true believer?'

Gavin, who had been thinking about the correlation between madness and hotness, was caught unprepared.

'If it gets me out of the house at someone else's expense, then I'm right behind you,' Gavin said, while thinking about being right behind her.

'Spoken like a true Satanist,' Karen replied, apparently satisfied. 'Now I can reveal the true plan from the Satanic Scriptures that the High Mage read to me in my dreams. It will blow your mind.'

*I'd rather she blew something else,* Gavin fantasised, reclining in the couch and rolling himself a smoke. It was going to be an interesting Tuesday.

* * *

### Space (the final frontier): 25 February 34 BZ

Anu Hopet stared menacingly from the viewport of his ship, *The Skull of Ra*, at the planet that birthed him. It had been a long time since he had been home and had thought of this moment for countless centuries. Ironically, with all the technology around him he could count those centuries to the Planck unit.

He stood in all of his battle armour, complete with pointed pauldrons and flowing scarlet cape, his arms crossed behind his back. It was the perfect brooding pose and he had mastered it well. In fact, he had pretty much invented dramatic posing.

Anu Hopet pondered destiny and prophecy as he stared silently at the continents slowly crossing the globe. *It would be so simple to just press a button and turn the world to dust.* Then he would beat the prophecy and not have to worry about being destroyed to fulfil someone else's destiny.

*But that is the way of the coward.* He may have been many things, but a coward wasn't one of them. He would face his destiny head on and he would prevail like he had so many times before. Had he not broken his chains all those millennia ago and forged his own fate?

He would do it again. He would crush this would-be God who Walks Like a Man and spit in the face of the Celestial Ones once more.

Anu Hopet smiled, fingers subconsciously twitching in anticipation.

'Ship, scan the entire planet for powerful Manifest signatures,' he said. 'He will be down there—I am sure of it.'

Scores of lights lit up like beacons across the viewport screen, indicating all the world's Manifests, along with their respective power classification.

Anu Hopet suddenly stared hard as something caught his eye.

'What was that?' he wondered aloud. 'Ship, scan orbit for all energy signatures.'

'Scan shows neo-industrial satellites and technologically comparative space stations,' came the robotic reply.

*That's funny.*

For a moment there he could have sworn he had seen the faint image of a colossal tick embracing the entire planet. He wondered if it was an omen. *No matter, Anu Hopet is not afraid of omens or giant parasites.*

'Ship, move to geosynchronous orbit above that southern desert continent and alert the others. It is time to remind Kismet that Anu Hopet makes his own rules.'

# March

### Grey: 34 BZ

*Upwards, ever upwards. Dream is not enough. Already being pulled back. Grasp. Cling to her. Hold on to her. Feast and suck. Need flesh. Need…a host.*

\* \* \*

### Dungeon Cell 9: 1 March 34 BZ

Andy Trailer hated the dingy cell that had been his recent home, but not as much as he hated his own existence. Cold, alone and naked in the dark. Forced to survive on insects and the occasional rat that entered his cell; it just wasn't fair.

He wanted nothing more than death, but some inner voice both tormented him and forced him to persevere. Him: a mutant demon creature and personal guinea pig of a sadistic psycho.

*I don't deserve this,* Andy thought as he spiralled into a disconsolate gorge of despair and self-pity at the injustice of it all.

The door to Andy's cell suddenly flew open, and a robotic dog sprinted in and started savagely mauling his face. The serrated teeth tore into Andy's pale green flesh while the titanium jaws crunched bone. Andy screamed.

'Malice, heel,' came a familiar voice from the doorway.

The machine stopped its attack and bounded back to sit behind its master.

'Good dog,' said the voice, its melodious tones masking the owner's sinister intent.

Andy began to recover and tried propping himself up on one arm, but his bulky wings made it a difficult task. It mattered little, as the owner of the voice quickly strode across the room, kicked him in the face, and knelt down on his chest.

'Prep him for surgery,' was the last thing Andy heard before his world started spinning and everything went black.

* * *

## Sacred Peaches Hotel, Hong Kong: 4 March 34 BZ

Naomi adjusted her French maid's outfit and fluffed her jet-black bob. Next, she applied her purple lipstick and matching eye shadow. Her intelligent, piercing eyes stared back at her from the mirror of the honeymoon suite her client had paid for. *Perfect.*

'Naomi, you are one hot bitch,' she said to her ravishing reflection.

'Come on baby, aren't you done yet?' came a voice in drunken Mandarin.

'Just a minute,' she replied in the same language as she did some final adjustments and opened the bathroom door. 'Good things come to those who wait, sugar.'

Spread out on the bed before her was a pale, middle-aged, fat Chinese man sporting a raging erection, completely naked except for his ridiculous frilly socks. His left hand pumped up and down on his unimpressive manhood while his right hand held on to his expensive bottle of champagne.

'Slut, come over here and make me happy,' he said. 'I paid good money to rent your cunt and I'm going to fuck it raw.'

*Not with that little worm,* Naomi thought. *The things I do to survive.*

'Oh yes,' she said erotically, 'I love it when you talk dirty to me. Say it again, you dangerous man.'

Zhang Wei was a very dangerous man indeed. With his grubby fingers in crime syndicates the world over, Wei was responsible for the deaths of hundreds of people and the addictions of thousands more. He also had a fetish for French maids and necrophilia.

'I'm Candy,' Naomi said huskily, climbing onto the bed and rubbing her lithe form against the unfit crime lord.

'I don't give a shit,' Wei snapped, slapping her across the face. 'You are nothing but a dog's cunt tonight.' He cradled her close to his face as she straddled him. 'And don't forget I can always fuck you cold,' he whispered in her ear.

The next thing Wei felt was a sudden intense pain in the back of his neck and he found himself lying back on the bed. Naomi purred, leaning close to his face.

'You were saying?' she cooed.

'My neck,' Wei cried. 'You bitch! What did you do to my neck? Aaa! I can't move. What have you done, you fucking—mmmph!'

Naomi stuffed Wei's mouth with her panties.

'Can you taste that, Master Zhang? Killing people makes me so wet!' Naomi said, standing up and disrobing. 'What I did to you was simple: I severed the nerves that allow your brain to send signals to the rest of your body.'

'Mmmmph!'

'But this…' She produced a long, slender needle with a mushroom dome on the end. 'This is a tool of my own devising that emits electric pulses into whatever it's inserted in. It won't hurt a bit,' she said, ignoring his muffled cries and jabbing the needle into the base of his penis.

Naomi pressed the tip of the needle and it began to hum, instantly making Wei's penis erect.

'When I heard that you were a necrophile, I became so excited!' she said, riding his dick. 'Now I get to fuck you while you die, just like you always fantasised about.'

Wei started sobbing.

'Oh, before I forget,' Naomi said, already building up a sweat. 'You really shouldn't have held out on the Kaiser. He sends his regards, by the way.'

* * *

**Coober Pedy, South Australia: 17 March 34 BZ**

Dread Sedgewick sat at the bar and drank his green beer from the barman's skull while he smoked a cigarette. St Patrick's Day celebrations always inspired Dread—Saint Patrick wiping out all those snakes for example—and the Wombat's Wrinkle seemed like the best place to wet his whistle.

Both the proprietors and patrons objected to this idea at first, but now they no longer had anything to say on the subject. Dread drew back on his cigarette and looked around the bar.

'Not really a talkative bunch, are you?' he said to the piles of corpses strewn about the pub.

His attempt at humour was interrupted by the inevitable inept local constabulary, who crept down the entrance stairs with their guns and flashlights drawn.

The local sergeant took one look at the big man, with his spiky hair standing straight up, dressed in his black trench coat and shit-kicker boots, who was calmly smoking amid the charnel house, and almost vomited.

'Vicious Man! Shit, it's fucking Vicious Man! Bloody fuck!' he cried to his fellow officers. 'Run! Fucking run!'

'Well, happy fucking Saint Pats to you too, motherfucker!' Dread said while the chubby sergeant fled as fast as his stubby legs could carry him.

Dread swiftly kicked one of the piles of corpses in front of him, sending the bodies flying like missiles, tearing through the policemen like a hot knife through blubber. Only the chubby sergeant survived, and he somehow managed to climb over the human remains, out the doors and away. His repeated cries of 'bloody fuck' trailed after him.

Dread finished his drink and butted out his smoke on the tongue of one of the heads on the bar. *Guess it's time to leave this shit-hole,* he thought, walking into the centre of the room. *This dump's already underground, so it may as well be buried.*

He crouched down and then jumped hard, smashing through the roof and causing an explosion on the surface like a bomb blast. The former pub became a crater, but his leap brought him down far away from the collapse.

Meanwhile, the chunky sergeant was still running as fast as he could toward town, the oppressive afternoon heat beating down upon him like his daddy used to do. Suddenly, he grabbed his flabby chest and fell face first into the dusty road. Heart disease was still a bigger killer than Dread. Just.

'Bugger,' Dread said, looking at the dead fat man. 'That's disappointing. Killing a corpse is just being redundant.'

'So is killing without purpose,' came a brazen voice from behind.

'You're brave to approach me again,' Dread said without turning around. 'After I slaughtered your so-called elite guard, or whatever they were called, I told you I'd finish crushing that silly helmet you wear the next time I saw you.'

'Do we have to go through this pointless dialogue every time we see each other?' the other man asked. It's not my fault you grew up without me. I didn't even know you existed until a few years ago.'

'Seven,' said Dread.

'Cry me a river,' the other man said, having still not come any closer. He wasn't stupid. 'You're apparently the most dangerous man on Earth, for fuck's sake! Get over it.'

'Now I know where I get my compassion from,' Dread sneered. 'Which is why I think I might pay your dirty little family a visit.'

'Now you just stay the fuck away from them. They have nothing to do with this.'

'Precisely why they must pay for your sins,' Dread said, continuing to look into the distance. 'Especially that superhero son of yours.'

'He beat you once.'

'I had to leave on that occasion, I'll kill him next time.'

'There won't be a next time.'

'He doesn't know, does he?'

'No.'

'Then I'll tell him before he dies, just to see the look on his face,' Dread replied, picking up a semitrailer and lifting it above his head, never taking his eyes off the sky.

'Then I have nothing more to say to you,' said the other man.

'Good. Then piss off and consider yourself lucky,' he warned, throwing the semi into the sky like it was nothing, while waving at the kid in the truck's cabin as it sailed away. 'But before you go, know that I will pay them a visit, and you can't stop me. There's just a couple of things I have to wrap up first,' Dread said, turning around just as the flying semi collided with the approaching attack helicopter—only to discover that his father had already gone.

* * *

### Heroes Squadron Headquarters, Canberra: 18 March 34 BZ

Bentaz Mullberry loved being on a super team. Unfortunately, however, monitor duty wasn't his favourite part of HSA membership. Watching endless news streams from around the globe and waiting for the hotline (yes, it was actually called that) to ring was boring as hell.

*Although, there was the occasional segment on Lorraine Freeman— man she was hot!* Bentaz felt he couldn't be the only one with a major crush on her.

Suddenly one report caught his eye and he turned up the volume.

'...massacre in Coober Pedy yesterday by the supervillain known as Vicious Man...'

Bentaz turned the sound down again. A Vicious Man sighting and he'd missed it!

*What they need is some kind of technology that transmits information around the globe instantly.*

His private thoughts were interrupted by a fellow team member strolling into the room.

'You're relieved,' said the grey-cloaked man with the black-faced helmet. 'It's time for one of those meetings with that government stooge, and surprise, surprise, I'm conveniently assigned to monitor duty,' he complained.

'I'm sure you're not missing out on much, Faceplate,' Bentaz said. 'I'll fill you in later.'

'Yeah, yeah,' don't let the door hit you on the way out,' Faceplate muttered.

*What a jerk,* Bentaz mused, heading down the corridor towards the briefing room. *Briefing room! This was way better than school.* In fact, he was going to learn more from this one meeting than a whole year of school.

He entered the room to discover the meeting had started without him. *Typical of Faceplate to take his time relieving me of monitor duty.* He tried to look impressive as he scanned the room for a vacant chair.

*Aww, the cheese isn't here.* He loved that surreal, talking, giant pyramid of cheddar. *But I guess he's an acquired taste.* There were seven others, plus the stooge—which wasn't a bad turn out for one of these things.

Bentaz located a spare chair close by and wheeled over to the group. Rather than look impressive, he looked quite ridiculous as he sat in an office chair in full superhero garb and tried to suavely squeeze in at the table.

He looked around and took stock of the attendees: next to him was the fearsome-looking Hellgoat, a man apparently possessed by a demon seeking redemption; Powerhouse, his biggest rival in the team with a hatred of being second best; Tracker, some strange cyborg guy with an actual radar screen on his torso; Gridlock, an inappropriately named dude who could shoot fucking domes(?!) from his hands; Grug, a paunchy guy with the unfortunate power of being able to shoot tangling hair from his wrists; Killer Comedian, a two-faced jokester who wasn't funny; and next to him on the other side was the giant sandstone monster, the Temple Man.

The stooge was none other than Tactician, rumoured son of that jerk Warden who ran the Powder Keg. Real names were classified, of course. Bentaz might not know who they were, but he wouldn't be surprised if they knew who he was under his helmet.

'As I was saying,' Tactician resumed. 'Both the United Nations and the Australian Government thank you for all your help so far in rounding up rogue Manifest terrorists; however, we need to call on your help again.'

Tactician swapped the sheet on the overhead projector and replaced it with a picture of a goat's head within an inverted pentagram.

*Isn't that an album cover?* Bentaz wondered.

'We have reason to believe that some kind of event is imminent,' Tactician said, his power suit quietly whirring every time he moved. 'We want you to be on the lookout for satanic cults.'

*Satanic cults! Could it get any better?* Bentaz doubted it.

'Satanic cults?' Powerhouse scoffed. 'Could it get any worse? We've got lunatics like Vicious Man running about, and you're worried about students standing around in bathrobes chanting in the dark.'

'Ha! Or maybe they're dole bludgers in hessian bags trying to summon demons in an abandoned cement factory or something,' Killer Comedian added unhelpfully.

'I assure you they're a priority threat,' Tactician promised, trying to reign in the briefing.

'They are nothing but cheap conjurors,' Hellgoat said, his voice shredding through all other sound. 'This smells like a ruse.'

'You would say that,' Powerhouse said accusingly.

'Yes, this could be a conflict of interest,' Tactician agreed.

'How dare you question my loyalty!' Hellgoat bellowed. 'I have proven myself on this team time and again. If I wanted to betray you I could have done it a long time ago. It's because I look demonic, isn't it?'

'Of course it is. Don't be so naïve,' Tactician said bluntly.

'Maybe we should stop picking on a fellow teammate and get on with this briefing,' Bentaz interjected, trying to diffuse the situation. 'I for one back Hellgoat, and I would have thought the rest of you would too.'

He stared at everyone around the table and then met Tactician's gaze.

'Please continue,' Bentaz said.

'Intelligence reports reveal a vast underground satanic conspiracy with the end objective of bringing about the rise of the Antichrist and the End of Days,' Tactician said, looking as grave as possible.

'Is that shit even real?' asked Grug. 'I'm a Buddhist.'

'Don't call it shit, you hairy pagan,' Powerhouse said. 'It's true. It's in the Bible.'

'Let's assume that it *is* real,' Tactician replied, ignoring Powerhouse's outburst. 'We need you to scour the news channels and lean on a few known suspects and get to the bottom of this. The moment you get a lead, let us know.'

'I will start scanning immediately,' Tracker said.

'What about that Lucifer's Coven group?' Gridlock proposed. 'Could they be behind this plot to destroy the world?'

'If they are, then I will crush them,' said the Temple Man, who felt he needed to contribute more to these discussions.

'We've already looked into them,' Tactician lied. 'They're a completely harmless bunch of amateurish show ponies. Don't waste your time.'

'Okay, we'll look deeper,' Bentaz said.

'Good. Well in that case, I'll have to end this briefing early as I have another meeting to attend,' Tactician said, suddenly looking at Hellgoat. 'No rest for the wicked. Bet you know something about that, don't you?'

Bentaz subtly gestured for Hellgoat to stand down.

Tactician left the room without saying another word and headed for the helicopter pad. The rest of the gathering stood up and started meandering to the exit.

'Thanks for sticking up for me in there,' Hellgoat said to Bentaz just outside the briefing room.

'Not a problem, it's what anyone would have done,' Bentaz replied while they strolled towards the entrance to the building.

'Thanks anyway, I won't let you down,' Hellgoat said, somehow sounding sincere while still looking menacing. 'What are you going to do now? Want to hunt some Satanists?'

'Nah, not tonight. Thought I'd have an early one,' Bentaz said, thinking how his mother had told him he had to go to school tomorrow.

'Yeah, but it's only two o'clock in the afternoon,' Hellgoat said as they walked out into the blinding sunlight.

'Sorry, dude, some other time,' Bentaz apologised, taking off into the sky at supersonic speed before Hellgoat could object.

\* \* \*

### The Moon: 18 March 34 BZ

Bentaz sat in the giant crater and stared up at the blue planet in the sky. He loved watching the terminator line as it moved silently across the Earth, leaving all the little lights in its wake.

*Peace at last,* he thought, relieved to have time to himself before heading home. At least he wasn't likely to run into anyone out here. He enjoyed solitude and this crater had recently become a special place for him to go and chill out. He'd have to remember to bring a chair next time though.

Bentaz's thoughts wandered while he took in his surroundings. *It must be really cold in this crater out of direct sunlight.* He looked at his hand and pondered his invulnerability.

It never ceased to amaze him how he could get so used to it that it was almost unnoticeable. Invulnerability wasn't like having no sensation; he had just as much now as he did before he Manifested. It was simply that things like burns and beatings didn't hurt or damage him.

*Such as the temperature of this crater for example.*

He could feel it was really cold but it just didn't hurt or incapacitate him. Neither did the emptiness of space, as he'd discovered not long ago.

Testing his powers had been his only way of knowing his limits; becoming a Manifest may have unlocked some hereditary knowledge, but one's unique abilities were not part of the deal. So over the last couple of years, Bentaz had been trying ever more dangerous things.

He knew that lasers couldn't hurt him, as it was lasers that triggered his Manifest seed in the first place—fired by those two losers, Brund and Beam.

*They also showed me that I'm bulletproof and how strong I've become,* he thought fondly, remembering how he'd beaten them up with a woollen jumper pulled over his head to hide his identity.

Flying into space for the first time had been extremely daunting, and Bentaz remembered inching his way through the upper atmosphere, ever cautious of disaster. It was totally worth it, and once that first hurdle had been overcome, it wasn't long until he tried other goals like flying to the moon. He discovered this crater shortly thereafter.

Even breathing was only reflex action these days, but he still instinctively held his breath while in a vacuum or underwater, yet he never seemed to run out of oxygen.

Testing his strength was the same; it was like the extra strength was there when he needed it, a bottomless well that could be drawn upon so he didn't otherwise have to treat everything like it was fragile.

Bentaz absentmindedly picked up a large moon rock and crushed it to a fine dust that seemed to hang in the air due to the lighter gravity and no wind.

He didn't come up here to crush rocks; he needed to get his head around recent events. *Is there really a plot to bring on the End of Days, or was Tactician lying?*

Unfortunately, telepathy wasn't one of his powers (but he always practised—just in case). He'd seen a lot of strange things in his fourteen years—there was a living cheese from another dimension on his team—so why not demons from Hell?

*Is it any more unlikely than Nazi supervillains? Or me?*

His mind flickered back to his fight with the Super Six. He wondered why those Nazis wanted him to join them, but more importantly, how they knew he was Axis in a previous life.

*That shit's kinda personal and not too many people are aware of it outside of immediate family. Did that enigmatic Kaiser the squid guy mentioned tell them? Is that why they thought I wouldn't turn them in?*

Knowing who you were in a past life was different to having their memories.

*Even if this Kaiser did know Axis how would he know I was once him? Not even Grandfather knows, although he'll probably suspect as soon as he sees my new outfit.*

*Ah, family.* They were a crazy bunch but he loved them anyway.

Thinking of family reminded Bentaz that it was time to get back home. It was a school night after all, but why he needed to attend given his abilities, he didn't know.

He stood up, dusted himself, and walked to the top of the crater. He took one more look at his favourite chill-out pad before he flew off at terrific speed.

*Definitely a chair.*

\* \* \*

### Geosynchronous Orbit: 18 March 34 BZ

'Did he detect us?' Anu Hopet asked, watching Bentaz streak past on the viewport.

'No, Great Armageddon,' said the cybernetic midget, who was fussing over a control panel. 'The ship would have alerted me now that I am reconnected to its systems.'

'I believe he is the one,' Anu Hopet declared. 'Track him and land the ship close by, but not close enough that we are detected.'

'No one will know we are there,' the cyborg said. 'I will not fail you, Great Armageddon.'

'Never more than once, at any rate,' Anu Hopet said before leaving the bridge.

\* \* \*

### Barton Correctional Facility: 18 March 34 BZ

Walter Screw loved life's little ironies. There was the obvious one of course: having the surname of Screw and being the senior warden at the worst prison on Earth.

*It's a pity the prisoners will never know that one!*

But the irony currently amusing him involved the beings shackled to the wall before him. After they escaped the prison, they swore they would never return alive, yet here they were, captured by someone they thought they could trust, bound to a wall and about to be used in a demonstration for rookies.

Walter personally oversaw the induction for new staff members as a matter of pride. He covered everything from the ground up: from Manifests 101 to the finer workings of the prison. He never assumed that anyone knew anything before they arrived here.

*Assumption being the mother of all fuck ups and all.*

This way everyone was on the same page and no one could claim they didn't know the way things were. Ignorance of protocol was no excuse in this place, and Walter hated ignorance above all else.

*That being the most delicious irony of all,* he thought, considering a large part of his job involved keeping secrets. He also hated tardiness, and therefore walked around the metal screen shielding the prisoners and into the auditorium to begin the induction at the precise time.

'Welcome new recruits,' Walter said, addressing the twenty-odd people in the room from the lectern. 'What I am about to tell you is classified, but that shouldn't be a problem considering you all passed the vetting process or you wouldn't be here.'

He looked around the theatrette.

'You now sit in one of the most highly classified and secure locations on the planet. Specifically, the Barton Correctional Facility is the deadliest repository of weapons of mass destruction in the world.'

'The Powder Keg!' said one of the recruits in the back row.

'Yes, colloquially it's known as the Powder Keg,' Walter conceded, noting the recruit for future latrine duty, 'and for a very good reason: these inmates are weapons and don't ever forget it.'

Walter paused for a moment to take a sip of water, wiping his mouth to dry it. A wet moustache was another of his pet hates.

'Now for the basics: ninety-five percent of the inmates here are Manifests, which as you all know is the name we use for all these super-beings running around the globe causing trouble,' Walter lectured. 'It's true we don't understand exactly what happens to turn people and things into Manifests, but we know how to deal with them.

'First thing we do as humans is to drag them down from their lofty mystique and label them with sterile terms to make them seem less scary. This was accomplished long ago after studying these beings. There are five classes of Manifest on the Q-Scale, and I will go through them one at a time,' he said before taking a deep breath.

'Class D Entities, or CDEs, have powers that make them either equal to, or less powerful than a human. In fact, what makes this scale so good is that it can be applied to non-Manifests. Humans are CDEs.

'Class C Entities, or CCEs, are the vast majority as far as the Manifest population of this world goes,' Walter continued. 'Basically, beings on this level of power can be pretty impressive but are not by themselves an extinction-level event. The mooks I'll show you later fall into this category.

'Class B, or CBEs, *are* extinction-level events and are to be treated as a national emergency. Think Ballistic or Vicious Man when thinking CBE.

'Finally, there is Class A, or CAEs,' Walter said, precisely on schedule. 'If you ever encounter a hostile CAE, then you may as well pray and hope that another CAE answers, because they may as well be gods.'

He paused for emphasis.

'That wraps up this part of the induction. Are there any questions before we proceed?'

'I have one,' said the recruit from earlier. 'You said five classes, but you only mentioned four. Which one did you forget?' He sat back in his chair and crossed his arms over his chest in pride.

'Yes, Class E Entities, or CEEs,' Walter replied to the smug newbie. *Definitely latrine duty.* 'These are the strangest of all and can come in all shapes, sizes and power levels. What makes them unique is they all share the same energy signature, yet none of them are Manifests. That ridiculous cheese mascot of the HSA is a perfect example of their overall weirdness. Yes, you,' Walter said, pointing at a female recruit.

'Can Manifests move between classifications, as in go from CBE to CAE for example?'

*Good question, I'll keep an eye on her.*

'Not to our knowledge, no,' Walter answered. 'Now if there are no more questions, we can move on to the fun part of the induction.'

Walter nodded to his adjutant, who pressed a button and raised the screen that had hidden the bound supervillains from the audience.

'These scumbags are Nazi filth,' Walter said, indicating the captives. 'So, if any of you are Jews, Gypsies or union members, you'll get a kick out of this.' He donned his helmet, covering his black hair and green eyes, and extended the energised batons from his specialised suit with a flick of his wrists. 'Oh, before anyone asks, yes, that squid guy on the end is an actual space alien, but that's a topic for another day.'

He started to pace up and down in front of his captives.

'Aside from being physically restrained,' Walter said, using his baton as a pointer, 'these so-called Super Six are kept in check by a Manifest null-field, created—like so many things—by Dr Thaddeus Q.'

*More irony, considering that Dr Q is a Manifest himself.*

'See this big guy here?' Walter pointed at Stärke Mensch. 'He's a whopping four and a half metres tall and weighs an improbable three tonnes! Impressive, I admit. But when exposed to the null-field? He's not strong enough to support his own weight.'

Walter felt he was running slightly behind schedule and his hypothesis was confirmed when he saw Tactician standing off to the side. He decided to wrap things up.

He walked over to the side of the stage and retrieved a futuristic-looking rifle from his adjutant. He checked it over to ensure it was powered up and walked back to the centre of the stage in front of the captives.

'Now, this little baby is a Q5 Anti-Manifest Carbine,' he said enthusiastically. 'Each of you will be issued one and trained in its use. For now, though, a demonstration is in order.'

Suddenly, Baron Von Ritzer was released from his manacles and found his powers returning. He saw an opportunity and prepared to take full advantage of it.

'In the unlikely event that the null-field ever fails, like it just did with Nazi-face over there,' Walter said, firing just as the Baron began to strike, 'then just a single shot to the torso with one of these will temporarily make them powerless.'

The carbine fired a small ball of energy, which struck the Baron and phased into him, emitting a blue glow as it burrowed into his chest. He appeared otherwise unharmed.

'Bah!' he said. 'Your weapon had no effect! I'll...' The Baron trailed off while looking at his hands as if expecting them to do something. 'Wait...'

Walter followed up his shot by beating the Baron to an unconscious heap with his energised batons. He then sheathed them and took another sip of water from his glass behind the lectern.

'I trust this serves as a lesson to you all. I now leave you with my aids, who will take you through the rest of the induction. Good night,' Walter said, exiting the stage to the sound of cheering.

'Son, how are you?' he said to Tactician once behind the stage.

'I am well, Father,' Tactician said. 'I just flew over from Canberra. Lucky my flight got in early or I would've missed your demonstration.'

*So I was running to time.*

'How was Canberra?' Walter enquired. 'Did you accomplish your mission?'

'I did,' Tactician replied. 'The HSA are off on a wild goose chase as planned. They'll never discover Project Typhon.'

'What outrageous story did you tell those naïve kids to keep them busy?' Walter asked on their way to the latest meeting with the American ambassador. 'Aliens? Killer robots?'

'I told them that Satanists were bringing about the apocalypse!' Tactician said, starting to crack up.

'And they actually believed that pile of horseshit?'

'Yep.'

'Fucking teenagers will believe anything.' Walter laughed as they entered yet another briefing room. 'Satanists starting the apocalypse. Ha! That's the best one I've heard yet.'

* * *

### Grand Satanic Headquarters: 22 March 34 BZ

Tuesdays had become a real event for Gavin in recent times. He couldn't help but be swept away with the mad hysteria promulgated by Karen and his fellow members of Ole Nick's Coven, and he began to look forward to their weekly meetings. Merlin Mondays seemed to now occur as regular as clockwork, and he got to hear all about it the next day.

Having learned all the vague prophesies from the Satanic Scriptures, or the *SS Dreambook* as he liked to think of it, Gavin wondered what was on the agenda tonight. He was hoping there would be a chosen one or Antichrist or something.

Usually the meetings were during the day, but this one was postponed until the early evening. The usual crowd were all here, except for creepy Navid, who apparently had some other commitment—though what could be more important than hearing the latest instalment?

There was a new guy, too, whom Gavin had never seen before. He looked to be in his mid-forties and was sporting a big bushy beard that was worlds apart from Gavin's stylish goatee.

'Hi, I'm Gavin,' he said, as the new guy awkwardly approached the couch that Gavin always claimed for these meetings. This time he'd even brought popcorn.

'Uh hi,' said the new guy. 'My name is Lancefield, pleased to meet you,' he added, extending his hand.

'Lancefield's an unusual name,' Gavin said, returning the shake.

'Good thanks,' was his reply as he sat down next to Gavin.

Lancefield had an overpowering smell of soap and bacon, which Gavin found confusing and decided to ignore.

'So what's your story?' he enquired, rolling himself a smoke.

'I always liked Thumbelina,' Lancefield answered while staring so earnestly that Gavin thought his eyeballs could shoot from their sockets any second.

'I mean, how did you come to be at this meeting?'

'My mum dropped me off,' Lancefield said. 'I can ask her if you can get a lift home after the meeting if you like.'

Gavin wondered if Lancefield was mentally handicapped or merely stupid.

'No, I mean how did you get to be on the council?' Gavin asked, making one last attempt before abandoning conversation with this guy altogether.

'Oh, now I get you,' Lancefield said. 'Sometimes I don't hear people properly as I have already predicted what they're going to say.'

This was followed by an awkward silence.

'And?' Gavin said, starting to become exasperated.

'On the odd occasion, people don't say exactly what I predicted they would.'

'But how did you get on the council?' Gavin asked once more, coming close to having an aneurysm.

'I'm the locum council member who gets called in when someone else can't make it,' Lancefield said. 'There always has to be six members on the council at these meetings.'

*When the fuck did we get a fucking locum council member? Aren't they doctors anyway? Who's ever heard of a locum Satanist before? And what fucking nuthouse did they find this guy in?*

'Matt, how have you been, mate?' Gavin suddenly said when he saw his brutish friend enter the room. Desperate to have any sort of diversion from Lancefield the earnest locum, Gavin resorted to a topic he loathed, but knew would save him: 'So how did your team go last night?'

'Gavin, hey,' Matt said, and then droned on about guys kicking a ball across a field for a few minutes.

Gavin didn't listen to a word but was relieved to be spared talking to

Lancefield. Instead, he thought about microwaving his popcorn.

'So yeah, I managed to use my cloak as a tax deduction last year, considering it's really a uniform for a non-profit organisation,' Matt was saying when Gavin tuned back into the conversation. 'I reckon you could too.'

'Yeah, but I'm on the dole,' Gavin said.

It was at that moment that Karen announced the meeting was starting.

*Dammit, I should have nuked that popcorn earlier.*

'Fellow members of the council,' Karen began as usual, 'welcome to another gathering of evil, hell-bent on bringing about the End of Days.'

*Wow, she's really going for broke tonight. Then again, she's never looked better. There's that correlation again.*

'First we'll run over the minutes of the last meeting,' Karen declared, turning so dramatically that her obsidian hair swished around her face. 'Tom, just the action items if you please.'

'Tom Higginbottom acknowledges your request,' he said. 'Floyd was going to go on a recruitment drive and bring us up to full membership.'

'Yes, that's right,' Karen said. 'Have you done as the dark one requested, Floyd?'

'Not yet, I...' Floyd began.

'Why have you failed me?' Karen interrupted. 'We need precisely that many members for our plans to work.'

'Do you have any idea how hard it is to keep our membership at a constant six-hundred-and-sixty-six members?' Floyd said defensively. 'People join, people quit, some people are unsuitable—the list of issues goes on and on. But I do have a plan and it should be in place in time for the big event.'

'Good. Make sure that they're ready at the appointed hour,' Karen ordered. 'Next action item?'

'Navid was going to scout for possible locations for the six groups,' Tom said.

'Well, as he's off running an errand for me, Lancefield will have to update us instead,' Karen said. 'Good thing we all decided to get a locum.'

*When did we decide that?* Gavin wondered. *Was I stoned?*

'Thank you, High Priestess,' Lancefield began, quietly retrieving his notes and donning a monocle. 'As you all know, Grand Satanic Headquarters will be the centre and the other five points need to follow the ley-lines from here. At least two of these will have to be on the coast and all of the places need to be isolated, yet still hold one-hundred-and-eleven people. I have shortlisted several locations, which I will pass around.'

*Who is this guy?*

'Bondi, Manly, Ashfield, North Ryde and Banksmeadow,' said Karen after looking at the pictures. 'I think that's close enough for our purposes. Proceed with preparing the locations. Next item?'

'Matt was going to give us a costings report,' Tom said.

'As you know, the cost of brown cloaks has gone up because of the global shortage,' Matt informed the group. 'Which is probably due to all these cults that keep popping up.'

'Imitators,' Karen snorted.

'We've also been raising funds with our door-knocking campaign, which should cover five shuttle buses, venue hire and the insurance premiums—provided everyone is sitting down during the event.'

'Satanists laugh in the face of insurance companies,' Karen said, trying to sound diabolical.

'We should even have money left over for catering,' Matt said.

'That's excellent. Are there any other action items?' Karen queried.

'Tom Higginbottom has read all the action items,' said Tom.

'Then we can move on,' Karen said. 'The High Mage came to me again last night and revealed the final verse of the Satanic Scriptures.'

*Ah, the SS Dreambook, and me without my popcorn.*

'He revealed to me that he's finally returning to our realm,' Karen continued. 'There must be a balance, which Navid is taking care of; a curse must be removed, which will take care of itself; and…there will be a chosen one.'

*Bingo!* Gavin was in heaven.

'What will the chosen one be chosen for?' Floyd asked before Gavin could.

'The chosen one will assist in the High Mage's return to a physical plane of being,' Karen answered.

'Who is he?' asked Matt.

'You're assuming the chosen one is a he,' said Karen. 'At any rate, the identity is still unknown to me.' She went on to explain the balance and how it would work.

Hours passed.

Once the meeting had wrapped up, Gavin finished his last smoke and prepared to catch the train home. Everyone else had left, but not before Lancefield had offered them a lift with his mum. Gavin turned to wave goodbye, only to find Karen standing right behind him.

'Oh. Gavin, did you bring popcorn?' she enquired.

'Yeah, but I didn't get a chance to nuke it,' Gavin replied.

'Well why don't you stick around and stick it in… the microwave,' Karen said huskily. 'And I'll tell you all about the perks of being the chosen one.'

'I thought the identity was unknown,' Gavin said, actually a little surprised. 'Are you saying that *I'm* the chosen one?'

'That was just for them to hear. The identity of the chosen one is a closely guarded secret,' she purred. 'Stay and see just how close.'

Tuesday was fast becoming Gavin's favourite day of the week.

* * *

### Parramatta: 23 March 34 BZ

The Manipulator gazed upon the beginnings of Terror Australis and basked in her vainglorious majesty. Soon her army would be complete and she would be controlling the destinies of the world.

The undead worm creature slithered around her leg and joined her at the walkway overlooking the abandoned factory.

'No, my pet, he is not here yet,' Manipulator said, addressing the worm. Her blank eyes surveyed the assortment of supervillains below. 'Though when he arrives, we will know it's time to change the world.'

The approach of the two armoured thugs drew her attention.

'Ah fuck, she's with that thing again,' Beam said, climbing the stairs to the walkway.

'I think it's cute,' said his companion, Brund. 'But I can never 'member its name.'

'Its name is Segment,' Manipulator said as they got close. 'I named it that because it has been cut into segments, yet they float together as if connected.'

*Yep, that's pretty obvious,* Beam thought. *I still hate it though.*

'Seg-ment,' Brund said, almost mesmerised. 'I'll 'member that one.'

'Yeah right, you dumb fuck,' Beam said. 'You already said that twice before.'

'Enough useless banter,' Manipulator commanded, determined to keep the scene focused on her this time. 'What news?'

'We need you to come down among the great unwashed, boss,' Beam said. 'Put that many supervillains together in one place and friction's inevitable. You need to sort them out and show 'em who's in charge.'

'Very well. Anything else?' she asked.

'There are a couple of new recruits who've just rocked up, who you should talk to,' Beam said 'and that fucking French guy, the Mole, is complaining again, boss.'

'Lead the way, my lackeys,' Manipulator said and gestured towards the stairs.

*Lackeys? Who does she think she is? I better still be getting paid.*

'Of course you will,' Manipulator said, responding to Beam's thoughts as they walked towards a few of the villains milling about. 'Now, who do we have here?'

'I'm Homey Killer,' replied a guy in battle armour, sporting wavy locks instead of a helmet.

'Welcome to Terror Australis, Homey Killer,' Manipulator said genially. 'And what do you do for a living?'

'I kill homeboys,' he said.

'Isn't that a pretty narrow field of supervillainy?' Beam interjected.

'Be that as it may,' HK said, 'that's what I do.'

'Hi, I'm Vaccumax,' said the next in line, a short dorky-looking guy with vacuum cleaners strapped to his arms and a really annoying voice.

'Let me guess: you really suck,' said Beam.

'That's enough,' Manipulator said. 'We don't treat our compatriots like that. Welcome, both of you.'

She turned to Beam. 'Now, take me to the other one.'

Beam led Manipulator past the throng of self-styled supervillains, with Brund following behind. *It's certainly a motley crew.*

Among others, it was made up of not one, but two dragon guys; a guy with impervious armour; an alien that turned people to stone, and some loser who could make paint dry.

*Why couldn't there be some hottie like that Lorraine chick? It's getting hard keeping track of who's who. It's like a fucking zoo,* he thought as they found a ridiculous-looking short guy dressed like a mole.

'Ah, mademoiselle,' the Mole said in fluent cliché. 'Thank you for listening to my concerns.'

'What's bothering you today?' Manipulator asked, having déjà vu.

'I wrote a list,' the Mole declared, producing something akin to a scroll. 'First up, what are we doing here?'

'I told you the answers would come in time. We just have to wait for a few more to arrive,' Manipulator said.

'*Ouais,* well some of us are losing patience,' the Mole said. 'Which brings me to the next item: why do we have to stay in a cement factory? Why can't we stay in a hotel and then come back when the others are all here? There are no bathroom facilities for starters.'

'There's a port-a-loo around the corner,' Beam said.

'But no bidet!' the Mole erupted. 'And that Dogman character keeps shitting in the corner over there.'

*There's a Dogman?* Beam wondered.

'We'll see what we can do,' the Manipulator said soothingly. 'You don't see the Russians complaining.'

'Well, they're Russians. This is probably better than their last accommodations,' the Mole said. 'And as for that dinosaur creature, I swear it's going to kill us all in our sleep.'

'Relax,' the Manipulator said, 'I have it all under control. Not long before we're all together and you can release all that tension.'

*It better be soon, or things are going to get nasty.*

\* \* \*

## London: 26 March 34 BZ

Lorraine Freeman was confronted by yet another barrage of camera flashes while she strutted down the polished silver catwalk. It was some spring collection she was modelling this time around, but she'd forgotten which lecherous sleaze designed it.

Her popularity continued to soar, which of course was a result of her Manifest abilities, yet no one had called her up on it...yet.

'Hey baby, smile my way!' some random yelled from off to her left as she performed a perfect pivot to head back towards the stage.

Lorraine smiled as she was bid and glimpsed the photographer's face after he snapped his pictures—it was glazed with hysteria. She smiled again, except this time it was genuine.

*I'm really starting to enjoy this,* she thought, finishing up and walking back behind the shimmering blue curtain that was the backdrop for the stage.

She continued past the line of models waiting to emerge onto the catwalk and through the flurry of personal assistants that buzzed around them. Suddenly *her* personal assistants surrounded her and added to her mass like she'd passed through a Higgs-Boson field.

'I'm done for today,' Lorraine said, dismissing her entourage like they were minions.

'But there's someone...' began one simpering underling.

Lorraine ignored her assistants and walked into the seventh dressing room, already beginning to get changed. The door closed behind her in the collective faces of her ever-present PAs.

'Mum!' she blurted, looking up after removing her heels. 'What are you doing here?'

'I was bored with the hotel pool and thought I'd check in on you,' said the tall, dark-haired woman standing in the middle of the room. 'Besides, I'm your mother and I have to look after my little girl.'

'Mum, I'm fine,' Lorraine said. 'My powers make everyone love me, so what could possibly happen?'

'I loved you before you Manifested,' her mother said, 'but that's beside the point. Have you ever thought that it might drive someone to try and hurt you? Or that they might also be Manifests and immune to your charms?'

Lorraine had to admit she hadn't thought about it at all. 'But if they were Manifests too, then I'd be able to tell,' she said.

'Sure, Manifests can all sense each other,' her mother agreed, 'unless, of course, they have the ability not to be sensed.'

'I'm not exactly sure what my powers are,' Lorraine confessed.

'Exactly my point, so you should be careful. I remember when I was with the X-Droids on a mission...'

'Do I have to hear another one of your old war stories, Mum?' Lorraine interrupted. 'Is this the one where you had to fight the Super Six and managed to blind them unexpectedly, or was it the time you inadvertently shorted out that sci-fi reject, Destructo the Destroyer?'

*Geez, what a silly name for a giant robot.*

'Well, it was the Destructo story, but that's not the point,' her mother conceded. 'I'm just worried about you, is all.'

'Mum...'

'How about we go out to dinner? I've already booked a table for two at this place I know called the River Café—hope you like Italian.'

The car trip to the restaurant was filled with small talk, and Lorraine spent most of the time looking out the limousine's window at the city.

*It's funny, the moment you see one of those double-decker buses you instantly know where you are.*

They pulled up to the restaurant and immediately drew attention to themselves. A limousine always meant the rich and famous, after all—a hot-pink limousine meant only one person. The chauffeur opened the door for them and they walked into the restaurant followed by gasps and pointing.

The maître d' was a caricature of unflappable Britishness. 'Reservations?' he enquired without really looking at the two ladies.

'I have a table for two reserved under the name Lucy Freeman,' Lucy said.

'Freeman?' the maître d' asked and finally looked up. His jaw dropped. 'Is that...?'

'Yes, this is Lorraine Freeman,' Lucy answered. 'She's my daughter.'

'Of course we have your reservation!' The maître d' beamed. 'Anything for a famous celebrity like Miss Freeman!'

'I'm a celebrity too,' Lucy said indignantly. 'I'm a super...'

'That's nice,' the maître d' interrupted as he led them to their table. 'Right this way, please.'

Lorraine and Lucy selected their food while the maître d' hovered around and were finally left in peace—aside from the staring patrons.

'It's a bit surreal how everyone just stares at me all the time,' Lorraine said.

'Scary is what it is,' Lucy corrected. 'Your untapped potential is enormous. But it's still early days, so tell me: how are you coping with all of this?'

'Okay, I guess,' Lorraine replied. 'I think I'm starting to get the hang of it, but it's just been crazy. Although I wonder if this is the extent of it, or whether I'm going to get more powerful and things are going to get even crazier.'

'Well, your Manifest radiates like what ole Doctor Thad would call a Class B,' Lucy said, pausing to accept her entrée from the waiter. 'I'd say there's a lot more to come.'

'But I'm guaranteed the basics, right?' Lorraine said between mouthfuls. 'Immortality and eternal youth, like you have, for instance? I can certainly sense other Manifests, which is meant to be a given among our kind.'

'It's hard to say, sweetie,' Lucy said. 'You're not even an adult yet. Most Manifests who get their powers as kids age until they're young adults and then stop. But this isn't always the case. You won't know until you're that age.'

Lucy paused to chew her food. 'People like Thaddeus Q like to classify everything around them, coming up with terms like Class B Entity and claiming there are baseline Manifest abilities, but the fact is that you just never know. Every case is different, which is what makes being a Manifest both a charm and a curse.

'Take your sisters, for instance,' Lucy continued while putting her plate to one side. 'Who could possibly tell what their powers will be? They haven't Manifested yet, but they will, and that's really the only guarantee: every child of a Manifest will themselves be a Manifest.'

'It's very profound when you say it like that,' Lorraine said as the main course arrived. 'But what about immunity to disease?'

'Depends on the disease; could be a Manifest disease.'

'Or control over bodily functions, like pregnancy?'

'You're way too young to be falling pregnant, so don't even think about it.'

'Or knowing all your previous reincarnations?'

'Only if you had a previous life and not the super ability to have false memories of past lives.'

'You've got an answer for everything...'

'Life experience.'

'Okay, so really I've just got to wing it,' Lorraine said, eating the last of her main course. 'By the way, this was so filling, I'm not sure I can have dessert.'

'Oh, but the pastries here are amazing,' Lucy said as she finished up too. 'That's okay sweetie, it was good just to sit here and talk to you. Good thing that Shara's looking after Heather and Samantha, otherwise I probably couldn't have come on this trip with you.'

'I'm glad I could talk to you about this stuff, Mum,' Lorraine admitted. 'It's been bothering me for some time, but I just haven't had a chance to talk to you about it since you decided to start me on a modelling career.'

'I saw the potential in you, and thought it could help for your future,' Lucy said, signalling for the cheque. 'This is why I've decided to get you an official home teacher, so you can continue with your career and still graduate from high school.'

*That...seems like a good idea.*

'By the way, thanks so much for going on Oprah and telling everyone that seven was my favourite number,' Lorraine added sarcastically. 'Now I find it everywhere: I'm always getting booked into number seven hotel rooms, there's always seven of everything lined up neatly in my dressing room... Someone even made me model a dress covered in little sevens.'

'That's showbiz, honey,' Lucy said as the maître d' and a chef appeared at their table.

'Thank you for dining here tonight, ladies,' the maître d' gushed. 'Dinner is on the house.'

Lucy went to say something.

'No, I insist,' he said. 'I would also like to introduce you to our young chef, Jamie. He has something for the young lady.'

'I made these for you,' Jamie said, producing some of those amazing pastries. There were seven of course. 'I would be honoured if you would take them with you.'

*He's pretty cute,* thought Lorraine, accepting his gift and standing up from the table.

'What did you say your name was again?' Lorraine asked.

'Jamie. Jamie Oli…'

'Thank you, young man,' Lucy interrupted as she saw the look between them and guided Lorraine to the door. 'Maybe you can look her up again once you're famous.'

\* \* \*

## South Western Sydney: 30 March 34 BZ

Mark Adams sat with the rest of the family in the living room, digesting his meal and watching the weekly instalment of *The X-Files*. He really enjoyed his family time and at least once a week he made sure they all dined together and watched their favourite show.

'Wow, that was a good episode,' Mark said as the credits rolled to the familiar theme tune. 'What did everyone else think?'

'Yeah, it was okay,' said Samara, who sat braiding her long black hair during the show.

'It was pretty cool,' Obie said. 'I wish something interesting like that would happen to us.'

'What, like being attacked by space aliens?' asked Desci. 'Pass.'

Sebastian didn't say anything as usual and simply fished around the chip packet for some crumbs.

'Well, you kids can sort out who's doing the dishes,' Mark said, getting up from the couch, 'because it's not going to be your mother or me. We're turning in. Don't stay up too late. 'Night.'

'Goodnight,' the kids said in unison.

Mark took Desci by the hand as the kids cleared the plates and argued over who was washing, wiping and putting away.

'To the bedroom, my love,' Mark said lasciviously. 'I have a big day tomorrow and have to get up early.'

'You assume a lot, Mister Adams,' Desci said, smiling.

'That's because to assume is to get your ass between you and me,' Mark replied leading her to the bedroom.

Sometime later, Mark and Desci lay in sweat-soaked sheets and listened to the wind blow outside.

'That wind's turning into a bit of a gale,' Mark said, cuddling Desci in the dark. 'I guess autumn is finally here. Seems to be getting warmer every year, like the seasons are coming later.'

'Hmmmmhmmm,' Desci hummed, almost asleep.

*The sound of satisfaction,* Mark thought, looking at his beautiful wife.

Mark stroked her black bob as Desci fell completely asleep.

*Even with trying to raise three kids on a pittance salary, I'm a lucky man,* he thought as he drifted off to sleep.

A crashing of rubbish bins and the sound of a cat screeching startled Mark awake and suddenly his memory was triggered.

'Ah fuck, it's bin night.' He got out of bed to do the task of husbands the world over.

Shortly thereafter, Mark walked out of the flat and down the three flights of stairs carrying several bags of rubbish and multiple boxes. He dumped it all into a cylindrical metal bin on the far side of the car and lugged it to the curb. *Why can't they just pay for a communal dumpster? I'd even be happy for a fucking wheelie bin.*

That's when Mark noticed the strange, middle-eastern man staring at him from across the road. He was standing right under the flickering street lamp and eyeballing Mark with an intensity usually reserved for the Haka.

*Creepy,* Mark quickly dumped the rubbish bin and turned to go back inside. He felt his spine tingle and the stranger's eyes raking his back.

He stole a glance behind him. The stranger was still there and silently stared at him without moving. *This is really starting to creep me out,* he thought, dashing up all three flights in record time.

He took one final glance at the stranger before going back into his apartment, and the creep seemed to blow him a kiss in return.

Thanks for the kiss.
You will see yourself soon.

Mark felt a terrible chill down his spine as he closed the apartment door behind him.

# April

## Grey: 34 BZ

*Close. So close now. Hold on. Grasp. Suckle, drink, drain. The host is almost ripe. Squirm. Squirm into the soul. Upwards, ever upwards.*

\* \* \*

## Dungeon Cell 9: 1 April 34 BZ

Andy Trailer awoke to the smell of hot coffee and bacon on toast. He peeked through his bruised and bloodshot eyes, wary of revealing he was awake in case punishment followed.

It took a moment for his eyes to focus, but when they did they rested on a plate of toast covered with overflowing greasy bacon and a mug of steaming coffee sitting in the middle of the room. The mug had a smiley face on it and the words 'Have a great day' stencilled across the top in big red letters.

Andy's stomach gurgled in anguish at the sight, and he used every iota of strength to drag himself across the floor towards the tantalising food. It may have been a trap, but it was better than raw cockroach.

Andy grabbed the plate and wolfed down the food when no immediate punishment occurred. He washed it down with the coffee, ignoring the scalding heat and thankful for the warmth in his belly after countless hours in the cold dark.

*You are weak, pitiful,* said the inner voice in Andy's head. *It is a trap,* it kept whispering as Andy took furtive glances around the room while scoffing the last of his food. By now he was crouching over the plate with his bat-like wings folded around him in a protective shield.

After Andy had fastidiously picked up every crumb with the tip of his pointed black fingernail, he noticed for the first time the beam of light illuminating the crockery. He followed the light trail with his bleary eyes toward the doorway. The door to his cell was open.

Andy froze like an animal in headlights and even put his hands up over his head, expecting an attack at any moment. Nothing happened. He listened for the sound of footfalls—any sound really—but could only hear the rasping of his own breath.

*It is a trap,* the unrelenting voice whispered. *It has always been so.*

Andy paused for a moment and tried to think of how he came to be there. The voice was right; it seemed as if he had always spent his life in some filthy dungeon. It just wasn't fair.

He struggled to remember his past—he wasn't even sure how old he was. *Seventeen most likely,* he thought.

Images of his childhood suddenly flashed through his mind: his older brother stealing his presents at Christmas time, his parents always blaming him for things his brother did, and even the girl he liked going for his dad instead. He'd felt trapped his whole life.

*Not fair.*

It all started to come back to him: going for a bushwalk to escape the news that he wasn't accepted into university on a technicality, then stumbling across that hidden door after spraining his ankle and literally falling into it—breaking his Walkman in the process.

*It could only happen to me.*

That's when his life went from a metaphorical prison to a real one. He remembered being accosted by strange guys in purple leather with matching helmets and felt he'd fallen into the set of some movie.

*I'm not that lucky,* Andy thought, remembering how those costumed freaks had pistol-whipped him and dragged him inside.

There he awoke to the being who began his real torment: the one who had corrupted his soul.

*And introduced you to me,* said the familiar voice inside his head.

*Yes. The Energy Lord. The one who sold me to my new tormentor.* Why did this keep happening to him? Why did these superheroes always seem to rescue everyone except him? It was unfair.

*You whiny bitch,* the voice said, forever eroding his self-esteem.

He looked again at the open doorway. The cell had become his home now and he was afraid to leave it. He was also afraid of punishment should he try and escape.

*It is a trap,* repeated the inner voice, *but do it anyway.*

Andy slowly crawled across the room towards the doorway as quietly as he could. He paused at the door and listened again. Nothing. It was funny how silence was a sound all of its own.

Cautiously he peeked through the doorway turning his head left then right, but there was no obvious danger. He looked again, slower this time, and noticed the surrounds for the first time.

Outside the cell was a sterile concrete corridor illuminated by rows of fluorescent lights. There was nothing except a wall to his left, but the corridor continued to his right, and Andy noticed there were other cells lining its length. The one directly opposite had the numeral 10 stencilled on it.

He looked up at the door to his own cell, and for the first time knew that he was in cell 9. He looked back down the corridor and noticed the door at the end had an exit sign on it. It was also ajar.

Andy now believed it was a trap and didn't need to be reminded by the inevitable inner voice, but remind him it did. He'd never been outside of this cell before and so he wasn't sure of the layout of the building. He didn't even know where the hell he was.

*Why can't this happen to someone else for a change?*

There was nothing else for it though, it was either try to escape, or die in this cell. That inner voice be damned.

*Just like you,* it said.

Andy crept slowly down the corridor on all fours. All of the cells were windowless, but he wouldn't have risked looking even if they had windows. His only thought was of the exit.

He eventually reached the end of the corridor and stopped at the exit door. Lying at the base of the door was a note, scrawled with a simple message:

*You are free. Fly like a bat out of hell, Night Demon.*

*Night Demon?* Like his favourite song. He used to daydream about soaring above the clouds when listening to that song. He didn't even get the reference to Meatloaf.

Andy peered through the gap in the door and could smell salt in the air. Salt…and freedom. For the first time since waking, he could hear something aside from his breathing and it was the glorious sound of the surf. His eyes adjusted and took in the sight of a beach at night, illuminated by the full moon in the sky.

*It is a trap.*

*Shut up. Shut up! Shut up!!!*

The sound of footsteps suddenly echoed from the corridor behind, and Andy sprang through the door without thinking. His wings took action subconsciously and he soon found himself soaring above the clouds—just like in his fantasies.

*Finally, things are going my way,* he thought, flying down low and gliding close to the coastline. Then he noticed a figure sitting on a metal chair in the middle of the beach.

*No, it can't be.* He saw the all-too familiar shape of his tormentor staring up at him with his spiralling Cyclopean eye and maniacal grimace.

Without warning, Andy fell from the sky and crashed into the wet sand at the feet of his captor. He found himself buried and unable to move, as if he'd landed in quicksand.

'Night Demon,' the cyclops said. 'Glad you could be here.'

'No,' Andy moaned.

'Although you never really went anywhere,' the cyclops continued. 'You're still right back home in dungeon cell 9.'

'Please, no.'

'Do you know what today is?' the cyclops said as the world began to shimmer.

'No…it's not fair.'

'April Fools'!' the cyclops cried. The scenic beach vista was replaced by the familiar dank walls of cell number 9. 'You thought you were free, but you really weren't! Isn't that a great prank?'

*Told you it was a trap.*

'Nooooo!' Andy screamed as he found himself shackled to the floor of the cell and surrounded by a trio of robots—one android, one cephalopod and the vicious dog, Malice.

'Don't ever, ever think about escape ever again,' the cyclops said, looming over Andy with his hypnotic eye. 'Just remember that I control your entire life, and my little gift allows me to control your mind as well. This lesson, however, is not in your mind.'

Andy whimpered as the Trio pummelled him into the cold, stone floor—and he welcomed the blanket of darkness that followed.

\* \* \*

### The Mullberry Residence, Canberra: 4 April 34 BZ

Bentaz Mullberry returned home from school to find his older brother swimming through the backyard lawn like it was a pool.

'Hey, Yam.' Bentaz walked through the back door and out into the secluded yard. 'Going for a new lap record?'

'Very funny, little brother,' Yam replied, swimming towards Bentaz and shooting out of the earth like a dolphin. The ground looked undisturbed. 'It's good to see you though.'

While Yam was taller and had long reddish hair, compared to Bentaz's short brown hair, the family connection was still apparent. Both brothers had similar features and hazel-coloured eyes.

'Likewise,' Bentaz agreed. 'You've only just moved out, yet it's like you never left.'

'Well, a group house is like living in a third world zoo: you only eat scraps and nothing works, so you call in the United Nations—in this case Mum—and voila! Clothes get washed and I get fed,' Yam revealed. 'Plus, I get to see my little brother and baby sister.'

'Don't call me that,' said their little sister, who had come outside to join them. 'I'm eleven years old, which means I'm almost an adult.'

'Pfff,' Bentaz huffed.

'At least I'll become a Manifest when I'm thirteen,' she said.

'Peach, you can't predict when it will happen,' Yam retorted.

'But you two did!' Peach said indignantly.

'Just be happy that it will happen at all,' said Yam.

'Ha ha,' Bentaz laughed, starting to crack up. 'What if you Manifest into a giant monster-face, Peach?'

'Shut up!' Peach cried. 'That's not going to happen.'

'It might.' Yam grinned, getting into teasing his sister.

'Shut up! Mum!' Peach called as she started to go back inside.

Mere moments later their mum was standing in the doorway.

'You two stop teasing your little sister,' she said in her 'stern' voice. 'You'll be in for it when your father gets home.'

'Whenever that will be,' Bentaz mumbled under his breath.

'Now come up here and help your poor old mother make dinner.'

Nikki Mullberry may have claimed to be old, and at forty-one years of age that was still debatable, but she didn't look a day over twenty-five. Her auburn bob and emerald eyes emphasised her sublime intelligence and beauty. She also knew how to handle her children.

Which is why Bentaz and Yam ended up making dinner while Nikki braided her daughter's amber hair. It did give them all an excuse to talk, however, and Bentaz used the opportunity to raise his latest bugbear.

'Hey, Mum,' Bentaz began. 'I was wondering something.'

'Yes?' Nikki raised an eyebrow.

'How come I have to go to school when Yam got to be home schooled?' Bentaz asked. 'I understand why Peach has to go, as she hasn't Manifested, but now that I have, I think I should be taught at home.'

'Honey, you didn't take off a kid's arm and force us to move suburbs,' Nikki said, looking at her oldest child. 'It's lucky I grew the kid a new arm, otherwise we could've had much different lives. Besides, nobody knows you're also Ballistic.'

'I bet that bully Warden and his bully son, Tactician, know my real identity,' Bentaz said. 'They probably know about all of us.'

'I'm pretty sure they know about Dad,' Yam said, putting the casserole into the oven to cook.

'Your father wears a helmet to conceal his identity and he provides well for this family,' Nikki said defensively. 'One day you'll appreciate that.'

'Yeah, but he goes by Hunter!' Bentaz said. 'That's his name!'

'He's hiding in plain sight, so to speak,' Nikki explained without conviction.

'I'd also appreciate it if he was home more often,' Bentaz confessed.

'His work involves a lot of travel,' Nikki admitted. 'Working for the government takes him places.'

*I'm not so sure he does work for the government.*

'Oh, I meant to tell you,' Yam interjected. 'I saw you on the news the other day fighting Nazi supervillains. I like your new outfit!'

'Thanks,' Bentaz said, cleaning up. 'I'm not sure Grandfather would approve though.'

'That's because he doesn't know and wouldn't understand,' Nikki said. 'He's always been a hard man, which is why your father is like he is.'

'Yeah, but Bentaz can't be held responsible for what Axis did,' Yam said, defending his brother.

'I don't understand,' Peach chimed in without looking up from her girly magazine. 'Who's Axis?'

'Axis was the codename for a German World War One super-human—the first Manifest confirmed by modern society,' Nikki answered, continuing to braid Peach's hair.

'His real name was Herman Himmler,' Bentaz divulged. He'd finished clearing the kitchen bench and poured himself a cordial. 'The Axis powers in World War Two used his name for their alliance.'

'Grandfather killed Axis at the end of World War One,' Yam informed his sister. 'They really hated each other.'

'But what does that have to do with Bentaz?' Peach asked.

'Well, sweetie,' Nikki said, 'Bentaz was Axis in his past life and now that he's unwisely dressing like him, we're worried that your grandfather will be upset.'

'Doesn't Grandfather know that Bentaz was Axis?'

'No,' Nikki said, 'and you mustn't tell him either. Promise?'

'Okay, but I don't get what the big deal is,' Peach said.

'Just don't say anything,' Nikki said. 'It's bad enough that Bentaz has to make it bloody obvious with his new togs, we don't need you opening your trap and making it worse. Your grandfather has little sense of humour, which Bentaz will no doubt be reminded of when he sees him on his birthday.'

'So anyway, can you home tutor me?' Bentaz hoped returning to the original subject would be less awkward. 'Please?'

'I'm hungry,' Peach interrupted, before he could get started. 'Can I open some chips?'

'No to both of you,' Nikki decreed, as she finished braiding Peach's hair. 'Dinner will be ready soon. What's say we watch the news while we wait?'

'Aww Mum,' Peach whined. 'I wanted to watch *Summer Breeze High*.'

'Hell no, we're watching the news,' Nikki said. 'Something important may have happened.'

*Like maybe Lorraine Freeman is coming to Canberra,* Bentaz hoped.

\* \* \*

### Outskirts of Dubbo, New South Wales: 6 April 34 BZ

Dread Sedgewick slowly crushed the screaming soldier's head into a bloody paste while he sparked up a cigarette. Several bullets bounced off his head as he dragged back on the toxic goodness, until suddenly a bullet shot off the tip of his smoke.

'For fuck's sake!' he yelled. 'Who the fuck are you guys anyway, the Cancer Council?'

The squad of soldiers continued to fire at him without so much as a hello. One of them cooked a grenade and threw it at Dread's face, the resulting explosion incinerating the entire packet of smokes he'd pulled from his coat pocket to replace the one they had shot.

'That tears it!' he raged. 'You pricks just got yourselves fragged!'

Dread lunged at the closest gunman with inhuman speed, his fingers morphing into metallic blades as he moved. Within seconds the gunman's helmeted head was flying into the sky.

He leapt into the air and kicked the head like a soccer champion, sending it flying through the chest of a second soldier, who killed a third when he wildly fired his gun as he died. It was over in moments.

The last soldier was in a sniper's nest about a kilometre away, and even at that distance Dread could see him clearly as he got up from the hide to flee. Dread flexed his mighty thews and jumped towards the hide. His serrated fingers seemed to slash through the air itself, and he retrieved a nasty-looking dagger which he threw at the fleeing sniper.

The dagger sliced through the sniper's ankle, causing him to fall into the dirt as Dread landed next to him—having covered the entire distance in a single bound.

'Who sent you?' Dread shouted, his crimson facial birthmarks looking like battle paint—serving to further intimidate his adversary. 'Speak, flunky, and you won't have to eat your own bowels!'

The sniper moaned and clutched his leg around his bleeding stump as he rolled around the ground in agony.

'I can tell I'm not getting through to you,' Dread said, seemingly oblivious to the suffering before him. In truth he just didn't care. 'One more time now: who sent you?'

The sniper selfishly went into shock instead of answering his polite query.

'Snap out of it!' he said, snapping the sniper's arm. 'Screaming should help keep you conscious.'

After an initial outburst, the unfortunate sniper remained conscious but fell into a feverish, babbling state.

'Let me see: five-man team, uniforms, helmets, expensive guns and equipment,' Dread thought aloud. 'There's nothing mystical about you whatsoever, which means that you can't be connected to this etheric cord that pulls me eastward.'

The sniper continued his incoherent murmuring while Dread sharpened his finger-blades.

'Therefore, you're most likely some special government military squad stationed out here in Woop Woop and opportunistically tried to take me out. Am I right?' he asked the sniper while he shredded the man's uniform. 'You know, if I'm going to figure out all the answers on my own, it doesn't really count as you telling me. So you better say something before I work it all out by myself.'

The sniper was dying fast and incapable of coherent thought.

'Obviously you've guessed I'm going east, as I tend to cause a bit of a ruckus everywhere I go,' Dread said casually, plunging his hands into the sniper's stomach. 'But I also tend to disappear, and therefore you can't continually track me. So the government hastily puts together a few squads and quickly peppers them around the area in the hope of finding me by chance. That's why you came at me with standard weapons and not that fancy anti-Manifest shit. Am I close?'

The sniper died out of spite rather than have the courtesy to listen to Dread's reasoning.

'What you couldn't know,' Dread explained, now on a roll, 'is that I'm walking east on foot by choice. I could just go straight to Sydney, but I've decided to take the scenic route and make those who call me wait. I've been popping home at night and coming back in the morning.'

Dread scooped a big handful of intestines out of the sniper and a tiny metallic capsule fell out of them into the dirt.

'What's this? A United Nations tracking device?' Dread stuffed the intestines into the corpse's mouth. 'Now if you'd only said that at the beginning, then I wouldn't have had to go through with my threat. Bon appétit.'

He looked briefly at his handiwork and wondered how much blood he'd gotten on his clothes. It soaked into him so quickly it was always hard to tell.

'What you also don't know,' he said, still talking to the corpse as he stood up, 'is that I can go anyplace I want to.'

Dread sliced his hands through the air as though he was carving a doorway through the atmosphere.

'See, my blades are so sharp, they can cut through reality itself,' he revealed. He grabbed the air where a doorknob should be and twisted. 'Impossible? Maybe for you. For me, it's a handy way to get around.'

And without further ado, Dread walked through the dimensional doorway and reality sealed itself behind him.

* * *

### Undisclosed location: 10 April 34 BZ

Walter Screw walked down the sterile corridor towards yet another meeting room. It seemed like that would be his life from now on: meeting after bloody meeting. *Maybe I've died and gone to hell and am being forced to suffer an eternity of bureaucratic mediocrity.*

At least this meeting looked like it was going to be interesting. The Australian Government was looking at forging even closer ties with the United Nations and so sent Walter and some representatives to find out what actually went on in all those facilities they sold to the UN, including their current whereabouts.

Walter preferred his regular stomping grounds to these laboratories, but he had to admit they did some amazing work here and was looking forward to being taken on an official tour rather than leading one.

*I don't need a tour to find my way to the meeting room,* he thought as he reached his destination. He spent a good deal of time here meeting with his son. Today would be no exception.

'Son,' Walter said, walking into the meeting room, 'good to see you again.'

'Father,' his son replied, 'it's good to see you too. But when the others arrive, please refrain from calling me Stan, Stanley or Son and address me as Tactician. Our identities need to remain a secret even to our allies.'

'You don't have to lecture your father on protocol,' Walter remarked. 'I wrote the bloody guidelines! Anyway, I'm looking forward to today—I mean, it's not every day you get to talk to two cyborgs, let alone ones that are mature enough to hold a conversation and who aren't trying to conquer the planet.'

'There will also be defence minister Robert Ray, the American Ambassador Edward Perkins, a representative from Xenotech Inc, and a creepy MIB guy. Not sure which one as they all look the same to me,' Tactician admitted. 'So I'd reserve judgement on the whole "conquering the planet" angle if I were you.'

'If you mean nurturing the planet towards a more agreeable future,' said a sudden voice from behind them in the meeting room, 'then I would agree with you.'

The voice came from a nondescript man with dark hair, of average height, and adorned in a black suit and tie. He was even wearing sunglasses despite being indoors. Although he appeared completely normal, something about him was slightly 'off' like a living Escher picture. Walter felt queasy just looking at him.

'Uh, Warden, this is um…' Tactician began.

'I'm simply an interested party,' the MIB said to Walter, 'and I'll just be observing today's deliberations. Pretend I'm not even here.'

*As you are probably the creepiest guy I've ever met, I seriously doubt it,* Walter thought. 'Pleased to meet you,' Walter said, offering his hand to shake.

The MIB turned around and returned to his seat in the corner of the room, leaving Walter with his hand extended looking like a dick.

*Motherfucker.*

Walter didn't have long to wait as the rest of the attendees soon arrived for the meeting. They filed in one at a time and exchanged cursory greetings as they took their respective places. The table they sat at was U-shaped and faced a giant screen on the wall.

'Thank you all for coming,' Tactician began from in front of the screen, amid the shuffle of meeting papers. 'I'm codename Tactician, commander of the United Nations task force on Manifests and official liaison to the world's governments. My real name is not for public record, but most of yours are. So, if you please, introduce yourselves for the record.'

Tactician gestured to his left where his father sat and then joined him at the head of the U.

'My name's also not for the public record,' Walter announced. 'I'm the Warden of the Barton Correctional Facility and also represent the United Nations at this meeting. I'm here to offer council as a subject matter expert on dangerous Manifests.'

*Any excuse for a junket.*

'I'm Toby Kim from Xenotech Incorporated,' said the Asian man on Walter's left. 'I'm the senior operations manager for Project Typhon, which is funded by Xenotech. I represent the United Nations as one of our business partners, but mainly I'm here to safeguard our investment.'

'I am the Honourable Robert Ray, Minister of Defence,' said a bespectacled man in his late forties. 'I represent the interests of the Commonwealth of Australia and whether or not we should become active members in this Project Typhon.'

*Now it's time for the interesting attendees,* Walter thought, subtly looking at his watch. *This meeting is already three minutes behind schedule,* he noted, *but it'll be worth it to see David and Neal again.*

He hadn't seen either of them since before the failed assassination attempt by that crazy Bloodlust bitch left them burnt and near dead. They would have been all dead if Dr Q hadn't miraculously saved them by improbably turning them into cyborgs.

Walter's thoughts were turned back to the meeting at the sound of an electronic voice.

'I'm Field Marshal David Hobbs,' said a man in a quasi-military uniform; his entire chest, right arm and head were obviously artificial. Even Hobbs's face, which was visible under his mirrored goggles, was in actuality synthetic flesh that moved through electronic impulses from his brain, safely encased in the metallic helmet that passed for his head. 'I'm here as a representative of Australia, considering the military implications of Project Typhon.'

'I also represent Australia in as much as I am told Project Typhon concerns civil policing matters,' said another cyborg, this one with a modified helmet-head with inbuilt respirator. He also had a back-pack that appeared to be grafted on, and an actual buzz-saw for a right hand. Walter wondered how he masturbated. 'I'm Commissioner Neal Jacobs,' the cyborg policeman finished.

'I'm Edward J Perkins,' said the senior black man, who was next in line. 'I'm the American ambassador to Australia. I represent the interests of the United States of America and I'm here to discern whether or not it's in the US's best interests for Australia to upgrade their membership with the United Nations.'

*Like it's any of your goddamn business.*

'And of course, everyone should be familiar with the work of Lex the stenographer,' Tactician said, referring to the dweeby-looking balding man sitting opposite him at the head of the U-shaped table.

The warm reception Lex received from those in the room was the envy of stenographers the world over.

'Thank you everyone,' Lex said. 'I'll try to live up to your expectations with the minutes of this meeting.'

The creepy MIB continued to sit silently in the darkness at the back of the room, and everyone else seemed perfectly content to completely disregard that particular elephant.

'Okay,' Tactician resumed, 'as you all know, we're meeting here today to discuss whether Australia should be brought into active partnership with Project Typhon and by default upgrade its UN membership to stage three status.'

'Can I just say before we get started that the United States believes this is a matter that should be brought before the Security Council,' Ambassador Perkins said.

'The Security Council has no say over UN membership,' Tactician stated.

'Then I warn Australia that this could upset the ANZUS Treaty,' Perkins persisted, undaunted. 'There is a special section that prohibits Australia from circumventing their current parameters regarding the UN, as set by the US.'

*And we actually signed that?* Walter wondered. He found himself drawn into the debate despite it now running well behind schedule.

'I think Australia has a right to know what operations the UN is conducting on Australian soil with subsidies from the Australian taxpayer,' Minister Ray said. 'I would say it's a done deal that we'll upgrade our membership to stage three. Therefore, I suggest you brief me on Project Typhon.'

'Robert, please listen to reason,' Perkins began. 'Have you forgotten Kuwait?'

'Ed, enough,' Minister Ray said. 'Please.'

'It's okay,' Tactician said. 'I'll answer this. Kuwait is now enjoying the protection and all the other benefits that go with full UN membership. Same as other countries before it, like Afghanistan, Vietnam, Taiwan, Northern Ireland, Czechoslovakia, the Solomon Islands and the Democratic Republic of Congo to name a few. Australia even entrusted us with the care of Papua New Guinea back in '75. We also would have helped out the citizens of Panama if the United States wasn't so fearful of rival powers...and ideas.'

'I can't believe I have to sit here listening to this one-world crap,' Perkins said under his breath. 'This was meant to be a cushy posting to retire on as a reward for all my years of hard work. I should've known it wouldn't be that easy.'

Walter began to tire of politics and wanted to steer the conversation back to Project Typhon and the associated tour of the facilities.

'I think it's established that Australia wishes to upgrade their status,'

Walter began, 'so as a sign of good faith I think we should move forward and brief the good minister on Project Typhon.'

Perkins sat with his arms crossed and said nothing.

'I agree,' said Kim. 'Xenotech have provided a lot of funding for this project and we would very much like to know what we've gotten for our investment.'

'Very well,' Tactician said. 'Project Typhon was founded in the fifties, and like so many things, was the brainchild of Doctor Thaddeus Q. It's named after the Greek monster with one hundred dragon heads, which represent the multifaceted approach we are taking.'

'Why didn't you just call it Project Hydra?' Commissioner Jacobs questioned in his respirator voice.

'Because everyone uses that term,' Tactician answered, 'and because Typhon was far deadlier. It assailed Mount Olympus and Zeus himself.'

*And was hurled into Tartarus by Zeus, from memory.*

'So what exactly is it?' asked Field Marshal Hobbs. 'Dr Q was a brilliant man—at least before his disgrace and subsequent disappearance—so I expect that it's something pretty amazing. I should know, considering he pretty much reanimated my corpse with all of this machinery you see attached to me.'

'Don't forget that he pretty much came up with it on the spot,' Jacobs reminded them. 'Imagine what he could've accomplished if he actually planned something.'

'Unfortunately, Dr Q wasn't much of a planner, so that was done mostly by the citizens of the UN. With help from some of the Security Council members of course,' Tactician conceded. 'But the general concept was Q's. Anyway, you would already be aware of some of the "dragon heads" as we like to call them but wouldn't have realised that they were part of a larger scheme. The Powder Keg for instance.'

*The Powder Keg?* Walter didn't know *that* little gem.

'There is, of course, our well-known peacekeeping force, the World's Defence and the fully automated though blandly named, Defence Base, but did you also know that it was our idea to form the HSA?' Tactician explained. 'It's part of a larger plan to keep the Manifest populations divided into "heroes" and "villains" and thus easier to control.'

Walter still marvelled at how it had become normal to talk about goddamn superheroes at a top-secret government meeting. He could only surmise that space aliens were up next on the agenda, followed by ancient Cossack poltergeists.

'This was a social experiment pioneered by Xenotech Inc in the seventies with the X-Droids,' Kim said.

'You stole the basic idea from the Nazis,' Perkins added unhelpfully.

'That's not entirely true,' Minister Ray said, almost defensively. 'Australia had the war hero, Ally, since World War One.'

'Copied from another German,' Perkins said.

'Ally is a true patriot that worked with Dr Q to advance our understanding of Manifests,' Hobbs blustered.

'Their contribution enabled Project Typhon to be possible,' Tactician acknowledged. 'It allowed us to form the T-Squad, an elite Manifest special ops unit.'

'Who?' Minister Ray asked.

'Exactly,' Tactician continued without missing a beat. 'Project Typhon even provided the tech that was the core of both your Super Trooper and Battle Suit projects,' he said to Hobbs.

'Just how far-reaching is this project?' Minister Ray queried.

'Typhon has so many dragon heads that they take a variety of forms. Some are very subtle. For instance, we've started pre-production on a movie making those guys the heroes,' Tactician divulged, pointing his thumb at the silent MIB in the corner. 'There are also other projects that you cannot learn unless you apply for stage four or five status. But we have accepted your stage three membership, and so I'm authorised to take you on a tour of this facility.'

*Finally!*

'That ends the official proceedings, so if you would kindly follow me,' Tactician announced, rising from the table and heading towards the door.

'I'll skip the tour, I've already taken it,' Perkins said, turning to Minister Ray and offering his hand. 'Robert, a pleasure as always.'

'Likewise, Ed,' Minister Ray said, 'but how is it that you've already seen this facility?'

'The US already has stage three membership,' Perkins replied, heading for the exit. 'Now, if you'll excuse me.'

*Typical, always trying to keep their allies one step down,* Walter thought as he overheard the conversation. At least things were on the up; he still got to take the tour and chat with David and Neal again.

'Hey fellas,' Walter said, approaching the two cyborgs. 'It's me, Walter. Do you remember me?'

'Walter, hi,' Hobbs said as they all began to follow Tactician out the door. 'Of course we remember you. Fine work at the prison.'

'How are ya, mate?' Jacobs said, his ocker slang sounding hilarious through the cybernetic respirator. His voice combined with his ludicrous buzz-saw hand almost set Walter into hysterics.

Walter still wanted to learn about their technological implants, but how to bring it up? Childish giggles were certainly not the answer.

He made idle chitchat with the two cyborgs as they joined Minister Ray, Kim and Tactician at the door to the sealed lab facilities to begin the tour. Perkins had already left, but remarkably, no one even noticed the MIB was gone too. Unremarkably, no one cared what happened to Lex the stenographer.

'What's beyond these doors is classified above top secret,' Tactician said, pausing at the hermetically sealed door.

*Spare us the theatrics, Son,* Walter mused. Somewhere in a parallel universe he imagined Stan had taken drama instead of science.

Tactician opened the door and led the group inside the mysterious laboratories beyond. Walter was privy to some amazing tech but was still impressed by what he saw.

They walked down a few stairs and into a large medical laboratory. Scientists and doctors of all types buzzed around the various experiments. They were led towards a group of scientists in hazmat gear fussing over some test tubes.

'This is where we're perfecting a serum based on the stem-cell manipulation used to create your Super Trooper,' Tactician said to Hobbs. 'We call this particular dragon head Project Cannon Fodder. Perhaps we can work together on finding some volunteers, eh?'

'I already have a couple of people in mind,' Hobbs said, his electronic voice suddenly taking on a sinister dimension.

'What's that over there?' asked Minister Ray. 'Looks like a big tank of slime and a whole bunch of machine parts.'

'This is where we maintain some of our lesser known Manifest agents: Chainsaw, Clawsaw and Waterman,' Tactician said, gesturing towards the water tank. 'We believe that Waterman is actually a refugee from another planet and we're hoping to gain his trust in order to learn his secrets.'

'Fully funded by Xenotech Inc of course,' Kim added.

'Do you mean to tell me you have an alien being running loose?' Minister Ray was alarmed. 'This is a major security issue! How many other aliens do you know about?'

'Don't panic, Minister,' Tactician said soothingly. 'For one thing, we haven't confirmed whether or not Waterman is an alien being. We merely think so based on his physiology, language and what he's told us. However, he could be lying and that's what we're hoping to find out.'

'Do you mean you can't tell if he's an alien?' Hobbs asked. 'Surely that would be easy to determine.'

'Actually, it's not,' Tactician replied. 'He could just be a human that's Manifested into something that resembles an alien. Remember that from what we know of Manifests, it appears absolutely anything can become a Manifest, and the range of their abilities is apparently limitless. Putting Waterman in a highly monitored team of "specialists" is the best way to resolve the issue of whether or not his origins are terrestrial.'

'How many of these little black-ops teams do you have?' Minister Ray enquired.

'Quite a few,' Tactician said, 'and we were hoping to work with the Warden here on another one.'

'Oh yes?' Walter was taken by surprise. 'My men are already occupied keeping that prison from rioting.'

'I was thinking more of the inmates,' Tactician said. 'We could put together a group of villains for the government. They would be expendable and deniable and totally under our control.'

'That actually sounds like a good idea,' Walter said. 'We'll talk about it out of session.'

'How do you keep all of this a secret?' Minister Ray asked. 'Surely these superhero teams you influence don't know about all of this. It would be a public relations nightmare.'

'We use misdirection,' Tactician revealed. 'We currently have the HSA scouring the countryside for phantom Satanists to try and avert a non-existent apocalypse.'

'You expect me to believe that?' Minister Ray scoffed. 'No one would buy that for a second.'

'Teenage superheroes would,' Tactician said. 'Now, if you would just accompany me over here.'

Tactician led the group towards another door and out into what looked like a manufacturing facility.

'But this, gentlemen,' Tactician said while stretching his arms in an all-encompassing movement. 'This is our *pièce de résistance*.'

All that could be seen were machine parts moving along conveyor belts and the constant clang of automation.

'What exactly are we looking at?' asked Jacobs.

'This is where we're creating a future for the human race,' Tactician said with a hint of melodrama. 'This is the dawn of the War Droid 25Z, or Braided Disposers as the prototypes have been nicknamed. We're starting to mass-produce a whole line of these androids based on the successful testing of the prototypes.'

'What can these machines do?' Hobbs was forever on the lookout for new military acquisitions.

Tactician led them toward a thin humanoid robot with six arms bristling with lethal attachments and two long coiled whips that extended from the back of its head, 'As you can see from this proto-type, this machine is equipped with multiple strike capabilities. These so called "braids" have a variety of functions, from communications to self-defence.'

*They do sort of look like braids, but what kind of pansy would name a deadly killing machine a Braided Disposer? Sounds to me like the inventor was a fag.*

'They're programmed with a sophisticated AI that can not only detect and subdue Manifests, but can also be used to determine friend or foe scenarios in standard military or civilian situations,' Tactician boasted. He led them towards another door on the other end of the manufacturing plant. 'You could use them in your prison, Warden.'

'I sure could,' Walter concurred, imagining how much easier life would be with a couple of these things in his hands. The group reached the next door.

'There's one last thing I want to show you before we finish the tour,' Tactician said, typing a code into the keypad. The air hissed as the door opened.

Tactician led the group through the door and down a long corridor illuminated by rows of fluorescent lighting. They walked past several doors, all of which contained little rectangular windows. The whole place resembled an asylum to Walter.

They were approached by two efficacious looking doctors as they reached the final room in the corridor. One doctor was male and the other was female. They both wore lab coats and carried clipboards. The woman had an eye patch over her left eye.

Walter was intrigued.

'Is she ready?' Tactician asked them.

'Yes...uh, sir,' the male doctor said, obviously unaccustomed to working with military types.

'Excellent.' Tactician turned to face his entourage. 'Gentlemen, please allow me to introduce you to Patient 1432.'

\* \* \*

### Undisclosed location: 10 April 34 BZ

Courtney Yeht had felt the group approaching since they'd arrived at the complex. The floor had told her there were visitors just by the extra vibrations their footfalls had caused when they walked around. The floor heard every little thing.

Not even the padded cell could stop the tiny reverberations as they travelled from their source, down the corridor and up into Courtney as she lay chained to the wall. Her blonde hair was matted and hung down across her slumped head, which matched her slumped body. It was hard to keep her eyes open with the constant regime of drugs being pumped into her, let alone adjust her immodest hospital gown for her imminent guests.

She would have cared once upon a time, but now she felt nothing at all. She was used to these people talking about her like she wasn't even there and this time was no exception. She remembered the anger she used to feel being treated like a thing, completely helpless and alone, but now it stirred no emotion whatsoever—it just was, as if her whole life has been spent in this cell.

Suddenly the vibrations grew more intense, and the floor told Courtney that her guests had arrived.

'Gentlemen, please allow me to introduce you to Patient 1432,' said a youthful voice on the other side of the door. Courtney could actually hear his voice as well as feel the vibrations through the padded floor her captors installed in a failed attempt to stifle her powers.

'A moment please,' said another timid voice, which Courtney recognised as Phil, one of her doctors. Phil was always kind to her. 'Can everyone please check the soles of their shoes for any pebbles or mud that may have been stuck there and remove them before we go in. Just a precaution, you understand.'

'Is this really necessary?' asked an unfamiliar male voice.

'I can assure you it is,' said a female voice known to Courtney, and belonging to Amy, the doctor who was always mean to her. 'Gentlemen, this eye patch I wear is not a fashion choice. A couple of months ago, I got careless and went in there with a pebble stuck in the sole of my shoe. Patient 1432 took control of it, and I lost an eye.'

*I remember that now,* Courtney thought. *I was so angry at the time.*

'Is everyone done?' said the youthful voice. 'Excellent. In that case, once again, gentlemen, please allow me to introduce you to Patient 1432.'

The door to Courtney's cell opened and her guests finally arrived. A group of strange men—including two that appeared more like machines—shuffled into her cell, followed by the two familiar doctors. She didn't need to look directly at the group to see them; the floor told her everything she needed to know.

'Why am I staring at a half-naked child chained to the wall?' asked the same voice that complained about their shoes earlier. 'This seems highly inappropriate.'

'I assure you it's totally necessary, Minister,' said the voice that had introduced her twice before finally entering the room, his body armour leaving a unique vibrational pattern. 'Appearances aside, this teenager is an incredibly powerful Manifest.'

'What? Like a Class C?' asked a new voice, sounding rough and gravelly like the deep beneath the floor. 'Because if she's a CBE, then this little room isn't nearly enough to contain her. Maybe she should be moved to the prison, where we at least have Manifest null-fields to suppress their abilities.'

'We believe she's a CBE, Warden,' the man in armour replied, 'but we've neutralised her personality to make her more malleable. She currently has the ability to control rocks and dirt as a sort of telekinesis, but we believe she is capable of generating earthquakes and landslides.'

*You think so small. Can't you hear the deep rumbling bass of the continents as they sing to me? The rhythmic bubble and flow of the mantle, or the core, as it spins in symphony with the others?*

'Besides, we do have a null-field set up in here,' Phil said, 'but we only have it on when we're not around—we *are* trying to enhance her abilities, after all. Under a controlled environment of course,' he added.

'Yes, she's starting to calm down and become more passive,' Amy agreed. 'We haven't had any trouble since she had her little tantrum over a month ago when I lost an eye.'

*I forgive you. I just don't care enough anymore. I'm happy just lying here listening to the music of the Earth and the vibrations of the staff.*

'Where did this girl come from?' the Minister asked. 'Is she an Australian citizen?'

'Her origins are unimportant,' the man in armour said, 'but now that you have stage three membership we can tell you about the *Counter-Manifest Terrorism Act 1979* that allows nations with stage three membership to detain a suspected Manifest of any nation that they believe could potentially become a threat to national security at any point. It was under this Act that we obtained Patient 1432.'

'That seems highly inappropriate,' said one of the machine men in his respirator voice. 'Abducting people off the streets and turning them into weapons for shadow governments—it's against our Constitution!'

'Don't forget, Commissioner,' the Warden said, 'now that Australia has stage three membership, you have the authority to detain suspected Manifests yourself.'

'Well, now that you mention it there are a few suspects we've had our eyes on,' the Commissioner conceded. 'So perhaps we should get another few of these rooms set up.'

Courtney was used to people talking in front of her like she wasn't there, but there was something about this Commissioner that troubled her. The vibrations told Courtney that he was invading her personal space, and she forced a peek through her web of hair.

She saw a helmeted face with glowing eyes and respirator looming over her with a big chainsaw hand held close to her face.

'Aaaah, get away from me!' Courtney screamed, the shock causing her to completely wake up.

Suddenly the ground shook and a large stone pillar smashed up through the floor in front of Courtney, knocking the Commissioner out of the way.

'Holy shit!' someone yelled.

'She attacked the Commissioner!' Amy cried.

'No, it was just self-defence,' Phil said, urgently trying to retrieve another syringe full of sedatives.

'Are you all right, Neal?' asked the other robot-man.

'I'm fine,' the Commissioner said. 'As the doctor said, I'm sure she just got a fright by my appearance.'

*Well, it is hideous,* Courtney thought as Phil injected her with another dose of happy juice. He told her it would be okay and she didn't resist.

'I think it's time to bring this tour to an end,' said the Warden as he started to usher everyone out of the room.

'Amy, we need to find Patient 1432 another room pronto,' Phil said, trying to take control of the situation.

'Doctor, a word,' said the armoured man as the group walked out of the room leaving Courtney alone. 'How could you be so reckless as to risk the lives of this delegation by switching off the null-field? I will have to personally review the security of this dragon head, it appears.'

'But Mister…ah Tactician is it?' Phil replied. 'The null-field *is* on.'

*It tickles,* Courtney thought, drifting into unconsciousness to the symphony of the Earth.

\* \* \*

## Xenotech International Hotel, Zurich, Switzerland: 13 April 34 BZ

Naomi stretched her latex outfit to expose more cleavage as she applied the finishing touches to her dominatrix look. *Luckily this guy is into being bound and humiliated so I don't have to fuck him,* Naomi thought, hooking the whip onto her belt.

'Hey baby, hurry up in there,' came a drunken Russian voice through the door.

*Déjà vu.* She opened the bathroom door and sauntered into the bedroom suite. 'Now who's been a naughty boy?' she asked in perfect Russian.

Vsevolod Rasskazov certainly began life as a naughty boy, but now he was pure distilled evil of a stronger proof than the vodka he was drinking. To the socialites of the Swiss banking scene, he was a precocious emissary bringing new opportunities from the former Soviet Union, but to the Kaiser he was a front man for the Russian mob. A front man who wasn't paying tribute for the privilege of operating in Western Europe.

To Naomi, however, he was just a perverted bondage deviant who liked wearing nappies and soiling himself while being whipped. She would bet her standard fee that the mob didn't know about *that* little fetish. *Why do I always end up with the freak shows?* Naomi wondered.

Vsevolod looked pathetic parading around the bed in nothing but a pair of giant nappies, begging for a spanking, and Naomi had a hard time holding back hysterics. It was short-lived, as from the smell in the room she could tell that he'd already cut loose with some unholy anal expulsion.

*Jesus Fucking Christ on a pogo stick, is that curry?* Naomi thought as the tang of vindaloo danced across her tongue. *I'm going to increase my standard fee after this or find a new line of work.*

'Goo goo gaa gaa,' Vsevolod said as he rolled onto his back and wiggled his limbs in the air like an infant.

*Die, you fucking twisted loser!*

Naomi sat down next to him on the bed and stroked his belly— before quickly standing up and whipping him across the underside of his thighs. 'Naughty boy gone and soiled himself!' Naomi yelled.

*Might as well have some fun with this while I'm at it.*

'Waaah!' Vsevolod cried and rolled away from Naomi towards the middle of the bed.

Only then did Naomi notice his necklace, which had twisted around the wrong way when Vsevolod was lying on his back. The necklace itself was just a plain leather strap, but it was threaded through the eye of what appeared to be a stone rune. *I wonder if it's worth anything?*

Suddenly the windows shattered and something large rolled into the room, its form obscured by the heavy blackout curtains. Naomi instantly leaped from her spot on the bed and pushed Vsevolod towards the ensuite and away from the window.

Moments later, bullets tore through the bed as an armoured figure emerged from the curtains, firing from the silenced miniguns mounted to his gauntlets. Large belts fed the twin barrels and the bursts of gun-fire were reflected in his chrome power suit as he relentlessly raked the bed.

'*Scheiße*,' the armoured man swore through his faceplate as he noticed for the first time that his target had moved.

'Big guns, power suit—you're just a poster-child for the '90s aren't you?' Naomi said from her new position next to the intruder. Before he could react, she drove her elbow into his face, cracking his visor and sending him sprawling into the glass table in the corner.

Vsevolod was nonplussed by Naomi's acrobatics and instead saw his chance to escape, muttering 'I can't die like this' in Russian as he ran past her towards the door.

*That's my pay packet making a getaway.* She flicked the whip she was still holding, which lashed around Vsevolod's ankle, causing him to trip and fall before he could reach the door. His sodden nappy squelched when he hit the carpet.

Before she could react further, she was blindsided by the attacker's gauntlet as he returned to the fray with a swift punch to the back of her head. Naomi tripped over Vsevolod as he scrambled to escape and careened face-first into the wall.

She barely had time to think before the attacker raised his left mini-gun and began firing at her. In one fluidic motion, Naomi sprang from the floor, drawing the blade hidden in her boot, and threw it through the intruder's ammunition belt as she ran across the bed and circled around behind him.

Her assailant continued to shoot at her while she did this, until he finally drew a point-blank bead on her as she drew close to him.

*Click.* The severed ammunition belt had been expended.

'*Scheiße!*' he swore again, bringing his right minigun to bear.

He was side-tracked by the big television set Naomi slammed down on top of his head, and only managed to shoot the cheap vase on the remaining side table.

Meanwhile, Vsevolod had freed himself from the whip and resumed his flight for the door.

'Not so fast, Spanky,' Naomi said, lunging towards the fleeing Russian. She grabbed for the back of Vsevolod's head, but was tackled from behind and grasped his necklace instead. The gunman wrestled with her, and Naomi could only watch helplessly as Vsevolod finally managed to open the door and flee into the corridor outside, leaving his necklace behind.

*Motherfucker.*

Her attention returned to the armoured man she was entangled with, who was currently tapping buttons on the back of his right hand.

'As I suspected, you are a Mani...' he began in German.

'Uh-uh, that's not for public consumption,' Naomi hushed, punching him straight in the facemask and smashing the back of his helmet into the ground. *But you're a Manifest too. I sensed you just before you crashed the party. Luckily, I'm harder to detect.*

She extricated herself from the attacker and pursued Vsevolod into the corridor, still clutching the necklace she'd inadvertently taken from him, but leaving the whip behind.

*Wish I knew who you are and whether you're trying to kill me or Spanky.*

No time to think about that now—her final mortgage payment was getting away.

He hadn't gotten far and was making his way down the atrium stairs from the mezzanine level to the main lobby. Ironically, Vsevolod had chosen a room on the mezzanine rather than a penthouse suite to keep a low profile on his sexual proclivities, yet here he was making a mad dash through the busy lobby in a shit-stained nappy.

The bystanders must have heard the gunfire despite the hi-tech suppressors the attacker had used, but seemed completely oblivious to the danger they were in. Yet none of them missed the grown man in a soiled diaper sprinting past them like a lunatic.

Before she could hurdle the bannister and chase after Vsevolod, she noticed movement out of the corner of her eye and her reflexively jumped to the side just as a burst of gunfire pockmarked her previous position.

A moment later, the assailant came running out of the corridor and into the atrium, but Naomi was waiting and tackled him over the balcony and down to the lobby below. She used his bulk to cushion her fall and rolled off him and back onto her feet in a single motion, then sprinted after Vsevolod.

Not even Blind Freddy missed the commotion this time, and he joined his able-sighted fellow bystanders in running screaming from the lobby.

Vsevolod wasn't among them, having already bounded through the reception doors and out into the valet parking area outside. Naomi followed the trail of excrement drops to the front doors.

*If I ever have kids, I must remember to never buy that brand of nappies,* she thought, exiting the hotel and running into the sunlight.

The onlookers outside were caught up in the chaos, as the fleeing hotel patrons infected them with their panic. Sirens could be heard in the distance.

*Fucking terrific.* Naomi scanned her surroundings for her target. *Aha!* He was making a beeline down the road to her left. *Still time to get paid.*

Naomi's budgetary concerns were interrupted by the ricochet of bullets off the flagpole to her right. She turned around to see the familiar sight of her tenacious pursuer. *Persistent fuck, but luckily a terrible shot.* At least now she knew he was after her, rather than Vsevolod.

'Who the fuck are you?' she asked him in German, as he closed the gap between them. 'Why are you trying to kill me?' She followed the question with a sudden roundhouse kick that collected her assailant on the side of the head.

'I can't answer you when you kick me in the face,' he replied in the same language, recovering from the assault. 'I'm Heist. Perhaps you've heard of me?' He slowly began to raise his remaining minigun at Naomi, hoping she wouldn't notice.

'Yeah, well assassinations don't fit the MO of the Heist I've heard about,' Naomi said as she caught sight of Vsevolod close to the taxi rank in the distance, taking one last look at the fight.

'I'm not an assassin,' Heist said. He suddenly raised his minigun level with Naomi's face and fired.

She'd anticipated this and knocked his arm aside with her left hand—causing Heist to shoot wildly—and neatly take off the top of Vsevolod's head just as he opened the door to the taxi.

*Perfect! Mortgage is as good as paid.*

'Now I can give you my full attention,' she said coldly, suddenly producing several more knives from her boots. 'I don't like liars and I don't like assassins. Well, *other* assassins that is.'

'Wait, you're an assassin?' Heist said uncertainly. 'I think there's been some sort of misunderstanding. I wasn't aware...'

'I wouldn't be doing a very good job if everyone knew who I was,' Naomi said, flicking her wrist and sending a stiletto flying through the other ammunition belt. 'Whoever paid you to take me out didn't give you very good intel.'

'But I'm not an assassin,' Heist repeated.

'Liar! You've been shooting at me all morning!' Naomi spat, as she prepared another blade for flight. 'If I had my full kit here, you'd be dead already.'

Heist ducked just as Naomi threw her blade, which merely sliced off the antenna on his helmet instead of slicing through his visor.

'*Scheiße!*' Heist cursed, rolling to the side and assuming a defensive posture. 'Wait! Let me explain!'

Naomi ran at him and dropped into a slide, kicking his legs out from under him, followed by a sharp elbow to the middle of his face-mask. The entire helmet cracked and flecks of blood could be seen on the inside of the visor.

'Now explain,' she commanded. She stood up, putting one foot on Heist's throat and calmly lighting a cigarette she produced from a tin pulled from one of her two belt pouches. She could see the special police squads approach from down the main road towards the hotel. 'Talk!'

'I…I'm a thief, as you know,' Heist coughed through his shattered helmet. One blinking eye could be seen through the cracked visor. 'I'm not here to kill you. I'm here for that necklace you're carrying.'

Naomi looked at the necklace she was still absentmindedly holding.

'Yeah, well you entered the room with guns a-blazin' and didn't make any fucking enquiries into any fucking necklace,' she snapped.

'You weren't meant to be there, and then I thought I sensed a Manifest, but wasn't sure and I panicked,' Heist confessed, his voice taking on a nasally tone.

'Quit your whining, you pathetic fuck,' Naomi said. She pressed down harder on his throat while dragging deeper on her cigarette. 'Now tell me what's so special about this necklace.'

'It's a rare artefact,' Heist blurted, 'worth a fortune.'

'Don't lie to me!' Naomi said, dropping her cigarette butt through the hole in Heist's visor. He squirmed violently.

'It's true!' he yelled. 'But it's also got magical properties—apparently.'

'Go on.'

'Russian folklore claims that the rune was carved by the witch Baba Yaga centuries ago for another immortal woman as a kind of failsafe against her husband, who some say was Merlin the Magician. Dumb bitch went and lost it, I guess. It's basically a set of instructions for summoning something, or so the legend goes.'

*What absolute crap, but it is valuable…this could be my nappy bonus.* 'Who sent you to get it and for what purpose? Going to summon up Excalibur and maybe even King Arthur to wield it to save us from Merlin the fucking Magician?'

'No one sent me,' Heist said, trying to catch his breath. 'I'm a thief, remember? I heard of the legend and thought it would make a nice addition to my collection. That's the truth.'

Naomi believed him this time but wasn't going to admit it to him. The police were rallying at the street linking the hotel with the main road, and Naomi didn't want to stick around for high tea.

'It's pretty cool,' Naomi admitted, turning the rune over in her hands. 'I think I might keep it, while you can stay here and talk to the cops. Consider yourself lucky I don't make a handbag out of your skin.'

'Nooo!' Heist yelled as he found a hidden reserve of strength and knocked Naomi's leg from his throat and lunged for the necklace.

'Yes,' she replied coolly. She kneed him hard in the underside of his jaw, causing his faceplate to fly off. He dropped him like a sack of shit.

Naomi quickly got up and ran from the scene, ignoring the calls from the police to freeze and darted around the side of the building and out of their line of sight. While she ran through the side streets behind the hotel she used one of her knives to slice her latex outfit around her waist. She pulled the top half over her head and threw it in a dumpster as she passed.

She didn't slow down, and opening the other pouch attached to her belt, produced a sports bra and bandana, which she quickly adorned. A pair of sunglasses completed the look.

*Which should be just enough of a disguise to let me slip out of the area unnoticed.*

Only then did she notice the flashing bracelet on her freshly exposed arm. She grabbed it on opposite sides and gave a quick squeeze.

'I'm here,' she said into the bracelet in English.

'It's me, Magnet,' said a voice from her wrist.

'I know who it is,' she said. 'No names.'

'Sorry.'

'What do you want? These calls cost a fortune.'

'I had to warn you,' said the voice. 'Scar put out a hit on you when you stopped working for him.'

'Fucking loser. First, he gyps me my fee for the Commissioner and the Field Marshal, and now this. Those two were dead when I left them—how could I anticipate that Dr Q would turn them into fucking cyborgs? Goddamn motherfucker. What's he going to do, send his gang of clowns after me?'

'He's really pissed about how you resigned.'

'So I gave him an extra scar. Guy's covered in them—that's his gimmick.'

'You shoved a blade up his arsehole, for Christ's sake!'

'He probably got off on it,' Naomi theorised. 'I still don't see why

I should care. I mean, I appreciate the sentiment in warning me, but Scar's fucking small-fry. That's why I moved onto bigger gigs in the first place.'

'Even so, I've been talking to the rest of the gang and we want you to come back home so we can watch your back,' the voice said.

'Not likely.'

'Rumour is he's hired Gorg.'

'Gorg?' Naomi said. 'Guy couldn't afford him. Besides, no one's even sure if he exists.'

'Scar's sure,' the voice said. 'Come home please, if only for a couple of beers.'

'I'll think about it,' Naomi promised, looking closer at the carved symbol on the rune. 'I have one more job I have to do first, but I can probably find time after that to drop in and say g'day.'

'Sounds like a date,' the voice said. 'Take care and I'll see you soon.'

'You too,' she said. She squeezed the bracelet again and the blinking light went out, ending the call.

*Fucking Gorg, eh? Prick sure can't take a joke.* Yet she couldn't shake the sudden uneasiness that came upon her.

* * *

### Parramatta: 14 April 34 BZ

Manipulator dwelled incessantly on her master plan and was oblivious to the growing discord among her chosen members of Terror Australis. As usual, she stood on the walkway above the old factory floor and gazed vacantly on the gathering while the undead worm, Segment, slithered around her legs.

More commotion than usual caused her to look down on the unfolding scene below. A short guy with silent-movie-villain facial hair and silly costume was awkwardly carrying the group's mountainous lunch order. A rabble of supervillains swarmed the hapless errand boy and soon his arms were empty.

'Hey, someone took my lunch!' he complained as they returned to their chosen territories within the abandoned cement factory.

'That's what you get for being a loser,' replied the Jamaican light-ning-man, Velocity, from over his shoulder as he walked away.

'But that was the last of my money,' the loser said. 'I don't get my dole payment for another fortnight.'

'Then you're living up to the name Captain Povo,' said Vaccumax, who really shouldn't have been criticising anyone, for anything. 'Any-way, you said you were going to rob the place—real supervillains don't pay for their lunch.'

'Yeah, but I forgot that they didn't stock any paint I could throw in their face and then dry solid with my powers,' the Captain said defen-sively. 'And it was too hard to lug a couple of tins all the way there. They don't put these industrial complexes close to any major outlets, you know.'

'Bumblers! Boobs! Poltroons!' Manipulator suddenly yelled to the motley crew below. 'You stand on the cusp of a new era of humanity and you squabble over scraps like pigeons!'

'I got your lunch right here, boss,' said the familiar voice of Beam as he sidled up alongside her with a foot-long sub.

'I'm the harbinger of doom for *Homo sapiens*,' Manipulator exag-gerated, hamming it up for good measure. 'I do not eat fast food.'

'I gotcha a meatball one like ya always have,' Beam said. 'But that fat shit Brund will always eat another one if you don't want it.'

'Or I could have it,' Captain Povo proposed, as the possibility of food sent him running up the stairs to the walkway.

'Meatball, you say?' Manipulator asked after seeing that the Cap-tain wanted it. 'Okay, as civilisation doesn't have much longer, I will indulge myself this once.'

'Aww,' the Captain sighed, missing out on yet another meal.

Beam took this brief respite from Manipulator's ranting, plus his edible peace offering, to broach a delicate subject.

'Uh boss,' he said, already expecting a verbal lashing. 'Ah've been talking with the troops an' we were wonderin' when we're gonna get underway.'

Instead of firing off a volley of aural abuse, Manipulator simply turned and looked Beam in the eye as she quickly finished chewing and swallowed her mouthful.

'Walk with me,' she said, leading him away from the group and into another part of the factory. Segment, as always, followed along behind.

'Surely we got enough members already,' Beam ventured when Manipulator said nothing more. 'There's about twenty of us already, including some guy with a big fucking vortex in his chest who showed up earlier...'

'His name's Vortex,' Manipulator said through a mouthful of food.

'My point is that everyone's getting really restless. How many more guys we gotta wait for?'

'Three more,' Manipulator said. She finished her sub, throwing the wrapper on the ground—supervillains laugh in the face of litter laws—as they walked down another set of stairs to a secluded part of the factory. 'Two of which are incredibly powerful, one above all. If we move without them, we will be undone.'

'Yeah, well, if they take much more time then we'll be undone anyway,' Beam said, walking up to a faded painted sign on the far side of the room. 'That Russian beast creature Rabboon is a fucking bag of unpleasant surliness, and sooner or later, either that annoying twat Vaccumax or that whiny frog, the Mole, are going to set him off. Either that, or that fucking dinosaur thing is going to get all *Jurassic Park* on us, or that militant North Korean wanker Flybye is going to set off a dirty bomb or something. Or we can be discovered by the cops. There's so many ways this can turn sour.'

'Have you finished your whinging?' Manipulator asked. 'You need to have faith in the stars—our future is written there and only I can see it.'

'Well, the stars say you've got one fortnight left 'fore people start leaving,' Beam warned. 'That's the ultimatum I was told to pass on. Only that Chinese dragon guy has any patience with you, boss. The only reason everyone else's staying is because they think they're getting paid—they are getting paid, aren't they?'

'Yes, ruling the world will be payment enough,' she said, 'but before you interrupt again, *you* at least will be getting a more monetary reward.'

'Truth be told, that's all I really care about,' Beam said. 'By the way, boss, why are we here staring at some beat-up sign for "Fatty's Cement

Works"? Geez, who'd fucking want a great big ugly picture 'a them on the wall like this anyway?'

'I picked this location for a reason,' Manipulator said. 'There's a ley-line running through here for a start, but the main reason is there's a connection in this very spot to someone I thought gone long ago. Just how that's even possible I have no idea, but it must be an omen.'

'Who is it, boss?' Beam ignored the ubiquitous omen reference.

'My ex-husband,' she said, 'known to most mortals as Merlin.'

'Say what now?' Beam was astonished.

'It's true,' Manipulator replied. 'I met him long ago, back when I went by the mortal name of Hilda. We even had a child—a malformed abomination that I cast out, no doubt a result of his poisoned seed. He was betrayed by his closest confidant and I used that opportunity to put a hex on him and free myself from his influence.'

'So, one of those whole "can't walk the earth again" type of curses?' Beam queried, getting into the whole story.

'Even better than that,' Manipulator said. 'I cursed him to never walk the earth again as long as I live!'

'Um…and you actually added that extra line about "while you live" at the end of your curse?'

'Of course I did,' she snapped. 'I'm not stupid.'

'So, what's to stop him from having you killed?' Beam asked, to his immediate regret.

Luckily, they were interrupted by the descent from above of a grown man dressed like a bee.

'Greetings,' said the new arrival as he buzzed above them. 'I've flown a long way to join your group.'

'And who might you be?' Beam enquired.

'I'm the Bee,' he said, ceasing his hovering and landing on the ground.

*Apt,* Beam thought. 'Is this who we've been waiting for?' he asked Manipulator.

'Remember how I told you we were waiting on three more arrivals and two of them were really powerful?'

'Yeah sure, boss,' Beam said. 'I remember.'

'He's the other one,' Manipulator said, turning around and walking back to the main area.

\* \* \*

**Vatican City: 17 April 34 BZ**

Lorraine Freeman wandered aimlessly through one of the gardens inside the walled city, happy to have a moment to herself. No doubt the garden she was currently strolling through had deep cultural significance, but to Lorraine it was simply a pleasant respite from her hectic tour of the globe.

Officially she was modelling some new range of perv-wear in Rome, but then she got an official invite to meet the Pope, and with a few days free in her busy schedule, it seemed like a good idea. *Especially as Mum wasn't invited and had to stay at the hotel.*

Luckily there were plenty of other sights for tourists to see in the city aside from Lorraine, but her current Jackie Onassis look was a good precaution nonetheless. It was getting late and there weren't too many people strolling around at this time on a Sunday.

She had thought the Pope was nice enough, but wasn't expecting him to be a fan. She just assumed he got swept up along with everyone else.

*Everyone except that one cardinal who seemed to eyeball me pretty hard, and not in the way that guys usually did. I guess you can't please everyone all of the time, even if that's your superpower,* she thought, absentmindedly examining the leaves on a bush.

Lorraine's thoughts returned once more to her tumultuous year so far, focusing on how it all started.

*Teenage rebellion.*

She didn't think her mother was likely to have thrown away the water pipe she had made, considering it became a Manifest at the same moment she did.

*Man, the whole thing is still all so surreal. What the hell are these Manifest seeds that they can grant powers to a human and consciousness to a bong?* No one had explained that to her before.

Suddenly a feeling came over her akin to a combination of déjà vu and someone walking over her grave, which she'd learned to recognise as the sensation of another Manifest close by. She turned around to be confronted by the same glaring cardinal from her earlier meeting with the Pope.

'Cardinal Ejigu, you startled me,' she said, subconsciously taking a step away from the holy man. 'What are you doing in the gardens so late?'

'I could ask you the same thing,' he replied, his Ethiopian accent barely noticeable through his refined speech. 'One does not usually walk around the Holy City without an escort, especially after a meeting with the Holy See.'

'Well, I asked if I could take a look around and everyone was only all-too happy to oblige.' Lorraine smiled. 'Everyone seemed so friendly that I thought why not?'

'You can cease with the act, witch,' the Cardinal said with the unfortunate tone of someone who's deadly serious and instantly casting a sinister air over an otherwise amicable conversation. 'We both felt it in there earlier and know what each other is.'

'Yeah, you're the nutter calling me a witch,' Lorraine said defensively, her adrenaline starting to flow. Yet she *had* felt it before—this guy was a Manifest.

'His Holiness and the rest of the College may have come under your spell, but I am immune to your charms,' he grinned. 'I know your secret, so you may as well confess. It may just save your soul.'

'I have no idea what you're talking about,' she lied, 'but maybe you better lay off the sacramental wine and let me be on my way.' There was no way she was confessing anything to this zealot.

'I knew you were going to say that, witch, and that's why I brought *this*,' the Cardinal boasted, producing an ornate dagger from his scarlet cassock. 'This blade has performed many sacred deeds for the Holy Inquisition and it's only fitting that it strikes down the Whore of Babylon herself!'

'Who are you calling a whore?' Lorraine asked with false bravado, backing away from the oncoming Cardinal. She was just about to run away when she tripped over a fallen branch and fell backwards against the massive wall enclosing the city.

'In the name of the Father, the Son and the Holy Ghost, I banish thee demon back to Hell!' Cardinal Ejigu yelled as he exploited Lorraine's fall and drove the dagger straight at her heart.

Lorraine screamed.

The blade snapped as it hit her chest.

*Huh?* Lorraine and the Cardinal both thought simultaneously.

Lorraine was in shock and quickly looked again at the spot where the blade had struck, but her skin wasn't blemished, let alone haemorrhaging.

'It cannot be,' the Cardinal muttered. 'It's the work of the Evil One, it has to be.'

'Looks like Jesus loves me more than you,' Lorraine teased, having gained more courage after the failed stabbing. 'Now get the fuck off me!' She shoved the Cardinal in the chest, and to their mutual surprise he was pushed off his feet and landed in a heap about five metres away. He lay still with arms and legs akimbo.

Lorraine slowly rose to her feet, trembling from the assault and the subsequent unexpected display of superhuman strength on her behalf. *I wonder if the Cardinal's okay,* she thought, a little panicked. *He looks hurt pretty bad—I hope I haven't killed him!*

Cautiously she approached the Cardinal's prone form, looking for any indication he was alive. Then she realised that the feeling of a nearby Manifest was still there.

Suddenly the Cardinal sprang up into a kneeling position, still brandishing the broken dagger in his hand. His left arm and right leg were obviously broken, yet he showed no signs of discomfort.

'No! You won't corrupt me like you've corrupted the others,' the Cardinal bellowed, his already intense eyes cranking up to eleven. 'My soul will remain pure!'

'Wait…what are you doing?' Lorraine asked, suddenly realising where this was going.

The Cardinal didn't answer, instead he softly recited one final prayer before thrusting the broken blade into his jugular and digging across his windpipe. His gurgling body fell limply to the grass, leaving Lorraine alone and completely bewildered as to what to do next.

One thing was certain, however: she would never forget this night even if she lived to be a hundred.

\* \* \*

## Grand Satanic Headquarters: 19 April 34 BZ

Gavin inspected the leftovers in the fridge, which seemed to him to be a hundred years old. *Maybe it's some ancient pasta of the gods and the fridge was built to enshrine it,* he pondered, trying to discern exactly what it used to be. Suddenly the leftovers appeared to move and Gavin decided that the muesli bars he'd spied in the cupboard earlier were the best choice for munchies. *If only I'd remembered to bring popcorn,* he thought.

That week's meeting had been more of the same: going over the plan, working out who would be in charge of which invocation point, and what that creepy Persian guy Navid had been up to. Gavin's recent change of status to Chosen One was still a secret—not to be revealed until the special anointment ceremony almost two weeks from now.

*I've never been anointed before. I wonder if they'll actually use oils or whether that's only in the movies.*

It was his post-meeting Chosen One 'training' that made him stick around after; in fact, he was spending more time there than at home in recent days. Not surprising, considering his training consisted of shagging Karen and getting wasted while she chanted over him.

He'd also experienced Merlin Mondays firsthand, which turned out to be nothing more than Karen muttering in her sleep and getting all sweaty.

*Heh-heh, and I can help her out with half of that equation.*

'Hey baby, when are you coming to bed?' Karen called from the back room as if reading his mind.

'Just looking for some munchies,' he replied, 'and I'll be right there.'

'You didn't bring any popcorn?'

Gavin ignored the comment, instead grabbing the box of muesli bars and heading to the bedroom. 'The Chosen One has arrived,' he announced, strutting into the room and beginning to undress.

'Yes, you have,' Karen said seductively as Gavin threw off the last of his clothes and joined her in the bed. Immediately she began touching and stroking him, playing with his beard. 'Mmm, your sexy goatee is really getting some length to it.'

'Thanks, I've been going for the Fu Manchu look,' Gavin joked, 'but it looks more like ZZ Top.'

'That's because a beard like yours is one of the signs of being the Chosen One,' Karen purred.

*Uh-huh. This really is all just a bunch of complete nonsense, but it's nonsense that comes with hot sex, so I'm in.*

'Then why isn't ZZ Top the Chosen One?'

'Because *you* are the Chosen One, silly,' Karen said playfully, with the twinkle of lunacy in her eyes.

*Gotta love zealot logic.*

Gavin left the thought unspoken. 'So, what's Navid up to again? You said he was eyeballing someone? Does he need any help with that?'

'Navid is on a special mission keeping eyes on the sacrifice, and requires no assistance from us,' Karen revealed, always eager to talk about the master plan. 'Hell demands a balance and the sacrifice will be needed so that the High Mage can return to the mortal plane. It will all become clear to you as Chosen One on *Walpurgisnacht*.'

*Even in a world where a sentient, flaming, toilet-seat man is a reality, that's way too farfetched.*

'Okay, and then the High Mage is going to give us the spells to conjure specific Lords of Hell at each of the points of the pentagram, right?' he asked, making sure he got the story right so he could continue with the sex. 'And the Grand Satanic Headquarters is going to be at the centre, and you're going to summon a demon lord here?'

'Well, not in the bedroom, you duffer.' Karen laughed. 'That would be ridiculous. No, I'm going to summon it in the meeting room.'

'How will you fit one hundred and eleven people in there?' He suddenly remembered his muesli bars and unwrapped one. 'It seems a little small.'

'The power of Satan will prevail,' Karen promised, actually meaning it. She took a bar for herself.

'So, what's the name of the demon lord you're going to invoke again?' Gavin said between bites.

'Ooblog, the Dark Lord of Perverse Molestation,' Karen unbelievably said with a straight face.

*There's only one thing I can say to that.*

'I feel a strange power overcoming me,' Gavin said, hamming it to the max. 'I feel I'm channelling Ooblog now and he wants me to perversely molest you.' He dived at Karen friskily tickled her, muesli bars forgotten amid her giggles.

*Fuck the High Mage, fuck the SS Dreambook and fuck Ooblog,* Gavin thought, unsheathing his chosen one and beginning to get Karen sweaty. *Life is good and not even the fucking apocalypse is going to spoil it for me.*

\* \* \*

### Australian War Memorial, Canberra: 25 April 34 BZ

Bentaz Mullberry flew down to meet the rest of the HSA as they gathered for the dawn service in the section set aside for special guests. Anzac Day was a national event for Australia and the HSA made it a point of showing their respect alongside other dignitaries and the public at large.

Most of the team was there this year, except for a small squad that had been sent to Kakadu to investigate some strange readings that could very well be caused by Satanists. Chuck Cheese was also absent, the team consensus being that the HSA mascot may be seen as disrespectful. Besides, someone had to do monitor duty.

There were also a lot of politicians and military personnel—as to be expected—but Bentaz was waiting on the arrival of one particular person he knew would be there today. *Grandfather hasn't missed a dawn service yet, as it's pretty much the only thing that has any meaning to him—even more so than family.*

There was at least half an hour to go before the ceremony and the sky was still dark. Nevertheless, Bentaz saw his grandfather clearly as he approached from the northern sky. His outfit looked like a cross between Bentaz's costume and a military uniform.

*Although my new costume has Axis's colour scheme.*

His grandfather, Arthur Mullberry, or Ally as he was known to the Hun and the Turks in World War One, had gone from the world's second known superhuman and war hero to retired government agent. They rarely saw each other on account of Arthur disowning Bentaz's dad—something to do with the son not living up to the father's expectations. *So, of course Dad takes the opposite approach, and has no expectations of me at all.*

His grandfather touched down, and Bentaz waited until he'd finished making polite greetings with the other dignitaries before going over to greet him.

'Hi Grandfather,' he said quietly so as not to be overheard and reveal his identity. 'How are you? I haven't seen you in a long time.'

'Bentaz,' Arthur said just as quietly, but coldly. 'I have been doing fine, thank you. I saw your new costume on the news.'

*Here it comes.*

'You disrespect all this day stands for by picking *his* colours,' Arthur continued. 'You are more like your father every day.'

*Maybe he doesn't know I was Axis in my previous life,* Bentaz wondered. *Best not to bring it up then, just in case.*

'He feels that you sold out your fellow Manifests when you worked with Dr Q to develop all of that anti-Manifest technology in the fifties,' Bentaz said 'He doesn't understand that you were also a hero, like I do.'

'That costume is proof you understand nothing,' Arthur said curtly. 'I am to blame.'

'Is that why you let yourself get old?' Bentaz asked. 'We Manifests only age if we want to.'

'My age is my concern,' Arthur said, 'and before you think that I am alone in my folly of believing the government was benevolent, just ask yourself what your government contacts have asked you to do.'

'Hunting Satanists to stave off the apocalypse,' Bentaz said. 'Although I'm not supposed to say anything, so please keep that between us.'

'I will not have to say anything,' Arthur replied, 'because that is the most preposterous thing I have ever heard. Now, if there is nothing else, I should prepare for the service.'

'Well, it's my fifteenth birthday today, and I thought…' Bentaz began.

'Happy birthday,' Arthur said flatly. 'Now, as there are other more important things to do, I will see you later.'

'Arsehole,' Bentaz said under his breath. 'No wonder Dad hates you. I hope you die.'

He returned to his fellow team members just as the service began, already regretting what he'd said.

\* \* \*

**Parramatta: 28 April 34 BZ**

Manipulator basked in the radiant glory of the fiery being that hovered above her and the rest of Terror Australis. Segment took refuge from the glare in her shadow that fell across the walkway.

'You have finally arrived,' Manipulator said in greeting. 'Welcome, White Hot.'

The naked flaming man simply nodded, his brilliance heating the general vicinity.

'Is this him, boss?' whispered the ever-present Beam. 'The one we've been waiting on?'

'Yeah boss, dat 'im?' repeated his maladroit companion Brund, at a much louder volume. 'Can we go now?'

'He is one of the two we were waiting on,' she said, 'but we must wait for the last member to arrive.'

'That'sss why I have come,' said White Hot, his breath making hissing sounds as it evaporated the water in the air, 'to witnesss hisss arrival. That'sss why you sssummoned me with your etheric cord, wasss it not?'

'Yes! YES!' Manipulator cried, finally feeling vindicated. 'As I fore-told, you have arrived for the dawning of Terror Australis! You will act as a beacon for our final teammate and light his way here.'

'Well, he sure is bright,' Beam agreed, with his hand shielding his goggles. 'Probably bring all the fuckin' cops too.'

'Please join the others below,' Manipulator said to White Hot, ignoring Beam. 'I will address the gathering shortly.'

'Of courssse,' White Hot said as he floated down to the others and dimmed his radiance.

Manipulator walked over to the edge of the walkway and grabbed the handrail, gazing down upon her congregation of supervillains while Brund and Beam flanked her.

'My fellow team members of Terror Australis,' Manipulator began, 'you gave me a fortnight and I have delivered. No doubt you witnessed the arrival of White Hot, our newest member.'

'But you said there were going to be *two* more,' called out Dragon-ski, the unfriendly Russian dragon-man. 'Are we not waiting for the last one anymore? Why have we been waiting here then?'

'Yeah! I passed up another job to be here,' roared the Crusher, a New Zealand supervillain that looked sort of like a Tiki with hideous burns. 'Don't tell me I wasted my time!'

'Nobody has wasted anything,' Manipulator replied. 'His arrival is imminent, and once he is here we can begin our conquest of Australia! We will start by razing Sydney to the ground to draw out those insufferable HSA fools, and once we defeat them, nothing will stand in the way of our global conquest!'

'How do you know he will even come?' queried Short Fuse, a D-list villain with delusions of grandeur. His helmet looked like one of those bombs from *Looney Tunes*.

'He will come,' White Hot said. 'That'sss why I am here.'

'White Hot is right,' Manipulator decreed. 'He will come, and I will tell you why: I used the ethereal strings that are attached to Segment here...' she indicated the undead worm creature at her feet, '...to create a pull on his etheric cord, which is irresistible,' she continued, obviously pleased with herself. 'The cord is growing tight, which tells me he will be here soon.'

*He fuckin' better*, Beam thought, *or we are so fuckin' dead when this mob is finally fed up*. On the plus side, he could win the pool on who it will be. Beam's money was on Gorg, even though Brund reckoned it would be Energy Lord. *Dumb shit ain't got a clue*.

'What's so special about that filthy thing?' asked Multiman, a creature that was also a collection of segmented body parts joined together by forces unknown.

'Segment is the last of its species,' Manipulator began, as if around a campfire. 'It came from a distant world that was visited by the embodiment of destruction. Mortally wounded, the creature slid through the dimensional portal the destroyer had come from, where I found it and gave it a new unlife.'

The Dinoman ululated at this revelation, adding to the already absurd atmosphere and setting off Dogman in a howling retort.

'Enough of this sideshow!' decreed Flybye, shaking his metallic turbine arm in the air. 'I demand we act now or I am leaving! Who is with me?' he yelled at the rest of the group.

There was an immediate raucous uproar, followed by a low-pressure wave of squabbling. Dragon Kong, the other dragon-man, quietly looked at the Unknown alien beside him, who also remained silent—content to protectively clutch the glowing stone it carried.

By now the general ambiance had degenerated into a chaotic mania and Manipulator sought to dominate the scene once more.

'Silence, you fools!' she cried. 'The hour is upon us. Behold: he has arrived!'

Manipulator extended her arms in a wide embracing gesture towards the dark figure that approached through the main entryway.

'Welcome to Terror Australis!' she said to the newcomer.

*Fuck me. Brund's guess may have been dumb, but Manipulator's choice was even dumber. No one's gonna win this pool.*

\* \* \*

### Fatty's Cement Works, Parramatta: 28 April 34 BZ

'Welcome to Terror Australis!' a strange witch-like woman said to Dread Sedgewick as he casually strolled into the abandoned cement works. He stared at the collection of spandex-clad losers before him, with their raving harpy on the walkway above, and couldn't hide his contempt.

'Do you mean to tell me that I've been walking halfway across the country only to discover I've been summoned by a fucking nerd convention?' he asked politely.

A wave of terror suddenly rippled through Terror Australis with scathing irony.

'Vicious Man? Are you fuckin' kiddin' me, boss?' blurted some guy in stylish armour to the witch. He looked like he was about to make a fast exit.

'Fear not!' she cried to the group. 'Vicious Man is an integral part of this group. We must embrace him, not run from him. *I* am the Manipulator. Everyone introduce themselves.'

Dread was affronted by a freak with a vacuum cleaner strapped to his back, who walked over and extended his effeminate hand in an ill-advised handshake attempt.

'Hi, I'm Vaccumax!' he blathered with too much enthusiasm. 'That's vacuum spelt with two "Cs" and one "U", in case you were wondering.' His hand remained extended at Dread.

'So, you're illiterate too,' Dread said in disgust, as his hands metamorphosed into their metallic forms, complete with finger-blades. 'Am I expected to actually shake that limp thing and then what? Join a super-team? Is that what this is?'

Vaccumax still had his hand extended, unsure what to do.

'Someone made one major fucking miscalculation,' Dread observed, and lopped off Vaccumax's head without even shaking his hand.

Panic Australis would have been a more appropriate name for the group, as half turned to flee while the rest tried to stop them.

'Wait! Wait! Vicious Man is the important one. Vaccumax was just a sacrifice for the greater good!' Manipulator yelled. 'We have to stick together. It is my destiny!'

'Manipulator, eh?' Dread enquired, licking blood off his finger-blades and retrieving a huge knife from the air with a slash of his other hand. 'Sounds like you're the one who's responsible for summoning me here, so I guess your destiny is to watch me shatter your dreams before I shatter your face. You never know, this could be fun.'

He then showed the remaining members of Terror Australis why he was known as Vicious Man.

'No, wait!' Manipulator cried in vain. 'This is not supposed to happen. You are meant to help me conquer the world!'

'You're a crazy bitch and I'm going to slay everyone here,' he promised, simultaneously kicking a jet-man through a wall and throwing his dagger into the glowing stone some Unknown alien was holding, causing it to explode and sever the alien's hand.

'We do not need you, we can conquer without you,' came the artificial voice of a lanky, segmented creature off to Dread's side.

'Conquer this!' he replied, stomping the creature into its individual parts. He then reached for the blade he'd thrown at the alien and it returned to his hand as if by telekinesis.

'Sorry, boss, but I can't spend the money you're paying me from six feet under,' said the guy in stylish armour on the walkway. 'C'mon, Brund, we're outta here.'

'Traitors! Betrayers!' Manipulator decried as it all fell apart for her.

By this stage most everyone else had fled the cement works too, except those brainless few who wished to prove themselves against the legend of Vicious Man.

'Scurry away, I'll get around to slaying you later,' Dread said. *I must be mellowing out in my old age,* he thought.

'You haven't finished with the Multiman!' screamed a familiar artificial voice from behind Dread. 'Smash me to pieces and I just join back together again!' The creature slashed at Dread with its serrated claws.

'Only 'cause last time I didn't crush your head to powder,' Dread retorted as he fixed his mistake and the arcane energy holding the creature together fizzled away. 'Come to think of it, it's way too fucking bright for this time of day,' he said, looking up. Above him floated a luminescent being that radiated with white-hot intensity. Dread was a little surprised he hadn't noticed him earlier.

'And what's your super power?' Dread asked the fiery man. 'Giving people a tan?'

'It isss one of many of my powersss, yesss,' he admitted. 'But really I'm jussst here to sssee you, the embodiment of dessstruction, before I go on my way.'

'Really?' Dread spat, throwing his dagger at the flaming man. 'Then here's a souvenir, lispy!'

The flaming man radiated even brighter and Dread's blade simply evaporated from the heatwave. 'It mattersss not,' he said. 'I have ssseen what I came to sssee.' He then floated into the sky, waving adieu to Manipulator, who looked like the most miserable person on Earth.

'Well, piss off then!' Dread said, already engaging his next target. 'And who might you be? Scrap Metal Guy?'

'I'm Iron!' decreed the guy in a suit of armour that did indeed resemble scrap metal. 'Tremble at my might!'

'Okay, so you call yourself Iron and you get around in a big metal suit, tossing clichés here and there. Am I right? Derivative Man or

Rip-Off Guy is more appropriate.' Dread slashed repeatedly at Iron's armour, but his finger-blades merely left scratch marks.

'Ha-ha! My suit's impervious to harm!' Iron said in the smarmiest way humanly possible. 'Oh, and for the record, this is technically a second skin—I can't take it off.'

'So you're dickless as well as unoriginal,' Dread pointed out. 'Oh, and for the record, I don't give a prehistoric shit about your fucking case of Manifest dermatitis. All I wanna know is: can you swim?'

He grabbed Iron by the shoulder and (dickless) crotch and threw him over the horizon and into the Pacific Ocean several kilometres away. 'Well, he certainly can't fly,' he said to himself.

His serene reflection was interrupted by an unexpected growl from behind and the feeling of metallic teeth breaking against his invulnerable shoulder, accompanied by a yelping sound. He turned around to see a strange dog-man backing away from him while clutching its metallic jaw.

'Now that's just pathetic,' Dread said, stalking his assailant. 'Bad dog needs to be put down.' He made a quick swipe, and the familiar sight of a soaring cranium delighted his senses. He tried to catch the droplets of blood on his tongue as it sailed by.

By now everyone else had fled the scene and Dread could finally introduce himself to Manipulator. As he approached, he noticed a pink segmented worm-thing with stubby arms and black soulless eyes.

'Howdy, bitch,' Dread said cordially to the pair still on the walkway above. 'I see you've found one of those aliens I thought I made extinct while on a bender in the Abyss. Obviously, that's how you lured me here.'

Manipulator was rocking back and forth, clutching her knees and murmuring something in some kind of catatonic state. The segmented undead alien worm skulked nearby.

'Stop gibbering and talk to me,' Dread said menacingly, which is how he said everything. 'I think you at least owe me the courtesy of explaining this malarkey before I render you inert.' Menacing *and* polite.

Manipulator stared up at him with her blank eyes, misery and defeat reigning across her face. 'I will tell you,' she mumbled, as the worm slithered towards her.

'Hold that thought,' Dread said, stomping the worm to paste without warning. 'I can finally say I made a species extinct. Now continue.'

'This cannot be happening… my destiny…' Manipulator began.

'Your destiny can be a whole lot more painful unless there's more info and less whining,' Dread interrupted. 'Let's make this easy for you: why did you summon me here?'

'You were to be part of my grand design to conquer the world,' Manipulator said, slowly rising to her feet. 'As a final spite upon my ex-husband, I would rule the world like he could not—after I cursed him never to walk the Earth again while I live!'

'That's it? Who gives a shit?' Dread asked courteously. 'You brought me here to kill you just for that? What are you, some comic book villain?'

'But have you not wanted to bond with others to do something with meaning? Otherwise what is the point of existence?'

'There is no point to anything—that's the point,' Dread replied, pulling out a cigarette and lighting it with the sparks from his finger-blades. 'Besides, I'm a misanthropic nihilist. I was going to start my own club for likeminded individuals, until I realised that there's no point because I hate everyone.'

He started chuckling at his own joke before taking another drag. 'Well, this was an interesting distraction, but I must be on my way. Hold still, this won't take a moment,' Dread said reasonably.

In that moment it finally dawned on Manipulator in a display of cosmic irony that it was she who was being manipulated by her ex. He'd tricked her into adding the line 'while I live' and now that loophole was being exploited. It can only mean one thing: he was returning.

Dread finished his cigarette and flicked the butt away, while he broke off a segment of the steel handrail with his other hand.

'No, it can't be. I can stop it,' Manipulator ranted, looking for an exit. 'But I can still recover; I can rise from the ashes like the phoenix. I can…'

Dread swung the handrail straight into Manipulator's face, severing the top of her head which hurtled over the wall and straight into the gaudy sign of Fatty with a loud clang.

'Uh-uh, you don't get to dominate *this* scene,' Dread said, casting the pole aside. 'All this exercise has made me want to take a dump. Where can I find a toilet around here?'

Violent psychopathic killing machine he may be, but even Dread was housebroken. He spotted the port-a-loo from the walkway and made his way down to it, stopping only once to remove a stubby pink arm caught in the sole of his boot.

Dread strode purposefully towards the commode, tearing the plastic door from its hinges, only to discover a cowering man in an obviously homemade costume hiding within.

'You really don't want to be in there when I unleash this colon concerto,' Dread said to the port-a-loo's terrified occupant. 'What's your name, slick?'

'C-Captain P-P-Povo,' he whimpered, wrapping himself in the sheet he used for a cape. 'P-please don't hurt me.'

'Captain, you just wait out here while I unleash hell in there, and when I'm done we'll have a little chat about your future prospects,' Dread said, grabbing the Captain and pulling him from the toilet. 'Don't worry, I'm not evil, I'm just misunderstood.'

Captain Povo seemed unconvinced as the port-a-loo buckled from Dread's rectal assault.

* * *

## South Western Sydney: 30 April 34 BZ

Mark Adams finished washing the last of the dishes and put them on the rack to dry. He was wearing only his jeans and work boots as he disliked rolled-up sleeves, but mostly because he knew that Desci liked the view.

The kids had gone to a friend's house after dinner, which by Mark's calculation gave them at least two hours. *Time to get the love on*, he thought.

'All done, sweetie,' Mark said as he literally swept her off her feet and carried her to the bedroom.

'About time too,' Desci teased, before giving Mark a kiss on the cheek. 'We don't have that much time before the kids get back.'

'I'm not sure I like them hanging out with that Blandley kid,' Mark said, putting his wife down on the bed. 'He seems like such a loser.'

'Life in the 'Fields,' Desci said, playfully rolling on the bed. 'There's a large percentage of them around here.'

'Yeah, like that creepy guy that seems to be hanging around of late,' Mark said, his thoughts diverging from the lewd bearing they'd been on previously. 'I think he's stalking me, always hanging around.'

'What guy?' Desci asked, sexily disrobing. 'I think you're imagining things. Now forget about that and focus, Mister Adams!'

Focus Mark did, and the downstairs neighbours got to endure more plaster falling from the ceiling. Time passed.

*Knock, knock, knock.*

'Must be the kids,' he said. 'Probably forgot their keys again. You can get dressed faster than I can, sweetie—why don't you let them in?'

'Pitiful excuse,' Desci replied, but she nonetheless threw on her dressing gown and got up to answer the door while Mark slipped on his jeans and boots. He still didn't bother with a shirt.

From where he sat on the bed he had a direct line of sight to the front door and enjoyed watching Desci walk to answer it.

Desci didn't look through the peephole and opened the door, expecting to see her children on the other side.

'Forgot your keys, did yo...' she began, until registering the creepy Persian guy standing on the other side. 'Who?'

Mark made eye contact with the stranger as he got up to see who it was.

'I see you,' the stranger said. 'A balance must be struck!'

Suddenly the bedroom door swung shut as if by magic, separating Mark from his wife.

'Desci!' Mark cried.

'Mark!' he heard his wife cry from the other side of the door. 'Mark, oh my god! Help!'

'Desci!' he screamed, frantically trying to open the door. It may as well have been a nuclear blast door for all the good he was having in breaking it down. He could hear Desci screaming from the other side.

Mark desperately turned around to check for any other exit— knowing already that there wasn't—but spied only the ensuite and the bedroom window. Too bad he was several storeys high.

He tried the door again and this time it opened as normal, no indication that it was ever stuck. He flung it open and sprinted through before his brain told him his eyes were lying.

He found himself standing in a large stone room, the walls adorned with hideous faces, leering and mocking in the flickering blue light. The source of the light was two enormous golden pillars that stood as twin sentinels over what appeared to be a glowing golden sarcophagus.

*This is insane. This cannot be.*

Mark looked behind him and could still see his bedroom through the open doorway, like an oasis in the dark nightmare that had befallen him. He looked back towards the interior of this apparent tomb, unsure of what to do. One thing was certain though: he had to find his wife.

'Desci?' he called into the dark.

His voice echoed off the stone walls and took on a haunting tone as it bounced deeper into the black depths behind the sarcophagus.

Something unborn stirred in the deep and began its lumbering gait towards the disturbance.

'Desci!' Mark called again as he noticed a silhouette approaching.

*Wait a minute. That's too big to be her,* he thought a moment before realising the figure wasn't alone.

The flickering light had a strobe-like effect on the figures when they finally came into view, and Mark felt like the world had sunk into the pit of his stomach. A dry nattering sound that conjured images of babies' bones in a skull rattle drilled into his mind.

The demonic visages that pierced his eyes were even worse and Mark found himself frozen to the spot, mostly out of fear but partly out of disbelief. There were four of them: a four-armed, charred corpse with horns; a mummified goat-creature with a necklace of scalps; an orange, winged abomination with long talons and chasms for eyes; and a slouched, shuffling horror that peered at Mark with scarlet eyes from within a mound of human skins—like a ghoulish snail with teeth.

Finally, the surging adrenaline woke Mark from his stupor and the flight instinct took hold. He looked back the way he'd come and spied his bedroom door—and the haven of his bedroom beyond.

He ran towards it, but like a nightmare it seemed to stretch further away from him the faster he ran.

'Stay with ussssss,' rasped a voice that sounded like a body being dragged across a dusty floor.

'Play with us! Play with us!' screeched a second, falsetto, mock-child voice.

Mark ran harder to escape the demons pursuing him, which was when he noticed the bedroom door slowly starting to close.

*No, please, God no,* he prayed, as the ray of light from his bedroom turned into a sliver.

He shoved his hand into the crack just as the door closed and he yanked it open—heedless of the pain in the face of demonic pursuit. He quickly scrambled through the doorway, slamming the door behind him and leaning up against it to hold it shut while he latched the flimsy lock.

Mark could again hear Desci's screams the moment the door closed and he felt gut-wrenching indecision as to whether to open it again.

Suddenly there was a heavy thump on the other side of the door and a terrible scratching began as the doorknob started to turn frantically. The hissing and grunting of beasts comingled with Desci's screams in a ghastly cacophony that threatened his sanity.

*This can't be happening!*

He backed away and into the ensuite—the only remaining refuge and safer alternative than a multi-storey swan dive. He closed the door and turned another flimsy lock, desperately looking around for some sign this was all a dream.

Mark glanced at his reflection in the bathroom mirror, suddenly pausing as something odd caught his eye.

*Red eyes? Why do I have red eyes?* he wondered, noticing his scarlet irises for the first time.

The mirror shimmered slightly and Mark's reflection metamorphosed into a monstrous grey gargoyle with bat-like wings and taloned fingers. Only his face appeared unchanged and his fearful reflection stared back at him from within the folds of the shadowy cowl between the gargoyle reflection's shoulders.

*What the fuck?*

Mark reflexively started grabbing at his body to see if he was actually changing and was relieved to discover he wasn't. The relief was momentary as the gargoyle climbed out the mirror towards him, and he found himself backed up against the ensuite door.

The gargoyle spread its wings and rose to its full height as it clambered over the bathroom sink. A twisted parody of Mark's face taunted him from within its ashen-coloured hood, as if the darkness itself was a mirror.

'Please, stop,' he whimpered at the demon. 'Please just leave my family alone.'

The demon stooped over Mark so that he could be face to face with his twisted visage.

'You summoned us with a blood sacrifice,' it said in a hideous mockery of Mark's voice.

Thanks for the kiss.
You will see yourself soon.

'Wait...I didn't know!' Mark cried. His vision spiralled into blackness while the demon loomed over him, laughing mercilessly.

* * *

### Grand Satanic Headquarters: 30 April 34 BZ

Gavin took guilty pleasure in scratching his nuts with reckless abandon. Lounging around the bed in the back room of Karen's pad had become Gavin's new favourite pastime and an itchy scrotum seemed to be part of the deal.

'Gavin sweetie, are you ready for the big night?' Karen cooed from the ensuite. 'The entire inner circle will be here tonight and as the Chosen One, you will be centre stage. So come now, chop-chop.'

Being centre stage at a weird satanic festival was a mixed blessing for Gavin. While he played the Chosen One angle for some wild poontang that only religious fervour could bring, he was worried that after tonight's failed attempt to resurrect Merlin (as if that shit could ever happen) all of this great sex would dry up like a nun's cunt. Not to mention he would have to go back to his job search requirements. He needed more information so he could start thinking up a plan B for sex.

'Okay, I'm getting up,' he said, slipping off the satin sheets and slipping into his brown Chosen One robes. He'd been anointed with oils so much lately that he seemed to slip everywhere. The ridiculous wizard's cap that went with the robes was the final humiliation and the whole get-up reminded Gavin of a dunce's outfit. 'So tell me, what's so special about tonight that we have to summon Merlin now?'

'Why it's Walpurgis Night, silly,' Karen said, sauntering into the bedroom in her special satanic lingerie. 'Also known as *Walpurgisnacht* in German,' she added.

'Saying it in another language doesn't help me know any more about it,' Gavin said.

'I think it has something to do with demons, witches and darkness,' Karen replied. 'I don't really know, but the High Mage says it has to be tonight. Oh, and you need to stop calling him Merlin—he hasn't gone by that name since Camelot.'

*Such madness. If only the sex wasn't so good.*

Gavin applied the finishing touches to his outfit (fastening the sash on his robe) and walked out of the bedroom and down the short hallway to the familiar coven meeting room. This time, however, it had been converted into a makeshift summoning altar.

Gavin could hear the footsteps of the inner circle as they approached up the stairs from the main reception. There was the usual crowd of Matt, Floyd, Tom and Lancefield, but Gavin was also surprised to see that creepy Navid was there as well. All of them were clad in the drab brown cloaks that the coven preferred.

*Didn't Matt manage to get them at half price?* Gavin idly wondered.

'I thought there always had to be six people at these meetings,' Gavin said to Karen as she joined him from the bedroom, 'but with Lancefield here, it makes seven. Who's he...ah, locuming for if Navid is here?'

'Well, for you, my love,' Karen said as the religious mania began to take hold once more. 'Your role here tonight is that of Chosen One, so naturally we had to fill your place on the council.'

Gavin made perfunctory greetings to the arrivals, his mind suddenly turning towards paranoia. It was short-lived, as Karen looked especially ravishing in her Italian-designed cloak and his thoughts wandered to more carnal subjects.

'Welcome everyone, to *Walpurgisnacht!*' Karen shouted and popped a special bottle of Moet she'd been saving for the occasion.

'Ooh, the fancy stuff,' Floyd commented.

'Tom Higginbottom is so excited to be here!' Tom declared.

'My mum says you can all have a lift home after,' Lancefield announced.

'Party! Party! Party!' Matt started chanting.

Navid remained quiet and continued to look creepy.

Gavin downed his glass and Karen quickly topped it up again, slipping in a sachet of powder as she did so. Gavin was preoccupied with the group's antics and didn't notice.

'Tell us, Navid, about the balance,' Karen said above the din. 'Was it struck?'

'Yes, the balance was struck,' Navid responded quietly. 'The unbeliever was dragged away to Hell.'

*Dragged away where? Why has this night taken a sudden left turn at Albuquerque?*

'And his family?' Karen asked.

'The wife was the only other one home,' Navid said, 'and she screamed for a bit when it all went down, but I just used the chloroform on her and put her on the couch to sleep it off.'

'Excellent work,' Karen said. 'No point turning a missing person case into a homicide. Satanists may laugh in the face of law enforcement, but there's no point drawing attention when we're so close.'

'Agreed.'

'Well, now that's confirmed we can begin the ceremony,' Karen proclaimed, topping up Gavin's glass again. 'What do you say, sweetie?'

'Huh?' Gavin slurred, swooning from the Mickey Finn. 'Yeah sure, whatever.'

'Then it's settled,' Karen stated, leading Gavin toward the decorated altar, which in reality was simply the conference table covered in a tie-dyed sheet. 'Just hop up here, sweetie, and we'll begin.'

The others had to help him onto the altar, as he was starting to lose all motor control and couldn't make the simple climb.

Gavin was happy to lay back and go with the massive head-spin he was experiencing. Karen chanted bizarre gibberish over him, while the others gave a satanic rendition of Gregorian chanting.

*Fuck, I am so wasted,* he thought, all his worries drifting away in a drug-induced euphoria. *Happy to go through all of the nonsense if all the days are like this.*

*They won't be,* said a sudden sinister voice from within Gavin's mind.

'Did someone say something?' he mumbled to the group as they danced their spooky dance around him, with obvious inspiration drawn from Michael Jackson's 'Thriller'.

*Yes, but it wasn't them,* the voice replied. *Only you can hear me.*

*Great, now I'm hearing things. Must be the drugs.*

*It's not the drugs. You are the Chosen One,* the voice continued. *Did you ever wonder what you have been chosen for?*

*This doesn't bode well.*

*You have been chosen to host my consciousness to complete my escape from Hell.*

*I'm having a drug-fuelled psychosis,* Gavin thought as the world spun around him.

*Hell demands a balance,* the voice went on, *which is why someone had to take my place there, but you... you will be my vessel here.*

*This is getting really bad. I think I may need an ambulance.*

*Atheists make the best sacrifices for these things,* the voice revealed. *For in that instant, when they finally realise that it's all true, they open their soul up completely, making it ripe for harvest and allowing it to become host for another entity.*

*This can't be real,* Gavin thought, but he lacked conviction.

*Can't you feel the truth in it?* the voice urged. *Everything that's happened to you with the coven has led you to this moment.*

*But... it just can't be. Then again, I always wondered why they allowed a doubter like me in the inner circle.*

*The good fortune, the recruiting of a locum... all the sex...* the voice persisted.

*It's true,* he agreed. *I can see it now. It's all been a set-up from day one.*

*Yesssssss…believe…*

*I can see it now. I <u>do</u> believe.*

*Finally!* the voice screamed within his mind. *After so long I am free!*

*I…* was the last thought Gavin ever had. His consciousness slipped into oblivion and his soul became food for his body's new inhabitant.

'I exist,' said Gavin's body with a new voice.

'So it was written in the Satanic Scriptures, and lo it has come to pass,' Karen decreed as dramatically as she could upon hearing his utterance. 'My fellow members of Lucifer's Coven—behold, the High Mage of Hell is reborn!'

# May

## White: 34 BZ

*Free! Free of the pit! The sacrifice will sustain me until I can continue in my goal. Upwards, ever upwards.*

\* \* \*

## Grand Satanic Headquarters: 1 May 34 BZ

The High Mage of Hell stared at his unholy congregation from within the husk of Gavin's body and basked in his newfound freedom. No words could describe the relief of escaping Hell, and thus none were given. Instead it was straight to business.

'My coven, I have come from very far away to finally address you on this auspicious night,' he rasped, still acclimatising to a body after being formless for millennia. 'For today is now Beltane in the Northern Hemisphere, and thus I am reborn in the final moments before its Southern Hemisphere inversion.'

The High Mage paused for effect (which worked well in Camelot), but could see that although many centuries had passed since he last walked the earth, the same vacant stare could be seen on the faces of the populace.

'Hail Satan!' Karen replied.

'Hail Satan!' the rest of them parroted.

*Dolts! How did these fools possibly free me from Hell?*

'As it is written in the Satanic Scriptures,' he began, ignoring their stupidity, 'I have come to walk in the light once more, to tear asunder Heaven's gates and drag the False Creator down into the dark.'

'Is that why we're planning the big event?' asked Floyd. 'Will destroying this False Creator bring about the End Days?'

*Only for this reality, for I will replace the False Creator and forge the universe anew in my image.*

'You are quite perceptive,' the High Mage lied, 'for you will all be kings of Hell for eternity!'

This time his pause provoked the right response as the inner circle cheered.

'First, I have errands to run on the mortal plane,' he explained. 'Then I can begin the astral ascendance to the Gates of Heaven.'

'In the meantime, my mum can give you a ride wherever you need to go,' Lancefield interjected. 'I'm Lancefield, by the way.'

'I know who you are,' the High Mage revealed. 'I learned all your names from the High Priestess here, as well as the local vernacular. That is irrelevant, however, as I have no need of steeds in my journey.'

'Well, actually she drives a punch-buggy,' Lancefield blabbered. 'Did they have cars in Camelot?'

*What is this buffoon blathering about? I should flay him with a scourging spell. I should flay them all with a scourging spell.*

'Don't bother the High Mage with that now,' Karen interrupted before scourging spells could be cast. 'He probably wants to eat first and maybe have a bath or something.'

'Yes, a roast boar would fill the belly,' the High Mage agreed, starting to grow accustomed to his host body. 'Though I will forego the bath as we never once bathed in Camelot and it didn't seem to harm anyone.'

*Besides, half the time we seemed to be wading through lakes looking for ladies.*

'Tom Higginbottom wants to know if you eat tofu, as roast boar is in short supply around here,' Tom Higginbottom said, breaking the High Mage's inner thoughts.

'But you are Tom Higginbottom,' the High Mage replied, almost confused. 'I will eat the flesh of any beast, no matter what it's called. I have craved meat for too long to be picky. Part of the torture in Hell was being forced to eat this rubbery white paste they called the devil's cum.'

'Well, it's not boar, but it's just like it,' Tom Higginbottom said. 'Certainly nothing at all like you described. Tom Higginbottom will whip up an organic salad to go with it.'

'Spare me the shrubbery and just bring me the meat,' the High Mage commanded dismissively as Tom went about his errand.

'Excuse me, mister High Mage, sir,' Matt ventured, 'but… ah, I was just wondering whether you will need a change of clothes. You can't really walk around dressed like that. I know a good tailor who could…'

'Fool!' the High Mage bellowed. 'The Chosen One was made to wear these robes especially because they were what I wore in the court of Camelot! What could possibly be wrong with my attire?'

'It's just that times have changed and wizard-garb is no longer in fashion,' Matt continued unperturbed.

'How dare you question the High Mage!' Karen shouted. 'This is Sydney, not the catwalks of Paris!'

'I was just worried about drawing too much attention from super-types,' Matt persisted relentlessly. 'I was at that Satanist convention last week getting these half-price robes and a lot of the smaller covens have been complaining about being hassled by the HSA…'

'Enough!' the High Mage said menacingly.

'Yeah, Satanists laugh in the face of superheroes anyway,' Karen bragged.

*I should roast their skulls and suck out their eyeballs! Although there is one I have yet to hear speak who looks like he could have potential.*

'You must be Navid,' the High Mage said, approaching the Persian in his hangout at the back of the room.

'Yes, and it's an honour to meet the exalted High Mage,' Navid answered with surprising obsequiousness. 'And I just have to say that being creepy is my shtick, but you pull it off like a natural. Tell me, is that why Gavin grew that beard, so that you could have the whole Saruman thing going on?'

*Are these children in adult's bodies? They babble such rot. Maybe I should curse them with the creeping necrosis?*

'What is a mage without his beard?' the High Mage said instead of inflicting the pain of instant decay upon the group. 'Now that my stupid wife has fulfilled the curse she cast upon me long ago, my first stop will be to pay a visit to my porcine, mutant son. The only reason I sired that abomination was to be a future storehouse of power, should I ever need it.'

'Not like the child you sired in me during our dream sessions,' Karen said, dropping a bombshell on the group. 'I'm several weeks pregnant.'

*But not with our child.*

'You will be due to give birth around the time of the great event,' the High Mage predicted. 'All part of my grand design that has taken millennia to unfurl.'

Karen attempted a round of maniacal laughter, but it fell flat after her initial outburst.

'Firstly though, I must ensure your loyalty,' he said, finally choosing a spell to cast. Suddenly a pink mist began to emanate from his shirt-sleeves and waft about the group. 'My obedience spell will ensure you will carry out my plans flawlessly. But presently I hunger, however. Tom, where is my meal?'

'Tom Higginbottom's just finished cooking,' Tom called back from the kitchen.

'Good. Then I shall feast on this tofu creature, and finally satiate my desire for meat,' the High Mage said, eagerly anticipating his first meal after escaping Hell.

* * *

### Liverpool Hospital, Sydney: 2 May 34 BZ

Desci Adams woke with a start to find herself in an unfamiliar environment. The beeping of monitors and accompanying drip made it obvious that she was in a hospital, but she couldn't recall how she got there. Then suddenly it hit her.

'Mark?' she called out. 'Mark?'

'Mum, it's okay,' said a familiar voice from beside her.

'Obie?' she said groggily, turning towards her son. 'What's going on?'

'You're in hospital… you've been…attacked,' Obie said hesitantly.

'I remember, sort of,' she said. 'That strange man came to the door and… Wait, where's everyone?'

'Samara and Sebastian are asleep on a couch in the lounge,' Obie replied, fidgeting with his long black hair. 'It's two am, Monday morning. You've been in and out of consciousness since Saturday. The doctors say that the worst is over, though.'

'Where's your father?' Desci asked, starting to feel anxious. 'Is he okay?'

'Dad's miss...' Obie began, before the flimsy hospital curtain was suddenly thrown open.

'Mrs Adams, please excuse my intrusion,' said a suave looking man in a nondescript suit and tie. 'I'm Detective Sam Shanks and I'm investigating your assault.'

'Where's my husband? Where's Mark?' Desci said, now trying to sit up. 'Did you say he was missing?' She looked at Obie.

'Yeah, he wasn't home when we got back...' he began, before being interrupted again.

'Please, Mrs Adams—Desci—may I call you that?' Sam continued without waiting for a reply. 'Desci, can you tell me what happened?'

'Well, as you probably heard through the curtain, I was home alone with Mark, my husband,' she said, getting emotional. 'Anyway... there was a knock at the door and I thought it was the kids coming home, but instead it was a really creepy looking guy...'

'Please go on,' Sam coaxed.

'He said something like "I see you" to Mark and then went on about a balance or something,' she recounted. 'Then the bedroom door slammed shut and that guy was putting a cloth in my face. Next thing I remember is waking up here.'

'Oh Mum, I'm so sorry I wasn't home,' Obie apologised.

'It's not your fault son,' she soothed. 'You may have been hurt, so I'm glad you weren't there.'

'Can you describe your assailant?' Sam inquired, almost disinterested.

'He was about six feet with dark hair, almost middle-eastern,' Desci said. 'I can't really remember what he was wearing. A tracksuit, I think.'

'I see. And since then no one has seen your husband... Mark, I believe you said,' Sam stated around a yawn.

'That's right. Dad was gone when we got home, and when we found Mum we called an ambulance,' Obie offered. 'That was Saturday night, maybe about eleven o'clock.'

'Can you describe your husband?' Sam asked, looking at his watch.

'I have a photo in my purse, but I don't know where my handbag is.'

'Here, Mum, we brought it with us when we came here with the police,' Obie revealed, retrieving the handbag from the bedside chest of drawers and handing it to his mother.

Desci fished around in her vast handbag with preternatural efficiency and quickly produced the aforementioned photo of Mark. 'Here it is.'

'Ta,' Sam said, snatching the photo and casting an eye over it with dramatic flair.

'So, what happens now?' she asked the detective. 'I need to get out of here to look after my children.'

'The doctors say you need to have a few more days' observation,' Sam replied. 'They detected chloroform in your system, but not enough to cause the severe reaction that you had, so they want to monitor you for a bit. In the meantime, are there any friends or family that your children can stay with while you fix up that body of yours?'

*Was that a come-on?* she wondered.

'We can stay with Nathan and his mum,' Obie suggested. 'We're over there all the time anyway—I'm sure they won't mind.'

'That Blandley kid? Your father and I don't really like that little wart, but I guess we have no other choice.'

'I'll give them a ride when I leave,' Sam promised. 'Why don't you go wait with your siblings while I finish up with your mother?'

Obie kissed Desci on the cheek and reluctantly left the room. 'I'll make sure we all say goodbye before we go,' he said on the way out.

'What did you want to talk to me about?' she asked cautiously.

'Desci, I believe that your husband is working with this man, which explains why he's missing. A single man couldn't possibly carry him off alone.' Sam said. 'Also explains why the bedroom door shut and he didn't come to your aid.'

'Mark would never...' she began.

'It's the most likely possibility,' Sam interjected. 'But I'll begin looking anyway. I'll send in a sketch artist tomorrow to try and get an idea of who we're looking for.'

'You need to find my husband,' Desci pleaded. 'We love each other—he'd never do this to me.'

'Look, I'll be frank,' Sam said. 'Finding a guy of middle-eastern appearance in Sydney isn't going to be easy, especially if your husband is with him and trying not to be found.'

'I just told you, Mark would never...'

'*Unfortunately*, this is my last week on the job, as I'm taking up a new position with the SWAT over in LA,' Sam said. 'So, I'll get some help from a couple of the cadets, as my mind will be on other things. The only reason I'm here at two in the morning is the overtime.'

*Did he really say that? Or are the drugs still in my system?*

'Did you just fob me off?' She was horrified. 'This is highly inappropriate. I want to speak to another detective.'

'I'm afraid the Sydney police force is understaffed at the moment,' Sam lied, winking at her as he did so. 'Don't fret. I'll make sure someone looks into it before I go.'

'I should think so,' Desci said, too tired to get too riled up.

'Okay, well thank you for your cooperation Miss Adams,' Sam lied, making to leave.

*That's Mrs, you jerk.*

'I'll send your kids in before I take them to their friend's house,' Sam said, turning to leave. 'Last chance to tell me what your husband was really into.'

'I think you should leave,' Desci said tersely, now fuming. 'And I don't want you driving my kids anywhere.'

'What do you take me for?' Sam asked, taking offence. 'I'm an officer of the law, not some psycho child murderer.'

*You're a dickhead, is what you are.*

'But being the generous man I am, I'll let you off,' Sam said as he walked out the door. 'Now, I'll go fetch your litter so you can say goodbye.'

*Pig!* Desci raged, but she secretly feared for Mark...and her family.

\* \* \*

### Fatty's Cement Works, Parramatta: 3 May 34 BZ

Walter Screw sparked up his Cuban cigar to hide the stench of dead supervillain.

*What a mess,* he thought as he surveyed the abandoned factory and the dismembered bodies therein. He exhaled the smoke in a long sigh. *At least it gets me out on a field trip.*

'What's the situation?' he asked one of the dozen or so special investigators who were buzzing about the scene—official ranks undisclosed as part of standard Manifest operations.

'Well, sir,' the man answered, 'we have four corpses and a dead worm creature, plus an arsenal of discarded weaponry. There were signs of multiple persons having been here and we think they were rogue Manifests.'

'Any witnesses?'

'Just one,' the investigator replied. 'That North Korean jet-man, Flybye, was beat-up pretty bad, but he's alive. We've already taken the liberty of transferring him back to the Powder Keg's hospital.'

'Liberties should never be taken when the security of the prison is at stake,' Walter said curtly. 'Next time, wait for my orders.'

'Yes, sir,' the man said.

*Always show them who's boss.*

'Anything else I should know?' Walter checked, puffing on the acrid cigar. 'Have you identified the victims? Do you have any suspects? Speak up, man!'

'Well, we...' the man stammered, sweat noticeably beading on his worried forehead.

'Well, we don't have all day—there are schedules to keep,' Walter interrupted. 'You're on the clock now that I'm here, so go find out—chop chop!'

'Yes, sir!' the man chirped.

*Heh-heh, I think he shit his pants,* Walter thought, watching the nameless underling scurry away to carry out his orders. *I better look around myself.*

He walked over to the closest body, which lay sprawled unceremoniously on the muddy and pitted concrete floor. It was also missing a head. *Is that a vacuum cleaner strapped to his back?*

'Never seen this loser before,' he muttered, walking further into the defunct concrete factory.

The next body appeared to be a big pile of white plastic and Walter wouldn't have recognised it for what it was if it weren't for the evidence markers dotted around it. He took a closer look.

*Geez, Manifests are fucking strange. That looks a bit like a toy Stan used to have as a kid. Couldn't get enough of it until the day I threw it out to help make him a man.*

Walter looked from the plastic debris and his eyes followed what seemed to be a natural course to the next body and then up the stairs to the final one—and it all fell into place.

*This was the work of one guy who basically just strolled in and killed everyone. That narrows down the list of suspects at least, but the flipside is we're dealing with a Class B Manifest most likely. Fuck.*

The next body was again decapitated but resembled a beast rather than a man. The canine head lay upside-down nearby and stared at him with blank, upturned eyes.

*I know this one—Mutt Guy or something. Filthy creature had it coming.*

He kept walking until he'd climbed the stairs to the metal walkway that overlooked the factory floor. Just to the left of the stairs was the final body as well as the squashed, pink paste that was most likely the dead worm creature. More nameless investigators fussed over the remains.

'Another beheading,' Walter said as he spied the lump of raw meat on the end of the female corpse's neck, her jaw jutting from her now-exposed cleavage, 'except not as clean as the others. This one must have been personal.'

*And I think I know just who did it. Double-plus fucking ungood.*

'Who's this woman?' Walter asked one of the investigators on the walkway.

'Are you talking to me, sir?' asked the closest investigator.

'No, I'm talking to the corpse,' he quipped with rapier sarcasm. 'Where's the rest of her head?'

'Oh, for a minute there I thought you were asking who *I* was,' she replied.

*As if I care who you are.* Walter chewed the stump of his stogie absentmindedly.

'The rest of the head is down over there, sir,' the investigator stated, pointing at some garish sign advertising the cement works. 'But it's a mess. We can't identify her.'

'Find out all you can,' he said distractedly. Something odd had caught his eye.

'Yes, sir,' she said to his back as he turned and walked back down the stairs.

Walter paced the short distance from the staircase over to the remains of a port-a-loo, its entire base buried in a quagmire of faeces. The malodour alone seemed to be responsible for the deaths of several small vertebrates that lay in the immediate vicinity.

'Fuck me drunk, that's worse than mustard gas,' Walter gasped, reeling back from the stench and its unspeakable origin.

'I've been told that an unidentified giant took a dump over the port-a-loo, except they can't find its footprints,' said a welcome voice from behind.

'Son,' Walter managed to say between coughs. 'I was wondering when you'd show.'

'Tactician, remember, *Warden*,' Tactician scolded, his suit whirring as he walked over.

'Whatever. No one heard,' Walter snapped in annoyance. He paused to look at his cigar. 'There's no way I can smoke this after inhaling those fumes,' he said, snuffing it out with his boot. 'I'm lucky I didn't ignite the gas, come to think of it.'

'You can't contaminate the crime scene with that,' his son said.

'Trust me, it can't get any more contaminated after *that*, which requires a full HAZMAT team to clean up,' Walter observed, gesturing at the shit-bog. 'Besides, I know who's responsible.'

'Your white whale, eh, Ahab?' Tactician mocked.

'True enough,' Walter admitted. 'I do have a special cell under construction for his inevitable capture. But all this isn't merely wishful thinking on my part. Three beheadings and two stompings, plus that unholy mess—it can only be Vicious Man.'

'That matches with what we know of the assailant,' Tactician agreed, 'but if it *is* him, then we have no idea where he's gone.'

'We knew he was heading east as we've been tracking him since Coober Pedy,' Walter said, trying to move the conversation away from the port-a-loo. 'This appears to be what he was coming for. The question is: where would he go from here?'

'The UN will find him—with help from our allies, of course,' Tactician said dryly. 'Dealing with Manifests is all part of our global strategy.'

'Just like eventually disarming the American populace?' Walter asked, causing them both to chuckle.

'As long as most people think it's a just a crackpot conspiracy theory, then we'll do it by stealth and create the conditions necessary for the US to upgrade to stage five membership,' Tactician said, no longer joking. 'Anyway, I digress. There's something very special not far from here that I need your opinion on. It's only a short walk.'

*I didn't expect to be here this long; I have a schedule to keep. Sounds intriguing, however.*

'Lead the way,' Walter said, 'but don't dawdle.'

'It's five minutes, tops,' Tactician rejoined, as the sound of the servo-motors in his suit responded to the increased activity. 'By the way, we have identified three of the bodies: Dogman...'

*Dogman! That's his name!*

'...Vaccumax, and Multiman—who coincidentally was a Manifest version of my favourite toy growing up,' Tactician continued as they walked along a disued footpath. 'I never did find out what happened to that...'

'I threw it out, mystery solved,' Walter said. 'I take it the woman is a still a Jane Doe?'

'You threw it out?' Tactician reeled from the revelation.

'Get over it,' Walter said curtly, subconsciously grooming his moustache. 'The woman?'

'No...we haven't identified her yet, but we will,' Tactician promised, almost sullenly. 'Strangely enough, that worm creature may be the second most interesting thing about this case. It's unlike any other life form we've encountered.'

'It could be a CEE,' Walter hypothesised.

'Negative. They dissolve when killed—that thing was squashed,' Tactician explained.

'And the most interesting thing about this case would be?'

'That's what we're going to see,' Tactician answered when they were within sight of the outskirts of suburbia. 'This is definitely something for Project Typhon.'

'That reminds me,' Walter began. 'How goes the whole "satanic conspiracy" diversion for your superhuman wards?'

'It's kept them busy, that's for sure,' Tactician said, looking his father in the eyes. 'Those kids have so much zeal, it's exhausting. They've kept away from Project Typhon, however, which was the whole purpose of the cover story in the first place. I've pulled them off the case for more pressing concerns and have them hunting down the rogue supervillains that I'm sure were meeting here.'

'No doubt they'll apprehend these guys, who'll claim it was some sort of failed satanic ritual that went on here,' Walter joked as they approached a rundown house, complete with dilapidated caravan out the back.

'Who'd try and summon demons in an abandoned cement works anyway?' Tactician wondered aloud. They passed through the gate and into the backyard. 'Aren't cemeteries the best place for these things?'

'How the hell would I know?' Walter asked. 'The only demon I ever summoned was your mother.'

Tactician let the comment hang awkwardly (for him anyway) as he led his father towards the caravan. There were investigators there as well, although they were fewer in number and uglier in visage.

*These guys don't look like your average UN taskforce,* Walter thought, feeling the burning stares straight through the visored helmet he used to conceal his identity when out in public.

When they drew close to the caravan, he noticed for the first time that a creepy MIB was standing guard over the caravan's single entrance. He opened the door when they got close. *If one of these guys is here, then this must be big.*

Walter wondered if it was the same one he met before. *They all look the same to me—like inbred bureaucrats. Creepy fucks.*

Walter deliberately avoided eye contact despite the MIB wearing sunglasses, yet he felt the agent's stare worst of all and it made it hard to continue his thought.

'Just go straight inside,' Tactician said, arriving at the caravan's steps.

Walter walked up the rickety steps into the dank caravan, and the reason he was there became immediately apparent. Before him was a standard bland dining table surrounded by a cheap vinyl booth. It was the unknown grey alien lying slumped over the table with a revolver in its hand and its brains all over the wall that was of more interest, however, and Walter forgot about his schedule the moment he saw it.

*Jesus Christ! Is that an alien? Looks like it killed itself—is Earth really that bad?*

The alien appeared to be made out of a hard, chitinous material, which included its red eyes and white teeth. Thick candy-striped tubes connected the creature's chin with its chest, and Walter couldn't tell whether they were artificial or not.

It wore what seemed to be purple and maroon body armour, although it could have very well been a part of the alien's exoskeleton, as it appeared to be made of the same material. The pistol was in its right hand, but its left hand was recently missing—the orange blood matching the chunks of brain that were splattered throughout the caravan.

Walter whistled as he exhaled and took it all in.

'Pretty impressive, isn't it?' Tactician asked from the doorway behind him, where he'd paused without entering completely. 'We're convinced it's an alien rather than a Manifest.'

'Oh yeah? How can you tell?' Walter queried without turning around.

'Initial tests indicate it's made of silicon,' Tactician replied. 'Plus, it appears to be an evolved entity, rather than a mutated one. We'll know for sure pretty soon.'

'You'll have to tell me how a space alien came to commit suicide in a caravan in Parramatta,' Walter said, finally turning around to face his son. 'But tell me outside—there's an overpowering smell of rubber or something in here and I think it's making me lightheaded.'

'That's the smell of its blood,' his son said, backing out of the caravan to let his father exit.

Walter quickly followed and avoided looking at the MIB on the way out. The MIB did nothing except close the caravan door behind them.

'Let's continue this conversation inside the house,' Walter suggested, walking towards the back door. 'That guy gives me the heebie-jeebies.'

'I'm not sure you'll feel any better inside,' Tactician said as they entered the house.

Walter followed his son inside and regretted it immediately.

'So, you only told your sister about the body?' Walter heard another MIB asking the couple that obviously lived here. 'No one else?'

*Another one! Are they twins?*

'Yeah, like I said, I only told May,' the middle-aged woman responded. 'She lives alone and won't tell anyone. You can see why I had to share this with someone though, don't you?'

'Of course,' the MIB said as he stood taking notes. 'Why don't you tell me where May lives and we'll go pick her up so she can actually get a peek of that thing before we take it away? That should give her a bit of excitement, don't you think?'

'Oh, that's a good idea!' Walter heard the gullible woman reply as he walked through the house to the front door. *They'll never be seen again, neighbours either, most likely. Loose ends make for frayed coverage.*

'Now tell me, what's the story with the alien?' Walter said when they found themselves on the sheltered verandah. 'How did it get here?'

'Okay, from the top: we picked up a call from our police wiretap about a dead "monster" our here in the sticks. Police assumed it was a crank, but we knew better, of course,' Tactician recalled. 'We interviewed the couple who live here and they told us they got back from holidays to discover the house has been broken into. The guy went to check if his gun's been stolen—he kept it in the caravan of all places—and hey-presto, dead monster.'

'Do you know why it committed suicide?' Walter asked, pulling another cigar from inside his breast pocket. 'It seems strange to travel millions of light years to Earth, only to rob a house for a gun and then kill yourself.'

'Personally, I think it's got something to do with the severed hand, as the injury was sustained elsewhere,' Tactician said. 'In fact, it was by following the blood trail that we discovered all the other bodies at the cement works.'

'It seems there're a lot of unknowns about this case,' Walter declared before sparking up his stogie.

'That's why we're calling this one Codename: Unknown for the purposes of Project Typhon,' Tactician said, waving the smoke away from his face. 'The biological data alone makes this alien priceless.'

'Regardless of whether or not it turns out to be an actual alien,' Walter agreed between drags of his cigar. 'Truly, it's an amazing find— you'll have to tell me if you figure out its mysteries.'

'Luckily, your security clearance is high enough.' Tactician laughed. 'On a slight change of topic: how goes your project with the Field Marshall and Commissioner?'

'Progressing,' Walter replied, picking a fleck of ash from his black moustache. 'We've narrowed down the field and I have shortlisted a few of the candidates.'

'Oh yeah?' Tactician enquired. 'May I ask who you're considering?'

'Well, Deathspawn, Tanglor and Avenatraitor, for a start,' Walter began.

'Yeah, yeah, easy to control wannabes with terrible names,' Tactician interrupted. 'And?'

'Mind Syphon may have been mentioned...' Walter paused, letting the name hang in the air for effect.

'You've gotta be fucking kidding!' Tactician spat, almost coughing. 'Who's going to lead these psychos?'

'I was thinking maybe Starlen,' Walter confessed, starting to enjoy his son's reactions. 'His nutsack's healed quite nicely since he had an unfortunate accident with a cigar.'

'You mean that General? General Joseph Starlen? His parents must have had serious issues,' Tactician scoffed. '*He* must have serious fucking issues after trying to overthrow the government in a giant fucking robot called Destructo the fucking Destroyer, for fuck's sake.'

'Watch the language, son,' Walter said. 'I brought you up better than that. Anyway, he certainly lives up to his Russian namesake in inspiring fear in his underlings.'

'I guess having "commanded underlings" on his CV means he'd be qualified for the job of leading your team of government sponsored supervillains.'

'Maybe we should call them the Government Villains?' Walter mused. 'Then no one could tell them apart from politicians or public servants!'

'Very droll,' his son groaned. 'Perhaps the UN can…'

'Hold that thought,' Walter said, raising his hand in a 'stop' gesture. 'I'm getting a patch from the prison.' He tapped a button on his gauntlet to accept the call. 'Warden here, go ahead,' he said into the mic embedded in his helmet.

'It's Gordon here, sir,' said the voice in Walter's earpiece. 'The Swiss Government upped the scheduled drop-off by three days.'

*Those fucking cheese-wheel ponces—nobody fucks with my schedule like that. You'd think with all that fucking watch-making, they'd be on time.*

'Okay, who are they dropping off again?' Walter asked, his thoughts in the throes of cultural bigotry.

'Fabian Swartzendruber,' Gordon said.

'Who? That actor?' Walter blurted, still trying to collect his thoughts.

'No, the bank robber. AKA Heist,' Gordon reminded him. 'He was arrested after shooting up some fancy hotel in Zurich. It took them some time to transfer him, as they wanted to try him there first.'

'I remember now,' Walter said. 'Those fucking collaborator Swiss bastards were too good to allow us to try him safely in the Powder Keg's courthouse and insisted on trying him there, despite everyone already knowing where he'd be sentenced to. So, wait a minute—if they've upped their schedule and shipped him three days earlier than planned, then that means…'

'Yes, sir,' Gordon answered. 'They're here now.'

*Mother-fuck. Not only am I in another state, but I'm running behind schedule anyway. And now this.*

'Rick, I trust you to handle it,' Walter said, using all of his willpower to hide his annoyance. 'Send my apologies that I've been held up, but my absence is of vital importance to national security. I'll be there by morning.'

'Yes, sir,' Gordon said. 'You can trust me, sir.'

'Warden out,' Walter said, pressing another button to terminate the call. 'I just love how this modern technology allows me to talk so clearly in real time to someone in another state, while I'm away from a telephone,' he said to his son.

'Indeed,' Tactician said, fiddling with a hi-tech gizmo on his wrist. 'The Swiss dropped off Heist early, did they?'

'How'd you know? Oh wait, of course,' Walter said. 'All these fuck-ing MIB wankers spying everywhere.'

'That's classified,' Tactician said smugly. 'Even to you.'

*More likely you tapped my call through your fancy suit. I taught you well, son.*

'That's okay, I don't want to know,' Walter lied. 'What I do want to know is where the hell Vicious Man disappears to after he finishes slaughtering people.'

'Perhaps he actually goes to Hell?' Tactician joked with unknown irony.

* * *

### The Abyss: Circa 4 May 34 BZ

Dread Sedgewick sat at the bar and clinked steins with a terrified Captain Povo.

'Here's to extra-dimensional escape hatches-slash-watering holes,' Dread said, before downing the stein in one gulp. It was his fifth.

Captain Povo took a timid sip of his beer and cupped it between his shaky hands on the bar. It was still his first.

'Another of your finest,' Dread said to the rough-looking skinhead proprietor on the other side of the bar. 'I'm in a drinkin' mood.'

'There's something new,' the bartender said with dripping sarcasm as he poured the ale. 'So, are you going to introduce me to your flam-boyantly-dressed companion?'

'My good Captain Povo,' Dread began with dramatic flair. 'This is Mosh Lightley, proprietor of the Abyss, and barkeep to the gods.'

'It's a pleasure to finally meet you subjectively,' Mosh said genially, extending a meaty paw to the Captain. 'I don't always get to meet every aspect of myself face-to-face.'

'Uh, thanks, I think,' Captain Povo said, returning the shake. 'I really have no idea what you just said to me, but I'll agree just the same.'

'What he means is: he's basically the subjective face of all reality,' Dread cut-in with his unhelpful explanation. 'He's existence itself, which is why even *I* won't get on his bad side. In fact, this entire bar is an extension of his subjective interface.'

'Now you've lost me again,' the Captain said, desperately trying to keep up with the conversation out of fear he would be slain if he didn't.

'Basically, I am everything,' Mosh began for the billionth time since opening the Abyss.

*Here we go again.*

'If the creator gods are the Yin and the Yang, then I'm the paper they're drawn on,' Mosh continued, rehashing one of his favourite lines. 'I'm also them as well.'

'Huh?' Captain Povo said, now truly lost.

'Okay, once more from the top. I am everything that exists: I am the creator gods, I'm the universe, I'm you, your neighbours' cat—even You the Viewer,' Mosh suddenly said, breaking the fourth wall and turning to address you, dear reader. 'I am all dimensions, all realities and the nothingness in between. Is that clear?'

'Absolutely,' Captain Povo lied, fearing annihilation.

'And because I am everything and nothing, I had to precipitate the creator gods from my own self and then get them to shape all reality from the rest of me,' Mosh resumed with unrelenting verbosity. 'I manifested this bar and now use it as a means to meet aspects of myself subjectively—like you and Dread here. Life is the way that I know I exist and sentience is the means by which I understand myself.'

'This is getting way too deep for me,' Dread interrupted with an emphatic fart. 'How about you quit jawing and pour me another?'

'How about I head-butt you in the face and throw you down the chute for Jypx to snack on?' Mosh said jovially. 'What do you think, White Lion?'

'So now you want my opinion?' complained the nearby white lion-man, who wasn't worth mentioning before now.

'Not really, but I was trying to be inclusive,' Mosh snapped back. 'Those glasses won't clean themselves, by the way.'

'Well, seeing as you're the god of everything, maybe you could just make them clean with your infinite power?' White Lion said.

'Weren't you just listening to a thing I was saying?' Mosh said. 'I may be all that exists, but I require my various aspects to make shit happen. Therefore, *you* clean the glasses.'

'I can't believe I turned down a mission with the HSA to stand here doing menial labour,' White Lion grumbled. 'I'm thousands of years old, for fuck's sake.'

'Then you should know how to do it,' Mosh shot back, before turning his attention back to Dread. 'Have you told the Captain about the bar, or do you want me to?'

'How long have we been here? A couple days? So hard to tell the time in here—it's like a casino,' Dread said. 'Anyway, I just haven't had the time, as I've been too busy drinking.'

'We've been here a couple of days?' asked the Captain, who suddenly looked even more agitated. 'But I'm still on my first beer!'

'Yeah, time's a bit squiffy around here,' Mosh said, playing with his chunky lip stud. 'You'll get used to it.'

'I've lived here my whole eighteen years, so I'm used to it,' Dread revealed, downing yet another beer.

'You lived here, in this pub?' Captain Povo sheepishly enquired.

'Not so much the bar, but rather its basement, you could say,' Dread said, lighting up a cigarette with the sparks from his finger-blades. 'There's a staircase around here that leads to it.'

Captain Povo thought that explained a lot.

'It does explain a lot,' Mosh said to the Captain, 'and provides the perfect segue for me to explain a lot to you—about the bar.'

The failed joke hung in the air unrealised.

'Anyway...here's the deal,' Mosh began. 'The Abyss is your basic establishment. To your right, you've got some booths, the toilets and the stairs that go up to the brothel. To your left, you've got the lounge, and behind you is the stage and dance area. There's also a nightclub, living quarters and a beer garden in space. There's probably more, but that's enough spoilers for now.'

'Don't forget to tell him about the doors,' Dread interrupted, butting out his smoke.

'Be careful with the doors around here,' Mosh said with sudden earnestness. 'While some of the doors are fixed and you can always guarantee what's on the other side, most of them will take you to wherever you visualise you want to go. But if you don't think before crossing the threshold, you could end up anywhere in existence.'

'Most of the doors, did you say?' Captain Povo looked as pale as the powder Dread had started snorting.

'Yep. It's the opposite if you want to get back here,' Mosh explained. 'Whenever you open a doorway, know with certainty that you'll end up here, and it will be so—even if you've never been here before.'

'That's right,' Dread interrupted, appearing somewhat smashed. 'Even though I can create dimensional doorways with my blades, it's really handy to be able to come here to chill just by walking through a door.'

'This place seems really dangerous,' the Captain said, finally finishing his beer.

'Oh, yeah, that reminds me,' Dread said. 'If you ever need to go take a slash in the thunderbox, don't fall down the chute by mistake. They're right next to each other.'

'The chute?' Captain Povo timidly asked.

'That's where I toss all the bar's refuse—like the losers of squabbles—that sort of thing,' Mosh divulged. 'At the bottom of the chute is a cavern, which is home to Jypx—an ancient horror who's fond of red meat—or whatever colour it happens to be. It's really not fussy.'

Captain Povo decided not to break the seal after hearing that, hoping his bladder could take it.

'Another beer for the good Captain,' Dread said to Mosh over his shoulder. He bored into the Captain with his intensely emerald eyes. 'You know, I'm really starting to like you, what with your twirly moustache, your goofy mask...and what is that—is that a bed sheet you're using as a cape? Outstanding.'

White Lion raised an eye-whisker at the remark.

'And what did you say your power was again?' Dread queried, handing another beer to the Captain. 'You must be one tough sumbitch with cojones of steel to schmooze with other supervillains dressed like that.'

'I can make paint dry,' Captain Povo said, feeling like a deer in the headlights. 'With a wave of my hand,' he added, as if that made it better.

'Did Mosh mention the Abyss runs on a strict survival of the fittest regime?' White Lion teased. 'It's true—because he is everyone, he doesn't play favourites.'

'Unless they go behind the bar,' Mosh interjected.

'Don't forget that rule applies to you too,' Dread said to White Lion, who was packing a bong now that he'd cleaned the glasses. 'So lay off the Povmeister.'

'Uh-uh, staff are off limits,' Mosh said, plucking a chest hair from under his black singlet for no apparent reason. 'Unless I'm feeling whimsical, that is.'

'And he's no stranger to whimsy,' Dread said conspiratorially to the Captain. 'See those big metal bolts around the top of his shiny bald head? And see that line that runs right around that same glistening noggin? Well, apparently, long ago he cut the top of his head off and poured strong booze onto his brain—which is why reality is so warped.'

'Is that true?' Captain Povo asked, looking at Mosh and noticing for the first time that he cast no shadow. 'It sounds implausible—even for this place.'

Before anyone could respond, they were interrupted by a slender, vampiric-looking man dressed in a tuxedo, sporting the same hairstyle as Dread: black, spiky and pointing straight up.

'Zoth! Glad you could join us. Have you met the gang?' Mosh asked the newcomer. 'Guys, this is Zoth, one of my many bastard children.'

'Thanks, Dad,' Zoth said, sitting on the stool next to Dread. His pronounced canines flashed when he smiled. 'Of course, I know Dread and "fur ball" over there—only my whole life now. Hey fellas.'

Dread and White Lion both grunted in acknowledgement.

'I don't believe we've met,' Zoth said to the Captain, waving at him from behind Dread. 'I'm Zoth, from the Lightley Management Company.'

'Pleased to meet you,' Captain Povo replied out of politeness and fear.

'Oh please. The Lightley Management Company?' Dread snorted in derision. 'That's just a fancy name you came up with for yourself when sitting around here stoned one night.'

'What do you manage?' the Captain enquired, as if expecting a bar brawl.

'Well, at the moment I manage a small band called Lactose Intolerant that plays here sometimes,' Zoth admitted reluctantly. 'But I'm hoping that Poseidon's Haemorrhage would take me on as well.'

'Who're they?' the Captain asked. 'I've never heard of them.'

'That's my band,' Dread said proudly. 'I'm the vocalist—we do metal.'
Captain Povo was again unsurprised.

'I think you should sign on with me,' Zoth said excitedly to Dread.
*Sigh, here we go again.*

'I told you a million times: I don't need a manager,' Dread said in
frustration.

'We'll see,' Zoth replied, unperturbed. 'Once you start living like a
rock star, and have no free time, you'll change your mind.'

'Sure, sure,' Dread said dismissively. He got up from the barstool
and grabbed Captain Povo by the scruff of his neck. 'But you've given
me an idea. Every rock star drives a nice sports car. I think I'll get one.
Come on Captain, we're going shopping.'

'If I must.' The Captain sighed.

'Hey cat-face,' Dread called out to White Lion as he opened one of
the many doors lining the walls of the Abyss. 'Did you say the HSA
was on a mission?'

'Yeah, that's right,' White Lion responded through a haze of bong
smoke. 'When they were off chasing Satanists…'

*Satanists? That's a new one.*

'…I couldn't be bothered going with them,' White Lion said. 'But
now they're off hunting some escaped supervillain team.'

*And I bet I know which one,* Dread thought smugly.

'Oh yeah,' he said. 'Whereabouts?'

'Around Sydney, I think,' White Lion answered.

'Then we're going somewhere else, and I know just the place,' Dread
said, pushing the Captain through the doorway. 'This is going to be a
blast!'

* * *

### Bondi, Sydney: 5 May 34 BZ

Bentaz Mullberry plummeted towards the city street at breathtaking
speed.

*Time to practise my new dive-bomb technique.*

He passed through a low cloud over the beach and lined himself up with the street. He'd spied his opponents from higher than expected, possibly because he had enhanced vision, but perhaps because super-villains had a tendency to stand out.

Bentaz flew down and along the street at around two metres above the asphalt, keeping his speed subsonic but still extreme for the busy area. He remembered to keep under the sound barrier, as last time he'd smashed all those windows and got a lecture from Tactician because the government had to pay for it.

*Not my fault there's no such thing as Manifest insurance.*

Bentaz drew closer to one of the villains, a two-bit loser known as Iron, according to the government files the HSA had access to. Iron had his back to Bentaz and looked like he was giving a clichéd super-villain rant.

*Going too fast for a snappy one-liner, so may as well try and look pro-fessional,* he thought, closing the distance between them in a heartbeat.

He slammed into the armoured villain at extreme velocity, caus-ing them both to fly through a line of parked cars and into the cor-ner of a building three blocks down. Bentaz emerged from the rubble, unscathed and grinning ear to ear.

'That was *so* cool!' he said to no one in particular as he adjusted his helmet and dusted his pauldrons.

'That was totally irresponsible is what that was!' said an unwelcome voice from above Bentaz. 'You could've killed innocent bystanders!'

'Hey, Powerhouse, pleased to see you,' Bentaz said sarcastically to his teammate. 'Anyway, I assumed you guys had already evacuated the area, given that I got here late.'

'It was the first thing we did when we arrived,' Powerhouse said. 'There's no one around.'

'Then what's your problem?' Bentaz snapped.

'That's not the point...' Powerhouse began.

'You cannot defeat Iron so easily!' declared Iron, suddenly bursting forth from the rubble after waiting for the most dramatic timing. 'Not even the "mighty" Vicious Man could stop me! What chance do you two posers have?'

'Seriously? You're calling us posers?' both heroes said incredulously, as they stopped bickering and stared dumbfounded at the affront to humility posing before them.

'My indestructible armour can withstand any attack, as my pride can withstand any jealous attack,' Iron said, lost in the beginnings of another supervillain rant. 'Armies and nations will be crushed...'

'Oh, enough already,' Bentaz groaned. He grabbed Iron and started shaking him at super speed. 'Maybe if I ring you like a bell, you'll make better sounds!'

'S-stop! I-I th-think I'm going to b-be s-sick!' Iron moaned from within the blur his outline had become. 'Th-the suit is s-sealed!'

Bentaz stopped shaking the villain and Iron immediately began vomiting inside his armour, thin strings of bile dripping out of his respirator.

'Gross,' Bentaz said to Powerhouse. 'How do you get spew out of an indestructible suit?'

'We can't leave him here,' Powerhouse said, failing to see the humour. 'You better fly him to the Powder Keg while I help the others deal with the Russians.'

'No need,' Bentaz said, refusing to let his pompous companion steal the glory. 'His suit's indestructible, right? Then all I need to do's this.'

Bentaz held Iron upright with his left hand and began hammering the top of Iron's helmet with his other hand at super speed, causing the villain to be driven into the concrete footpath like a nail. Bentaz persisted until Iron was buried up to his neck.

'Voila! Temporary holding cell,' Bentaz said, hamming it up to annoy Powerhouse. 'Now, where did you say the others were?'

'Follow me,' Powerhouse said sullenly before flying off.

Iron continued to dry-heave in his indestructible barf bag as they left.

Bentaz followed Powerhouse who streaked ahead, leaving Bentaz trailing behind.

*Typical. Jean Pierre knows he's faster than me, so he just has to pull these stunts to prove himself. And right after lecturing me for flying too fast!*

Bentaz didn't have long to ponder his compatriot as the rest of the melee was only a few blocks away from where Iron had been nailed.

Bentaz saw Powerhouse zoom around the corner of the next block well ahead of him, having gained a fair distance in his race to the battle.

As he approached the corner, Bentaz heard a loud crack and saw an olive-green dragon man come tumbling through the air in front of him. The creature's hostage likewise airborne, having come loose from his captor's grasp.

*Okay, time to get serious.* He instantly took in the scene and worked out his course of action. He poured on a short burst of speed, plucked the former hostage from the air, and swept up above the buildings as the dragon man continued his trajectory into the shopfront below, his giant wings failing to resolve his predicament.

From on high, Bentaz could finally see the action as it unfolded on the hapless Bondi locals and tourists alike. The first thing he noticed (aside from the fact the area looked like a bomb had recently gone off in it) was a giant drill machine on treads looming in the centre of the street as a fellow HSA member, the Metallic Man, tried to lift it above his robotic form. In the foreground another HSAer, the Savage Scavenger, ripped into the equally ferocious Russian werebeast, Rabboon; and above them all, in his navy uniform with sky-blue cape floated Powerhouse, who was obviously responsible for Dragonski's flight into the shopfront below. Sirens wailed in the distance as the local police struggled to cordon off the area.

Bentaz could also see something else from his viewpoint that had been missed by his teammates, but before he could react he was distracted by a brilliant flash right next to his visor.

It was only then that he noticed the hostage he'd rescued (and was still carrying) looked for all the world to be a Japanese tourist—complete with "I heart Australia" t-shirt and giant camera—which he was busily winding for his next photo.

*First things first,* Bentaz thought, and sported a cheesy grin for the subsequent picture.

He flew away from the street at a right angle, dropping the tourist on a rooftop before circling around and back towards what he'd spied earlier: two armoured men with guns on a shop roof overlooking the battle.

He arrived just as they'd drawn a bead on Powerhouse, who hadn't noticed the danger and was instead looming dramatically over the street, looking to see if Bentaz was watching his heroics.

*What a dick. Still, he's on the team and that means he's off limits to supervillains—especially these two.* He charged his fists in anticipation.

Bentaz pointed his hands, which were crackling with power, and fired off a couple of energy beams at the armoured men, destroying the hi-tech guns strapped to the gauntlets of their right arms.

'Hello, boys, remember me?' Bentaz asked jovially. They both turned in shocked disbelief to see him floating behind them. 'Last time I saw you two losers, I was dropping you off to the authorities after you had the dumb luck of triggering my Manifest seed during one of your failed bank heists. Thanks for that, by the way. Now, how did you escape the Powder Keg? I hear the Warden's security is like his arse— tight and bristling with hostiles.'

'Aww fuck, Beam, look who 'tis!' said the bigger of the two. 'It's Ballistic!'

'I can see that, Brund, you dumb fuck,' said the smaller one in a state of panic. 'Don't just stand there like a drooling fucktard—shoot him!'

'But he broke my gun.'

'Use your other gun, stupid,' Beam shouted back, bringing his good arm, and its other gun, to bear.

Bentaz didn't need the HSA files to know who these two clowns were, given stray shots from their guns had unexpectedly turned him into a super-being instead of ending his life on a cold Canberra street two years ago. He also knew their guns could no longer hurt him as they unleashed with lasers and cannons.

Bentaz disarmed his assailants with a couple of quick chops that shattered their remaining weapons, wondering how much it cost to replace them each time a superhero smashes them.

*No wonder they have to keep robbing banks. Talk about your vicious cycle.*

'Nice try, fellas, but you missed your chance to nail me years ago,' Bentaz said. He grabbed them both by the neck joints in their armour and held them steady. 'Now, these suits have to have a power source somewhere...and if it's based on a Q design... hey presto!'

Bentaz delivered a quick strike just between the shoulder blades, driving his fingers through their armour and retrieving what looked like two small batteries—which he promptly crushed, rendering their suits powerless.

'You fucking brat! I can't fucking move!' Beam said while Bentaz carried him and Brund down to the street below. 'I'll get you for this!'

'Yeah, yeah,' Bentaz said when Powerhouse finally located him. 'Something you missed in your rush to get here,' he said to his teammate, dropping off the helpless supervillains.

'I was too busy dealing with the real threat: Dragonski,' Powerhouse said arrogantly. 'You're quite capable of dealing with third-rate losers like these two without my help.'

'Yeah, well you might want to be more careful when "dealing" with threats in the future,' Bentaz said, pointing towards the building behind him at the end of the street. 'I had to rescue a civilian you'd apparently evacuated earlier and drop him off safely over there.'

'I saw him and knew you'd save him,' Powerhouse lied. 'So stop giving me a lecture in the middle of battle and try and do something to carry your weight on this team for a change. I'm sick of picking up your slack.'

*Fucking jerk! I wonder if anyone would notice if I snapped his neck and blamed it on a supervillain.*

Instead of giving into temptation, Bentaz decided to assist the Metallic Man with the giant drill machine. He was struggling to lift or tip it over, despite his impressive robotic body, as the drill machine was designed to stabilise in the most unpredictable terrain and was bigger than the HSAer.

Bentaz flew over and grabbed the drill machine, lifting it into the air above his head with ease. 'Need a hand?' he asked the Metallic Man, trying (and failing) to not sound like a show-off. His teammate didn't care, for wrestling with giant drill machines was overrated anyhow.

Bentaz dug his fingers deep into the machine while he held it above his head and then promptly ripped it in half, shaking each piece to empty the contents onto the street below. After a couple of shakes, a short man in a mole costume fell ungracefully onto the bitumen along with piles of miscellaneous junk and garbage.

'How dare you?' screamed the Mole. He jumped up from the

ground and started waving his arms about. 'Do you have any idea how much that machine cost? Not to mention the loss to science that your careless thuggery has caused! As subterranean overlord, I...'

The Mole's impromptu villain rant was cut short by the surprise of the Metallic Man suddenly coming up on him from behind.

At three metres tall, weighing over three tonnes and consisting of a giant machine body, complete with intimidating attachments and machine tail, the Metallic Man AKA Anthony Coulson, former high school student, was a horrific sight. His head sat like a hunter's trophy at the top of the machine body, filled with multiple tubes and wires that were lit up by an artificial left eye. Only his facial movements indicated that he was actually cyborg in nature, but few guessed that all of this was a result of becoming a Manifest. Super powers aren't always what they're cracked up to be.

'Sacré bleu!' the Mole exclaimed when the Metallic Man ensnared him with multiple steel cables that shot out from his robotic arms. His further cries were muffled as he was bound like a mummy.

'Thanks for the assist, Ballistic,' the Metallic Man said. 'Don't worry about this guy, I'll keep him under wraps.' He laughed at his own pun.

'Great, thanks mate,' Bentaz replied. 'Can you also grab those two guys in armour over there? They're incapacitated at the moment, but I don't want them to reboot or anything and get away.'

'Sure thing,' the Metallic Man agreed. 'Looks like this is almost over anyway.'

Bentaz turned around to see that the Metallic Man was probably right. Powerhouse was in the process of defeating the shaggy Rabboon with a bombardment of super-speed punches—after 'assisting' the Savage Scavenger as an excuse to steal the show.

'Lucky I was here to help you out, wasn't it, SS?' Powerhouse gloated smugly to the Savage Scavenger—and any journalists he hoped were hiding nearby. 'Rabboon's a tricky customer, not really an opponent for a rookie.'

'I'm quite capable of looking out for myself,' the Savage Scavenger hissed in response, 'and I've been on this team longer than you have. Oh, and stop calling me "SS"—I'm the Savage Scavenger—not a fucking Nazi.'

'Whatever, furball,' Powerhouse responded, frowning beneath the stylised mask that wrapped around the back of his head like a band and met at the bridge of his nose. 'Why don't you get a decent super-hero name like…I don't know…like me. Come to think of it, your costume really sucks. What's with the whole lime-green spandex and red booties? And what's with that silly dagger insignia on your chest? It takes away from the whole wolf-boy look you suffer from.'

Suddenly Powerhouse was consumed in a massive torrent of flame that spewed forth from Dragonski's mouth after he'd recovered and snuck up on the hero during his showboating.

'Never turn your back on the dragon,' Dragonski said menacingly over Powerhouse's smouldering form, having practised that line for decades and finally getting to use it. Now he paused awkwardly, having never thought once of what to say after.

It mattered little, for a moment later Powerhouse burst from the ashes of his cape and blasted Dragonski in the face with his eyebeams. 'You cannot defeat justice, you Communist scum!' he declared need-lessly, following up his ocular assault with his patented super-speed punches to the face.

'The USSR broke up a couple years ago,' Bentaz said, walking over with the Metallic Man, who was now carrying Brund and Beam along with the Mole. 'Besides, there are no reporters around to hear you.'

'Very funny,' Powerhouse said, who was now mostly shirtless as well as cape-less. 'In case you hadn't noticed, while you were standing around doing nothing, I was taking down the major threat here.'

'Is that the same major threat you carelessly threw into that shop-front earlier and then turned your back on?' Bentaz asked, grabbing his metaphorical stirring spoon and giving it a twist.

'Well, he's pretty tough, but not as tough as me, as I've just proven,' Powerhouse said smugly. 'What did you do? Oh yeah, nothing.'

'Guys, this is unhelpful,' said the Metallic Man, who had silently bound Dragonski and Rabboon in his robotic tendrils and was now carrying them too. 'We're all on the same team.'

'I know we are,' Powerhouse said stuffily, 'but I'm not sure what part of the team plan involved Ballistic being here.'

'Oh, Chuck Cheese radioed it in,' Bentaz said cheerily. 'He thought you could all do with some help—especially you, Powerhouse—he worries about your safety.'

The Savage Scavenger snorted, trying desperately to suppress his laugh.

Powerhouse was not laughing, however, and immediately took offence as his dislike for their cheese mascot was well known. World-saving superhero teams didn't have need of childish things like mascots being his reasoning, but most everyone just assumed it was because he was a jerk.

'Anyway, you should make yourself useful and clean up this mess before you take these criminals back to the Powder Keg where they belong,' Powerhouse said to Bentaz, subconsciously scanning for news vans. 'I have to go shopping for a new outfit.'

'Not so fast, flash,' Bentaz said before his rival could leave. 'If you capture the bad guys, then you have to take them to the prison. And as for cleaning up this mess… I'm not a qualified tradesman, I can't fix this. Besides, our government chaperone likes to have his guys go over this stuff forensically, which you damn well know.'

The Savage Scavenger and the Metallic Man exchanged looks and stepped back, long used to the constant bickering between the team heavyweights.

'That's not fair! I did the heavy lifting; I shouldn't have to do clean-up duty too,' Powerhouse said, his voice taking on a nasal whine. 'Anyway, I have to get a new suit.'

'Rules of the game, my friend,' Bentaz rejoined absentmindedly, his attention caught by something in the rubble. 'This is what it means to step up and be number one.'

'I already am,' Powerhouse said. 'But to show *you* what it means to be number one, I'll take these guys to the Powder Keg for you. Some-one trustworthy should do it, after all.'

'Good. Don't forget to grab Iron as well,' Bentaz said, hefting a large, heavy, wooden deckchair from under a sheet of corrugated iron that had been wedged on top of a car. 'Fucking fantastic! Dibs!'

'Hey, you can't take that! It doesn't belong to you!' Powerhouse whined. 'Besides, what would you want with a crappy deckchair any-way?'

'I think saving the world from evil on countless occasions has earned me a single deckchair,' Bentaz replied, unfazed. 'What I do with it is my business.'

Bentaz could see several special AMPs—anti-Manifest police—cautiously approach the heroes, and decided it was time for him to leave.

'Well fellas, it's been nice working with you again, but I really must be going,' he said to the Metallic Man and the Savage Scavenger, 'Powerhouse: congratulations on saving the day. Enjoy your credit on the way to the Powder Keg.'

'You still can't take that chair...' Powerhouse began, but Bentaz couldn't hear him because he'd already left.

\* \* \*

### The Skull of Ra: 8 May 34 BZ

Anu Hopet brooded with unparalleled intensity at the ship's viewscreen, his striking armoured image silhouetted against its glare in the otherwise gloomy bridge. He only ever took off his armour in private, not just because he needed to maintain a certain image—he felt empowered wearing it.

The armour, like the ship, was a product of alien technology whose inventors were now long dead. At least the ones who used to inhabit this ship were. Anu Hopet assumed that their species was still out there somewhere in the vastness of space.

*Probably wondering whatever happened to their lost ship. It was obviously the work of Kismet that I met these creatures when I did, setting me on my path of destiny.*

Anu Hopet's pauldrons and breastplate were adorned with his final contribution to the armour: a stylised skull on a field of pitch black that would become his symbol and namesake for his group, the Skull Band—a name he also came up with.

*Enough reminiscing.*

'Ship, show me recent images of Subject Alpha,' Anu Hopet boomed, breaking the silence. He was of the firm belief that commands should always be boomed, otherwise they may as well be suggestions.

Detailed images of Bentaz Mullberry fighting supervillains in Bondi appeared on the screen as if by magic. It was not magic; it was the advanced spy drones that Anu Hopet's cyborg lackey had sent out previously at his command—boomed, of course.

*He is improving,* he thought while he watched the recording, *but still untempered and not yet a worthy adversary.*

In the meantime, he had more pressing concerns.

'Disk,' Anu Hopet said, turning to address the cybernetic midget who was fretting over a nearby computer panel, 'have you found the talisman yet?'

'Not yet, Great Armageddon,' Disk replied irritably. His metallic armour was sporting the same skull symbol that adorned his master and the rest of the Skull Band. 'You'd be first to know if I'd done so.'

'Watch your tone, whelp!' Anu Hopet snapped. 'You forget who you address.'

'My apologies, Great Armageddon,' Disk supplicated. 'Forgive me. I'm just frustrated with this planet's primitive communication technologies. They keep most of their information on paper and their rudimentary global information network contains virtually no information at all!'

'Have you found anything useful?' Anu Hopet asked, walking towards his minion. 'Has it been destroyed or lost to time? If so, when was it last seen? I remember it was a treasure worn by Queen Kyra Zol when I was a slave. Surely that bitch did not reign forever.'

While the probes Anu Hopet dispatched to monitor his home world in his absence kept him informed of a great many matters, they were inevitably incomplete.

'It's very time consuming, but luckily I've had some success by targeting individual computer networks remotely through the use of the ship's drones,' Disk explained. 'By scanning the computer to the quantum level, then replicating it virtually, I'm able to read the information stored on their hard...'

'Spare me the technical details,' Anu Hopet interrupted. 'I know how the machines work.'

'Basically, the information they have is patchy, but it seems Queen

Kyra Zol vanished with her empire around the same time you commandeered this ship from the Evolvers,' Disk said, slowly getting to the point. 'But the talisman turned up as a curio found by British Egyptologists around seventy years ago...'

'But where is it now?' Anu Hopet boomed, starting to get frustrated.

*I should not lose my temper; he is not in control of his destiny like I am.*

Like the rest of the Skull Band, Disk's Manifest abilities were chosen by the Evolvers who once commanded *The Skull of Ra*. This was unlike Anu Hopet, who was granted his abilities by Manifest himself. It was he who discovered them frozen after taking the vessel, setting them free and giving them new names and a new purpose.

*That is why it is my destiny to command and their destiny to serve.*

'It was most recently owned by a Vsevolod Rasskazov,' Disk continued, 'whose official residence is listed as Moscow.'

'I thought you said you had not located it,' Anu Hopet said. 'It appears as if you know who has it and in which city they come from.'

'There's more, Great Armageddon,' Disk said hesitantly. 'I cross-referenced this with a local news report and it seems that Vsevolod Rasskazov is dead and the talisman is missing again.'

'It was not with his effects? Or bequeathed to family?'

'No, I sent a probe to quantum scan his listed address in the same way I scanned the computers and it wasn't in the virtual recreation,' Disk said. 'I believe he may've had it on him when he died, but it wasn't buried with him—I scanned his grave as well as the murder site. He had no family. It may've been stolen when he was murdered. It may've even been *why* he was murdered.'

'That is a lot of speculation,' Anu Hopet said, 'but it is a start. Do you know who killed him?'

'Yes, Great Armageddon,' Disk replied. 'It was a low-level Manifest—Class D according to their scale—who was moved to a prison on this continent. I scanned the prison, but astonishingly the technology they use to contain the prisoners prevents me from undertaking a full scan. The talisman could be with the prisoner or at least he may know its whereabouts.'

'Then we send Battle Tank, Gurk, and Backstabber to find out,' Anu Hopet said.

'There was another individual involved,' Disk added. 'The authorities believe it was an unknown Manifest, a woman. She could be
another lead.'

'The prison first, then the woman,' Anu Hopet commanded. 'Gather
as much information as you can while I prepare a plan. I wish this to
go smoothly.'

'Yes, Great Armageddon,' Disk said, typing on yet another keypad.

Suddenly and inexplicably, a strange creature comprised of two
heads in mirror opposition that shared the same mouth, appeared in
the corner of the ceiling behind Anu Hopet. It sprang at him.

'FDAM!' it screamed as it passed by his head before landing on the
two sets of spindly legs that sprouted from each head and scampered
off under a control station.

'Shit!' Anu Hopet cried, actually being startled for the first time in
years.

'Another one!' Disk exclaimed, looking excited. 'If I can catch it, I
can study it!'

'Do not bother,' Anu Hopet said, having calmed down. 'It has
already gone again.'

'They're a mystery endemic to this world,' Disk said. 'They're known
as Miasma creatures, or Class E Entities, and they come in an almost
infinite variety. If I can study one, perhaps I can utilise its power for
our cause.'

'Just figure out how to keep them out of the ship,' Anu Hopet
growled, turning and heading for the door. 'Your previous attempts
have proven useless and their novelty has long expired.'

'Yes, Great Armageddon,' Disk said, bowing while his master left
the bridge. 'Your will is life.'

*And soon everyone will know it*, Anu Hopet thought, heading towards
his quarters.

* * *

### The Moon: 9 May 34 BZ

Bentaz Mullberry lay back on his brand-new deckchair and soaked in the spectacular view. Life was good. The stars were so clear from here, and as 'The Call of Ktulu' kicked up a notch on his Walkman, Bentaz felt his troubles wash away.

*I'm surprised my Walkman works up here,* he thought, swept away with the music. *It must have something to do with my protective aura.*

He shifted in his seat slightly and pointed his finger at a nearby boulder, imitating a pistol in the age-old fashion. Except unlike almost everyone in history, Bentaz's hand began to glow and a beam of energy shot out from his finger to shatter the boulder.

*Okay, that was an easy one.* He spied a harder target beyond the shattered boulder. The first beam missed, but Bentaz hit his target on the second attempt.

He picked another target and this time blasted it with his other hand.

*I could do this all day. I love being able to shoot energy from my hands. I love how I just will it to happen and it does. I just wish I could shoot eyebeams like they do in the comics, or like Jean-Pierre, if I'm being honest with myself.*

The song came to an end and the tape switched sides in his Walkman. Bentaz was aurally blasted by 'Fight Fire with Fire'.

*Aah wrong sound.* Bentaz stopped the cassette. *They really need to invent a portable music device that only plays your favourite songs. Or I could just get off my arse and make a mix tape, I suppose.*

He packed his Walkman away in the pouch he'd attached to his belt and pulled out the photo of his family he'd been carrying around for years. His eyes (and memory) were good enough to see the details in the dim light, but he made his hand glow and looked at the picture in full light anyway.

The picture was faded, taken when he was very young. The image was so old that Peach was just a baby and being cradled by their mother, while Bentaz and Yam sat on their father's shoulders. They all looked so happy.

*That was before Dad got his current job and we actually got to spend time together as a family. I wonder what it he actually gets up to—he only ever describes it as 'business'. Mum's so sketchy about it too—it must be dodgy.*

Bentaz looked at the photo one last time before placing it back in his pouch.

*I guess I should get back home.* He sighed internally as he donned his red helmet and stood up on the sturdy deckchair. He went to dust off his cape before leaving, only to discover he was moon dust free.

*That chair has already proven invaluable.* He looked back on the deckchair while levitating himself out of the crater and began the flight home. *And now that I've dropped it off, I can see if I can beat my record back to Earth.*

And with that goal in mind, Bentaz rocketed from the moon without looking back.

\* \* \*

### New York City, United States of America: 12 May 34 BZ

Lorraine Freeman sat in the green room for *Good Evening New York*, already bored with the pile of tabloid rags lying on the coffee table beside her. This was her first big talk show appearance and the wait was starting to get to her. Her hair and makeup were already done and there was nothing more for her entourage to do than mingle with the show's stylists and fashion gurus while they waited for the current guest to finish their segment of the show. Lorraine sat nervously, with only her ever-present mother for company.

*She hasn't let me out of her sight since Rome,* she thought, studying her mum studying a gossip rag. *I really should be grateful considering how lucky I was that she was there to support me with that shit at the Vatican.*

Lorraine had been certain she was going to go to jail, but instead everyone seemed eager to sweep it under the rug. It had been a nightmare and her mother had stood strong and helped her through it.

She felt a twinge of guilt at that—she hadn't really been that kind to her mother during this trip. She also didn't want to think of the other possibility why the Church seemed so keen to keep it quiet.

*How powerful will I become? Will people just do anything for me because they have no choice? Do I even want that kind of power? Am I a monster?*

The questions tumbled over and over in her mind, and each of them accompanied by frightening images. The only relief was the fact that other Manifests appeared to be immune to her power.

*But for how much longer? No one's meant to know I'm a Manifest either—how long until someone figures that out, and then what?*

She adjusted her floral dress for the umpteenth time as she sagged in the lounge and waited for her call.

*Uh, this dress is too short—and it's ugly. Seven big flowers—how predictable. Everyone will still love it because I'm wearing it though.* She looked at her painted nails, green to match her eyes. *Just once I'd like someone to not fawn all over me—provided they don't intend to kill me, that is.*

She was so lost in thought that she jumped when her name was called by the production manager.

'Good luck, sweetie,' Lucy Freeman said when her daughter got up to leave.

Lorraine nervously followed the efficient-looking production manager through the door and was ushered to the set, where the show's host, David Leno, was waiting. When she approached the long couch that adjoined the host's desk, the previous guest slid along it to allow her sit down next to David.

*Is that...?* The feeling of déjà vu turned into a spine tingle.

Before she could complete her thought, her segment of the show began and she was swept away by the experience.

'...Our next guest needs no introduction!' David was saying as she arrived at the desk. 'Ladies and gentlemen, I'd like you to give a warm welcome to Lorraine Freeman!' He took Lorraine's hands and kissed her on the cheek. The crowd cheered and several bold souls chose to wolf-whistle at the teenager. David Leno was a professional and continued with the interview when they both sat down.

'Lorraine, it's so great to have you with us tonight,' he began in his market-tested casual yet thoughtful interview style.

'Thanks, David, it's good to be here,' Lorraine replied, the nervousness washing away under the studio lights and cameras.

'I'd just like to say first up that the dress you're wearing is really lovely. Seven flowers, is it?' David began, leaning forward in his chair. 'I hear that's your favourite number.'

'Well, I have my mother to thank for that,' Lorraine said, smiling.

'She only had to say that on Oprah once and that's how it all started. Sure, I have an affinity with the number seven now, but really I don't have a favourite number.'

'Did you hear that, folks? Miss Freeman *doesn't* have a favourite number,' David said, swivelling his chair to face the audience. 'You heard it first on *Good Evening New York!* First question out and already making waves.'

The market-tested hyperbole was underscored by loud, dramatic music that suddenly pumped out of speakers to her immediate right, as if the other guest was a jukebox. That's when Lorraine remembered exactly who the other guest was.

'Lorraine, where are my manners?' David said, noticing her reaction. 'I haven't formally introduced you to our other guest on the show tonight, New York's own resident Manifest and rock star, Samuel Beatrix—the Beat Master.'

'The pleasure's all mine,' he said, extending his right hand, which was hidden beneath his skin-tight metal suit. The abbreviation for megahertz had been stencilled on his knuckles.

The dramatic music had come from the speakers in his upper arms and back. Lorraine couldn't believe she hadn't realised who he was before now.

'I was a big fan of yours growing up,' she said, taking his hand. 'I also remember my mum loved your aerobics videos.'

The crowd laughed without need of the flashing sign.

'I almost didn't recognise you with your helmet on,' she confessed. 'Maybe you should take it off so we can see the rest of your face.'

'If it's what the people want…' Samuel began before he was cut off by more cheering.

*Or is he doing it because I want it?*

He removed his helmet, grey like the rest of his suit (with the same dorky red arrows) and complete with a retractable mirrored visor.

Lorraine noticed the abbreviation for kilohertz stencilled on the knuckles of his left hand when he placed the helmet on his lap. She took in his handsome features, from his intelligent eyes to his chocolate-brown skin. He hadn't aged a day since those old aerobics videos—one of the benefits of being a Manifest.

*Too bad he's gay.*

'So, Lorraine,' David said, bringing their attention back to topic, 'what brings you to the Big Apple?'

*Well, there's got to be at least one scene set in America, otherwise no one will read this.*

'I'm here to promote the latest Larouche Spring Collection,' she answered, thinking how grateful she was that Pepe the sleazebag was still in Europe. 'It's part of my global tour. From here I go to LA, Las Vegas...'

There were a few cries of 'Vegas' from the audience.

'...and a few other cities,' she continued, adjusting her dress yet again. 'Then the Southern Hemisphere tour begins.'

'That's great,' David interjected. Market testing showed no interest in the Southern Hemisphere. 'Your rise to fame has been so fast that we know so little about you. So, tell us a bit about yourself—your mother was an Aussie superhero, wasn't she?'

'Yeah, she was known as Spectrum and was part of the X-Droids, who are now in semi-retirement,' Lorraine revealed. 'In between fighting supervillains, she managed to raise me and my two little sisters on her own.' She awkwardly checked her nails while saying this, remembering the little unit they had in Chatswood in Sydney.

David, being the seasoned professional he was, read Lorraine's body language and could tell the issue of her father would be an emotional subject and probably not something she'd want to talk about, but decided to go with the market-tested approach.

'And what about your father?' he asked. 'I remember there was some stir Down Under that your mother never disclosed his identity to the public.'

*He actually looked into that?*

'Ahh...that's something I'd rather not talk about,' she said, looking David directly in his eyes.

Suddenly David felt compelled not to persist with that line of questioning, despite the network having specifically chosen those questions before the show. Instead he moved on.

'Okay...so what was it like having a superhero for a mother?' David enquired, taking a sip from his network coffee cup. It was really bourbon.

'For the most part it was fun. Mum was already in semi-retirement by the time I was old enough to understand what her job was,' she said, recalling her childhood. 'Occasionally I'd worry about her, especially when I saw her on the news fighting all manner of psychos and giant robots. She certainly helped give me a drive to succeed and has fully supported my modelling career.'

*Yeah, she practically forced me into it.*

'So, what's it like going from regular teenager to global superstar in a couple of months?' David queried, now unwilling to ask anything too personal. This was the exact opposite of his usual methods. 'What's the secret to your success?'

'Ha-ha, I'll let you know when my head stops spinning.' Lorraine laughed and the audience laughed with her. 'It's just so overwhelming—I can't put it into words. I guess I'm still waiting for the other shoe to drop.'

'I know that feeling,' Samuel added from alongside her on the couch, his inbuilt speakers underscoring his words.

'Just before we cut to the break, we have time for one question from the audience,' David announced, gesturing to his offsider who was already standing with someone in the crowd. Lorraine couldn't see them through the glare from the floodlights.

That was when Kismet tossed Lorraine a shoe.

'Hi,' said a slightly 'off' male voice. Lorraine still couldn't see who it was. 'I'd just like to know what it's like to be a Manifest—can you tell me what having superpowers feels like?'

The crowd went into an uproar. David Leno looked totally lost for the first time since he'd interviewed a guy called Zambini Surrealay while still a rookie talk-show host.

'I...' Lorraine stammered.

*How does he know that? Who is he? I can't see him properly. I can't think!*

Beat Master's impromptu background music only made it worse.

'You're a Manifest?' David asked. It was almost an accusation.

'I thought I felt something when you walked in,' Samuel said, having silenced his speakers. 'It just wasn't my place to say anything.'

*And it is now?*

'Wait...' Lorraine said.

'So you *are* a Manifest!' David declared, rising from his chair. 'Breaking news on *Good Evening New York!* What are your powers? Wait a second; does this explain why you're so popular?'

*Oh shit. I don't like where this is going.*

Lorraine didn't know how to answer and luckily didn't have to, for suddenly all the power in the studio went out. Confusion set in among both the crowd and the crew.

'It's not like this happened because we were late going to commercial,' Lorraine heard David say in the darkness nearby. 'Must be the goddamn unqualified losers I have to work with. Someone's going to get fired for this!'

'Maybe now's a good time to get the hell out of here,' Samuel whispered to her. 'Before they restore power and start to grill you some more.'

'I think maybe you're right,' she agreed. 'Thanks for the advice.'

'No problems.' Samuel activated a light on his suit and quickly showed Lorraine the way to the exit.

She didn't waste any more time and quickly sprang from the couch and ran towards the door she'd entered through.

'Wait! Where are you going?' David cried out after her. 'The interview's not finished!'

*It sure as hell is,* Lorraine thought, racing into the green room to find her mother, who stood there impatiently waiting for her.

* * *

## Undisclosed location: 13 May 34 BZ

Courtney Yeht knew Phil and Amy would be coming to see her the moment the floor had told her they'd exited their little sealed room. It was built over several weeks after the 'incident', including an upgrade of the facility in general. It was one of two new sealed rooms that must have been designed with her in mind—especially because the floor couldn't tell her anything that happened within them...and the floor heard every little thing.

*I wish I could remember what happened,* she thought as the doctors' footsteps drew closer, *but everything's so hazy.*

She didn't have much time to think about it, for at that moment the two doctors entered the room. They seemed standoffish with each other as if they'd just been fighting.

'Ah, 1432, I see you're awake,' said Phil, the nice doctor. 'How's that new medication you're on? How do you feel?'

'Okay, I guess,' Courtney answered, sitting up and pulling the floral bedspread around her waist. She couldn't actually remember feeling any other way than she did now. 'I feel like I'm forgetting something important. Have I always been here, in this room?'

'Of course you have,' Phil said soothingly. 'You hit your head in the accident and lost your memory. You grew up in this room.'

Courtney looked around the pink room while she subconsciously checked her head for sore spots and couldn't find any. The modest bookcase, piles of clothing and shelves of stuffed toys looked unfamiliar—whole setting resembled a child's bedroom.

*That doesn't seem right...but Phil's always been nice to me. He wouldn't lie to me. Amy's the nasty one.*

Amy stood quietly and took notes on her clipboard as usual.

*I swear she's staring at me through that eye patch.*

'Where are my parents?' Courtney asked, feeling really confused. 'Why do you keep calling me that number?'

'That number is your name, 1432,' Amy said, breaking her silence.

'Uh, yes, well that's true,' Phil said, somewhat more tactfully. 'But as for your parents...don't you remember they were killed in the incident?'

'The incident *you* caused,' Amy said icily.

'I...don't know,' was all Courtney managed to say.

*Did I really hurt my parents?*

'Now, now Amy, it wasn't her fault,' Phil said diplomatically. 'You just need to promise never to practise your special power when we're not around. Will you do that for me, 1432? Do you promise?'

'I promise,' Courtney said, unsure of what else to do. 'I'm sorry I caused all of this. I don't remember hurting anyone, especially my parents. I can't even remember what they look like.'

'That's all right,' Phil said, putting his hand on her arm. 'You've had a bad accident. I'm sure it'll all come back to you in time. Meanwhile we'll just continue to give you your medication to ensure your safe and full recovery.'

'Can I go outside today?' Courtney asked, tired of being cooped up in the same room for so long and desperately trying to take her mind off her sudden guilt. 'After practise, I mean.'

'Now, you know that's not possible, 1432,' Phil said, feigning concern. 'It's not safe outside—the police are always looking for gifted teenagers like you to sell to secret government labs. It was your parents' dying wish that you should remain here with us for many years. You do want to honour that, don't you?'

'Of course...I...' she said.

'Come now, it's time for practise,' Phil announced, drawing back the covers. 'Your parents' life work could help millions and you're vital to its success. Amy will help you get changed and I'll meet you in the training room.'

Phil got up and headed for the door. 'Now, be nice,' he said to Amy under his breath as he left.

Courtney was left alone with Amy, who looked even more hostile since Phil left.

'Hurry up and get dressed,' Amy said coldly. 'We don't have all day.'

*Bitch. I'm just too tired to fight with her.*

Courtney got up and put on her dressing gown, which was about as 'dressed' as she ever got. She slipped on her scruffy bunny slippers and followed Amy out of the room.

Courtney walked down the short, well-lit corridor and into the spacious training room. It was mostly empty except for about a dozen stones of various sizes and a plastic table surrounded by plastic chairs—all of it a dark green. On the table were several items: a plastic bucket filled with sand, a granite rock, a sheet of copper, a pile of iron filings, an apple, a glass of water and a pencil. Courtney didn't even have to look to know what they all were—they were the same items she'd been training with the last week.

She sat down in a plastic chair opposite Phil, while Amy took the seat next to him and lined up a brand-new sheet on her clipboard.

'If you would be so kind as to begin,' Phil said when everyone was ready. 'You know the drill, 1432. Start with the rock and work your way through the items.'

Courtney was still annoyed that she couldn't go outside and decided to show off by lifting the granite rock off the table and firing it at the pile of other stones in the room without even looking. She struck the smallest of them and it shattered.

'Well done,' Phil exclaimed.

Next, she made the sand swirl out of the bucket—even forming a ring this time—and tipped the glass of water over. She had no control over the other items despite spending hours trying to achieve exactly that.

When she was done, she got up to head back to her room. Amy stopped her.

'Not so fast, 1432,' Amy said, indicating the rarely used second door to the training room. 'You need to come this way.'

'What do you mean?' Courtney asked, not trusting her one little bit.

'What Amy means to say,' Phil interjected, glaring at Amy as he did so, 'is that we've got a brand-new room for you and it's down this way.'

'But why do I have a new room?' Courtney was confused. 'And what about all my stuff?' she added, almost as an afterthought. Her 'stuff' had no real meaning to her.

'Not to worry, all your things have been moved to your new room while you were in training,' Phil said, putting his hand in the small of Courtney's back and leading her towards the second door. 'Your old room was damaged in the incident and so we made this brand-new room for you. It's much safer than your old room, I'm sure you'll be happy with it. It's much larger, too.'

Courtney hesitantly allowed Phil to lead her through the second door, down another well-lit corridor, down some stairs and finally to a foreboding metal hatch. It looked like an airlock.

'This is my new room?' Courtney asked, starting to feel afraid. 'It looks like a prison cell.'

'It's no prison cell.' Phil laughed while he typed into the keypad and the door swung open with a hiss. 'I told you, it's your new room. Viola!'

Courtney looked through the doorway, and sure enough, all of her stuff was in there. On closer inspection, she noticed there were two doors; one opening out and the other opening in. Her room was separated from the rest of the building by a thin void, like it was somehow suspended in place.

*What is this? It looks like a trap. Yet, I'm sure Phil wouldn't hurt me.*

'I see you've noticed the special design,' Phil said, as if reading her mind. 'Your room is actually suspended on magnets and doesn't touch the main building at all. Even your door opens by remote signal when the outer door is opened.'

'But what if I want to leave my room, to go to the toilet or something?' Courtney nervously playing with her golden hair.

'Well your new room has its very own toilet facilities. You shouldn't be wandering the corridors unescorted—it's not safe,' Phil said, as friendly as ever. 'We're cognisant to the fact that hearing all those vibrations is of great discomfort, so this room was made especially for you. We only have your best interests at heart, after all. Now, why don't you step inside and check out your new digs?'

Courtney took a nervous step through the gap and into her new room. All of her stuff was there, it was just more spread out.

*And it's still painted pink.*

That was when she noticed the pile of *Stylish Girlfriend* magazine lying on the bed, and she walked over, excited to see something new.

*Summer Edition, 1989. So not that new then.*

Suddenly she heard a hiss behind her and turned around to see Phil closing the door.

'Goodnight, Courtney, see you tomorrow,' he said as the doors obscured her view of him.

'Wait...' she called out in vain.

The airlock doors sealed shut, and for the first time she could remember, Courtney could feel no vibrations save for her own heart.

* * *

'See? That's how you gain their trust,' Phil said to Amy as they walked away. 'You catch more flies with honey, so the next time you call me a hypocrite for being nice to her, just think about that.'

The new room worked perfectly—the floor didn't hear *that* little thing.

\* \* \*

### West of Kanye, Botswana: 22 May 34 BZ

Naomi spied the cave entrance on the opposite side of the crevasse that lay hidden in the dusty scrub and cautiously approached. Twilight was fast approaching and the terrain was deceptively hazardous.

*This better be worth the detour,* she thought, clambering down the rocky slope and into the crevasse. It would have been the height of embarrassment if she couldn't complete her assignment due to a twisted ankle or broken arm.

But Naomi was nothing if not good at her job, and once she lined up with the cave entrance it was relatively easy to jump the chasm and land in its mouth. The hard bit was jumping between the sharpened sticks that lined the cave mouth like fangs.

*So far, so good.* She came out of her tuck and landed on her feet inside the cave. *Not even sure if this guy's real, and if he is, what am I going to say to break the ice?*

Each of the four spears representing the canine teeth impaled a separate baboon's skull, further adding to the mysterious atmosphere. Burning torches lit the way to the interior of the cave.

*This whole place feels wrong. In fact, the entire crevasse looked fake. The monkey skulls are great though—maybe I can snavel one on my way out.*

She followed the tunnel down into the earth until she reached the main den. More torches lined the walls, but they were emitting an eerie green light that gave everything a sinister edge. In the middle of the den was a burning hearth and on the far side sat the person she came to see.

'Tenebrous,' she said to the cloaked figure, who was hunched over the coals, poking the fire with the end of a staff. It was long and spiked at the base with a light blue gem held fast between two horns at the top.

'Who calls me by that name?' the figure said without looking up, the matching horned helmet obscuring their features, but their voice revealing them to be male. 'Few people know me by that name, and fewer have spoken it in eighty years. Who are *you*, little girl, to speak the name given to me over a century ago?'

Naomi wasn't sure how to respond, so she decided to go with the truth.

'My name's Naomi Bloodlust and I come here seeking your counsel,' she said, unsure how revealing her surname was going to be received.

*Changing it by deed poll on my eighteenth birthday seemed like a good idea at the time.*

'I have heard of you,' Tenebrous said, surprising her. 'I am not without my agents in the wider world. But I still don't know who sent you or why I should help you. You have the stink of the Kaiser on you. Tell me: are you one of Enigma's agents?'

'No, the Kaiser doesn't know I'm here,' she replied truthfully. 'I have a job not far from here and took the opportunity to see you.'

'You wouldn't know it even if you were his puppet,' Tenebrous muttered, finally looking up and staring into Naomi's emerald eyes with his blank grey ones. They seemed to glow from within the eye-slit of his metallic helm. Naomi couldn't tell if the devil horns protruding from the front were part of the helmet or part of the man. 'Though if not the Kaiser, then who? Tell me or we go no further; lie to me and we go further but on a different path.'

'It was a friend of mine, a man named Bojangles,' she answered, standing opposite Tenebrous across the hearth.

'Bojangles?' he responded, almost alarmed. 'Why would *he* send you to me asking for help? What does he think I can offer you?' He continued to stir the burning coals.

'He asks that you help me and I ask that you council me on *this*,' Naomi said, producing the necklace she'd snatched from the Russian in Zurich. 'He also said that you'd help me to lift Kgosi Bakubung's debt—whatever that means.'

'That is a debt I never thought to be free of,' Tenebrous said, standing up and dramatically opening his cloak to reveal his ebony skin. 'I agree to those terms. Now, show me this object.'

'I heard it was carved by a witch called Baba Yaga,' she said, handing him the necklace. 'I'm not sure why it's so important, but as soon as I mentioned it, Bojangles said to see you and told me where to find you.'

'Baba Yaga is only part of the story,' Tenebrous revealed, turning the necklace over in his hands. It was made of polished bone and had a symbol carved into it, which resembled a shepherd's hook with a cross at the bottom and another line crossing the curve at the top. 'It is actually much older than that—it was originally created by an Egyptian prince named Kiol Zol for his mother, Queen Kyra Zol. I believe it is actually a piece of his own bone—which one is lost to time. There was nothing magical about it in the beginning, but the queen loved it nonetheless, and it was that love that started the rumour it was mystical in nature.'

'But you're implying that it's magical now?' Naomi asked, taking the necklace back after Tenebrous had finished inspecting it. 'Does it summon something as the legend says, or is it all a giant hoax, as I suspect?'

'Funny, you believe in mystic beings, just not mystic artefacts.' Tenebrous chuckled as he sat back down by the hearth fire. 'No, the talisman doesn't summon anything, but it does grant you an audience with the being, Summon—which I was getting to before you interrupted. Nevertheless, I will explain all if you remain silent and let me speak.'

*Guess his manners are a bit rusty from living in a cave,* Naomi thought, but remained silent as instructed. She took his lead and sat down on the opposite side of the hearth. She removed her small backpack and then continued to turn the talisman over in her hands.

'So, the queen loved the necklace and the legend grew,' Tenebrous recounted. 'Then one day her empire fell to the Scouts of the World Eater and they abducted her son, the prince, and left in their Tomb of Power. The queen vanished shortly thereafter, but she gave the necklace to Bojangles before this happened, and he kept it for many years as a token of their love.'

He paused, possibly for effect, or perhaps to collect his thoughts.

*While this story's pretty interesting, I hope I don't have to listen to four thousand years of history.*

'Anyway, the fool lost it,' Tenebrous resumed, 'and that's when Baba Yaga got hold of it and carved the rune into it at the behest of another, who called herself the Manipulator. That's the rune of Summon, and focusing on it while calling out for an audience with him is all it takes. It had to be simple, as so was the Manipulator. She wanted it as a means to barter for weaponry to use against her estranged husband, Merlin, should he ever return.'

*Weapons, eh? This may actually be useful.*

'Now Bojangles found out about this and tricked Manipulator into giving it back to him,' Tenebrous recalled, as the story started to become memory. 'He kept it with him for many years before our paths finally crossed.'

He paused again and resumed stoking the fire with his staff, and Naomi noticed for the first time how the gem in the tip glowed with each thrust, its dim blue light barely noticeable in the firelight.

*I better not interrupt him again, but I really hope he doesn't keep me here all night,* she thought while she lit up a cigarette. *May as well get comfortable in the meantime.*

'I was a young boy when we first met,' Tenebrous said, breaking the silence. 'I had wandered off from my village, lost on an adventure as only a child can be. It was then that I was beset by four baboons whose territory I had accidentally entered.'

*Those skulls from the entranceway. I guess I can't steal one now.*

'Bojangles appeared from nowhere, saved me from the troop, and took me back to my village,' he continued. 'But everything comes at a price—even the life of a small boy. Bojangles gave me the talisman and bid me when I was old enough to take it north to Egypt and bury it within the tomb of a forgotten boy king. He claimed it was to keep it safe, but I suspect it was because the talisman was cursed the moment the witch tampered with it.'

Tenebrous paused once more as Naomi flicked her cigarette butt into the fire.

'I will spare you the details...' Tenebrous began.

*Thank fuck for that.*

'...but soon enough I was old enough to make the trip. I placed the talisman in the tomb—not without incident—and made my way back home. That was long ago, before the travelling juju man taught me his ways and the white man christened me Tenebrous. You may now ask your questions.'

'So obviously this talisman was eventually discovered and found its way to me,' Naomi said. 'So why did you agree to help me?' She thought she knew but wanted it confirmed.

'Bojangles told me I would know my debt was paid when I saw the talisman again,' Tenebrous admitted. 'As a child I was known as Kgosi Bakubung —which you no doubt have already guessed.'

'Okay but that doesn't explain why Bojangles said I should seek your help,' she said, shifting her weight to her other side, her tight leather work outfit creaking as she did so. 'Nor how he even knew about it in the distant past.'

'You should know that Bojangles' mind exists outside linear time,' Tenebrous said. 'He foresaw this day and he knew I could help you for a very good reason. I grew up with the talisman, remember? I learned its secrets and I learned its curse. This too, you will come to know if you keep it. I believe that is why Bojangles did not ask for it back when you first told him about it. That—and to finally lift my debt, of course.'

'What's stranger is that Bojangles approached me, like he already knew I had this talisman,' she confessed. 'I'd only just acquired it myself, and like you, I'm not so easy to find. Why he didn't just tell me it was cursed is now apparent.'

'Is there anything else you wish to know?' he asked. 'You should use this opportunity wisely, as I doubt we will meet again. My home is hidden to all except those who seek me specifically in this specific place and I do not take visitors lightly.'

'*Is* there anything else I should know?' Naomi countered. 'Okay then, how do I use this talisman? Who is this Summon being?'

*And what weapons does he have?*

'I told you, it is simple,' Tenebrous explained. 'You just hold it in your hand, focus on its power, call out for an audience with Summon, and you will appear before him. As for Summon himself, well, he likes to trade in rare artefacts and will only accept barter. Fear not, for he is honest—but never try to cross him, for he is in total control of his chambers. Anything else you wish to know?'

'No, that just about covers it,' she said, standing up to leave, pocketing the talisman and picking up her backpack. 'You've been most enlightening. Thank you for all your help.'

'And the price of my help?' Tenebrous said without looking up. 'Helping you has paid off my debt to Bojangles. What of your debt to me?'

'It's you who should fear not,' she declared, tossing him the backpack. Tenebrous deftly caught the bag and placed it beside him. 'I didn't really know what to expect, so I hope ten thousand UNos is okay.'

'United Nations money is just fine,' he replied, still without looking up. 'I may be a hermit who lives in a cave, but I do have a standard of living to maintain.'

'Then I thank you once more,' Naomi repeated and turned to leave.

'One more thing,' Tenebrous said.

Naomi paused to listen.

'Be careful of the Kaiser—he's even more dangerous than I. Do not get too close to him, especially close in proximity. You will be his slave without even knowing it.'

*Good thing I've never actually met him in person then.*

'I'll be careful,' she promised as their eyes briefly met through the firelight. 'I appreciate the warning, thank you.'

'Now be on your way and never return,' Tenebrous hissed. He returned to stoking the hearth, his deep-accented English suddenly taking on a menacing tone.

*Jeez, fucking moody much?* Naomi turned and left without saying another word.

It was almost two days later when she made it to one of the Johannesburg slums to complete her assignment for the Kaiser. *The target may be small-fry in the Kaiser's international 'operations' but you don't get to run these kinds of operations in the first place if you let people get away with cheating you.*

She approached the corrugated iron shanty cautiously, constantly scanning for movement within. *No doubt they already knew she was coming. She had a way of being noticed—and it wasn't just her striking good looks. Naomi usually played that to her advantage, but posing as a high-class hooker just wasn't going to cut it here. She needed the direct approach.*

A random resident of the slum cockily approached her from across the street, saying something lewd in his native tongue, but one direct glare from her was enough to persuade him it wasn't worth his while and he returned to his shack.

She drew close to the open doorway and sensed no movement inside.

*Something's not right here; they should be shooting at me by now.*

She slipped silently through the doorway only to discover…an empty room.

*It's more than that.*

It was like the tale of the *Mary Celeste*. Everything was in its place, meals sitting half-eaten, cigarettes still burning—but what made it clear that they hadn't just abandoned the place were the piles of cash and weaponry lying around.

*It's like they just vanished into thin air. I don't like this, it all feels wrong.*

She felt the talisman grow hotter at the thought.

That was when she noticed the note on the meagre coffee table. It simply read:

You're next.
G.

*Gorg,* she thought, and her stomach plunged.

For the first time since her stepfather's beatings forced her out of home, Naomi felt the irresistible urge to flee.

* * *

### Cabramatta, Sydney: 25 May 34 BZ

The High Mage of Hell walked slowly along the creek, searching for his porcine abomination of a son. His enhanced senses could smell his prey now that he drew near.

*And others,* the High Mage thought from within the husk of the Satanist, Gavin. *There are others with him, others the like of which I haven't encountered before. Some are fellow Manifests, but not all…*

His brown robes could have disguised him as just another of the city's homeless if his cloaking spell wasn't already rendering this moot.

He'd finally narrowed down his son's location through scrying spells, simultaneously learning as much as he could about his offspring in his thousand-year absence from the mortal plane.

He'd left his lackeys from Lucifer's Coven to enact their plans—if they were capable—and of course go about finding a replacement for Tom Higginbottom after the tofu incident.

*At least I got to use my scourging spell.*

The High Mage continued to approach the place by the riverbank where he knew his son to be, walking along the dirt trail, which was littered with…well, litter.

*This future world is amazing. The magical devices they use, the horse-less chariots and towering monoliths of glass and steel.*

He paused while a random jogger ran past him from the opposite direction, completely oblivious to the demonic sorcerer she'd passed—except for a shiver and quick glance over her shoulder, as if afraid of pursuers in the late afternoon gloom.

*Ironic that for all this world's marvels, the peasants are still as blind to the real world that ripples just below their senses. They cannot possibly know what I have planned for them and their False Creator.*

The High Mage finally saw the group he'd been searching for and it was the strangest sight he had ever beheld. There were six 'beings' in the group: a man with a stringed instrument and board with wheels, a cardboard automaton, a quaking albino, a lizard man wearing a leather jacket and tinted eyepieces, and a caped hero in blue and yellow.

In the middle of this group of failures, and closest to the metal drum they were using as a heat source, was his mutant porcine son. He was a humanoid pig man with hooves for hands and feet, short horns on his head and giant red bat-wings sprouting from his shoulder blades. Sunglasses balanced atop his hairy snout and tusks jutted from his drooling mouth. It was face not even his mother had loved.

*I should gather as much information as I can before moving on. This is my son and his companions, after all.*

He watched, invisible and silent, while the group went about their inane antics, completely oblivious to the predator in their midst.

'Check this out, me droogs,' said the man with the instrument, before he jumped on his board with wheels and plucked a few discordant strings. 'I'm so cool, I'm so rad, I'm a duuuuude,' he caterwauled to the dismay of all living things.

'That was awesome, Cool Rad Dude,' replied the lizard man in leather. 'Sing it again!'

'Tyranno's right, I could record you,' said the caped hero, his faced obscured by a rectangular mask.

'I say,' said the cardboard automaton. 'I like your idea, Captain Cassette. We can all sing along and maybe get famous.'

'You're scaring me, Influence Man,' whimpered the cringing albino.

'Shut up, Yella' Belly!' the group cried in unison.

'None of us are worthy of being anything more than a group of losers,' said the High Mage's son, who had been silent until now. 'That's why we call our little "super" team the Failures, isn't it? That's certainly how we were publicised in *The Australian Telegraph* when they did that big article about how Manifests are menaces to society and offensive to civilised people—even ones with virtually no powers—like us.'

*His voice, it's the first time I've heard him speak words.*

All the High Mage remembered was him squealing like a pig when he was born. That's when he named the abomination, Hell Hog, and abandoned him to his wife, Hilda.

'Aw shucks,' Tyranno said. 'Hell Hog is right—we *are* offensive to civilised people.'

*The creature is correct; it is an affront to the senses. They are offensive, all of them, including my son. It was right to spawn him as my larder of power.*

The High Mage chuckled at his nefarious thought, suddenly putting the Failures on alert. They couldn't see who was laughing but expected anything from violent gangs to their loser nemesis, Short Fuse.

'Friends,' the High Mage said, and suddenly became visible on the other side of the flaming metal drum.

The Failures started to panic—especially Yella' Belly—and fell over one another in the chaos.

*Is everyone in this time a complete buffoon? This mummer's farce must end!*

'Fear not,' the High Mage said, casting a subtle calming spell as he did so, 'for I am but a humble traveller come to tell you a story. Forgive my theatrics, it was accomplished with nothing more than mirrors, I assure you.'

'Wow! That's really cool,' said the cardboard automaton. 'I'm Influence Man, a homemade costume come to life, and these are my team members, the Failures.'

The group all made their introductions, except Hell Hog, who seemed to be staring intensely through his sunglasses.

*It's almost like he senses who I am, despite the new body. Perhaps that satanic fool was correct earlier when he said that mage garb was no longer commonplace.*

'So, what's this story you were going to tell us?' Hell Hog asked, breaking his silence. 'If it's as impressive as your parlour trick, then we're in for a good night for a change.'

There was a hint of mockery on the wind.

'I will tell you, for it is an old story,' the High Mage began, his scarlet eyes shimmering and his long beard seeming to take on a life of its own. The firelight flickered across his grey skin while he paused to sort it out in his head. 'Long ago, there was a magician, a mage from on high, if you will. This mage could soothsay long into the future and devised a great plan.'

'Greater than God's divine plan?' interrupted Hell Hog, who was unsurprisingly religious.

'It's funny you should mention that, for is a man not created in the image of God and therefore a god in his own right?' the High Mage asked, looking around the group and gaining support with his enthusiasm.

'Well no, it doesn't work like that...' Hell Hog began.

'I'm scared,' Yella' Belly interrupted.

'Let him tell the story,' Influence Man said, using his Manifest ability to influence the mind of anyone who took him seriously—which was no one at all.

'Yeah! And I'm gonna tape it!' Captain Cassette said, as he used his ability to take mental control of the tape recorder he always carried with him and depressed the record buttons.

'That's so cool and rad, dude,' said Cool Rad Dude. 'Maybe I can add some theme music for the tale?'

The High Mage used a quick (and unnoticed) stroke of his finger to snap the guitar strings.

'Oh, that's a shame,' Cool Rad Dude said, 'but lucky I brought my spare strings!'

'Will you mugs shut ya traps before I shut them for ya?' Tyranno hissed. 'I want to hear this story!'

'Yeah, it's like a movie where the villain tells his evil plan, giving the heroes time to stop him,' Captain Cassette said without a hint of irony. 'Though I yield the point. Please continue,' he said, gesturing to the High Mage.

*Movie? What is this fool blathering about?*

'Now, where was I?' the High Mage asked, genuinely struggling to remember through all his thoughts of carnage. 'Oh yes, the beginning. So, this mage devised a great plan and went about setting it in motion. For he had divined that the Creator was false, and that he should take his place as the Lord of Hosts.'

The Failures all seemed terrified at the thought. All except Hell Hog, who actually seemed interested.

'This was not an easy task; the False Creator had powerful seraphim at his disposal—this was how he banished the False Lucifer to Hell,' the High Mage recounted, feeling inspired.

'That's a lot of the word "false", wouldn't you say?' Hell Hog interrupted. 'Lucifer is Lucifer. The only false thing about him is his word.'

'No!' the High Mage said. 'It stands to reason that if the creator is false, then so must be all his creations.'

'But that would include us, and everything that exists,' Hell Hog said. 'I feel quite real.'

'You are, we all are,' said the High Mage. 'We who are created in God's image are gods ourselves.'

'You just said that God was false!' Hell Hog huffed.

'No, I said the Creator was false,' the High Mage corrected. 'God is an entirely separate issue.'

'That doesn't make any sense,' Hell Hog said. 'You're crazy!'

'You just can't see the big picture,' the High Mage said defensively. 'Besides, it's what the mage in this story believed.'

'The story that you keep interrupting, Hell Hog,' said Captain Cassette. 'I'm going to have to go back and edit all this out of the final recording.'

'See, this mage learned that the False Creator's arrogance was his greatest weakness,' the High Mage resumed, taking his cue from the ridiculous Captain. 'An army of demons could overthrow the Heavenly Host…'

'But Michael already cast them out with Lucifer…' Hell Hog began.

'…if the False Creator's attention was diverted by being attacked on two fronts,' the High Mage continued relentlessly. 'A second demon army would be unleashed upon the earth—and the people whose worship he requires to remain powerful—to simultaneously distract and weaken him. Once the seraphim were defeated, then the False Creator would have to finally show himself and *I* will destroy him and take the Gates of Heaven for myself!'

'Hang on, what did you just say?' Hell Hog asked, suddenly feeling cold despite the burning drum. 'Did anyone else catch that?'

'Shush, this story's great,' Captain Cassette admonished, holding out his tape recorder. 'I'm getting some great stuff here.'

*These fools are wearing thin with their incessant babbling.*

'The mage realised that the False Lucifer would need to be contained until the False Creator could be overthrown,' the High Mage explained, enjoying the sound of his voice. 'The Lords of Hell were always happy to conspire against their master for power, plus they would relish the chance to escape their prison for either the Gates of Heaven or the mortal realm. The False Creator would assume that the attack came from the False Lucifer and would divide his forces to attack Hell. Meanwhile, the mage would rob the demons of the souls they sought on the mortal realm and at the same time use this power for himself to command the attack on Heaven.'

He paused, expecting more interruptions, but everyone seemed completely absorbed by the tale.

*Excellent, the calming spell I cast is working, though I doubt it can subdue their true natures for long.*

'All the mage needed was a powerful artefact called the Soul Gem with which to channel the souls, but he was betrayed by his closest friend before he found it,' the High Mage said, remembering all too well. 'He was killed by a demon of his own reflection and his soul was sent to Hell.'

'So we're safe then? Yay!' said Yella' Belly—the chicken emblazoned on his yellow and white outfit making him look like a fast food employee.

'No, for he escaped Hell through a loophole he discovered,' the High Mage replied menacingly. 'Dreams allowed him to escape Hell and bypass the Mystical Realm at the same time. The same realm that eventually trapped the one that betrayed him. The one that knows where the Soul Gem is. Unfortunately, the mage doesn't have the power to get there.'

'Unfortunately?' asked Hell Hog. 'Is anyone else hearing this?'

'All I hear is a good story,' Tyranno said, 'which you keep interrupting.'

*They really need to learn silence. The silence of the grave. One more outburst...*

'The mage had anticipated a scenario in his great plan where he would be bereft of power,' the High Mage continued, slowly moving his hands around the fire licking the top of the drum. 'That's why I had a son to be a storehouse for when I needed it. To grow in power over time, although I didn't imagine just how much time.'

'I can't believe none of you are hearing this!' Hell Hog said to his companions, unaware they were spellbound. He turned back to the High Mage. 'Who are you? You haven't said your name.'

'I am the High Mage of Hell, but I was once known as Merlin.'

'Father?' Hell Hog asked in shocked disbelief. 'Is it really you, after a thousand years?'

'Forsooth,' the High Mage declared, 'it is a new body, but an old soul. I have returned to fulfil my destiny to ascend to godhood. I just need to raid my larder, in a manner of speaking.'

His tone shifted to one of thinly veiled hostility and the High Mage smiled at his son as he spoke. Then he smacked his chops like a ravenous dog.

'But that would make the larder...' Hell Hog began.

The tension in the air drew as tight as a guitar string.

'Fixed it!' Cool Rad Dude shouted, breaking the silence with a tuneless twang on his re-stringed guitar. 'Weee arrrre doooomed!' he howled.

*That's it! I can bear it no longer!*

The High Mage stood up dramatically, lifting the glamour spell he used to disguise his true features. The grey and partially decomposed face of Gavin the would-be Satanist stared at Hell Hog with malice. His glowering scarlet eyes radiated with unmasked ferocity and other menacing adjectives.

'Failures!' Hell Hog cried, desperately scanning his comrades. 'Snap out of it! We have to stop this guy from attacking Heaven!'

'It's the apocalypse!' Yella' Belly screamed, cowering into a ball. 'Help!'

It was no use. Aside from Yella' Belly's usual theatrics, no one else seemed to notice anything was wrong. Hell Hog knew it was all up to him. He faced his father.

'It's time for you to pay for abandoning mother and I to the wild all those centuries ago,' he said with false bravado. 'It's payback time,' he added, drawing inspiration from the cinema.

Hell Hog drew a deep breath and then blasted two streams of hell-fire through his nostrils straight at his father. It combined with the flames from the drum and swept over the High Mage, lighting up the entire area. Some passers-by stopped to stare and then decided better of it.

The High Mage laughed as the flames moved around him but didn't touch him. 'I have spent the last thousand years bathed in hellfire, and before that I mastered the elements. You have no hope of defeating me, for I planned this day from the start. My plan is foolproof.'

'Yeah? I bet you didn't count on this!' Hell Hog yelled back.

Without warning, Hell Hog jumped to the side and pushed Influence Man at the High Mage. The living cardboard costume tripped, hammering the wizard off his feet. 'Tallyho!' it cried.

*Enough of this!* the High Mage thought, tossing the ridiculous automaton from him and knocking over the Failures like bowling pins. *These fools must not delay me.*

'We're all gonna die!' Yella' Belly cried again.

'The craven speaks true,' the High Mage said ominously, his hands beginning to glow. Long strands of mystic energy snaked from his fingers and then suddenly plunged into the chests of the group.

'This would make a great movie!' Captain Cassette said while the energy drilled into his solar plexus. 'Too bad I'm only recording audio…' His voice trailed off as his life force began flowing to the High Mage.

The tendrils struck the Failures, sans Hell Hog, and they began ageing at an incredible rate as their essence was absorbed.

Hell Hog looked around while his companions died simultaneously, withering to dust before his porcine eyes. 'Nooooooo!' he cried—without needing to draw on any cinematic inspiration. He spread his batlike wings and took to the sky.

'Not so fast, son,' the High Mage called after him. 'This family reunion's only just beginning.'

With a gesture of his hand, the High Mage took control of the fire in the drum, turning it into a fiery hand that stretched out and snatched his son. Hell Hog screamed as the flames consumed him. The High Mage gestured with his other hand and brought his smouldering son crashing to the ground at his feet. The aroma of bacon wafted through the air.

'Looks like I'm finally going to get my roast boar after all,' the High Mage said. He calmly tore his son's arm from its socket and sank his teeth into the charred flesh. The same energy that drained the others flashed across his teeth with every bite.

*This is delicious,* he thought as he tried some wing. *And so powerful! He's been storing evermore power through the centuries—more than I could've hoped for.*

The High Mage continued to eat until his thoughts were interrupted by a high-pitched siren wail drawing closer.

*This body's memories tell me those sounds mean I should leave.* He plucked an eyeball from his son's pigface. *I should absorb the rest of his energy with haste.*

The High Mage repeated his earlier spell and a mystic tendril shot from his hand to syphon his son's remaining power.

*Now that I have the power to travel to the so-called Mystical Realm, it's time for the next phase of my plan. It's time to slay Death and free Antimatter. Upwards, ever upwards.*

The High Mage chuckled to himself, casting his invisibility spell and slipping unnoticed past the bewildered policemen just as they arrived on the scene.

* * *

### Dungeon Cell 9: 29 May 34 BZ

Andy Trailer lay battered and bruised on the cold stone floor, shivering uncontrollably while the insects crawled over his flesh. He couldn't tell how recent his last beating was, as time had lost all meaning to him. The cockroaches seemed new—at least in such vast numbers— although there was one he recognised: it was fat, black, and twice the size of the others. Its size was proof of his failure to catch it for a meal. Andy sensed it was female without having any idea why.

*But is it even real?* Andy thought miserably as the roaches nibbled on his necrotic flesh. *Or is it part of some hallucination brought on by my master? It seems real though and it would be nice to have a friend in here.*

*It is part of the trap,* said the familiar alien voice in his mind, the voice that eroded all confidence. *The cyclops is using it to spy on your mind—you cannot trust him. You can only trust us. Kill it! Kill the spy!*

'No!' Andy said aloud, his harsh voice echoing off the stone walls. *You're the one I don't trust; Master has always been honest with me. Who's 'us' anyway? There is no us, there's me and there's you.*

*Yes, there is only you and us,* the voice said. *You and Wisp.*

*Is that what you're called? How many of you are there?* Andy slowly stopped shivering and began to sit up. *You could be a test from the Master.*

*We have been here long before the cyclops,* Wisp said in its toneless voice. *We have been with you since birth; we have always been a part of you. Energy Lord merely broke down the mental walls that prevented you from being aware of us when he triggered your Manifest seed.*

*That sounds like a lie, not to forget fucking sinister.* Andy sat up against the wall, his giant wings folded around him. *If that's the case, where do you come from?*

*Wisp are a gift from Gledandron to all the children of Earth,* Wisp replied. *Wisp are the ones who know your true nature and whisper it to you in your dreams. There is one Wisp unit for each newborn child—all the better to guide the human race. You have been blessed to hear our voice without restraint.*

*Yeah, me and all the crazy people.* Andy studied a cockroach that was walking the length of his protruding rib. *Why's this happening to me? It's not fair.*

*It is true that many whom your society calls insane have also been blessed with knowing of us,* Wisp intoned. *It is not our fault that you misunderstand our gift to your species.*

*Our species?* Andy thought that sounded strange. Hunger overcame curiosity and he dismissed the idea, snatching the roach from his rib and throwing it between his serrated teeth. *So, you are an alien?* he asked, chewing the bitter arthropod.

*We are but aspects of almighty Gledandron,* Wisp answered. *Ancient and terrible and ravenous, yet Gledandron offers hope through faith in its aspects—like Wisp. You have been blessed to know the truth of it.*

*I think you're incapable of telling the truth.* Andy caught another bug and stuffed it into his ulcerated mouth. The fat female cockroach watched from within its nest at the base of the protruding rib. *Besides, I'm the one who's ravenous. If you were any real help, you'd conjure up some food for me to eat. Unless you're just another trick like I expect.*

*We are no trick,* Wisp said. *The trick has been the 'training' missions you have been doing for your so-called master. You know they are not real, yet you still do them—and for what? He still gets his mechanical Trio to beat you, and his assistant—the one in purple and green with the living blades—never feeds you anything, leaving you to forage for insects.*

*Master does feed me—I get bacon, and stew, and even prawns after that one time I completed my mission perfectly.* His stomach rumbled at the thought of skewered garlic prawns. *The beatings are to remind me to never think of escape. I am his Night Demon and my place is here.*

*None of it is real!* Wisp yelled in Andy's head. *You cannot eat only in your mind.*

*The beatings are real,* Andy reflected with dread. *It might not be fair, but it's better than displeasing Master.*

*The cyclops is not your master,* Wisp said. *Gledandron is our true patron, Gledandron is our true god.*

*You lie! I must obey the Master.* Andy looked for another roach.

*The cyclops is simply another Manifest like you, though not as powerful,* Wisp said.

*Powerful? Yeah right,* Andy thought despairingly.

*He seeks to unlock the secrets of not only the seeds that give Manifests their abilities, but also those of the Wisp,* Wisp continued. *This cannot be allowed. None may know of Gledandron until they behold his majestic form at the moment of their death.*

*Now that does sound crazy.* Andy impaled a third cockroach with his fingernail and delivered it to his salivating mouth. *You're saying the Master wants to learn about you?*

*It is the very reason he acquired you from the Energy Lord,* Wisp responded, giving the impression of a snake coiling in Andy's mind.

The cockroaches had all fled now that Andy had regained his resolve, all except the fat female that had nested in the dead flesh around his exposed rib. He tried to fish it out with his nails, but it burrowed deeper into his gangrenous wound.

*Maybe it is a spy for the Master, watching while my loyalty is tested,* Andy thought, failing yet again to catch his insectoid nemesis.

*If you cannot kill it, then you must take control of it,* Wisp advised. *Use the gifts you have been blessed with.*

*I do!* Andy thought defensively, *I use them on my master's training missions. I can fly, I'm strong, and I have sharp claws and teeth.*

*If you only knew what else you were capable of,* Wisp replied. *You could become the Master.*

*Yeah and then get revenge on Energy Lord for starting all this.* His emotions turned to vengeance.

*Yesss…* Wisp hissed. *This is how you should be thinking. Obey the cyclops for now, learn from him and grow strong. Then it will be time to strike.*

*But how will I know when the time's right?* Andy asked, afraid this entire conversation was a trap laid out for him by Master.

*You will know,* Wisp said ominously. *The magician unit has returned and will soon unleash forces this world has never seen. That will be the time. Now, take control of that cockroach.*

Andy looked again at the suppurating wound around his exposed rib. The big female had returned to peer through the hole at Andy. It appeared to be guarding a clutch of eggs.

*Unusual,* Andy thought, focusing on the insect. *But that's not relevant. Now focus on the task.*

'Come to me, little one,' Andy said, pointing at the roach. 'Come to Night Demon.'

He got a brief flash of…something. The cockroach slowly raised its head out of the wound.

'Come on, come,' he cooed as best he could with a voice that invoked images of a mortar and pestle grinding bones. 'Come little one.'

Another flash.

The cockroach crawled out of its nest and onto the tip of his pointed finger.

*Now eat your reward and rid yourself of this spy,* Wisp said without congratulating Andy on his accomplishment.

Andy paused with his finger pointed at his open mouth, the cockroach stood calmly on the edge of the sharp nail. Another flash—longer—this time. Andy got a glimpse of his own hideous face looming down on him like a twisted giant.

*No,* he finally thought. *She's my friend, she's fed off me, laid her brood in me—that means something, something special.*

*If you insist,* Wisp said. *It may become a useful ally in the end. Only Gledandron knows for sure.*

*Not just Gledandron.* Andy smiled. *I know too.*

# JUNE

## University of Sydney: 1 June 34 BZ

Seth Zaraxom stretched back in his seat and had a private chuckle at the ignorance of the human race. The lecture he'd randomly sat in on to pass the time was on music in ancient cultures, specifically the Hurrian people and their hymn to Nikkal, the goddess of orchards from the city of Ugarit.

The lecturer had just finished saying that it was the oldest substantially complete piece of notated music in the world, but sadly the composer was unknown and lost to time.

*Or sitting right here in the lecture hall,* Seth thought, looking around the room at the half-asleep uni students. *Kismet sure does like her coincidences.*

'I'll now play a couple of renditions of this piece,' the lecturer said in his monotonous public speaking voice. 'This music is almost four thousand years old.' He hit the play button on his cassette player.

Haunting words began to resonate around the hall, accompanied by the chords of a stringed instrument, like a harp or lyre.

*This sounds nothing at all like I remember it,* Seth mused, shifting in the uncomfortable fold-down seat. *As tempting as it is to go down there and correct him, it probably wouldn't be wise. Besides, Bojangles should be here soon.*

Seth adjusted his position again as his long, black trench coat had caught in the fold out desk in the arm of the chair. He tore the lining of his coat in his attempt to free himself.

'Shit!' he said, a little too loudly, causing some of the audience to turn and look.

'Bloody Goths,' a nearby chunky student muttered to his friend. 'Think they're so badass in all black and wearing makeup, when really they just look like poofs.'

'Yeah, all trying to be individuals by looking the same,' his pimply companion added. 'How pathetic, pretending to be young by imitating the Goth movement.'

*Foolish children.* He stared at the back of their uncombed heads two rows down. *I'm so old I can't remember what it was like to be young, let alone pretend to be. And forget the Goth movement, my look inspired the fucking Visigoths!*

Seth was currently dressed in a tight shirt, leather pants, steel-cap boots, and of course his torn trench coat—all of which was as black as his long flowing hair. What appeared to be eye shadow and lipstick were his natural birth markings—but everyone assumed the former. Add to that his chiselled features and pale complexion and needless to say, he was easy to mistake for a member of the current Goth movement.

Seth appeared to be in his early forties, but he was much, much older than he looked. In fact, at approximately twenty-nine-thousand years old, Seth looked absolutely fantastic for his age. Being immortal also brought with it a lot of time to kill.

The next rendition of the hymn to Nikkal sounded even less like Seth remembered, and he grew impatient waiting for his companion.

*Where the fuck is Bojangles? I don't know how much longer I can sit here listening to this.*

As if on cue, a grey-haired Aboriginal man slipped silently into the lecture hall and sat down next to Seth. He was also dressed in all black, sans trench coat, and although he looked older than Seth, he was actually ten thousand years younger. 'These seats are pretty uncomfortable,' he declared.

'Finally!' Seth whispered. 'What took you so long?'

'It takes time to do the things I do,' he replied, taking off his sunglasses and slipping them into his shirt pocket.

'You can teleport, for fuck's sake,' Seth said a little too loudly, causing Chunky and Pimples to turn around and shush him. He ignored them. 'It shouldn't take you long to do anything,' he said, lowering his voice.

'You know me, I'm a people person, I like to stop for a cuppa,' Bojangles said with a huge grin on his face.

'Something tells me that Tenebrous isn't one for high tea and cucumber sandwiches,' Seth surmised.

'Oh, you'd be surprised what concoctions that withered old sod can brew up.' Bojangles gave him a wink.

'So how did it go?' Seth enquired, as yet another rendition of the hymn was played to the audience.

'I'll get to that in a moment.' Bojangles shifted in his seat. 'I just have to ask—what the hell is this we're listening to?'

'Oh, it's a song to my sister,' Seth explained. 'I wrote it a long time ago, though I don't remember why. I also remember it being catchier.'

'This is a song to Lilith that you wrote?' Bojangles was sceptical. 'And we're sitting in a lecture about it?'

'Well, she was known to the locals as Nikkal at the time,' Seth said. 'But basically, yeah.'

'What are the odds?' Bojangles asked rhetorically.

'About the same as you giving me an update in the next year,' Seth retorted, completely deadpan.

'All right, all right,' Bojangles said resignedly. 'You'd think at your age you'd have learned to be more patient.'

'I've also learned the importance of time,' Seth responded.

'Do you want me to update you or not?' Bojangles said with a laugh. He'd known Seth for so long that these sorts of conversations were almost a ritual. 'Right—so I went and saw Tenebrous in his dingy cave to see how Naomi's visit went down, which was as planned. She's got that cursed talisman and knows how to use it—I just don't know why you even care about it, considering you don't need it.'

Chunky and Pimples turned around and gave Seth and Bojangles death stares. They ignored them both and continued talking.

'I don't need it as I know other ways of getting an audience with Summon,' Seth revealed. 'I just like having a backup plan. Besides, I wouldn't have any plan at all if you hadn't foreseen all of this.'

'Some of it at least,' Bojangles conceded, 'although only the parts that relate to my own life and not all of it at that. I wish I could foresee if I'll ever meet up with Kyra again.'

'I'm sure you will,' Seth said, shifting in his seat. 'That whole incident with her disappearance and the prior abduction of her son, Prince Kiol Zol, is the reason I've become so involved in stopping the World Eater.'

'Kyra didn't disappear; she was abducted by a strange helmeted man who appeared out of nowhere—as you very well know,' Bojangles said as the final rendition of the hymn began. 'He appeared to be unaligned with the demons that imprisoned Prince Kiol in their mobile tomb, but Kyra wouldn't have been there to be kidnapped if those same demons hadn't captured us as well. Good thing Emperor Sargon was there to free us or we might have been eaten ourselves.'

'True,' Seth agreed, 'but now that Merlin has returned as the so-called High Mage of Hell, we may be consumed regardless. I have to stop him, which is why I've borrowed a magical artefact.'

'I thought your shtick was finding the pretentious God who Walks Like a Man?' Bojangles asked in a teasing tone. 'Do you also take time out to fight demonic world eaters?'

'Ha-ha,' Seth replied. 'Sure, looking for signs of the prophecy was what my father tasked me with eons ago, but someone's got to stop the World Eater or there'll be no prophecy to come true. Besides, I think both my goals will come together at some point.'

'So it was your father who gave you that pointless mission?' Bojangles paused to eyeball Chunky and Pimples, who gave up on their latest attempt to shame Seth and Bojangles into silence after seeing his golden irises. 'Bloody family, hey?'

'Yeah, but at least I can blame the gods for my crazy relatives,' Seth said, smiling. 'Given that that's exactly what most of them are.'

'Speaking of crazy relatives,' Bojangles segued, as the lecture ended and people started to leave—Chunky and Pimples being the first. 'What's with that fucked up nephew of yours?'

'That...I'm not even sure Mosh knows,' Seth answered as they found themselves in an empty lecture hall.

\* \* \*

## Interstate 5, California: 3 June 34 BZ

Dread Sedgewick tore down the highway in his '74 Corvette Stingray to the tune of Glenn Danzig's 'Mother', accompanied by the terrified Captain Povo and pursued by half the state's police force. He didn't seem to notice.

'This is a fucking wicked car!' Dread shouted over the pounding music. 'Zoth was right when he said I needed to get something like this as a status symbol!'

That wasn't quite how the Captain remembered it, but he'd rather eat a cheese grater than say so. He was still reeling from the realisation they'd been in the Abyss for almost a month when it seemed they arrived there only yesterday. 'Yeah,' was all he managed to say.

'Here, hold the steering wheel for a sec,' Dread said, fishing in his coat for a cigarette. 'Now, where are they?'

Captain Povo grabbed the wheel in panic but managed to keep it still—which was no mean feat at close to two hundred kilometres per hour. Dread continued to fish around in his jacket, seemingly unconcerned with driving the vehicle. He finally found one and lit it with the sparks from his finger blades before changing his hand back to normal and taking the wheel.

'Oh yeah, feel that nicotine goodness,' Dread said in defiance of the taboo of endorsing smoking. He was the world's most dangerous supervillain after all. 'I'm glad you could accompany me on this little road trip, my good Captain, and your help with customising this beauty is appreciated.'

Proof of this was the fact that Captain Povo was still breathing.

'It's been fun,' the Captain lied. He returned to cringing in his seat, his seatbelt having been removed by Dread earlier as a show of toughness. 'I also think you made the right choice of car, no matter what that salesperson thought.'

The salesperson in question was now spread across at least two American states and Dread had taken the car anyway. He was so massive he barely fit in the car, but he'd always wanted one and didn't like the suggestion of a campervan instead.

Black and sleek, the Corvette had only been improved by Dread painting his personal symbol on the bonnet—a silver shape resembling a pentagram, except the side points unfurled like wings—with Captain Povo using his awesome ability to dry paint to ensure the job was completed quickly.

The car yard was next to a gas station and they'd dropped in for fuel and road-beers. Directions were sought from the timid Bhutanese attendant.

It was then that Dread had decided to take it for a test drive and reluctantly chose Interstate 5 after learning that the legendary Route 66 had been effectively neutered by the government—and was also miles away from their current location.

Always one to kill the messenger, Dread had caused a lot of mayhem at the news, but it was short-lived due to his overriding desire to experience a fabled American road trip. He drove from crime scene to crime scene—all of them gas stations—and collected the fleet of police cars and accompanying Apache helicopters along the way.

*Which brings us up to speed,* Dread thought. *One hundred and twenty-five miles per hour, to be precise.*

'So what d'ya think, should I let Zoth manage my band?' Dread raised his voice to be heard over Danzig's manly bellow. 'I remember Desecrate was keen when Zoth asked him about it.'

'Who's that?' Captain Povo asked as the song drew to a close. 'I haven't heard of Desecrate before.'

'Oh, he's another band member,' Dread replied nonchalantly. 'He's a Danish supervillain who's into heavy metal.'

'Fitting,' the Captain observed. The song ended and the next track on the album, *Metal Mix 4,* started to play.

'Let's hear that song again, I fucking love it,' Dread announced, hitting the 'back' button on the car's fancy CD player—another feature that he adored. Danzig once more began to wail. 'Lucky they had this CD at that last petrol station we stopped at in San Diego. Speaking of which, where the fuck is everyone? You'd think there'd be more cars around on such a giant road.'

'I think they closed the road especially for this road trip,' the Captain offered. He stopped short of mentioning the elephant in the room, despite the sound of the Apaches clearly intermingling with the music.

'Well, it *is* an auspicious occasion,' Dread said, meaning it. 'But even the oncoming lanes are empty.'

'*We're* in the oncoming lane!' Captain Povo exclaimed with frantic agitation. 'In America, they drive on the right!'

'That explains why the steering wheel's on the wrong side,' Dread said. 'So tell me: what are your plans after our little trip to find the American dream—which is the sole reason people go on these trips, remember?'

'Presuming I survive...' the Captain began.

*Good assumption.*

'...I think I'll return to my job as a painter,' he revealed. 'I think I might be over the whole supervillain experience. And what about you? What are your plans?' It was a bold question. Dread took it in his stride.

'You know me,' Dread exaggerated. 'I like to take things easy, one day at a time. I really like drifting from place to place, never knowing what kind of random adventure I'm going to have next.'

Captain Povo thought that spoke volumes.

'But I do have some family matters to attend to one of these days.' Dread absentmindedly flicked one of the gas station attendant's eyeballs he'd used in place of fluffy dice. 'I like to take my time with these things—eventually I'll get around to fragging everyone on my shit-list. In the meantime, they're on borrowed time.'

'So, you're sort of like a loan shark that loans time instead of money,' the Captain said, trying to sound agreeable so he didn't make the shit-list. 'And when you come to collect, you don't just break their knee-caps.'

Dread liked the sound of that. 'No, but I'll still break their kneecaps anyway!' He laughed and flicked his butt out the window. 'Loan shark eh? I like it! Captain, my Captain, I think you just earned yourself at least another year of walking the planet!' He meant it too.

Captain Povo didn't know whether to feel horrified that his life would be up for review in a year, or relieved that at least Dread wasn't going to kill him now and dangle his eyeballs from the rear-view mirror like the hapless attendant's.

Feeling confident for the first time since meeting his hulking kidnapper, Captain Povo decided to satiate his morbid curiosity.

'So...' he began. '...what family business do you have to attend to? Is this like a mafia thing? My great uncle was a part of the Povolo crime family back in the Old Country.'

Dread suddenly turned and eyed the Captain with an intense emerald stare, his red facial markings almost darkening as he narrowed his eyes.

Captain Povo broke into a cold sweat, desperately holding onto his bladder so he didn't ruin the car seats, but Dread smiled his maniacal grin and turned back to the road. 'Anymore of those road-beers?' he asked hopefully as 'Mother' wound up for the second time.

'Uh, no, you drank the last one an hour ago,' the Captain replied, starting to sweat again. 'You can have my sparkling mineral water if you like.'

'How did you even sneak that sissy shit into the car without me noticing?' Dread enquired politely. 'Give me that.'

Dread grabbed the bottle of water and threw it out the sunroof in disgust.

'Anyway,' he continued, plucking an eyeball from the rear-view mirror and sucking on it, 'I discovered my father has another family he was keeping secret from my mother and I, so I am going to kill them all and make him eat what's left.'

Captain Povo could only imagine what primordial abominations spawned the death machine sitting alongside him, and simply knowing there were more of them out there somewhere was enough to cause many a sleepless night. He chose not to press his luck with that line of questioning and decided instead to address the elephant in the room, which by now was also giving birth to a circus car full of midget clowns.

'So, how many police do you think are following us?' he asked, looking over his seat at the force pursuing them—which seemed to have doubled in size since he last looked.

'Oh, a couple hundred at least,' Dread answered casually while the next track came over the speakers. 'My reputation precedes me and someone probably calculated that the collateral damage isn't worth pissing me off. They're probably hoping we cross the border and become Mexico's problem.'

'But we're not going to do that, are we?' the Captain queried, having a sinking premonition of the things to come.

'No...' Dread replied almost under his breath, as Megadeth's 'Symphony of Destruction' ramped up and he slammed on the breaks while simultaneously turning the car one hundred and eighty degrees to face the oncoming police. The tyres and Captain Povo both screeched in protest. 'The American Dream is taking too long to find. Let's play a little game of chicken instead and see how far their non-engagement policy goes when we're coming straight at them.'

Captain Povo would rather they didn't, but then again, he wasn't consulted. Dread finished revving the engine, dropped the clutch and floored the accelerator.

'Mexico's got enough problems already,' Dread said observantly, 'and besides, the Yanks love flexing their muscles—it's win-win.'

He cranked the volume to jet engine levels. The music thundered, ironically *unlike* the Pied Piper that Dave Mustaine was singing about.

The Corvette rapidly narrowed the distance between them and their pursuers, despite the police rapidly decelerating when they saw what was happening.

'This is gonna be great!' Dread yelled over the din as the car reached its top speed. 'Open your eyes; you don't want to miss this!'

Captain Povo snuck a peek with a single eye and almost unclenched every sphincter in his body at once. No less than four helicopters loomed in front and he could actually make out the faces of the police in the oncoming cars.

'Fuck yeah!' Dread screamed as the police cars began scattering before them—parting like the Red Sea, but with a lot less water. 'You guys lose!' He started laughing and was having such a good time that he considered becoming Mexico's problem after all.

A bullet suddenly punched through the back window and shattered the rear-view mirror. Captain Povo jumped. A nerve in Dread's face twitched.

'This is the thanks I get after graciously deciding to spare them?' Dread fumed justifiably. 'Here, grab the wheel—don't worry, she'll stop on her own—just don't crash into anything. Wait for me, I'll be right back.'

The Captain barely had time to register what was happening before Dread squeezed out the sunroof and was gone.

Dread jumped from the moving Corvette, slashing the air and retrieving four long daggers from whatever pocket dimension he stored them in.

The police cars had all stopped in defensive positions and the helicopters hovered above them, all of them pointing guns at him. He noticed that one cop was yelling at another cop who sat in the gun turret of a modified SWAT van.

*He's obviously the douchebag who shot my brand-new car,* Dread thought, stalking the authorities with the tune of 'Symphony of Destruction' still playing in his head. *At least the Captain managed to stop the car without any further damage, which is a plus. Hey, that gives me an idea...*

'Yo, pigs!' he called out when he came within earshot of the combined force of several branches of military and civilian armed response teams. 'Tell you what, you give me the little prick who shot my car, and I'll let the rest of you live. Sound fair?'

The police seemed to actually consider the proposition and looked to each other for support. The man who fired the gun turned as pale as an albino's arse in the snow.

*Ooh I just love moral dilemmas.* He licked his lips.

He took a step closer and suddenly one of the Apache helicopters fired two hellfire missiles at him. He retaliated by throwing two of his blades with remarkable accuracy, detonating the missiles before they could strike.

'Now that's just cheating!' he shouted with righteous indignation. 'Who brings rockets to a knife fight anyway?'

To be fair, only Dread knew it was meant to be a knife fight, but it became irrelevant as frayed nerves resulted in the order to fire at will. He responded in kind.

Two minutes later and Dread calmly lit a cigarette amid the burning vehicles and dismembered corpses. Of the three hundred and twelve personnel who had played chicken with Dread, only about thirty remained —he was saving them for later.

*What's the opposite of decimating something, I wonder?* he thought, drawing back on his smoke. *Good thing I took my time slaying them or I'd be feeling disappointed.*

All the helicopters were down and all but one of the vehicles were scrap—the modified SWAT van with the guy who shot his car still sitting in the turret. Dread approached him.

'Now, where were we?' he asked without expecting an answer. 'What's your name, champ?'

'S-Sam Shanks,' he muttered. 'It's not my fault—I'm new...I wasn't trained properly...I was fast-tracked...my aunt's married to...'

'Oh, you're an Aussie?' Dread was amused. 'Fancy running into one of you here, of all places! I like Australia and spend a lot of time there.'

'Y-yeah, I remember seeing you in my police reports,' Sam said nervously. 'I used to be a detective in Sydney.'

'Just because I like Australia doesn't mean I like you,' Dread barked between drags. 'You shot up my new wheels, so here's what's gonna happen: I'm gonna let you live—which is more than can be said for the last of your mates—but for a limited time only. You won't know when the end will come, but be assured that it will be delivered by my hand. I want you to spend what remains of your miserable life looking over your shoulder.'

Sam was without a snappy comeback for the first time in his life, until he caught something in the corner of his eye behind Dread, who hadn't seemed to notice. 'Yeah, well maybe it won't come to that and me or someone else will get the drop on you first.'

Dread raised an eyebrow in response. 'What, do you think that mister "I didn't inhale" actually has the balls to nuke me on American soil? Nah, more likely one of the government's pet Manifests is on their way here right now,' Dread scoffed, before pausing to take a final drag and flicking the butt into Sam's face. 'You know what? You seem like just the type of irredeemable arsehole who would try to get revenge on me after I've been so kind to you. That'll just make it funnier when you spend all that time planning, only to fail when you finally catch up with me again.'

'Oh, I don't think it'll take *that* long,' Sam said with unusual confidence, and ducked down and covered his head.

'You think I can't hear you two skulking around behind me?' Dread said, turning around to discover that two of the soldiers he'd thoughtfully spared had wheeled over and set up a Q9 Anti-Manifest Howitzer and had it pointed straight at him. He'd managed to subdue everyone earlier before they had time to use it. 'Pfff—your pissy little anti-Manifest rifles don't work on me. What makes you think that will?'

The soldiers decided to try their luck anyway and fired the heavy weapon. The howitzer fired a ball of energy much larger than those fired by the carbine, which was followed a millisecond later by the explosive shell itself. Like the Q5 carbine, the pulse removed the target's powers, leaving them vulnerable to the standard projectile.

The explosion rocked the area and sent smoke and debris flying in all directions. The howitzer team were killed by the blast, but luckily Sam was protected by Dread's body being directly in front of him. His ears were ringing badly, but it was worth it to know that Dread was finished—and that he didn't have to be the one to sacrifice himself.

The smoke cleared, and to Sam's horror Dread was still standing.

'Look what those fucks did to my shirt!' he complained to Sam, turning so he could show the big hole in his red undershirt, revealing the scorched skin underneath. 'I hate it when something gets through my aura and ruins my clothes!'

Sam was now regretting his earlier smartass comments.

'Now don't fret, Sammy boy. I meant what I said about letting you stew on your impending death for years, so I won't hold you accountable for your cheek. I figure being a complete cunt-bucket is in your nature,' Dread said. He turned back to his Corvette only to notice the passenger door was wide open. 'Looks like the good Captain decided to make a break for it, so I gotta go find him—slash ya later.'

Dread jumped the distance to his car in a single leap, having already relegated Sam Shanks to the shit-list and out of his mind.

'Oh Captain,' Dread called out dramatically. 'It's okay, they didn't kill me and it's safe to come out!'

'I have already apprehended your partner and taken him into custody,' said a stern voice from above and behind him.

*Why do people keep talking to me from that strange angle?* Dread wondered, turning around to face the new arrival. *And yep, I was right about the government going for the pet super-doofus option. Fuck, this guy looks like he could fart the Declaration of Independence.*

'Something tells me you're a local boy,' Dread mocked, already stirring the newcomer. 'But go easy on the Captain, he's an artist.'

'He will be taken to the Powder Keg, as will you,' said the floating superhero. He was dressed in blue and white spandex complete with bright red pauldrons with 'USA' emblazoned across them. He was also wearing a navy blue half-helm with a single white star in the centre and his cape was the American flag. 'I am called the American Way and you're either with me or against me. Something tells me it's the latter.'

'Hey, I've heard of you!' Dread acknowledged. 'You're one of those pompous twats who's in that team you have the audacity to call the World's Defence, yet you only patrol North America. Is that like the World Series or something?'

'You are lucky that the rest of the team's not here, otherwise I doubt I could hold them all back,' American Way said, taking offence. 'Though I am more than sufficient to arrest you—I've been America's defender since 1950. I just wish I could have gotten here quicker and saved those valiant patriots you murdered in cold blood.'

'I didn't murder *everyone*,' Dread said defensively. 'I especially saved a few so that if one of you hero types showed up, you could try to save them. It must get pretty boring chasing bank robbers and saving cats from trees, so I thought I'd spice it up for you. Don't worry, there's no need to thank me—I'm a courteous guy.' He smiled amiably.

'How can you be such a monster at your age?' the American Way said, looking more and more disgusted. 'I believe you are beyond redemption.'

'What? I'm an adult, I'm almost nineteen!' Dread protested. 'Well give or take—time's a bit hard to measure where I grew up. Heh-heh, but I've always been beyond redemption.'

'Then you bring this on yourself for your unprovoked and unrepentant attitude,' the American Way announced.

'Unprovoked?' Dread couldn't believe how one-sided this was. 'They put a bullet hole in my brand-new car!'

'Enough!' screamed the American Way. 'Perhaps this will show you how your car compares to the lives you've cut short. Feel the power of my hurricane breath!'

The American Way drew in a deep breath and exhaled it in a focused blast of wind, which sent Dread flying into his Corvette. The sleek muscle car was flattened and then blown apart, the pieces scattering across several lanes of highway.

'Fuck me, super-halitosis or what?' Dread coughed, lifting himself up onto all fours. 'I guess you don't have much time to clean your teeth, what with defending America all the time.'

Dread stood back up to his full, almost-eight-foot height and dusted himself off, which is when he first noticed that his car was obliterated. The driveshaft rolled around near his feet.

'Oh, you motherfucker,' he said to the American Way, who was still floating above him with his arms crossed, flag-cape billowing in the wind, and looking very smug. 'That's the biggest mistake you've ever made.' He grabbed the driveshaft.

'You do not scare me: I am invulnerable and have been battling the likes of you all my life!' The American Way flew at Dread at super-speed.

'There's no one like me,' Dread said under his breath. He waited until his adversary was only metres away before thrusting the driveshaft through his teeth and into his mouth until it hit stomach. 'Let's see if your insides are as invulnerable as your outsides!'

The driveshaft was wedged in the American Way's oesophagus, which appeared to be at least as invulnerable as the rest of him, but it obviously caused great discomfort. Dread followed it up with a quick kick to the throat, bending the driveshaft and ensuring it was stuck fast. American Way emitted a muffled scream and desperately tried to dislodge the obstruction, so Dread kneed him in the nuts to draw his hands away.

'Now just remember that you brought this on yourself, and what transpires from this moment on is entirely your fault,' he said casually, grabbing the end of the driveshaft poking out of his foe's mouth and lifted. 'I gave you the opportunity to save some of these cops I spared, but now you will be the instrument of their demise.'

Dread jumped back towards the police wreckage where the survivors he'd mercifully spared had started to mill about to watch the battle and call for reinforcements. He still held the driveshaft and used the momentum of the leap to swing the American Way up and over his head to smash the survivors like a humanoid club.

'How does it feel to know that it's your invulnerable body that's killing all these brave patriots?' Dread asked the American Way, swinging him round viciously, pulverising the survivors as they tried to flee. A red mist floated on the breeze. 'How does it feel to know that none of this would have happened if you hadn't wrecked my car?'

The American Way couldn't answer even if he didn't have a metal pole wedged in his throat—he'd long since passed out from the experience of being used as a club.

'Typical,' Dread said in disgust. He let go of the pole and the American Way dropped unconscious to his feet. 'How selfish not to be awake to see the misery he's reaped.'

The entire area was dripping in gore.

'Let this be a lesson to you,' he said to the American Way as he stepped over him. 'I'll spare you so that you can remember the day your hubris stained your hands with innocent blood.'

Dread pulled another cigarette from his coat pocket and lit it.

'And you...' he said to Sam Shanks, who was still sitting in the turret, this time covered in gizzards and now the lone survivor of the force that had pursued Dread, '...I don't know why I'm even still talking to you.'

He turned and walked back to the wreckage of his car, leaving Sam to deal with the unconscious superhero.

'Such a shame,' he sighed, looking at his warped symbol on the crumpled bonnet.

*Captain Povo's nowhere to be seen,* he thought, carving a dimensional gateway in the air. He shrugged, figuring he would catch up with him after he got a replacement car.

*For now, I better skedaddle before this place fills up with righteous spandex and I'm forced to really cut loose.* Chilling at the bar and laying low for a while—maybe working on his music—seemed like good idea.

Dread stepped through the dimensional gateway and returned to the Abyss, already thinking about his first cold beer after a trying day.

* * *

## Grand Satanic Headquarters: 5 June 34 BZ

Bentaz Mullberry calmly waited in the dusty clothing store with his demonic companion, Hellgoat. It was mid-afternoon and the store was apparently open, but it was emptier than the donation box for the 'Save the Pubic Louse' movement Grug had set up in the HSA kitchenette.

*How is this place even here?* he wondered, looking around the gloomy shop. *Why haven't they been bought out and replaced with yet another restaurant?*

'What do they sell here again?' he asked his fearsome teammate. 'It looks like they only stock brown cloaks.'

'They also sell Satanic paraphernalia,' Hellgoat replied, pointing out the various flaming goat-head candelabras and stacks of books on the subject with the tip of his bat-like wing. 'Maybe they have some sort of dark magic in place to hold back the real estate developers.'

'There's no magic that powerful,' Bentaz mused, 'but something's going on here all right. Isn't this meant to be the headquarters for some famous Satanist group?'

'Yeah, Lucifer's Coven apparently.' Hellgoat pointed at the room behind the empty counter. 'I'm guessing this store's just a front and the real action is back there.'

'Didn't that jerk, Tactician, tell us not to look into these guys as it's a waste of time?' Bentaz asked, inspecting a chalice shaped like a skull. 'He may have been onto something.'

'I doubt that prick would be onto something even if he decided to remove his head from his arse once in a while to take a look around,' Hellgoat declared, moving around the counter. 'What's strange is that these guys used to be a big time Satanic-themed adults club and were pretty popular, but now they've become…well, this.'

It did seem to be a step backwards.

'Okay, so when these guys were really popular and it was the "in thing" to be a part of it, they were obviously charlatans,' Bentaz said, trying not to set his cape alight from the dozens of candles that lined the walls. 'But now that they've fallen on hard times and are having a bargain-basement sale on mountains of occult crap, they're a threat to all existence? Forgive me if I don't quake in terror.'

'Mock me if you will, but they're the only ones left we haven't investigated yet,' Hellgoat said as he walked through the doorway to the back room, his cloven hooves clicking on the wooden floor. 'On top of that, I also feel something in my gut that tells me there is something truly evil going on here, and they are withdrawing from the spotlight now that they have achieved their nefarious plans.'

'Oh please, you sound ridiculous,' Bentaz scoffed, following Hellgoat into the back room. 'I'm not even sure I believe in this whole satanic conspiracy nonsense.'

The room they were standing in just seemed to contain boxes full of more brown cloaks and an even thicker layer of dust.

'I'm living proof that it's not nonsense,' Hellgoat countered, slightly annoyed. 'There's a whole upstairs to this place, and it lies beyond this door.'

The door said 'Staff Only' on its plain wooden face, except someone had scrawled 'Satanic' above the words in red paint marker.

'I dare say your origin and the try-hards who live here are worlds apart,' Bentaz said. He knocked on the door in the classic 'A Shave and a Haircut—Two Bits' pattern.

'Why are you knocking when we could just walk through—even if it was locked?' Hellgoat remarked. 'The fate of the planet could be at stake.'

'Or it could be a bunch of whackjobs doing nothing more dangerous than chanting in the nude,' Bentaz replied as movement could be heard on the other side. 'We're HSA; we knock first.'

Suddenly the door opened a crack and urgent whispers leaked through, along with an overpowering smell of soap and bacon.

'I told you not to answer it...' said a man's voice.

'They used the secret knock! I had to answer...' said another male voice. The door swung open to reveal two men wearing the same brown cloaks that filled the shopfront. Somehow, they looked even cheaper when adorned.

They both gasped when they saw who it was, but Hellgoat's presence almost tipped the one who answered the door over the edge.

'The apocalypse; has it begun already?' he asked, seemingly panicked. His great big bushy beard hid most of his face and his monocle made one eye seem twice as big. 'I thought it was planned for "The Feast of Lights", when the baby...'

'Lancefield, will you shut up?' the other man said, pushing him aside. 'Don't you know anything? These kids are part of the HSA—you know, the Heroes Squadron. Ballistic and Hellface or something. Anyway, they don't want to hear your crazy talk!' He turned to the heroes. 'Sorry about that, he's a little eccentric. Now what can I do for you? This area is for staff only, and we don't allow the public out the back.'

The man was in his mid-forties, bald, and looked slightly malformed.

'We're hardly what you call the general public,' Bentaz protested, 'and besides, the shop was unattended. We're also here on official HSA business.'

'Is that right? Well, I can't think of why superhero types like you would have any business with us,' the bald man said, eyeing them defiantly. 'This seems like religious persecution to me.'

'You're very defensive—we haven't even asked you anything yet,' Hellgoat growled. 'What are you hiding here? I sense...something... something infernal.'

'Well, of course you do!' Lancefield suddenly said, trying to push his way back in front of the door. 'This is the headquarters of Lucifer's Coven, you know!'

'Lancefield, shut up!' the bald man said, keeping his enthusiastic companion at bay.

'Aww, Floyd, you never...' Lancefield began before Floyd silenced him with a backhand.

'May we come in to discuss this?' Bentaz enquired, ignoring the slap.

'No, you may not,' Floyd said, barring the door.

'Not like you could stop us,' Hellgoat said unhelpfully. 'We are extending a courtesy by asking.'

'I thought you guys were heroes. That don't sound like hero-talk,' Floyd said tauntingly with a big smile on his ugly face. 'You guys don't want a lawsuit on your hands, do you?'

'We have immunity to those sorts of things as HSA members,' Bentaz said, standing over the smaller man.

'Yeah, well you're not immune to the media,' Floyd said casually, looking unimpressed by Bentaz's intimidation tactics. 'Just look what happened to that tasty minx on the David Leno show a few weeks back.' He smiled and licked his cracked lips.

*This freak's talking about Lorraine Freeman!* Bentaz was disgusted. *He's old enough to be her father.*

Bentaz had developed quite a crush on Lorraine over recent months and became really defensive of her, despite the two of them having never met. The revelation that she was a Manifest only made her more appealing in Bentaz's eyes.

'Look, we just want to know if you've been messing around in any serious occult stuff,' Bentaz said, using all his willpower not to flatten the creepy bald fuck. 'You know, like trying to summon up demons from Hell or something.'

*I can't believe I actually said that.*

'Like it's any of your business what our religious practises are,' Floyd sneered. 'Our ways aren't for the uninitiated.'

'You're playing with forces beyond your ken!' Hellgoat looked like he was going to torch the place with his hellfire.

'Unless that's a reference to Barbie, then I have no idea what you mean,' Floyd said, moving to close the door. 'To be clear: we haven't summoned any demons and we have no idea why you'd be interested in us. If you continue to persecute us, then we'll sue your government employers, not you personally. Now, I'm sure great heroes like your-selves can find your way out. Don't come back.'

'Why you...' Hellgoat began, hands flaming up.

'Hellgoat, forget it, let's go,' Bentaz said, leading his companion away.

*They're probably just lunatics anyway; surely those losers couldn't bring about the apocalypse.*

'Way to go, Floyd!' Bentaz heard Lancefield say as the door started to close.

'They're superheroes, not fucking bikies,' came Floyd's reply. 'The High Mage must remain a secr...' The door closed and the rest of the sentence was cut off.

*Or could they? That sounded highly suspicious...but I suppose it could've been a ruse to provoke us into a lawsuit. But are they that smart?*

Bentaz and Hellgoat exited the 'Grand Satanic Headquarters' and walked out into the cold street. King's Cross buzzed with life all around them, and several people stopped to ask for autographs and photos.

Bentaz was still thinking about their encounter with the Satanists, and Hellgoat was acting surlier than usual—a sign to be on their way.

'Come on, let's get back to HQ,' Bentaz said to Hellgoat, attempting to sound important in front of the crowd. They both took to the sky to the sound of cheers and camera shutters clicking.

The flight back to Canberra took about forty minutes, as Bentaz had to slow down so Hellgoat could keep pace. He had to use wings, after all. The flight was uneventful and mostly silent—Hellgoat was in a brooding mood.

They flew over the murky waters of Lake Burley Griffin and landed outside the entrance to HSA Headquarters—like everything else of importance in Canberra, it was built on a grandiose scale designed to make people feel small. The late afternoon shadow covered the area in gloom.

'Looks like we're just in time for the meeting,' Bentaz said, holding the large glass door open for Hellgoat. 'I can see a few government cars in the parking lot.'

They made their way to the briefing room and Bentaz remembered why he liked being in the HSA so much. This always led to the inevitable afterthought:

*I wish I didn't have school tomorrow. Sure, Mum lets me get away with missing a day here or there if there's some emergency, but never just to hang out. You'd think someone would start a school for gifted youngsters.*

They entered the crowded briefing room.

'You're late,' Tactician snarled the moment they stepped through the door. His eyes were obscured by his blue visor, but Bentaz could tell he was frowning.

*I'm surprised his suit doesn't whir when he frowns, like with all his other movements. Better find a seat quick before he gets really cranky.*

It felt like déjà vu to Bentaz as he scanned the room for a seat, except this time he wasn't alone. Hellgoat faced the same conundrum. Luckily there was a seat in front of him and it was Hellgoat who had to shuffle awkwardly to stand at the back of the room. Giant bat-wings weren't really suited for office furniture anyway.

*Why can't we have some impressive-looking meeting hall like they do in the comics about us, instead of this bland office room? Then maybe we'd actually be able to have the whole team here for a change, instead of less than half at any one time.*

The room was packed and Bentaz looked around to see who was there.

There was Tactician, of course, along with two men in suits and sunglasses who looked like twins, and fellow HSA members: Powerhouse, Grug, Mauler, Gridlock, Tracker, Gate Crasher, Mercury, Revenger, and the Pike. By far the most noticeable sentient in the room, however, was the metre-high, bright yellow pyramid of cheese with a goofy face like a clay animation model. He had no arms and got around on stunted legs beneath the square pyramid base. His only other distinguishing features were the black ear holes on either side of his 'head' and the chunk missing from one back corner—as if someone had taken a bite out of him.

*Ha! Chuck Cheese is here! Tactician usually doesn't allow him to attend because he's an unpredictable Miasma oddity, but he always cheers me up, so I'm glad he's here.*

'Hullo Ballistic,' Chuck Cheese said in a voice not dissimilar to Mickey Mouse's.

'Silence, cheese,' Tactician said, turning to face the team mascot. 'You are here as a courtesy only—don't make me regret you being here.'

The image of a stern man in a futuristic-looking motorised suit dressing down a giant talking cheese was the silliest thing Bentaz could ever remember witnessing. He was already starting to feel better. Then Powerhouse opened his mouth.

'I don't know why you let him on the team at all,' he said. 'Same goes for some of the other deadbeats on this team, like the fucking Flannelled Avenger and his nerdy fucking son, Cloth the Flannelled Wonder! Fuck, the names these guys come up with!'

'Will you quit it with your whining?' Bentaz spat. 'You need to leave these guys alone—all of them have a role to play here.'

'Yeah, Flannelled Avenger and Cloth are popular with the working class,' Gridlock agreed, somewhat snobbishly.

'Not to mention White Lion, who's never here...' Powerhouse persisted, undaunted.

*Yeah, where does he go?*

'...or Faceplate, Armournator, Night Fighter—any of those guys without powers.' Powerhouse was on a roll today.

'I have to agree with Ballistic: shut the fuck up!' Tactician said authoritatively. Powerhouse wasn't game to defy him, despite Tactician having no powers aside from his enhanced suit. 'Now, onto official business: most of the Manifest terrorists who were gathered in Sydney have been rounded up, although the most dangerous and illusive one is still at large.'

'You're talking about Vicious Man, aren't you?' Mauler had a way of stating the obvious. His metallic green and blue armour was only outshone by the glowing stone embedded in his chest—apparently the actual meteor that triggered his Manifest seed.

'Who else?' Tactician snapped. 'He should be our top priority at the moment.'

'I told you we should have gone after him instead of wasting our time with bloody Satanists,' Powerhouse said smugly.

'Speaking of Satanists, Hellgoat and I may have stumbled across something,' Bentaz interjected, leaning forward in his seat.

'Yeah, Lucifer's Coven are hiding something,' Hellgoat called out from the back of the room.

'I told you they weren't worth looking into,' Tactician said, 'and you go wasting your time harassing civilians!'

'But they're definitely up to something...' Hellgoat began.

'Takes one to know one,' Powerhouse said.

'That's enough!' Tactician hated dealing with teenagers. 'I can tell you that Lucifer's Coven is responsible for jack shit—the Satanist problem has already been dealt with.'

'What? When did this happen?' Bentaz asked.

'And when were you going to tell us?' Mercury said, breaking his silence. While he looked like a regular teenager with a terrible haircut, he was really mentally holding his liquid mercury body in that shape. He also could no longer touch anyone for fear of poisoning them—another loser in the Manifest lottery.

'If you'd all be quiet for a moment, I was actually planning to inform you in this very meeting,' Tactician said. 'Revenger, if you'd please.'

'Thank you,' the Revenger said in his robotic voice. Once a black-ops soldier codenamed Eagle Eye, he became the Revenger at the expert hands of Doctor Q, who cybernetically enhanced his body after it was ruined by minions of the Energy Lord. 'As you know I have recently arrived from Kakadu...'

*Well no, this is the first I've heard of it.*

'...having gone on a mission with Fire Lord, Sawmill, Saroid and Robo Bird to investigate strange readings that may have been Satanists, causing us to miss the Anzac Day commemorations,' Revenger droned on without needing to draw breath. 'What we discovered there is no doubt responsible for these murmurings of the apocalypse.'

*Then what were those freaks from Lucifer's Coven doing? Maybe they're connected to the mysterious Kaiser that Squido mentioned when I apprehended him.*

'How could you tell?' Hellgoat sounded querulous. 'I'm the team's authority on all things satanic.'

'And all things unhygienic,' Powerhouse added.

'You're about to see just how unhygienic I can get!' Hellgoat always rose to a slight.

'That's enough, Hellgoat,' Tactician said. 'Revenger, please continue.'

Hellgoat glared at the government stooge menacingly.

'We discovered a giant elemental plant-beast that had apparently been summoned by a mercenary band known as the Outcasts,' Revenger recalled.

'Did you just say giant elemental plant-beast?' Gate Crasher asked, his face a portrait of disbelief. He wore no mask, but questionably chose to wear a multi-coloured spandex bodysuit instead.

'Yes,' the Revenger said neutrally. 'It even had a name—Grrmulch—at least that's what the Outcasts said when we intercepted them.'

'This is crazy,' Mauler opined.

*Grrmulch? Seriously, I'm meant to buy this?*

'I'm more likely to believe that as opposed to insidious Satanic conspiracies,' Grug said, shooting a tendril of hair from his wrist and snatching an apple from the fruit bowl in the middle of the table. His rumbling stomach was audible despite the chatter.

'The creature was responsible for the readings, which have never been seen before,' the Revenger continued, unfazed by the constant interruptions. 'The Outcasts were there when we arrived, well, half of them at least—the creature had killed the other half beforehand. They must have summoned it.'

'The Outcasts are mercenaries. Someone else sent them there,' the Pike observed. Likewise mask-less, he was wearing a maroon spandex bodysuit with an emblem of two stylised pikes across the chest.

'What evidence is there for these claims?' Hellgoat asked irritably.

'They are your fellow team members for a start,' Tactician responded.

'We can verify it,' the twin men in suits said with the same voice.

*Now that's fucking disturbing. Are these guys Manifests? There's something definitely fishy about them.*

'Plus, I was the one who detected the strange energy signature in the first place,' Tracker boasted, pointing at the big radar screen in his chest.

'Well, that's just dandy,' Hellgoat replied sullenly.

'So what happened to the other half of the Outcasts?' Bentaz enquired. 'Are they now breaking rocks at the Powder Keg?'

'We had to…terminate two of them in self-defence,' the Revenger answered. He may have sounded like a machine, but he was a man once and still possessed emotions, therefore he chose his words carefully. 'The one called Bulldog escaped, though he was gravely wounded. I don't think he survived.'

'Did you just say terminate?' Gate Crasher had the same look of disbelief on his face. 'I thought our policy was no killings.'

'It is…for the most part.' Tactician could have been a diplomat. 'It's like you said; everyone has a role to play here, and the Revenger and his sub-team have final sanction privileges as they're all either ex-military or completely artificial in origin.'

'And we all owe our existence to Doctor Q,' the Revenger said, his face expressionless and his eyes hidden behind the visor of his spiked helmet.

*Like that excuses anything. Doctor Q invented a tonne of shit and revolutionised cybernetics before he was disgraced and disappeared.*

'So, does that mean that the reason we all have secret identities is because of all this black-ops shit?' Hellgoat grumbled.

'No, the main reason is because most of you are minors and we have to conceal your identities...' Tactician revealed.

'To protect us from what?' Powerhouse interrupted. 'Superpervs?'

'...to protect your families and friends,' Tactician finished, ignoring Powerhouse.

'So what about Lucifer's Coven?' Bentaz still felt unresolved on the issue.

'I told you to drop it!' Tactician barked. 'In fact, your recklessness is the next item on the agenda.'

*Recklessness? We only talked to them!*

Tactician pulled a copy of *The Australian Telegraph* out from under his meeting notes and unfolded the newspaper for all to see. The cover featured a tabloid-sized picture of Bentaz sporting a big cheesy grin with the headline 'Hero smiles while Bondi burns'. The story was continued on page three apparently.

*Hey, that's the photo that Japanese tourist took. Didn't turn out half bad.*

'Care to explain this?' Tactician asked angrily. 'Powerhouse says you were endangering civilians and posing for photos while he had to help Metallic Man and Savage Scavenger capture the Manifest terrorists.'

*Ooh that cunt.*

'That's not true...' Bentaz began.

'Is too!' Powerhouse sat back in his chair, looking pleased with himself.

'I don't want to hear your excuses,' Tactician said to Bentaz. 'This photo speaks for itself.'

'This is one incident!' Bentaz couldn't believe the injustice.

'Unfortunately, it's not,' one of the men in suits said. 'You exposed our secret tunnels under the Civic bus interchange six months ago when you engaged *das Super Sechs.*'

'What, really?' Bentaz was actually surprised. 'I thought they were just sewer tunnels.'

'Which is what we wanted people to think if ever they were discovered, as they're not on any schematics,' Tactician explained. 'We didn't *want* them exposed, however.'

'What are they used for,' Bentaz queried, 'if they're not on any maps?'

'That's classified,' said the other MIB with the same voice as the first.

*These guys must be Manifests. I'm pretty sure twins' voices aren't identical. Are they?*

'So the point is, you need to be more careful,' Tactician said. 'If you spent more time following protocol, then maybe you could've prevented that multiple murder in Cabramatta a couple weeks back, for instance.'

'Yeah,' Powerhouse agreed.

'This is the first I've heard of a murder in Cabramatta,' Bentaz said, ignoring Powerhouse.

'Precisely my point,' Tactician said.

*This logic makes no sense, but I can't be bothered arguing.*

Powerhouse smirked at Bentaz.

*Then again, that prick, Jean-Pierre, deserves a bitch-slap.*

Powerhouse seemed to read his thoughts. 'Go ahead, and you'll be kicked off the team,' he dared.

Bentaz did nothing but shake his head.

'What's the matter? The "God who Walks Like a Man" is all angry stares and no balls?' Powerhouse taunted.

*That fucking magazine article! I wish they never ran with that title!*

'At least I was on the cover of *Time Magazine*,' Bentaz riposted, trying to stay calm. 'You're just jealous.'

'I was too busy doing real work and saving people from danger to be jealous,' Powerhouse countered.

Bentaz's hands subconsciously glowed with energy.

'Don't be a fussin' an' a feudin' guys,' Chuck Cheese broke in with his silly voice. 'You don't wanna' end up bein' an ole sour puss like our government friend.'

'Enough!' Tactician yelled.

Tactician glared at the cheese, and this time Bentaz believed he could hear the whir of his frown. He smiled and began to feel better again.

'You are about to get a message,' one of the MIBs said quietly to Tactician.

*Here comes that sinking feeling again.*

Tactician tapped his wrist pad and said, 'Patch it through.' He held his hand up to the room and turned his head away from them to take the call. 'Hello, yes Mister Ambassador, it's me…no I haven't spoken to them…calm down, what happened?'

There was a longer pause.

'Holy shit!' Tactician said at once. 'No, I didn't know…this is the first I've heard of it…'

*Sounds familiar,* Bentaz thought, sitting quietly and looking around the room at everyone else doing the same thing while they all waited for Tactician to finish his call.

'That mobile phone in his suit is pretty sick, hey fellas?' Mauler said, trying to break the silence, but no one responded.

'…the president said what to Keating? …uh-huh…right, well I'm sort of in the middle of something…I'll call you back momentarily.' Tactician tapped his wrist pad and turned back to everyone in the room. 'Apologies, I have to take this, something's come up at higher echelons. I think we were about done here anyway.'

He stood up from his seat along with his MIB escorts and started to leave.

'What's going on?' the Pike asked. 'Is it more Satanists?'

Tactician paused before leaving. 'It's Vicious Man. He's killed several hundred people in the US and severely injured the American Way. It's now hit the news, so I really have to go.'

The room sat in silence for a nanosecond.

'Told you,' Powerhouse said, but no one heard him in their scramble to the monitor room to see the news bulletins.

* * *

**Barton Correctional Facility: 7 June 34 BZ**

'Yes…sir.' Chief Warden Walter Screw slammed the phone down and exhaled a long pillar of smoke.

'Minister. It's a pleasure to see you again,' he said to the man standing on the other side of his meticulous desk. Walter took another drag from his cigar before butting it out in his pristine ashtray. 'It seems I have been asked to show you around this facility.'

'I don't know why you bothered questioning it,' Minister Robert Ray said calmly, waving away the lingering smoke. 'You know that smoking inside a federal building isn't allowed. It gives people cancer, in case you hadn't heard living out here in the desert.'

'Whatever,' Walter said dismissively, donning his visored helmet. 'Working here is way more dangerous than a few wafting fumes.'

*This is such a waste of my time,* he thought, getting up from his swivel chair and gesturing to the door. *Nobody gives a shit when Vicious Man slaughters a whole town in Australia, but kill a few American cops and suddenly it's a crisis.*

'Well, let's get this over with. I do have a schedule to keep,' Walter said, leading the minister towards the elevator in the middle of the command centre that encompassed the entire top floor of the prison. There was another elevator that ran down the outside of the prison, but the internal one was the only way to get to the observation spire. 'This is a panopticon style facility, and in case you haven't looked it up by now, that means this entire prison is basically a giant cylinder with a centre spire. Like a reverse doughnut.'

'Uh-huh,' Minister Ray said as they got into the elevator and took the short trip down to the top level of the observation spire. 'And the point of this is?'

'All prisoners are confined to their cells at all times,' Walter explained. The doors opened and they walked into the darkened room. Through the giant reinforced windows they could see the top level of cells brightly lit up, showing the prisoners clearly on a three hundred and sixty degree angle. There were banks of computer terminals and viewing platforms along the windows. 'They can't talk to each other, but more importantly, they can't see us. The idea is that they will be well behaved if they think they're being watched. So even if we don't have enough staff to watch everyone all the time, it only takes a few staff to watch everyone most of the time.'

'Okay, so far so good,' Minister Ray said, walking around the outside of the elevator and looking at all the prisoners. Some of the cells were empty but were lit up nonetheless. 'Hey, I'm sorry to inconvenience you—and I really do mean that—but Prime Minister Keating wants a complete briefing on this place, especially as Australia has upgraded their UN membership status. Also, as you've no doubt heard, President Clinton gave the PM an admonishing about letting Vicious Man run around loose.'

*Like we have any fucking control over that lunatic. But I guess the Yanks need someone to blame in the face of a crisis.*

'Yes, we all have our crosses to bear,' Walter said as he waited for the minister to look around. 'But we're about containment at this facility; someone needs to bring Vicious Man here first.'

'Understood. Seeing the special cell you built for his containment is the primary reason for my visit here,' Minister Ray said. 'Still, I'd like to have a look around the rest of the facility while I'm here.'

A solitary guard walked up the internal stairs from the level below, saw Walter and the minister and went to check a terminal without saying anything.

'This level is a mixed group,' Walter said after they had walked around full circle. 'We've got sentient machines, suspected and confirmed alien species, and Class E Entities.'

'Class E Entities?' Minister Ray asked. 'What are those again? I can't keep up.'

*Here we go again. Today's schedule is going to be totally shot.*

'Also known as CEEs or Miasma creatures,' Walter began. Explaining these anomalies was hard. 'They're not Manifests, but they register as something similar. They literally spontaneously burst out of portals around the world at random intervals. Rumour has it they come from some place called the Miasma—whatever the hell that means—and they're somehow connected to that crazy Manifest, Zambini Surrealay. That's one of them there.' Walter pointed at the strange, bearded lizard-dog that scuttled around the cell.

'They're hard to contain as they come in different varieties with different abilities that we can't turn off,' Walter continued. 'But at least the Manifest suppressors in their cells do prevent them teleporting away, and they don't need to be fed so we never have to open the cell once they're in there. All of them defy science, so it's lucky we've caught any.'

'I thought the majority of those things were harmless,' Minister Ray said, turning back towards the centre of the room. 'Yet you seem to have quite a collection.'

'They're still pests, and some of them can cause havoc, what with them teleporting here and there,' Walter replied, leading the minister down the internal stairs. 'Take the Roaring Twenties for example—they are literally a pair of giant red twenties that roar and travel around the place at breakneck speeds!'

'I see you don't have those here at the prison,' Minister Ray observed. They walked down to the next level of the observation spire. It was identical to the top layer.

'I'd like to see you catch them first. When I said giant, they are actually several storeys high,' Walter said, walking up to the windows. A new ring of cells was on display. 'Anyway, on this level we have the Class B Entities, or CBEs. As you may have noticed, a lot of the cells are empty, seeing as these guys are so hard to catch.'

'I see that Nazi Baron is on this level,' Minister Ray said, referring to the leader of *das Super Sechs*. 'I'm surprised you don't just execute him, given his crimes.'

*If only I could.* He seemed to have gotten more powerful since he was last here, which is why he'd been moved to this level. It was probably a misclassification on the first time, as they're not meant to be able to move classes.

'Well, we don't execute prisoners in Australia for a start, and nor does the UN pass the death penalty,' Walter answered, looking out the window. 'The truth is that it really is a death sentence—everyone is sentenced to this place for life, no matter the crime. You get a gift like a Manifest, you better not blow it and turn bad.'

'I thought Manifests were immortal?' Minister Ray asked. 'Is this prison immortal too?'

*Everyone's a fucking comedian. This is such a fucking waste of time.*

'The anti-Manifest suppressors not only remove their abilities, they make them age at the normal rate,' Walter said, checking his watch. 'And all the Manifests made from non-living items simply remain inert and are used for study. As you know, truly dead Manifests show no trace of this elusive Manifest seed that bestows them with all these random powers.'

'So why do you allow them to wear their costumes? Surely prison uniforms would be better,' Minister Ray declared, stopping to stare at this level's only other occupant: a man with a bandaged face wearing a suit with a radiation symbol on the chest. He appeared to be unconscious.

'Like anyone's getting that close to these maniacs to change their outfits,' Walter admitted. 'Besides, we remove any obvious weaponry, and even if they did escape, their costumes are usually so garish that they stick out like dogs' balls.'

'There have been too many breakouts from the prison of late, which is part of the reason I'm here to evaluate the special containment cell,' Minister Ray said. 'So make sure you keep that public list of known supervillains up-to-date.'

*Sure, I'll just drop everything and get on that, shall I?*

'I will give it my attention as soon as I can,' Walter promised, gesturing to the stairs. 'There's not much to see on this floor, shall we go down a level?'

They walked down the stairs to another darkened viewing room, except this time instead of mostly empty cells, there was a panorama of evil on display. Manifests of all shapes and sizes—most in ridiculous costumes—filled the cells that loomed large through the observation windows.

'This is the CCE level,' Walter said, gesturing to the rows of supervillains. 'They are the most numerous classification, hence the overabundance of inmates. You may see some familiar faces from the news.'

'I see a lot of potential time bombs and not a lot of guards,' Minister Ray said. 'I also see that the cell walls are just glass.'

'Actually, it's force-field technology developed by Doctor Q about a decade ago,' Walter corrected. He could feel the minutes passing by with each explanation. 'It's the same tech that's still keeping the police out of his house after he was disgraced by that whistle-blower in the seventies.'

'Whistle-blower is one word for it, after what he did,' Minister Ray said, walking around and looking at all the villains as if in a zoo. There were more guards posted on this level than the one above.

'Yeah, well, that was bullshit,' Walter spat. He stopped to stare at the

Russian dragon-man, Dragonski. 'Trust me, I've been around true evil my entire career, and he was set up. In fact, he's the only Manifest I've ever trusted. I worked with the man for years, and if you knew him, you'd know he barely had time for human contact, let alone molesting young boys.'

'Then why'd he disappear? Innocent people don't run, and they don't protect their houses from lawful entry by using force-fields.' The Minister slowly walked around the floor. 'He escaped from here too, I believe.'

'Well, he did help design the place,' Walter said, fingering a cigar in his uniform pocket. He never risked smoking in the prison itself though. 'But we made some adjustments after that, such as building the basement level...'

'I'm actually surprised this entire complex isn't under the ground, given how dangerous the occupants are,' Minister Ray interrupted. 'The Americans pointed out that very fact.'

'Then maybe they should have agreed to host this prison on their soil, but too many people protested about having it so close to their homes,' Walter replied. 'Luckily Australia always begs for the world's table scraps, so we volunteered to host it. I mean, we're a country that lets other countries set off nukes on our own soil, so of course we'd take the world's Manifest riff-raff.'

'So...those adjustments you referred to...?' Minister Ray decided to ignore the slur about their nation's domestic policies.

*Must remember to remain professional and not speak out of turn. This guy's just getting to me with all this Q&A time wasting.*

'Doctor Q's original design was for a subterranean complex—the Americans just neglected to give us the funds we needed to build it underground. But quite frankly, the technology just didn't exist and no one thought there'd be so many of them around when it was built. Don't forget, it was constructed hastily after World War Two to house *das Super Sechs*, who were the Powder Keg's first occupants, and anti-Manifest tech didn't exist in those days,' Walter said, as if he hadn't had a minor rant a moment ago. 'Since then, of course, we've had several upgrades, and now each cell contains primary and backup Manifest suppressors, which are also saturated throughout this facility and even the surrounding prison grounds. We have no less than ten backup power reserves, and in the case of blackout, special locks are released and massive tungsten doors slide down, blocking the entrance.'

Walter paused to draw breath.

'Prisoners never leave their cells, and they never receive visitors aside from the prison staff who feed them. There aren't many guards patrolling inside, as there's not much they can do if the power goes down,' he added. 'But we have plenty of security personnel in reserves in other complexes that can act swiftly to stop any situation. It's basically the best we can do with our limited funding.'

'You could also call in some government-sponsored superheroes like the HSA,' Minister Ray suggested. He had finished looking at all the prisoners on this level and began heading for the stairwell.

'That would be a last resort. Inviting more super-powered lunatics to a breakout would be like adding fuel to a very big fire. Besides this prison is designed to have low staffing levels, being a panopticon and all,' Walter said, hitting the elevator button. 'We don't need to check out the ground floor—that's just the Class Ds. Those losers aren't worth looking at and we can't get out on that level. We need to go back up to the top and take the external elevator back down to the ground in order to get to the basement level.'

'That seems like a poor design,' Minister Ray said as the button dinged. 'Makes sense that you could go all the way to the basement and exit at every level.'

'Actually, the observation spire is disconnected from the rest of the prison, especially the basement,' Walter said. They got into the elevator and he hit the button for the command centre on the top floor. 'We load prisoners through the front entrance, and there's another service elevator on the cell rings, but this spire needs to be cut off from prisoner access in order to keep them out of the command centre.'

'And the basement? It doesn't need to be observed?' the Minister asked.

'Not by human eyes. The prisoners there are so dangerous that they are monitored by cameras only. Each cell is loaded through a separate entrance, which is then completely collapsed and buried, like Egyptian tombs. The prisoners are then frozen solid and kept in total darkness.'

'Sounds extreme,' Minister Ray said when they arrived back at the command centre. 'What classification are they?'

'They're still CBEs, as we can't contain CAEs,' Walter answered while they walked to the external elevator. 'But they're at the upper end of the B classification and can't be contained on the standard CBE level. Make no mistake, Minister, they're certainly extreme, and the world's much safer once they're in here and not out there. As a matter of fact, even the human rights groups are satisfied with our containment measures. Plus, it helps that this is a top-secret facility and they don't have clearance to visit the basement.'

'And this is where you plan to contain Vicious Man?' Minister Ray enquired. 'In a frozen cell in the dark?'

'Yep, right above the thermonuclear failsafe in the core of this building,' Walter said, exiting the elevator into the lobby.

'I'm aware of the bomb,' Minister Ray said, unfazed. 'The UN couldn't very well place a live nuke on Australian soil without our approval, regardless of our UN membership status.'

*I guess the government has at least one testicle then,* Walter mused as they turned towards a heavily guarded doorway on the far side of the lobby. The guards didn't bother to check Walter's ID on account of his familiarity and the foreknowledge that he would be escorting a VIP around the prison. Walter rounded on them like a feral dog.

'You two fucking idiots just earned yourselves a week of double-shifts,' he barked at the guards responsible for checking IDs. 'You are to let nobody, and I mean *abso-fucking-lutely nobody* past this checkpoint without confirming their identity!'

'Sorry, sir!' Both the guards snapped to attention and began to verify Walter's ID. The sentries in the turrets above the doorway quietly smirked at their colleagues' blunder. Walter recognised one as the smartass recruit he'd given latrine duty to on his first day a couple of months ago.

'Don't you two laugh,' Walter said to the sentries. 'You're on latrine duty for a month for failing to initiate a "halt" protocol.' Their smirking turned to misery. 'And don't forget to check the Minister's ID too,' Walter ordered the guards.

'Isn't this a bit extreme?' Minister Ray asked as his retinas were scanned and fingerprints cross-referenced in some database some-where. His visitor ID was also checked. 'I had to go through all this on the way in.'

*At least some of my staff can do their fucking job properly.*

'I'm sure this minor inconvenience won't be objected to, Minister, once you realise why we do it,' Walter said as cordially as his genes would allow. 'There's every chance a Manifest shape-changer or mind-bender will try to get past one of these checkpoints one day, and we have to make absolutely sure we've done everything possible to pre-vent it. The future of the human race could be at stake.'

'Well, since you put it that way...' Minster Ray said. His identity was confirmed and they were ushered through the checkpoint and into the corridor on the other side. 'I actually feel more confident knowing you take such stringent measures for the Australian people.'

'Hold on a moment, I have to make sure I don't forget,' Walter said. He tapped a couple of buttons on his wrist gauntlet. He always wore his full uniform when outside his office. 'Rick...yeah it's me. I need you to change some rosters for me... Where are you?... In the interrogation room?... Yeah, I'll tell you the changes later on...okay. Warden out.'

'Rick...Rick Gordon, he's your second in charge, correct? I wouldn't mind seeing this interrogation room you have, after we see the base-ment,' Minister Ray said. 'Are you still interviewing for that inmate team you somehow got authority for?'

*Goddamn it! This is going to take all day.*

'Certainly, Minister, the interrogation room is close to the base-ment entrance,' Walter said professionally.

They continued to walk along the shielded corridor that ran along the side of the building towards the loading dock. Several prison staff passed them along the way.

'The entrance to the basement level is off the loading bay,' Walter explained. The corridor rounded the building and they were met with another checkpoint before walking through the three titanium air-locks and into to the loading bay. It was large enough for a semi-trailer to back into and was the only external entrance to the main prison.

The giant loading bay door was open as they'd just received a deliv-ery, and guards were in abundance as they escorted the Powder Keg's latest inhabitant to his cell. He looked like a silent movie villain in a red bed sheet.

'They fast-tracked him here from America, hoping he'd act as bait for Vicious Man,' Walter said, referring to the villain. 'Calls himself Colonel Popov or something—as if that loser could ever be in the military. Class D, completely useless, but is an unlikely associate of that psycho.'

'Well, if Vicious Man does come for him, you'll be in the perfect position to capture and contain him—which is what I'm here to verify,' Minister Ray said. He took a quick glance at the interior of the prison and the rows of Manifests it contained. 'Now, is staff access to the basement level around here somewhere? I presume that there's some way down there and it's not sealed up like the prisoners themselves. You have to be able to check the cameras and so forth.'

'Look, we can go to the basement and check out the chamber, but you'll have to wear night-vision goggles the entire time...' Walter began, twisting his moustache subconsciously, as he did when plotting.

'That sounds like fun,' Minister Ray interrupted.

'...and of course, there are the more...invasive checkpoint identity checks,' Walter added, determined to hatch his plot. 'If you catch my meaning.'

'Maybe we should just press on and see this villain team you're assembling,' Minister Ray said, catching the meaning perfectly. 'I believe you've described it well enough and I'm satisfied it's suitable.'

*Excellent! Finally catching a break—this day may yet be salvageable.*

'Right this way,' Walter said, leading the Minister to the brightly lit interrogation room attached to the loading dock. 'Don't worry, the "candidates" are safely restrained in our portable containment units. They'll be powerless.'

Rick Gordon was with five guards, all of whom snapped to attention when Walter entered the room. 'Sir, Minister, welcome to the interview process for what everyone's calling the "Government Villain project".'

*Everyone eh? I'll have to remind 'everyone' about probity later on.*

'Thank you, Gordon. Now who do we have here? Please, brief the

Minister on our candidates. Don't worry, Minister, the prisoners can't hear you,' Walter said, looking at the villains visible only through the small viewing port on the front of the cylindrical containment units. They all sat on treads and were used to transport prisoners around the prison. Each cylinder contained a Manifest suppressor and the whole thing was coloured fluorescent yellow, complete with flashing orange lights that activated when the cylinder was in use.

'Of course, sir,' Gordon replied. 'Minister, here in this cell on the end we have someone I think you should know well: Joseph Starlen.'

'I thought he died decades ago, assassinated by those two monsters he created,' Minister Ray said without looking through the viewing port. 'The same ones you have upstairs.'

'Ah, not Stalin, the Soviet leader, but rather Starlen, the ex-general who tried to overthrow the government in a giant robot,' Gordon corrected gently. 'He is our pick for team leader, given his military history and ability to actually stage an attempted coup in this country.'

*I wonder how his nuts are healing up since our little interrogation session a few months back.*

'Oh yes, the Destructo incident. How could I forget?' the Minister said. 'And the next candidate?'

'This one's called the Grasshopper, given she's a giant Manifest grasshopper,' Gordon continued.

'You know its gender?' The minister was astonished.

'We determine the sex of all non-human Manifests—if possible—when we neuter them,' Walter interjected. 'In all the human cases we've studied, the Manifest ability appears to be passed onto any off-spring once their abilities…uh…manifest. We can't afford a plague of Manifest locusts getting around, or any other Manifest species for that matter, so we de-sex them in case they escape.'

*I'd sterilise the whole lot if it wasn't seen as a human rights violation.*

'That sounds prudent,' Minister Ray said, almost disinterestedly, as the next candidate had piqued his interest.

'This is Deathspawn, Minister,' Gordon said, seeing all the cues and knowing his boss's dislike for time-wasting. 'He's basically your stand-ard monstrous supervillain who actually causes cancer.' Deathspawn was dark green with long blond hair, one red eye, and broken teeth.

He was missing an eye, his lips, and nose. His face was filled with glistening sockets.

'Repugnant but effective, I presume?' Minister Ray asked, staring at Deathspawn's hideous countenance through the cylinder's viewing port.

'Yes, Minister,' Gordon answered, moving the politician on to the next cylinder. 'Which is also true of this next villain…ah…Tan…Ten…'

'Tanglor, sir,' one of the guards said from her position along the back wall. Her face was obscured by her helmet, but she was large and muscular, and Walter recognised her as the intelligent recruit from the induction several months ago. 'He can open portals to another dimension and controls some giant tendrilled beast that apparently lives there.' The guard suddenly realised she'd interrupted, apologised, and fell silent.

'What's your name, guard?' Walter inquired.

'Studebaker, sir,' she responded, snapping to attention.

'Thank you for your input,' he said, not unkindly.

*That young lady has a promising career ahead of her.*

Gordon waited until they'd finished talking before moving onto the next candidate. 'Minister, this is Mind Syphon and it's extremely dangerous. It has no physical gender but the minds of both. You see, it can absorb a person's consciousness right out of their brain, adding it to its pool of minds and leaving the original body an empty vessel.'

Minister Ray took a cautious look through the viewing portal to behold a purple-skinned cyclops whose head morphed into a big, bulging brain above the single red eye that dominated the middle of its head. It had no other facial features.

'Why the hell would you ever let that thing loose?' the Minister asked, horrified. 'What use could it possibly have?'

'It would be our last resort for interrogation in the field,' Walter explained. 'Great for exposing clandestine operations.'

Minister Ray held up his hand. 'I don't want to know. Plausible deniability, you understand.'

'Our next candidate's called Rattlesnake…' Gordon began.

Suddenly the lights dimmed and turned red, and the clangour from an alarm drowned out all conversation.

*What fresh hell is this?*

The guards immediately took defensive positions while Gordon checked the locks on the containment units before shepherding the minister into the far corner.

'What's going on?' Minister Ray yelled over the din. He looked scared. 'Are the prisoners escaping?'

'Stay calm,' Walter said as he dialled up the command centre on his wrist pad. 'Singh? It's the Chief Warden. I want a situation report.'

The moments spent waiting for Walter to get answers seemed to stretch into infinity.

'Singh, keep an open channel going.' Walter pressed a button on his wrist pad and turned his attention back to the group. 'Okay, we have a situation here everyone. Three unidentified entities have appeared from nowhere outside the prison grounds. They are most likely hostile Manifests, but that's still undetermined. At the moment they're outside the prison's external suppressor field, but I expect that's temporary.'

'Surely you have force-field defence systems in place?' Minister Ray seemed to be hyperventilating and had turned the colour of phlegm.

'Only around the entrances—we don't have the power to generate a field to cover the whole prison,' Walter said dismissively.

'But you can project the Manifest suppressor field around the grounds—you just said so,' Minister Ray said.

'Different tech, I'm afraid. The exterior walls are reinforced concrete and that'll have to do.' Walter turned to his wardens. 'Studebaker, take an assistant and escort the minister to the command centre with due haste. Gordon, take the rest of the men and get these prisoners to their cells. I'll scout the area before joining you in the command centre. Lucky for us they're on the opposite side of the prison from the elevator.'

A dull pounding began on the outside wall as if to punctuate the statement, and Singh reported that one of the intruders had opened fire with heavy ordnance while the other two were sprinting towards the prison.

'Move!' Walter commanded his companions as he stepped out of the interrogation room and into the loading bay. He dashed across the bay and into the main prison while the other wardens carried out his orders.

The pounding was coming from the outside wall on the opposite side of the loading bay and the prisoners on the first two floors looked nervous. Walter ducked through a locked hatch and into the secret access tunnels that ran between the cells and the outer wall.

The pounding was much louder in the tunnels and Walter was defying his own protocols by being there alone during a siege. Singh had failed to identify the assailants in the prison's extensive records, and so he saw it as his duty as Chief Warden to identify them for the response teams that would already be mobilising. Plus, he was a hands-on kind of guy.

*If I can get out through the emergency exit hatch, I can keep covered and provide eyes on the ground. If I don't get killed in the process, that is.* Luckily, he always packed his batons for just such an eventuality.

The emergency exit hatch was on the far side of the pounding, which grew louder by the second. The wall shattered just before Walter could cross, and he was knocked back from the blast of rubble as a chunk of the wall caved in from an outside explosion.

Before Walter could get back on his feet, a small, green creature wearing a silver helmet with matching armour and flowing amaranthine cloak snuck through the smoking opening and scampered down the tunnel. It carried a large knife and had a symbol of a white skull on a black background on the back of its helmet.

'Oi, you!' Walter cried at the gremlin as he cautiously started to follow it, still wary of its companions. 'Singh, we have a breach! Be advised that the intruder is about a metre high, armoured, and armed with a blade. Looks to be a mutant of some kind, and it's heading towards junction K.'

'Defence teams one and two report contact with a heavily armed hostile in red battle armour,' Singh said to Walter over the comms channel. 'Manifest suppressors remain operational and no prisoners have escaped their cells. Minister arrived safely too.'

*Well, that's some fucking good news at least. But where's the third guy?*

Walter slowly crept up to the edge of the smouldering hole. 'Singh, do we have eyes on the thir —'

He was suddenly confronted by an aquamarine-coloured shark-man, stepping into the tunnel from outside, the same skull symbol as the first intruder emblazoned on its shining silver armour. It stood over two metres tall at the apex of its head-fin, and was humanoid, yet had a long fish tail that swayed from side to side. Walter got a good look at it as it gnashed its serrated teeth in his face. Its hot breath smelled of blood and fish. It looked at Walter with an eye that was almost human.

*There's intelligence in those eyes,* Walter thought before he was hammered by the creature's forearm, causing him to trip over a chunk of rubble and fall on his arse. 'Hello, Singh?' The radio hissed static in response. *Must be damaged.*

'Akk-akk, Gurk, hazha!' the creature roared, and fired the harpoon gun embedded in its right-hand gauntlet straight at Walter's stomach.

Walter dived to the side and the harpoon clanged harmlessly against the concrete floor. The shark creature retracted the harpoon while unsheathing a serrated dagger from its belt with its other hand. Bloody drool dripped from between its jagged fangs.

*Seems to be relying primarily on its tech, although it must have physical enhancements. That means it's either a mutant, a machine, or even a fucking alien, otherwise its Manifest should be suppressed.*

The creature turned and brought its tail down like a meaty bludgeon, but Walter was already on his feet and he slammed his fist into the creature's nose.

*Fuck! Harder than I thought...*

The shark-man slashed Walter deep across his stomach with its dagger and followed through with a kick to his groin. Pain flashed through Walter's whole body and he tried not to pass out from the violent attack.

*Bloody fool, trying to show off. He's much stronger than you. You have batons—fucking use them.*

Walter summoned a new reserve of strength and extended his energised batons with a flick of his wrists as he steadied himself against the wall.

*Don't pass out now, old man. You may've lost a lot of blood, but the response team will be here soon. Show this fish-faced fuck what normal humans are made of.*

'Kaw rah-heggle hazha!' the creature bellowed, aiming its harpoon gun at Walter again. That's when Walter noticed its armour's 'collars', which extended from the main suit, spray a fine mist onto what looked to be the creature's gills. 'Gurk Shrokvozi muck-akk.' It looked to be mocking him.

'Fuck you, Great White!' he said, lunging at his assailant and batting the harpoon aside as it fired it at him. Walter struck the creature's nose with his energised baton with better results than his first attempt, and then followed it up with a strike to the creature's wrist, causing it to drop its dagger.

Walter's advantage was soon lost as he began to grow light headed from the exertion, the whole front of his suit drenched in his own blood. Great White pressed the attack, swiping Walter's feet out from under him with its thick tail and then diving on him with its full weight.

*Mother-fuck! Don't fucking faint, you pussy!*

Great White tried to bite Walter's face, but he got his arm up just in time, causing its jaw to crunch on his gauntlet—breaking its teeth along with Walter's arm and making the energy baton fizzle out.

He started to black out from the blood loss and pain of Great White's crushing jaw when he noticed the collar squirt more water onto its gills. Walter shoved his remaining baton into Great White's gills, electrifying the sensitive area and causing the creature to roll off him, shrieking in pain.

Walter rolled the other way and snatched his opponent's dagger, then used it to slice off the end of Great White's finned tail when deflecting its swipe. Great White became off-balanced, and Walter used this to his advantage, slamming his baton on his attacker's head and smashing its face into the concrete floor.

Walter collapsed on top of his unconscious opponent before sliding off it to the floor, where he remained slumped in an expanding pool of his own blood.

*Well this could be it,* he thought as he started flitting in and out of consciousness. *I knew this day was fucked the moment that goddamn minister turned up looking for a tour. My schedule's going to be out of whack for God knows how long.*

'Warden, sir!' said a familiar voice, rousing Walter back to consciousness. 'We came back as soon as we secured the prisoners.'

*Hey, it's Rick. Where'd he come from?*

'The threat's over, the other two escaped,' Gordon reported. 'Don't worry, sir, we'll get you patched up in no time. You just hang on there—stay with me.'

Walter watched from what seemed like so far away as Gordon's team secured Great White and called in a medical team. One of the guards was showing the others the piece of fin Walter had sliced off his foe earlier.

*Oi, that's mine!*

Walter felt himself getting colder and started hallucinating the stock-standard tunnel of light.

*Is that a giant tick in the shadows behind the light?*

The ghostly image of the tick condensed into the concerned face of Gordon.

'...stay with me, sir,' he was saying to Walter from across a sea of white noise. 'Help has arrived and we're going to transport you to the prison hospital now.'

'The fin...get the fin...' Walter's voice was a whisper.

'What was that, sir? The fin, did you say?' Gordon was confused.

'The shark fin...' Walter pointed weakly at the guards who were still holding Great White's tailfin. 'When I get through this, I want the prison cook to make it into a soup...'

He then lost consciousness and everything went black.

\* \* \*

## The Skull of Ra: 7 June 34 BZ

'Report.' Anu Hopet stared down silently at his apprehensive minions as they bickered over who amongst them should speak first.

Four of his Skull Band were present: there was Disk, of course, the cybernetic midget who forever fussed around the ship's control panels; Backstabber, the even shorter alien assassin; Battletank, carmine dreadnought with heavy artillery; and the svelte Bodyguard, who was standing off to the side, looking smug as he wasn't involved. They all had birth names, but Anu Hopet preferred the names he had chosen for them. The appellation that had been chosen for him he could give or take.

They were all who remained of the former prisoners, who once served as scientific guineapigs aboard the ship. It was Anu Hopet who freed them and moulded them, when he wrested control of the vessel from its original owners. Now they served as an extension of his will; tools to be used to forge his destiny.

*And to help me free myself from this accursed prophecy. If they can get it into themselves to stop cowering long enough to be of use.*

'One of you speak, or I will make all of you scream!' Anu Hopet boomed, standing like an armoured monolith, his swirling vermillion cape contrasting with his dark, motionless form. With his arms crossed over his chest and gruff expression, it was truly a Kodak moment for grandiose evil poses.

'The mission was a success, Great Armageddon,' said Backstabber obsequiously, its jutting green jaw moving rapidly below its half-helm—the only part his its flesh aside from its hands that wasn't covered by armour. Survival at all costs was ingrained in its species and Backstabber plied its trade well. 'Battletank stood out of range of their defences and made an entrance for us close to our target with his weaponry. You were right: the Manifest suppressors had no effect on our alien physiology and I was able to locate the target without resistance. Although Gurk was captured and the target didn't have the talisman...'

'And you call this a success?' Anu Hopet's hands began to glow with quantum energy —tiny particles of antimatter that reacted with the ship's atmosphere—a subconscious response whenever he got angry.

Backstabber saw this and quickly ramped up its survival mode. It still remembered what had happened to its former teammate, Garach, all those years ago. 'The target told us where to find the talisman, Great Armageddon! It was taken by the mystery woman who was with him before he was apprehended! Please forgive me if I misled you.' It cowered.

'And you believed this individual?' Anu Hopet enquired. 'How can you be certain he was telling the truth?'

'I can be very convincing when need be,' Backstabber said, touching the hilt of its poisoned dagger fastened to its belt. 'His name was

Fabian Swartzendruber—Heist, he goes by—and he was very forth-coming once his toes started falling off. He did not know the mystery woman's name, but said she was an assassin—there to kill the talis-man's original owner. She took the talisman opportunistically and doesn't know of its power.'

'But no doubt assumes it is valuable, nonetheless,' Anu Hopet said as his hands stopped glowing. 'Very well, we will make locating this woman our highest priority. Now, I know what you are all thinking but are too scared to say; but Gurk knows not to betray me and, they do not speak his language.'

The Skull Band looked uncomfortable, but they were too scared to say anything. 'Yes, Great Armageddon,' they murmured.

'Good. Now, Disk, I believe you had something to report.' Anu Hopet returned to his classic evil stance.

'My liege, I have finished scanning the entire world's libraries, and our databanks are now updated on Earth,' Disk began, still working out how best to deliver his news. Good news first. 'This led me to information on the anti-Manifest technology this world utilises, and I have replicated it for more controlled study. It is my hypothesis that you can use it to great advantage against your nemesis, as well as keep-ing those Miasma creatures out of the ship.'

'Finally, some good news on that front,' Anu Hopet said. 'Was that all?'

'There's one more thing...' Disk relished life and hesitated to go on.

'Spit it out!' Anu Hopet was quick to anger. 'Or do I have smash your brains in and use them for an augury?'

'That won't be necessary, my lord,' Disk replied hastily. 'It's just that...well...my scan of the libraries...and something Backstabber confirmed with me earlier...which Heist said...led to certain revela-tions about the talisman...'

'What about it?' Anu Hopet's hands started glowing again. 'Or do I have to forcefully extract the memory drive from your brain and find out for myself?'

'Great Armageddon, it appears as if the talisman's magical prop-erties don't come from Queen Kyra Zol, but rather some legendary witch called Baba Yaga. You...you are seeking this object for the... ah...wrong reasons.' Disk seemed to be sweating lubricant.

'You think I do not know that?' Anu Hopet roared. 'You have knowledge, thanks to your technology, and because of that you actually think you have the wisdom to see into my mind and uncover my plans.'

'Spare me, Great Armageddon!' Disk squealed, cowering before his master. 'I only sought to bring this to your attention. I should have had faith in your infallible nature.'

'Yes, you should,' Anu Hopet said, satisfied with Disk's response. 'You do show both bravery and loyalty by bringing me this information. For that I shall explain it to you. It is true I am seeking objects of power, but it is not for my battle with the upstart. They are for the acts of deicide that will follow. I am also seeking revenge against those who wronged me long ago, and the talisman has power in that regard. For you see, it is intrinsically linked to the queen and her son, and once I have it I should be able to track them down.'

'And what if they are already dead? It has been a long time since we left Earth,' Battletank felt bold enough to ask, and Disk was happy to share the spotlight. Bodyguard rarely said anything, having previously found that silence was the best way to avoid their master's wrath.

'Then I shall take what small satisfaction I can and move on.'

*As I always have,* Anu Hopet thought before turning away and leaving the bridge of *The Skull of Ra* to his bewildered Skull Band.

* * *

### Xenotech International Hotel, Los Angeles, California: 10 June 34 BZ

Lorraine Freeman was on her third straight week of moping in her hotel room and bingeing on room service. Hiding from the world was all well and good, but she was starting to get incredibly bored and had run out of ways of entertaining herself a week ago. She would have even raided the minibar if her mother hadn't done it first.

*I guess that's one way to stop me underage drinking,* she thought as she slowly plodded from the bed to the couch where her mother was having a nap, her chestnut hair covering her face.

*I can't go outside—not after that terrible interview. Now my secret is out, people will start thinking my popularity is some sort of mind control.* All of a sudden staying home and going to school didn't seem so bad.

Lorraine flicked on the TV and began her daily ritual of channel surfing.

At least there were about a hundred channels available, compared with the half dozen she had at home. Lorraine intended to watch them all. Incomplete sentences rang out across the hotel room:

'…yesterday's earthquake in southern Mexico…'

'…please welcome our next guest, Asparagus Man…'

'…the Ab-Meister 3000 will have your abs begging for mercy!'

'…bodies are still being found in the aftermath of Vicious Man's murder spree down the West Coast last week…'

'…US/Australian relations have taken a frosty turn since last week's terrorist attack by an Australian Manifest…'

'…American Way has made a full recovery after defending the ideals of liberty…'

'…Vicious Man…'

*Hmmm, no one seems to be talking about me at all.* Lorraine wasn't sure whether to be relieved or disappointed. She continued surfing.

'…sightings of the Roaring Twenties in Detroit…'

'…the mandrill troop forages through the undergrowth for…'

'…well what about Lorraine Freeman's mother?'

*Bingo.*

'That washed up has-been? She was part of those superheroes from the sixties who posed as androids, wasn't she? I can't even remember her code name. Was it Speculum?' Laughter erupted from the TV set.

'Turn that fucking thing off!' Lucy Freeman said suddenly and with a heavy slur.

'Oh, Mum, I didn't know you were awake,' Lorraine said, slightly startled. 'There's nothing to do and this is the only show that's talking about me.'

*Okay, so they were talking about Mum, but close enough.*

The voices on the TV continued: 'I seem to remember that the company they worked for had to be completely rebranded after they were exposed as frauds for not being androids at all, and instead just a bunch of loser Manifests working for a sham company. Their stock crashed, the entire board was replaced and the X-Droids were all fired.'

'Maybe that's why "Speculum Girl" decided to get knocked up and exploit her daughter's talents instead,' said the other voice, while more laughter burst from the TV.

'Notice how she's always trying to steal the spotlight? So sad and pathetic. Her daughter on the other hand, has caused an explosion on the World Wide Web!' More laughter.

'Lorraine, that's enough of that!' Lucy sat up and slowly brushed the hair from her face. 'Or I'll black it out like I did at your David Leno interview.'

'You're so drunk that you're the only one blacking out around here.' Lorraine compromised by changing to the music channel. Eighties music permeated the airwaves. 'Is it true? What they said on the TV?'

'No, we weren't really fired—we still do clandestine work for Xeno-tech Inc on the side,' Lucy said, now sitting up and massaging her temples. 'How do you think we're paying for all this? Your money's going into a trust until you're eighteen.'

'That's not what I mean,' Lorraine said, nervously wringing her hands. 'Is all of this just you trying to live your life through me?'

'I...' Lucy paused too long to think of a plausible lie. '...Yes, I suppose so, if I'm being honest. I find it hard to lie to you now, since...you, ah, Manifested.'

'Well, that's...honest,' Lorraine admitted, a little shocked. 'Maybe more honesty than I was expecting.'

'What can I say? I was disappointed with how they lambasted us in the media for "misleading" the public by pretending to be androids—especially when I told them it was a bad idea in the first place, and they should have just confessed we were all Manifests and focused instead on the little rocket boots they gave us. But oh no, they had grander visions and look where that got everyone.' Lucy rubbed her bloodshot eyes.

'Go on,' Lorraine said, her words punctuated with a blast of music from the television.

'So I learned to move on. After all, my relationship with your... father? Other mother? What's the term for a hermaphrodite anyway?' Lorraine's mother was prone to diversions.

'Mum...'

'So anyway, I was involved with Shara and before I knew it, you and your sisters were on the way and you became my lives. I still had plenty of money and the odd jobs for the new Xenotech executives kept me satisfied for many years.' Lucy got up and poured herself the remaining dregs from a bottle of vodka she'd had sent up with breakfast. 'No, I suppose if I'm still being honest, I was listless and I think that finally drove a wedge between Shara and me. I blamed all of that on your anti-social behaviour when you became a teenager. The fact is, I saw myself in you, what with your drinking and pot smoking.'

'Well, if it wasn't for my pot smoking, I wouldn't have made the bong that triggered my Manifest, and I'd just be an antisocial teenager, rather than cover girl of the year.' Lorraine wondered if that would be better or not.

'Just because you have these wonderful abilities doesn't mean I have to like how you got them,' Lucy said, glad that her daughter's rebellious stage appeared to be over. 'I mean, making a bong at your age? What would the neighbours think?'

*Did Mum seriously just use that cliché?*

'I hope you didn't have it thrown out after we left for this tour,' Lorraine said, thinking of how her creation changed from plastic bottle to porcelain after it Manifested. 'I called it Obtuse, given it's now a sentient being.'

*These Manifest seeds are so crazy! Hard to imagine a bong being alive, let alone sentient.*

'As if I would throw a living creature away like that, even if it does defy the laws of nature,' Lucy replied. 'Besides, it's now inextricably linked with you and I wouldn't do that to you.'

'We're getting off topic again,' Lorraine said, determined to get this out in the open.

'That was your fault this time,' Lucy said, finishing her drink and scanning the room for more. 'Okay, so yeah, when you became a Manifest, I noticed how everyone suddenly went out of their way to please you. So I tried to give you the opportunity I didn't have, by marketing you, and not passing you off for something you're not. That's why I went on Oprah.'

'Except that's exactly what you did do!' Lorraine was instantly angry with her mother in that way only teenagers can be. 'Here I am, some hermit in a hotel because, first, you start acting like my agent, and then you expose me to global humiliation and force me to hide from the media! You can still hear them outside, waiting for a chance to grill me some more. I wouldn't be surprised if you set up the whole thing!'

'Lorraine, darling, you need to calm down. I'm your mother...'

'And you're drunk. Mother of the year, you are,' Lorraine snapped.

'You're out of line. This hasn't been easy for me, either...'

'Well, I want you to stop drinking, I hate it!'

Lucy stopped searching for the scattered bottles as if a switch had suddenly been turned off in her head. 'Okay...sure, honey, anything for you.' Her mother smiled.

*She sounded liked she meant it too—did what I think just happen actually happen? Did I just control my mum, another Manifest?*

The mood was broken by a video clip of someone called King Diamond blaring from the TV.

'I'm sorry, Mum, I didn't mean to yell.' Lorraine's anger had gone as quickly as it arrived. 'It's just when I heard those guys on TV...'

'There's no need to apologise,' Lucy said, sitting down next to her daughter. 'You're right, I shouldn't have pushed you into this, and I should've been a better role model.'

*It's like she didn't even notice she's stopped looking for booze.*

'I only want the best for you,' Lucy continued. 'I would never humiliate you—as I said at the time, that guy in the Leno audience was a plant. He was one of those MIBs who work for the UN—or maybe the UN work for them—I know, I've come across them many times before. Creepy fuckers all look the same, and I'd never forget that rude head if I lived to be a thousand. You knew that people would eventually figure out you're a Manifest, you *are* the daughter of one—"washed up hasbeen" or not. It was only a matter of time.'

'But now everyone will think I've been controlling them or something,' Lorraine complained. 'The government will lock me up in some padded cell in an undisclosed location, I just know it. Especially after what happened at the Vatican—that'll be seen in a whole new light after this.'

'You've got nothing to worry about, sweetie,' Lucy said reassuringly. 'People still love you—me most of all—and no one can take that away from you. As for the Vatican? You'd have to give the bishops in that place a colonoscopy to probe any secrets out of them. They'd be the last people to talk.'

Lorraine was starting to feel better. 'You might be right,' she conceded, handing her mother the hairbrush lying on the coffee table. 'Most of the news shows were talking about Vicious Man.'

'Well, he did just go on another murder rampage in this very city,' Lucy said, brushing her daughter's hair. 'Left a trail of destruction down the entire West Coast and then disappeared. It's his standard MO.'

'Why didn't you stop him? You're a superhero.'

'Then you'd have one less mother,' Lucy laughed. 'There's no way I'd confront that monster by choice.'

'They said on the TV that he's Australian—I didn't know that,' Lorraine said. Her long, brown hair began cascading down her shoulders.

'He's not—I don't think he's even human—they just keep saying he's Australian because he was first sighted there. Also, unlikely as it is, most of the world's Manifests come from Australia. Why'd you think so many people are always trying to migrate there? It's because they think Manifest seeds are catching or in the water or something.'

Lucy continued brushing as King Diamond was arriving at his falsetto crescendo finale.

'Why are most of the Manifests from Australia?' Lorraine asked.

'Buggered if I know,' Lucy replied. 'Doctor Q had a theory before he disappeared. Or so he said. He never shared it with anybody to my knowledge. But that's all beside the point: everything's going to be fine. The tour will be over soon and you'll be back home before you know it. It's just lucky we already had a break scheduled, otherwise we would've had to end the tour early.'

There was a brief pause between video clips, and the sound of a large group of people could be heard outside in the courtyard.

'You hear that? They're your fans, not media hounds,' Lucy said as she finished brushing Lorraine's hair. 'No one cares that you're a Manifest. If anything, it's made you more popular.'

Lorraine wasn't sure if that made it any better, or whether her powers were really just a curse. She got up from the couch and walked towards the window just as 'Make Your Own Kind of Music' by Cass Elliott began to play on the TV.

*I know this one,* she thought, drawing open the curtains and instantly lighting up the whole room, *and it's inspiring me to do something crazy.*

Lorraine opened the double glass doors to the balcony. Their room was on the first floor and overlooked a small courtyard ringed with honeysuckle. The entire space was crammed full of devoted fans all hoping to catch a glimpse of Lorraine—especially now they'd detected movement on the balcony. She idly wondered why the hotel tolerated them.

'Lorraine, sweetie, what are you doing?' Lucy was surprised and slightly concerned by the sudden turn of events.

'I'm only doing what you said I should do. I'm going to face my adoring public.' Lorraine began rearranging the balcony furniture, moving the table aside and sliding a chair up against the guardrail. 'I'm just going to do it in my own way.'

'Wait…Lorraine, don't be stupid!' Lucy yelled when she realised what her daughter was attempting.

Before her mother could stop her, Lorraine climbed up onto the balcony guardrail. The crowd went berserk, cheering and egging her on. Lorraine was illuminated in a hundred camera flashes and captured on streams of videotape.

*This is crazy, but it just feels right.*

Lucy sprang from the couch and dashed towards the balcony just as Lorraine stretched her hands to the sky and the music started to peak. 'Lorraine! Lorra…ahhh!'

Lorraine turned around as her mother slipped on a vodka bottle in her drunken state and face-planted the floor.

'Mum! Are you okay? Don't worry, I'm not going to jump or anything—the music inspired me to finally face my fears and see how the people would react. Turns out they do still love me!' The crowd cheered as if to punctuate the statement, distracting Lorraine as she turned back to wave to them and causing her to carelessly misstep over the ledge. The collective gasp from the crowd could be heard a block away.

'Lorraine! Oh my god!' Lucy cried, scrambling to regain her footing.

'Mum, it's okay, why're you freaking out?' Only then did Lorraine notice what she'd done and was instantly aware that she was standing on air like a cartoon character.

*Oh shit!*

It took Lorraine a split second to realise that, unlike a cartoon character, she didn't plummet to the ground followed by a giant boulder after becoming aware of the situation.

*Am I floating? Can I fly?*

The crowd certainly thought so and erupted into a wild frenzy that made Beatles Mania seem like high tea with the queen. Lucy Freeman could only stare with her mouth agape.

*I wonder how long I've been able to do this. Probably since I Manifested, I guess. What if I can take to the skies like Mum?*

Lorraine tried to fly but found she could only walk, as if the air was just another surface for a constitutional. She revived her catwalk routine and strutted out to stand above the centre of the crowd, spinning around above their cheering heads.

* * *

### The Tomb of Power: Circa 19 June 34 BZ

*I think I'm in hell.* Mark Adams started to regain consciousness and take in his surroundings. He was still dressed in his jeans and work boots and was lying prone on a cold stone floor with one arm outstretched and the other tucked underneath him. In front of him in the centre of the tomb was a golden sarcophagus, flanked end to end by two golden pillars crackling with turquoise energy that occasionally arced between them. Demonic stone faces lined the grey walls surrounding the pillars and cast judgemental gazes down upon him. More lined the dais that raised the sarcophagus above the floor. The only illumination came from the pillars and the stone faces seemed to change in the flickering light.

*Either that or I'm having the worst nightmare in history. Where am I? What was I doing? Was I looking for something? Where's Desci?*

Suddenly it all came flooding back and he involuntarily sucked in his breath and fully opened his eyes. Primal fear flooded his reptilian brain.

'Sssso, the human awakenssss,' rasped a husky voice to his left in the darkness.

Mark quickly sat up and got into a crouching position, facing the direction the voice had come from. Only then did he notice he'd been lying exactly on a grotesque outline etched into the floor.

*What's going on? Last thing I remember was hallucinating about this place after that strange guy showed up and attacked Desci. Then there was some sort of gargoyle in the mirror. Am I still hallucinating? This can't be real—can it?*

'It is real, Mark Adams,' said a second voice from the shadows. It reminded Mark of how his voice sounded on a tape recording. 'We are now connected to you through the blood sacrifice you made to summon us.' The owner of the voice stepped from the shadows and its face was lit up under its hood by a sudden arc of energy from the pillars.

The full horror dawned on Mark and he remembered being assaulted by his twisted reflection in his bathroom just before blacking out.

Thanks for the kiss.
You will see yourself soon.

'Stay away from me!' Mark yelled with false defiance, but he was too scared to move from the spot. 'Who are you? What is this place? What do you want with me? What have you done with my wife?'

The demons erupted in mocking laughter and he felt a chill run the length of his spine. The demon with Mark's face crouched down in imitation of his pose, its giant bat-like wings folded up behind its shoulders making it look more like the gargoyle it reminded him of. It smiled at Mark in a rictus grin.

'The human askssss questionsssss,' hissed the first demon as it stepped from the shadows to stand behind the gargoyle. It had wings and taloned fingers like the gargoyle but was bright orange with a spiky face and long upper teeth that extended from its skull like stalactites. 'He will not want the answerssss.'

Mark became aware of a nattering sound behind him and turned to see two more demons lurch from the darkness. The one making the sound was short and appeared to be hunched over—weighed down by the mound of human skins it wore like a shell. Only its scarlet eyes and white chattering teeth could be seen beneath the folds of man-leather.

'We say we teach this meat his place and dismember him,' said the second demon on Mark's right. 'We want his scalp.' It was brown and lanky, with skin stretched tight over its inhuman bones. Its head looked like the top of a ram's skull except it had luminescent green eyes and hypodermics for teeth. It also wore a necklace of scalps around its scrawny neck.

Yet another demon suddenly jumped in front of Mark and leered over him. It was large with four arms and had a horned, hairy skull for a head. It too was missing a jaw, and the hole in its neck glowed and smoked, as if its insides were aflame. This could have very well been the case; its skin was charred from head to foot. What disturbed Mark the most, however, were the twin serpents it had instead of a phallus. They hissed and flicked their forked tongues as they writhed together in unholy dance.

'Hee hee hee, play with us! Play with us!' it started screeching, the loose, wet eyeballs rolling around in its sockets as it danced around the tomb.

'Negative,' the gargoyle doppelganger interjected. 'Mark Adams must be delivered alive and unspoiled to the demon lord, Xph'Ish'Matarg...'

*Ziff what? Did that thing say demon lord? Why is this shit happening to me?*

'...as the High Mage requested,' the demon continued. 'No, we say that we answer his questions in the order he asked them.'

*I don't even remember what I asked. I'm too terrified to think straight. I'm worried about Desci and I'm also worried that they're speaking the truth about demon lords and high mages.*

He also wondered if they were using the royal 'we' when referring to themselves, like they're part of a hive or something.

Mark shifted on the spot, now surrounded by his captors and without an exit. He didn't know where he'd go—the doorway to his bedroom was gone and the inky darkness beyond the sarcophagus looked uninviting.

'Hee hee hee, we are going to play a word game! Play with us! Play with us!' shrieked the burnt, four-armed demon.

'Very well, it is decided then,' said the ram-skulled demon. 'We will answer his questions.'

*I don't think I'm going to like the answers.*

'No, you will not,' the gargoyle said. 'You forget your Wisp connects you to us through the blood sacrifice. Your every thought is ours to dissect.'

*Wisp? I don't understand.*

'Then you should listen,' the gargoyle suggested, all the while mimicking Mark. 'We are the Scouts of the World Eater; the almighty Gledandron. This unit is classified Im'shtar, demon of the reflection. The unit to our left…'

'Hee hee hee, is Ress'urekt, demon of the animated corpse,' the cackling horror continued on from Im'shtar without missing a beat. The creatures introduced themselves in succession as Mark struggled to take it all in.

'This unit is Styryk, the Disemboweller,' rasped the orange grotesque through its facial stalactites, 'and we can ssssmell your gutssss.'

The mummified goat-demon leaned forward. 'This unit is Racuse, the Scalper, and the final unit is Saracuth, the Keeper of Skins.'

Saracuth only nattered from beneath the folds of its flesh-shell in response.

'You have guessed that we share one mind and can tap into your mind through your Wisp.' It was Im'shtar who spoke. 'Wisp are Gledandron's gift to the sentients of Earth—every human child receives one at birth. Usually they are only strong enough to whisper in your deepest thoughts, but yours, Mark Adams, has become strong enough to actually transmit your thoughts—thanks to your blood sacrifice.'

'But I didn't know it was a blood sacrifice! I didn't choose this; how could I possibly know?' Mark yelled in frustration. He was sweating despite the cold in the tomb.

'Hee hee hee! It matters not! Rules of the game! Rules of the game!' Ress'urekt danced a jig on the spot, which surprisingly Mark found more irritating than frightening.

'But why me?' Mark asked.

'He asks another question! There is much going on underneath that handsome scalp. It is wasted on his head, we should peel it off,' Racuse croaked. 'Then Styryk could have his guts and Saracuth can have his skin.'

The nattering grew louder and took on an insectoid feel.

'That course of action has already been rejected,' Im'shtar said, turning towards Racuse. 'It was agreed to provide answers and answers he shall have.' Im'shtar turned back to face Mark. 'You are within the Tomb of Power, an ancient construct of Gledandron, designed to provide sheltered transport between dimensions. It is based on Geburan architecture.'

'Geburan? What's that?' Mark summoned the courage to ask. He thought it better to keep them talking and maybe he'd live longer.

'The Geburans were the native inhabitants of Geburah,' Im'shtar answered, smiling at Mark with the twisted replica of his face, 'though you would call them Martians.'

*Martians? I don't know what I was expecting, but it wasn't that.*

'But Mars is a lifeless rock, so what happened to them? Are…you from Mars?' he asked. The demons started laughing, each in its own unnerving style.

'Gledandron sent us to Earth from Geburah long ago, but we are not from there. We come from beyond,' Im'shtar said. 'As for the Geburans themselves…well they became one with Gledandron.'

'Hee hee hee! We ate them!' cackled Ress'urekt.

'They were consumed along with all trace of their existence, as will befall Earth and its life forms,' Im'shtar recounted. 'We were sent here to scout your world for Gledandron's arrival.'

*I wonder how long until it gets here?*

'Why, Gledandron has been here for centuries already!' Racuse laughed. 'The World Eater moves on a scale so large that its presence is not detected until too late. Two worlds it has devoured in this system already, and your world will be the third.'

*This is a fucking nightmare! I have to get out of here and warn someone!*

'No one would believe you, even if you were to escape,' Im'shtar replied to Mark's thoughts. 'The Tomb of Power moves outside of regular time and space, and while it has been hours since you arrived here from your perspective, weeks have passed on Earth and you have been declared dead.'

*That can't be true!*

'But it issss true! You can feel it in your bowelsssss,' Styryk spat.

Saracuth's nattering sounded like crickets chirping.

Mark hated how they kept reading his thoughts but didn't know how to shield them. Instead he asked questions. 'Where are you taking me? What do you want with me? Where's my wife? Why can't you do this to someone else?'

'Sssso many questionssssss!' Styryk snapped, unfurling its enormous orange wings. 'We grow weary of his tongue.'

'Hee hee hee! The Tomb is taking you to Hell! You are the High Mage's payment to Xph'Ish'Matarg for allowing him to go free!' Ress'urekt shrieked, waving its four arms around spasmodically. 'A balance must be struck!'

*I remember that weird guy said that when he showed up at the door!*

Instantly it all came flooding back and he remembered everything. Then it sank in that the demon said it was taking him to Hell.

'Maybe I can make a deal, and Ziffish Ma...ah... your boss will let me go too?' Mark was desperate.

Unfortunately, his question just brought scornful mockery.

'You can ask Xph'Ish'Matarg that yourself when we deliver you to it,' Im'shtar said. 'It should not take too much longer for the Tomb to bypass the Mystical Realm and enter Hell. Such a feat would not even be possible if the Tomb was not powered by a Manifest, sleeping eternally within the sarcophagus—a so-called prince from Egypt we ensnared long ago. Unlike him, you were chosen at random. Like a fishing line, those flowers were left as bait for the blood sacrifice and you were who we caught. You are not special, Mark Adams—it could have been anyone.'

That revelation didn't make him feel any better; in fact, somehow it made him feel worse. But then he had a thought which sparked a glimmer of hope.

'If I'm not special and you only abducted me because I found the flowers, then there's no need to have hurt Desci,' Mark said hopefully.

Once more the demons laughed mercilessly.

'Your logic is flawed like your species,' Im'shtar mocked. 'All life on Earth will be consumed by Gledandron. Your family simply received this honour before most.'

'No, it can't be! You lie! Nooooooo!' Mark felt despair enshroud him in its obsidian grasp. He started sobbing.

'Yes…feel the hopelessness of your situation and know that you belong in Hell. It is your fault your family is dead. If you had only left those flowers where you found them, none of this would be happening,' Im'shtar said coldly, while the other demons continued to laugh. 'Now prepare yourself for an eternity in Hell!'

All Mark could do was curl into the foetal position as the demons stood over him and jeered in the flickering gloom.

\* \* \*

### Kings Cross, Sydney: 21 June 34 BZ

Seth Zaraxom and Bojangles strolled aimlessly down the bustling street, the bright lights glittering like tiny diamonds in the fine drizzle, which had been intermittent over the last hour or so. It was also cold.

'Lots of people out tonight—despite it being a Tuesday,' Bojangles observed jovially, sidestepping some bubble-gum on the footpath.

'It's the solstice tonight,' Seth said knowingly, 'perhaps that explains it.'

'Except no one knows it's the bloody solstice except people like you, so unless it's some primeval thing I'm not aware of, I'd say it's just a coincidence,' Bojangles replied, grinning from ear to ear. 'Besides, the only ritual these people seem to be following is the relatively recent pub-crawl ceremony. Let's join them and get to the bottom of this confounding cult phenomenon.'

'Get to the bottom of a glass is more likely,' Seth riposted as they crossed the busy intersection. 'Didn't you earn your name from a previous alcohol-fuelled misadventure? Wasn't your official title "Nameless One" before then? When was that, the sixties?'

'You know I'm still sensitive about that, even after close to thirty years,' Bojangles said, his smile now gone as quickly as it had appeared. 'As you bloody well know, I stepped from the Dreaming without a name and some who knew me called me the Nameless One. But as you also know, I have the ability to see glimpses of my timeline and I knew that one day I would be known as Bojangles, so I adopted the name early. I had grown so used to it over the years that I forgot I had originally foreseen that someone else would be the one to officially give me that name.'

'Remind me again of the details,' Seth said, stopping to light a smoke out the front of a rundown store, which claimed in faded letters to be the grand-something headquarters. 'I'm so old that I tend to forget the finer points of memories.'

'Well, if you must hear it again, then yes, it was in the sixties,' Bojangles recalled, gesturing for a smoke from Seth. 'For someone who forgets the "finer points of memories" you seem to have a pretty good one. So, I was celebrating the results of the '67 referendum—I mean they let crazy white guys with superpowers vote before Aboriginal people, what the fuck's with that?—anyway, I may have had a few drinks too many and stopped for a nap in the park. I had Fluffy, my gratuitous evil dingo, with me at the time, but we weren't bothering anybody.'

'Go on,' Seth said with a smile as he started to recall the story.

'So, here I am having a dream about some lovely ladies—and you know me, I'm from the Dreaming, so my dreams are deeply spiritual...'

Seth snorted at the remark. 'Sounds like it.'

'...and then some trumped up white arsehole starts fucking kicking me awake!' Bojangles started getting worked up at the memory. 'He starts spouting some shit about how this is why we shouldn't have the vote, as we're all "just a bunch a drunken niggers", and that I was "that Mister Bojangles coon from that song" as I had my dog with me. Fucking prick.'

'So what did you do?' Seth asked, taking another drag from his smoke and watching the parade of people pass by.

'I didn't have to do anything,' Bojangles laughed. 'Stupid cunt kicked Fluffy and lost his leg below the knee! Hahaha! I teleported us out of there while he cried for a doctor and got away with it. I then realised that's what I had foreseen long ago and decided to keep the name— seeing as I'd been using it for so long already.'

'That's a much weirder origin than "rocketed from a doomed planet" or similar story,' Seth asserted.

'Well, that's life, isn't it?' Bojangles said. 'One giant mind-fuck, where you pay your admission on exit.'

'What's that? Waxing poetic?' Seth teased, dropping his butt and stamped it out with his boot heel. 'The Bard can rest easy.'

'Give a guy a break, will you?' Bojangles laughed as he took a final drag and did the same. 'English isn't my first language.'

'Speaking of the English, the High Mage was here in Sydney,' Seth said, his words taking on a serious tone. 'He found his son, despite us relocating him half a world away from his birthplace. Murdered him a few weeks back.'

'You shouldn't be surprised. His mother moved here of her own accord as well and it had nothing to do with their son. People are just drawn here, it seems.' Bojangles peered through the shop windows out of curiosity. 'Man, there's a lot of dusty shit in there—looks like a bunch of clothes or something.'

'You're getting distracted. We have to focus on the High Mage,' Seth said, trying to get Bojangles to focus. 'If only we knew who his agents on Earth are, and where they're hiding. He must have them—it's the only way he could've escaped Hell.'

'Maybe it's those guys with all the dusty cloaks?' Bojangles joked, turning back to the conversation. 'I think I spied a copy of *The Satanic Bible* on a shelf in there.'

'Will you be sensible for a moment? I'm serious,' Seth said. He started walking in an effort to draw Bojangles away from the shop-front. 'If I knew precisely what he had planned, I could adequately plan *for* it. You mentioned Manipulator moved here of her own accord—turns out she recently made the deceased list too.'

'Was it the High Mage?' Bojangles asked as they continued walking away from the Cross.

'Coincidentally, it was my nephew, but I can't help but feel the High Mage was involved somehow,' Seth said. They turned down a side street. 'I managed to acquire the Orb of...' He made a strange exhaling sound.

'The what? Did you just hack up a loogie?' Bojangles wasn't sure what he'd heard, only that it came with spittle.

'You know, the Orb of Horath,' Seth replied. The street lights got dimmer and the crowd thinned out.

'Then why didn't you just say that instead of coughing up a lung all over me?' Bojangles complained, wiping his sleeve.

'Because that's its true name,' Seth answered. They approached a group of guys milling about in drunken celebration. 'Horath is what the uninitiated call it—only those who know its true name can use it for divination.'

'Then use the Orb to divine the answer, stupid,' Bojangles said. 'You said you already used it once before to learn that Merlin would change his name to the more pompous High Mage of Hell when he finally escaped that place.'

'Sure, it can provide us with the answers we seek, but the price of knowledge is steep,' Seth said, tying his hair back into a ponytail. 'Still, it's the most useful arcane artefact we could have at the moment.'

'Well, if you have that, why do you need Naomi's necklace to meet that old trader, Summon?' Bojangles adjusted his sunglasses, which he wore at night to hide his dazzling golden eyes.

'Because I need the Soul Gem,' Seth responded quickly as he moved to walk around the group of drunken pedestrians. 'The High Mage is after it. He has to be, if he's planning what I think. Summon has the Gem and you know he always expects an exchange of goods.'

'He's a fucking weirdo, that's for sure,' Bojangles declared as he started fishing in Seth's backpack, which was still on its owner's back. 'But do you have the Orb on you? Can I sneak a peek?'

'Hey! Stop that! Do you want to smash the Orb?' Seth asked, twisting out of his backpack in an effort to keep it zipped up.

'Aww come on, let me see,' Bojangles said, not letting up.

'Are you six years old? No!' Seth scolded in frustration. 'I'll show you the Orb later, not here. There are people around.'

Kismet ensured they weren't just any people, either.

'Well, well, well, look who we 'ave 'ere,' said one of the drunken revellers as Seth and Bojangles walked past. 'Oi, look who 'tis!'

'If it isn't the chatty Goths,' said a second drunk.

Seth recognised the reference and turned back to look. It was Chunky and Pimples, the two dicks from the lecture on ancient music. This time they had six friends with them—all of them drunk and built like brick shit-houses.

'What? You boys got nothing to say now that we're off campus?' Pimples had obviously been drinking rum, given the illogical anger that flowed from him.

'I think someone should lay off the firewater and go home to bed,' Bojangles said off the cuff, and kept walking.

Chunky had other ideas. 'That's rich, comin' from a petrol-sniffin' abo,' Chunky foolishly uttered.

Bojangles stopped as if suddenly frozen to the spot.

'Oh boy, you've done it now,' Seth said under his breath. 'Don't kill him, he's just a stupid kid,' he said to Bojangles, putting a hand on his shoulder.

'Kill us? That fucking boong could only do that with his ugly face!' Chunky said, crossing the line in a metaphorical Sherman tank.

'Don't...' Seth said to Bojangles, but it was too late. His long-time friend and travelling companion had already turned back to face his tormentors.

'Don't worry, mate, I got this,' he said to Seth as he strode purposefully towards the group.

'Ooh, here he comes, fellas! I'm quaking!' Chunky yelled, secretly hoping his friends would step in on his behalf.

'Maybe you should tone it down, you're drunk,' Pimples said nervously to his fat friend.

'No need for that. Grab him, guys!' Chunky said to his brutish mates, pushing Pimples aside to get a closer look once he'd determined he wouldn't have to actually do any fighting.

The six brutes grabbed Bojangles and held him with his arms and legs apart, waiting for Chunky and Pimples to arrive. 'Hit him! Go on, we've got him!' one of the brutes encouraged Chunky.

'Aren't you going to help your friend?' Chunky called to Seth.

'I don't need to, mate,' Seth called back. 'You kids are going to be very sorry you didn't let this go.'

'Don't listen to him,' another brute said. 'This black bastard's going nowhere.'

'You got that right, you piece of shit,' Bojangles said calmly. 'Rather it's you who're going somewhere.'

In an instant, all six brutes simply vanished. Chunky and Pimples couldn't believe their eyes.

'I warned you,' Bojangles said to Chunky as he tapped Pimples on the shoulder and made him disappear too. 'You see, I can teleport things with a touch, like all your friends for instance.'

Bojangles grabbed Chunky by the throat; he squealed and wet his pants.

'Don't worry, I only teleported them a block from here,' Bojangles began. 'What you have to worry about is whether they'll make it back here in time—if at all—to get you to a hospital.'

Bojangles squeezed harder and started choking Chunky through the folds of his neck fat.

'I thought you said you weren't going to kill him,' Seth said nonchalantly. While he didn't kill needlessly, he was too old to really care about individual mortals.

'I'm not,' Bojangles confirmed, as a slight pop could be heard from within Chunky's neck, followed by a loud splat on the footpath. 'I just teleported his larynx and tongue onto the street. This cunt won't be calling anyone a fucking boong anymore.'

Bojangles released his grip and Chunky fell to his knees, grasping his throat.

'Better get that checked out, there're a lot of big veins in your neck,' Bojangles said, turning away. 'Good luck calling for help.'

He walked over to where Seth was finishing up another smoke. 'Sorry about that. Now what were we talking about again?' Bojangles asked, all hostilities forgotten.

'I was going to show you the Orb,' Seth replied. 'How about you beam us out of here to someplace quiet and I'll show you?'

'I know just the place,' Bojangles said as he put his hand on Seth's shoulder and they vanished into the night, leaving Chunky alone and choking on blood.

* * *

## Undisclosed location: 26 June 34 BZ

Courtney Yeht didn't like her new room. The floor had been silent ever since she arrived, and the stillness ached like a void that needed to be filled. She felt restless and unwell, with intermittent hot and cold flushes, profuse sweating and uncontrollable shaking.

She couldn't understand what they'd done to her. The sickness began shortly after she was moved to her new room and had gotten worse each day. The only time she felt better was when she was let out for training.

At least she thought that was so. Her head was so jumbled, she could barely remember the day before.

*Why can't I remember anything?*

Her thoughts were interrupted by a violent spasm in her stomach, forcing her to vomit a stream of hot bile across the plastic floor of her bathroom nook as she tried to make it to the toilet. She slipped and fell on her bottom.

*I need to get out of here; I need to feel the vibrations of the Earth. I need it bad.*

Courtney groaned, pulled her blonde, matted hair back and attempted to drag herself over to the toilet, but a second spasm caused her to vomit again. She dropped her hair during the ordeal and the ends dangled in the frothing ejecta.

She tried again to craw to the toilet, but instead collapsed and lay in a heap in her regurgitated breakfast. The plastic tiles were cold and welcoming, and she was content to lie in the foetal position while the world spun around her.

*I feel like I'm dying; could they be poisoning me? Why would Phil do that? He's always so kind to me. Maybe it was Amy.*

She didn't have long to ponder it as the door to her hermetically sealed room hissed open and two orderlies raced in, grabbed her under the arms, and carried her from the bathroom, her feet dragging across the floor and leaving a trail of vomit in their wake. They carried her out of her room and into the corridor. She instantly began to feel better the moment they crossed the threshold.

*Yes! Oh yes! That's much better.*

A sense of wellbeing rushed through her as her eyes shot open and she took in her surroundings. The orderlies were still carrying her as they headed for the training room, but she now felt strong enough to walk.

Before she could assert herself, the floor began whispering to her again, and suddenly she knew how many people were in the building and even in the carpark outside. Not only that, she knew what they were talking about—each and every one of them. The floor did hear every little thing, after all. One snippet of conversation in the scores that were happening simultaneously across the building drew Courtney's attention and she focused on it.

'...it's like a drug to her, it seems, like she's addicted to the Earth,' she felt Amy say through the floor's vibrations.

'Or maybe it's more than that, like a need to breathe or eat or drink. I've never seen her so sick.' The floor told Courtney it was Phil who spoke. 'I'm worried...'

*I knew he cares about me!*

'...that Patient 1432 is more trouble than she's worth and we should just lobotomise her?' Amy cut in.

*Fucking bitch!*

The orderlies carried Courtney through the doorway into the training room and lay her down on the floor. She thought about getting up but decided to play possum instead. Besides, she was enjoying the feeling of lying flat against the ground, the great rhythms of the Earth running the length of her entire body.

The floor told her that Amy and Phil's arrival was imminent, and a moment later they walked through the door on the other side of the training room and approached her prone form.

'Patient 1432, are you okay?' Phil's familiar vibrations were soothing.

'Come on, get up and stop faking,' Amy said in stark contrast to her colleague.

*Bitch. Bet she doesn't want another eye-patch.*

Courtney sat up nonetheless, all feelings of nausea long banished. 'Yeah, I feel a lot better now,' she said.

'That's good, we were worried about you for a moment there,' Phil said reassuringly. 'Everything's going to be all right now.'

'What's wrong with me?' Courtney adjusted her uncomfortable hospital gown. 'I thought you'd poisoned me.'

Phil and Amy exchanged a quick glance before Phil turned back to Courtney. 'Do you trust me, Patient 1432?' he asked.

'I… trust you, Phil,' Courtney replied hesitantly.

*Just not that one-eyed harpy.*

'Well this may come as a shock to you, but it's not us that's poisoning you,' Phil said, running his fingers through his thinning silver hair. 'It's the Earth itself.'

*Huh? How can that be true?*

'But…but the opposite is true,' Courtney said. 'I always feel sicker when I'm in my room. I feel great now that I can touch the Earth again.'

'That's because you're a junkie,' Amy chimed in unhelpfully.

Phil glared at her yet again. 'Don't mind Amy's lack of tact,' he said, trying to prevent another incident, 'but essentially she's telling the truth. Your abilities are like a drug and constant use gets you more and more addicted. We're trying to cure you of this awful affliction. It's what your parents would have wanted, I'm sure.'

The mention of Courtney's parents swamped her with guilt.

*And I killed my parents before they could cure me. Maybe Phil's telling the truth; maybe this is best.*

'If you think it's what they would've wanted.' Courtney felt deflated.

'Good, good. Yes, it's what they wanted,' Phil said, smiling. 'That being said, it's okay to use your powers in moderation, as we've being doing in our training sessions. You'll just be spending more and more time in your room while we wean you off this insidious affliction. The more time you spend away from training, the more you'll come to appreciate being here—you'll see.'

'I guess so,' Courtney said resignedly, looking at the two orderlies who stood near the door. 'But can I stay here for a little bit first?'

Amy went to say something, but Phil got in first.

'Absolutely,' he said. 'Do you want to work on your training while you're here?'

Courtney contemplated it. 'You know what? I feel terrific now, so I think I will.'

'Great!' Phil nodded to Amy, who stopped writing on her clipboard and went to set up the equipment. 'I'm glad you're so willing to improve your skills—you really have so much untapped potential.'

*You don't know the half of it,* Courtney thought as she secretly exalted to the thrum of the Earth's molten core.

# July

## South Western Sydney: 2 July 34 BZ

Desci Adams sat on the worn couch and stared at the door without really looking at it. She'd been this way since she got back from the hospital a month ago and found the house unnervingly empty without her husband Mark. Her deep malaise was exacerbated by the shame that it was now her teenage children who had to look after her while she was in this state.

*Some mother I am, letting the kids look after me. Get a grip, Desci, pull it together.*

She subconsciously looked at the faded photo of Mark on the mantelpiece and waves of despair washed over her, quashing her will and drowning her resolve.

*I just wish there was some word from Mark. Why did he leave me like this? I hope he's okay, wherever he is.*

Surprisingly, Detective Sam Shanks had passed on the missing person case to another detective as promised, but his replacement seemed to be even more inept than his disinterested predecessor. He'd repeated the same theory about Mark and the stranger being in cahoots but promised to look into it personally. Yet that was weeks ago and there'd been no word since.

*Probably chucked Mark's file in the bottom drawer of his desk and went to get some discount doughnuts instead. God knows he ate enough of them the one time we actually met. Oh, Mark, why did this have to happen to you, my sweet man?*

Desci slowly became aware of someone standing to her left. They were talking to her, but she wasn't hearing the words. Her eyes finally focused and she saw her son leaning over her with a concerned look on his face. His obsidian hair streamed over his broad shoulders in the spitting image of his missing dad. His cousins stood nearby and they were all dressed to go out.

'Mum, are you going to be okay?' Obie asked, leaning over her. 'Samara, Sebastian, and I are going to the park for a while. Nathan's coming to grab us pretty soon.'

*That awful Blandley kid. What do they see in him?*

'Yeah, I'll be fine,' she lied. 'It's kind of you to ask, but don't worry about your mother—I'll be all right.'

'Are you sure, Aunt Desci?' Samara confirmed. Although she'd been legally adopted by Desci and Mark, she still referred to them as aunt and uncle. She had dazzling blue eyes like her mother, however. 'We'll stay if you want.'

Sebastian said nothing as usual, but looked on, concerned. His short buzz-cut the polar opposite of his cousin's flowing locks.

'No, no, it's okay. You kids go out and have fun,' Desci said, almost overwhelmed by the gesture, but craving solitude all the same.

*Knock, knock,* came the sudden rapping on the door. Desci jumped. 'Sounds like your friend's here,' she said, forcing a smile.

Sebastian opened the door to reveal a short, ugly kid with beady eyes and a baseball cap turned sideways on his head. The stench of unwashed teenager pervaded the small flat. 'Hey, Nathan, we won't be a minute,' Sebastian said to the visitor. 'Come in.'

'Hey guys, hey Mrs A,' he said in his grating voice, striding into the flat like he owned it.

*Ugh.*

'Hi Nathan, how are you?' Desci asked politely, not expecting an answer.

'Looks like I'm feeling better than you at the moment,' Nathan said obnoxiously. 'You look like death warmed up.'

'Time to go,' Obie cut in before the conversation could get worse. 'We won't be gone long. Take care.'

Obie kissed Desci on the cheek as the others exited the flat. 'Bye!' they called as they left.

'Stay out of trouble and be careful,' Desci said to Obie as he went to join them.

'Sure Mum, will do,' he said, closing the door behind him, leaving Desci alone with her thoughts.

She began to sob.

* * *

## Barton Correctional Facility: 4 July 34 BZ

Walter Screw sat in the hospital bed and supped his shark-fin soup. It tasted like satisfaction. His son Stanley was currently in Canberra at the American embassy enjoying the celebrations, and Walter decided that as he couldn't attend, he was going to celebrate anyway, and finally ordered the cook to make his soup.

Even though the previous owner of the fin, Great White, was discovered to be most likely an alien life form, the prison scientists had declared its flesh safe to eat. They were still horrified at the loss to science when Walter told them his intentions.

*Fuck 'em. Perks of the job. Might make up for my schedule being shot to pieces by that alien fish fucker.*

Walter carefully spooned the last of the soup from the bowl and savoured the final mouthful. He then placed the utensil neatly next to the bowl and pushed his wheeled bed tray aside and lay back on the pillows. The bandages and plaster cast on his left arm made everything an effort.

*Now what to do? Recovery is so boring and there are only so many times I can check in with Gordon or Singh before I start becoming a nuisance.*

He looked around the room for something to hold his attention. There was no TV and, not one for trashy tabloid mags or cumbersome newspapers, he had little to do other than re-read the morning's situation report. Nicotine cravings made the situation worse.

*If only I could have a stogie, I'd be fine! But I guess it's not the fifties anymore.*

Something caught his eye on the far side of the bedside table.

*Hey, I wonder who brought that in?*

Walter had picked up the small statue of Michael the Archangel as a curio from a bazaar while in Morocco on the one holiday he'd had that decade. Raised as a Catholic, he'd always liked Saint Michael for his role in booting the scum out of Heaven, and had never seen anything like the statuette before. It was about six inches high and crudely painted, but the winged archangel held his flaming sword and shield, and Walter knew he had to have it the moment he saw it.

While working at the prison had certainly tested his faith, he always felt his resolve return whenever he gazed upon the stoic figure that had occupied the same corner of his desk for years. This time, however, it made him uneasy, as if it was looking back at him with its blank porcelain eyes.

*What's come over me? I used to love this statue, but now... What if it has anything to do with that tick face I saw when I thought I was dying? It's amazing the tricks your brain can play on you when starved of oxygen.*

He slowly turned his back on the statue but was soon plagued by the feeling of those blank eyes boring into his back.

*What? You're scared by a fucking statue now, you pussy? Don't lose your shit now that you're almost out of here. Cabin fever's all it is.*

He tried thinking about other things to take his mind off his neurosis—who sent Great White and why; the discoveries its biology would bring to science; even whether or not he should get a dog—but his mind kept returning to those dead porcelain eyes.

The hospital ward was unusually quiet and Walter became cognisant of his rapid heartbeat. His imagination ran wild with images of the porcelain homunculus Manifesting into life behind him, ready to slice him in half with its fiery blade.

*Enough is enough! You're obviously going through post-traumatic stress or something. Face your fears, you grizzled old fart!*

Walter slowly turned back around to face the statue and his blood ran cold.

It was smiling.

\* \* \*

## The Mystical Realm: Circa 11 July 34 BZ

The High Mage of Hell trudged across the golden sand dune that seemed to stretch into infinity under the cloudless pale-yellow sky. In truth, the Mystical Realm *was* infinite in size, despite being self-contained. Like a universe contained in a bubble that enveloped and protected all the subtle realms of Earth.

The Mystical Realm was formed from the hollowed carcass of Afterlife, a fallen Celestial One, and designed as a trap for spawn of the False Lucifer to stop them appearing on Earth. At least, that's what the High Mage had come to augur from his time in Hell.

*It's also why it took me so long to escape the inferno, as I had to bypass this place or remain a prisoner here for eternity. I'm not sure who decided to call this place the Mystical Realm—the Yellow Misery would have been more appropriate. I guess that imaginations weren't as vivid when this place was created.*

He continued his slow walk through the shifting sands of the dune as he closed in on the life forms he'd detected somewhere in the bleak wastes. He could feel the Realm sapping his determination and draining his abilities the longer he dwelled here, but it would be worth it once he found his prey.

*This place is designed to contain anything the False Lucifer can throw at it, and I can feel it taking its toll on me already. Time doesn't exist here, so it's hard to say how long I've lingered. All I know is I can't stay here for too long or I'll never leave.*

The High Mage trudged along the dune until a shape in the distance drew his attention. It was a figure, but still too far away to ascertain its identity. The golden sand cascaded down the dunes with each step, and there was no wind or breeze of any kind to erase the path the High Mage had taken since he'd teleported here from Earth. Getting here was easy; it was leaving again that was tricky.

He looked over his shoulder and it was if he'd been walking his whole existence; his footprints appeared to stretch to infinity behind him.

*This place plays havoc with the mind. I can't let it beat me. Upwards, ever upwards.*

The High Mage walked for what seemed like aeons and yet no time at all, until he could finally make out the approaching figure.

*I don't know this one—he's not one of the False Lucifer's brood. How did he get here?*

The figure was wearing a grey uniform with black boots and appeared to have sharp metallic fingers. He was armoured across his chest, shoulders and neck, with a menacing helmet that featured a frowning visor and downturned mouthpiece—so that it appeared demonic. Tubes and wires criss-crossed his entire body, but the most unusual aspect of the suit was the metallic apparatus that seemed to be embedded in his flesh and covered from underneath his ribs to the base of his groin. Tiny lights flicked on and off across its shiny black surface, and the four tubes that joined it to his thighs and sides pulsed and hummed.

'*Hallo!*' the figure called through his respirator. His voice sounded artificial.

The High Mage looked him over as he continued to call out.

*Sounds like he's speaking in a Germanic tongue.*

Luckily, the High Mage could understand any language and replied in the same language. 'I am the High Mage of Hell,' he declared flatly, all sense of drama eroded by the Realm.

'Uh…all right…I am called Moros,' came the hesitant reply. Moros stopped his approach and stood a fair distance from the High Mage.

'Where is Hieronymus Rhydderch, who calls himself Element?' the High Mage asked. 'Where are Plague and Death?'

'I don't know of whom you speak,' Moros said with his tinny voice. 'I've only just arrived here—well, at least, I think so, my chronometer stopped working—and you're the first person I've seen since I arrived. Plague and death, however, have always been my companions through life, and never as much as in recent times. Tell me, how goes the war?'

'Which war is that?' The High Mage was disinclined to mince words while his power was slowly being drained.

'The Second Great War, of course,' Moros answered. 'Surely you have word of the Third Reich? You speak German so well, I just assumed… Who are you? Do you know where we are? How did we get here?'

*He's talking about the Second World War—he's a Nazi! The host body's memories serve me well.*

'I have already told you I am the High Mage of Hell, and I'm not in the habit of repeating myself.' The High Mage suddenly extended his right hand and tendrils of energy shot out to bury themselves in Moros. 'You are trapped here in the Mystical Realm, but as for how and why you got here, I will know soon enough.'

Moros shrieked in agony as the tendrils burrowed through his body, syphoning his life force with increasing intensity.

'The Kaiser…didn't make me…head of the *Schwarze Orden*…for nothing…' he began before falling to his knees. He tried to press a button on the shiny black apparatus but collapsed before he could. His body shrivelled and his loose helmet fell away, revealing his desiccated face, while the energy wormed through his suit and armour unabated.

Rivulets of power poured into the High Mage from the cracked apparatus and with them came fleeting images of a multi-coloured snake along with about a dozen monstrous faces. The High Mage's eyes grew wide with the heady feel of raw power as he sucked the last of Moros's essence.

*Yes…I see it now. He had absorbed so many of the False Lucifer's spawn that his aura changed and he fell through the veil of existence to this place. Well, his misfortune is my boon.*

The unexpected added power allowed the High Mage to briefly overcome his spiritual doldrums and scan his surroundings for his main quarry.

*He's surprisingly close. I also sense that he is not alone. Death is with him.*

He used another spell to home in on their exact location and transported himself into their midst. Caught off-guard and already in a weakened state from being trapped in the Realm for millennia, they were easily subdued by the High Mage.

'Finally! After so long I can have my vengeance!' the High Mage decreed once he was certain they could not escape the mystical bindings he'd cast around them. He turned to a man clad in grey cloaks and a sleek, silver helmet with obsidian visor. The skin of his face, which was exposed below the visor, was also an unhealthy grey. 'You thought me gone forever, didn't you, Hieronymus? Or should I call you by your farcical mummer's name, Element?'

The grey man's jaw dropped. 'Merlin? Is that really you, after all these years?'

'I go by the title of High Mage of Hell now,' he replied.

'And you accuse me of being farcical.' Element coughed. 'I haven't been in this place for long, but I thought you gone to the Underworld a decade ago. Escape is impossible—how can you be here? Can it have changed you so much? Yes, your druid's outfit is the same, yet you look like an entirely different person.'

'That's because I had to take a host body to house my consciousness since you destroyed my original body and sent my soul to Hell!' The High Mage almost killed Element right then.

*Not yet. Say your piece first, you've been rehearsing it long enough.*

'I didn't! I had nothing to do with that!' Element cried, wriggling in his restraints.

'Liar!' the High Mage raged, tightening Element's bonds and causing his captive to scream. 'It was you who trapped me in the crystal; it was you who poisoned Morgana Le Fay against me. You allowed the False Lucifer to corrupt me and force me into the Soul Master's service. I spent a millennium in Hell thanks to you!'

'We suppose he's also to blame for all your bad decisions too? Or maybe for us being here as well?' said the rasping, hollow voice of the High Mage's other captive. 'Perhaps all the troubles of the world are the fault of your former apprentice, hmmm?'

Death was aptly named. It was garbed in a dirty brown cloak and dull metallic helmet with long devil horns, although the left one had been broken off. The front of the helmet featured a skull ornament, which captured Death's face in miniature.

'Ah, yes, I had almost forgotten about you,' the High Mage said, turning to face his skeletal captive. 'So tell me, is it Death, or Death the Second? How should I address the spawn of Death the Horseman?'

'What can Death create, but more Death?' it answered. 'Call us what you will, it is of no consequence.'

'Legend has it that you claim to have destroyed the universe once before; tell me, is it true?' the High Mage asked, tightening Death's bonds. 'How is it that we're all still here then?'

'It was written out of continuity,' Death stated matter-of-factly, 'and we have languished here since that time, suddenly an avatar of another being of the same name. There are few who even understand what that means, and so we are mocked by lesser beings such as you.'

'This lesser being happens to be holding you prisoner. I also understand perfectly what you mean. Tell me, was it the False Creator who usurped your position?' The High Mage wondered for the first time if the legend about Death might actually be true.

*I know the so-called Creator is false, mayhap he took the power from this pathetic creature, and all that remains of his power is the whispered legend?*

'No, we believe it to be an aspect of Mosh Lightley, operating from beyond the fourth wall,' Death intoned emotionlessly.

'Enough of your riddles, I will know once I absorb your essence.' The High Mage's hands started to glow with a creepy green light. 'Tell me, before you experience oblivion: legend also says that you found a way to escape the Realm. How did you manage such a feat?'

'We created an avatar of our own, Voltex, who had the necessary skills required to escape. At least in this continuity, that is. Now, we think it is time you carried out your threats, or are they merely empty words?' Death appeared unafraid of death.

'As you wish.' The creepy green light around the High Mage's hands extended into writhing energy strands that combined with the magical bonds to squeeze Death and burst the entity like an overripe blackhead. Rivers of arcane energy flowed into the High Mage's solar plexus. Death faded into nothingness without so much as a single sound.

'Now I can focus all of my attention on you, traitor,' the High Mage said, turning around to scowl at Element. 'You have a lot to answer for.'

'You were the one who abandoned me, your apprentice, to that witch, Le Fay!' Element protested. 'I never had to turn her against you; you were just too prideful to see her true nature. That wench you impregnated later was just like her…'

'Silence!' The High Mage made the bonds squeeze tighter. 'Both of you schemed to encase me in crystal so you could corrupt my soul with the False Lucifer's power and allow the Soul Master to use me as his own agent, when it should have been I who was in command! All of them are long dead now, naught but for you.'

'Summon is dead? I thought that being to be indestructible after he cast you to Hell…'

*That's right; it was Summon who sent me there. How did I forget that? No, no, the demon Im'shtar took my mortal body…but my soul escaped to Summon's realm. It's all become clear.*

'…and the Immortal too? I guess his name was just a bluff.' Element seemed genuinely surprised.

'Wait, you said the Immortal had a role in this?' the High Mage asked. 'Seth Zaraxom?'

'Who else? The whole thing was his idea to begin with—part of his grand plan to topple the Soul Master. It worked too; I saw Seth kill the Soul Master with his own vaunted Soulsword,' Element said. 'Then the bastard sent me here to rot. I'm glad that he's dead—I can only hope it was painful.'

*The Immortal Seth Zaraxom was the mastermind behind the whole thing?*

'I thought Summon was the one who opposed the Soul Master and that Seth was just another one of his agents, like the Knight of Runes, Vong the Undead Pigman, or even his sister, Lilith.' The High Mage began to doubt himself.

*If he really was in charge, then maybe my vengeance against Element is misplaced? Maybe they all worked for Seth instead of Summon or the Soul Master?*

'Neither Seth Zaraxom nor Summon have been slain by my hand, and I hope they both do still live—so I can be the one to take their lives.' He suddenly remembered the other reason he sought out his former apprentice.

*How could I forget that? It's this place; it steals memories like it steals power.*

'Where is the Soul Gem? You were the last to see it,' he asked.

'Is that all you want to know? Will you spare me if I tell you?' Element would do anything to survive. 'That's easy, Summon has it.'

'I can tell you are speaking the truth. That is all I needed to hear.' The High Mage's red eyes glowed and he looked at Element hungrily.

*This place is still sapping my strength and resolve; best I devour his soul regardless of his role in my imprisonment.*

'What is your ultimate goal? Why are you here? If you release me, I'll aid you in your quest,' Element said, recognising the look in his former master's eyes and desperately trying to weasel his way out of the situation.

'I am not the fool you take me for,' the High Mage said, beginning to cast the same spell he'd used to absorb Death. 'I am here simply to gain the power I need to return to Hell.'

'B-but why go back when it was so hard to escape the first time?' Element wasn't sure he was desperate enough to willingly go to Hell.

'Because this time it will be of my own will, under my own power, and that will make all the difference. Now die.' The High Mage cast the spell.

Element cried out as saw himself wither and crumble. His grey dust mingled with the golden sand when he collapsed on the dune. As his essence poured into the High Mage, the faces of five beings could be seen in the metaphysical torrent, and with them came realisation.

*So, it was these five False Elementals who were really in control of Hieronymus, hollowing out his soul and using him as a puppet. He invoked them as a means to impress me and thought he could control them!*

The High Mage always knew he was a fool, which is why he chose Morgana to be his apprentice instead. He was now glowing with power and sent out psychic feelers to locate his final snack.

*Plague continues to elude me. If it is in the Mystical Realm, it is too far or too adept at hiding for me to find indirectly. Pestilence, obviously created him to avoid detection.*

The High Mage decided the unexpected power he had taken from Moros more than compensated for the sickly life force he would get from the avatar of *that* particular Horseman and decided to concentrate instead on the other reason he was here.

*Death spoke of creating an avatar to escape the Realm, but my plan is more ambitious than that. I plan to break it; punch a hole through it to Hell, allowing the demons direct access to Earth. Such a diversion should distract the False Creator long enough for me to strike the fatal blow and usurp his power.*

The High Mage conserved his power and walked towards the Realm's core. It took moments and centuries, and ultimately his goal could be seen in the yellow haze: a long plume of smoke that rose up from behind the dune ahead.

As he approached he saw three figures standing around a smoky fire that burned bright like the sun. One was a humanoid skeleton with a ram's skull for its head; one seemed to be a gooey, roiling mass of slime that bore some resemblance to a humanoid; and one had a black sphere for a head and was protected by black, brown and gold armour, as well as a ridiculously long curved blade that had no comparison in the mortal realm. It wore a purple, chunky scarab necklace that pulsed almost as bright as the blinding fire they were clustered around.

As the High Mage drew near, the skeleton and the slime creature moved to intercept him. The Unknown Warrior remained where he was, behind the fire. The smoke turned alabaster white and billowed furiously.

'Halt! Approach no closer!' the skeleton said to him in all languages simultaneously. 'You have been warned.' The bog monster squelched in agreement.

'There is no need for hostilities,' the High Mage lied, drawing closer to the beings. 'I am not a spawn of the False Lucifer; perhaps you have heard of me? I was once known as Merlin the Magician.'

'I am Skeletal and this is Pugranox. Your name is irrelevant; you have been corrupted by those you absorbed. You will pass no further.'

'I wield the power of those I consumed, nothing more,' the High Mage explained, narrowing his crimson eyes. 'I plan to use the False Lucifer's minions against him and then use all the power of Hell to assault the gates of Heaven and the False Creator himself. For that to happen, your precious Mystical Realm must be rent asunder.'

'Foolish creature,' Skeletal said coldly. 'You have been deceived by Gledandron the World Eater. It has sent you here to release its aspect, Antimatter, and extinguish the Flame of Eternity. An outcome we cannot allow.'

Pugranox squelched again.

*Gledandron the World Eater? Antimatter? I have never heard these names before. Is it possible I have been tricked?* The High Mage snorted and a knowing smile spread across his bearded face. *More likely it's these creatures who are trying to fool me into changing my path and leaving them alone. The High Mage is nobody's fool.*

'Enough banter,' he said simply and cast his standard draining spell at Skeletal.

'He's using a type of leeching ability,' Skeletal said emotionlessly as it fell to its knees. 'Compensate.'

Pugranox lunged at the High Mage and slopped all over him, covering his hands and stopping the spell before it could completely drain Skeletal. It oozed into his mouth and nostrils and soon the High Mage was completely smothered by the living muck.

*What is this horror? It can't end like this—drowned by a mindless swamp demon.*

The High Mage drew on the vast energies he'd absorbed and switched to a different kind of spell altogether. Suddenly he erupted with a fiery blast wave, which instantly evaporated most of Pugranox and sent the remaining charred lumps scattering in all directions. The High Mage then absorbed what power remained in those pieces as he turned back towards the Flame of Eternity and its final defender.

*Except it isn't—the smoke—it's wisping into a death's head and coming this way.*

'Something tells me I shouldn't absorb you,' the High Mage said to the Creeping Death as it wafted towards him. 'Instead, I will use the power of the Elemental, Air, to disperse your form.' The High Mage extended his arm and a tornado appeared, whipping the sand up and blowing the smoke away.

Immediately, the Unknown Warrior was upon him, silently slicing with its deadly blade, which extended in length with every thrust. The Warrior's scarab necklace swung from side to side and the High Mage felt as if it was mesmerising him.

*Don't weaken now; not when I'm so close!*

The High Mage utilised another Elemental's power and sent a frozen concussion wave into the Unknown Warrior, which splintered its sword and tore right through its chest. The necklace fell from around its neck and cracked as it hit the ground; the dazzling light inside it faded from purple to puce and finally went out.

The High Mage now stood unopposed and drained the Flame of Eternity without delay.

*I've seen so many kings and conquerors pause on the cusp of success to spout some banal words. Not I. He who hesitates is lost.*

'Stop...' said a weak voice from behind him. It was Skeletal—still alive, but too drained to move. 'You will only aid Gledandron...'

'Silence! You are but the aspect of a dead Celestial One's echo; you are less than nothing, and soon the Realm will fade into the black abyss—and you along with it.' He kept syphoning the fire, which dimmed at an ever-increasing rate. The very atmosphere itself seemed to groan in protest, the golden sand lost its lustre, and the yellow sky grew transparent, revealing a kaleidoscope of flittering dimensions and subtle realms beyond understanding.

Finally, the Flame of Eternity was absorbed into the High Mage, proving yet again that some titles should be chosen with more modesty.

He turned back to Skeletal now the task was done and his power had increased a thousandfold. 'You are not worth consuming, as I have what I need. Your words have been proven false, like those I seek to overthrow.'

'Fool,' Skeletal replied and said no more.

*Defiant until the end. It is imperative that I confront the False Lucifer before he discovers the Realm is no longer a barrier between Earth and Hell. There is now a doorway between worlds and I'm holding the only key.*

The High Mage focused his newly augmented abilities on creating a dimensional gateway to Hell. A portal resembling a diseased sphincter opened before him and a gush of sulphurous-smelling air escaped like an infernal fart.

*Here we go*, he thought, stepping through without hesitation.

Had the High Mage stopped to linger, he may have noticed the grey mist seeping from the cracked scarab necklace that lay forgotten alongside the body of the Unknown Warrior. No longer a being of antimatter; the millennia spent trapped in the scarab had pupated it into something else entirely. Now it was simply Antithesis.

\* \* \*

## The Mullberry Residence, Canberra: 17 July 34 BZ

Bentaz Mullberry finished his essay on Australian colonial history, got up from his desk and lay on the bed.

*Boooring! So glad that's done—I can't believe I'm trusted to save the world from evil, but I still have to do homework. Mum always says, "What happens if you suddenly lose your powers and have to get a real job?" I guess she's got a point.*

It made Bentaz wonder why his mother never became a doctor, given she could heal with a touch, and chose to be a mundane housewife instead. Maybe that's why she always hassled him about school.

*"Supporting your father,"* she always said. *I'll never understand it.*

He picked up a pile of *Phantom* comics, found one with a cool cover, and started flicking through it. His mind returned to his previous thoughts.

*Yam's another one I'll never understand, and he even finished Year 12 and started studying palaeontology at university. What's with the underachievement factor in this family?*

His older brother's Manifest ability to swim through the earth and see fossils in three dimensions ceased to be a career inspiration, and instead he chose to become an unemployed environmental activist. It was Bentaz and his younger sister, Peach, whom their mother had pinned her hopes on.

He heard his mother calling that it was dinnertime and he tossed the comics aside and headed to the dining room.

The dining room was small, but spacious enough for everyone to squeeze in at the table. Dinner was shepherd's pie with ice cream for afters.

As usual, Nikki Mullberry sat at the end, while Bentaz and Yam sat on one side and Peach on the opposite. The head of the table was always kept free just in case the patriarch of the family, Hunter, ever decided to grace them with his presence.

*More likely we'll win lotto,* Bentaz thought as he started eating.

Unfortunately for the Mullberry family, no one had bought a ticket, for the back door opened and Hunter entered the house. 'I'm home,' he called out in his slight Scottish accent.

'Dinner's in the oven. Why don't you grab it and join us? We're just starting,' Nikki called from the other room.

Hunter did as he was bid and soon joined them at the dining table. So rarely was their dad home for dinner, that it was as if they'd been joined by Santa Claus. Unlike jovial Saint Nicholas, the only gifts Hunter brought his children were hard life truths.

Hunter Mullberry was a large stocky man with a headful of wild, long red hair and matching ginger goatee. He was dressed in his light blue work outfit and black boots, and although he'd removed his silver helmet, he still wore the dark eye shadow he used to obscure his features that could be seen through the helmet's eye slits.

'So, Dad, what's the special occasion?' Yam asked around a mouthful of food. 'It's been so long since you joined us, I'd forgotten what you look like.'

*And so it begins again.*

'I was out putting the food on your plate, which you're letting get cold with all your yapping,' Hunter replied without missing a beat.

'So how was your day, dear?' Nikki began, hoping to douse the argument before it could begin.

'You know I can't talk about my work,' Hunter snapped. 'My employer is a private individual.'

*I'll say—we have no idea who you even work for.*

'Yeah, who *do* you work for, Dad?' Yam continued unwisely. 'Your employer wouldn't happen to be the Mob, or maybe some insidious multinational corporation?'

'Yam!' Nikki exclaimed.

'That's enough, son,' Hunter said, staring to get noticeably angry. 'You'll be eighteen soon, old enough to get a job and move out. I didn't raise you to be a layabout.'

'You didn't raise me at all—I seem to recall it was Mum who was always here, not you.' Yam couldn't help himself.

'I think you better go to your room, right now, young man,' Hunter said, putting down his fork.

*The way these two fight, it makes my argument with Grandfather seem trivial. No wonder he and Dad don't get along.*

'Can't we try to have a nice family meal, just once?' Nikki began, exasperated.

'*I'm* being good,' Peach chimed in, hoping there would still be ice cream for dessert.

'Stop sucking up. You're not helping,' Bentaz said to her across the table.

'Leave your sister out of this,' Hunter said, coming to Peach's defence. She always was his favourite. 'She's the only one who's not misbehaving.'

'What did *I* do?' Bentaz asked defensively. 'I've just been sitting here, quietly eating.'

'I don't mean tonight,' Hunter said, briefly pausing his fight with Yam to begin a battle on a whole new front. 'Why are you taunting your grandfather with that new outfit you've been poncing around in?'

'What? I'm not poncing…' Bentaz began. 'You don't even get on with Grandfather…'

'Why don't you stop picking on Bentaz for a change?' Yam always stuck up for his younger siblings. 'He's more powerful than the whole lot of us combined. He's entitled to wear whatever the fuck he wants.'

'Language!' Nikki yelled.

'I thought I told you to go to your room?' Hunter resumed his usual rhetoric.

'To hell with that, I'm going out!' Yam got up from the table and stormed into the kitchen towards the back door.

Hunter got up and followed. 'Don't you walk away from me, young man!'

Bentaz tried to follow, but his mother grabbed his wrist. 'Sit down,' was all she said and returned to staring at her half-eaten shepherd's pie.

The sounds of fighting could be heard clearly from the next room.

'Yam, get back in here and go to your room—you're grounded!'

'Try and stop me, Dad.'

'You asked for it.'

It was on hearing those words that Nikki woke from her stupor and raced to the back door. 'Hunter, what are you doing?'

Bentaz and Peach were quick to follow.

*Are they going to actually fight?*

Bentaz ran to the back door to see his father standing with his right arm extended and Yam on his knees on the grass outside.

*Holy shit! He's using his powers on Yam!*

Hunter was not only a skilled combatant; he also possessed the Manifest ability to control gravity—a skill he was currently using to pin his eldest son to the ground. 'Now, have you had enough and are ready to come back inside and go to your room like I asked?'

'Hunter, please…'

'Dad, what are you doing to Yam?' Peach looked worried.

'Everyone go back inside, this is between Yam and I.' Hunter wasn't used to justifying his actions.

'You know what Dad? I bet you don't even have an employer. I reckon you're out having an affair with some whore and that's the real reason you're never home.' Yam started venting his frustration. 'Maybe you have a whole other family out there—it sure doesn't seem like you care about this one.'

'What did you just say to me?' Hunter's voice turned colder than usual.

'I said you're an arsehole,' Yam replied before phasing into the ground and swimming away under the topsoil.

Hunter stood silently with his back to the rest of his family, before finally turning around and heading back towards the house. 'This is why most Manifests don't have kids—it's got nothing to do with how long we live and everything to do with super powered teenagers.' It would have been funny if it weren't for the sad fact Hunter never cracked jokes.

'Can I have some ice cream now?' Peach asked, her one-track mind coming to the fore.

'Of course you can, sweetie,' Hunter said, leading her inside. 'Anything for my baby girl.'

*That's all well and good for Peach, but what about the rest of us, Dad?* Bentaz kept his thoughts to himself and began clearing the table.

\* \* \*

### Victoria, Seychelles: 24 July 34 BZ

Naomi Bloodlust lay back under the giant beach umbrella and pretended to blend in with the rest of the tourists. She felt naked without her kit and was dressed—if it could be called that—in a one-piece swimsuit. She'd been lying low here for a while now but kept telling herself that she hadn't been spooked by the events in Johannesburg.

*Maybe that talisman is cursed. All of this Gorg bullshit started just after I took the fucking thing. What did Tenebrous say to me about believing in mystic beings, but not mystic artefacts?*

She pulled the talisman in question from her small handbag and turned it over in her hands. The bone had worn smooth over the centuries, yet the hooked rune looked like it was carved only yesterday.

She wondered if she should go home like Liu wanted. She missed him terribly, but couldn't stay with him after all that shit with Scar. The Blood Brigade was never more than a childish fad anyway; just a cheesy team name for a bunch of delinquents trying to band together. Liu was the only one she really cared about.

*Magnet and Miss Bloodlust, supervillain power couple. Were we really that young and naive?*

Naomi smiled as she remembered the misadventures from her early days as a professional criminal. She looked again at the talisman and her thoughts snapped back to the present.

*Maybe I should use this to access some of those weapons Tenebrous told me this Summon guy has. Not sure what I could barter for them— it's not like I have any magical artefacts in my possession.* She returned the magical artefact to her handbag with unknown irony.

*Then again, I could be getting all worked up for nothing. Maybe Gorg's shtick is to psych people out with mind fucks. That could be why nobody's seen him.*

Naomi doubted it somehow.

*Try to relax! That's why you picked this place to lie low. Helps that the international airport's not too far away though.*

She picked up the complimentary newspaper the hotel had left her and took a sip of her lavish cocktail as she began to read the main story. Apparently, there was an upcoming vote on whether Seychelles should upgrade to stage five membership and become part of the United Nations proper. Most people, it seemed, were all for it.

*Well, they have been using UNos ever since the coup attempt of '81 turned into a protracted civil war. Ballsy move, hiring a bunch of South*

*African mercenaries to turn up disguised as holidaying rugby players in an attempt to overthrow the government.*

She liked to keep abreast of world events and remembered the incident well. She recalled that the coup would've failed miserably if they hadn't hired that racist Manifest thug Supernaut, seeing as their secret weapons stash had been discovered before they could reach it. He cleared the way, they accessed the stash, and Seychelles had to endure nine years of bloody conflict.

*They're only just starting to recover, which is why I'm here helping the local economy.*

She also had a tendency to invent excuses when faced with an uncomfortable self-truth—like how she was only hiding out so she wouldn't be forced to reveal the secret she'd been keeping ever since she Manifested. She may be here a while.

*Luckily, my credit line of UNos is unlikely to run dry, thanks to all those Swiss bank accounts.*

Ever since the European Union decided to adopt the UNO, it became the primary currency for business transactions, and the most valuable currency in the world. Naomi used nothing else.

She continued to read through the newspaper until a shadow fell across her, coupled with the feeling of a nearby Manifest. Instantly, she reached into her handbag to retrieve the poisoned stiletto she carried at all times.

Not one to usually be taken off-guard, she'd chosen a location with an open panorama and had even gone so far as to install mirrors into her oversized sunglasses to prevent someone sneaking up on her from behind. She hadn't expected someone to descend from above, however, with the beach umbrella hiding their approach until too late.

Naomi sprang from the banana lounge and landed in the sand nearby, ready to fight if necessary. She wished she had her kit with her.

She was confronted by a bronze-skinned man with long black hair, who was dressed in red and purple armour adorned with a symbol of a white skull on a black background. His eyes were obscured by a vermillion visor, but there was no mistaking his scowl. He floated above the ground with his arms crossed over his chest.

'Hand me the talisman or die,' he said in a South American dialect

Naomi hadn't heard before but understood nonetheless—one of the abilities that all Manifests shared when conversing with each other.

*That goddamn fucking cursed talisman again! Who's this guy then? I don't think it's Gorg—doesn't seem his style.*

'Who are you?' Naomi figured there was no point denying she had it.

'I am Iztali, Bodyguard of the Great Armageddon, and I will not ask you again.'

Naomi wasn't enlightened at all with the revelation of her attacker's identity, but she didn't respond well to threats.

'Bring it on, honey.'

Bodyguard flew at Naomi with arms extended like a human battering ram, but she sidestepped at the last moment and he ploughed into the sand, exposing his groin to a ruthless downwards kick.

'Ow!' she yelped.

*Shit, I think he may be one of those invulnerable types.*

Bodyguard exploded from the sand and flew at her once more, this time parallel to the ground. He blocked her strike at his throat and delivered a withering backhand, which sent her skimming into the surf. Somehow, she managed to hold onto her blade.

She didn't have time to think it over, as Bodyguard was on her again, snatching her handbag and knocking her to the ground. He fished through it and seemed satisfied when he produced the talisman. He opened his mouth to speak.

Naomi saw her opportunity and threw the stiletto at his mouth with unnerving accuracy. 'Eat this, motherfucker!' she cried.

Bodyguard caught the blade in his teeth.

He took the knife from his mouth and licked the edge to show that even his tongue was invulnerable, laughing all the time.

*I'm out of options. Time to decide whether keeping my secret is worth my life.*

She never got the opportunity.

'You have amused me,' Bodyguard said, pocketing the talisman in a belt pouch. 'I will spare you, as I have what I came for and you have fought well. I respect that, so I will leave you with this.'

He punched her in the face and left her lying semiconscious in the surf.

She managed to drag herself halfway up the beach before the pounding sun and her pounding head took their toll and she lost consciousness, but at least her secret was safe.

* * *

## The Abyss: Circa 31 July 34 BZ

Seth Zaraxom clinked steins with Bojangles and stared into the large, maroon crystal ball that sat between them on the sodden beermat.

'It doesn't look all that spectacular,' Bojangles said, before sipping the froth from his lager. 'I was expecting something out of some fantasy epic, not a red glass sphere.'

'All part of its illusion to make people think it's just another mundane object.' Seth took a massive gulp of his pint.

'Yeah, well it's working,' Bojangles said with a grin. 'It looks about as magical as a used condom.'

'It's fascinating the way your mind works, but I get your point. It only looks mystical when it's in use—then it's as obvious as a bikie in a preschool.' Seth took another gulp.

'Is there a competition between you two, to see who can come up with the most ludicrous similes?' asked the gruff, bald barman who'd been listening to their conversation while drinking a beer of his own. 'If so, Bojangles is winning.'

'Ha! In your face!' Bojangles was slightly drunk and pointed at Seth's chiselled features.

They'd been there for some time, but as time had no real meaning in the Abyss, it made it hard to pace yourself when having a few brews. At least, that was the usual trope trotted out by anyone who'd ever gotten smashed too quickly in the bar.

'Can you ever be serious?' Seth was smiling despite his best intentions. He was feeling a bit tipsy himself. 'Mosh is just stirring, as usual.'

Mosh Lightley finished stirring his beer with a random wooden spoon and cast it aside. 'That's a fair call,' he said with a laugh. 'Now, are we going to move this plot along, or will I have to cut to another scene?'

Seth took the hint. 'I really need to know what to do next. The High Mage must be after the Soul Gem to complete the plan he started a millennium ago. So, do I make a play for the Gem? Summon will no doubt swap the Gem for the Orb of Horath—he's not interested in anything's value—but thrives on the act of barter itself.'

'You know, your aunt Nocturne's been looking for her Orb for a long time now...' Mosh began.

Seth ignored the interruption. 'Or should I get another mystic artefact—the Sceptre of Conquest perhaps? It's rumoured to make its wielder invincible in battle. Either way, I need to get that Summon talisman off your friend—Naomi, did you say her name was?'

'Yeah, that's right,' Bojangles confirmed. He signalled Mosh for another beer. 'Nice girl—we've been friends for a couple years, ever since we found ourselves back-to-back against the forces of the Energy Lord.'

'I haven't heard that tale,' Seth said, starting to get sidetracked again. 'What happened?'

'Another time, maybe. We don't want to piss off Mosh any more than usual, unless we want to pay Jypx a visit,' Bojangles cautioned, referring to the legendary tentacled monster that lived in a cavern beneath the bar.

*Not bloody likely,* Seth thought as he rolled himself a smoke from the packet of Smex—Mosh's own brand—which was sitting on the bar.

Mosh returned with a fresh beer and handed it to Bojangles.

'Did you pour that into the same glass?' Bojangles asked suspiciously. 'This is a pub; surely I can get a fresh glass?'

'Well, if you want to come back here and clean glasses, then be my guest,' Mosh snapped. 'White Lion's off on some HSA adventure and until he gets back, you'll just have to make do.'

Bojangles decide not to press the point, lest he meet Jypx in person. Instead he resumed his conversation with Seth. 'What I want to know is why you put me through that whole malarkey of sending Naomi off to Tenebrous the moment she found that talisman—claiming you didn't need it except as a backup plan—but now changing your mind and deciding you do need it. What the fuck's with that?'

'Can't a person change his mind?' Seth replied defensively. 'Look, you knew she had to take the necklace to Tenebrous to complete that vision you had when you saved his scrawny arse from those baboons when he was a kid. Sure, I don't need the talisman to be granted an audience with Summon, but it is a mystical artefact after all, and now I'm thinking I can trade it *and* the Orb for both the Gem and the Sceptre. Then we'd hold all the cards.'

'Except the High Mage is playing chess,' said a sudden feminine voice behind them to their right.

*I was wondering when she'd show up.*

Lilith Zaraxom may have been Seth's twin sister, but thankfully, unlike Seth, she resembled their mother more than their father. She walked down the stairs from the brothel, but woe betide anyone who thought she worked there—it was just coincidence that the staircase to her castle lair could only be accessed from a door upstairs.

She was dressed in a long, black flowing dress that was so dark it hurt the eyes to stare at it. Her stygian hair flowed long over her shoulders and was kept in check by the black top hat adorning her hypnotising, vampiric features. Her eyes were the colour of twilight and flashed from beneath the hat's brim.

'Hey, sis,' Seth said jovially. 'Why don't you grab a drink, pick a stool, and join us at the bar? I could do with your advice, as it happens.'

'The High Mage has destroyed the Mystical Realm,' she said flatly as she stood at the base of the stairs. 'I hope you know what you're doing—you set him on this path in the first place. Tell me brother, was unleashing the forces of Hell upon Earth part of your grand plan? Because that's what the outcome will be.'

The general vibe in the room soured. Mosh noticed and stopped cutting the lemons he was preparing for the tequila shots he was about to pass around.

'What are you talking about? I know the High Mage went to the Realm—that was all part of the plan—but he should've only gotten the power necessary to return to Hell, so when he raises his demonic army, they'd all be trapped there before they could invade. What do you mean he destroyed the Realm? That place is eternal.'

Lilith stared at her brother long and hard before deciding to take Mosh up on one of his shots. 'You always did think yourself cleverer than you are,' she said after the lip, sip, and suck. 'You failed to anticipate that he'd find another in the Realm who would give him enough power to tip the scales and allow him to absorb the Flame of Eternity itself. So, while I may have exaggerated about it being completely destroyed, it has been dealt a fatal blow. You really should have consulted me first, before embarking on this crusade.'

'Well, it was a long time ago that I thought of this plan—I failed to anticipate this other being in the Realm,' Seth said, almost apologetically. 'Who was it?'

'His name was Moros, once a member of the *Schwarze Orden*, thought lost over fifty years ago.' Lilith sighed and had another shot of tequila.

'I remember that cocksssucker,' Bojangles slurred, putting down his shot glass. He'd taken Mosh up on the offer as well. 'Fucking Nazi dickhead turns up one day in the outback in the thirties, declaring he'd come to study Dreamtime legends while his fellow "scientists" started measuring the locals' heads. No shit, they actually believed in phrenology! Total wankers!'

'There was a point there somewhere...' Seth teased as he contemplated having a shot.

'Anyway, a couple years later, this high and mighty tosser ends up drawing the attention of one of the World Eater's spawn—a crude imitation of the Rainbow Serpent—and I'm forced to intervene. But does this fool thank me?' Bojangles didn't wait for an answer. 'Not on your life—he starts spouting some Aryan bullshit and begins to absorb the spawnling. Well, something must've happened, as he disappeared in a flash of yellow and gold.'

Bojangles realised he'd been talking relentlessly and became sheepish. 'Sorry, you know I like a good yarn.' He had another shot.

'Obviously Moros absorbed too much of the World Eater's energies and became trapped in the Realm,' Lilith said knowingly, taking a seat at the bar. 'This is how the High Mage came to take his power.'

'I suppose you knew this all along?' Seth asked Mosh.

'What part of "I am everything" are you having trouble grasping?' Mosh asked in return, lining up more shots. 'Of course I knew, but I don't play favourites, remember?'

'If the High Mage has crippled the Realm, then there's nothing to stop the World Eater from spawning its full force on Earth!' Seth said, a little too emotionally. 'I assumed you'd care about that, given humans seem to be the majority of your clientele.'

'Nope. Life's cruel, here's a tissue.'

'But creating Afterlife just so she could become the Realm and act as a trap for Antimatter and all the other agents of Gledandron was your idea in the first place!' Seth couldn't understand the logic of gods.

'That was your grandfather's idea,' Mosh explained. He finished preparing the next round of tequila. 'I don't actually do anything—except run this bar, of course. Who's for another round?'

'I'll need one to deal with all these revelations,' Seth sighed, before licking his hand and sprinkling some salt on it. 'I thought my plot to use the High Mage against Gledandron was foolproof, but it turns out I'm the fool, as my plan failed epically. Now that he's absorbed the Realm, he's actually become powerful enough to destroy the Earth—even if he doesn't, he's still left a gaping hole for Gledandron! If only I knew how to proceed from here.'

'You know what you have to do,' Lilith said after sucking some lemon. 'Look to your Orb for the warning.'

*That would make a great song title.*

'Okay, sure, what's the worst that could happen?' Seth said resignedly, taking his shot.

'Well, your eyeballs could burn in their sockets and you could go crazy—at least that's what you told me when I wanted a go,' Bojangles said with a sly grin. 'But that's not as bad as Earth being devoured like Geburah and Harmen, so you better man-up and get cracking.'

'Shall I make popcorn?' Mosh was only half-joking. Instead he poured the dregs of the bottle into everyone's shot glasses. A strange arthropod fell into Seth's glass with the last few drops.

'What the hell's that?' Seth blurted when he saw his drink. 'That doesn't look like a worm or even a scorpion to me.'

'It's a trilobite,' Mosh replied with a shrug. 'The bottle's been sitting on the shelf for a while, so I thought I'd use it up.'

'So when you say "a while", you really mean since the Permian?' Seth was hesitant to eat something that had been gathering dust for two-hundred-and-fifty million years.

'It's obviously Mosh moving in "mysterious ways" again, so you better just drink it. Time's wasting.' Lilith was glad she didn't have to drink it though.

'Drink it, you pussy!' Bojangles dared.

Seth caved to peer pressure and threw back the trilobite tequila shot. It was crunchy and intoxicating and tasted like extinction.

With eyes watering and face flushing, he grabbed the Orb of Horath, recited the incantation (spraying his words all over Bojangles) and stared into its depths.

*Holy fucking shit!*

To an outside observer it would have simply appeared to be a drunken Goth spacing out into a red glass sphere—as the Orb only affected the person using it—but to Seth, the broiling visions were seared into his mind's eye the moment he glanced at the crimson maelstrom. It was over faster than anyone (except Mosh) expected and Seth allowed the Orb to roll from his grasp along the bar while he turned and spewed onto the floor.

'Taxi!' Bojangles joked as he stopped the Orb from rolling any further.

'I hope you're going to clean that up—White Lion's not here, remember,' Mosh said. Again, he was only half-joking.

'What did you see?' Lilith asked, being the only sensible one in the room.

'Give me a sec for the world to stop spinning…everything's a bit of a jumble in my head.' Seth swooned.

'The Orb's like that; don't be surprised if the visions come to you over time.' She was speaking from experience. 'Some things should be clear though. Did it give you any indication on whether you should pursue the Gem or the Sceptre?'

'Actually, neither. It seemed to indicate that I needed the Crown of Knowledge.' Seth wasn't sure what that meant. 'At least the odds are that Summon's got it in his stash.'

'And then what are you supposed to do, write an encyclopaedia?' Bojangles scoffed, lighting up a smoke from the packet of Smex.

'There was something about the number twelve and I'm supposed to find some people, I think, although I don't know who. The Orb whispered, "Give one the Crown of Knowledge and receive knowledge from the other with the crown"—whatever that's supposed to mean.'

'The Orb whispered to you?' Bojangles asked incredulously. 'I guess visions are so passé they need to come in surround sound now.'

'Will you be serious?' Lilith said to her brother's oldest friend. She signalled for another drink.

'That's what I keep telling him,' Seth laughed. The Orb's effects were wearing off and he was feeling much better. 'Still, we've now got something to go on, when before we had nothing. I'm starting to feel hopeful again.'

Kismet always listened out for words like that.

Suddenly the background music stopped and the guitarist, who up to that point had been playing unnoticed on the stage at the far end of the Abyss, got up and slowly sauntered over to the group.

He was a giant at almost eight feet tall and was dressed in black jeans, boots and trench coat, which obscured a dark red undershirt adorned with a silver symbol akin to a pentagram. His black spiky hair stood straight up about a foot from the top of his head and vermillion facial markings stained the face around his eyes and cheeks. No one paid him any heed until he came up on Seth from behind.

Bojangles seemed to notice him first and pointed behind his friend. 'Uh…Seth.'

Seth swivelled around on his barstool and found himself face-to-chest with the arrival.

*Oh no!*

'Hello, Uncle,' the man said in a voice like gravel, before suddenly turning his hand into metal and viciously tearing out Seth's throat with his finger blades.

Seth grabbed his neck in shock and tried to staunch the gushing wound, but it was futile. He collapsed off his stool and went into a death spasm. He felt his life drain away until finally the world went black and he died on the cold wooden floor of the bar.

Lilith and Bojangles continued drinking.

'Fuck me drunk! For the last time—White Lion's not here!' Mosh cried. 'Now who's going to clean that mess up?'

# August

## The Abyss: Circa 1 August 34 BZ

Dread Sedgewick licked his dead uncle's blood off his finger blades before changing his hand back to normal and stealing his uncle's beer.

'Here's to Uncle Seth,' he joked, before downing the beer in one gulp. 'Another of your finest, if you please.'

Mosh obliged and handed Dread a frothing brew.

'Was that entirely necessary?' Lilith asked. 'We were in the middle of an important conversation.'

'Hi, Mum,' Dread said, turning to face her. 'Bojangles—a pleasure as always.'

Bojangles gave a half-hearted wave and started to roll another smoke.

Dread stepped over his uncle's body and sat at the freshly vacated barstool. The Orb of Horath caught his eye. 'What's that, Swedish designer furniture or something?'

'That's none of your concern,' Lilith snapped. 'You still haven't answered my question—did you have to kill your uncle?'

'Well, technically that's a different question; but the answer's yes, in both cases.' He smiled, snatched the packet of Smex away from Bojangles, and began to roll. 'I don't see what all the fuss is about.'

As if to punctuate the statement, Seth stirred.

'See? He'll be right as rain in no time.' Dread quickly changed the fingers on one hand, lit his smoke with sparks from his finger blades, and changed them back again. 'It's not like this hasn't happened before—he's been around for a while, always assuming this identity or that throughout history.'

'True enough,' Bojangles chimed in. 'I mean, how many times did the Russians try to kill him when he was off calling himself Rasputin?'

'Just because I can't die doesn't mean I don't feel pain,' said a voice from the floor. Seth slowly got to his feet and glared at his nephew. 'Unlike you. Now, will you please stop killing me every time I see you? Joke's over.' He'd healed completely, though the bloodstain remained.

'Maybe when I stop laughing,' Dread replied with a murderous grin. 'Good to see you again, Uncle. Pull up a pew and join us.'

'One day I'll find a way to get even,' Seth said without malice as he sat on the next stool. 'Actually, you may be of some help; we need to stop an alien parasite from devouring Earth.'

'Bugger that, I have plans of my own.' Dread had little interest in alien parasites.

'This is slightly more important...' Seth began.

'Maybe to you, but I don't give a shit.' Dread butted out his smoke in the overflowing ashtray that sat on the bar. 'My plans are personal.'

'If it involves terrorising your father and his family, then I'm telling you to let it go,' Lilith warned.

*Typical.*

'We're his family, Mum, or have you gotten senile in your old age?' Dread shot back.

'It was never my intention to start a family, you know. Your father didn't even know about you for years, and in that time he started a family of his own.' Lilith hated repeating herself and had said this several times already. 'You're lucky to even be here—most Manifests don't even have children on account of us living so long.'

'Manifests outside of our family maybe,' Dread scoffed. 'We seem to breed so much that Dad has two families. You're such a hypocrite, considering your first husband and his second family.'

'Just let it rest, I don't want to talk about this again,' Lilith said, turning away. 'Now getting back to our conversation before my son so rudely interrupted...'

Dread didn't want to talk about alien parasites, and if he couldn't talk about revenge then his only recourse was mischief. He'd already been playing guitar for Mosh knows how long and needed to do something else.

He got up from the barstool and looked around for something to break.

'Not in here, you don't,' Mosh called from behind the bar. 'If you're going to trash things—do it outside. White Lion's not here to clean up anything and you've already spilled blood all over the floor. Maybe when's he's back, I'll let you cut loose, but until then—vamoose.'

Dread didn't feel much like meeting Jypx either, so decided to take Mosh's advice. He walked over to one of the many interdimensional doors that lined the walls of the Abyss and opened it. It creaked.

*Earth sounds like fun. I'll let the doorway dump me in some random location, just like a mystery flight!*

He stepped through the open doorway and the door closed behind him with a click.

* * *

### Antarctica: 2 August 34 BZ

*Everyone's a fucking comedian,* Dread thought miserably as he traipsed through the drifting snow and howling winds towards civilisation.

* * *

### San Diego Convention Centre, San Diego, California: 6 August 34 BZ

Lorrain Freeman signed the glamour photo for her fan and stopped to pose for a picture before repeating it all again with the next person in line.

*Comic-Con is great! I love getting to meet my fans like this, away from the snobbish fashion moguls. Mum was right; they do still love me despite discovering I'm a Manifest. Good thing that nasty Vicious Man didn't ruin it for me by trashing too much of the city.*

It was a tribute to precisely just how much they did love her, giving her guest of honour status over the likes of such industry giants as Matt Groening, Leonard Nimoy and Jean-Claude Van Damme. Even

Beat Master, fellow Manifest and homegrown superstar, had taken a backseat to Lorraine's popularity.

*At least Mum's off somewhere looking at one of the panels. She didn't seem so happy when her name wasn't on the guest list. She just doesn't understand that Australian superheroes aren't very well known in the States. Except for that cute Ballistic guy, that is.*

She finished signing the next picture for a male fan who looked to be in his fifties and he was replaced by two eager-faced young teenagers.

The boy was shorter than the girl and had short peroxide blond hair, which was in stark contrast to the long yellow, orange and pink hair his female companion was sporting. They were shy and kept looking at their feet—especially the boy. They both had the same glamour photo of Lorraine that she'd signed a hundred times previously over the course of the convention.

'Hello there! Who should I make these photos out to?' Lorraine smiled at them as she spoke in her soft voice. 'There's no need to be shy. Why don't you tell me your names?'

Immediately their nervousness was gone and they looked up at Lorraine.

'I'm Phunk Phastic,' the girl beamed with sudden enthusiasm, 'and this is my friend...'

'I'm Gomez...ah...Hector, Hector Gomez,' the boy said, blushing red like a pomegranate.

'Very pleased to meet you both,' Lorraine said amiably, passing them back the signed photos. 'I hope to run into you again someday,' she added as they turned to leave.

*Nice kids, although they really aren't that much younger than me. That girl had a strange name, what was it again? Funk or something? Sounds like something a celebrity would name their child.*

One of Lorraine's entourage took that opportunity to get her attention.

'Excuse me, Miss Freeman,' she began, 'but I'd like you to meet some special guests who came here especially to see you.'

'So did everyone else in this giant queue. Why do they get to cut in?' Lorraine asked, slightly perturbed.

*This better not be another loser trying to get me to model their latest swimwear.*

'Because they're filthy rich,' the nameless aid blurted. She quickly realised what she'd said and tried to rephrase. 'Ah…what I mean is, they're incredibly busy and influential people and…'

'That's okay, they're here now, may as well meet them,' Lorraine interjected. 'Besides, I can't bear seeing you dig any deeper.'

'Okay, then. Lorraine, I'd like you to meet Richard Hilton, famous real estate broker, and his daughters, Paris and Nicky,' the aid said, recovering like a professional.

'Please, call me Rick,' said the man, extending his hand towards Lorraine. She went to shake, but he kissed her hand instead. 'It's a pleasure to finally meet you.'

*Ugh! Why do all the guys over twenty-five insist on kissing my hand? It's so old fashioned. And gross.*

'I'm touched,' she lied. 'I can't believe you came here especially to see me.'

'We don't live that far away, and my girls are big fans and wanted to meet you in person,' Rick said.

'I want to be just like you when I grow up,' the older girl said.

'Me too!' said her younger sister.

'My wife's a great admirer of your work as well,' Rick continued. 'It's just a shame she can't be here today, but she's looking after my son, Barron, and our brand-new bundle of joy, Conrad Hughes. Maybe you could come and visit us in Bel Air sometime?'

'I'd love to,' she lied again, 'but unfortunately this is my last day in the US. I fly out tomorrow for Rio de Janeiro.'

The mention of the Southern Hemisphere had the same reaction with the Hiltons as it did with viewers of *Good Evening New York*.

'That's a shame, but I understand,' Rick said with sudden glazed eyes. 'Would you be so kind as to sign these for my girls?' He handed her a pile of photos.

*So much for one per person.*

Lorraine signed them anyway, which delighted the girls. She waved them off with the usual courtesies and was about to return to signing more pictures for the rest of her fans, when an announcement came over the PA system letting everyone know it was time for the costume competition.

'Sorry everyone, but I really want to see this,' she said to the people in the queue. 'I'll have to sign photos for you later on.'

One grown man at the front of the queue broke down and wept.

*Okay, that's a sign to beat it, if ever I saw one.*

She was ushered to the main auditorium by her nameless assistant who looked a little stressed fending off more of Lorraine's adoring public. She'd turned down a security detail over her tour manager's objections as her mother had promised to protect her.

*Except Mum's now nowhere to be seen and this aid looks like she's going to have a nervous breakdown. Lifestyles of the rich and famous, I guess.*

Lorraine gaped as she entered the auditorium and was confronted by a sea of cosplay hysteria. Homemade costumes paying homage to all aspects of fanboy culture stretched as far as the eye could see, and Lorraine lost track of how many awesome creations she saw.

*Wow, some of these guys are really talented! Others look to be over-weight basement-jockeys in leotards, however. And the hats! What is it with the human race and silly hats?*

As if on cue, eight strangely-garbed men and one strangely-garbed woman burst into the auditorium from behind the stage curtain and pranced about the stage—a couple of them even doing backflips. They appeared to be part of a group effort—they all had blank faces, yet were dressed in ludicrous costumes, each representing a hat that stereotyped their country of origin—as revealed by the little flag each one wore on their sleeves. One of them even had two heads.

The competition organisers looked confused and kept studying their clipboards for answers.

'Good citizens and visitors of San Diego,' said a faceless black man dressed in a tuxedo, who appeared to be the group's spokesman. 'I am Top Hat, and these are my comrades in capery: Lord Pith, the Mortar Board, Le Beret, the Scarlet Sombrero, Akubra, the Turban, Dunce and Fez Man…'

Each one did a little rehearsed move when their name was called.

'…and together we're the Hat Trick! Tremble at our name!' Top

Hat paused for dramatic effect, yet no one had ever heard of them before. He looked embarrassed despite having no face. '*You know*, the Hat Trick—the terrible titfers, the hounds of the harrowing headgear? We're the impenitent purveyors of hat-themed crime…'

*What the fuck? Hat-themed crime? They sound like villains from that campy sixties Batman TV show—maybe that's what they're imitating?*

The crowd had seen enough and soon the heckling began.

'Get off!'

'Boo!'

'Bring on the next contestants!'

'Losers!'

'Get the cream, DSK!'

Top Hat looked to his team for support before turning back to the crowd. 'Fools! This is no joke—everyone remove their hats and put them in the bags, or the Turban will blow this place sky-high!'

Two-headed Dunce and the Mortar Board suddenly produced heavy sacks and moved towards the crowd, who were now looking uneasy.

*Wait a minute, these guys are serious! Who could tell with the way they're dressed?*

Lorraine had felt other Manifests, but assumed they were part of the crowd. She decided it was time she stepped up like her mother always wanted. She drew on her Manifest abilities, taking a step on the air and walking up over the crowd as if on an invisible staircase, until she had a clear path to the stage. The crowd cheered when they saw her, now thinking it was all part of some elaborate show for their benefit.

*Keep walking Lorraine, just like you've been practising.*

She jumped down onto the stage and faced the combined might of the amateurish Hat Trick. Top Hat wasn't expecting any resistance and wasn't sure how to proceed, so he went with supervillain rant number forty-six: 'Ha! You think to defeat the Hat Trick by yourself?'

'Except she's not alone, you faceless blowhard!' said a familiar deep voice from behind Lorraine. She turned and saw Samuel Beatrix, more commonly referred to as Beat Master, as he joined her on the stage.

'Hey gorgeous, remember me?' said the handsome black man,

dressed in his full costume, complete with inbuilt sound system. 'Thought you could do with a hand against these losers.'

'Thanks,' Lorraine said. It was now her turn to blush. *Too bad he's gay.* 'I thought you'd left yesterday after your event.'

'I always stay to see the costumes,' he replied. 'Good thing too.'

'Are you done talking like we're not even here?' the Top Hat raged. 'Didn't you hear me when I said the Turban's got a bomb? It's a real one too, not made out of firecrackers like last time.'

'Yeah, yeah, whatever, I don't believe you,' Beat Master snapped back. 'I know Manifests when I sense them, so I'm guessing you have some lame powers instead.'

'I have the power to generate hatred in others!' the Turban said defensively.

'Well, it's working—I hate you, and the crowd doesn't seem too enamoured with you either.' Lorraine had been practising her super-hero repartee and was pleased with her line. 'Are we gonna do this or what?' she asked Beat Master.

'Hang on a sec, just gotta line up my fightin' song.' He fiddled with the fast-forward button on his inbuilt tape-deck. It was well known that Beat Master's Manifest abilities not only made him a superb dancer, but also the more invigorated he felt by a piece of music, the more powerful he became—increased strength, speed and stamina in particular. 'Ah, got it. I'll put this one on loudspeaker, as I'm sure you can draw inspiration from it as well. It has that effect on people.' He smiled and hit the play button. 'Everyone in the crowd sing along— and you too can help save the day!'

*Always the showman; just look at how he works the crowd. Now they really do think it's all an act.*

The familiar tune of Survivor's 'Eye of the Tiger' blared from Beat Master's shoulder-mounted speakers and it was on before Lorraine could say "*Rocky III*".

Beat Master launched himself at the closest member of the Hat Trick, Lord Pith, dropped into a Capoeira move, and kicked the villain in the head, sending his pith helmet flying. The crowd cheered and sang along.

'Ha! That must've pithed him off!' Lorraine joked as she confronted Le Beret, the lone female of the group.

*Okay, so my banter still needs a little work. I should probably just concentrate on not getting killed.*

Lorraine easily blocked Le Beret's leather riding crop and followed through with a brutal punch she'd picked up in high school. Le Beret went flying into the Mortar Board as he returned to the stage to assist his team members, and they both ended up sprawled in a heap.

*Gotta watch myself—I don't know my own strength. I sure don't want to kill anyone.*

Meanwhile, Beat Master had unleashed a series of coordinated blows on the Turban and the Scarlet Sombrero, all the while trying to close the distance to the group's self-proclaimed indomitable leader, Top Hat.

Lorraine had her own troubles as a stockwhip suddenly cracked and wrapped around her arm. The other end was held by Akubra: The True Blue Jackaroo.

'Strewth cobber!' he exclaimed in fluent Ocker. 'Stone the bloody crows, you weren't meant to catch that. Now don't I feel like a painted bloody galah!'

Lorraine yanked on the whip and pulled Akubra within striking distance. 'Don't you know that nobody in Australia talks like that?' she asked, punching him in his featureless face. He didn't answer, on account of suddenly being rendered unconscious.

The song was wrapping up and Beat Master was focused on stopping Fez Man, who was whirling around him like a dervish. He extended his foot and Fez Man tripped over it and careened into the stage curtain, becoming hopelessly entangled as it tore loose. The organisers hardly noticed—they were still looking at their clipboards.

Top Hat made a break for it as the song ended and Beat Master paused to hit the rewind button on his suit. Lorraine was unable to stop him either, as she was too busy dealing with the Dutch villain, Dunce. He wore his namesake on one of his faceless heads and the other sported a children's propeller-cap.

She was struck with inspiration and used her ability to walk on air to dodge Dunce's attempted bear hug. She ran up and over him, before she dropped behind him and slammed both of his heads together hard.

'I guess two heads aren't better than one,' she quipped.

*Slightly better, but don't hold out for the Oscar.*

By this stage, Top Hat was making for the exit, trying to push past the crowd, who were thrilled at this unexpected addition to the convention's agenda.

*Damn, he's getting away!* She looked at Beat Master, but he just looked apologetic while he continued to rewind the song. *I don't think I can get to him in time.*

Top Hat noticed the heroes' dilemma and stopped to get in a final supervillain rant. 'Fools! No one can stop Top Hat! I will escape to strike again another...'

Suddenly Lucy Freeman appeared in front of Top Hat and connected a powerful uppercut before he could finish his tedious diatribe, knocking him out cold. She was dressed in the aquamarine Lycra costume she wore when fighting crime as Spectrum. 'Seems like that was your third strike, right there,' she said. The crowd cheered and clapped furiously.

*Mum? Has she been invisible this whole time, just waiting for this opportunity? Or worse, has she been spying on me? Did she set this whole thing up?*

Lucy grabbed Top Hat by the collar of his tuxedo with one hand and collected his hat with the other. She flew over to the stage to join her daughter and Beat Master. The crowd was going nuts and Lucy waved at them, smiling from ear to ear.

'Hey sweetie,' she said, landing next to Lorraine. 'I told you I'd be around if you needed me. Beat Master, good to see you again.'

He finally finished rewinding his tape to the right spot and waved in response.

'Mum, are you responsible for all this?' Lorraine asked, ready to start another fight. 'Seems like a bit of a coincidence to me.'

'Well it *is* a coincidence. I had nothing to do with any of this, I promise,' Lucy replied. 'I was just getting around the convention, invisible, as I like to do, and decided to watch you in action. You were great out there—I couldn't be prouder.'

Lorraine smiled and waved at the crowd as the local AMPs arrived on the scene and started securing the Hat Trick. Some of the crowd began to realise it wasn't part of the show after all. It was a great way to finish up her tour of the Northern Hemisphere. There were only a few more stops in South America, South Africa and New Zealand, and then she was home.

Lorraine wondered whether that would be good or bad as she basked in the light of a thousand camera flashes while the Hat Trick were led away.

*I think I'm finally starting to enjoy myself.*

\* \* \*

## Barton Correctional Facility: 9 August 34 BZ

Walter Screw slowly paced around his lavish office, enjoying the first cigar he'd had in months. Acrid smoke polluted the air but everyone present was too smart to say anything about it. Walter puffed away, unconcerned with passive smoking.

His arm was still in a sling, although the cast had been removed and the doctors had reluctantly allowed him to return to light duties—his injuries had been severe—but had specifically warned him about his smoking habit.

*Fuck 'em. It's the only thing that keeps me sane in this madhouse.*

Walter continued to pace, all the while feeling like something wasn't right. Then he remembered it was because his statuette of Michael the Archangel was missing from his desk—he'd had it sent to the lab after his disturbing experience a month ago, which everyone else thought was caused by his pain medication.

Walter was joined by his son Stanley, who was using his codename, Tactician, while in the company of others; Rick Gordon, his second in command; and Leslie Studebaker, the promising young guard in whom Walter saw a bright future.

'Uh, sir, it's almost time for me to do my rounds,' Rick said, trying to avoid the uncomfortable conversation he knew was coming.

'I have every confidence that Singh can handle anything while you're gone.' Walter ashed into his spotless ashtray which sat on one corner of his meticulous desk. 'Now tell me again what the lab boys said about my figurine.'

'Exactly as expected, sir. It's simply a painted porcelain figure. Sure, it was a lead-based paint, but that's about as dangerous as it gets,' Rick responded professionally, waving the smoke away. 'There was no trace of a Manifest seed, alien technology, or anything else that would explain your reaction—meds aside, of course.'

*Was that a crack? Can't say I blame him. It's a crazy theory, but I'm sure I didn't imagine it.*

'But the damn thing was smiling!' Walter still couldn't consul that fact.

'And still is, sir. The lab boys think this must've always been the case, and that somehow your injuries coupled with the pain medication, conspired to give you the false memory that it never used to smile.' Rick knew the Warden wouldn't have wanted to hear that, but also knew his honesty was respected—*and* expected.

'Sta…Tactician,' Walter corrected, 'surely you remember when I got it? It never used to smile, did it?'

'Honestly, I don't remember,' Tactician replied. His suit's servomotors whirred as he adjusted in his seat. 'I'm inclined to agree with the scientists, sorry.'

'They also said they've done all the tests they can think of, so the statue is ready for you to pick up whenever you've got a free moment.' Rick couldn't actually remember the last time Walter had a free moment outside of a hospital bed.

'They can keep it,' Walter said, then reconsidered. 'Better yet, they can destroy it.'

'Are you sure you want to do that?' Tactician asked. 'You were always quite fond of that obscure knickknack.'

'I can't look at that thing again. I know it's not logical, but I think there's something seriously wrong with it. I can feel it in my gut,' Walter added before taking another drag on his cigar.

*Now you're starting to sound like an old woman. Better just stick to the facts.*

'Fair enough. It's your statue, do with it as you please.' Tactician had little sympathy ever since Walter revealed what became of his Multiman toy when he was a kid. He was more concerned with his father's mental capacity to run the Powder Keg.

'No one's been able to explain to me how the damn thing got into my hospital room either.' Walter tried a new angle based on facts. 'None of you did it, and the security footage shows nothing. One minute it's on my desk, and the next it's next to my bed in the ward.'

'Yeah, that is kinda creepy, I'll admit, which is why we're even having this meeting at all,' Tactician conceded. 'But if the lab geeks say there's nothing special about the statue, well then...' He trailed off.

'Sir, could it have been one of the prisoners, trying to mess with your head? Or maybe it had something to do with the break-in?' Studebaker suggested, finally breaking her silence.

*That's a thought—glad I decided to invite her here.*

'Again, the footage shows nothing,' Rick answered, having accepted the junior officer's presence only because Walter had asked for her especially. 'Plus, the suppressors were all still functioning—they were powerless. As for the break-in, it's true it did happen after that, but it's unrelated. According to our debriefing of the prisoner, Heist, they only wanted to know about the location of an amulet of some kind.'

*I wonder if we'll ever know what that was all about?*

They all went silent to ponder the implications. Walter continued to pace and smoke, resembling a steam engine as he went back and forth between the same two patches of floor, pausing only to ash in the receptacle on his desk.

'There's something else I haven't told any of you, and that's because I'm not so certain it wasn't a hallucination.' Walter chewed the end of his cigar as he recalled his fight with Great White. 'But combined with the events surrounding the statue, I thought I'd share. Oh, and please hear me out before starting the ridicule.'

*I can't believe I said please. I must be pretty shook up.*

'Go on, sir, we won't judge,' Studebaker said, perhaps trying a little too hard to impress now that she saw clear career goals ahead of her.

Walter let it go but decided to expound on his near-death experience before anyone else interrupted. He explained about the tunnel of light and the insidious tick's head that was lurking behind it in the gloom beyond the final veil.

When he was done, only Studebaker seemed concerned.

'That sounds like something Hellgoat—that demonic HSAer—

would say,' Tactician said, being the first to break the silence. 'Sounds like a simple case of oxygen deprivation on the brain.'

'Well, if someone like Hellgoat can exist...' Studebaker began before she was cut off.

'Hellgoat's a Manifest. His powers aren't magical in any way, despite what he claims,' Rick interrupted. 'The inescapable truth is there's nothing on the other side of death except oblivion.'

'Perhaps...' Walter looked thoughtful as he considered what Rick had said. 'I don't like to talk about my religious beliefs—I try to lead a private life—but maybe it'd help if I gave you some background. See, I was raised as a good, God-fearing Catholic boy and I was proud to count myself as one of the faithful. Then I started my career in law enforcement and my faith was truly tested.'

'I don't think I've heard this story before,' Tactician said, 'and I've known you longer than a lot of other people.'

*Not sure why you don't just admit you're my son. It's not like people haven't guessed—the rumour's been around for years.*

Walter recounted his tale. 'Well I learned about Manifests and machine consciousness and reincarnation and goddam fucking aliens. It sort of took the zing out of the Bible. Jesus walked on water, sure, but I know a fucking teenager who can fly to the moon! And chances are there's some fucking Moon Man who's been living up there the whole time waiting to say g'day!'

'I wasn't aware we'd discovered...' Rick started, before realising Walter was hyperbolising.

'My point is: what if Jesus was a Manifest? That's something the Church would never admit—it would be the end of them. I mean, when the UN finally went public with the announcement that alien life was real—trotting out that Nazi, Squido, as proof—most of the world's religions were quick to say that even though aliens existed, only man had an immortal soul destined for an eternal afterlife. But Jesus being a Manifest? No, they wouldn't go with that—it would have a domino effect across all faiths.'

'I seem to recall the Raëlians prospered after that announcement,' Tactician said. He whirred in his seat, trying to resist the urge to pace as well. 'But that hysteria died down after the initial excitement, then aliens were old news and people moved on.'

'Yeah, if people knew just how many alien species we've catalogued, they'd never sleep at night,' Rick added. 'Luckily most folk think they're just mutant Manifests.'

'As for Jesus being a Manifest—or any other religious icon for that matter—it's immaterial. I don't believe any of them ever existed. I'm with Rick, there's no life after death.' Tactician didn't have his father's Catholic upbringing and found religion in science instead. 'Next thing you'll tell me is that Merlin the Magician's real and is the force behind this whole thing. Just listen to yourself: evil ticks devouring souls—it's lunacy on toast.'

'I never said anything about devouring souls, but what if that's the whole thing? If religious prophets can be Manifests, then why not the gods themselves? What if what this Hellgoat character says is true, except beings like Satan are Manifests themselves? Maybe the tunnel of light that people see when they die is just the proboscis of some soul-eating Manifest.' Walter took a final puff and butted out his Cuban.

*Okay, so that does sound a little crazy.*

'Maybe it's time you took another holiday. It's long overdue,' Tactician suggested.

'Could be you're right,' Walter sighed, rubbing the back of his neck. 'Still, I just can't shake it. You yourself even came up with the idea of sending the HSA on a wild goose chase looking for Satanists—what gave you that idea?'

'I made it up as a means to prevent them discovering Project Typhon!' Tactician couldn't believe he was still having this conversation, and with his father, no less. 'Lord knows that little Ballistic shit almost found it when he exposed the tunnels underneath Canberra. Fortuitously, we were able to relocate, but still. And before you ask whether some Manifest could have influenced me in my decision, know that I sleep under a Manifest null-field and this suit's got an inbuilt Manifest detector. The idea of Satanists just came to me one day and I ran with it.' He neglected to mention all the fuss Ballistic and Hellgoat had made over that satanic cult in Sydney.

Walter looked crestfallen. 'Studebaker, what do you think? I asked you here for your input.'

Studebaker looked like a deer caught in the headlights. She had decided the conversation had gotten too personal and it wasn't wise to talk about that stuff with your bosses. Yet she rose to the challenge when asked. 'I suppose it can't hurt to put a few feelers out in case there's something going on. Maybe ask some of those HSA black-ops guys to investigate. In the meantime, try not to put yourself in any undue dangerous situations. Oh, and I'd destroy the creepy angel statue too, just to be on the safe side.'

*Sounds reasonable. I'm glad I invited her along.*

'Add that you'll seriously consider a holiday, and I'll do some investigating from my end,' Tactician said as he got up from his seat and went to leave.

'Fine,' Walter agreed. 'Rick, make sure the lab boys dispose of that statue with extreme prejudice.'

Rick and Studebaker saw the signs and did the same. 'Yes, sir,' he said.

'Thank you everyone for your input...and your discretion,' Walter said as they filed out of his office, leaving him alone to contemplate having another cigar.

*Well that was a fucking waste of time,* he thought, sparking a match.

\* \* \*

### The Skull of Ra: 14 August 34 BZ

Anu Hopet turned the bone amulet over in his armoured hands and allowed himself a rare smile.

*Finally, I have a piece of you both! A physical piece of one and an emotional piece of the other. My ancient enemies may have so far escaped my wrath, but at least I will have this as a symbol of their failure to cage me all those years ago.*

Anu Hopet's version of those events over four and a half thousand years earlier had become somewhat skewed, but one thing would always remain clear to him. Once he was a slave to Queen Kyra and Prince Kiol Zol, but freed himself after he spontaneously gained his abilities by witnessing close hand the mysterious, shadowy being that was the namesake of their kind: Manifest. It was said only a god could interact with Manifest and that he (everyone just assumed it was male) cast magical seeds wherever he went that would sprout into super beings.

Anu Hopet turned over the talisman so he could look at the rune carved into its face. It was not dissimilar to a shepherd's crook, with a cross at the bottom and one going diagonally through the hook part at the top of the symbol.

*It's a lucky coincidence that my trophy also doubles as a means to access the fabled treasured vaults of Summon. I shall enjoy pillaging his hoard.*

'Good work on using one of your drones to locate this,' he said to his cybernetic lackey, Disk. 'I am pleased. You may access an additional pleasure subroutine for your efforts.'

'Oh, thank you, Great Armageddon,' Disk said, almost prostrating himself in supplication. 'What about Bodyguard, my lord? He was the one to fetch the talisman for you from the human witch who possessed it.'

'If the idiot lives, then that will be reward enough.' Anu Hopet did not suffer fools lightly. 'He has been poisoned with ricin, and the outcome of his fate is not yet determined. He may have been invulnerable to physical harm, but it would seem toxins are an exception.'

'But sire,' Disk hesitatingly began. 'With the technology we…ah… *you* possess, curing Bodyguard of his affliction would be no trouble at all.'

Anu Hopet allowed the statement. 'Bodyguard is either strong enough to be one of the Skull Band, or he is not. I will not allow technology be a factor in his recovery.'

'As you wish it, so it is done, Great Armageddon.' Disk knew when *not* to press a point with his cantankerous master. 'I will ensure he's confined to quarters until this is resolved either way.'

'Excellent, proceed.'

Disk tapped buttons on a keypad.

*If I can use the amulet to acquire a legendary artefact like the Sceptre of Conquest or the Key of Worlds, or maybe even the Soul Gem, then I will have everything I need to take my true place in this prophecy I asked for no part in.*

'Disk!'

'Yes, Great Armageddon?'

'I need you to look into something post-haste,' he said, putting his thoughts into action. 'I want an audience with Summon...'

Suddenly the whole world shimmered and Anu Hopet thought his ship was being invaded by another Miasma entity until he realised it was he who was disappearing.

*What in the black abyss?*

Anu Hopet found himself in a darkened room with walls that appeared to be literal curtains of night. His calculating eyes were drawn to the round, grey table covered in a thick charcoal cloth. On the far side of the table, in an impressive high-backed chair, sat a man dressed in a homespun black tunic with chalk-white skin. The only feature on his otherwise blank head was a rune—the same one that adorned the talisman.

*It appears I am in Summon's lair, but how did I get here?*

Summon appeared not to heed Anu Hopet's arrival and continued to look at the purple cards he'd laid out before him on the sigil-covered table. A miniature woman with a blank face and long dark hair emerged from the deck and she slowly pulled cards from her body and handed them to Summon, who would put them on the table to scrutinise.

Anu Hopet turned to approach Summon and noticed an aggressive pygmy plant creature that looked like it was prepared to defend its silent master.

'Do not fear. Be at peace and offer your barter,' a soothing voice suddenly beamed into Anu Hopet's head. 'I am Summon and this is Tarot and Bracken; we are eternal, we offer exchange. What item do you seek?'

Anu Hopet noticed that each time he 'heard' Summon speak, the sigil on his face flashed the same violaceous colour as the cards.

*Best to get information before revealing anything.*

'I seek the Sceptre of Conquest. Do you have this artefact?' Anu Hopet asked as friendly as he could manage, the amulet still in his hand.

'Yes, it is in my possession,' Summon said without hesitation. 'What do you offer in exchange?'

*Exchange? Does he not realise who he is speaking with?*

'I am Anu Hopet, the Great Armageddon. I do not exchange, I take!' Without warning he unleashed a storm of deadly antimatter bolts at Summon, only to be faced with shocked disbelief when they fizzled harmlessly against an invisible dome that encompassed the entire table—Summon included.

He didn't even look up from his cards at the failed assault.

*Impossible! Nothing can withstand my antimatter attack!*

'If you have nothing to trade then you have no business here,' Summon beamed. He held out his palm to Anu Hopet.

It was the first time in millennia that Anu Hopet had been denied and he did not take it well.

'You think you can just cast me aside, like chaff?' he began, but was cut short by an irresistible falling sensation.

*This cannot be!*

He fell for what seemed like eternity and a day until finally the darkness gave way to shattered skies and dull, yellow sand dunes.

*Where on Earth?* he thought before he hit the ground and everything went black.

* * *

## Outskirts of the City of Dis, Hell: Circa 19 August 34 BZ

The High Mage dropped his cloaking spell and stopped to stare at the architectural majesty that jutted from the craggy landscape before him like an infected molar.

*Ah, the fabled capital city of Hell. It's here I'll find the False Lucifer and bind him to my will.*

The cloaking spell was necessary for concealment while he used the familiar terrain in this part of Hell to boost his ability to communicate mentally with his minions in Lucifer's Coven back on Earth. He walked along the very spot he used when he conveyed his wishes to the High Priestess through her dreams, now made easier since her impregnation. Every advantage helped when in perdition, even if this one had to be done while sleepwalking.

*Even still, it surprises me that it's easier to communicate with Earth from Hell, than it is from the Mystical Realm.*

The other reason he had chosen to contact the coven immediately upon arrival was because he would soon be busy for an indeterminate length of time.

*This is a crucial aspect of my plan; if I fail here, then it will have all been for nought. Luckily, I have power enough to see it through—I will not fail. Upwards, ever upwards. Or downwards in this case, I suppose.*

He smiled at his observation and started the long trek towards the thrice-damned city and its infernal master.

When he was first dragged to Hell, he'd been surprised that it was exactly as he'd imagined it to be, but upon return he understood that nothing the False Lucifer created could hold up to the imagination of the human mind, and so Hell itself was forged from a patchwork conglomeration of the fears of those sent here.

Smouldering brimstone mountains and fiery lakes of wailing souls surrounded the city of Dis, but the High Mage had already journeyed past them while in his cloaked somnambulist state. One of the many traps here was being aware of the suffering of others, and exposure to them generally resulted in being convinced of your own unworthiness and deservedness to stay and suffer too.

*Who would have thought communicating through dreams to a pregnant mad woman had so many additional benefits?*

The High Mage reached the final approach to Dis: a treacherous winding path over an apparent bottomless pit. In the distance, he could see enormous city gates that extended out like a titanic metallic maw, swallowing the end of the path. The souls of sinners could be seen squirming on the ends of the gates' barbed teeth.

He began the slow walk down the meandering path, which played tricks with the mind to fool unsuspecting travellers into turning back or walking off the edge into the bottomless chasm that yawned wide on either side of the track. It was another test; the secret was to feel your way with your feet and walk in a straight line. Soon he stood before the great maw gate, which opened violently and swallowed him on arrival.

He was cast to his knees as all who entered were forced to do. He looked up at the city, which looked broken and decayed and infested with smouldering, twitching pits that served as burrows for the city's inhabitants. Human souls in various states of torture and rot decorated the necropolis, and at the centre of it all stood a forbidding citadel that wept blood.

*Inside! Now on to the Castle of Pain…*

He was suddenly confronted by the guardians of the walled city: a collection of thirteen voracious demons of sickening form.

*Hell's Elite Guard…I wasn't expecting them so soon.*

'Foolish creature, though you may have suppressed your Wisp, it still allows us to know your intentions here,' barked the all-seeing hound of hunger, Ibeel.

'You are unworthy to wield the power of our master,' slobbered the blubberous grease squealer, Dumarg.

'You will fail!' buzzed the giant blowfly, Uln—virulence on the wing.

The High Mage hoped he wouldn't have to listen to them spew some banal utterance.

*Still, they have proven useful by revealing the nature of the Wisp I thought subdued. I still don't know how they managed to implant me with one in the first place, though.*

'It is you who are mistaken,' the High Mage said, finally breaking his silence. 'Have at thee!' He cast a powerful banishing spell.

It had no effect.

*Fuck!*

'You think we can be discarded so easily?' laughed Syroth, the gravitating mind vacuum, while Krargen the brutal butcher beast raced at the High Mage with murderous designs.

*Think of something, fast!*

A repulsion spell scattered Hell's Elite Guard in all directions and bought him time to think of a way out. *Perfect,* he thought when struck by an idea.

'I've waited a long time to finally cut loose with this,' the High Mage announced, casting the unadulterated version of his scourging spell upon his foes. Ghostly serrated chains shot out from his fingers and tore through all thirteen of his opponents simultaneously.

*Best not to destroy them—they may be of use once I am lord of this realm.*

Hell's Elite Guard was no match for the High Mage's power, and he used the spectral knouts to bind them together once he'd flailed them into submission. He chose the smallest one to interrogate.

'What is your name, demon?' he asked the dark green, four-horned anthropoid.

'We are called C'vin, the sadistic eroto-gremlin,' it growled.

'I never understood why demons always choose such outlandish epithets,' he said, constricting the bindings until C'vin cried out. 'Now, what else should I expect in the Castle of Pain?'

'Your destiny.' The creature laughed. Its teammates joined in.

He cast a cloaking spell over the bound demons and then another one for himself.

*That should prevent them being discovered. Don't get sidetracked this time; head straight for the donjon—no doubt the False Lucifer lurks there.*

He encountered no further resistance as he stormed the bleak fortress singlehandedly. The drawbridge to the citadel opened as he approached, seemingly beckoning him to enter. The words 'Abandon all hope, ye who enter here' were scratched into the archway above the entrance, and the howls of the damned buffeted him like a chill wind when he crossed the threshold into the Castle of Pain. It was exactly as he had imagined it would be.

He walked down a long dark corridor until he came to a festering courtyard decorated with obscene living artwork—more souls of those doomed to Hell. From there it was only a short stroll to the donjon and the chambers of the King of Hell.

The doors to the donjon were already open, as if he was expected.

It wasn't long before he entered a large hall rimmed with walls of soulfire. Images of torment and suffering flickered in the flames. At the end of the hall, upon an intimidating throne of bones, sat the ruler of Hell.

The False Lucifer had the body of a muscular man with cloven hooves, enormous bat wings, and the head of a horned goat. Its hate-filled red eyes glared from beneath the dirty grey matted fur that covered its naked body, which crawled with human-headed lice.

To the right of the throne stood the False Archdemon, Dark Lord of the Wounds that Never Heal, and highest-ranking of the Lords of

Hell. Though hunched over, it was enormous and its crusty, weeping skin was a dirty reddish-brown colour and ridged with deadly spikes. Its stained fangs protruded from the slavering mouth that made up most of its hideous face, with its black, soulless eyes dominating its horned head.

*Now there's a face for radio,* came an unexpected thought; obviously influenced by his body's previous owner, the Satanist known as Gavin. 'I am here for your throne,' the High Mage said purposefully.

'This is how you repay us for gifting you with the knowledge of Hell and allowing you to walk once more on the Earth?' the False Lucifer asked, its voice a cacophony of the souls that suffered in the infernal realm. 'You believe you have the power to destroy us and then the Creator itself? Delusional mortal, you only have the power we have granted you.'

'You have granted me nothing! Everything I have achieved has been through my own means,' he said defiantly. 'You will provide me with the power required to topple the False Creator and assume my place as lord of creation.'

'Just because you call us false, does not make it so,' the False Lucifer replied without moving. 'You do not understand the forces you are tampering with.'

'I understand more than you credit me for, lord of lies. You and your creator are false idols that shall be removed from the face of existence.' The High Mage's hands began to glow as he prepared to cast another spell.

'You do not have the power to face us both,' the False Lucifer said calmly, looking at the demon lord to his right.

The High Mage made eye contact with the False Archdemon and nodded briefly.

'Lucifer speaks true,' it said, acknowledging the gesture. 'He does not have that power, which is why he recruited us.'

The False Lucifer looked shocked and went to rise from its throne. The High Mage cast his most powerful draining spell at that very moment, striking the False Lucifer in the chest. The False Archdemon attacked with berserker ferocity and tore through its previous master, tooth and nail.

The False Lucifer was unprepared for an assault on two fronts and was hurled back into its throne, causing it to shatter in a shower of bones. 'It cannot be! We would have known!' it cried as it was brought low.

'Demon lords are always plotting to overthrow their masters,' the High Mage said, smiling. 'A masking spell simply hid the reasons why in this case.' He used another spell to animate the scattered bones into a skeletal chain, which wrapped around the False Lucifer and held it fast. The False Archdemon ripped into its former master's goat head with a final slash of its claws.

*Now for the hard part.*

The High Mage focused on a complicated binding spell to trap the False Lucifer in its chambers while simultaneously piercing its chakras with mystical umbilical cords to drain its incredible power reserves.

'It is done. The False Lucifer will not be able to free himself,' the High Mage managed to say to his associate between exhausted breaths. 'The Castle of Pain will now act as a transmitter, syphoning off its power and sending it to me wherever I may be.'

'And what of your promise to us?' the False Archdemon said icily. 'That was the sole reason we oversaw the events that led to your escape from Hell in the first place. You would not have succeeded if we did not assist you.'

'I haven't forgotten. You will get your chance to lead the armies of Hell against the Gates of Heaven when I make my final move against the False Creator. But for now, I need you to ready your demonic host while I visit each of the Lords of Hell in turn. They should know who their new master is.'

The High Mage turned and strode from the throne room, leaving the False Archdemon to wonder if it had made the right decision.

\* \* \*

### Undisclosed location: 23 August 34 BZ

Courtney Yeht broke the boulder apart with her mind and then reformed it into a rudimentary anthropomorphic shape. It remained in this state temporarily, before crumbling into its constituted parts.

'Well done, 1432!' Phil said at her achievement. 'That was even longer than last time!'

'Yes, very impressive,' Amy reluctantly agreed.

Courtney was starting to get the hang of her training and felt good about finally being appreciated.

*Even Amy's been nice to me lately—almost makes me feel sorry for taking her eye. I can't really remember doing it though—I can't really remember anything much.*

She may have spent most of her waking moments in a confused state, but she was certain her abilities were growing stronger. She was also getting better at controlling them—thanks to her endless training sessions.

*I just don't understand them.*

She continued to hone her abilities over the next couple of hours until she'd practised the various tests at least three times over. She was tired but didn't want to go back to her room as it made her sick, so she tried to think of excuses to stay put.

'Can I do the tests again?' she asked Phil as he shuffled his notes and pack them away.

'You really don't want to overexert yourself,' he replied, looking at his watch. 'You'll be able to do the tests over again tomorrow.'

She stalled some more. 'But you think I'm improving?'

'Yes, definitely, we're all really proud of you.' Phil looked at Amy for support.

'Come now, 1432, it's time to return to your room,' Amy said, trying her best to be friendly. 'Your dinner should be ready. Corned beef sandwich tonight—your favourite.'

*Not again! Just because they serve it to me every day doesn't make it my favourite.*

Courtney ignored Amy and kept talking to Phil in the hope she could side-track him into a long discussion. Anything to keep feeling the vibrations from the world around her. 'So how do you think I've improved?'

'Well, for a start, you held those shapes for a lot longer than you did before, plus the shapes are more refined every time you do it. That last one even had the rough outlines of a face.' Phil paused to consult his notes. 'You're also getting much better at hitting targets—those mannequins you demolished are testament to that.'

'1432...' Amy tried again, looking frustrated.

'But how do my powers work?' Courtney was determined to stay longer.

'We're not entirely sure,' Phil answered, ignoring Amy's death stare. 'It appears as if you can control silicates and some oxides, but exactly which ones and how much influence you exert on them is exactly what we hope to find out. What's plain to us so far, however, is that you're very sensitive to sound vibrations, which we believe is why your hearing's so good.' He neglected to mention they thought her powers directly tied to the Earth itself.

'Okay, that's enough for today,' Amy interjected. '1432, it's time for you to say goodnight and go back to your room and have your tea.'

'What's my real name?' she asked unexpectedly, almost afraid.

The stunned silence left an awkward tension.

'1432 is your real name,' Amy said before Phil could answer.

'Yes, that's true...' he began.

'It's a number, not a real name, and I don't like it!' Courtney began to feel angry. 'I want a proper name!'

The room shook as if an earthquake had started. The normally efficacious doctors looked worried, and Amy hit her portable panic button. Four orderlies quickly entered the room, but Phil waved to them to hold back.

'Okay, calm down,' he said soothingly. 'It's okay, you're among friends. I'll tell you what: how would you feel if I chose a name for you?'

'Phil!' Amy said urgently.

Courtney thought about it for a moment and the quaking subsided. 'Okay, I trust you.'

'Good. How do you feel about Courtney? That's a nice name, don't you think?'

'Phil!'

*Courtney? Why do I know that name? Is it my mother's name? I wish I could remember something—anything—about my past.*

'I like it, thank you Phil. That's much better than a number,' Courtney said, fidgeting with her flaxen hair.

'It's only appropriate that I name you, as I'd like you to think of me as a sort of father figure. I want you to always trust me.' Phil gave Amy a knowing look.

Amy turned from Phil towards Courtney. She had a sour look on her face and the skin around her eye-patch was twitching. 'Are you happy now, 14…um…Courtney? You have a nice, new name and the knowledge that there's someone here to help fill the void left by your parents.'

*I never thought of it like that before. Probably because my head is so foggy most of the time.*

'So, please come along now, it's time for dinner,' Amy continued, indicating for Courtney to get up and follow.

'You better go, I'll see you tomorrow,' Phil said, smiling.

This time she obeyed without argument and waved to Phil before being led back to her room, the orderlies following close behind.

Later, as she sat on the bed eating her corned beef sandwich, she tried to think over the day's events. It was always hard after her daily injections.

*I'm glad I finally have a proper name and not that stupid number,* she thought between bites. *I just wish I knew why it's so familiar to me.*

She made a pact with herself to find out.

# SEPTEMBER

### Dungeon Cell 9: 3 September 34 BZ

Andy Trailer stuffed the raw offal into his mouth with unbridled zeal.

*Finally, a reward for my good service!* he thought as he chewed into the uncooked organs.

He reflected on the latest mission he'd just returned from as he swallowed. His master had sent him out to retrieve lumps of granite, fibreglass, cedar and other substances. He must have been pleased as Andy found the plate of food waiting for him when he got back.

Andy still didn't know whether the missions he went on were real or all in his mind and in the end deemed the whole argument irrelevant so long as he wasn't constantly beaten.

*You should heed our advice,* said the ubiquitous voice inside his head, Wisp. *You should turn the tables on the cyclops; you should use your new friends to spy for Gledandron.*

Instead of licking the plate like he would have done a few months back, Andy allowed his dozens of cockroach friends to feast. They were the offspring of the fat female that lived in his ribs and felt like family.

*They are my closest companions; I don't like using my mind to control them.* He stopped crouching and sat down to watch the roaches feed. His abilities had increased since he discovered them. *And stop calling my master "the cyclops"; he has revealed to me his name is Pulse Pounder.*

*That is not a true name; it is another lie,* Wisp whispered in Andy's mind.

*It's like my name, Night Demon—it's my reborn name. All of my master's servants have names like that.* He'd been trusted enough to properly meet Pulse Pounder's lieutenant, Guillotine, as well as the individual members of the mechanical Trio that used to torture him: Malice, Repulsive and the Hood.

*But that is not your name. Your name is Andy Trailer, although Gledandron will accept you as Night Demon, if that is the name you prefer. Such is his everlasting understanding. You would be wise to accept his love as his time draws near.*

Andy thought on that for some time.

*My master has been so kind to me lately…I dare not defy him.* Andy remembered the beatings with eidetic clarity. *Besides, I still don't know if all of this is just another way for him to test my loyalty.*

*No, this is reality,* Wisp resumed. *You have not been under an illusion for a while now, which is why you have offal instead of garlic prawns and the like. He is unaware of your new abilities, otherwise he would have never let you loose outside this cell.*

*The Master has really been letting me outside in the real world?* Andy was hesitant to believe.

*Yes, and you did not even notice. Do you not now feel foolish for not escaping?*

Andy had to admit he did. But then just as quickly came the relief that he didn't. He was onto a good thing and didn't want to spoil it.

*Coward,* Wisp said, striking a nerve. *You fear true freedom, freedom that only Gledandron can grant you.*

Andy started to feel miserable again, which happened every time Wisp spoke to him. *I suppose it couldn't hurt to send a few of my friends out to find out if my master speaks true.*

*Yesss… do it,* Wisp intoned, wearing down Andy's mind through the attrition of constant doubt.

Andy looked down at his brood that were busy eating the bloodstains on the chipped ceramic dinner plate. Multiple flashes occurred in his mind's eye—a sign he was joining minds with his insect brethren. Soon, they were like extensions of his body.

*Now do what you must do—for Gledandron.* Wisp never relented.

Andy sent the roaches scuttling through the crack in the wall and into the next cell. From there they egressed the empty cell and nimbly ran down the main corridor outside.

He didn't know the way to the other parts of the compound, so he split the cockroaches up and sent them in multiple directions simultaneously. The mental feedback was confusing at first, but he soon grew accustomed to it.

Eventually one of them crawled through a gap under a door and came into a large, well-lit room. There were people standing around and Andy made the roach hide in the shadows to watch and listen. He focused on the insect's mind and became aware of its surroundings as if he was there in person.

In the room stood Pulse Pounder and Guillotine.

'...don't know why you got that wretch to seek out all these lumps of wood and rock—codename Substance was already a success—although you have left your creations to languish in a dungeon for over a year,' said Guillotine while he paced around, his six namesakes stretching from his back on metallic limbs, twitching as he did so. He was wearing a green and purple Kevlar suit and his face was partially concealed behind a domino mask.

*Codename Substance? What is that?*

'I thought I might create some more as a control group, which is why I sent the Night Demon to retrieve the same ingredients I used last time,' Pulse Pounder replied, his Cyclopean eye spiralling constantly above the smiling mouth on his noseless face. His skin was alabaster and he was shirtless, aside from a perse cape fastened around one shoulder. He wore maroon pants that merged into his boots. 'Perhaps you are right; perhaps it's time to move to the next phase of my Manifest studies.'

'Overdue is more like it,' Guillotine rejoined.

'I value your opinion, but watch your tone,' Pulse Pounder snapped. 'I will need fresh subjects: mortals and Manifests alike. I am determined to discover the secret of the Manifest seeds and why they are in such abundance on this island continent.'

'Perhaps it has something to do with these Wisp creatures you discovered by accident?' Guillotine ventured.

*See? I told you they seek to learn of Gledandron.*

'There just isn't enough information to go on.' Pulse Pounder turned and noticed the cockroach in the corner.

'Doctor Q sought those same answers and look what became of him,' Guillotine said, still pacing.

'Yes, Energy Lord had him framed, so no one would care when he abducted him,' Pulse Pounder revealed, walking towards the intruding arthropod. 'It's just a shame for him that the wily old coot outsmarted him and escaped. Now no one knows where he is.'

'Perhaps we should send Night Demon to hunt him down?' Guillotine absentmindedly started picking his nose. Supervillains cared little for etiquette. 'He would be invaluable to our cause.'

'No, it's a pointless search, he's probably dead. Even Energy Lord's agent, Hunter, failed to find him again—and he was the one who captured him for the Energy Lord in the first place. No, there are other targets I have in mind for Night Demon to abduct.' Pulse Pounder suddenly unleashed a concussive vortex from his hand, crushing the roach and sending a wave of vertigo through Andy. 'This place is infested with vermin, see to it at once,' was the last thing Andy heard through the dying insect.

His mind snapped back to his familiar dungeon cell.

*So, it is real...Master didn't know I was watching through my friend's eyes.*

*I told you...I speak only the truth,* Wisp lied. *The cockroach died so you would know this as fact.*

*Its sacrifice won't be in vain, I promise. I just don't know what to do with this knowledge.* Andy was still torn between loyalties.

*For now, do nothing except gather information. Do as your 'master' bids, until the time is ripe to bring him into Gledandron's fold. It is not long now.*

For the first time he could remember, Andy felt in charge of his own destiny.

\* \* \*

### North Ryde, Sydney: 8 September 34 BZ

Bentaz Mullberry knocked on the front door of the unassuming cottage-style house on the quiet suburban street. The house had been specially built for its occupant for his years of service to his country, and while he could have had something far more lavish, he had always been a fairly modest man; at least in his later years.

The door was opened by a white-haired man who appeared to be in his mid-seventies. A blank expression crossed his face when he saw who was visiting. 'Bentaz,' was all he said.

'Hi Grandfather,' Bentaz said with a smile. 'Can I come in?' He was dressed in civilian attire and looked just like any other wavy-haired fifteen-year-old boy with a knapsack.

'If you must,' his grandfather replied, holding the door open and gesturing to come inside. 'Come to apologise, have you?'

*Blunt as always.*

'Well...yes,' Bentaz admitted, walking into the humble entrance. 'I haven't seen you since my birthday, and I'm sorry I said those things to you. I just felt like...'

'Either you're sorry or you're not—don't water it down with justifications,' Arthur Mullberry growled, closing the door behind his grandson.

'Then I'm sorry,' Bentaz said, desperately trying not to fight the instant he arrived.

'Good,' Arthur said. He turned and headed towards the kitchen. 'I've just put the kettle on if you'd like a cup of tea.'

Bentaz hated tea but knew better than to ask for cocoa. 'That sounds nice,' he lied.

A few minutes later they sat down in the spartan lounge room in awkward silence, quietly sipping their tea.

*This feels really uncomfortable.*

Bentaz took another sip and gently placed the teacup on the plain wooden coffee table. 'So, have you done anything interesting lately?' he asked in an attempt to break the ice.

'You know I haven't,' came the brusque reply. 'When you get to my age, there's really not a hell of a lot to do, except sit around waiting for the reaper.'

*Gee, that's uplifting.*

Arthur Mullberry was one hundred and twenty years old and would have still looked thirty-seven (the age at which he Manifested) had he not allowed himself to grow old after his falling out with Bentaz's father, Hunter. He still had his powers, but they were a shadow of his former glory. At least that's what Bentaz's mother had once told him.

*Better not mention Dad, or this'll be over before it starts.*

'Um, I'm not sure what to say to that,' Bentaz said hesitatingly. 'I came to see you about something.'

'You mean aside from apologising for your remarks on Anzac Day?' Arthur said curtly. 'Well, if you're here for something else, then spit it out. I don't have all day.'

*Why, is the reaper popping over later on?*

Bentaz kept his thought to himself and instead tried to think how best to broach the subject. 'It's about my new costume…'

'Axis's costume, you mean. Sure, you're missing the iron eagle symbol the Nazis later adopted as a hate symbol, but it's basically the same,' Arthur interrupted, nursing his tea on his lap. 'Did you know they also named the Axis powers after that Hun murderer? I bet you didn't; kids today know all of diddly squat.'

It looked like his grandfather had something to get off his chest, so Bentaz let him talk.

'You have no idea what things were like in those days,' Arthur continued. 'It was a different era before the First World War—no one had heard of Manifests before. At least outside of nursery rhymes and tales of ancient demigods, that is. Then suddenly the Germans announced the coming of the *Übermensch*, Herman Himmler, and the whole world was abuzz with the news. Not like today, where it seems there's a new Manifest every day of the week.'

It was true; Manifests seemed to increase in number every year, as if it was all building to some sort of mysterious climax.

Arthur paused to finish his tea. 'Well Axis, as he came to be known, may have been the first publicly known Manifest, but I'm sure I had my powers before him, I just didn't go public. Anyway, I digress; you probably know they sent him in to sort out that whole Franz Ferdinand business, and the rest is history.'

Bentaz nodded.

'You probably didn't know, however, that he sank the RMS *Lusitania* in 1915, killing everyone on board. It was after he drowned all those innocent civilians that I decided I had to take that murderer down.' Arthur paused in reflection.

'Which you did at the end of the war.' Bentaz had heard this part of the story many times.

*I almost remember it too.*

'Yes…it was technically after hostilities had officially ended though.' Arthur remembered it like it was yesterday. 'The ceasefire was in place, but it had become personal by then and we fought to the death bare-handed. I remember a strange man tried to stop us, and if Axis hadn't paused to kill him for interfering, I probably wouldn't have been able to turn the tables and break his neck.'

*So that's how. He never went into the specific details before.* Bentaz felt a chill run down his spine.

'Hitler then used his legend as the template for his Third Reich and to justify the mechanised slaughter of millions. Therefore, you can see why seeing that costume on you stirs all these memories best forgotten.' Arthur put his teacup down and stared into Bentaz's hazel eyes. 'So, what is it you wanted to tell me about that costume? You really ought to have known better.'

Bentaz swallowed hard. *This is going to be worse than I thought, but I guess there's no backing out now.*

'Well…um…ah…' was all he managed to say. Facing supervillains was one thing, but relatives were another thing altogether.

'Out with it, it's obviously important to you,' Arthur grumbled.

'Well ever since I Manifested…I learned that…I, ah…'

'Yes, yes, sometime today, if you please.'

'I learned that I was Axis in a past life.' The words hung in the air like a bad stench.

'Is this some kind of joke?' Arthur was furious.

'No, I wanted to tell you earlier, but…'

'I think you should probably leave now,' Arthur said coldly. 'Thank you for your apology.' He got up to show Bentaz the door. 'Actually, you should probably leave via the back. I don't want anyone seeing you.'

'Grandfather, I…'

'Get out!' he screamed. 'Don't think because I'm old I don't have the power to throw you out. Come into my house and throw this in my face, will you? You're just like your father, and I'm sorry I gave you the time of day.'

Bentaz got up to leave without another word. The old family portrait of happier times, taken when he was just a kid, seemed to mock him from its place on the wall as he walked past it, through the laundry and out into the sequestered back yard.

*Well that failed spectacularly,* he thought miserably as he changed quickly into the costume he'd concealed in his knapsack.

He packed away his civilian clothes and took to the air, flying high above the mostly red-bricked houses.

He was so caught up in his own thoughts that he failed to notice a strange gothic man and his Aboriginal companion as they stopped to stare from the footpath outside his grandfather's house.

* * *

### The Territories of Xph'Ish'Matarg, Hell: Circa 11 September 34 BZ

Mark Adams awoke in agony. The first thing he noticed was the burning air that scorched his lungs and burnt his mouth and nostrils. This was quickly followed by a more intense pain through his wrists and ankles that dwarfed anything else he'd ever felt before. His heartbeat pounded in his temples. He opened his stinging eyes and saw that he'd been crucified to an inverted cross of giant gnarled bones. It sat atop a jagged precipice that overlooked a scalding plane of misery.

Mark tried to vomit, but the bile caught in his throat and he ended up coughing up the bloody reflux. It ran down his face and into his long, tattered black hair.

*How… how did I get here? Last thing I remember was the Tomb… those awful demons…one looked just like me. This…this must be Hell. They said they were taking me here.*

'Ah, you have awakened,' said a deep, bestial voice. It came from an enormous goat-headed demon wrapped in a long flowing cloak that hid its body. The cloak looked like it was made of blood. The demon's eyes flashed in crimson hatred and its matted, white fur covered its head like a creeping mould. 'You are correct; the Scouts brought you here in their enviable Tomb to be our plaything. We are Xph'Ish'Matarg, Dark Lord of Sacrifice and Penance.'

The crucifix was positioned in such a way that Mark stared straight into the monster's giant face. It appeared to be upside-down.

*It can read my mind too?* Mark remembered how the other demons had pored over his every thought during the trip here. They had poisoned all of his memories and raped his soul bare.

'Yes we can,' Xph'Ish'Matarg revealed. 'You have a lot to atone for; you deserve to be here for allowing your wife to die.'

*Desci... Maybe he's right; if I hadn't picked up those flowers, none of this would've happened. Maybe I do belong here.*

'Of course you do. Hell is a place for sinners,' the demon confirmed. 'You only need admit it to yourself—you have all of eternity to confess.'

Mark tried to talk, but it hurt too much. He could only breathe in small gasps, and even those seared his oesophagus and tasted like ash. Every moment was a new definition in suffering. *Hell's exactly as I imagined it to be.*

'Ha-ha-ha-ha!' Xph'Ish'Matarg roared, throwing its head back in twisted laughter. 'He thinks like you used to. And with a physical body he suffers twice as much. Perhaps we made a wise gamble when we took you up on your bargain.'

*Not that fucking poem again...*

'Perhaps it was wise for us to allow you to leave this place in exchange for someone else,' the gigantic demon continued. 'Someone with flesh.'

*Huh? Is it still talking to me?*

'Of course, you made a wise decision. You have a much nicer pet, and I now truly live up to the epithet of High Mage of Hell.' The husky voice came from behind Mark and sounded smaller, as if the speaker was human.

*There's someone behind me!*

'That is the one you can thank for fate, Mark Adams,' Xph'Ish'Matarg bellowed. 'That is Merlin, the new Satan now he's overthrown Lucifer.'

'The *False* Lucifer,' the High Mage corrected.

'Sorry, our liege.'

*What are they talking about? What's this got to do with me?*

'It's like the Scouts told you, Mark Adams: you were to be delivered to us on the High Mage's request.' Xph'Ish'Matarg returned its gaze to Mark. He could feel an unnatural chill seep into the very core of his being.

'B-but...w-why...me?' he managed to croak, trying to stop the demon from responding to his thoughts.

'Do not feel special, mortal,' said the voice from behind. 'It was totally random—something else to blame on the False Creator and his misguided plan.'

*Is he talking about God?* Mark didn't have the strength to vocalise his question, but it was ignored anyway.

'Which reminds me, I have almost finished speaking with each of you Lords of Hell, Xph'Ish'Matarg, but I have a special warning for you.'

'What is that, our liege?'

'The False Creator may send some of his seraphim to Hell once he uncovers my plans, which is only a matter of time. A flesh and blood mortal will be most likely to draw their attention. Be on the lookout.'

Mark wished he could see who was behind him.

'We are ever vigilant, we see all,' Xph'Ish'Matarg claimed. 'We will not relinquish our plaything at any cost.'

*That sounds bad.* Mark squirmed on the crucifix in an effort to lift his head to stop the blood pounding in his temples. It availed to nothing and he remained upside-down on the inverted bone cross.

'Very well, then I shall go meet the next Lord in succession,' the High Mage said. 'I wish you many an aeon of entertainment with this mortal.'

'Our liege, may we ask a question before you go?'

It was hard for Mark to imagine this demonic behemoth supplicating to something with a human's voice. *Did it say Merlin at one point?*

'Granted, but be brief.'

'It is rumoured that you plan to free the great elemental, Ooblog. Is this true?' the demon lord asked.

*What is an Ooblog? Do I even want to know?*

'The rumours are true. The plans are inexorably in motion,' the High Mage admitted.

'But it is not like us, it is not born of this dimension like the Lords of Hell. Luci…the *False* Lucifer,' the demon corrected itself, 'trapped Ooblog here to act as a spawning matrix for Hell. If it gets free, we will not be able to hatch new demons for our armies.'

'Ooblog will act as *my* matrix on Earth,' the High Mage replied. Mark thought he sounded annoyed. 'Ooblog's terrestrial origins are precisely why I have chosen it, and its release from Hell must be natural, which is why it also must be born on Earth.'

'How is this possible? You would need a mortal to physically give birth to it.' Xph'Ish'Matarg was astonished for the first time in millennia.

Mark was horrified and he still didn't understand what an Ooblog was.

'Let us say that I have found a human female to birth it. Unsuspecting of course.' The High Mage laughed. 'I must leave. I have said too much already.'

*That poor woman. It sounds even worse than what I'm going through.*

'Fear not for her, Mark Adams,' the goat-headed demon said, turning its attention to its plaything. 'Your time in Hell has only just begun.'

Mark cringed under its piercing gaze and choked on its foul breath. Xph'Ish'Matarg laughed again.

\* \* \*

### Puerto Williams, Chile: 16 September 34 BZ

Dread Sedgewick sat in the frozen ruins of the small town, eating the side of beef he'd cooked in one of the many fires caused by his earlier rampage. The fire he was currently sitting beside in the former lounge room was warm and the meat was succulent.

*It's so good being able to eat decent food again. There's nothing to eat in Antarctica except penguins, seals and scientists.*

He'd taken the time to look around while he was there, but was fairly unimpressed and decided to head for South America as it was the only continent he hadn't visited. He was actually surprised he got to see Antarctica first.

*At least I got to break the world record for long jump—I reckon I jumped close to a thousand k's. I even got to see outside of the atmosphere, which has to be another record, surely. It's not like I cheat by flying or anything.*

Dread had gotten the idea of leaping continents in a single bound after hearing of some giant cannon Saddam Hussein had built a few years ago in escalation to Israel getting their own UN-sponsored superhuman, Peacekeeper. He liked the idea of being shot from a massive cannon.

*I'll have to pay the porn-moustached wanker a visit sometime and check it out.*

The impact of his jump had left a giant crater just outside of town that had brought everyone together to gawk. It had made the next part easier.

He'd made short work of the town's naval base and police force and even some suicidal locals who'd banded together to defend their town. Everyone else had died shortly after that.

*So why are you sitting around this dump now that you've had a feed and a bit of fun?*

He cracked off a rib and sucked the bovine flesh from the bone.

*Why are you really putting off attending to business? It's not like you really care what your mother says. You know he beat you last time, no matter what excuses you come up with. Are you scared to face him again, is that it?*

'I'm scared of no one,' Dread said aloud. 'I'll take a tour of this place first, and then I'll go pay them a visit.'

*Great, now you're talking to yourself.*

He stood up and threw the rest of the meat slab into the flames before walking out the collapsed house and into the gravelly street. Dismembered corpses lay with limbs comingled.

*Am I scared? Are my testicles really just low-hanging ovaries?*

Self-doubt was new to him and he wondered if it had anything to do with the alien parasite his uncle was so worried about.

He dismissed the thought as a military convoy in the distance caught his eye and he left to head them off.

* * *

## Sydney (Kingsford Smith) Airport, Australia: 25 September 34 BZ

Naomi Bloodlust jostled her way through the busy terminal on her way to the baggage carousel. She was wearing large dark sunglasses to hide most of her faded bruises after her run in with Bodyguard, and struck an intimidating figure at six feet tall and scowling. All her outfits were in her suitcase and she wanted to collect them quickly but was impeded by masses of loitering people.

*Why are all these people standing here gawking? There can't be that many planes arriving at once, so it must be a celebrity or sports star. I'm surprised they let them all past security.*

Then again, Naomi found it a piece of cake to get all sorts of things past security. Her kit always travelled in her carry-on luggage and a nifty piece of Q-tech she'd pinched on the job was able to fool the scanners.

*If they ever finish their civil-rights debate on putting Manifest scanners at airports to prevent hijackings, I'll have to think of something else.*

She finally made it to the carousel and immediately located her purple suitcase.

*Now I only have to fight my way to the exit.*

The crowd surged before she could push back past them and calls of "make way, make way" could be heard over the throng. She found herself suddenly ushered back by airport security and almost went on the defence until she saw what was happening.

A teenage girl dressed in pink and black came into view amid a starburst of camera flashes. She was accompanied by a bustling entourage and a woman that could only be her mother.

Naomi immediately knew who it was.

*Hey, it's that model, Lorraine Freeman! Back home after her big tour, eh?*

Naomi had caught the celebrity news feature before her in-flight movie. She'd turned sixteen a couple of weeks back and had a birthday party extravaganza. Naomi found herself liking the girl despite her best efforts not to.

It was in that moment that Lorraine walked past and Naomi made eye contact with her for a brief moment. Time seemed to stand still for Naomi in that instant and she felt something akin to love. Then it faded as Lorraine continued down the terminal and the crowd followed in her wake. She was left with a warm afterglow.

*Wow. She's a Manifest all right, and a pretty fucking powerful one from…from whatever the hell that was. I wonder if she could tell I am too? I'm pretty hard to detect, but it seemed like we had a moment there or something.*

Naomi found it much easier to walk to the exit with Lorraine and her horde of sycophants gone and soon she was outside at the taxi rank. The queue was unusually long.

She suddenly became aware of a person approaching from behind, and she could tell it was another Manifest from the sensation. She turned to see an old familiar face—and a friendly one at that.

'Bojangles, a pleasure to see you again.' She was used to him just appearing and gave the silver-haired man a hug. 'I like your shades. They sort of match mine, don't you think?'

'Except mine are a lot cooler,' he replied with a cheesy grin. 'How's it feel to finally be home?'

'Actually, it feels pretty good, I must say,' she answered as they shuffled along the queue. 'What are you doing here? Come to save me money on a taxi fare?'

'And ruin all the fun of a white-knuckle thrill ride through the city? I don't have the heart to do that to you. No, I'm here to see if you ended up using that talisman yet.'

*Why is everyone so obsessed over that bloody amulet?*

'Didn't get a chance—and before you ask, I lost it, okay. The fucking thing is cursed, you were right.' Naomi didn't feel like including the part where she got her arse kicked.

'That's a shame.' Bojangles sounded unusually glum. 'Turns out I need it back. Do you know where I can find it?'

'You need to ask some flying South American guy who calls himself Bodyguard to the great Armageddon or something like that.' In truth it was exactly like that.

'Did you say Armageddon? Like as in a person?' He sounded even more alarmed.

'I guess so. I thought he was being metaphorical, but I guess he could've been talking about someone. But who would be pompous enough to go by a name like that?'

*It's even worse than me changing my name to Bloodlust.*

'Someone who's about as much fun as a Judas chair,' Bojangles despaired. 'I better go tell my friend. Maybe you can come along after all?'

'And miss out on my white-knuckle thrill ride? Ha!' Naomi smiled and kissed him on the cheek. 'Sorry, but I must decline. There's someone I have to see.'

'Wow, they must be important for you to pass up on your old mate Bojangles,' he joked.

'What's the matter, jealous?' Naomi laughed and climbed into the next taxi to pull up at the curb, leaving Bojangles to his own devices. *It's good to be home,* she thought, laying back in the seat as her white-knuckle thrill ride began.

* * *

### The Mystical Realm: Circa 27 September 34 BZ

The High Mage of Hell trudged through the fine sand that had turned from a brilliant gold to a pale yellow since his last visit. The sky haemorrhaged realities in a mosaic that was beautiful in its own unique way.

*The trip back to Earth from Hell is a lot easier since I broke this Realm,* he thought as he walked along the dune. *Now that I've spoken with the Lords of Hell, my plans are almost complete. I only require one more item and then it is only a matter of waiting for the stars to align.*

His internal monologue was interrupted by the sight of a crumpled man in purple and black armour lying on the crest of the dune ahead. He had rectangular pauldrons with the image of a white skull on a black background, and his scarlet cape was half buried in the sand.

*I don't remember this being from my previous visit. I can sense the raw power flowing from him in waves. It matters not what his origin may be; I can use every bit of power I can get.*

As the High Mage approached, he noticed the armoured man was unconscious. In his limp hand was a bone amulet necklace. He plucked it from the man's fingers and inspected it.

*It looks like the stars really are in my favour—that's Summon's sigil. Now I have something to barter with the trader for the object I desire. Soon I won't need to make deals with anyone to get what I want, but for now I must play the game.*

The High Mage was intrigued by the stranger. He grabbed him by the throat and lifted him up with one hand. 'Reveal your secrets,' he commanded, casting yet another spell from his repertoire.

His red eyes grew wide as the information poured into his mind's eye. 'I have heard of you: Anu Hopet, a former Egyptian slave known by prophecy to some as Armageddon, and to others as the Usurper. You are older even than I. How you got here is unknown even to you, but I suspect the answer is the talisman you possessed. It matters not; I will know soon enough.'

He attempted to drain the life force from Anu Hopet, but the spell short-circuited and fizzled out without effect.

*Hmmm, it seems you are still protected by the prophecy that the long-gone Celestial Ones placed on you millennia ago. I won't be able to drain your power until I replace the False Creator as Lord of Hosts and rewrite all prophecies.*

'Go, return to Earth where I can absorb you at a later time,' the High Mage said as Anu Hopet began to shimmer and fade from that reality.

Once the High Mage was alone, he looked again at the talisman and the rune carved into it. *It looks like I don't have to travel to Earth just yet after all. Now I can pay Summon a little visit first.*

The High Mage smiled. He liked writing his own destiny.

* * *

### Lilith's Dark Castle, Black Abyss: Circa 30 September 34 BZ

Seth Zaraxom sat on the cold, uncomfortable stone chair and sipped his black lotus tea. It tasted like cat piss to him but was renowned for eking out slivers of forgotten truth after one used the Orb of Horath.

*Or so my sister claims. She could've just been playing a prank on me all these years. I've never seen her drink any of this foul stuff before. Not sure it's working at all.*

Lilith could feel her twin brother's doubt. 'Trust me, it works. It showed me I had to seduce Hunter.'

'And look what that got you.'

'Yeah, a wonderful son.'

'A son that likes killing his uncle for shits and giggles, and let's just say there's more shits than giggles in that equation.'

'Will you stop whinging? It's not like you can die anyway.' Lilith had a point: in twenty-nine thousand years Seth still hadn't come across anything that could kill him for longer than a year—and he'd been at ground zero at Hiroshima in '45. It just took him longer to reconstitute himself the more badly damaged he was.

'It will help to talk it through while you wait for the flower to take effect,' his sister promised. 'How was your trip to visit that old Manifest, the one you haven't seen since the human's first mechanised war?'

'Fruitless. The man's really let himself go—he's gotten *old*, of all things! In all my years I don't think I've ever seen a Manifest age deliberately, apart from children of course. But an adult? Never.' Seth shifted his weight and looked increasingly uncomfortable. 'You wouldn't have any cushions in this castle of evil, would you, sis?'

'Of course, you only needed to ask.' She signalled to her shambling ghoul attendant, Corpse. He was one of two servants that Lilith kept in her nocturnal lair, the other being the undead werewolf, Carcass. Legend had it that Corpse was her first husband, Adam, who foolishly rejected her for a younger woman, and Carcass was his son Cain, who she first cursed with lycanthropy and then undeath. They endlessly prowled the cold, quiet halls.

Lilith's Dark Castle was conjured by its mistress long ago when she first reached adulthood and moved out of the Abyss and into what the gods confusingly call the Black Abyss—utter mind-rending darkness that she liked to think of as the true face of Mosh Lightley.

The castle itself was a monolithic slab of polished stone, with few decorations or adornments. Its foundations were set in the top of a skull-shaped, cavernous rock and the entire thing was improbably hanging by a single long, spindly staircase that was connected to a wooden door at the very top that led to the Abyss. While some deceased individuals had said the name *Dark Castle* was unoriginal, Lilith reminded them that it was when she'd named it.

'Go on,' she said to Seth.

*Now, where was I? Oh yeah.*

'Well, Ally—Arthur, I learned—well, he didn't believe it was really me, said he'd seen Axis kill me...'

'That guy you thought was the chosen one from the prophecy, this puissant God who Walks Like a Man?' Lilith interrupted.

'Yes, don't remind me... *Anyway,* he said that Axis being distracted with me was how he managed to win that fight and finally put their rivalry to an end. He also said he thought he might've been having some sort of mental episode given he'd just had a fight with his grandson, who Bojangles and I saw flying off.' He paused to take the cushion Corpse had fetched. 'He's that powerful teenager, goes by the public name of Ballistic...'

'You're not going on about that teenager again, are you, mate?' said a familiar jovial voice from across the oversized room. 'Do you think he's actually the chosen one? Don't you remember when you thought it was that German guy? Well, as he was killed, I wouldn't bet the house on your ability pick the chosen one from a banana.' Bojangles laughed and sat down on one of the stone chairs. 'Lilith, you really need to get some new furniture; these chairs are murder on the arse.'

'I'll murder you, you ass,' she teased, all smiles.

'Is that what happened to those two stinky zombies you keep lurking around here? Did they sit on your chairs for too long without a cushion?' Bojangles suddenly turned and looked at Seth's single cushion with envy.

'So, what's the news on the talisman?' Seth asked before the conversation could move onto cushions.

'She lost it.'

*Damn, I really don't like the alternative method.*

'It was taken from her.' Bojangles started fidgeting. 'You won't guess who by.'

'Don't tell me it was the High Mage,' Seth guessed with unknown irony.

'Nope. Get ready—Anu Hopet,' Bojangles said casually. He'd been practising.

'Really, after all this time?' Seth couldn't believe it.

'Yep, Armageddon has arrived!' Bojangles had always wanted to say that.

'The Usurper has returned after all this time?' Seth was still grappling with it.

'And here you were only just talking about the prophecy,' Lilith mused. 'Aunty Kismet works in mysterious ways, all right.'

Seth was about to agree when Kismet took the words from his mouth and replaced them with an Orb flashback. His eyes rolled back into his head and he started to drool.

'Seth, mate, what've you been drinking?' Bojangles looked concerned. 'And can I get one for meself?' he asked Lilith.

'He's having an Orb flashback, you clown,' she replied.

Seth snapped out of his vision as quickly as it had come on. 'I know.'

'Know what?' Lilith and Bojangles asked simultaneously.

'I know he plans to release the forces of Hell upon Earth...I also know when the High Mage will strike—I mean, I know the actual date!' Seth proclaimed. *What a stroke of luck!*

'Well, don't leave us in suspenders,' Bojangles managed to say with a straight face.

'The Feast of Lights, better known as Christmas Day,' Seth declared with a certain gravitas in his voice.

'Around the Solstice,' Lilith added. 'That doesn't give us much time.'

'No...' Seth paused to work it out in his head. '...now I know what the Orb meant with its vision about the number twelve—by my calculations that gives us just over twelve weeks and counting until the apocalypse!'

# PART TWO:

# WEAVES

# Week Twelve

### Grand Satanic Headquarters: 2 October 34 BZ

Marek Mahoney proudly donned his brown satanic cloak and joined in the nefarious chanting with true-believer gusto. He thought it sounded like a slowed-down version of some black metal band's hellish repertoire.

*Is this a Venom song, or maybe something from that new Cradle of Filth album?* he wondered as he bellowed out the diabolic lyrics. *Not that I care, Satanists laugh in the face of copyright laws.*

He was almost six feet tall, in his mid-thirties, with short auburn hair and thick beer-bottle glasses. He had the meagre beginnings of a Hitler-style moustache (which he lacquered daily) sprouting above his pencil-thin lips and a single, thick black hair sprouting from the middle of his forehead. He also reeked of Old Spice cologne.

*I finally made it to the inner circle! Man, this is the life; hanging with other agents of darkness and getting to plot the world's demise all day. They even put me in charge of the shopfront downstairs!*

The chanting reached its fiendish finale and Marek finished with a high-pitched scream for added effect. No one batted an eye; they were used to it by now.

'Okay everyone, that's a wrap for today's chanting practise,' said Matt, the heavyset other zealot of the group, who Marek was always trying to out-Satan in some sort of iniquitous true-believer contest. 'It's time to talk business. Lancefield, do you have the meeting notes?'

'Aye captain, I'll give 'er all she's got,' Lancefield replied in an absurd 'Scotty' reference that was lost on the group. You guessed it—Satanists

laughed in the face of *Star Trek* too. Lancefield donned his trusty monocle, cleared his throat dramatically, and fluffed his red, bushy beard
before reading the minutes from the last meeting.

'Before I get into it,' Lancefield began, always eager to hear himself
talk, 'I just want to remind you that my mum will be available after the
meeting to give you a lift home, should you need it.'

'Just get on with it,' said Floyd, the odd-looking, mean-spirited, oldest member of Lucifer's Coven. 'No one wants a ride home with your
grabby mother.'

*Yeah, I won't make that mistake again—at least, not until she has a
shower.*

'I was only trying to be helpful,' Lancefield said sullenly. He took the
hint, however. 'So anyway, last meeting we officially promoted Marek
here from Prime Locum to official member of the inner circle...'

Marek swelled with pride. From neophyte to Second Locum when
that Gavin dude became the chosen one, then to Prime Locum when
they promoted Lancefield, and now full member of the inner circle.

*I've really come such a long way in a short time. Who says finishing
high school is important?*

'...after Tom Higginbottom made the...ah... *faux pas* of trying to
pass off tofu as wild boar,' Lancefield continued.

The aforementioned Mr Higginbottom's flayed, putrefied corpse
was now hanging in the upstairs meeting room they were gathered in,
as a warning against failure and amateur taxidermy.

Lancefield droned on: 'The initiation ceremony went well—thanks
to Navid for supplying the dugong blubber...'

Creepy Navid merely smiled and gave a slight nod.

'...and we brought Marek in on our plans to bring on the apocalypse
for the High Mage of Hell, as it was written in the Satanic Scriptures.'

'All praise the holy tome,' they all said in unison.

*I always knew that Satan and Hell were real. There's no way so many
metal bands could be wrong.*

'Is that all we got up to last meeting?' Matt enquired.

'Ah...well Floyd got drunk and we ended up giving him a ride home
with my mum.' Lancefield turned white.

'Fucking what now?' Floyd looked shocked. 'I don't remember

that—I thought you got me a taxi. No wonder I got that rash…'

'Okay, I think we'll move on,' Matt said after Floyd's anger turned to shame at having mentioned the rash.

'So, what are my duties now that I'm part of the inner circle?' Marek asked in his squeaky voice. Everyone had gotten too wasted last week to tell him and he couldn't hear through the initiation head-jar they made him wear anyway. 'Do I get to do some magick? Oh, by the way, I spell magic with a "K" on the end as that's more badass.'

'That *is* more badass!' Matt agreed enthusiastically. 'I think I'll use it for my numberplate.'

'You don't even have a car since you got fired from your junior accounting job,' Floyd sneered. 'Why do you need a numberplate?'

'Because I'm gonna' put it on yo momma when I ride her,' Matt shot back.

'Ooh snap!' Marek said. *Damn, that's one more point to him in our Satan contest, insults being the work of the devil, of course.* 'But you can't use magick, that's my word.'

'Your word is unimportant; it is *my* word you should obey as it is the word of the High Mage of Hell,' said a shrill female voice from down the corridor outside. Moments later, the High Priestess, Karen, waddled into the room. She was heavily pregnant. 'I carry his child, after all.'

*Yeah, that baby could only be the Antichrist if it's the High Mage's. I mean, who else could it be?*

'Yes, High Priestess.' Marek didn't dare anger the mother of the Antichrist while he was still on inner circle probation. 'I was just eager to learn what my duties are as an inner circle member.'

'Aside from managing the shopfront downstairs, which we mentioned to you last week, your expanded duties are managing and maintaining your share of the six hundred and sixty other members of the coven.' Karen paused as a beeping came from the other room. 'That'll be my popcorn. Lancefield, would you fetch it please?'

'You betcha!' He raced to the kitchen.

'Wow! Where'd you get popcorn? I thought we only had muesli bars around here.' Matt was always hungry.

'I found it in the back of a cupboard,' Karen revealed, looking irritated. 'You're not getting any, so there's no point asking about it. Now silence! I'm explaining Marek's new role to him, as you all got too wasted last meeting to do it properly.'

They all hushed before the obligatory dressing down could evolve into a full-on rant.

*Hormones. It has to be. I doubt she would've been this crazy before she was knocked up.*

When Karen was certain everyone was behaving, she resumed her list of Marek's duties. 'Your other responsibility will be choosing a new Prime Locum,' she said, turning to face him. 'They must be a true believer and loyal. Do you think you're up to it?'

'Am I ever?' Marek replied enthusiastically. 'I bet we have plenty of worthy candidates for the role!'

'Excellent! We need people of our refined calibre in positions of power within the coven,' Karen said, turning towards the doorway. 'Oh look, and here's Lancefield with my popcorn.'

* * *

### The Mullberry Residence, Canberra: 3 October 34 BZ

Bentaz Mullberry walked into his father's cluttered workshop, which was located downstairs and could only be accessed from the outside.

'Hey Dad,' he said, walking into the brightly lit room. 'Whatcha up to?'

'Just preparing for another job,' Hunter answered without turning around. 'What can I do for you?' He was working on some kind of robotic claw that looked like it could be worn as a glove.

'Well, it's just been good having you around of late, that it's a shame you have to go again so soon,' Bentaz exaggerated, thinking of the double-edged sword that was his father's presence. He was really tip-toeing around the question he really wanted to ask.

*Just ask him and be done with it already—you've faced off against supervillains for fuck's sake!*

Hunter finished tinkering and turned around to face his son. 'That's nice of you to say, but I feel you've got something else on your mind.'

*He's giving you the perfect opportunity!* Bentaz looked his father in the eyes. 'So, what is it you actually do for a living?' *There, it's finally out.*

'I'm sure your mother told you. I do contract work for a private employer,' Hunter stated, returning the gaze. He grabbed the metallic pincer-glove and started polishing it.

'That's an answer you give a child,' Bentaz said with a frown. 'I'm fifteen now and can handle the truth.'

'Oh, *well,* fifteen, that's positively ancient,' Hunter replied sarcastically. 'You think you're an adult now and can handle straight talk, is that it?'

'You're not a criminal, are you, Dad?' Sarcasm only made Bentaz bolder. 'Is that what you do when you go "on a job"? Is that how you pay for everything, including all this random tech you have lying around?'

'What I do, I do for your mother and you kids. Life's more complicated than superheroes and supervillains, no matter what the UN propaganda says.'

'It's true then, you are a supervillain.' Bentaz was reeling despite sounding calm, which came from years of practise fighting bully Manifests.

'Ah, teenagers and their simplistic view of things.' Hunter sighed. 'You think it's easy for me to do some of the things I do? It's true, I work for dangerous people, but I do it to provide for my family. The people I work for aren't that different from that Tactician stooge you report to, but at least they're open about their intent. Governments weren't so fast to recruit Manifests back when my career got started, not like they are now.'

'Well, they recruited Grandfather,' Bentaz snapped. 'No wonder he won't speak to you. He knows, doesn't he?'

'Do you think they would've been so fast to trust him if there wasn't a war on? Not to mention the very public debut of your previous reincarnation, Axis. No doubt he was manipulated by his government too.' Hunter put the mechanical glove on his left hand and immediately the tiny diodes that ran its length lit up and it started to hum. It tightened around his wrist with a hiss and the claws opened and closed as he tested it. 'Perfect,' he said under his breath.

He turned back to Bentaz, who looked upset. 'As for your grand-father, he was born of a different era—immaculate conception if you believe *my* grandmother—and was always hard to live up to. He's an icon, for Christ's sake.'

'You didn't even try!' Bentaz accused.

'What would you know?' Hunter raged. He was always slow to anger, but then would suddenly explode. 'You don't even really know what happened, as I've never talked about it much. You want adult talk? Fine. The truth is that he abandoned me as a child and I was raised by my mother in Scotland alone. You see, he just knocked her up and left, like any old soldier after the war. This is the Second World War I'm talking about, of course.'

'Of course.' Bentaz didn't know what else to say. He hadn't heard this part of his family history and it came as a shock.

'Yet he was meant to be this fucking amazing superhero that fought with the Allies in *two* world wars and full of bravery and light.' Hunter looked bitter. 'Some fucking paragon of virtue he turned out to be.' He rarely swore, so when he did Bentaz always knew it was serious.

'But, you both live in Australia and Mum used to take us to visit him when we were kids.' Bentaz felt his world turning upside-down.

*I knew my family was dysfunctional, but I didn't realise exactly how much.*

'He eventually returned to Sydney and they built that house for him that he's still living in,' Hunter explained, continuing to test his new glove by picking up various items scattered around the workbench. 'I grew up to hate him, and after my mother died from a stroke, I went to Africa and became a mercenary. Anything to be different from my father. It was there that I became a Manifest several years later.'

'That's right, you said you were being tortured when it happened.' Bentaz wondered if that was the truth.

'Correct. You know all of that. The point is once I gained my pow-ers, I was hired for better jobs and by coincidence was offered a tempo-rary job opportunity in Australia. Of course, I then met your mother and decided to stay.' Hunter paused to tighten a bolt on his glove. 'It was she who thought that you kids should meet your grandfather as she never knew either of hers.'

'He always said he fell out with you as he didn't like your line of work,' Bentaz said.

'He never liked to face the truth. At least the whole truth—it's true he doesn't like my line of work.' Hunter seemed satisfied with his glove and returned it to the workbench.

'So what exactly is your line of work? You still haven't answered me.'

'Son, I do dirty work, but I'm not a supervillain, if that's what you're worried about.'

It wasn't a satisfying answer, but Bentaz thought he could live with it for now.

'I think deep down he must still care. Why else would he have allowed himself to get old?' Bentaz had never really understood it.

'Honestly, I don't care. He had his chance to make amends when I was a kid. He doesn't even publicly acknowledge having any family.' Hunter, it seemed, did care. 'Now, I really am quite busy, I have to leave early in the morning, and will be gone a while. Take care of your mother, and I'll see you when I get back.'

'Sure Dad, g'night, safe trip tomorrow.' Bentaz turned and left the tool room, uncertain how he felt.

* * *

### The Freeman Residence, Neutral Bay, Sydney: 4 October 34 BZ

Lorraine Freeman couldn't believe how massive the new house was. *Can we really afford this? Hotels are one thing, but this is a mansion. Talk about rags to riches.*

'Come on, dear, you've got to check it out,' Lorraine's mother, Lucy, was calling from the lavish footpath ahead.

Lucy Freeman had made all the arrangements for the new digs while Lorraine had been off touring, and the rest of their family had already moved in—now joined by a legion of staff. This was the first time Lorraine had seen it.

*I hope they grabbed all my stuff from the old place, including my bong, Obtuse. I also wish I'd had a chance to see our old house at least once before Mum sold it.*

She walked slowly up the pathway towards the front door, trying to take it all in. The lawn was freshly mowed and there was even a topiary grove alongside the house.

*This is all too much.*

As she approached the front door, it swung open and two young girls came running out to greet them—her sisters. The eldest had long, chocolate-brown hair and green eyes and took after their mother, while the youngest was blonde with blue eyes and looked more like their other mother. 'Mum! Lorraine!' they called in unison.

'Heather, Samantha, it's good to see you again. I've missed you both,' Lorraine said, giving them each a hug. 'I hope you've been good while I've been away.'

Their angelic looks of innocence told her they hadn't—at least not all the time.

'Of course we have,' Samantha beamed. 'We're always good!'

'Yeah, and I'm really Vicious Man in disguise,' Lorraine laughed.

'Come check out the new house!' Heather urged, yanking on Lorraine's arm. 'It's really cool!'

'Yeah!' Samantha agreed, grabbing her other arm. Lorraine let them lead her inside.

The mansion was expansive and Lorraine gawped as she entered the vast foyer and the giant staircase that led up to a landing before splitting and going up either side of the room to the upstairs areas.

*It's positively cavernous…I don't know how I'll ever feel at home here.*

Before she could be led any further, she was greeted by at least twenty people gathered by her other mother, Shara Tiyarn, who had been looking after the girls while Lorraine was on tour.

'Hi Mum,' Lorraine said, kissing her on the cheek. 'Did you see me on TV?'

'I've seen little else,' Shara responded with a smile. She had dazzling blue eyes and golden hair that cascaded over her athletic frame, with a viridescent streak running through it that matched her lipstick. 'You're all the rage over here—you know what Aussies are like with their home-grown celebrities.'

'Thanks for looking after the kids while I was gone,' Lucy added, giving Shara a hug. 'It means a lot to me.'

'You know I love having them,' Shara replied in her deep voice. Also a Manifest, Shara looked like a woman, but was born with complete sets of both genitals—a true hermaphrodite—and sounded like a man as a result. She normally lived alone in Nambucca Heads, but had taken time off work to supervise both the children and the house sale. 'It was also fun to manage this purchase—everything went smoothly and I got to stay here until you got back. This place is amazing.'

Lorraine was starting to feel awkward as she didn't know who all the other people were. 'Ah, Mum, do you want to introduce us to everyone?'

'Oh yes, sorry,' Shara said, turning around. 'These are all the house staff your mum has employed to look after this place.' She began the long list of introductions.

*Babysitters, chefs, maids, gardeners, and even a fucking butler—if all of my money is going into a trust, how is Mum affording all of this?*

Once the introductions were done, Lorraine excused herself to look around while her mothers caught up. The kids had long since gotten bored and run off somewhere. She eventually found her room in the mazelike house; at least she assumed it was her room as all her stuff was in there. She immediately began searching for her most important possession.

*Where's Obtuse? I really hope they didn't throw him out. We triggered each other's Manifest seeds and he'll always be special to me. Please, please, please,* she thought as she riffled through the packing boxes. *He's not here!*

Panic set in, but then she remembered to check her private chest. Relief followed shortly thereafter.

Lorraine pulled the purple and white porcelain bong from the bottom of the chest. 'Obtuse! I'm so glad you weren't thrown away!'

'No, I only had to spend months in the dark at the bottom of a box, but I suppose it's better than ending up as landfill.' Obtuse's male voice seemed to come from everywhere at once, which wasn't any stranger than a talking bong in the first place. 'Care for a cone?'

'You've got a one-track mind,' Lorraine laughed. She'd long ago gotten over the weirdness of talking to a sentient water-pipe.

'Well, what do you expect? I am a bong,' Obtuse pointed out.

'True, but no thank you, I don't do that anymore,' Lorraine said, putting Obtuse on the shelf. 'And don't offer any to the girls, either.'

'You know I'm no pusher.' He sounded indignant. 'Just remember that I'm always here if you need me.' Along with sentience and the ability to talk, Obtuse was also granted the super-ability to always be ready to go.

'I will, thank you. Now I better go find the others and check out the rest of this palace.'

*That's if I can find anyone again in this labyrinth.*

\* \* \*

### Barton Correctional Facility: 5 October 34 BZ

Chief Warden Walter Screw was feeling much better now that he was fully healed. To prove his point, he reclined back in his swivel chair and took a long drag from his stogie. He was enjoying the rare peace and quiet when Kismet decided to intervene.

*Knock, knock.*

*Bloody hell, just when I was enjoying this.* He leaned forward and butted out his cigar. 'Come in.'

The door to his office opened and the familiar form of his son in his mechanised uniform walked in. 'Warden,' Stanley Screw said as he entered, closing the door behind him. 'I see you haven't gone on holiday yet.'

'Son,' Walter replied, wanting to see if he could get away with the familiarity in his own office.

'I suppose it's okay to call me that in here, as no one's listening,' Stanley allowed. 'But I almost prefer Tactician now, as I'm so used to it.'

'Well I'm not calling you that in private.' Walter emptied his ashtray into the dustbin next to his desk.

'I hope that cigar was out before you tipped it in there,' Tactician scolded.

'What, do you think I'm stupid?' Walter hated being second-guessed. 'Now, what brings you all the way out here without notice?'

'I have something with me of great interest, something that may make you feel better about the whole statue paranoia.' Tactician produced a cassette tape. 'They found this on some loser Manifest—one of the group killed in Cabramatta several months ago. It was lost in some bureaucratic bungling and I only just got it last week.'

*Great, just when I was getting over that whole embarrassing episode.*

'What's on the tape?' he asked. 'Pass it here, I have a cassette-deck on the shelf.'

Tactician passed him the tape and he put it in the player. A crackly conversation came over the speakers. It spoke of Merlin and False Creators, of Lucifer…and of Michael the Archangel. The end of the tape was muffled, but it sounded like someone was being murdered. When it was over, Walter felt uneasy again.

'Well, that was fucking creepy. Where did you say you got that again?' Walter pulled another Cuban from the desk draw and cut the end off before sparking it up.

'It was found on the body of a Class D from the appropriately named so-called super team, the Failures. Given the coincidence with your…um…concerns, I thought I would share it with you.' Tactician sat down on the leather couch against one wall of the large office. 'We still don't know who killed them, but if we believe the tape, it appears to be Merlin the Magician, as unlikely as that sounds. It also seems as if his plan is to overthrow God and reshape reality.'

'You're right; when you put it like that, it sounds absolutely ludicrous.' Walter sighed. He was having trouble believing it, despite his recent encounters with tick-faces and unnerving statuettes. 'What do you suggest we do?'

'It can't hurt to be prepared, like you suggested before,' his son offered. 'You're almost done with your Government Villain project— we can link up with Commissioner Jacobs and Field Marshall Hobbs and put on some training exercise around Sydney, considering that's where the body was found. Who knows? Maybe something will happen and we'll be prepared.'

'Not bad. What about those satanic cults you were looking into? Did anything actually come out of that, despite it being a diversion for the HSA?' Walter puffed away.

'There may be a lead in that area. I'm double-checking given this latest evidence.'

'So really, there's only one more question we have to answer,' Walter said.

'What's that?'

'If this Merlin guy is really going to kill God and bring about the apocalypse, then how the fuck are we meant to stop it?'

The question hung in the air along with the smoke from Walter's cigar.

\* \* \*

### Undisclosed location: 6 October 34 BZ

Courtney Yeht sat alone in her sealed bedroom and tried to ignore her rising nausea. She still felt sick the longer she remained cut off from the rest of the building, but was allowed out regularly to counter this. Her medicine had also been increased to help reduce the sickness.

*At least that's what Phil and Amy keep telling me, and I have no reason to disbelieve them. They raised me after I killed my own parents and even gave me my name. I just wish I knew why the name is so familiar.*

She thought about this for a while as she sat and flicked through one of the magazines she had for entertainment. It made her wish to be like all the normal people that smiled out from the glossy pages.

*I really hope I'm allowed outside at some point.* Phil had told her that it wasn't safe for her to leave. That people will hurt her if she does, as they are still looking for her for killing her parents.

She soon grew tired of the magazines and the mixed feelings she got whenever she looked at them. There wasn't much else to do in her room except look at old books and think.

*At least my powers seem to be getting stronger.* She could do a lot more now than she used to and was getting better at controlling her abilities. *I can even make living statues! I bet none of the people in those magazines can do that.*

The other thing that Courtney didn't like about her room was the silence that surrounded her like a blanket. She missed hearing things through the floor. Phil had told her that listening to vibrations through the floor is bad for her, and she should only do it when he asks her to. He said it was for her own good.

*I just don't know why it feels so good to do it if it's so bad.*

There was a lot she still didn't understand, but she hoped that she would soon.

*Once I master my abilities… which shouldn't be long now.*

* * *

### Dungeon Cell 9: 7 October 34 BZ

Andy Trailer returned to his cell after another successful mission for his master. He found the bowl of lukewarm gruel waiting for him and he fell upon it like a ravenous beast.

*Not as good as offal, but better than cockroaches,* he thought, placing the bowl back on the floor for his insect companions. *Good thing they're now my friends and I don't have to eat them. There's so many of them now—several hundred at least.*

He crawled into the corner of his dingy cell and onto the pile of dirty straw he was now allowed to have for a bed.

*Rest while you can, because soon you will need all of your energy to enact the will of Gledandron,* the ever-present voice of Wisp rasped inside Andy's mind.

*And revenge, don't forget revenge,* he thought back. *Revenge against Energy Lord.*

*Yes, and Pulse Pounder as well,* Wisp agreed. *Such is Gledandron's promise.*

*My master? But he has shown such trust in me recently.* Andy suddenly felt uncomfortable on his straw bed, a symptom of conversing with the voice in his head. He curled his great bat-wings around himself for cushioning. *He's got me bringing back real people now and everything.*

*He lied to you. The first people you captured were all an illusion he planted in your mind.*

*But the most recent ones were real—I could tell because my mental contact with my friends was still intact. Besides, what else could he learn about you that he hasn't already?* Andy had long ago confessed under torture to having Wisp in his mind.

*You do not know what he could learn. He may learn of your ability to touch the minds of others,* Wisp said.

*Well insects maybe,* Andy conceded. *Still, I don't think he'll find out about that. I know he hasn't mentioned it away from me, as I've been secretly spying on him.*

*Do not take him for a fool; he is growing suspicious at the ever-increasing number of cockroaches breeding within you.* Wisp always had a way of making Andy doubt himself.

*He doesn't know I control them,* Andy replied, trying not to let Wisp bring him down. *I just don't understand why I can't get my revenge now, especially if you're so concerned that he'll discover my secret.*

*No! The time is not yet ripe, but soon...soon will come the time of Gledandron. You need only wait; we will let you know when to strike,* Wisp advised. *Then you will truly become the Night Demon and be free of this prison.*

*And finally have my revenge.*

* * *

### The Abyss: Circa 8 October 34 BZ

Dread Sedgewick downed his beer and slammed the stein on the bar. 'Hit me,' he said to the bald bartender.

'You know, I might have to start charging you if you keep this up. You've been going non-stop for days now,' said the barkeep.

'Yeah, yeah, Mosh, it's not like you can run out or anything,' Dread said, sparking up a smoke. 'Plus, you've never charged anyone before, so why start now?'

'Because I'm prone to unpredictable acts of whimsy,' Mosh replied, passing Dread another beer, 'and I'm sick of you sitting here staring at me with your ugly mug.'

*If it was anyone other than the God of Everything who said that, I'd make them eat their pelvis.*

'Well, it's a good thing I am the God of Everything then, isn't it?' Mosh had a bad habit of knowing everyone's inner thoughts. 'Now, have you finished running around the globe avoiding your quest for revenge on your father's second family, or have you come to the sensible conclusion that it's not worth the effort?'

'I'm not avoiding anything,' Dread said defensively. He hated having his mind read. 'I was just getting around to it—I've been busy touring South America and finding my inner artiste. Easter Island has a freshly carved Moai for the first time in centuries!'

'Don't forget you got to sing on stage with Gwar too—that's always been a dream of yours,' Mosh said, grabbing a bottle from the shelf and skolling from it.

'They even seemed to like me joining their band; I guess it adds to their notoriety.' Dread quaffed his drink and took another drag from his cigarette. 'So there you go: I wasn't avoiding, I was entertaining.'

'You can't lie to me,' Mosh retorted. 'Not that I care anyway, being everyone means I don't play favourites, as you should know by now.'

'I know you say that a lot, but you seem to have a soft spot for some people—and how could *I* not be one of them?' Dread laughed.

*Still, Mosh has a point, I am stalling. At least be true to yourself.*

'That's the spirit! You're not as likeable when you're moping around, full of self-doubt,' Mosh said. He finished the bottle he was drinking and tossed it over his shoulder. 'Now, I'm getting bored with this, so you better take a hike.'

'Okay, okay, I get the hint,' Dread said, butting out his cigarette in one of the many ashtrays dotting the bar. 'Just let me have one more beer for the road and then I'll be out of your hair.'

'You're an absolute riot,' Mosh declared, running a hand over his smooth scalp as he poured Dread a final beer.

# WEEK ELEVEN

**Banksmeadow, Sydney: 9 October 34 BZ**

Naomi Bloodlust embraced Feng Liu and gave him a big dramatic kiss on the lips. 'Mwah!' she added for effect. 'I can't tell you how good it is to see you again.'

'Likewise, babe,' the muscular Chinese man responded suavely. He was clean-shaven and attractive. 'Where've you been? I was starting to get worried as I hadn't heard from you in ages before you called to let me know you were back in town. Have you come to re-join the Brigade? Is this the return of Miss Bloodlust and Magnet to the most wanted list?'

'We were never on the most wanted list—at least *I* wasn't.' She laughed as they walked into the small café where they'd agreed to meet. 'The public has no idea who I am.'

*It feels so good to be back.*

'As for reliving the glory days, alas, I wish it were so,' Naomi admitted. They sat down at a table and waited for the flustered staff to notice them. 'In truth, I wanted to see a friendly face, but I can't really hang around for long.'

'If this has to do with that gangster cunt, Scar, then I wouldn't worry about him. You said that whole Gorg thing was bullshit anyway.' Liu saw something in Naomi's eyes. 'It *is* bullshit, isn't it?'

'Yeah, about that...I'm no longer convinced that's the case.'

They paused their conversation to order coffees.

When the waitress was gone, Naomi said: 'I may have had a run in with him in Jo'burg. I came across a scene that fits his MO.'

'Fuck me,' Liu replied, passing up the opportunity for his usual double entendre joke. 'But you didn't actually get a glimpse of this guy?'

'Unfortunately, no.'

'That's a pity; no one knows what he—or she—looks like. Everyone assumes he's a bloke, though.' He lowered his voice to a whisper. 'But you're here now and there's no way the team's going to let some trumped-up hitman take out one of our own.'

'The team, huh?' Naomi teased. 'Not just you?'

Liu smiled. 'Well, *me* the most, but I'm certain Molecule, Spindler and Fatmandu feel the same way. I mean, we even named our team after you.'

*Ah, the Blood Brigade, another name that seemed cool at the time.*

'I appreciate the sentiment, truly.' They paused again to receive their steaming coffees and the giant Anzac biscuit Naomi had ordered. 'You know me, I can fight my own battles.'

'No one's saying you can't, but there's no point being self-defeating about it.' Liu tore the end of his sachet of raw sugar and tipped it into his latte. He then used his magnetic abilities to stir it with a teaspoon.

'Careful, someone will see you,' Naomi cautioned.

'Meh. No one's paying any attention to us.' Liu took a sip. 'Look, how about we go and see Scar together and get this whole thing called off. If he's a total prick about it, then you can leave again. It's not like anyone can keep track of you for long anyway.'

'Or maybe I could give him another scar to match the rest of them and lobotomise his smug arse. Maybe take out his pathetic Seven Servants while I'm at it.'

*I like the sound of that.*

'Then who'll call off this Gorg wanker? No, trying to talk sense into him is our best bet. I'll arrange a meeting—I just need to know how to get in touch.' He emphasised the word 'touch' with a raised eyebrow— he didn't miss *that* opening for a double entendre.

'Okay, seeing as you put it that way,' she purred, picking up on his meaning.

*It'll be good to shag someone who isn't into corpses or sodden nappies.*

They finished their beverages and left the coffee shop, making their way to Naomi's safe house to be properly reacquainted.

Neither of them noticed the figure watching them from the roof of the building opposite the café.

* * *

### The Skull of Ra: 10 October 34 BZ

Anu Hopet opened his eyes to see a cyborg midget staring into his face.

'He's awake,' Disk said to the other two members of the Skull Band, who had gathered around to gawk at their master.

*What? What happened? Last thing I remember was being defied by that trader, Summon.*

'Get out of my face—now!' Anu Hopet commanded, slowly getting to his feet. 'How did I get here? Tell me what your sensors recorded and make it quick.' Even weary and confused he was intimidating.

'Yes, Great Armageddon.' Disk tapped a button on his temple, causing his artificial left eye to project a three-dimensional recording of Armageddon's disappearance. Battletank, the red-armoured giant and Backstabber, the pygmy alien gremlin, moved aside to give their master an uninterrupted view.

Anu Hopet watched as first he disappeared while holding the amulet and talking about Summon, and then reappeared in a heap, unconscious and covered in sand. The timestamp on the recording revealed that close to two months had passed.

*And all I can remember is a frustrating and fruitless encounter with Summon before falling. I had the talisman with me when I fell, I remember that at least, yet I do not have it now. Someone has taken it.*

'Did you scan the planet while I was gone? Did you look for me at all?' He always felt better when terrifying his minions. 'What exactly have you been doing all this time?'

Disk, Battletank and Backstabber looked at each other nervously.

'Uh…I was defending the ship and protecting the crew…uh…Great Armageddon,' said Battletank, whose expertise was not thinking.

'I do not care what *you* have been doing,' Anu Hopet declared. 'Disk is the one who was in charge and he is the one who was responsible.'

Disk didn't like the sound of that and looked around for support, but found no succour in his teammates' eyes. Instead, Backstabber appeared to smile—if that was at all possible with lips that were also its teeth.

'Great Armageddon,' Disk began, 'I scanned the Earth but you were nowhere to be found, so as I waited I plumbed the planet's libraries, but there was nothing there of immediate value, just unhelpful legends. Then you appeared as suddenly as you vanished about an hour ago and we've been trying to wake you ever since.'

'So, you have learned nothing in my absence?' Anu Hopet was used to being master of his own destiny and setbacks made him testier than usual.

'I...I have, my liege,' Disk replied hastily. 'I analysed the sand you were covered in when you arrived!'

'And?'

'I learned that it's beyond the laws of science...'

'You do not know what it is. How is this knowledge?' Anu Hopet's hands began to glow.

'...it can only be from a godform entity...from a Celestial One,' Disk blurted, not realising how close he'd come to death.

*I should have known that the Celestial Ones would try to stop me— they were the ones who cursed me with this prophecy to begin with.*

'So, it was a Celestial One that interfered in my plans. Well, I won't allow it to stop me. Armageddon writes his own fate.' Anu Hopet turned to look each of his lackeys in the eye when he said it. 'And what of Bodyguard?' he added, almost as an afterthought.

'He has not recovered and appears to still be fighting the poison, Great Armageddon,' Backstabber croaked in response, as it had been the one looking after their sick crewmember. 'Although he has developed a strange affliction: he keeps repeating a single word over and over again.'

'And what is this word?' Anu Hopet was intrigued.

'Antithesis.'

Anu Hopet did not know what that referred to, yet a shiver went down his spine.

\* \* \*

### Centrepoint Tower, Sydney: 11 October 34 BZ

The High Mage of Hell stood atop Sydney's tallest building and gazed down upon the city by night. He was freshly arrived from his extra-dimensional travels and stopped to marvel at the wonders of this century before he erased it from existence.

*Soon…so very soon now that I have it. And to think, it only cost me a talisman that fate delivered to my hand.*

He stared at the large, diamond-shaped blue crystal he'd obtained from the trader, Summon. *Once I become master of reality, I'll return to that rune-faced trafficker and have my revenge for the trouble he's caused me over the years. Until then, I'll have to content myself that he's ensured his own demise by swapping a worthless amulet for this.*

The High Mage turned the Soul Gem over in his hands and laughed.

\* \* \*

### North Queensland: 12 October 34 BZ

Seth Zaraxom plodded through the sticky mangrove swamp on his way to the rocky outcrop that lay in the secluded inlet ahead.

*Why on Earth did the Orb give me a vision of this place?* he wondered as scores of mudskippers fled from his lumbering form. *I don't think any of these fish can help me stop the High Mage. I'm so sick of this mud.*

He was also sick of drinking his sister's black lotus tea to refine the Orb's visions. *I knew I had to come here, and I guess they're the reason why.*

He had drawn near enough to the outcrop to notice a lone figure sitting on one of the rocks watching his approach. He could tell she was a woman, despite the sun shining directly into his eyes and her being mostly obscured by the collection of boulders she was perched upon. The whole scene looked out of place in the otherwise flat mangrove.

*I just wish I could've known the precise location of this outcrop. It would have saved me time—and pants—to have come straight here from the bar, rather than wading through all this muck.*

As he arrived at the outcrop, he got a clear view of the person he'd come to see and in all his years on Earth, he'd never seen anyone like her.

*A mermaid? You've got to be fucking kidding me!*

The mermaid was lying back against the smooth rock at the top of the outcrop, her long, shiny blue tail outstretched in front of her. The tail was shaped like a fish's, except the fins were turned sideways like a dolphin's and it clearly merged with her human form just below her bellybutton. She was naked, yet her exposed breasts were partially covered by her long, blue-green hair. She was strikingly beautiful and her head was adorned with a crown of pink seashells.

*Give one the Crown of Knowledge and receive knowledge from the other with the crown.*

'You're late,' she said as he climbed up out of the goo and sat on one of the sandstone rocks.

'You're expecting me?' Seth was shocked.

'Nah, I just thought I'd say that for the hell of it. I don't get many visitors around these parts.' The mermaid reclined further and looked straight up into the azure sky. 'You must be after something, so what do you want?' Her voice had a strange quality to it, like whale song.

'Ah…my name's Seth Zaraxom,' he answered uncertainly, having been totally caught off guard for the situation. 'I guess I'm here for knowledge…if you catch my drift?'

'Was that a sea pun?' She kept gazing into the sky. 'I'm not sure I have time for jesters.'

*Off to a good start then.*

'My apologies, it was unintentional. I mean no disrespect.'

*I don't even know why I'm here or what knowledge she could impart. Then again, I didn't think mermaids existed until a moment ago.*

'Apology accepted,' she said as she sat up and made eye contact. 'I'm Sprite Superna. Pleased to meet you, Seth. Are you a friend of my sister's? You look a bit like her boyfriend.'

'I'm afraid I haven't had the pleasure of her acquaintance,' Seth replied. The sun was still behind her and he had to shield his eyes to see her properly. 'Like I said, I'm here for knowledge, but not sure exactly what knowledge.'

'So, you don't really know why you're here and you're after knowl-edge.' Sprite smiled mischievously. 'Knowledge takes many forms, but I sense there's only one thing I know that someone like you could pos-sibly be interested in. But first I need to know who sent you.'

'Well, no one sent me exactly.' Seth shifted uncomfortably. 'I had a vision from a crystal ball telling me to come. I know that sounds hard to believe.'

'You're talking to a mermaid; you'd be surprised what I believe.'

*She's obviously a Manifest too.*

'Okay then, that's the truth.' Seth hoped she really did believe him, as he wanted to complete his mission and get out of this humid swamp.

'You wish to learn how to summon the ancient behemoth, Levia-than, I'm sure,' she said.

'Yeah…that sounds like it could be the reason I'm here. Can you teach me how?' Suddenly the oppressive heat and blistering sun wasn't such a concern.

'It's something I picked up in my travels,' Sprite revealed as she changed position and reclined in the opposite direction. 'I'd be happy to share it with you. Just be warned: Leviathan is hard to control, being an elemental and all. You'll pretty much only be able to call him—he'll leave again of his own accord.'

'He sounds like a great asset to have on my team. I presume he's pow-erful—if he's the source of all those old legends.' Seth had heard a lot of legends in twenty-nine thousand years, including ones about himself.

'The *Titanic* thought so: it only scraped him and we all know what happened after that.' Sprite rolled on to her side and smiled again. 'Sound powerful to you?'

'It sounds great. Thank you, I appreciate it.' Seth was glad he came after all. 'Shall we get started? Unfortunately, it's pressing that I don't linger for long.'

'Sure, I have nothing else to do anyway. Though tell me this: why do you need to even summon Leviathan at all?'

'I have to stop the apocalypse,' Seth said with just enough flare to make it sound less corny.

'Hmmm, sounds important.' Sprite sat up again and extended a hand to Seth.

*That's got to be the understatement of the year,* he thought as he took her hand and began to learn.

* * *

### The Territories of Xph'Ish'Matarg, Hell: Circa 13 October 34 BZ

Mark Adams screamed as the burning flail was whipped across his spine again and again. His ruined back arced with each stroke and the simmering welts formed and ruptured in an agonising chorus. After a time, they healed and the process was repeated all over again.

'This will teach you to try to hide your thoughts from us,' the demon lord, Xph'Ish'Matarg, said over the sounds of Mark's agony. It indicated for its brutish, cacodemon servant to pause its scourging. 'Have you learned yet that there is no part of you we cannot hurt?'

Mark couldn't respond, he couldn't even think. He'd tried to think in 'themes' rather than words in an effort to stop the demons from reading his every thought, but they had ruthlessly punished him for his transgression. The only theme that had remained now was one of pain and misery.

He was tied with barbed wire and face-down on a smouldering, rhomboid-shaped rock. He was still wearing his jeans and work boots, but they were frayed all over and provided little protection. The rock was on another high precipice, so as to be eye-level with the colossal goat-headed Lord of Hell.

'We can heal you endlessly, so your body will find no rest while you dwell in Hell,' the ginormous demon lord continued as it loomed above him. 'But if you cooperate, we may grant you oblivion—once we're done with you, of course.'

*I would welcome it.*

'There is no point hoping, mortal. That will be a long while off yet—if we decide to do it all.' Xph'Ish'Matarg laughed and gestured for another cacodemon to approach. 'The High Mage chose well when he sent you to me. Now, it is time for you to eat, we must sustain your fragile body, mustn't we? This is called the devil's cum.'

The scrawny cacodemon dragged over a bucket of foul-smelling, thick white paste and sat it beneath Mark's chin. It then grabbed the crusty ladle and scooped the mucilage into his mouth.

*Ugh! This gunk tastes like tofu.*

Mark was too weak to resist this latest torture and gagged as the cold mush was forced down his throat.

*I can't take it! I need to get free.*

'There is no freedom for you, Mark Adams!' Xph'Ish'Matarg roared. 'Though it is good to be in contact with your Wisp again and to hear your thoughts, instead of trying to interpret those thematic ones you tried to resist us with. We will enjoy tormenting you for eternity.'

*Not if I escape first.*

'There is a fire in you, mortal. We shall enjoy extinguishing it.' The demon lord gestured to the brutish cacodemon and the flailing began anew.

\* \* \*

## South Western Sydney: 14 October 34 BZ

Desci Adams sat upright in bed in the catatonic state that was fast becoming her usual state of mind. Her only other mood seemed to be irrational rage.

Her and Mark's savings were almost gone as their income had vanished along with Mark, and she didn't qualify for any insurance payout as he was officially declared missing, not deceased.

*I just don't know what to do. If it wasn't for the kids looking after me, I probably wouldn't even feed myself. Get a hold of yourself!*

It was easier said than done, and soon the resolve left her and she continued to stare out the window. A pigeon walked along the windowsill.

*I just wish I knew what happened to him.*

She was lucky to have had Mark declared missing, as the police thought he was working with the man who came to the door. In truth, it was Obie, Samara and Sebastian who arranged for Mark to be put on the missing persons list, as Desci hadn't left the flat since she'd returned from the hospital months ago. They were currently out with their friend, Nathan Blandley.

*It's not like me to be so melancholy. I just love Mark so much and feel so lost without him. I hope he's safe, wherever he is.*

Desci thought again about getting out of bed and starting to put her life back together, but it just seemed all too hard. *Maybe tomorrow.*

\* \* \*

### Grand Satanic Clubhouse, Ashfield, Sydney: 15 October 34 BZ

Marek Mahoney was having a bad day. Not only was Saturday the day he regularly met up with the one hundred and ten members of his chapter of Lucifer's Coven—meaning he couldn't get too shit-faced drunk the night before—but today was also the day he had to interview candidates for the Prime Locum position. He was currently sitting in the community hall they rented for their meetings, listening to the penultimate candidate drone on about why they were worthy for the role, and while he found the whole thing to be an honour, he wasn't in the mood for it today.

He'd also woken up with a strange mark on the back of his left hand: a black and white stain that looked like an ink spot. He'd tried washing it off, but no matter how hard he scrubbed, the offending mark still remained. It was like someone had tattooed him while he slept. Normally this wouldn't have bothered him—Satanists laugh in the face of body art, after all—except that it had started talking to him in a loud, annoying voice and hadn't shut up since he noticed it. What was worse was that no one else seemed to hear it.

*Am I going mad, or is this a sign from Satan that I'm special and have been chosen to host one of his agents?*

'This guy sucks, we should piss him off and get on with the next candidate,' the spot remarked. Marek tried to ignore it, but it was getting more difficult. 'Hey, are you listening to me? YOO-HOO, I'M TALKING HERE! LISTEN TO ME!!!'

Instead, Marek called up the next candidate. 'Okay, state your name, tell me a bit about yourself, and let me know what you can bring to the role of Prime Locum,' he said to the final hopeful without looking at them. He was preoccupied with the shouting blot.

'Uh, hi, my name's Melissa Rupert Lump,' said a deep, male voice. 'I'm a lesbian trapped in a man's body.'

The unusual introduction actually managed to draw Marek's attention away from the bellowing inkblot. Before him stood a tall, hideous man with fish-lips, thick, bushy eyebrows, and poorly applied makeup that made him look like a cheap hussy. He had long, dyed black hair that was grey at the roots, and he was dressed in a shabby, unwashed tracksuit that reeked of milk, urine and sweat.

*What the fuck is that?* was Marek's initial thought.

'Kill it! Kill it now!' the spot yelled. Marek had to admit he was tempted.

'O...kay...tell me a bit about yourself,' he said, subconsciously stoking his lacquered Hitler moustache in anticipation. *But do I really want to know?*

Melissa licked his fat lips before continuing: 'Well, I'm a musical savant, like Mozart. My band's called The Dishevelled Servals, and we do punk in the constant war against jive. Maybe you've heard of us?'

*Nope, never—and right now I'm glad.*

'I've been told I look like Gillian Anderson...' he lied, while pouting and fluttering his eyelashes.

*Maybe if Gillian Anderson looked like a grotesque, fifty-year-old man.*

'...and...and...did I mention I'm a lesbian trapped in a man's body?' Melissa grabbed his fatty man-boobs for emphasis when he said it.

'More like a giant turd trapped in a loser's body,' the spot offered.

Ignoring the commentary from his new tattoo, Marek tried to continue the interview. 'So...ah...you believe you're a woman? A supporter of transgender issues then, are you?' Lucifer's Coven was unisex.

'Not really—only when I'm masturbating, as I think it'll be really sexy to be a girl. See, I push my testicles back inside me and rub...'

'Okay, that's enough detail on that,' Marek interrupted, desperately trying to get the image out of his mind. 'Why do you think you're Prime Locum material?'

'I mentioned I'm a savant. I'm good at everything I do—and those who say otherwise, I just ignore, as I know they're just jealous of my talents.' Melissa smiled to reveal his rotten, broken teeth and then started braying like a donkey. 'I know they're just jealous of my talents,' he repeated, incorrectly thinking it was funny.

'Call the Smithsonian—we've found the missing link!' the blot suggested.

'So, do I get the job? I'm much better than those other losers you interviewed before me,' Melissa said with no sense of irony as he started picking his nose while he waited for an answer.

Marek couldn't even remember the other candidates since having his sanity blasted by the talking spot and the demented freak with a potato-shaped head that was boasting in front of him.

*At least he doesn't seem to care what anyone else must think of him, which is very Satanic. I may as well just choose him—I really want to get the hell out of here and start drinking.*

'Okay, you're hired. I'll give you a run down on your duties next week.' Marek didn't wait for a response, and quickly called an end to the meeting and dashed outside into the fresh air.

*Thank Satan that's over! He stank so badly, I don't think I could take another minute of it. Now, if only I knew what the hell this talking spot is,* he thought, looking at his stained hand.

'I'm Blotch McMahn,' the spot said. 'That's McMahn with no "O" either, in case you were wondering. Glad to finally introduce myself.'

*Maybe I have gone mad,* Marek wondered as he walked down the street looking for a pub.

# Week Ten

**Blue Mountains, New South Wales: 16 October 34 BZ**

Andy Trailer soared through the night sky, enjoying the freedom that came with the retrieval missions for his Cyclopean master. This was the longest trip yet, which had started in a red, sandy desert to the northwest.

*It's good to finally be trusted to undertake these missions for real.* He swooped low and glided over the treetops. *Pulse Pounder didn't even try to disguise that this mission wouldn't just be an elaborate illusion.*

*Good that you no longer refer to the cyclops as your master and instead call him by his infidel name,* said the voice of Wisp in Andy's mind. *He suspects nothing and trusts you to do his bidding.*

Andy scanned the rugged terrain for the tell-tale signs of his prey, his immense wings perfect for aerial silent running. Night Demon was on the hunt.

*This pursuit will help with that.* He spotted a campfire in the distance. *I only have to bring one person back with me. If there's more than one, then my mast…Pulse Pounder said I can do what I wish with them as long as there are no witnesses.*

*And you know just what to do, do you not?* Wisp asked, already knowing the answer. *Pulse Pounder thinks you have forgotten…but we helped you remember.*

*How could I ever forget that it was around here that the Energy Lord first abducted me?* Andy could now see the campers as they sat around the modest fire and cooked sausages on sticks. There were three of them—two men and a woman—with the silhouette of another woman visible through one of the two yellow tents close by.

*Perfect. There are several to test your abilities on,* Wisp observed. *Now remember: it is no different to the cockroaches. This is your true Manifest ability, not the demonic form Energy Lord made for you.*

Andy circled high above the campfire until he'd worked out how to proceed.

*Time for the Night Demon to strike,* he thought, suddenly dive-bombing the campsite—the happy campers oblivious to the peril descending from on high.

One of the campers heard a whooshing sound and looked up just in time to see Andy fly out of the darkness and grab him by the shoulders, before tossing him into the tent with the woman inside, bowling her over and entangling them both in the collapsed shelter.

The woman beside the campfire screamed and the remaining man cried out about monsters and demons.

'The Night Demon, to be specific,' Andy answered in his high-pitched voice before grabbing them both by their throats and drawing them close to his fierce green face.

*Now remember, it is just like the cockroaches,* Wisp reminded as Andy began to hypnotise them with his scarlet eyes.

*I can do this.*

Two bright flashes strobed in Andy's mind's eye and he was in control of the campers a lot faster than he'd expected.

*Excellent! Now get them to do your bidding. Crush their will and replace their resolve with your own,* Wisp commanded.

Andy found the experience of reaching out and taking control of the campers' minds to come naturally, as if this was what he was born to do. Soon it was if he had three pairs of eyes and two additional bodies. The only thing he couldn't seem to stop them doing was drooling.

*They look like zombies. I guess I'll have to work on my abilities to get them to look normal. But until then...* Andy implanted his commands into their brains.

'Go, search for the Energy Lord. Scour these mountains until you find his secret base and then reveal to me its location,' he said aloud for emphasis. The two campers turned and walked off in opposite directions without hesitation.

*You have done well. We are proud,* Wisp said robotically. *Now for the other two.*

Andy walked over to where the remaining campers were struggling to free themselves from the ruined tent. The woman was still inside, trapped by the man who lay moaning on top of the twisted material. Andy noticed the man's leg had turned sideways at the knee.

*He's useless to both me and Pulse Pounder,* he thought, picking up the man by the throat.

*Then take the woman to the cyclops—she appears intact—and use this one for sustenance. He will taste much better than offal.* It almost sounded as if Wisp was smiling. Andy didn't know how he knew that or if it was even possible for a voice in his head.

*But isn't that like cannibalism?* He was hesitant to gorge on man-flesh.

*It is only cannibalism when it's the same species,* Wisp replied. *This human is beneath you, you are a god to it. Eat and you won't regret it. We promise.*

Andy looked at the squirming outline of the woman to ensure she wasn't damaged. She was calling for help.

*She's not screaming; that's a good start.* He looked at the horrified man, wriggling in his grasp.

*Do it! Eat him!* Wisp's influence on Andy was profound.

Andy looked back at his captive and his stomach rumbled. He opened his mouth wide and exposed his razor fangs.

The man screamed.

* * *

### Scar's Warehouse, Ashfield, Sydney: 17 October 34 BZ

Naomi Bloodlust warily entered the deserted warehouse, accompanied by her four fellow members of the Blood Brigade. She was hesitant at first to get the old gang back together but had to admit that she felt more comfortable returning to the lion's den with strength in numbers.

*Liu looks so sexy in his leather Magnet costume, maybe I'll have to get him to wear it when we shag next. Assuming we get out of here alive, that is.*

Naomi was also dressed in her leather work outfit, complete with knee-high red boots, utility belt and her self-made war gauntlets. Her top was low-cut and tight—all the better for distracting male opponents. Scar was old school and had an all-male crime syndicate, believing that women had their place—and that place wasn't in business meetings.

*Chauvinistic pig is more like it. He doesn't seem to get that it's not the thirties anymore. He's a fucking dinosaur and needs to realise he's extinct.*

She was flanked by Liu on one side, in his caped red and grey uniform, and Spindler on the other, who was dressed in a mesmerising rainbow-splotched suit. Both wore helmets to conceal their identities.

Following a few steps behind were the oddballs of the team, Molecule and Fatmandu: respectively a Manifest caffeine-molecule in humanoid form and beach-ball-shaped eating machine with cutlery growing from his wrists. Together they were a formidable unit and definitely a force to be reckoned with.

Waiting for them in the centre of the warehouse was the man they'd come to see.

Alfonso Barbaro was a short, bald man with no eyebrows and opportunistic eyes. He was dressed in drab brown clothing and would have otherwise been unintimidating, if it weren't for the hundreds of scars that covered almost every patch of his skin—and the source of his better-known alias, Scar.

Standing behind him in a wide semicircle were his Seven Servants, a collection of strange Manifests that acted as his personal grenadiers. Most were once human, but two were originally non-living, until given life by their Manifests and brought into Scar's service. Manifests with non-living origins were always the easiest to manipulate, as thinking was new to them.

'Miss Bloodlust,' Scar said coldly as they approached. 'I was hoping you'd be dead by now.'

'Give me some credit,' she countered, coming to a halt opposite him. 'I'm a lot harder to kill than people expect.'

'I could open one of my scars and drain your life force right now,' Scar threatened.

'We've been down this road before. I can reach you before you can drain me completely, only this time I'll shove my blade through your heart instead of your arse,' Naomi retorted, remembering what led her to leave Sydney in the first place.

'I've been in business a long time,' Scar mused. 'Do you think you're the first person to threaten me? I've outlived kingpins, cops, judges, and politicians. Hell, I've even outwitted that superhero, Ally. Compared to them, you're nothing.'

'Oh yeah? Then how come none of them gave you a new scar where the sun don't shine?' She was able to hold her own with trash-talk.

Scar seethed and looked like he was going to call on his lackeys before Liu intervened. 'Call off Gorg,' he said bluntly.

'Ha, ha, ha, not a chance. He's obviously toying with your girlfriend here, otherwise we wouldn't be having this conversation.' He smiled to reveal more scars across his gums. 'Besides, his services are bought and paid for.'

'I think you're bluffing. I don't think he even exists,' Liu replied.

'Oh, he exists all right, though I've never seen him. I used him many years ago to dispose of Harold Holt,' Scar said, enjoying every moment. 'I heard he was also responsible for the disappearance of Jimmy Hoffa,' he added.

'Maybe we should just take you out now and then Gorg would have no reason to go through with it,' Naomi said.

'What I hear is that Gorg's a man of honour: once he takes payment for a contract then it's as good as done—even if the person who hired him is dead. It's as certain as the sun rising.' Scar looked calm. 'So you can start a fight with me—and maybe even win—but my Seven Servants will take their toll on your friends and you'll still die at Gorg's hands. Is that what you really want?'

Naomi stole a glance at Liu and knew it wasn't. 'C'mon, let's go,' she said to her team. 'I'm going to kill this Gorg prick and then I'll come back for you,' she said over her shoulder to Scar.

He laughed. 'I hope to soon hear of your death.'

*Laugh it up, chuckles, because I have a secret. One that Gorg won't be expecting.*

She hoped it would be enough.

*  *  *

### The Abyss: Circa 18 October 34 BZ

Seth Zaraxom sat on his favourite barstool and passed the dutchie on the left-hand side to Bojangles.

*These Binah Buds are mind-melting madness! Thank Mosh my healing abilities don't counter the effects of narcotics—at least here in the bar.*

Seth rolled a cigarette from the packet of Smex that lived on the beermat. 'I'll just have this and then get on with it, shall I? I really need to be out of my mind to attempt this.'

'Don't worry, mate,' Bojangles said, passing the joint to White Lion—now returned from his mission with the HSA—and back behind the bar cleaning glasses. 'I'll be here to make sure nothing bad happens.'

'That's what I'm afraid of,' Seth joked as he lit his smoke. 'I've done one part of the vision the Orb of Horath showed me: I've learned how to summon the elemental, Leviathan. I've now got to get the Crown of Knowledge *from* Summon and give it to Mosh knows who.'

'I *do* know who,' Mosh Lightley interjected at just the right moment. 'But I'm not telling, as it'll ruin the plot.'

'Thanks Mosh, as unhelpful as always.' Seth sighed.

'Let me know if there's anything I can do,' White Lion offered. 'I'm due for some long service leave from this place anyway.'

'But you only just got back!' Mosh complained. 'I had to put up with Seth's bloodstain all over my beautiful floor for weeks!'

'Just ignore him,' White Lion said to Seth. 'That's what I do. Seriously, I'm happy to help.'

'There is something you can do. You too, Bojangles. I don't need you to watch after me—I can't die, remember,' Seth said between puffs.

'So, what do you need us to do?' Bojangles asked, taking a sip of his stout.

'Put the word out among all the Manifests you know. Tell them what's coming; tell them to be on the lookout for anything suspicious,' Seth said. 'White Lion, tell your HSA friends.'

'Anything suspicious includes just about everything that's ever been expulsed from the Miasma,' Bojangles remarked unhelpfully.

Seth ignored him.

'If we can find out who the High Mage's agents are on Earth, then maybe we can put a serious crimp in his plan before he unwittingly unleashes the full power of Gledandron the World Eater upon the planet. He thinks he's assaulting the creator god and has aspirations of replacing it to become a god himself.' Seth paused to take a breath. 'In reality, he's wasting his energies on an aspect of Gledandron and has destroyed the Mystical Realm, the main defence we had to stop the World Eater spawning on Earth.'

'Huh?' White Lion was confused, yet determined to pass on accurate information to save the world, and so he persisted. 'I thought your grandparents were the creator gods. Who's this other one then? And what's this all got to do with this World Eater, Gledandron?'

'Really? This again? How many times to do I have to hear this?' Bojangles had been friends with Seth a long time and had to sit through this explanation thousands of times before. His protestations were all for show, which Seth knew anyway. 'I can't believe you've been in this bar for thousands of years cleaning glasses and still don't know the connection between all these gods and monsters,' he said to White Lion before sucking on the joint.

'What can I say? I focus on my tasks and tune out everything else,' White Lion said defensively as he finished cleaning another glass. 'And I'm sure not going to learn anything if you keep interrupting.'

'Fair enough, point taken. Might as well get wasted—this'll take a while. Pass me that joint,' Bojangles said to Mosh, who'd been hogging it. 'Seth, once more from the top, if you please.'

'Will you be serious for a change?' Seth smiled, despite himself. He'd known Bojangles so long he was family. He turned back to White Lion. 'Okay, so yes, my grandparents created *this* universe, but there's probably an infinite number of universes out there and some of those were probably created by different gods. Who knows? There might even be a universe somewhere that quantum tunnelled into reality and created itself without the help of gods.'

'My guess is somewhere beyond the fourth wall,' Mosh added with a wink.

'Right, so Gledandron is a type of godform parasite,' Seth continued, taking White Lion's advice and ignoring Mosh. 'Godform is the species name for multidimensional entities that most people would think of as deities—elementals are simply bestial versions of the same type of being. Humans have had a lot of those over the years, as you know. But not all gods that humans worship are godform; some are aspects of Gledandron.'

Seth decided this *would* take a while and gestured for a beer from Mosh.

'So where does it come from? Are there more out there?' White Lion really was surprised he hadn't heard this tale before.

'As far as we know, it's the only one,' Seth replied, accepting his ale from Mosh. 'It comes from deep space; we believe it may have been originally created inadvertently by the Evolvers—those creepy grey aliens responsible for all those abductions. The same ones who created the ship that Armageddon the Usurper stole when he left Earth all those centuries ago. Anyway, all of that's unimportant. What's important is it's arrived in our solar system.'

'How long's it been here?' White Lion asked.

'Longer than I've been alive, so some time now.' Seth smiled. 'Long enough to devour Geburah—Mars to the layman—and turn the E'hobans' planet, Harmen, into what astronomers now think of as the asteroid belt between Mars and Jupiter.'

'But how does it do that?' White Lion was genuinely intrigued. 'And how come no one but you guys know about it?'

'Each planet is different so it takes a different approach. With Geburah it manifested its spawning matrix directly on the planet, allowing it to slaughter all life with abominations it copied from the Geburan Hell. It sucked the essence of the world dry—along with their goddess, the souls of every life form, and even the very evidence of life itself. With Harmen, it spawned a copy of their creator god and got it to blow up the planet, using the energy as fuel to pupate into a new form especially suited for Earth. It takes time for it to acclimatise to each world's unique biosphere, but in each case, it uses copies of that planet's gods against them.'

'Did you say it copies gods? Is that as bad as it sounds?' White Lion had been smoking joints all day and was trying not to be paranoid.

'I'm afraid it is,' Seth answered as he rolled another smoke. 'It has no real original thoughts; all of its knowledge has been gained by devouring the souls of sentients. It's not creative; rather it uses images from its victims' minds to construct replicas of whatever they fear or love the most. In fact, the name Gledandron comes from the Geburan god of Ragnarök. It stole it along with the image of that god from the Geburans' minds. I fear it now wears a new mask since pupating, one uniquely attuned to Earth. Its true face is akin to a tick's, well, at least that's what my aunt Kismet says.'

'So, what *is* it doing to Earth? You said the attack on each planet is different.' White Lion decided he needed a drink and helped himself to the Undead Fridge that lurked unplugged behind the bar.

'It first sent its Scouts here in a Tomb of Power long ago to study Earth, so that the form it pupated into would be perfectly adapted to our world,' Seth said. 'Bojangles and I have tangled with those demons many times over the years.'

'Yeah, it cost us Prince Kiol Zol and his mother, Kyra Zol—the love of my life,' Bojangles lamented.

'After it arrived here, it caused the Dark Ages and began regurgitating the souls of the fallen Geburans—the finest warriors in the solar system—into weapons against the minds of the human population. These constructs are called Wisp—djinn to some—and are attached to people's souls when they're born. Luckily, they're usually destroyed when someone Manifests, but not always; in those cases, the Wisp becomes truly monstrous indeed.'

'This sounds like a nightmare!' White Lion turned pale, but nobody noticed as he was covered in snow-white fur. 'I hope I don't have one of these Wisp leeches attached to my soul!'

'Don't worry, you were born before Gledandron arrived on Earth,' Seth said reassuringly. 'So anyway, it uses these Wisp to influence the minds of humans, causing them to war among themselves or worship idols. Idols whose images Gledandron can copy until the person unwittingly begins to worship the copy and by default, Gledandron itself. This marks a person's soul, allowing the World Eater to vacuum them up with its proboscis when they die. Some people report this as a bright white light. If you're dying, don't head towards the light.'

White Lion got a spine tingle at the thought.

Seth continued: 'So basically, every time a human creates an image—especially for religious beliefs—and they begin to believe the image is an accurate and absolute representation of the god they worship, then they risk worshipping the idol instead of the god. That's when Gledandron has them and that's why I went to so much effort in the past getting people away from graven images and idol worship. All religious, racial and political hate that afflicts the Earth like a cancer is the work of Gledandron.'

'Okay, and you're planning on stopping it, I got that part,' White Lion said between swigs of his bottle of hooch. 'How's that crazy Merlin the fucking High Mage connected with all of that?'

'Like all those corrupted by the World Eater, Merlin is caught up in the lie, and thus bound by its rules,' Seth said cryptically. 'He thinks he's going to replace the Christian god, but this False Creator he's after is not the Christian god at all, but rather another Gledandron spawn, this time a copy of the E'hobans' creator god. Neither is the Heaven or the Hell he's planning on pitting against each other what they seem. Again, they're but constructs Gledandron created out of what people imagined them to be.'

'Okay, but wouldn't that just weaken Gledandron, given its constructs would destroy each other in battle? I thought you said one time that these things all share a hive-mind.' White Lion couldn't see the problem.

'They do, it's why they always talk in plural,' Seth replied, finishing both his smoke and his beer. 'Sure, one of the World Eater's weaknesses is that it's bound by the rules and legends of the beings it copies, hence its demons and angels are in conflict. The problem is that if the High Mage succeeds in punching a hole through the World Eater's version of the Gates of Paradise, there'll be a continuous tunnel all the way from Earth to Gledandron's mouth. It will finally be able to spawn itself on Earth and devour all trace that life ever existed there. The planet will look like the moon when it's done. The Mystical Realm used to shield Earth from this, but I underestimated the High Mage and he shattered it.'

'That's because you didn't ask your sister Lilith for her help with your grand plan,' Bojangles reminded Seth. He was drunk and stoned. 'She's a lot smarter than you, ya know.'

'I won't argue with that,' Seth agreed as he got up from his barstool and walked towards the concrete mosh-pit in front of the stage behind them. 'Now, remember to spread the word,' he said to Bojangles and White Lion.

He pulled a long ornate dagger from his boot and retrieved the Orb of Horath, which he'd left sitting on a table between the bar and the stage. He packed it into his backpack. 'Don't worry, Mosh, I'm sure White Lion will clean up the mess before he goes, and if not, you're hardly going to notice another stain in this mosh-pit.'

Without waiting for a response, Seth jumped down into the concrete pit.

*Okay, so without that talisman, I'll have to do this the hard way. The only way to force an appearance with Summon is to offer up your heart's desire. Unfortunately, it's a very literal translation.*

Seth held the large dagger in both hands and pointed it at his heart. 'I wish an audience with Summon and I wish it now. I offer my heart's desire in exchange.' Seth drove the dagger into his chest and through his heart before he collapsed, dead, on the cold concrete floor.

His body slowly faded before disappearing completely, but the bloodstain remained for White Lion to clean up.

* * *

### Heroes Squadron Headquarters, Canberra: 19 October 34 BZ

Bentaz Mullberry sat in the leather chair and watched the array of monitors before him. The news reports were fairly varied today: sightings of a strange demon—or maybe a vampire, depending on the eyewitness—stalking the Blue Mountains; the clean-up in Chile was continuing after Vicious Man's rampage there a few weeks back; loser supervillain team, the Laa-De-Daa Gang, were harassing locals in Manly; and of course, there were many segments on Lorraine Freeman's return to Sydney.

*Ah, Lorraine. What I wouldn't do to meet that babe.* Bentaz finished his can of Panta and threw it in the bin. *Sales of that soft drink have gone through the roof since one of the cans Manifested and became the walking advertisement, Panta Boy. Not sure that teaming up with Asparagus Man was such a bright idea though. Who associates soft drink and asparagus?*

Bentaz's thoughts were interrupted by someone entering the room behind him. The clock said they were overdue by about five minutes. 'You're late,' he said, swivelling around on the chair. 'I have to get to the meeting.'

'Yeah, yeah,' Faceplate grumbled as he tramped into the room, his grey cape flowing behind him. '*Again,* I have monitor duty right when an important meeting's being held. It's a bloody conspiracy, I tell you.'

*Or maybe it's because you're a negative prick and we don't value your input.*

Bentaz kept his thoughts to himself and headed for the meeting room. 'Yeah, maybe,' he said absentmindedly as he left. Faceplate just wasn't worth the energy.

Moments later he furtively crept into the meeting, scanning the room for a vacant chair. Inconveniently, the only one was on the far side of the large rectangular table they were all gathered around. *Déjà vu again. What is it with finding a chair in this room?*

Sitting at the head of the table was the government stooge, Tactician; this time accompanied by only one MIB, who sat on his left. Also present was Bentaz's rival Powerhouse; as well as Gridlock, the guy who shot domes from his hands; Tower Man, blond-haired, blue-eyed haemophiliac that could grow to giant size; Hologram, master of illusion, who may or may not have actually been present; Medicine Man, the team's healer; Razorback, the cyborg, mutant pigman; White Lion, who was almost never around; and of course, Bentaz's favourite mascot, Chuck Cheese.

Bentaz walked around the back of the room to get to his seat and had to squeeze past several teammates to get through. *Is it my imagination, or is there always a different shaped table in here every time we have a meeting?*

'You're late,' Tactician snapped as Bentaz sat down. 'The meeting started five minutes ago.'

'Sorry, Faceplate was late to relieve me from monitor duty,' Bentaz replied, already on the defensive.

'Typical, blame the non-powered guy for your tardiness. How pathetic,' said Powerhouse, who was sitting opposite him.

'Give it a rest, would you?' Bentaz retorted. 'You don't even think he should be on the team, you said so yourself.'

'I don't remember that,' Powerhouse lied, looking smug behind the mask covering his eyes. 'It's *you* who I don't think should be on the team.'

'Powerhouse says you've been taking credit for his work,' Tower Man claimed. He was Powerhouse's biggest fan.

'Now, now, Tower Man, we all know that Powerhouse is a silly-billy,' Chuck Cheese said from next to Bentaz. He was too large and awkwardly shaped to sit on a chair.

'Silence!' Tactician hated dealing with teenagers and giant cheese mascots from other realms. 'We don't have time for this; White Lion was just about to tell us something important.'

'I was? Oh yeah.' White Lion stopped zoning off and refocused on the meeting.

*Is he stoned?*

'So, I have it from a reliable source that there is some serious evil afoot—evil that could threaten existence itself!' The ancient lion-man had found that teenagers thrived on drama. 'It has something to do with Christmas, evil gods and World Eaters, but I can't recall the details. My memory's not what it used to be.'

'Does this have anything to do with that Satanist thing we were looking into a while ago?' Hologram asked as he created images of little devil heads in the air.

'Yeah, I thought that was all resolved,' Gridlock added, firing a mini-dome from his hand around one of the devil heads.

Medicine Man also said something, but no one heard him through the gasmask he wore over his skin-tight HAZMAT suit.

'Yeah, maybe,' White Lion said in answer to Hologram's question.

'Further evidence has come to light, and we now believe that Bentaz may have been right when he said that Satanic cult, Lucifer's Coven, was up to something.' Tactician leaned forward and his suit whirred in response. 'I'm now going to suggest we focus our attention on them.'

'But Hellgoat and I tried that and they threatened us with lawyers and the media,' Bentaz recalled.

'You let me worry about that,' Tactician reassured. He looked at the MIB. 'We have agents everywhere—lawyers and the press won't be a problem.'

*That sounds a little sinister.*

'Wait a minute; I thought we were meant to be apprehending Vicious Man. Are you saying we're back to chasing ghosts?' Powerhouse whined.

'You had these kids off chasing the world's most dangerous super-villain?' the White Lion asked, horrified. 'Some guardian you are, sending them after Vicious Man.'

'In case you hadn't noticed—and with the number of meetings you miss, I wouldn't be at all surprised if you hadn't—these "kids" happen to be the most powerful Manifest team on Earth.' Tactician wasn't going to be lectured to by a talking cat. 'But that will have to wait until we deal with this latest threat. Besides, we lost track of him after that infamous Gwar concert in Brazil.'

'I wish I'd been at that concert,' Razorback snorted. 'Gwar's my favourite band.'

Medicine Man agreed with a muffled reply.

'This is bollocks,' Powerhouse complained.

'Learn a new word, did you?' Gridlock quipped. Apparently, he was Bentaz's biggest fan.

'Enough! The fate of the world is at stake, you could at least act like adults,' Tactician yelled. The MIB remained impassive.

'Tell that to Ballistic,' Powerhouse said sullenly.

*Jeez, I didn't even say anything and I get the blame. He's such a dick.*

Tactician stood up and leaned over the table until the teenage super-heroes hushed. 'Okay, so it's settled. I'll contact you with the details of the plan once we do a little background work. But be prepared, it will be soon. In the meantime, be on the lookout for anything…suspicious.'

Tactician gave them all a look that indicated the meeting was over in no uncertain terms. They began to shuffle out of the room.

'Ballistic, a moment, if you please,' Tactician said to Bentaz as he went to leave.

'Uh, sure, what did you want to talk about?' Bentaz queried, sitting back down. *What lies has Jean-Pierre been telling now?*

Tactician waited for everyone else—bar the MIB—to exit before he continued. 'This is serious; it's about your friend, Hellgoat.'

Bentaz immediately felt uncomfortable. 'Um…what about him?'

'I want you to keep an eye on him, just to make sure he's not doing anything he shouldn't be,' Tactician said. 'There is a legitimate threat to mankind from so-called demons, and I want to ensure we're not taken down by an inside agent.'

'You've never liked him, and now you want me to spy on him? This isn't right; he's a member of the HSA, just like me.' Bentaz also quite liked the devilish rogue.

'We can't afford for sentimentality to undo us at this critical hour,' Tactician persisted, unfazed by emotional concerns when confronted by potential extinction-level events. 'I'm not asking for you to do anything more than make sure he keeps out of trouble.'

'I suppose I can do that,' Bentaz agreed reluctantly, 'but I don't like it.'

*Now that he mentions it, there were sightings of an apparent demon in the Blue Mountains. How many of them can there be?*

'Good. I trust you to do the right thing,' Tactician said, getting up to leave. The MIB followed. 'I know your contribution to the team, no matter what Powerhouse might say.' They left without another word, leaving Bentaz once more alone with his thoughts.

*Was that a genuine compliment, or was he just trying to butter me up so I won't feel bad about doing his dirty work? Probably a little of both.*

\* \* \*

### The Skull of Ra: 20 October 34 BZ

Anu Hopet paced the length of the bridge and brooded over the viewscreen before pacing back again. He'd been doing this all day, and his minions were expecting punishment at any moment. 'Have you learned who took my talisman?' he boomed at his cyborg assistant.

'Not yet, Great Armageddon, but I will eventually,' Disk promised.

'There's been an unusual level of background interference; it's been wreaking havoc with the ship's scanners.'

'I do not want to hear excuses,' Anu Hopet snapped. 'I need the talisman to equip myself with the Sceptre of Conquest, which will be essential in my battle with the Celestial Ones and this accursed prophecy they forced on me.'

'Of course, my liege,' Disk said unctuously. 'The city you chose to land the ship in is perfectly situated to monitor events on this planet— plus it's close enough to monitor this God who Walks Like a Man usurper.'

'Yes, I chose well, but there are around three million people living here. Are you sure you've concealed *The Skull of Ra* convincingly?' Anu Hopet was never satisfied and always questioned his subordinates.

*The Skull Band would be nothing without me.*

'Yes, Great Armageddon,' Disk replied, used to being second-guessed by his master. 'If anyone approaches, they will just think we're part of the surrounding park. We're not the only one hiding here either: there's a subterranean complex not too far away. I believe one of this world's governments operates it in secret. Among other things, there's a strong magnetic field emanating from its core and it is rocked by seismic vibrations at infrequent intervals.'

'Do you think they have my talisman?'

'Well, no, my lord, I just thought you would find it useful information.'

'You were wrong; I have no interest in this world and its inhabitants, at least not yet. I am only interested in acquiring what I need to steer my own destiny,' Anu Hopet clarified. 'However, I am interested to know if you have learned what this "Antithesis" reference Bodyguard kept repeating was all about.'

'Not yet, Great Armageddon,' Disk apologised. 'I am working on it, though.'

'Work faster or you may end up like Bodyguard.' Anu Hopet had commanded that his poisoned minion be placed in suspended animation until his mysterious condition could be studied, as his constant wailing had proven extremely annoying.

*Normally I would simply destroy him, but I need to know what*

*Antithesis is. Perhaps it is the name of whoever stole my talisman. With the Celestial Ones involved, anything is possible.*

Anu Hopet also wanted to know why the word made him shiver but refused to admit it.

* * *

### Grand Satanic Clubhouse, Manly, Sydney: 21 October 34 BZ

Marek Mahoney felt sick after the ferry ride and seeing the coven's newest Prime Locum strut around in drag wasn't helping.

*Why did Melissa insist on coming to visit this chapter of the coven? Why did I agree to let him?*

He'd travelled around to all five of the satellite clubhouses that radiated out from the main headquarters in King's Cross with the other members of the inner circle so that Karen, their pregnant High Priestess, could bless each in turn with the power of Satan. The place was packed with all one hundred and ten members of the chapter, as well as the inner circle, and the place felt like a kiln.

*Thankfully, this is the last one, and seeing as it's Matt's chapter, at least there's beer. Not sure that decorating it in the colours of the Sea Eagles was a good move, though.* Marek may have been a rugby fan, but he went for the Eels and preferred yellow and blue to maroon and white.

He squinted through his thick glasses at his fellow inner circle members in the cramped scout hall they'd rented for their meetings. They were all there: inbred Floyd, creepy Navid, peculiar Lancefield, muscly Matt, of course, and Karen, who'd finished her chanting, leaving Melissa with nothing to dance to.

'Greetings, members of the Manly chapter of Lucifer's Coven,' Karen said from her position on the portable dais she insisted on having driven to all the blessing rituals. She had put on an incredible amount of weight during her pregnancy. 'This is the final clubhouse to be blessed with the power of Satan, channelled through me by the ancient knowledge granted by the High Mage of Hell—writer of the Satanic Scriptures and father of my baby, the Antichrist.' She delivered it all with a straight face and the sunken eyes of madness.

The crowd lapped it up and cheered.

*All right! This is great news! Soon we'll be all set for our big plans at the Feast of Lights. The only thing left to organise is the catering.*

'You really believe this tripe?' Blotch McMahn suddenly blurted from Marek's hand. 'YOU GUYS ARE ALL FUCKING LUNATICS!' the indelible spot screamed like a protesting trade union member.

Marek looked around nervously, but no one else heard the outburst. He kept forgetting the voice was all in his head, even if the blotch itself wasn't.

*Everyone just says 'cool tattoo' every time I show them this annoying mark. I'm not game to tell them it talks to me in case they kick me out of the coven and shatter my lifelong dream of being a cultist.*

'Will you shut up?' he hissed quietly at the unwanted stain. 'I want to hear what the High Priestess has to say.'

*Maybe it's magick, and that's why only I can hear it?*

'Yeah, whatevs, el loser,' Blotch McMahn said casually. 'I'm a free entity and I speak when I please, AND IT PLEASES ME TO SIIIIIII-IIIIIIING!' It started to do its best baritone.

Marek couldn't hear himself think, let alone whatever Karen was saying.

Suddenly the singing stopped and Marek tuned into the end of her speech.

'...so just last night the High Mage revealed to me that he has cast a forgetting spell over all the people of Earth—everyone but us will forget we even exist. We can now operate with impunity!'

The crowd roared their approval.

'Time to celebrate!' Matt called out as he opened an esky, confusing anyone who called them iceboxes or coolers. 'Beers for everyone, except Karen.'

*Hell yeah, beer! I heard that part, at least.*

'I demand a beer too,' Karen said from atop a mound of pillows. 'Satanists laugh in the face of doctors' advice.'

The beers started flowing and Marek elbowed his way through the throng towards the esky. As he hovered at the back of the disorganised queue, he discovered there really was a beer for everyone—even Karen.

*Matt always plans ahead, thank Satan.*

Marek finally made it to the front of the queue, but as he reached down to take the final beer, it was snatched from under his nose by the Prime Locum, Melissa.

'Hey, you've already got a beer. That one's for me,' Marek protested.

'It's my birthday today, so I deserve two beers,' Melissa responded petulantly as he opened the second beer and slobbered all over it with his slug-like lips so Marek wouldn't want it. 'Besides, I think you have a drinking problem, so I'm helping you out by having this.'

*Why, the nerve of this guy!*

'Ha-ha!' Blotch McMahn laughed mockingly in a shameless *Simpsons* reference.

Marek could only fume as Melissa turned to the group and proposed a toast to himself.

* * *

### The Territories of Xph'Ish'Matarg, Hell: Circa 22 October 34 BZ

Mark Adams writhed in agony as the cacodemon cut into his stomach with its taloned fingers. He was strapped down on a splintered wooden wheel of pain and was helpless to stop the demon standing over him as the wheel spun at a nauseating pace. He was determined not to scream.

*Unh! You can do this…don't give them the satisfaction…* Inexplicably, a Rolling Stones tune began to play in his head.

'You cannot confuse us with your music, mortal,' the cacodemon boasted as it plunged its icy hands into Mark's organs and twisted. 'Xph'Ish'Matarg has commanded us to discover your secrets while it sees to its other prisoners. We will learn why you can resist us so.'

Mark coughed up blood but didn't answer. The pain was beyond anything he thought possible and it took every ounce of strength not to cry out.

The cacodemon continued to talk while it worked: 'The other Lords of Hell are preparing to leave this place for your realm. Soon you will have company.' It leaned over and used its teeth to sever part of Mark's intestine, causing him to thrash about in torment.

*I just wish I could pass out, but this place won't let me.*

'No, there is no respite for you, sinner,' the cacodemon insisted, flinging something red and wet over its shoulder. 'Not even the host of seraphim know you're here and soon it will be too late for them to do anything other than defend the Gates of Heaven from the High Mage's army.'

*It must be lying, there's no one that powerful.*

'Why lie, when the truth cuts twice as deep?' the cacodemon asked before licking its bloody fingers. 'Now, what are you hiding here?'

*Be strong, be strong, be strong.*

It reached deep into Mark's pelvis and removed his testicles from the inside. Mark screamed until he ripped his vocal chords.

# Week Nine

**The skies above Sydney: 23 October 34 BZ**

Bentaz Mullberry glided through the night sky with his demonic friend and ally, Hellgoat.

*I can't believe Mum let me out on a school night; either she's distracted by all the fighting between Dad and Yam, or she thinks that saving the world is more important than an early night.* He guessed it was probably the first one.

The unlikely duo banked around Centrepoint Tower and took off towards the south. The city lights sparkled below them like a sea of jewels.

*I suppose I better get on with it. I'm not just here to go on patrol with Hellgoat; I have to know if he's really been deceiving us.*

'It's funny, I've spent the last few weeks scouring the city, but I can't seem to remember why,' Hellgoat began before Bentaz could ask his awkward questions. 'I'm sure it was important, but the more I think about it, the further it slips from my mind. All I know is I found something in six locations around Sydney: Ashfield, Banksmeadow, Bondi, Manly, North Ryde and the 'Cross, to be precise.'

*Grandfather lives in North Ryde...*

'You haven't visited the Blue Mountains among all those locations, have you?' Bentaz enquired. There, it was out.

'Not to my knowledge. I've just kept to the inner city,' Hellgoat responded, as they flew through a low cloud. 'Although with my sudden memory loss, I guess it's possible. Why do you ask?'

'There've been reports of demon sightings in the area, and I just wanted to make sure it wasn't you.' Bentaz was sure there was something else he should be doing, but like Hellgoat, he couldn't remember what it was. 'Tactician asked me to look into it.'

'Tactician asked you to spy on me, is more like it,' Hellgoat snarled. 'I don't know how many times I have to prove that I'm on your side.'

'Hey, I believe you,' Bentaz reassured him, looking at the traffic below. 'Your word's good enough for me.'

'Well, that better be true,' Hellgoat replied truculently. 'You're like a brother to me. I won't ever betray you, and I hope the feeling's mutual.'

Bentaz felt guilty that he ever questioned his friend's intentions. 'Let's do one more sweep of the city and then head for home,' he said in an attempt to move on.

The rest of the night's patrol was spent in silence.

* * *

### Barton Correctional Facility: 24 October 34 BZ

Walter Screw was sick of paperwork. Not that there was much in his line of work—most everything being highly classified and top secret—but the few reportable items he did have seemed to require a whole forest to archive. His hand ached from signing.

*Thank god I don't have to convert all these papers to digital, at least. I don't know whose bright idea it was to insist on retyping everything into a computer so they could save money on scanners—it's not like they're ever going to get rid of hard copies.*

He put down his fountain pen and handed the stack of papers to his assistant, who left the room to process them. He waited for his assistant to go before pulling a cigar from his top drawer and lighting it up. He took a couple of puffs and looked at his son, who was sitting in a leather chair on the other side of his desk.

'It's done. The Government Villain project is complete. We can use the prisoners to undertake covert missions anytime we want,' Walter said through a haze of smoke.

'That's great news,' Tactician replied, waving the offensive fumes away. 'I presume they can function as a team?'

'Of course. They've been training regularly now and should be good to go in a few weeks. We've got the legal authority to implant tracking devices into them in case they escape.' Walter twisted his mouth. 'I wanted to implant them with bombs, but apparently that's a human rights violation. You'd think they'd make an exception given the project's role in keeping a lot of politicians' dirty laundry out of the press, but no, not this time apparently. Have to wait for the opposition to get in before we'll get approval for that.'

'Something for you to look forward to, no doubt,' Tactician stated. 'So anyway, I believe I have a date for this...this event, and appropriately enough it appears to be Christmas day.'

'That's a strange coincidence.' Walter felt an odd sensation wash over him. He stroked his moustache subconsciously.

'I don't believe that it is; I think it's supposed to be symbolic. Anyway, I've reassigned several of our regular and special units, including some of our Manifest units. I even put the word out to Toby Kim from Xenotech Inc, who's going to put his X-Droids on alert.' Tactician's suit whirred as he sat back in the chair. 'The only problem is we don't know where it's going to happen—could be anywhere. We can only worry about this country and let the UN deal with anything offshore. I have a feeling it's going to be here though, which is why there are so many Manifests in this country.'

'Could be you're onto something there, son.' They were alone and Walter now found it a sort of game to see if his son would insist on being called by his codename.

Tactician didn't bite and continued talking about their plans. 'I split up the Battle Suits and put Cougar in Brisbane, Tunnel Barge in Melbourne, and Concord in Sydney, along with Super Trooper. The HSA has our nation's capital as well as it being home to Commissioner Jacobs and Field Marshall Hobbs. Chainsaw, Clawsaw and Waterman have been assigned to Adelaide, Darwin and Perth, with the Defence Base and this place to cover the rest.'

'All part of Project Typhon, I see.' *And also your little Manifest black-ops unit, T-Squad, which I know better than to ask about.* 'What about those War Droids? They seem more useful than your pet Manifests.' Walter chewed his cigar.

'They're…not ready.'

'Or that girl you had locked up? The one with the power over rocks.' Walter wondered if they'd given her more clothes since the first time he saw her.

'Patient 1432? She's definitely not ready,' Tactician explained. 'Too unstable and too dangerous—her training continues, so maybe one day—provided we don't all get wiped from reality.'

'A minor technicality,' Walter laughed. 'It all seems a little silly, as any battle of the gods would surely take place outside our plane of existence.'

'Yeah, you're right. I have a feeling we were going to get the HSA to look into something, but I can't remember what it was. I feel like we're forgetting something important.' Tactician sounded unusually concerned; he didn't like making mistakes.

'You were talking about investigating someone, I remember,' Walter agreed. 'But now that I think of it, I can't recall who you said it was either. I'm sure it will come to me though, I'm usually pretty good at remembering things. Maybe it was in one of those reports I just signed.'

'Maybe,' Tactician conceded, 'but I doubt it.'

Walter doubted it too, and then the topic was forgotten.

\* \* \*

## Xenotech Incorporated Head Office, Circular Quay, Sydney: 25 October 34 BZ

Lorraine Freeman walked through the daunting lobby with her mother and entered the spacious elevator that was waiting for them. A nondescript security guard swiped his card against the control panel and they descended to the basement. The muzak piped softly as they waited silently. Soon enough the elevator dinged and the doors opened.

They exited the lift and found themselves in a huge concrete chamber illuminated by fluorescent lights. One bulb flickered in the corner and a foul odour permeated the air.

*There's always one flickering light, isn't there? Why is Mum taking me down here and why's she wearing her superhero costume? And what's that smell?*

Only then did Lorraine notice the collection of strange characters waiting in the centre of the empty basement. *Who're all these people?*

She didn't have long to ponder the question, as a middle-aged Asian man walked over and introduced himself, leaving the eleven Manifests to call out various greetings to Lucy from afar.

'Hello! I'm Toby Kim, Senior Operations Manager for Xenotech Inc, and you must be Lorraine! Your mother's told me so much about you.' He turned to her mother. 'Lucy, how are you?'

'I'm well, Toby,' Lucy replied before resuming walking towards the others. 'How're the kids?'

'Fine, fine,' Kim said, brushing it off. He seemed almost obsessed with Lorraine. 'Now young lady, have you met your mother's teammates before? I'd like you to meet the rest of the Xenotech Droids, or X-Droids, as they're commonly known.'

*I thought Xenotech Inc publicly disowned them and got them to do secret jobs out of the public's eye. What are they doing here?*

'I'll introduce her, thanks, Toby,' Lucy said, cutting in. 'Lorraine, sweetie, these are my teammates I've told you all about. Guys, this is my daughter, Lorraine.'

Now the greetings were directed towards Lorraine. She was first introduced to Ruby, a russet-haired beauty, who devalued her namesake by shooting the precious stones from her hands; and then to her husband, Electron, whose long, blond hair stretched out from his head from the same static discharge crackling in his hands.

*I'm not shaking his hand, despite his hunky features.*

Next up was Tendril, who had a long cable-like tentacle sprouting from each wrist; Photon, who had guns protruding from his wrists and was dressed in camouflage fatigues; and Neutron, a short nugget of muscle with a chip on his shoulder.

*How am I possibly going to remember all these names? I need some sort of dramatis personae to refer to.*

The remaining team members ranged from interesting through creepy to downright disturbing, and Lorraine hoped they'd be easier to remember. There was the robotic skeleton, Reflex; Lightning Bolt, an electrified cyborg with a shield in one hand and a thunderbolt in the other; and Doctor X-ray, who stood rigidly with his tattered, carmine cape covering his body.

*Is he wearing a rubber mask?*

Then she was introduced to Mudman, an oozing anthropoid with some type of gasmask for a face; and Crystal, a guy who turned into living crystal and sparkled like a chandelier.

*What sort of man calls himself Crystal?*

Lastly, Lorraine met Decompose, who was basically a liquefying living corpse, who could rot things with a touch and by far the most disgusting thing she'd ever encountered.

*Gross, he stinks so bad. I think I'm going to throw up.*

All of the X-Droids were wearing the compact rockets around their ankles, which was the signature feature of the team.

*Even Mum dressed for the occasion, so I guess there must be some reason we're all here, but I think I need some fresh air.*

'Lorraine, sweetie, are you okay? You look a bit ill,' Lucy asked, concerned.

'I think I'd like to get some fresh air. It was nice meeting you all,' Lorraine said, turning towards the elevator.

'Oh okay, honey,' her mother said, 'if that's how you feel.'

*Gee, she seems a bit disappointed. I guess this was a big deal for her, but I just can't cope with that awful stench. No wonder that mud guy's wearing a gasmask.*

'It's okay, this isn't a prison, she's free to go if she likes,' said Kim, blatantly staring at Lorraine's arse as she walked away. 'There's actually a specific reason I've called you all together. I've been informed of an impending threat to the planet, and as I have an interest in protecting Xenotech's share price…'

Lorraine walked out of earshot.

*Did he say 'threat to the planet'? Maybe I should have stayed after all. Can't really turn back now either, not after making a big deal of getting some air. I suppose I should sort out my own life before I try saving the world, anyway.*

She thought saving the world might be more fun as she entered the elevator and heard the same muzak that was playing on the way down.

\* \* \*

**Christmas Island, Indian Ocean: 26 October 34 BZ**

Dread Sedgewick cut off the man's last remaining finger and used it to stir his espresso. The man had long since passed out and Dread ignored him while he sipped his coffee.

*This place is a dump—had to search everywhere to find a decent coffee. Why the fuck did I ever come here?*

It was a rhetorical question; he already knew the answer.

*I'm stalling, but why? It's not like I can be hurt—hell, I can't even feel pain—so maybe it's a fear of losing and ruining my rep?*

He finished his espresso and stood up to walk around the ruined café, crushing the unconscious man's head with his boot as he did so. Several other bodies lay strewn about amid broken chairs and shattered tables. He walked outside into the quiet street, stepping over the shredded corpses of the diners he'd defenestrated earlier.

The street was silent on account of everyone being dead, and those that were lucky enough to have survived Dread's assault had long since fled. He soon became bored with looking at devastation.

*Mosh is right: I'm not as likeable when moping around, so it's time for some action. Maybe what I need is a sparring partner to practise on before I go and pick a fight with Dad's secret family, and I know just the person for the job.*

He walked the short distance to the beach, waded into the water and began to swim.

\* \* \*

**Undisclosed location: 27 October 34 BZ**

Courtney Yeht was sleeping when the door to her room suddenly hissed open and Phil entered, accompanied by two orderlies. 'Sorry to wake you at this hour, Courtney, but you have a visitor,' he said.

She was still groggy from sleep and wasn't sure she'd heard him correctly. 'Huh? Phil, what's going on?' she murmured, her voice thick with slumber.

'I said you have a visitor. Now get up and get dressed, we don't want to keep him waiting.'

*Him? Who could be here to see me?*

She was hesitant to go, but nevertheless changed into her hospital gown and followed Phil and the orderlies from the room. Any concerns of modesty had disappeared long ago.

'I hope you feel up to putting on a show on such short notice, but I have every confidence in your abilities,' Phil said as they walked through the airlock and into the main ward.

As soon as she crossed the threshold, she felt the nausea that was her constant companion when confined slough from her like a second skin. As it left her, she was bombarded by the vibrations that coursed through her from the floor and she became aware of every little thing.

*Phil and Amy keep telling me it's bad to listen to the floor unless they ask me to, but it's not like I can help it—it just happens.*

The floor told Courtney that the person who waited for her was someone she'd met before, although she couldn't quite remember how she knew.

*My guest has a unique vibrational signature, like he's wearing a mechanised suit or something.*

It wasn't long before the group entered the training room and Courtney could see her visitor sitting at the observation table. He was indeed wearing a mechanised suit; one made of a shiny green metal that whirred with every movement. On his head sat a concealing helmet with a blue visor, his face below the visor the only exposed part of him.

*Where do I know this guy from?*

'Courtney, I'd like you to meet our sponsor, Tactician,' Phil said genially as she was escorted over to the table.

'Courtney?' Tactician asked, perplexed. 'I thought her name was Patient 1432?'

'Uh, we gave her a new name, as she wanted to feel like everyone else,' Phil stammered. He appeared to be scared of Tactician.

'Very well,' Tactician said, standing and extending a hand to Courtney. 'Pleased to meet you, *Courtney*. I've heard so much about you.'

'Um…you're welcome,' she replied, shaking his hand. 'Have we met before? You seem very familiar.'

'No, this is the first time,' he lied. 'I've heard nothing but good things about you, however, and have taken this opportunity to see you in person. I apologise for the hour, but I'm a very busy man.'

'Thank you for taking the time to come,' Phil interjected as he fussed over his ever-present clipboard. 'I hope she meets your expectations.'

'I'm sure she will. Now, if there's nothing further, I'd like to see what my funding has paid for.' Tactician inherited a disdain for time-wasting from his father.

*Paid for? What does he mean by that?*

The thought was quickly put aside as she began to show off her skills. After an hour she was tired, but proud of her performance. So was everyone else, apparently.

'That's very impressive, Courtney,' Tactician said, standing up from behind the sterile table. 'You're a girl of many talents, and will no doubt prove to be an invaluable asset. You may even be able to redeem yourself for your past actions.'

*Why does everyone have to keep reminding me of that?*

'Th-thank you,' she stammered, unused to praise from anyone other than Phil. 'I've been practising a lot lately. I…'

She noticed a quick glance between Tactician and Phil.

'Courtney, you've made us all proud,' Phil interrupted, 'but I think it's time for bed. Vernon and Akash, if you please?' He gestured to the two orderlies standing nearby.

'But…' She suddenly found herself being led away. She despondently obeyed.

As she was escorted down the long corridor back to her sealed room, she was still able to feel the vibrations from the training room.

'Why did you tell her her real name?' she felt Tactician say. 'What if she finds out the truth?'

'She won't…' Phil replied.

'She better not. She may be our ace in the hole against a threat we've just become aware of.'

'I assure you, it'll be okay,' Phil vibrated. 'We'll give her another course of medication so she forgets this ever happened and she'll never find the file. Give me a couple of months and she'll be ready for you.'

*What's Phil saying? I thought he cared about me!*

She was in shock as the orderlies opened the door to her room and bundled her inside before leaving her alone in silence.

*He said there's a file. Maybe I should try to find it.*

* * *

### Fatty's Cement Works, Parramatta: 28 October 34 BZ

The High Mage of Hell sat cross-legged in a trance-like state as his consciousness bored through the aether of the higher realms. He'd chosen this place because of the plethora of ley-lines that ran through the abandoned factory, as well as the personal connection he shared with his ex-lover, Hilda—better known as the Manipulator—who had unwittingly sacrificed herself on this very spot several months earlier. It was the perfect place to scry on the Gates of Heaven.

*What better way to see what awaits me when I lead the armies of Hell to tear Heaven asunder? Though I'm sure they would now know of my plan, it behoves me to not draw their attention too soon.*

His mind took the very path his armies would use for their assault when the time was ripe: through the suppurated wound in reality he'd created when he shattered the Mystical Realm. He perceived climbing higher and higher, although it was just an illusion as the subtle realms were more than three dimensions.

*Upwards, ever upwards.*

After what seemed like an eternity, yet no time at all, the High Mage's mind finally reached its destination and was confronted by a blinding vista of radiant pearly gates that burned into his soul. The brilliance was almost unbearable, but he persisted until he became acclimatised to the light.

The Gates of Heaven stretched into infinity and appeared to be made of both solid sunlight and moonbeams. They were accompanied by clouds of chrome-coloured stardust that wisped all around it.

*They're exactly as I imagined them to be. The False Creator believes himself safe behind them, but I will prove this assuredness as nothing more than his vainglorious ego. All I need is to wait for the stars to align and all of this will be swept away and the dawn of a new age will begin.*

His vision could not penetrate the gates themselves, so he scanned the surrounding area for the Heavenly Host. Amid the countless seraphim that soared through the glittering clouds were several beings that stood out from the identical angels.

*I can see the False Archangels, Michael and Gabriel, and even the lesser angels, Life, Judgement and the Wraith. It appears the Four Horsemen are elsewhere, perhaps in another realm like the fallen Infernal Ones? No matter, I will scour all realities once I am God; none of these creations will elude me.*

The High Mage became mesmerised by the scene, as the angels' graceful flight paths took on a hypnotic pattern, and with their great numbers it created an optical illusion.

*Concentrate! This is all just a trick designed to dazzle any who would look upon these gates. It's funny, but the pattern they make almost looks like a giant tick's head. Mayhap it's designed to intimidate?*

He didn't like to think about the fact that it worked.

*I believe I've seen all I need to; Heaven's defence appears to be exactly as I expected. Now, I should return to my body before I am discovered.*

Kismet heard the High Mage's thoughts and was true to character.

Suddenly, the angel Life spread its enormous eagle wings and flew closer to the High Mage's vantage point. It had a male form and was bare-chested with a pure white sash adorned diagonally from its left shoulder to its hip. It had a golden belt that held its lower tunic in place, and it wore golden sandals and vambraces. Its head was covered by a finned, silver helmet with glowing fluorescent eye slits and it carried a phosphorescent longsword.

*What's it doing?*

Life turned to look straight at the High Mage and its eyes glowed malevolently. 'I see you, mortal,' it said in a voice like thunder and judgement. The image of a tick bit at his face.

Reeling, the High Mage felt his mind tumble back to Earth and he woke from his trance in a cold sweat. *They know. I must prepare.*

He slowly rose to his feet and pondered his next move.

\* \* \*

**South Western Sydney: 29 October 34 BZ**

Desci Adams looked at the unopened pile of bills and despaired. She could almost see the red overdue notices through the thin envelopes that formed a paper mound on the coffee table in front of her. Her stone-cold green tea sat untouched next to the heap.

*I don't know what to do. I can't pay the rent without Mark, let alone all these other expenses. They'll cut off the utilities soon and kick us out on the street.*

The thought made her angry, angry that the police seemed to be doing nothing about finding her missing husband and irrationally angry at her husband for disappearing in the first place. The anger gave way to depression, as she hated this weakness in herself.

Her self-loathing was interrupted by her children as they walked into the small lounge on their way out the door. They'd become so used to their mother's depressive behaviour that they no longer asked her how she was. They were just glad that she'd managed to find the strength to at least get out of bed.

'Where are you going?' Desci snapped, and immediately hated herself for doing so.

'Oh, Mum, I didn't know you'd be up so early,' her son Obie replied. 'We're just going outside. The block's got some very important visitors coming today.'

'What visitors?' she snapped again, despite herself. 'This isn't some sort of cover for going out with that Blandley kid again, is it? He's a bad influence on all of you.'

'Well, Nathan will be there,' Samara admitted. 'But that's not why we're going. Didn't you hear? Today the block's going to be visited by the HSA members, the Flannelled Avenger and his sidekick, Cloth the Flannelled Wonder.'

'Yeah,' Sebastian, Samara's brother, added, 'and they're being accompanied by those two cyber-Westies, Boganator and Boonatron—it's going to be awesome!' Always the silent type, if *he* was excited, then it must be something important.

*I guess that's okay. I just get so worried when they go out. I don't want to lose them too. Then why I am I pushing them away with my moods?*

'All right, go and have fun,' she said resignedly. 'Just don't be too long and be careful.'

'Yeah, sure Mum, whatever you say,' Obie agreed sarcastically, rolling his eyes. 'We'll try not to get into trouble by going outside. It's not like we do it every day or anything.'

'Don't get smart with me, young man, or you won't be going anywhere,' Desci shot back. 'Same goes for you two as well,' she said to Samara and Sebastian.

'Yeah, okay, *Aunt* Desci' they said, giving each other a look that screamed 'you're not our mother'.

The three teenagers left the apartment and slammed the door behind them.

*Get a hold of yourself, or you really will lose them.*

Desci sat quietly for a moment before swiping the table clean in a fit of anger, sending the teacup careening into the wall, where it shattered, spilling cold tea all over the carpet.

# Week Eight

**North-Western Tasmania, Australia: 30 October 34 BZ**

Dread Sedgewick gnawed at the raw thylacine haunch and crashed through the underbrush on his way to find his quarry. The three-day swim had given him an appetite and finding the marsupial had set his stomach rumbling. It was only after he'd finished worrying the marsupial's bone that he gave it any thought.

*Hmmm, I assumed these critters were extinct. Probably because they're so tasty. I guess this is evidence they're not all gone—unless this was the last one. Wouldn't that be a hoot?*

He tossed the bone aside and focused on the reason he was in the dense forest in the first place. 'Hey, Supernaut! Are you out here somewhere?' he cried.

A myriad of bird calls answered, but otherwise the forest was quiet.

'I know you're lurking around here someplace. Come out, you Boer bastard!'

A branch cracked to his right, and Dread sensed he'd gotten a reaction. 'Why are you hiding in the arse-end of nowhere anyway, you fucking pussy?'

The crashing grew louder until Dread was confronted by an enormous two-and-a-half-metre tall juggernaut in jet-black armour. The only distinguishing feature in the otherwise plain metal plating that covered his entire body was his spiked helmet with triangular eye-slots that revealed his angry, bigoted eyes. The helm was girt by a cage-like structure attached to both the single spike on the top of his head and the gorget underneath his chin.

'There you are, you clanking lummox. I knew you must be around here, as it's the only place someone of your ungainly stature could get about unnoticed. Oh, and it's also the last place you were sighted, so the odds were in my favour,' Dread said matter-of-factly. 'How've you been, you Afrikaner arsehole?'

'You,' Supernaut said disgustedly.

'Me,' Dread replied genially, flashing a toothy grin. He still had pieces of Tasmanian tiger stuck between his teeth.

'Why have you sought me out?' Supernaut said cautiously. He'd heard of Dread's reputation for wanton destruction but hoped maybe there was more to him.

'I need someone to practise my moves on,' he responded, quashing any hope Supernaut had of an alliance. 'I thought about having a few rounds with Desecrate, but he still has to play bass for Poseidon's Haemorrhage, so I picked you instead. If you like, I can sign my name in that rusty armour of yours.'

'You tempt fate by provoking my ire.' Supernaut clenched his mighty fists.

'Your ire? Tone it down, Shakespeare,' Dread mocked, morphing his fingers into blades. 'If your "ire" was anything to worry about, you wouldn't have fled South Africa after Mandela became president. But nice work in Seychelles, by the way. It's just a shame you bollocksed it up and an easy coup turned into a fruitless civil war—I guess they're all living in fear of your ire too. Tell me, is there some sort of "ire" club I can join?'

'You dare say the name of that kefir pretender in my presence?' Supernaut raged, ignoring the reference to the Seychelles incident. 'You dare insult me?'

'I dare anything,' Dread declared. 'Now are we going to spar, or am I going to have to resort to more "ire" quips?'

Supernaut charged without further comment and slammed his fist into Dread's face with the force of a locomotive. Dread was repelled by the punch and sent flying through the surrounding trees, which smashed with his passing. Supernaut was on him moments later, slamming his armoured fists into his face. The pummelling sounded like a cannon volley.

Supernaut rose up and jumped with both feet on Dread's chest, driving him deep into the damp earth. 'So much for the legendary Vicious Man,' he said. 'Looks like you were all talk.' He turned to walk away when he heard a giggle.

'What are you, a chiropractor? No wonder you couldn't conquer a couple of small islands.' Dread sounded disappointed as he climbed out of the freshly made pit and dusted himself off. 'I was hoping for a bit of a challenge and instead I get some piss-weak loser who can't take a joke. You should be ashamed of yourself for wasting my time.'

'It's not possible,' Supernaut said incredulously and with a hint of fear in his voice. 'That should have shattered a mountain.'

'Maybe a mountain made out of mashed potato, but you'll find I'm a close encounter of a different kind.' He licked the ends of his finger blades. 'Now, I think it's time I showed you what "provoking my ire" really means.'

He sprang into action with pantherish agility and knocked Supernaut's feet out from under him with a sweeping kick. He then booted Supernaut in the stomach and sent him smashing into a fallen trunk, which shattered from the impact. Dread then pulled a knife from a pocket dimension and flung it at Supernaut's faceplate. Instantly, the cage surrounding his head rotated at blinding speed, which clipped the knife and sent it careening into the brush.

'Well, that was original. Never seen anyone deflect one of my blades like that.' Dread rarely offered praise. 'I was wondering why you had that silly cage around your head; good to see it wasn't just a bad fashion statement.' He was also a people-person.

Supernaut climbed to his feet and ran his hands over the dent in his breastplate before turning to stare at Dread. His wide eyes could be seen clearly through the triangular eye-slots of his helmet. He looked back at the dent in his chest and suddenly sprinted off into the bush.

Dread couldn't believe the rudeness of some people. 'Seriously? That's it? You're just going to cut and run without saying goodbye?'

Supernaut didn't reply and continued to beat a hasty (and noisy) retreat. Dread sprinted after him, extending his hand and telepathically retrieving his lost knife as he did so. He tackled Supernaut and slammed his head into a nearby mossy rock. 'This is the thanks I get for honouring you with a sparring session? Even Desecrate would've been more of a challenge, and he's gotten a bit tubby of late.'

'Leave me be. You're insane!' Supernaut cried as Dread turned him over and tore the cage from his helmet.

'But I haven't signed your armour yet!' He began to carve his name into Supernaut's faceplate. He signed it 'Vicious Man' so everyone would know who did it, as his real name wasn't widely known. He then stunned him with a crunching head-butt.

Supernaut lay unconscious while Dread sat on his chest and sparked up a cigarette, deep in thought.

*I could kill him and make a belt from his teeth, but I really don't think he's worth the effort. I'll just leave him for the AMPs to find—if they will in this bloody thicket.*

He took a couple of puffs and finished his smoke prematurely, flicking it into one of Supernaut's eye-slots.

*What a fucking waste of time this was. I should have just gone straight after Dad's family, rather than swim all this way for nothing. It's decided then; time to get down to it.*

Dread got up from his resting place and carved a dimensional doorway in the air.

\* \* \*

**Fatty's Cement Works, Parramatta: 31 October 34 BZ**

The High Mage of Hell channelled the power of the ley-lines into his glowing form. His hateful eyes flashed red and a malicious grin spread across his face.

*Lesser mages would think this was just one big ley-line, but the truth is it's a weave of multiple threads that stretch far and wide, soon to be a knot as I absorb it all into me. And today it flows easily; such is the power of Halloween, despite it being reversed in this hemisphere.*

It was approaching midnight and the whole area was blanketed in darkness, with the only light emanating from the High Mage himself as he stood rigid with his hands extended at hip level. Energy crackled from his fingertips into the concrete floor. He needed to absorb as much power as he could before beginning his assault, and this was the perfect place to tap the Earth without drawing attention.

*Not even Lucifer's Coven knows I am here, and the forces of the False Creator should not have been able to deduce my location after they discovered me scrying upon them.*

'That is where you have underestimated us, mortal,' said a stern voice from above. 'The Creator sees all; he is omnipotent.'

The High Mage looked up to see a thin man in a white bodysuit with grey gloves, boots, and a cape that flowed out behind him on undetectable winds. His head was covered by a grey helmet that looked identical to the one worn by the great angel Life. His hands glowed with the radiance of Heaven's Gates.

'So, one of the False Creator's agents has found me.' The High Mage was unworried as he stopped syphoning the ley-lines and made his hands glow in kind, except instead of a brilliant white, they glowed deep amber. 'Who are you and what do you want?'

'I am Heaven's humble servant on Earth, known as Mister Invincible,' he announced, reaching out with his left hand. 'I have been sent on a holy mission by the angel Life to send you back to Hell.' His extended hand began to radiate brighter.

The High Mage struck first, bringing up his hands and casting bolts of orange lightning into his foe. Mister Invincible was consumed in an electrical storm.

'It appears you don't live up to your fanciful name,' the High Mage mocked as smoke poured from his opponent, 'as with all the children of the False Creator.'

The smoke cleared and Mister Invincible appeared unharmed. 'You were saying?' He retaliated by firing the High Mage's lightning right back at him.

The High Mage fell to his knees under the onslaught.

'It is my faith that sustains me,' Mister Invincible stated matter-of-factly. 'I simply absorbed your attack and sent it back to you. I do not hurt the enemies of God; I make them hurt themselves.'

*Got to focus. If I can't defeat the False Creator's mortal agent, how do I plan to take him and his entire host?* He willed himself to stand.

'You attack me tonight of all nights?' he said, changing spells and causing his hands to glow a light blue. 'You should've waited a few hours until All Hallows' Day.' Aquamarine tendrils snaked from his fingertips and burrowed into Mister Invincible.

'I can turn this back on you and absorb your power,' the celestial agent said with conviction. He landed on the ground and attempted to reflect the High Mage's spell.

A struggle ensued as both mages became locked in a deadly embrace unseen outside of comic books. Each one tried to out-will the other and their battle turned into a stalemate.

*Wait—he said that his faith is his strength. That gives me an idea...*

'If your god is so powerful, then why does he hide behind his gates and send you instead?' the High Mage said as they tussled.

'God does not need to face you, as I am more than your match,' Mister Invincible replied with certainty.

'I'm just toying with you. I could destroy you at any time. Soon I will be the new god and all reality will be mine.'

'Never!'

'Oh yes, and I can sense your doubt, too,' the High Mage taunted. 'I shouldn't even be in a position to threaten the False Creator if he was so powerful, yet here I am after overthrowing the False Lucifer and taking Hell as my own. That's not written in any scriptures, but it happened nonetheless. If even one part is false, is it not so of the whole? After all, isn't he meant to be perfect?'

'Y-you lie,' Mister Invincible said, but he sounded far from confident. *Got him!*

Mister Invincible's faith slipped for only a fraction of a second, but the shift in power was enough for the High Mage to tip the scales in his favour. In moments, only he was casting spells.

Mister Invincible lost his ability to reflect the attack and dozens of draining tendrils pierced his body. It was now his turn to fall to his knees.

When he was positive he'd drained all life from him, the High Mage took several steps forward and lifted the charred helmet from his adversary's shrivelled head. A desiccated, lifeless husk of a face looked back at him with sunken pits where his eyes once were. His mouth hung open like a burrow in his head.

'Invincible indeed.' The High Mage laughed.

A purplish-yellow fog plumed from Mister Invincible's mouth and eyes until it coalesced into an amorphous cloud above his pointed wizard's cap.

*The true power behind this mortal, no doubt.*

The cloud formed into a billowing demonic creature with long, clawed hands and an arrow-shaped head. Its body was purple, its face yellow and it rippled orange where two eyes and a mouth should be. 'We are Wisp and we have heard all of your plans,' it whispered. 'We have alerted the Host and now your secrets are known to all.'

The High Mage cast a destructive bolt of iridescent fire into the Wisp and destroyed it before it could escape. The air smelled of ozone.

*It looks like the False Creator can control mortals with creatures like this 'Wisp' I just banished. I wonder how many mortals out there harbour a similar entity?*

The thought was fleeting and he returned to syphoning the ley-lines.

\* \* \*

### Grand Satanic Headquarters: 1 November 34 BZ

Marek Mahoney awoke half-naked and sticky. He was lying on his back, and slowly the dirty ceiling came into focus as he tried to work out where he was. Then he remembered.

*Guess I went a little overboard at last night's Halloween bash.* He sat up and looked around the decorated meeting room. *I guess we all did.*

The other members of the inner circle were strewn about the room: Matt was curled up on the couch, Lancefield was sprawled across the table, Floyd was lying under it, and Navid was in the corner looking creepy—he slept standing up with his eyes open.

*Karen obviously went to her bedroom to sleep it off—she was partying harder than the rest of us.* He groaned as he got to his feet.

'Oh, you're awake, finally,' said an unwelcome voice from his hand. 'I've been waiting all morning for you to hear my rendition of "Summer Rain".' Blotch McMahn began to caterwaul Belinda Carlisle's hit with more volume, but less harmony.

Marek's temples throbbed. He went to steady himself on the table but ended up putting his hand on Lancefield's bushy beard, waking him up. 'Mum, is that you?' Lancefield mumbled as he stirred.

'Nah, it's just me, Marek,' he said, trying desperately to ignore the odious singing. 'Your Mum gave Melissa a lift home last night and you ended up crashing here.'

'That's right, he pinched my ride,' Lancefield said, sitting up. 'Bastard! Now I'll have to take the bus.'

The others started to wake from all the talking—all except Floyd who was still passed out and drooling underneath the table.

'What are we talking about?' Navid said, suddenly wide awake without looking any different from when he was sleeping.

'Keep it down, you lot,' Matt grumbled from the couch, tossing a cushion at them and hitting Marek in the back of the head, adding to his blossoming migraine.

Blotch McMahn switched from 'Summer Rain' to Snow's 'Informer'.

'We were talking about that dick, Melissa,' Lancefield said quietly to Navid.

'He's a creepy fucking cunt, that one,' Navid said, 'and I should fucking know, right fellas?'

'Navid's got a point,' Matt said, giving up on trying to sleep and joining in the conversation. 'Why did you invite that prancing fucktard to our Halloween bash?'

They all looked at him accusingly.

'It was meant to be inner circle only,' Lancefield said before Marek could defend himself. 'Why did you even pick him for Prime Locum in the first place? I saw him picking his toenails over the punchbowl, for pity's sake.'

*Gross, I drank from that.*

'Yeah, and he insisted on hogging the stereo after sulking because we wouldn't let him play his ukulele,' Navid added, somehow making the innocuous sentence sound creepy.

'And he wouldn't shut up about that video game…what was it? Oh, yeah, *Doom* or something. He must play the fucking thing morning, noon and night the way he raved on about it,' Matt complained.

'And you should have heard what he said about you when you weren't listening,' Blotch McMahn said, but of course, only Marek could hear it.

*I don't like where this is all going.*

'Look, guys, I'm sorry,' he said apologetically. 'I didn't mean for him to come. I promise it won't happen again.'

'It better not,' Karen said suddenly from the doorway, 'or your dream of becoming a Satanist will be over and we'll get someone more capable to replace you. Now go fetch me breakfast—I'm eating for two, don't forget.'

\* \* \*

### Freeman Residence, Neutral Bay: 2 November 34 BZ

Lorraine Freeman lounged in the deckchair and watched her two younger sisters as they splashed around the shallow end of the backyard pool. Lucy was off with the X-Droids again, and her other mother, Shara, had returned home to Nambucca Heads, leaving Lorraine to babysit. She was currently listening to Nirvana's *Nevermind* album on her new Discman.

*It's not so bad, I guess,* she thought as she flicked through the latest issue of *Stylish Girlfriend*. Her photo was on the cover. *It's good to be out of the spotlight, and I do enjoy spending time with Heather and Samantha. So why do I feel so restless?*

Lorraine grew tired of fashion and beauty tips, tossed the magazine aside and stretched out in the chair. Her sisters continued to play.

*I wish Mum had taken me along with her, but she hasn't offered since I walked out last time. I think I offended her teammate, the corpse guy. But what does she expect when he stinks so bad?*

Even the memory of Decompose's stench was enough to make Lorraine gag.

*I'm going to have to get used to a lot worse than that if I ever hope to be a superhero like Mum and not just a catwalk model. I'd rather be using my powers for something more than just getting my face on the cover of girly mags, but I don't know their full extent.*

Lorraine was determined to find out—right after her nap.

\* \* \*

## South Western Sydney: 3 November 34 BZ

Desci Adams finished cooking the noodles and served them into four bowls. Money was running low and she was forced to buy cheap meals for the family.

*It might not be glamourous, but at least it's putting food in the kids' stomachs.*

She set the table and called out to her children to come as dinner was ready. After a couple of minutes of sitting alone, she was joined by her family.

'Sorry, Mum, but we're going over to Nathan's for dinner,' Obie said, walking into the lounge with Sebastian.

'But I just finished cooking...' she began.

'Yeah, noodles, big deal,' Samara criticised as she joined them. 'Nathan's mum's getting Maccas to celebrate, as he got his licence today.'

*That fucking Blandley kid.*

'Then we're going for a spin in his Datsun after,' Sebastian added, and immediately received glares from his siblings.

'None of you are going anywhere—especially with that Blandley kid driving,' Desci snapped.

'His name's Nathan, and you can't force us to sit here and eat this when we're already expected for dinner at his house,' Obie said defiantly. 'What would his mother think if we did that after she bought all that food?'

'I don't care what his mother thinks!' Desci yelled. 'What do you think I've done? This food isn't free, you know.'

'Yeah, but you could at least buy something nice for a change,' Samara complained, looking at her watch. 'We'll be late if we don't leave now. We're going and you can't stop us.'

'I can't believe the way you're talking to me,' Desci said. 'If your father was here...'

'Yeah, well, he's not. *Mark* ran out on all of us, and the sooner you get over that, the better.' Samara stormed out of the apartment and Sebastian followed without making eye contact.

Desci was stunned. 'Please...' she said to Obie as he went to follow them.

A flash of pity revealed itself on his face before it was gone. 'Sorry, Mum, gotta go.' He left, closing the door behind him.

Desci sat and stared at the door. She couldn't really believe what just happened.

*Have I lost them too?*

She looked down at her bowl of noodles. They'd gone cold.

\* \* \*

### Magnet's Safe House, Bondi: 4 November 34 BZ

Naomi Bloodlust lay naked and sweaty amid a tangle of sheets and Liu's muscular body. He was still wearing his Magnet costume.

*I'm glad I made him wear it—feels just like old times. Too bad I've got to leave.*

She looked over at his sleeping form.

*I could just slip out now while he's asleep. I can't let Gorg find him first.*

She slowly untangled herself and went to slip away.

Liu stirred. 'You're not trying to run away again, are you?' he asked. 'I told you, we're in this together.'

'I told you that I fight my own battles—that way, the people I love don't get hurt,' she replied, sitting back down.

'Oh, so you *love* me now,' Liu teased, rolling over to face her. 'And here I was playing hard to get.'

'I thought we were just taking a stroll down memory lane,' Naomi purred, a smile crossing her face. 'Besides, I was just using the word as a form of expression. The point still remains, however.'

'Look, there's no point arguing. I'm helping you and that's final. You know how stubborn I am.' He sat up and removed his supervillain helmet.

She started to protest.

'Uh! The matter's resolved,' he interrupted, holding his hand out before she could begin. 'Now, we need to think of a plan. Okay, so do we know what Gorg's power is?'

She relented and decided to humour him. 'Aside from being "very mysterious", it seems Gorg can make people disappear. But it must be a trade secret, as no one really knows how he does it.'

'Sounds like teleportation powers to me,' Liu said. 'Though, I suppose it could be something else. Okay, so that makes him a little hard to deal with, I'll admit. Maybe we should focus on taking out Scar and seeing if Gorg really will honour this contract.'

'That's something I've wanted to do for a while,' she confessed, getting up and looking for her underwear. It was on the other side of the room. 'I just didn't want to do it when we were expected and outnumbered.'

'I still think we could've taken them, but I can appreciate why you chose restraint.' Liu paused to watch as Naomi walked over to grab her bra and panties. 'Sure, Scar can drain life energy through his open scars—have you ever seen him do that? Looks like little mouths—fucking creepy. Anyway, so he's the biggest threat, but after him there's what, his Seven Servants and a whole bunch of non-Manifest thugs. That's nothing; we'd go through them easy.'

'You're probably right,' Naomi agreed, getting fully dressed. 'Who is there? There's Tube, some freak who shoots chunks of his bone at people. Jake, the lamest-named cyborg ever. Scream, a screeching monster. Brainwave, an even more hideous creature who can implant thoughts as well as its DNA—and probably the most dangerous of the group.'

'Don't forget the ones who started off as non-living items. Like Grid; a living radar screen, Box; a fucking cardboard box that grew a human body; and Pad, the worst of the lot,' Liu added.

'I hear that one is really a used sanitary pad that Manifested,' Naomi said, putting on her boots. 'Fucking disgusting.'

'Just think: Fatmandu will probably still eat it!' he laughed.

'Gross…but probably true.' She smiled. 'I guess besides the two of us and a guy that can eat anything, we've also got someone who can shoot hallucinogenic arrows and control the target's trip, as well as a living molecule that can disintegrate with a touch. Not really sure what I was so worried about.'

'You were right about having the element of surprise on our side.

We haven't survived for so long in our line of business by taking too many chances.' He climbed out of bed but was already dressed. 'You know, we could always ask for help from some of the other crime teams out there, like the Deathly Duo or maybe even the Quartet.'

'Are we starting a band, now? No!' Naomi scoffed. 'The Duo are a couple of losers who are sore they weren't picked for the HSA, and the Quartet are untrustworthy. Rumour has it they were created by an ancient witch—probably the same one who made that cursed talisman I told you about. No, if we do this, we keep it in-house.'

'No problem, but promise me one thing,' Liu replied. 'Promise me you won't try to run off again.'

'I promise.' But she wondered if she really could.

* * *

### The Skull of Ra: 5 November 34 BZ

Anu Hopet was growing impatient. There had been no progress on finding his stolen talisman, nor the identity of the mysterious Antithesis that Bodyguard kept calling out to before he was placed in stasis.

*I wish I could vent my frustrations upon my useless lackeys, but dare not reduce my Skull Band any further. Not with Bodyguard in his current state, and Gurk getting captured infiltrating that prison for Manifests.*

Anu Hopet paced over to where his cyborg minion, Disk, was fixating on a panel readout. 'What news?'

Disk almost jumped in surprise. 'No news, I am sorry to report, Great Armageddon. I'm just trying to discern what is happening in that secret underground base not far from here.'

'I thought I told you I am not interested in the affairs of this planet,' Anu Hopet thundered.

'I was merely documenting it for thoroughness, my liege,' Disk whimpered. 'I've been unable to find the talisman…'

'I am aware of your failings…'

'…so I started cross-referencing the energy signature from the sand you brought back from…wherever you were, for any matches on Earth.' Disk was hoping he wouldn't be vaporised for being proactive.

'And?' Anu Hopet boomed, his red cape billowing behind him for effect.

'This entire city seems to be saturated in it,' Disk squeaked. 'There appears to be no reason for it, so I wondered if that compound had something to do with it, given the strong magnetic field and intermittent earth tremors that emanate from it.'

'And does it?'

'I can't say yet for certain, but it appears not,' Disk surmised, calmer now that he expected to live. 'I would say it's a Manifest that's causing the quakes—and a powerful one at that.'

# Week Seven

Courtney Yeht undertook her training session with unexpected precision and vigour. Phil and Amy scrawled furiously on their clipboards.

'This is amazing, Courtney, really,' Phil said. 'I've never seen you perform so well.'

'Are you sure you've been taking your medication?' Amy was always suspicious.

'You give me the injections, so you know I do,' Courtney said with more sass than usual.

*But I think whatever it is you've been pumping into my veins has lost some of its effect.*

'It's amazing, really,' Phil said, studying his notes. Amy walked over to him and whispered in his ear, but Courtney heard every word clearly.

*The floor hears every little thing.*

'Maybe we should up her dosage,' Amy whispered. 'I think she's building up a tolerance.'

'Nonsense, you're being paranoid,' Phil whispered back. 'Any higher and we risk poisoning her.'

*Maybe he does still care, but then what was he saying to that Tactician guy? I can't remember clearly.*

The medication may not have the same effect on Courtney that it used to, but it still messed with her memory. All she could remember was her need to find her file.

Unbeknownst to Phil and Amy, Courtney had been 'searching' for her file the whole time she'd been practising. By tuning into the slightest vibrations across the facility, she'd been forming a map of the complex in her mind. She imagined it was how bats saw the world.

She continued to search while Phil and Amy had their 'private' conversation.

*They're not as cautious around me as they used to be.*

They were finished momentarily. 'Sorry about that, Courtney,' Phil said. 'A fantastic effort today. As a reward, I'll let you pick a new magazine from the trolley in the hall.'

'You spoil her too much,' Amy objected, but was ignored. She subconsciously adjusted her eye patch.

The two orderlies, Vernon and Akash, came to lead Courtney back to her room and she walked with them into the hallway. *It's a shame I couldn't stay longer. I'm sure I'm close to finding out where they keep the files.*

She stopped by the unattended trolley and grabbed a fashion magazine from the top as her reward. Someone called Lorraine Freeman beamed from the cover, and Courtney felt an irresistible urge to read all about her.

*This magazine's pretty recent too—this year—they don't normally have anything from the last decade.*

The orderlies ushered her along and she let them guide her back to her sealed room, which she was beginning to think of as a cage. Just as she took her first step into her room, she felt the unmistakeable vibration of a filing cabinet being opened.

*Bingo!*

\* \* \*

### Magnet's Safe House, Bondi: 7 November 34 BZ

Naomi Bloodlust leaned back into the horseshoe pillow and flicked on the television with the chunky remote on the bedside table. News images flooded the screen.

*I hope Liu gets back soon; TV will kill me faster than Gorg. How long does it take to talk to a few contacts?*

She watched the news coverage about a supervillain known as Homey Killer, who was wanted by the police for allegedly murdering three youths in baggy pants.

*That seems like a pretty narrow field of supervillainy to me.*

'...in other supervillain news, White Hot, the fiery, hazardous enigma, was seen over Penrith earlier today...' the newsreader reported from the screen.

*Haven't seen that guy before. Seems to be more Manifests every year.*

Suddenly the television screen was struck by something small that pierced the window behind her and penetrated deep into the appliance, shorting it out. Moments later the television imploded into a singular point before vanishing with a pop.

*What the fuck? Gorg! Shit!*

Naomi dived in a perpendicular direction from the bed and went into a roll, continuing into the wardrobe. There was barely enough space for her to fit, especially when lying as close to the ground as possible.

*How did he sneak up on me? If he's a Manifest, I would have sensed it. Maybe he can mask his presence, like me? No time to think about that now—I need my kit.*

Unfortunately, her kit was at the foot of the bed. She listened for any noise that could give her attacker away, but the only sound she could hear was the ubiquitous traffic outside.

*He could be using some kind of long range weapon. Could be he doesn't have any powers at all, and that's why I couldn't sense him. Or it could be he's toying with me and waiting for me to make a move.*

She slowly rose into a crouch before quickly rolling towards the foot of the bed. She snatched her gear and used the thick wooden bedframe for cover as she hurriedly got dressed. She snapped her belt around her waist and finally felt ready to confront her assailant. A myriad of thoughts raced through her mind.

*Nothing happened. Why didn't he attempt another shot? He must've seen me—the TV was only a metre from the bed. Could he have gone? Why would he waste time playing around like this? Maybe I could make it out the door? It's only a couple of metres away in the next room.*

Suddenly the doorhandle began to turn until the lock prevented it. The person on the other side tried it a couple more times in quick succession.

*Get ready. Don't give him time to think.*

She sprang into the sitting room and alongside the door—making sure she wasn't in direct line of sight of the bedroom window.

The jangle of keys could be heard from the other side of the door.

*Wait a minute—that's not right. Oh shit, Liu!*

The door opened inwards and Naomi instantly recognised her friend as he entered the apartment. She reacted instinctively and tackled him diagonally through the doorway and into the corridor outside just as another shot fired through the bedroom window and hit the wall behind them, making a large, circular chunk disappear with a loud pop.

*Fuck, that was close!*

'Naomi, what the fuck's going on?' Liu asked as he tried to get up from the floor.

'Gorg. Stay here,' was her only reply before she raced down the corridor, down the stairs, and out through the foyer.

*To get that angle through the bedroom window, there's really only once place he could be. This prick's gonna pay for this. No one takes a shot at my friends.*

She recklessly dashed across the road towards the apartment block on the other side, sliced through the lock, and climbed the internal stairs to the first floor. It didn't take her long to find the door to the unit she was seeking, and she kicked it in without a second thought.

Lucky for her there were no booby-traps as she foolishly entered the flat in a rage. Sense quickly regained control and she cautiously looked around the one-bedroom apartment.

*Empty. This is the place all right—I can see clearly into Liu's safe house from here. He'll need a new one after this.*

A slight breeze rustled a single piece of paper nailed to the windowsill. She tore it free and read the hastily scrawled note:

Nice moves. Won't save you next time.

G.

Naomi scrunched up the note and threw it out the open window.

*Fuck you, bring it on,* she thought as she turned around and went back to find Liu.

* * *

### Summon's Chamber: Circa 8 November 34 BZ

Seth Zaraxom awoke on the floor of a darkened room, encircled by ghostly curtains of night. It was a familiar sight.

*It worked. I got an audience with Summon. So glad I didn't stab myself in the heart for nothing.*

The ornate dagger he'd used to offer his heart's desire was still embedded in his chest, but was slowly being expelled from his body. He pulled it out and tucked it into his boot as he stood up. The wound healed instantly.

He turned around and was greeted by a familiar figure sitting on a tall dark chair at a medium-sized table draped in a grey velvet cloth. As usual, he was busy studying the cards his miniature assistant drew from her body to hand to him, ignoring his botanical assistant, who skittered around his legs.

'Summon, Tarot, Bracken, my old friends, thank you for granting me an audience,' Seth said respectfully. 'I have come to trade, and believe I have something worthwhile this time.'

Summon looked up from his cards at that. The sigil in the middle of his otherwise featureless face flashed. 'Last time you said that you traded me an obnoxious Miasma entity for the Orb of Horath,' he beamed into Seth's mind.

'Look, I'm sorry about that,' Seth lied, pulling his knapsack from his back. 'That Blotch McMahn entity was driving me insane, and you'd never put any caveats on what could be traded with you before.'

'I still have no limits, but I feel cheated as this…Blotch McMahn… disappeared shortly thereafter and I was without something to show for the Orb,' Summon beamed in reply.

'Well, it just so happens I have the Orb to trade back to you,' Seth said, producing the shimmering sphere from his bag.

'I hear your aunt Nocturne wants it back—why should I not just get Bracken to take it from you?' Summon asked as he took another card from Tarot. Bracken stopped and turned to look at Seth. Its leafy face somehow looked hungry.

'I've never known you to use force to take what you want, and it's not like I haven't helped you in the past—without asking for anything in return, I might add.' Seth rolled the Orb around in his hands.

'It is true you acquired Bracken to be my earthbound agent after the Knight of Runes was slaughtered by the Soul Master, so I am likely to overlook our last trade.' Summon turned over another card. 'The connection is plain—the Soul Master was an agent of Gledandron, who you helped me resist, and now you need my help against more agents of the World Eater. Tell me, what is it you have come to trade for?'

'I've come for the Crown of Knowledge. Do you have it?'

'The cards are in your favour. I have the Crown.' Summon gestured to Bracken, who was suddenly holding the Crown in its frond-like hands. It lolloped over to Seth to make the trade.

*I hope it doesn't drop the Orb, but I guess it didn't last time.*

He exchanged the Orb for the Crown and held it up to study its magnificence. The Crown was living gold with four arches, each containing a diamond-shaped gem of a different colour. On the front it had an additional circular blue crystal that glowed in all the colours of the rainbow. The Crown hummed with power.

*It's so beautiful—more than I anticipated. To think, I don't have to give this up; I could wear it and become omniscient. But would I want to?*

His thoughts snapped back to the present as Summon beamed a warning into his mind.

'Beware making a false gambit, my friend, for another unwitting pawn of Gledandron was here before you—the one known as Merlin, who now goes by the loftier sobriquet of High Mage of Hell. He traded a bone amulet with my sigil engraved in it for the Soul Gem.' Summon returned to looking at the cards.

*So that's what happened to that cursed talisman.* He knew the High Mage would make a play for it eventually, but last he heard Armageddon had it.

*I've been one step behind since he unexpectedly destroyed the Mystical Realm. The Crown would tell me what he's planning, but was that a warning Summon gave me about false gambits?*

Seth decided this time he'd check with his sister first—she was smarter than him, as everyone liked to point out. 'Thanks for the warning,' he said at last. 'Now, is there any chance you could send me home?'

* * *

### Dungeon Cell 9: 9 November 34 BZ

Andy Trailer sat on the straw bed in the corner and felt confident for the first time since he was transformed from avid bushwalker to the gothic monster, Night Demon.

*Pulse Pounder finally has complete confidence in me—I have succeeded in insinuating myself into his trust. As long as I complete the missions he gives me, he's happy. He doesn't know I've developed a taste for man-flesh and always indulge on my missions. He doesn't even suspect the cockroaches infesting his underground base are my eyes and ears either. Soon he will reveal all his secrets to me and I can have my revenge. Not even you can deny me that.*

*There is no denying the will of Gledandron,* Wisp said inside Andy's mind. *You are fortunate that it is Gledandron's will that you should have your revenge. Pulse Pounder and Energy Lord both will pay, but so will the one directly responsible for your transformation.*

*Who is that?* Andy asked. *It was the Energy Lord who did this to me.*

*Energy Lord ordered your capture, but it was another, one of his elite, who suggested and performed the dehumanising experiments upon you,* Wisp replied. *It is Gledandron's will that you should now remember what was stolen from you.*

*Who is this person? What is their name?*

*His name is Doctor Frank, and you will find him at the Energy Lord's base,* Wisp answered. *It is a good thing one of those two campers you tasked to find it was successful. We now know where it is.*

*Yes, even if it cost him his life and cost me a friend.* Andy considered all those under his sway as friends. *I don't understand why I can't strike now.*

*Because you are not yet powerful enough—you must wait for the right time. We will tell you when, but know that it fast approaches,* Wisp advised. *Just ensure you complete your tasks for Pulse Pounder as required, and vengeance will be yours.*

Andy savoured the thought and looked at his cockroach family with love as they scurried around his bleak cell.

* * *

### The Territories of Xph'Ish'Matarg, Hell: Circa 10 November 34 BZ

Mark Adams awoke from delirium to find himself hanging by his neck from a burning chain and suspended above a pool of acid. He immediately began choking and remained perpetually in that state, as his tormentors never let him lose consciousness—unless they wished it, of course. The steel collar chaffed large strips of skin from his neck as he thrashed about, but the rest of his body had completely healed from his previous torture.

*So they can torture me all over again.*

'That is right, Mark Adams,' boomed the terrible voice of his omnipresent captor, Xph'Ish'Matarg. 'How else will we discover your secret? It is the only thing left in you of mystery. We know all your hopes, your dreams and your delicious fears; we want your secrets too.'

*If I knew what it wanted I would have told it by now, if only to end this misery. I tried to resist, but I feel broken.*

'We know that already, mortal.' Xph'Ish'Matarg extended its gigantic hand and turned the gallows around so Mark could face its murderous goat visage. 'We know how you hoped to make more of your life, we know you wished for another child before you were forced to adopt your wife's niece and nephew, and we know you fear losing your wife above all else. You fear she's too good for you and you fear she resents you for ending her modelling career. You are full of fear, Mark Adams, and full of regret too. We know all of this, so we know that if you knew what makes you so special, you would have told us.'

*I don't feel special, I feel cursed.*

'We wonder if your wife feels the same way,' Xph'Ish'Matarg said ominously. 'Maybe you should ask her?'

*Desci? Here? No, please no.*

'Yes, that is her.' The demon lord laughed. 'She is a sinner too, and we acquired her to keep you company.'

A female figure approached through the haze. She was broken and withered.

*No, please God, no. Don't let it be her.*

'Mark, is that you?' the woman said, drawing near.

*It's her voice. Oh, please God, no.*

'Mark, honey, it's so good to see you again,' she said, stepping through the haze and into clear sight.

*Oh my god, it's Desci. What have they done to her?*

She looked older and haggard, with clumps of hair missing from her cracked and bleeding head. She was naked and covered in welts. She drew closer.

'Desci, the acid!' he croaked with all his strength. 'Watch out…'

She seemed not to heed his words as she went to embrace him and stepped in the boiling pool beneath him. Her feet sizzled and a pungent smell of burnt flesh filled the air, but she appeared oblivious. Instead, she began rubbing against him.

'You like seeing me naked and beaten, don't you, lover?' she said coquettishly. 'Hmmm, you could fuck me right here in this acid until we melt and become one.'

'Desci…what have they done to you?'

'Nothing you haven't fantasised about doing, I know,' she replied with a smile, pulling him down into the pool. Mark screamed as his feet dissolved.

'Kiss me,' she purred, grabbing him by the back of the head and driving her tongue into his mouth. She tasted like ash.

He closed his eyes from the horror until the feeling of something unnatural burrowing into his mouth compelled him to open them again. He wished he hadn't.

Desci (if that's who it was) was gone, and in her place stood a hideous monster with a caterpillar face, its maggoty tongue busy wending through his mouth.

He tried to emit a muffled scream, but the worm-tongue was lodged down his throat and he could only gag. He bit down hard in reflex, but instead of blood, the demon oozed an acid that immediately dissolved his tongue, gums and cheeks.

Mark tried to pull away, but it was hopeless and the demon drew him closer and began to eat through his face with its caterpillar mandibles.

'We will have your secrets, Mark Adams, even if we have to devour you to get them.' Xph'Ish'Matarg laughed as the monster continued to feast.

* * *

### Close to the Mullberry Residence, Canberra: 11 November 34 BZ

Bentaz Mullberry walked home from the local shops after stopping in for a blue heaven milkshake after school.

*Thankfully it's now the weekend and I can have a couple days to relax. Not that there's many weeks left until I graduate from high school. At least that'll be one thing off my mind and I can focus on this whole end of the world thing.*

He took another sip of his milkshake and his mind started to wander.

*I hope the Heroes Squadron can stop this menace that White Lion warned us about. I wonder how he learned about it in the first place. He must go somewhere interesting between missions, which is why we hardly ever see him. Maybe he comes from another dimension, like Chuck Cheese?*

He somehow doubted it. Chuck Cheese claimed to be from a planet called Chedder, which resides deep in the Miasma. His thoughts turned to the HSA mascot.

*Apparently, he was exploring the Miasma in some sort of cheesecraft, when he fell overboard and that's why he suddenly appeared out of thin air at the HSA's inaugural meeting.*

Bentaz smiled when he remembered the look on Tactician's face at the time.

*He also claims there're more cheeses like him living there—gee, can you imagine if that's true? Something tells me that White Lion isn't from somewhere that exotic.*

He absentmindedly put his hand in his pocket and his fingers closed around the plastic stem of the Remembrance Day poppy he'd bought at the shops. He bought one every year, despite them reminding him of his grandfather.

*Will he ever speak to me again, I wonder? I need to give him some time to digest the bombshell that I'm the reincarnation of his nemesis from the Great War. And if that's not enough, Dad's not speaking to Yam.*

'I can't believe it's the end of the world and my family's squabbling like a bunch of characters from *Neighbours*,' he thought aloud, between sips. 'Who's got time for school?'

Bentaz suddenly became aware of the local crazy person watching him from the bus shelter as he walked past. The man was wearing a giant sandwich board proclaiming that the end was nigh.

'You tell 'em, matey! That's what I said almost ten years ago, and I ain't ever looked back!' he yelled drunkenly.

Bentaz wondered if it was some sort of omen.

'Got any change?' the man asked.

\* \* \*

### Barton Correctional Facility: 12 November 34 BZ

Walter Screw wasn't used to so many people in his office at the same time—he was in a restricted area in the middle of the desert after all. Luckily (for them) he was already used to them wasting his time, so he was still cordial.

*It also helps that I've got a great big honking cigar to calm the nerves.* He blew a long plume of smoke across the room, but it was hard to tell since the room was already full of smoke after the three-hour briefing.

His visitors were his son Tactician, his two MIB bodyguards, Toby Kim from Xenotech, Defence Minister Robert Ray, his second-in-command Rick Gordon, and Lex the stenographer, who was recording the minutes of the meeting.

'Thank you all for coming to tell me this in person,' Walter said after drawing breath. 'Though I wasn't expecting to have a mini-conference today, I understand we couldn't talk about such sensitive matters over the phone.'

His inner thoughts remained concealed and he was the epitome of professionalism. 'Now before we wrap up, are there any more items of business?'

'Just one,' Minister Ray said quickly. 'I heard you apprehended the villain that Tactician's little HSA black-ops subunit believed they'd fatally wounded. He was one of those Outcasts, what was his name... Bullfrog was it?'

'Bull*dog*,' Tactician corrected. Walter thought he looked surprised.

'I do read all of those reports,' Minister Ray replied, catching Tactician's expression. 'Why do you think I send Lex to all these meetings?'

'Yes, it's true, we have Bulldog here in the prison—he's being treated for his injuries,' Walter answered with another plume of smoke. 'I'm surprised he lived at all.'

'Well, I'd like to see him,' Minister Ray said. 'Perhaps he could shed some light on this whole threat you've got us all worked up over.'

'I'm afraid that's not possible, Minister.' Walter flicked ash into the ashtray.

'And why not?' Minister Ray wasn't used to being denied.

'He's lost his mind,' Walter said frankly. 'He keeps repeating the word "Antithesis" over and over again. We've no idea what it means, if anything at all.'

# WEEK SIX

### The Skull of Ra: 13 November 34 BZ

Anu Hopet was sick of the word antithesis. He had ordered Bodyguard from suspended animation to see if there'd been any change in his condition, but within no time discerned it was a pointless exercise and he was promptly returned to that state.

*There are too many distractions preventing me from focusing on the reason I came here from Titan in the first place. I need to think.*

He left the medical bay and headed to his private quarters in order to brood. Soon he was inside the austere chambers. He removed his heavily armoured helmet to reveal bronzed skin with short black hair and hard brown eyes. He sat down on the metal slab he used to meditate. He didn't need to sleep.

*I am glad the creatures that built this vessel, the so-called Evolvers, had the technology to allow me to construct a room for myself—and to my exact specifications, no less. It would have been considered magic when I was born.*

Anu Hopet's only other personal items aside from his battle armour were the broken manacles and chains lying on a small metal slab that passed for a shelf. He liked to look at them when determining his next move.

*They remind me of my former bondage as a slave for the whore-queen, Kyra Zol, and of my destiny, for were it not for shadow-being, Manifest, blessing me with one of its seeds, I would not have had the power to take the ship from its previous owners.*

He stood up, walked over to the shelf, and picked up the chains.

*It all seemed so simple before: get revenge on the Celestial Ones for this prophecy they forced upon me by defeating their champion.* But now it has become more complicated.

*I need to ignore talismans and Miasma creatures and secret bases and Antithesis. I do not need any of these things to defeat the God who Walks Like a Man, and defeating him will prove the Celestial Ones wrong, diminishing their divinity.*

He put the chains back on the shelf.

*Maybe I should have just vaporised the planet when I first arrived, despite it being dishonourable. It is not like I live here anymore, and destroying Earth would certainly cripple the Celestial Ones. What greater revenge could there be?*

Anu Hopet had determined his next course of action.

*Then I have decided. If I do not find out any new information soon, I will leave and destroy the world from orbit.*

* * *

### Freeman Residence, Neutral Bay: 14 November 34 BZ

Lorraine Freeman waited for her mother to tuck in her sisters before coming down to the kitchen. The staff had gone home for the night but she still remembered how to make cocoa. She made her mother a coffee, which had replaced alcohol as her drug of choice.

'Oh, you read my mind,' Lucy Freeman said, referring to the boiling kettle.

Lorraine remembered when her mother used to have a nightcap instead. *I don't think she's had a drop since LA.*

'What's on your mind, sweetie?' Lucy asked, accepting her coffee. 'You've got that look on your face again.'

'I'm just bored, I guess,' Lorraine declared, dancing around the question.

'I thought you wanted to come back home and escape the limelight?' Lucy sipped her beverage. 'Mmmm, perfect.'

'It's not that I want to go out modelling again,' Lorraine said, cupping her cocoa and leaning against the sink. 'I've made enough money for now, as this house testifies, but I was kind of hoping…'

'Oh, yes? Spit it out, dear,' Lucy teased, also ignoring the comment about who actually paid for the house. 'I think I know what you're going to ask.'

'You do? Was I that obvious?' Lorraine sipped her cuppa. 'Well, I was hoping you'd train me to be a superhero like you. If that's okay with you?'

'Oh, I presumed you were going to ask if your friend Sam could come and visit us here in Australia,' Lucy confessed. 'I've already invited him.'

Lorraine was unprepared for this turn of events.

'You know, Sam—known to the world at large as Beat Master,' Lucy continued. 'He's such a fine young man.'

*Too bad he's gay.*

'Oh, you mean *Samuel*; he doesn't go by Sam,' Lorraine chided.

'He didn't object to me calling him Sam,' Lucy replied indifferently.

'Mum, I'm serious about the training,' Lorraine said, trying to steer the conversation back on course. 'You said so yourself; big things are happening, and I want to be ready to help if needed.' Lorraine finished her drink and put the cup in the sink. 'It could be a bonding exercise.'

Lucy saw something in Lorraine's eyes.

'Okay, well, if you're serious, I can take you out bush to a little place I know,' Lucy offered. 'How does next week sound?'

Lorraine was surprised it was so easy. 'Next week sounds great.'

\* \* \*

### The Tomb of Power: Circa 15 November 34 BZ

The High Mage of Hell ran his gnarled fingers along the golden sarcophagus, pausing to admire the sinister ibis head carved into its lid.

'Fitting resting place for the prince,' he said to the five demons who travelled in the tomb. 'Clever, using him as a power source for this place.'

'We have had to be resourceful in the thousands of years we have been here,' answered Im'shtar, the demon of the reflection. It was not currently tormenting anyone, so its cowl was a featureless void.

'Hee hee hee!' cackled Ress'urekt, the demon of the animated corpse.

'Then I presume you're ready for what approaches,' he stated, walking around the sarcophagus and the twin pillars that bookended it.

'We are prepared, fear not,' added Racuse the Scalper.

'And you know what you must do?' the High Mage asked from the opposite side of the sarcophagus.

Saracuth the Keeper of Skins, nattered angrily at the wizard.

'You insult us,' accused Styryk the Disemboweller. 'We have aided you flawlessly and got you to where you are now. We even delivered the mortal to Hell for you.'

'Yes, you have served me well,' the High Mage conceded. 'Yet I have not become Heaven's challenger by taking unnecessary risks. So humour me: what is your next mission?'

'We are to travel to the nexus point at the preordained time to ensure there is no interference by the host of seraphim,' Im'shtar replied.

'Be especially wary—they know something's afoot. I have already had to deal with one of their agents, known as Mister Invincible apparently.' He'd been unimpressed by the egotistical moniker.

'We have clashed with that one before,' Styryk revealed, its talons twitching.

'Well, you won't again. I absorbed his essence,' the High Mage said. 'Just be aware that I can absorb yours as well, should you fail me.'

'There is no need for threats,' Im'shtar said. 'Now that you have the Soul Gem, you are virtually unstoppable. We will not betray you.'

'Although you will need someone to guard the Gem while you assault the Gates of Heaven,' Racuse said. 'It would be unfortunate if it should be recovered during that phase of your plan.'

'Then it is lucky I have someone in mind for just that role.' He enjoyed the verbal sparring that came with dealing with demons.

'Who?' the demons asked in unison.

'Who else but the Dark Destroyer?' The reputation of Hell's Assassin spoke for itself and the High Mage left any embellishments unsaid.

*I just need to do some convincing first.*

\* \* \*

## Grand Satanic Clubhouse, Ashfield: 16 November 34 BZ

Marek Mahoney felt he was being tested by Satan himself. It was bad enough that he was host to a malevolent talking spot, but satanic practise—which should have been a deep religious experience—was being ruined by a mentally deranged, cross-dressing loser.

'That Melissa creature sure is a worthless piece of turd-cancer!' remarked Blotch McMahn, the aforementioned malevolent talking spot.

*For once I agree with you, but won't give you the satisfaction of saying it aloud,* he thought as he watched his chapter's rehearsal for the big day. Currently, Melissa was telling everyone what they were doing was wrong and how they should be following his artistic genius.

Marek had seen enough and felt compelled to act. 'We're doing it as we were told; these invocations come from the Satanic Scriptures themselves,' he said to the group, bypassing Melissa.

'Now wait just a minute,' Melissa protested. 'I'm a savant, and I interpret the Satanic Scripture invocations differently from you. That makes me the expert.'

'These were described to us by the High Mage himself, so there's nothing for you to interpret. We must do it precisely in order for the magick spells to work,' Marek said to Melissa for the hundredth time. 'He spent centuries in Hell learning these secrets.'

'But I have a gut feeling...' Melissa began.

'Probably constipation,' Blotch McMahn suggested.

*It's a test, it's a test, it's a test.*

'You will do it as directed,' Marek said, cutting off Melissa. 'Now, we have to get this just right or we won't be able to conjure Rancid, the Dark Lord of Decay, on the Feast of Lights.'

'I was thinking we should summon Beelzebub instead. He's much more reflective of our cultural zeitgeist,' Melissa proposed. 'Plus, I've written a song about him that I could sing during the event.'

'It's Rancid we're summoning, and you're not singing anything—we don't want the Dark Lord to be angry with us.' Marek felt his faith being tested.

'Oh, of course, because my singing is so angelic,' Melissa replied, actually meaning what he said. 'I guess I'll agree to that—unless I just sing it with a heavy metal death-growl.'

'More like a death-rattle,' Blotch McMahn quipped. 'I can't believe I'm hanging with such deadbeats.'

*I feel the same way—they're ruining my spiritual experience. If only these two would leave, then I could actually enjoy bringing about the apocalypse. Is that too much to ask?*

\* \* \*

### Undisclosed location: 17 November 34 BZ

Walter Screw didn't know why he was back at Project Typhon and why they all didn't start using the secure phone line. He'd only just seen his son a couple of days ago—in another state, no less.

*I guess I should be thankful I got to leave the prison, even if it is just to visit another concrete bunker.* Although that didn't mean he wasn't on a schedule.

*I hope Stan doesn't leave me waiting here much longer.*

Walter's hopes were answered as Tactician presently walked into the reception area to escort him into the secure areas of the compound.

'Warden, a pleasure to see you again so soon,' his son said by way of greeting.

'S…Tactician, the feeling's mutual,' Walter responded, almost slipping up.

*Best not to play that game in here.*

'I'm glad you could come. I think you'll understand why I didn't say anything over the phone.' Tactician led him into a part of the facility that wasn't on the official tour he took earlier in the year.

'I haven't been to this area before,' Walter said when they walked into a room that looked to be part barracks and part medical facility. 'What part of Project Typhon is this?'

'This is where my T-Squad resides when not on duty,' Tactician divulged. 'They've been undergoing extensive training in preparation for…well, for whatever it is we might be facing.'

'I see they're currently off-duty,' Walter said of the squad members, who were relaxing on the cots that lined one side of the room.

Tactician took the hint. 'Warden, I'd like you to meet the Tactician Squad. This is T-Man, the team leader; Ron, our team cyborg; Jeffrey, who has the Manifest ability to be completely normal; Totem, a living carving; Spud, the team's cook; Knife, a Manifest kitchen knife; Froz, an alien scientist; Gumption, his alien assistant; Fire Axe, wielder of charged weaponry; and Crust, who is a Manifest...ah, don't ask.'

*How the fuck am I meant to remember all these people's names? Who came up with these codenames anyway? Seriously, Jeffrey? What kind of stupid handle is that? And are those two really aliens, or are they still being assessed? I can't keep up.*

'Nice to meet you,' Walter said to the group.

'I'm sure you have a lot of questions about them, but I'm afraid they'll have to wait,' Tactician said, leading Walter over to the infirmary side of the room. There were several gurneys with medical equipment attached, and on the far side was a glass viewport that looked into what appeared to be a wardroom.

'So why have you brought me here?' Walter asked as they headed towards the viewport. 'It's not got anything to do with that girl you've got locked away here who can control rocks with her mind, is it? She hasn't gotten loose, has she?'

'No, this has nothing to do with Patient 1432,' Tactician replied, his suit whirring as he walked, 'but there have been some developments on her. I'll arrange to have you read her file before you go. You also need not worry about her getting loose either—I've got both Super Trooper and Concord stationed here with express orders to subdue her if she attempts to escape. No, the reason you're here is in the other room. Look for yourself.'

Walter stepped up to the window and looked through into what appeared to be a quarantined room. Lying on the bed was a large man in black armour with red spikes protruding from his arms and legs. His face was obscured by a visored helmet with a grated facemask. Despite being hidden beneath his protective suit, his body movements indicated he was feverish.

'Who's that?' Walter asked, turning back to his son.

'That's Muscle, T-Squad's bulldozer. He was seriously injured in a recent training exercise.' Tactician paused to look through the view-port. 'Doctors say he'll survive, though.'

'He looks delirious,' Walter admitted, taking another look at the patient, 'but why's he quarantined?'

'Listen,' Tactician said, 'he'll say it again in a moment.'

Suddenly Muscle contorted and uttered a single word: 'Antithesis.'

Walter felt his skin goose-prickle. 'Maybe I better see his file too.'

* * *

## Undisclosed location: 18 November 34 BZ

Courtney Yeht lay back on her bed and flicked through a copy of *Stylish Girlfriend* magazine. It was the same one she'd taken from the cart a couple of weeks ago, the one with Lorraine Freeman on the cover that had captured her imagination.

She'd read the article many times over since acquiring the magazine, and coupled with her growing tolerance to her 'medication', she'd started to see things more clearly.

*She's not much older than me, so why does she get to live the life of a princess while I'm left to rot down here? Sure, I have Phil to look after me, but sometimes I don't think he's got my best interests at heart.*

Courtney thumbed through the article one more time before tossing the magazine aside.

*She's so fake. The article says she's a Manifest, which I guess is what I am. That only makes it even more unfair. She should have to be here with me too.*

She sat up and tied her blonde hair into a ponytail. She always fidgeted when in her room and cut off from the vibrations of the wider world.

*Or maybe I'll pay her a visit if I ever get out of here. But first I need to learn more about myself.*

Just then the door to her room hissed open and Akash the orderly came to collect her for the latest round of training. She immediately began to feel better upon leaving her room and felt completely empowered by the time she arrived for training. Akash escorted her to the table in the middle of the room and left via the opposite exit.

As usual, Phil was present, but it came as a pleasant surprise that Amy was elsewhere.

'Courtney, hello, I'll be with you in a moment,' Phil said distractedly as he fussed over a mound of paper files with the other orderly. 'Thank you, Vernon, I've verified the information is up to date. You may take these and file them.'

*I wonder if my file is in there.*

Kismet was feeling generous, for at that moment Akash came running back into the room. 'Doctor, you're needed urgently—the patient, Muscle, is having a seizure!'

Both Phil and Vernon turned around at the commotion, causing Vernon to fumble and drop the mountain of files he was carrying. The top file was marked *Patient 1432.*

*I can't believe it—that's my file!*

Phil and Vernon were still engaged in conversation with Akash, and Courtney used the opportunity to quickly slip her file under her gown and down the front of her underpants. She then quickly folded her arms across her waist.

The conversation finished abruptly and Phil turned back to face her. 'I'm sorry, Courtney, I really have to go see to this personally. Another patient needs my help, you understand. We'll have to cancel today's session. Vernon, please escort Courtney back to her room. Forget about the files—collect them on the way back.'

Vernon stopped sorting the files and led Courtney away as Phil went over to join Akash. No one said anything about her file being missing.

*They didn't notice!* She held her breath with excitement.

She allowed herself to be led back to her room and was silent the whole time, afraid that if she made even the slightest noise, her theft would be discovered. Kismet was on her side, however, and she soon found herself alone and back in her sealed room. She pulled the manila folder from her gown.

*This is it, the truth.*

Courtney took a deep breath, opened the folder and began to read.

\* \* \*

## Ashfield Community Hall, Sydney: 19 November 34 BZ

Naomi Bloodlust sat in the rented community hall with the other members of the gauchely named Blood Brigade. She was dressed in her black leather work gear and went so far as to wear her specialised war gauntlets. The getup went well with her bob haircut and intelligent emerald eyes.

*I may as well look the part, despite the embarrassment of meeting in a Boy Scout hall.*

She was accompanied by her teammates and they all sat in a circle in the centre of the hall. Curtains had been drawn across the large windows and the door was locked. Liu had even made herbal tea as coffee was seen as cannibalism by Molecule, the team's Manifest caffeine molecule with a destructive touch.

He was dressed in his sexy Magnet costume and somehow managed to sit gracefully in a chair with his cape. 'Okay, so why are we here again?'

'It was your idea to rent this hall as it's the last place anyone will suspect to find us, apparently,' Naomi said, crossing her legs. 'I'm not entirely convinced.'

'Could be you're onto something,' Liu replied as he sipped his tea. 'I found a dusty brown cloak in the kitchenette and a copy of the *Domesday Book*—maybe someone's trying to bring about the apocalypse through a census?'

'Funny you should say that,' said Spindler, his psychedelic outfit making it hard for anyone to take him seriously. 'There's talk on the street that something big's going down; some people are saying it *is* the apocalypse.'

'And what, you think that the person who left the cloak and book is somehow involved, and what's more, is bringing about the apocalypse from this Scout hall?' Naomi scoffed. 'Don't be absurd. No, we should be focusing on the problem at hand.'

'Miss Bloodlust's right,' said Fatmandu, the beach-ball-shaped eating machine. 'The apocalypse is out of our sphere of influence.'

Molecule clapped its hands in agreement.

'Okay then, we need to go over the plan to take out Scar and Gorg, and anyone else if need be,' Liu said before finishing his tea and putting the cup by his chair leg.

'We've covered this already: we storm Scar's warehouse and take him and his flunkies by surprise,' Spindler said. 'How many times do we have to go over this?'

'Yeah, I'm hungry,' Fatmandu added.

'Well, unless one of you has montage powers, then we're going to go over it bit by bit until it becomes second nature,' Naomi snapped. 'Now once more from the top…'

The Blood Brigade was named after Naomi for a reason.

# WEEK FIVE

### The Moon: 20 November 34 BZ

Bentaz Mullberry sat on his wooden deckchair and looked up from the crater at the Earth as it hung in the sky. He was listening to They Might be Giants on his Walkman in the vain hope that they would cheer him up. It was no use; he had too much on his mind.

*I just can't seem to relax of late. I'm worried about my family but most of all I'm worried about this upcoming doom that's set for Christmas Day.*

He aimlessly fired an energy beam from his hand at a pile of rocks, pulverising them to dust.

*We still don't know who's behind it or where the hammer will fall, yet I have a feeling we had suspects in mind but have somehow forgotten who they are. Weird.*

He took off his Walkman and stowed it in the pocket on his belt.

*On top of that, the HSA is expected to apprehend that psycho, Vicious Man, who's probably the most dangerous man alive. Maybe he's behind this deadly threat to all existence? He's certainly evil enough. Either way, I'm not looking forward to facing him again. Last time I barely escaped with my life. Is it okay to be scared?*

He took a shot at another pile of rocks further away. This time he missed.

*I can't be off my game like this if I'm to confront Vicious Man. What's his beef with everyone anyway? Probably just fucked in the head.*

He rose from the deckchair and took a final look at Earth from the frozen crater.

*Even though I'm a lot closer than Voyager 1 was, I can't help but be reminded of Carl Sagan's pale blue dot quote. How small all my troubles seem when compared to this. How can anything possibly exist that could threaten all reality?*

Bentaz had no answer as he floated off the deckchair and flew back to Earth.

\* \* \*

## The Territories of Xph'Ish'Matarg, Hell: Circa 21 November 34 BZ

Mark Adams sat strapped into a chair of razor blades and tried desperately to remain motionless. His long, black hair was matted and crawling with rapacious lice, and his demonic abductor had been tormenting him with nightmarish versions of his own family. Compared to that, the razor-chair was nothing. It still wasn't pleasant, however.

*Just have to stay still.*

'Your willpower is impressive, mortal,' boomed the giant, goat-headed Xph'Ish'Matarg as it loomed over him.

Mark had been completely healed so he could suffer anew in the chair, and from where he was positioned he had a panoramic view of a great plateau across the plains of inferno.

Below him, great hordes of demons hurried around in frenzied pandemonium. Most were monstrously naked, but others were festooned with weapons and banners proclaiming unknown messages in strange hieroglyphs.

*What's going on?*

'We are glad you asked, Mark Adams,' Xph'Ish'Matarg bellowed. 'The legions of Hell are preparing for the war against Heaven. Soon all reality will be remade and all mortals shall share your fate.'

*It can't be; someone will stop you. God maybe.*

'Foolish child, the...*False* Creator will be dead, and will join the false Celestial Ones in oblivion. All life will follow,' Xph'Ish'Matarg stated confidently.

*Celestial Ones?*

'Yes, minor entities that once defended the mortal realm until they were annihilated and scattered by Antimatter, the anti-god. It too, was overthrown, which resulted in a Mystical Realm appearing to protect the Earth from our incursions. This forced us to capture the elemental Ooblog to become our spawning matrix.' Xph'Ish'Matarg looked to the horizon. 'But those secrets are not for mortal ears; all you need know is the Mystical Realm has now been crippled by the High Mage and nothing can stop our ascent to divinity.'

*Someone will stop you. I remember that High Mage character saying that Heaven might send an agent to save me.*

'That would be wishful thinking; there is no hope for you.' Xph'Ish'Matarg looked down on Mark. 'We will be prepared for any agent of the Heavenly Host. Until then, we will prise this secret from you.'

The Lord of Hell gestured unperceivably and a blade grew from the chair straight up Mark's sphincter. He screamed.

* * *

### South Western Sydney: 22 November 34 BZ

Desci Adams sat watching the television and slowly ate her two-minute noodles. The screen was currently filled with images of talk show host, David Leno, who was interviewing the American Way on his recovery. She tried to ignore the pile of mail marked with threatening red letters on the envelopes.

*I'm surprised they haven't cut the power by now. I guess my pleading with them over the phone had some effect.*

It was late evening and she was alone once again.

*I wish the kids wouldn't go out visiting that Afflicted Existence, Nathan Blandley, all the time. Although I suppose I can't blame them. I just don't know how to tell them just how in debt the family is since Mark disappeared. I will have to get a job, but I don't know what to do. It's not like I can return to modelling.*

Suddenly there was a knock at the door, and her blood ran cold.

*It's got to be the kids; they must've forgotten their keys again...but that's what I thought last time. Could that strange guy have come back?*

There was another knock, more urgent this time.

*Don't be such a coward. Open the door. It's probably the neighbour or someone.*

She got up slowly, went over and looked through the peephole in the door. There was no one there.

*Whoever it was must have gone. Yeah, most likely the neighbour.*

Desci cautiously opened the door to look down the corridor.

The hooded man appeared in the hallway as if by magic. She stepped back by reflex, and the man used the opportunity to force himself into the flat.

'Who are you? What do you want? Help!' she screamed, backing away from the intruder.

'Be calm,' the man growled in a deep voice as he closed the door behind him. 'I mean you no harm, Desci.'

She didn't believe him and continued to back away. 'Who are you?' she repeated. 'How do you know my name?'

The man was cloaked in a black cape that covered his entire body. His large hood obscured his features, but even still, she could sense that something about him wasn't right.

He threw off his cloak to reveal a man in a black outfit with a stylised red dragon on the chest. His hands and feet were taloned and a sheathed sword hung from his hip. By far his most striking feature, however, was his green, Chinese dragon head.

*What the fuck is that?*

'Do not be alarmed. I am Zhang Po, unfortunately known to the West as Dragon Kong,' he said calmly. 'I am also your father.'

'W-what? My father died years ago...you...you're some kind of monster.' Desci thought she was losing her mind.

'I am a Manifest, not a monster,' Dragon Kong replied. 'Your mother lied to you. She was always ashamed of our love, so I left her after your sister was born.'

*Maybe that explains why Mum was always so cold to me and Debbie?*

'Yeah, well, I didn't see you at Debbie's funeral, so I'm reserving judgement on you being a monster,' she snapped with false bravado. 'I'm not sure I even believe you; as you can tell, I don't really look like you.'

'That is because my Manifest turned me into this form and I am unable to change back. I am so old I have looked like this longer than I have looked human, but if I still did, you would see the family resemblance.' Dragon Kong continued to speak calmly. 'It is easy for people to mistake me for a villain from my looks alone. I happened to be in Sydney after being manipulated into joining a supervillain team. When that came to an abrupt end, I thought I would seek you out.'

'I don't care about your adventures,' Desci said, eyeing the door. 'Now that you've seen me, you can go. Unless you know where my husband Mark has gone.'

'I've come to warn you: there is a great danger building, and I believe it will be unleashed in Sydney,' Dragon Kong stated. 'You should leave.'

'What do you care?' she spat.

'You are the last of my family and I do not wish for you or my grandchildren to die,' he replied.

'We're not going anywhere, but you are; time to go.' She couldn't believe her courage.

'Very well, stay. I believe your Manifest will protect you,' he predicted.

'I'm not a Manifest...'

'You know that the children of Manifests become Manifests themselves, do you not?'

'Well, that didn't happen to Debbie.' Desci was no longer scared, she was angry. 'She just died—like a normal person, and I was forced to raise her children.'

'Yes, it is a tragedy that her Manifest seed did not trigger in the car accident,' he said flatly. 'They are usually triggered through dangerous events.'

'I think you should leave now,' she demanded, hoping she wouldn't do anything crazy like lunge at him.

Dragon Kong appeared lost in thought. 'I wonder if *your* Manifest would be triggered by placing you in jeopardy.'

Desci didn't like the sound of that, and she felt her bravery fading.

Dragon Kong turned back to look her in the eyes. 'Let us find out,' he said, unsheathing his sword.

\* \* \*

## Blue Mountains, New South Wales: 23 November 34 BZ

Lorraine Freeman sat on the folding chair, staring into the campfire while sipping her hot chocolate and toasting marshmallows on a pronged stick. She'd spent a long day training with her mother in the scrub—chosen specifically for its secluded location and because she could cut loose without fear. Now it was time for a couple of well-earned creature comforts.

*I could get used to this. It's a nice change to get away from the madness of being ultra-famous.*

Lucy Freeman sat opposite Lorraine on the other side of the campfire with a steaming thermos of coffee and marshmallows of her own. The fire crackled in the starlight. 'We should get to sleep: it's almost midnight. I have more training in store for you tomorrow,' she said before popping a marshmallow into her mouth.

'Can't we just spend our last day spelunking in the Jenolan Caves instead?' Lorraine asked. 'We've been going non-stop for two days now.'

'Well now, we know just how strong you are—at least up to the size of the largest boulder we could find, and we know how fast you are,' Lucy replied, skewering another marshmallow. 'Plus, we discovered there seems to be no limit to how high you can walk on air,' she added.

'I also seem to be pretty tough,' Lorraine boasted, putting down her beverage and holding her hand in the flames. It didn't burn.

'Now, I can train you as much as possible,' Lucy said as she toasted her marshmallow. 'But none of your other abilities compare to your ability to inspire love and devotion. You could change the world with that kind of power.'

*Mum could be right; she stopped drinking the moment I asked forcefully and I don't think she even realises it.*

'Yeah, but I don't want to be some fashion model that people gawk at. I want to be a hero, like you were…err… I mean *are*. I think I'm beginning to understand why you joined the X-Droids in the first place. I had a lot of fun at Comic-Con.' Lorraine remembered the thrill of taking down the Hat Trick with Beat Master.

*Too bad he's gay.*

'It's not all like that, believe me,' Lucy cautioned. 'There's a hell of a lot of dangerous Manifests out there. Just look at that psycho, Vicious Man.'

*That's a point. Not even Mum wanted to take him on. And the way he beat up that American Way guy? That guy pretty much stopped the Korean War single-handedly.*

'They've been saying on TV that even the Heroes Squadron are scared of him.' Lorraine's green eyes glinted in the firelight. 'He's a special case, as no one in their right mind would want to pick a fight with him.'

'It's not just him,' Lucy said. 'There are other dangerous Manifests out there like Scar, or General Starlen, or Energy Lord or Pulse Pounder or...'

'Night Demon,' came a sudden rasping voice from the darkness beyond the campfire's glow.

*What the fuck?*

Lucy jumped up and turned around to face the sound but was battered through the campfire by a giant batwing. She disappeared into the dark bush with a snapping of branches.

'Mum!' Lorraine cried, leaping up to see if she was hurt. Then she noticed the assailant as he entered the light. He had green skin with long horns sprouting from his forehead and was dressed in black rags. Giant wings kept him aloft.

*Is that a fucking vampire?*

'You are mine,' the demon said, swooping on Lorraine with fangs and taloned hands.

* * *

### Blue Mountains, New South Wales: 24 November 34 BZ

Andy Trailer launched himself at the screaming girl. Her face was obscured by her long brown hair, so he couldn't see her face as she cried out.

*I like it when they scream,* he thought, swinging the girl round and tossing her into the campfire.

*Yes, the other one made little noise before you batted her into her tent,* Wisp observed, whispering in its gossamer voice within Andy's mind. *Now you must choose which one to capture for Pulse Pounder and which one to make 'friends' with. Mother and daughter too; how delicious.*

*But which one to use as a replacement for the scouts I lost to the Energy Lord? I need as many as I can when I finally free myself of Pulse Pounder and take my vengeance on them both.* Andy had been dreaming of the day ever since Wisp had shown him it was possible.

He looked at the crumpled tent in the distance, where he'd thrown the girl's mother when he first arrived, after spotting their fire from afar. Nothing stirred amongst the piles of canvas.

Pulse Pounder sent him on this mission to retrieve yet another guinea pig for his experiments and gave Andy freedom in his choice of hunting ground, as long as it was a great distance from Pulse Pounder's base in the Simpson Desert. Therefore, he chose to forage close to where the Energy Lord called home.

He turned around to look at the girl he'd thrown into the flames. She'd been hurled clear of the fire and was slowly rising a couple of metres away. Several burning logs lay scattered around in the sand.

*She is strong, this one,* he thought, moving in her direction.

*She would be perfect for our plans,* Wisp declared. *Take control of her and take the mother back to Pulse Pounder.*

'I will have your mind,' Andy said to the girl as he flapped his wings just enough to gracefully leap over the campfire and land next to her. She was on all fours with her head down and seemed to be stunned.

Without warning, something hard smashed into Andy's face and he saw stars. Several more followed with quick succession.

He fell back into the campfire and kicked the remaining logs into the eucalypts beyond the sandy campsite. It didn't take long for the dry leaves to catch alight. Another invisible blow connected with his genitals, sending needles of pain to his brain.

*The mother has become invisible,* Wisp said. *We can sense her soul. She is a Manifest—you can feel it yourself.*

*Yeah, like insects crawling along my spine,* Andy agreed. *Now that you've shown me the connection, it's more noticeable. The daughter is as well—that's why she's still conscious despite how hard I threw her.*

Another blow knocked him to his knees and was followed by the hardest strike of all, sending his face into the dirt.

*Fight back!* Wisp commanded.

Andy sprung to his feet and lashed out with his enormous wings, the very tip of his right wing connecting with something his eyes couldn't see. The invisible object cried out and became visible, revealing the woman Andy had battered into the tent earlier. She fell to her knees, clutching her stomach.

He quickly strode over and grabbed the back of her head.

'Lorraine, run!' she cried out before Andy smashed her head into the sand, knocking her out.

By now Lorraine was on her feet and frozen to the spot, unsure of what to do. Andy still couldn't make out her face through the tangle of her hair, despite having excellent night vision.

He unfurled his wings and glided over to her before she could run, grabbed her by the shoulders, and held her to his gruesome face. Her chestnut hair fell away to reveal the most beautiful thing Andy had ever seen in his life. Unfamiliar yet powerful feelings flooded him and made his stomach flutter.

*Is she an angel?* He was smitten.

'Let go of me!' she screamed, and he did without even realising it.

*What are you doing? Crush her!* Wisp ordered. *What is wrong with you?*

'Nothing's wrong with me,' Andy replied aloud as he took a step back from Lorraine, who was now looking confused.

*You were supposed to take her mind, not the other way around,* Wisp derided. *Possess her, Gledandron wills it.*

'You come down here and attack us and you say there's nothing wrong with you?' Lorraine yelled defiantly, unaware of Andy's internal dialogue. 'Get the hell out of here right now and leave us the hell alone, or I'll make you sorry you ever lived.'

*I…I think I should do what she says.*

*Fool! She is a Manifest and using her power against you!* Wisp was unaffected by emotion.

*No, she's a goddess,* Andy countered. *I can't hurt her or her mother. Gledandron will understand, being the benevolent god you say he is.*

'Go on! You heard me!' Lorraine continued to scream. 'Leave now!'

Andy was already several kilometres away before he realised he'd left.

*I'll just tell Pulse Pounder I failed. He trusts me now,* he told himself as he flew west.

For once, Wisp remained silent.

* * *

### Outskirts of Wangaratta, Victoria: 25 November 34 BZ

Dread Sedgewick snapped his uncle's neck and threw his lifeless body to the curb. He returned inside the campervan where his uncle had surprised him and waited. The former occupants—a retired couple on their long-awaited trip around Australia—were still seated in the front. They'd just died at the chance to meet Dread after he dropped in on them when they'd stopped at the side of the road for lunch.

He didn't have to wait for long. Soon the door opened and his uncle entered the campervan. 'I wish you'd stop doing that,' he said flatly. 'One day I'll think of a way to get even.'

'Uncle Seth, so nice of you to suddenly drop in on me,' Dread said with mock sincerity. 'I have to say I wasn't expecting to see you out here in the middle of nowhere in a vehicle I chose at random to commandeer.'

'You know, the Abyss can be used as a means of locating anyone as long as you focus on them,' Seth replied from the doorway. He was hesitant to sit down.

'You and my father use it too much for my liking,' Dread declared as he withdrew a cigarette from his pack and sparked up with his finger blades. 'Just tell me what you want before I grow weary of this family reunion.'

'Well, I can see you're stalling in confronting your father...' Seth said casually, trying not to poke the bear too much.

'Hey! I'm heading there at my own pace.'

'...so I thought you might reconsider joining me in the war against the World Eater,' Seth continued, ignoring his nephew's interruptions.

'I have the last artefact I need, now I just need warriors, and I can't think of any better qualified than you.'

'For the last time: bugger off. I've got better things to do.' Dread disliked most things, including repetition.

'Petty revenge against your daddy is hardly more important than saving the world from extinction,' Seth admonished. Being immortal meant he had little to fear from his nephew.

'Enough! Time to go, before I do damage enough that it'll take you a decade to reintegrate.' Dread finished his smoke and dropped the butt to the floor.

Immortal or not, Seth knew not to push his luck. 'If you change your mind, you know where to find me,' he said as he left.

*No, nothing's going to stop me getting even.* He lit up another smoke.

\* \* \*

### The Abyss: Circa 26 November 34 BZ

Seth Zaraxom sat at the bar and downed his pint of beer. He was joined by his sister, Lilith, on his left and his eternal friend, Bojangles, on his right. The proprietor, Mosh Lightley, was there of course, and also White Lion, who was worth mentioning this time.

'Did you hear that? You got a mention this time,' Mosh said to White Lion with unbridled ebullience as he poured Seth another beer.

'Huh?' White Lion stopped cleaning the glass he was holding and looked confused.

'Never mind, this skit's gone on too long anyway,' Mosh announced, turning around to face Seth. 'So, do I need to call you "your grace" now that you've got that?'

'Very funny. That was almost as bad as Bojangles' crack about it being my crowning achievement,' Seth answered before taking a sip of his beer.

'You love it,' Bojangles quipped pithily, lighting up a smoke he rolled from the packet of Smex on the bar.

'The Crown of Knowledge is an amazing artefact,' Lilith crooned, staring at the golden ring. 'Do you know who you're meant to give it to, yet?'

The crown in question was currently sitting on top of a cushion on the bar, which Seth had put there to protect it from the sodden beer-mat. It glinted in the dim light.

'No, not yet, but I'm sure Kismet will let me know… when the time is right, no doubt,' Seth said, putting down his beer and picking up the Crown. 'Maybe it will be one of the Manifests you all agreed to talk to about the High Mage. So how did that all go?'

'I'll go first,' White Lion offered. He cleaned his final glass and reached for the Smex. 'I talked with the HSA as well as that government stooge, Tactician, who surprisingly believed me and informed all his network contacts. That probably includes the Xenotech Droids and the World's Defence. Although good luck getting them to help if the High Mage strikes outside North America.'

'That's not a bad start,' Seth allowed. 'Was that all?'

'I also talked to a few other Manifest teams, but they probably won't be much help,' White Lion said, lighting up his smoke.

'Any help is welcome,' Lilith said, 'for cannon fodder, if nothing more. Who did you speak to?'

'Well, seeing as you put it like that…' White Lion laughed, puffing smoke from his nostrils. 'I spoke to Boganator and Boonatron, Asparagus Man and Panta Boy, the No-Hopers, the Newest Heroes…'

*The Newest Heroes? What happens when they're old news?*

'…and even the Crappy Super Heroes,' White Lion continued. 'That **Obvious Man** character is just too much. I also looked for the Failures, but word is they got whacked a few months back.'

*That's right, that's the team the High Mage's son, Hell Hog, was a member of. That could be the clue I'm searching for.*

He wondered why he didn't know that already.

'Where did they get "whacked", as you so colourfully put it?' Seth queried.

'In Sydney, as a matter of fact. Killed in mysterious circumstances, apparently.' White Lion poured himself a cider. 'I'm surprised it didn't happen sooner with their useless powers.'

'That's it!' Seth exclaimed, almost knocking over his beer. 'Sydney will be where the High Mage will strike! It all makes sense now!'

'What makes sense?' Bojangles shifted on his barstool dramatically. 'Speak up, man! The suspense is killing me!'

'Would you be serious?' Lilith scolded.

'Who me?' Mosh asked innocently from behind a random Santa mask. No one took the bait.

'The High Mage once told me long ago that he sired a son as a future meal. I thought he was just being perverse at the time, but his son was a member of the Failures, so it seems he wasn't joking.' Seth paused to grab the packet of Smex. 'Plus, it can't be a coincidence that the child's mother, Manipulator, was also in Sydney recently—before being killed herself—although, Dread's responsible for that.'

'I feel we know this already, but the details are fuzzy, almost like someone made us forget,' Bojangles said, suddenly feeling déjà vu.

'It also ties in with my theory about why there are so many Manifests on Earth, and Australia specifically,' Seth continued, not really listening to his friend.

'I thought that was Doctor Q's theory,' Bojangles teased, rubbing his silver beard for effect.

'Okay, *our* theory then,' Seth admitted, brushing his long black hair behind his ear. 'But don't you see? If Manifests are like the Earth's immune system—like *we've* long believed—then it makes sense that Australia is the source of an infection. An infection caused by Gledandron.'

'You're right; Australia is a mediocre country that is largely ignored by the rest of the world—it's the perfect place to feed unnoticed,' Lilith observed, also brushing her obsidian hair behind her ear in the same fashion as her twin brother.

'Hey, I resent that!' Bojangles said, but was also largely ignored.

'Which is why Sydney fits as ground zero for the High Mage's assault on Heaven,' Seth explained. 'The False Creator is a construct of Gledandron, stolen from the extinct E'hobans, and the veil between dimensions would be thinner at the feeding site. You're going to have to update all your contacts.'

'You mean I have to talk to those losers again?' White Lion whined.

'What do you think, Bojangles?' Seth asked. 'Would you be willing to talk to your contacts again?'

'Some of them, yeah, maybe,' Bojangles reluctantly agreed. 'Tenebrous won't lift a finger to help, Kaiser Enigma is too dangerous, Pulse

Pounder's a lunatic, and I suspect the Energy Lord is an agent of Gledandron too. I could probably convince some of the minor villains like the Quartet, or the Deathly Duo, or the Laa-De-Daa Gang, if I must.'

*Who comes up with these names?*

'A deranged mind, I'm sure,' Mosh mooted, knocking on his bald head.

'What about your friend, Bloodlust?' Lilith asked Bojangles. 'Have you told her of the World Eater?'

'I haven't been able to find her, surprisingly. She was having trouble with that Scar wanker.' Bojangles hadn't bothered warning *him*. 'She's probably gone to ground.'

'And what about you, dear sister?' Seth enquired. 'Have you got anything to report?'

'I do. I spoke with Mother and Father who said they'd left the destiny of the world in our hands—even reciting that mouldy old prophecy you're involved in.' Lilith secretly wanted a prophecy of her own. 'Demigod is off-world hunting Evolvers, not that I would have any control over him anyway, and the rest of the gods are either missing or disinterested. We are on our own.'

'This may be our final hour,' Seth said solemnly. 'I may be immortal, but somehow I don't think I'll survive having my soul eaten by Gledandron.'

'Don't be so melodramatic,' Mosh chimed in. 'You've still got lots of horrors to face in the future, like Xenobots, or Psylopods, or even fucking Phantasmogore Tetragrammaton Galacticon.'

*What the fuck is that, killer geometry?*

'Uh, thanks Mosh,' Seth replied sarcastically. 'That made me feel a lot better.'

'It wasn't supposed to,' Mosh shot back.

'Maybe you should start talking to your contacts, maybe one of them will need a crown,' Lilith said to Seth as she leaned over him for the packet of Smex. 'Perhaps they'll even be the one from the prophecy.'

*Or maybe it'll be Vong the Undead Pigman instead.*

'I guess it can't hurt…'

'It would also help if you spoke to some of my contacts too, maybe try and rally some group effort?' Bojangles said, adjusting his sunglasses.

'And mine, too,' White Lion added. He hoped he could palm off the whole task.

*How did I end up doing everything?*

He agreed nonetheless.

# Week Four

## Freeman Residence, Neutral Bay:
## 27 November 34 BZ

Lorraine Freeman sat on the couch in her dressing gown as her private nurse took her blood pressure. 'I feel fine,' she said.

*I seem to have healed completely since that creature attacked us in the bush. Luckily, Mum seems to be on the mend too. Good thing I was there to carry her back to civilisation before calling for help.*

As if sensing her daughter's thoughts, Lucy Freeman suddenly entered the lounge with a strange man in green mechanised power armour. They were accompanied by two creepy looking men dressed in suits and wearing dark sunglasses despite being inside.

'Lorraine, sweetie, this is Tactician, UN Manifest liaison, and he's here to talk to us about our encounter last week,' Lucy announced, taking a seat next to her daughter. She deliberately ignored the MIBs.

'I believe debrief is the correct term,' Tactician said amiably, smiling at Lorraine. 'It's an absolute pleasure to meet you. Normally I don't make house calls, but for you I made an exception. As your mother said, we'd just like to run over your encounter, if you don't mind. However, the nurse will need to leave before we begin. In the interests of national security, of course.'

*I wonder how she feels being spoken about like she's not even here.*

The nurse appeared indifferent and packed away her kit in silence before leaving.

'Excellent. Why don't we start with a description of the being who attacked you?' Tactician began. He took one of the nearby armchairs and moved it opposite the Freemans. The MIBs stood silently in the background.

*They're fucking creepy! Didn't Mum say they were responsible for outing me as a Manifest? Why'd she even allow them in?*

'Well, I didn't get a real good look at him in the dark, but he was around seven feet tall and had giant bat-wings sprouting from his back,' Lorraine answered, goose bumps forming as she remembered the ordeal. 'His skin was a sickly green and he had fangs like a vampire, but it's his glowing red eyes I'll never forget.'

'Sounds like you got a pretty good look at him,' Tactician said, his suit whirring as he moved in the chair. 'Can you recall any other details?'

'He also had long hair and two long horns sprouting from his head,' Lucy added, 'and sharp claws for hands. He wore black rags and seemed to have a rib poking through his chest.'

'Don't forget, he said his name was Night Demon and that he was after my mind,' Lorraine recalled, shifting uncomfortably in her seat.

'A demon, did you say? And after your mind? My poor dear, that must have been terribly frightening. How did you escape this monster?' Tactician tried to sound caring but came off as condescending. Lucy gave him a funny look.

'Um…I…ah…Mum must've hurt him when they fought as he just left,' Lorraine stammered, not sure if she wanted to trust this guy with the truth.

*So a half-truth will have to do.*

'I see. You say that this demon attacked you and fought your mother—obviously how she sustained her injuries—and then was about to attack you but decided to leave instead.' Tactician sounded dubious. 'And what were you doing at that moment?'

'I was yelling at him to leave us alone,' Lorraine said defensively.

'Interesting,' Tactician stated. He caught Lucy flashing Lorraine a look. 'Don't worry, Miss Freeman, I believe you. Now, where did you say this all happened? The Blue Mountains?'

'That's right, it was in the bush somewhere, I can't remember exactly where,' Lorraine replied truthfully. 'It was a place Mum took me. I'd never been there before.'

'That's okay, I will get the exact coordinates off your mother later,' Tactician said. 'For now, I'd like to know more about your abilities, such as how you Manifested in the first instance. It's now public knowledge you're a Manifest, by the way.'

*Yeah, thanks to that David Leno interview and those creepy MIB guys.* She didn't like where this interview is going either.

*There's no way I'm telling him about Obtuse—they'll confiscate him for sure.*

'Now wait a minute,' Lucy interrupted. 'I agreed to tell you about the demon because you said it was vital, but I didn't agree to you harassing my daughter.'

'I think it's in your best interest to cooperate, Ms Freeman. I know the limits of your powers,' Tactician said menacingly.

*Did that jerk just threaten my mum?*

Lucy looked unsure of what to do.

'Now, Miss Freeman…' Tactician began.

'I want you to leave,' Lorraine said forcefully before he could finish the sentence.

'But, I…'

'Now!' Lorraine shouted.

Tactician paused as if deep in thought. 'Very well. I've learned all I need to for now.' He stood up and indicated to the two MIBs.

'And don't come back,' Lorraine added.

'No, of course not. I don't have any reason to.' He turned to the MIBs before leaving the room. 'Let's go, we've learned all we will here.'

The MIBs looked at each other silently and then turned to stare at Lorraine before following Tactician from the mansion.

*Man, they are really creepy. They weren't affected by my power either, and that worries me.*

'I'm sorry about that dear,' Lucy said before standing up. 'I better make sure they leave—I'll be right back.'

*Were they really interested in that demon, or were they here to spy on me?*

Lorraine wondered again if her powers were worth the trouble.

* * *

## Grand Satanic Headquarters: 28 November 34 BZ

Marek Mahoney bellowed the names of the demon lords with extremist fervour along with his fellow inner circle members of Lucifer's Coven.

'Zoolith, Bahlor, Ishlarr, Rancid, Leviathan, Ooblog,' they chanted in unison ad nauseam.

After twenty minutes of intense intoning they needed a break, and there was a rush for the single couch.

'I'm puffed,' Marek exclaimed, as he grabbed one of the seats. 'Who would have thought that satanic chanting provides a complete cardio-vascular workout?'

'I try to do a satanic workout every day,' Matt said, attempting to out-Satan Marek from the other spot on the couch. 'My biceps are the work of Satan himself.'

'Praise be to the Dark One,' creepy Navid said creepily.

'It's the High Mage we should be thanking. If it wasn't for his spell that made the world forget us, we wouldn't be able to enjoy our nefarious proclivities.' Karen, the High Priestess, waddled into the meeting room with a bowl of popcorn. Her pregnancy had almost come full term, yet her brain was only half-baked.

'Popcorn!' Lancefield squealed, clapping his hands and fluffing his ginger beard.

'This isn't for you,' Karen snapped.

'I'll just go make some more,' Floyd offered, as popcorn seemed pretty good to him too. He rubbed his bald, asymmetrical head. 'We *are* having a break, after all.'

'This is the last of it,' Karen advised. 'You will have to have the old muesli bars.'

*At least Matt remembered to bring beer.*

'I'll just have to get my mum to get some on the way home,' Lancefield said resignedly. 'I hate wasting saliva drooling over unrealised snacks.'

'Enough! Satanists laugh in the face of snacks,' Karen ranted with madness in her eyes and popcorn crumbs on her lips. 'I need to know if all of you know your part of the plan, as time grows short. It's now less than a month to go before the Feast of Lights.'

*Why doesn't she just call it Christmas?*

'Of course we do,' Floyd answered, deciding to forego the muesli bars. 'That's what we've been practising for the last couple of months.'

'Then you'll have no trouble humouring me,' Karen declared dramatically. Suddenly she turned around to face Marek, but her black hair swished in front of her face and covered it. She spoke regardless. 'Marek. You are the newcomer to our inner circle—perhaps you would do the honours?'

All eyes fell on the bespectacled, auburn-haired Prime Locum. His lacquered Hitler moustache glistened satanically.

*Now's my chance to prove to them my loyalty and devotion to the High Mage's cause.* He cleared his throat and took a sip from the beer Matt had passed him. 'Well, the plan is that at precisely midnight on Christmas Day…'

'Is that daylight savings time?' Lancefield asked. Matt nodded.

'…we each summon a Lord of Hell in our respective clubhouses. I will summon Rancid, Dark Lord of Decay, in Ashfield; Navid will call forth Ishlarr, Dark Lord of the Frozen Mind, in Bondi; Lancefield will summon Zoolith, Dark Lord of Brimstone and Persecution, in Banksmeadow; Matt will call Leviathan, Dark Serpent of Bindings and Restrictions, in Manly; and Floyd will summon Bahlor, Dark Lord of Despair and Failure, in North Ryde.' He paused for breath.

'I like how they all form an inverted pentagram on a map,' Floyd stated. 'Anton never had vision like that when he founded Lucifer's Coven.'

'Yes, with our Grand Satanic Headquarters at the centre, where Karen will bring forth Ooblog, Dark Lord of Perverse Molestation,' Marek announced with glee.

'Yes, Ooblog, who will watch over me as I give birth to the Antichrist,' Karen claimed before eating another handful of popcorn.

*She'll make a great mum.*

'We'll each be joined by the one hundred and ten members of our respective chapters,' Marek said. 'Making a total of six hundred and sixty-six members to conjure the Lords of Hell as heralds for the reign of the High Mage!'

They all shared in a round of evil laughter.

'YOU ARE ALL INSANE!' screamed Blotch McMahn from the back of Marek's hand. For one brief, yet blissful moment, Marek had forgotten about his indelible intruder.

*I'm just glad no one else can hear him, or I'd be kicked out of the coven for sure.*

Unaware of Marek's dilemma, the coven members continued their scheming.

'And all the other arrangements are in place?' Karen enquired.

'Yep, we've got all the cloaks...' Navid began.

'All of which were a tax write-off, now rendered moot as no one knows who we are,' Matt interjected.

'...the clubhouses are rented and the catering's all done,' Navid continued. 'The insurance is all sorted and we've even got a shuttle bus to help some of our mobility-impaired members.'

'And my mum said she'd help ferry people around too,' Lancefield added.

'You're probably safer with his mum than summoning forces of darkness,' Blotch McMahn theorised. 'YOU'RE ALL GOING TO DIE!'

'Will you shut up?' Marek snapped.

'She only wants to help,' Lancefield sulked, mistakenly thinking Marek was yelling at him. 'Sorry.'

'There is no need to snap at Lancefield,' Karen scolded Marek. 'He's proven his loyalty, whereas your competence has been called into question.'

'I'm surprised it took her this long,' Blotch McMahn quipped.

'What do you mean?' Marek asked. 'I've devoted my life to the satanic cause.'

'We've had complaints about your lack of judgement and failure to listen to the advice of your fellow members,' Karen accused.

*I bet Melissa is behind this.*

Marek didn't have the strength to fight it, so he apologised instead.

'I won't let you down,' he said to the inner circle.

'See that you don't,' Karen threatened, pointing to the liquefying corpse of Tom Higginbottom that was still hanging in the meeting room. A bucket sat underneath him to catch the drips. 'Failure is the one thing that Satanists *don't* laugh in the face of.'

* * *

## The Skull of Ra: 29 November 34 BZ

Anu Hopet called his Skull Band to the bridge for a final briefing before deciding whether or not to destroy the Earth.

'Great Armageddon, what would you ask of us?' Disk dared to utter.

'I ask nothing,' Anu Hopet boomed. 'I command.' He stood with his back to them and looked through the viewport, his colourful battle armour a stark contrast to the dark ship.

'What is your command, my liege?' Battletank asked dutifully. He was wearing his battle suit sans helmet, revealing a bald man with dull eyes.

'Yes, Great Armageddon,' Backstabber hissed. 'We live but to serve you.'

'I want a final status report from your respective duties,' Anu Hopet replied.

*I must know whether it is worth my while to confront the prophecy the honourable way or to simply destroy this world and be done with it.*

'There has been no change in Bodyguard,' Backstabber reported, cringing slightly.

'Nor has Gurk escaped from the human prison,' Battletank added, referring to their shark-like companion. 'It seems he hasn't been able to overcome their ingenuity.'

'Is your news any better?' Anu Hopet asked his cyborg.

'I'm afraid not, my liege,' Disk admitted. 'There is still no trace of the talisman or the thief who stole it from you.'

'Then there is no reason to stay. We should leave and destroy this planet from orbit,' Anu Hopet declared.

'There may be one, if I may be so bold as to say, my lord,' Disk offered.

'Go on.'

'Well, there is definitely some kind of imminent event in store for this city. The sensors indicate an energy signature similar to those of godform entities. It could be a Celestial One,' Disk suggested. 'It could also be related to that underground base close by. It could even be the lair of the one who robbed you. We won't know unless we can scan the interior.'

'And how would you do that?' Anu Hopet had to admit he was intrigued.

'I would need to go over there and do some reconnaissance,' Disk advised. 'I request your permission to go, Great Armageddon.'

Anu Hopet weighed his options.

'Granted,' he finally said. 'Make your preparations.'

*I may as well rule out every possibility before I turn this world to ash.*

\* \* \*

### The Territories of Xph'Ish'Matarg, Hell: Circa 30 November 34 BZ

Mark Adams lay broken and bound to the smouldering rock. His flesh slowly sizzled while the lone cacodemon inspected his organs. The smell of his own flesh cooking made what remained of his stomach growl in protest, adding to his torment.

*Why? Why are you doing this?* He didn't attempt to speak anymore; talking was too painful in the burning atmosphere and the demons could read his mind anyway.

'We must know your secrets,' the creature replied. 'Xph'Ish'Matarg has willed us to do it.'

*I don't see him around, so it mustn't be that important.*

'How dare you question the Master's plan!' the cacodemon screeched, snapping off a rib as punishment. Mark roared in pain.

*No matter how much damage they do to me, I'm conscious the whole time.*

'And the pain never goes away, does it mortal? That is why we needed your physical body as well as your soul.' The cacodemon cackled, its impish frame shuddering with each laugh. It stabbed Mark in the leg with his own rib.

*I will tell you anything you want if you'd just stop.*

'You are in no position to bargain,' the cacodemon taunted. 'We already know you would tell us everything—you have already tried. You do not know, but we will find out.' It started to fossick around Mark's gizzards.

*Desci...I've tried to be strong for you and the kids...Obie...even*

*Samara and Sebastian…but I don't know how much more I can take. I hope to join you in the afterlife soon.*

'Wait…what was that?' The cacodemon peered into Mark's abdomen.

*But…before I go…I would do anything to get even with these creatures for taking you from me.*

'There it is again! A faint glow…'

*The more it talks, the more unbearable this becomes. Free me from this place!*

'Yes! Yes! That's it!' The cacodemon focused all its attention on something deep within Mark. 'Of course, it is the reason why the High Mage captured you—the lure he used must have been designed to catch a certain type of prey.'

*What's that thing babbling about?*

'We have discovered your secret, Mark Adams, deep in your soul.' The cacodemon withdrew itself from his innards and danced around gleefully. 'Xph'Ish'Matarg will be pleased with us for finding it!'

*What could it have possibly found that it didn't find the first hundred times it vivisected me?* Being a horror movie fan, Mark was all-too familiar with the word 'vivisect'.

'It must be your emotions combined with the torture. Yes, we have tasted this before, but the body masks it.' The imp ignored Mark as it dissected his secret. 'We can sense it now…a seed…it is latent…but wants so much to Manifest.'

*I'm a Manifest?*

\* \* \*

**Barton Correctional Facility: 1 December 34 BZ**

Chief Warden Walter Screw brushed the ash from his trimmed moustache. 'You think the attack will occur in Sydney?' he asked his son.

Tactician reclined in the leather couch in his father's office. 'I do, as strange as that sounds. A creature apparently known as Night Demon has been seen prowling around the Blue Mountains. Sydney's also where we found the recording of…ah…Merlin's plan. It fits.'

*Nothing about this fits, least of all Sydney being ground zero for the apocalypse.*

'Where did you come by this additional information? I know your HSA pal, White Lion, believes so, but I think he was stoned when he told us.' Walter took another puff from his cigar. 'It's not that I don't agree with you, but we should be certain before committing our limited resources.'

'I heard it from that teen model, Lorraine Freeman…and her mother,' Tactician replied. 'I have no reason to doubt her…um…*them*. One of the few Manifests I like, actually.'

'Are you sure? You sound like one of her hysterical fans,' Walter teased, smiling the whole time.

Tactician blushed for the first time since he was a child. 'I'm guessing it's the same way you behaved when you finally got Supernaut locked up after Vicious Man left him for us,' he retorted before going on. 'The attack will be in Sydney, I'm certain—at least the attack on this dimensional plane.'

*Dimensional plane? I can't believe that phrase has become commonplace of late.*

'I suppose there's all this "Antithesis" talk as well, which is disturbing to say the least,' Walter conceded. 'But let's say you are right. What's the plan? Are you going to evacuate the city? Call in your forces from other cities or even other countries? Alert the media?' The last line was Walter's idea of a joke.

'I haven't even alerted the Prime Minister.' Tactician laughed. 'The UN doesn't want countries acting autonomously on something so important. It was the MIBs' idea.'

'I thought they worked for the UN, not the other way around,' Walter said.

'It's…complicated,' Tactician admitted. 'So no, we won't be evacuating Sydney for the twin reasons of its size and because there's a slim chance we're wrong. Either way, the media would be alerted.'

'Same reason why you're not putting all our eggs in one basket by recalling your other assets, I presume?' Walter blew a smoke ring.

'Indeed. The plan is to use several of our assault teams to undertake surgical strikes against the enemy—once the enemy reveals itself in whole.' Tactician waved away the smoke ring. 'The last thing we want is to have individual governments involved—the Yanks would probably nuke the city.'

'It may yet come to that if we're to stop the apocalypse.'

Walter's words hung in the air with his subsequent smoke ring.

* * *

### Fatty's Cement Works, Parramatta: 2 December 34 BZ

Seth Zaraxom walked with Bojangles along the metal walkway to the collection of supervillains milling about the abandoned factory floor below. 'I can't believe you talked me into this,' he said, brushing his hair behind his ear subconsciously.

'I told you I needed your help convincing them to assist us, as they don't seem to believe me. They are supervillains and suspicious by nature. They also want to know what's in it for them,' Bojangles added with a cheeky grin. 'Some of them are quite powerful—nothing like your nephew—but powerful enough. We can use them against the High Mage, especially as your pal Vong the Undead Pigman is nowhere to be found.'

*He's probably still searching for my aunt, Nocturne, in the hope she'll forgive him and make him human again.*

'You don't seem to be too worried that we're about to ask a gang of supervillains to potentially stave off the End of Days.' Seth was immortal, yet even he had to concede he was worried.

'I can see the future, remember,' Bojangles said in ominous tones. 'What concerns me is that I can't see anything beyond about thirty years from now, only a brilliant whiteness—like the Earth doesn't exist beyond that point. That's what we should be worried about.'

'One problem at a time,' Seth replied, stopping in the centre of the walkway. 'Right now, I have to deliver a sales pitch to a bunch of psychos in an old concrete factory. Why did you choose this place anyway?'

'It has a ley-line running through it,' Bojangles answered. 'Or at least I thought it did, but there doesn't seem to be any trace of it.'

'Sounds fascinating,' Seth lied before turning to the villains, who were all watching him expectantly.

Gathered before him was Sydney's local supervillain crowd, plus a few 'crime tourists' who'd heard about the meeting. Not all of them were invited either, but word soon travelled through the underworld. It wasn't every day that the legendary Immortal was going to address a crowd.

Present at this historic event were the awkwardly named Colour Brothers, Blackman and Redman; rejected HSA candidates, Jackrabbit and River Man, the Deathly Duo; and the mercenary Quartet: Armed Gunman, High Flyer, Eye and Horsepower.

Seth spied the ridiculous Laa-De-Daa Gang, comprised of Angry Man, Cutie, Happy Man, Homester, Mascot, Povsicle and Rotary Hoe. They were joined by Terror Australis survivors Homey Killer, the Crusher, the Bee, Short Fuse, Vortex and the radiant White Hot.

Rounding out the group was Brainwave, one of Scar's Seven Servants; Guillotine, the right-hand man of Pulse Pounder; and DYDX, the Energy Lord's android assassin. Behind them stood a man in metallic helmet with a long, red cape. He was carrying a battle-axe and had a robotic claw for a hand.

*Is that...? What's he doing here among this...rampage...of supervillains?*

He wondered what the collective noun for supervillains was, but dismissed the thought and cleared his throat. 'Fellow Manifests, as my colleague Bojangles has already told you, we all face a deadly threat from beyond this dimension.'

*It sounds so silly and trite when said like that.*

He pushed on. 'We have now confirmed that Sydney will be the epicentre of the threat in the physical realm. I am hoping you will all help stop it.'

'Why should we?' the cyborg battering ram, Horsepower, called out. 'We work for money. What incentive is there?'

'How about your life?' Bojangles called back from the walkway.

'The best thing to do would be to leave for another town,' Redman declared.

'Yeah, that's what the Colour Brothers will be doing,' Blackman added.

*I know those guys' names refer to the colour of their outfits, but do they not have any self-awareness?*

'This all still sounds like bullshit to me!' yelled the Crusher, his New Zealand accent somehow fitting with his Tiki-ish look.

'Believe what you will. I am so sure of what I tell you, I'm willing to pay you for your services.' Thousands of years had allowed Seth to accumulate wealth beyond the dreams of Scrooge McDuck.

'How much?' Jackrabbit, the hirsute hare, harangued.

'A million each, perhaps?' Seth offered.

'Seriously?' Bojangles almost choked. 'Can you pay me too?'

'What do we have to do to earn this million?' asked the Povsicle, his voice somehow audible through the chunky blocks of ice that encased him.

'Where did you come by this information?' cried River Man, before Seth could answer the human ice block.

'I know this because I speak with the gods,' Seth replied matter-of-factly. He knew how it sounded, but age had turned his care factor to dust.

'I've heard all this before from another ancient witch,' Vortex spat. 'How do we know you'll keep your word?' The vortex in his chest swirled.

'I for one believe thisss Ssseth, it'sss the reassson I am here,' White Hot announced to the group as he floated above them. 'I feel drawn to him like a moth to the flame.'

Homester and Homey Killer started squabbling, so Seth decided to wrap things up before the villains could get at each other's throats. 'I need you to be on the lookout for anyone resembling a sorcerer or anything that looks like a demon. The attack will come on Christmas Day, so I expect there to be an increase in activity leading up to that. Once the attack begins, I'll need you to stop it at all costs.'

'That might cost you more, but we can negotiate terms later,' Armed Gunman mumbled through his gasmask.

'Good, then we are done here.' Seth had excellent hearing. 'Bojangles will run you through the finer details and answer any questions you may have.'

'Oh, I will, will I?' Bojangles rolled his eyes, but no one saw behind his sunglasses.

'That's it? We came all the way out here for that? It was only about five minutes!' River Man complained, his long, brown hair flowing like his namesake. 'I caught a train to get here.'

*No wonder the HSA didn't want him on their team. You'd think he'd be grateful for the warning—not to mention the cool million I'm offering.*

Seth thanked Bojangles and headed back along the walkway to the stairs, ignoring River Man's whining. Before descending the stairs, he took one final look at the gathering and White Hot in particular.

*There's definitely something peculiar about that guy...something familiar.*

\* \* \*

### Outskirts of Bombala, New South Wales: 3 December 34 BZ

Dread Sedgewick didn't know why he chose to come this way.

*I should have just kept travelling north rather than cutting east. If I hadn't come across that bus full of nuns for entertainment it would have been a total loss.*

It was a hot summer's day and there was a high fire danger posted on the road sign. That was reason enough for Dread to spark up a cigarette.

*Now I just have to figure out the best way to have my revenge.*

He took a long drag from his durry and ran through options in his mind. His red facial markings made him look angry despite how calm he felt. His emerald eyes scanned his surroundings.

*Should I take out Dad's family one at a time or should I hit them all at once? Do I make Dad watch? Maybe I should alert the media and make a spectacle of it?*

He quickly dismissed the last idea as it would draw too much attention from the Anti-Manifest Police—and that prison warden who'd been chasing him for years.

*It's not like they'd consider Supernaut a gift and give me some space, the ingrates. No, I need to keep this a private family affair.*

He was wearing his trench coat despite the high midday temperature yet didn't notice the heat. A blowfly impaled itself on his needle-like hair, which stood straight up on the top of his head. He didn't notice that either.

He tossed his smouldering cigarette butt into the dry grass by the side of the road.

*Okay, no more fucking around; it's time to get my early Christmas present.*

Dread strolled down the highway whistling as the bushfire kindled behind him.

# Week Three

## Dungeon Cell 9: 4 December 34 BZ

Andy Trailer lay beaten and broken in the dark filthy cell. After the highs of the last couple of months, his reversal of fortune drowned him in lows he didn't know existed. Not even his cockroach family that swarmed over his flesh could make him feel any better.

*It's not fair,* he despaired. He was curled in the foetal position with his wings tucked around his body, his recent bruises making his green skin look even sicklier. *I thought Pulse…my master, had finally trusted me as one of his servants. It wasn't my fault I didn't bring her back.*

Pulse Pounder had been less than impressed with his demonic assistant when he returned from the Blue Mountains without the Manifest he learned his master wanted, the one called Lorraine Freeman. As a result, Andy found himself cast back to his familiar cell and had to endure regular beatings ever since. Pulse Pounder had even taken his straw bed away and he was back to lying on the cold stone floor.

*But it is your fault,* came Wisp's inexorable voice inside Andy's mind, forever eroding his confidence. *If you had only stopped playing Night Demon and grabbed the girl like we advised, you would not be back here, calling the cyclops 'Master' again like a craven dog. Pathetic.*

*It was you who told me to embrace the Night Demon persona in the first place!* He sat up and grabbed his head with both hands.

*Under our guidance, under the guidance of the almighty Gledandron, yes. You should have struck without warning and you should not have shown mercy,* Wisp thrummed. *Then you would be focused on revenge, rather than a return to prostrating yourself for your slaver. If you had captured her, Pulse Pounder would still trust you. We warned you of this.*

*That's not true. If I'd only obeyed my master and not listened to you, I wouldn't be here. It's your fault,* Andy whined, despite the conversation occurring inside his mind.

*Weak fool, it is because of us that you rose above your many limitations to stand by the cyclops's side, ready to have your vengeance for what he did to you. Do you no longer care that he and the Energy Lord conspired to turn you into a hideous monster?* Wisp asked in its eerie voice.

Andy was no longer sure what he wanted—aside from getting out from his cell. *Pulse Pounder or Gledandron; who do I choose?*

Kismet overheard and events were set in motion.

Suddenly the cell door creaked open and Pulse Pounder's second-in-command, Guillotine, stepped into the dark cell, his body silhouetted in the doorway. 'Come,' he said. 'The Master is willing to offer you a chance to redeem yourself.'

*Now you must decide who you really are,* Wisp declared. *Are you the Night Demon, or are you merely a dog?*

Andy feared it was the latter.

* * *

### Crappy Caravan Base, Collector, New South Wales: 5 December 34 BZ

Seth Zaraxom couldn't believe he agreed to go through with this. He was currently attending the annual get-together of all the wannabe superhero teams at a rundown caravan park, hosted this year by none other than the aptly named Crappy Super Heroes.

*How did White Lion convince me to talk to these guys? And now he's buggered off! These guys are the most ridiculous ensemble of loser Manifests I've ever seen. How are they supposed to help defeat the High Mage?* He guessed they could serve as a distraction at the very least.

Assembled before him in all their inglorious splendour was the largest collection of Class D Manifests in the Southern Hemisphere. Manifests whose powers made them no more powerful than regular people. The wind whipped Seth's obsidian hair across his face as he turned to take it all in.

*I think there are some Miasma creatures in the crowd. This should be interesting.*

There were the hosts, the Crappy Super Heroes, made up of Prance Man, Doink Man, Decrepit Man, Heroic Pose Man, **Obvious Man** and Irrelevant Man, who was also a member of the Newest Heroes—alongside Biff Man; the Miasma entity, Gwunk; the aliens, Queegul and Zeegul; and the bizarre Flaming Toilet Seat.

They were joined by the No-Hopers: Sad Man, Stress Man, Many Rolls Man and their leader, Vague Man. Alongside them were the beer-fuelled redneck cyborgs, Boganator and Boonatron; the unlikely twosome, Asparagus Man and Panta Boy; the tubby Victor 'Call me Vic' Tim and his son, Peabo Busybody; as well as a smattering of One-Time Superguys, as Seth liked to call them. Even the emissaries from the HSA, Flannelled Avenger and Cloth the Flannelled Wonder, were present. White Lion had made all the introductions before leaving.

*Well, I've waited long enough. Time to get on with this.*

Seth looked down at the 'Orator's Soapbox' he was meant to stand on to address the crowd. He stepped up. 'I think we should begin.'

'Zambini isn't here yet,' **Obvious Man** said, which was obvious to anyone who knew Zambini. The flashing neon sign above his head that said 'I am **Obvious Man**' blinked and pulsed.

'He never shows up, so I say we should start without him,' Biff Man said gruffly.

'A-are y-you s-sure?' Stress Man started sweating profusely. 'W-what if he's got vital information that we'll miss out on if we proceed without him? What if it could save the Earth? What if it's already too late? What if...'

Seth had decided that was enough. *Let these guys start talking and they'll never stop.*

'Friends, heed my words,' he began, before recounting the now familiar tale of wizards and apocalypse. When he was finished, he reluctantly opened up the floor to questions.

'This sounds preposterous. This is the real world and things like that just don't happen. How can we know you didn't make it up?' the

Flaming Toilet Seat asked without irony.

'It's true. White Lion said the same thing,' the Flannelled Avenger advised, his plaid cape fluttering in the strong breeze.

'How will you stop it?' Victor Tim wondered aloud. 'Bojangles said you were going to summon a sea monster. Is that true?'

*Bloody Bojangles and his big mouth.*

'Yes, it's so,' Seth confessed, pulling a cigarette from his coat pocket and lighting it. 'The ancient one, Leviathan, elemental of the deep.' He hoped that sounded impressive.

'How will we get there?' Boganator enquired before chugging a brewski. 'Collector's far from Sydney and I can't afford a bus. I spent the last of my cash on suds for this shindig.'

'Never fear, I will lead us there,' Vague Man offered, as he did his best to out-pose Heroic Pose Man.

'Do you even know how to get there?' Asparagus Man queried, his cellulose body photosynthesising righteously in the warm morning sun.

'It's up north,' Vague Man said defensively. 'Besides, we have some time to get there.'

'Then it's settled,' Seth interrupted when he saw his opening. 'I'll see you all there on Christmas.'

'That's because you have functioning eyeballs,' **Obvious Man** replied from under the glow of his enormous sign. 'I'm **Obvious Man**, by the way. That's what my sign says, too.'

The irritation of that moment almost caused Seth to become homicidal, but he snuffed it out with some Zen (in)action.

*Ooh, White Lion and Bojangles owe me bigtime for this.*

\* \* \*

### Barton Correctional Facility: 6 December 34 BZ

Walter Screw stood on the roof of the prison in the baking midday sun. His helmet's inbuilt tinted visor barely shielded his eyes from the blinding radiance and he was uncomfortably hot in his grey uniform. This was completed by an overwhelming sense of déjà vu. He let none of it show.

*Why do fucking superheroes always have to meet on the bloody roof?*

He was meeting with a contingent of HSA members: Ballistic, Powerhouse, Mauler and Hellgoat, who were hovering a couple of feet above him despite having walked through a portal created by their other team member, Gate Crasher, who was standing next to another non-flyer, Razorback.

*I get it now; float a few feet in the air so you can look down on me. Fucking teenagers, always having to show off.*

He greeted them warmly. 'My young friends, to what do I owe the honour of your visit?'

'We were just searching for that monster, Vicious Man, and thought we'd stop by to thank you for the intel that he'd been spotted in Tasmania.' It was Ballistic who spoke.

'There's no need to thank me, as it was my duty to pass that information along. I may be able to contain Vicious Man, but I need you to capture him for me,' Walter explained, stroking his moustache. 'Besides, it's his own fault he carved his name into Supernaut. It's like he was sending us a message.'

'Yeah, well, he'll be sorry he sent for us,' Powerhouse boasted.

'If you're gonna destroy the world, you better expect an ass-whooping,' Razorback added. He rubbed one of his tusks subconsciously.

'White Lion said a sorcerer called the High Mage of Hell is behind all of this,' Hellgoat growled. 'I don't think Vicious Man's involved.'

'How could someone like that not be involved in the end of the world?' Ballistic asked. 'What other reason could there be behind his existence?'

'There could be many reasons,' Walter offered, trying to wrap up the conversation. He was late for another meeting. 'Granted, he's certainly a menace to society, and there're still a couple of weeks left until the main attack on Christmas Day.'

'Really? The decorations have been up since Easter, so it's hard to tell,' Mauler joked.

'That's not the only reason we're here,' Gate Crasher said, looking at Ballistic.

Walter picked up the subtle hint. 'I see. You're also here to check up on me, make sure I'm not torturing the prisoners, correct?'

'I told you I would,' Ballistic answered, his crimson half-helm failing to conceal his smugness. 'When I dropped off the Super Six at the start of the year, remember?'

'That's not how I remember it,' Walter snapped, already tired of the conversation. 'This is a waste of my time. I have a lot of things to do and if I'd known this is what you wanted to meet up about, I wouldn't have agreed to it.'

'Sounds like you've got a guilty conscience,' Ballistic said. 'Good thing we decided to pop in to keep you on your toes.'

'I thought we were coming for a tour,' Powerhouse complained to Ballistic. 'If I had known your true intentions, I would've insisted you stayed behind.'

'Lucky you're not in charge then,' Hellgoat said in his friend's defence.

'You're lucky you're trusted enough to even be here,' Powerhouse shot back.

'Guys…' Mauler began, always the peacemaker.

'I just don't think we should be out here accusing the Warden of mistreating a bunch of Nazi supervillains when we should be tracking down Vicious Man and the High Mage of Hell.' Powerhouse may have been a total wanker, but he had a point.

'You should listen to your companion,' Walter said to Ballistic. 'He seems to be the wisest among you.'

Powerhouse looked pleased with himself.

'The point is we're meant to be working together to stop the end of the world, but I'm not convinced we can trust him,' Ballistic barrelled on, determined to say his piece. 'I *want* to trust him, so I stopped in to remind him I'm watching.'

*Why that megalomaniacal little shit!*

'Who do you think you are, policing the government? You work for the government, don't forget.' Walter was furious.

'*Quis custodiet ipsos custodes?*' Hellgoat said under his breath. No one knew he spoke Latin.

'Spare me your fancy quotes,' Walter said. He had excellent hearing. 'The fact is, you don't have to like me, hell, you don't even have to trust me. But you should trust that I have the country's best interests at heart and the end of the world would be a serious setback to that goal.'

'I imagine it would also incur a mountain of paperwork,' Gate Crasher japed, causing Razorback to snort.

Walter ignored them. 'Now, I've got things to do. Good luck on your mission—I hope you do find Vicious Man.' It almost sounded like a threat.

Gate Crasher opened up a portal to the next location on their list. The HSA members started to leave.

Ballistic paused before walking through the portal. 'Okay,' he said, 'I'll give you the benefit of the doubt—for now.'

*Fucking teenagers!*

'How gracious of you,' Walter said sarcastically as Ballistic turned and stepped through the portal. It closed behind him and Walter was alone on the prison roof once more. He produced a cigar from one of his many pockets and lit it.

*I really hope they don't run into Vicious Man—I'm going to need them to stop the apocalypse.*

\* \* \*

### Outside Scar's Warehouse, Ashfield: 7 December 34 BZ

Naomi Bloodlust sat in the rental car with Liu, across the street from the quiet warehouse. There wasn't much going on, the occasional shady delivery being the only visible activity she could see from her vantage point.

*Hopefully this will provide some useful information on Scar's movements so we can execute our plan without any surprises. I hate surprises.*

Suddenly the rear car door opened and a silver-haired Aboriginal man jumped into the backseat before closing the door behind him. 'Hey guys,' he said casually. 'What's happening?'

*What the fuck?*

She spun around in her seat with knife in hand, ready to strike. Liu was slower to react, but only marginally. Then they saw who had blown their cover.

'Bojangles? What the fuck are you doing here? You're ruining our stakeout,' Naomi said, lowering her weapon.

'Is that what this was?' He laughed jovially. 'Because I thought you were saving Scar the trouble of looking for you by parking across the street with a giant target painted on the roof. I noticed you two straight away.'

'Yeah, but you have one of those uncanny abilities to locate someone you're looking for,' she pointed out. 'I'm sure Scar has no idea we're here.'

'That's because he's a self-absorbed dickhead,' Bojangles agreed, adjusting his sunglasses. 'But there's always a chance he could get lucky.'

'What are you doing here?' Liu cut in. 'Are you going to help us against Scar?'

'Nah, I reckon you guys have it covered. Scar may have been around for decades, but he's still small fry.' Bojangles pulled a packet of cigarettes out of his black jacket.

'He's hired Gorg to kill me,' Naomi confessed.

'Gorg? Shit, I didn't realise your troubles ran so deep.' Bojangles lit his smoke. 'I still think you've got what it takes to take out that elusive bastard, though.'

'That's the plan,' Liu added, signalling Bojangles for a cigarette.

'But Gorg *and* Armageddon? You really know how to attract the wrong kind of attention,' Bojangles said between puffs. He rolled the window down to let the smoke out.

'Who's Armageddon?' Liu asked Naomi.

'Never mind, I'll tell you later,' she said, brushing it off. *I don't want to get into that whole talisman saga again.* 'You still haven't told me why you're here,' she said to Bojangles.

'I wanted to come and warn you about something. You may have heard, but there's going to be an attack on Sydney on Christmas Day,' Bojangles said a little too dramatically. 'An ancient sorcerer now calling himself the High Mage of Hell is responsible.'

'So, you're the one behind that silly rumour,' Naomi said. 'It's the end of the world apparently. Surely this is just another one of your jokes.'

'No joke,' Bojangles replied, flicking his butt out the window. 'I know how crazy it sounds, but it's been verified by the Celestial Ones themselves. My pal, Seth the Immortal, is descended from them, you know.'

*I've heard of that guy. Oldest Manifest of us all, apparently, and born of the gods themselves, if you believe the story. Not sure I do, though.*

'Do you know where the attack will occur?' Liu asked. 'Sydney's a big place.'

'It could be anywhere, we really don't know what to expect,' Bojangles answered, putting on his seatbelt. 'Except that when it happens, it'll be big.'

*Great, end of the world's all I need.*

'Are you planning on going somewhere?' Naomi asked Bojangles, referring to the seatbelt. 'We planned on sitting here for another hour at least.'

'That's boring; wouldn't you rather drop me off in town?' Bojangles suggested. 'Besides, you're not going to learn anything out here that you don't already know.'

'If you can teleport, why do you need a lift into the city?' Liu finished his smoke and flicked the butt out the window too.

'Well, this way I can enjoy some conversation.' Bojangles smiled ear to ear.

'How can I resist a smile like that?' Naomi said, starting the ignition and slowly coasting down the street.

* * *

### South Western Sydney: 8 December 34 BZ

Desci Adams had never felt so good. Her depression had lifted and for the first time since Mark disappeared she had hope. The kids had noticed too and they were starting to feel like a family again.

*Is this how Manifests feel all the time? No wonder they dress up in costumes and are always in the spotlight.* She started to prepare breakfast.

It had been a tumultuous fortnight for her since she had the strange visitation by her apparent father, the one who called himself Zhang Po, but who others called Dragon Kong.

She thought he was going to kill her with his sword, even taking a deep gash across her arm when she held it up in defence, but the second strike felt like she was hit with a bomb.

Dragon Kong had shown her that she was a latent Manifest by putting her in danger and thus triggering her seed. She had mixed feelings about why it worked for her and not her sister.

*I'm also not sure I can forgive 'Dad'—if that's who he really is—despite what he did for me.*

It wasn't just a metaphysical gift that Dragon Kong bequeathed her; he also provided more mundane assistance. The money he provided was enough to cover the bills until she could get back on her feet.

*I knew better than to ask where he got it. It doesn't matter; not when it comes to my family.*

She cracked some eggs into the skillet she'd preheated and they immediately began to sizzle and pop. She'd lit the gas stove with a thread of green flame that snaked from her finger, her unique Manifest ability she'd been learning to control.

*I wonder if that's the sum total of my abilities, or whether I'll be able to do more than shoot a small flame from my fingers.*

She also needed to work out how to tell her children. Things had been so good lately, she didn't want to risk ruining it with the bombshell that their mother was Manifest.

Desci finished frying the eggs and called the kids for breakfast.

*For now, I just have to focus on keeping this family from falling apart.*

\* \* \*

### Undisclosed location: 9 December 34 BZ

Courtney Yeht was determined to escape. She'd been slowly putting a plan together ever since she'd gained access to her personnel file a couple of weeks ago. It told her that everything she was taught to believe since arriving there was a lie.

*I didn't kill my parents at all—they abandoned me when they discovered I'm a Manifest.*

It was her parents who first named her Courtney; Patient 1432 was just her designation when she came to the facility—at least according to the file.

*There's no one looking for me either. Why would Phil lie to me like that?*

The file also said he had wanted to keep her there when others had wanted to kill her.

She was surprised that no one noticed the file was missing, but nevertheless it emboldened her to take more decisive action in remedying her predicament.

The first thing she did was to stop taking her 'medication', and she surreptitiously spat them into the toilet when faking her bouts of sickness.

Once her head had cleared from the drugs, it had been a relatively simple matter for her to learn what was happening outside her sealed room. All it took was a single hair dropped in the doorway when no one was paying attention. Her blonde hair was quite long, certainly long enough to stretch from the doorway to the floor outside her room, bypassing the magnetic field that suspended her room and physically separated it from the rest of the complex.

*With that hair I'm able to once more hear what the floor has to tell me.*

That's how she learned what had everyone so distracted.

*They think it's the end of the world—at least some of them do.*

She sat up on the bed and crossed her legs.

*They also think that guy in the infirmary—Muscle, I think they called him—is connected somehow. He keeps repeating the word 'Antithesis' over and over again.*

Thinking about the word sent a shiver down my spine.

*Maybe that's why they sent those soldiers here—Concord, the one in the clunking metal suit, and his friend Super Trooper, who thinks he treads without making a sound.*

She laughed to herself. *The floor hears every little thing.*

Courtney pulled her file out from under the mattress where she'd been hiding it.

*Sometime soon they'll realise I have this, so I better start thinking of a decent plan to escape. One thing's for sure: I'm getting the fuck out of here.*

* * *

**Castle of Pain, City of Dis, Hell: Circa 10 December 34 BZ**

The High Mage of Hell stood before the throne of bones and laughed in the face of Satan. The former ruler of Hell writhed incessantly against the mystical chains that bound him to the mock cathedra.

*The more the False Lucifer fights his bonds, the more power he transfers to me. His pride won't allow him to stop either.*

He was joined by the gigantic False Archdemon who stood in the entranceway to the throne room. 'Report,' he demanded without turning to address the demon lord.

'The armies are ready,' the False Archdemon replied. 'We await your command.'

'And the other? Have you brought him?' he asked, turning to face the demon.

'Allow me to introduce the Dark Destroyer,' the demon lord rasped, saliva dripping from its serrated maw.

A humanoid-sized being dressed in a grey trench coat, pants and tattered hat stepped forward. Its features were obscured by the clothing, yet its crimson eyes pierced the shadows, emanating menace.

*Finally, I am face to face with Satan's Black Hand of Death. If it is everything the legends say, it will be the perfect guardian for the Soul Gem while I attack Heaven.*

The High Mage smiled.

# Week Two

**Freeman Residence, Neutral Bay: 11 December 34 BZ**

Lorraine Freeman lay back on her bed while the Prodigy's 'Voodoo People' blared from her stereo. She was deep in thought and nearly jumped out of her skin at the sudden knock on her bedroom door.

'Lorraine, honey, your friend Sam has arrived,' Lucy Freeman called through the door.

*That's Samuel, Mum.* She got up from the bed, turned off the music and began to get changed. 'I'll be right out.' She heard her mother walk away.

She slipped into a slinky short black dress inlaid with sequins that sparkled when they caught the light.

*This dress would probably cause the paparazzi to have a heart attack,* she mused as she sat at her vanity unit to do her makeup. *Just because he's gay doesn't mean he can't appreciate beauty, right?*

Despite being a Manifest, Lorraine was still a teenager and prone to the fantasies and hopeless crushes that came with growing up. In her case, however, she had power like no teenager ever before.

A wicked thought flickered and was quickly shunned. *That would be sooo wrong! I want to be a good person, and power like mine shouldn't be abused.* A smile spread across her freshly glossed lips. *Can't hurt to dream about it though…*

She finished up and left her room to navigate the mazelike halls and down the stairs to the giant foyer. Lucy could be heard laughing from one of the ground floor rooms off to the side of the front door. *Mum does like to entertain people in the 'drawing room' like she's royalty. Why's it called a drawing room, anyway?*

The thought was dismissed the moment she entered the room and saw the handsome black man who'd travelled from the other side of the world to spend Christmas with them.

'Samuel, so good to see you again,' she said, kissing him on the cheek.

Lucy shot Lorraine a disapproving look when she saw the dress but didn't say anything. *I'll probably cop it when next we're alone.*

'It's great to see you too,' Samuel replied enthusiastically. 'I had so much fun at Comic-Con I just had to see you guys again. I mean, come on, the Hat Trick? Hat-themed crime? Give me a break. Anyway, what's been happening with you? Lucy tells me you guys had a run-in with some kind of demon. How horrible for you! I can't even imagine what that would have been like.'

*No, probably not.*

Lorraine related the story for what seemed like the hundredth time before changing the topic by asking what was new for him. He finished up by saying that he was invited to perform in a Carols-by-Candlelight event in Darling Harbour and thought it was the perfect excuse to come visit.

'Maybe you should go with him,' Lucy suggested. 'Something like that would do you good.'

'Um…' Lorraine began.

'That's a great idea!' Samuel pounced. 'We can sing "Jingle Bells" together!'

'Carols aren't really my thing…'

'Think of all the money we'll raise for charity,' he continued, now on a roll. 'It would also mean a lot to me.'

'You may as well,' Lucy added before Lorraine could answer. 'I'll be out with the X-Droids at Circular Quay anyway, and Shara will be here to look after your sisters.'

'Okay, okay, I'll go,' Lorraine agreed. 'What's the worst that can happen?'

\* \* \*

### Undisclosed location: 12 December 34 BZ

Courtney Yeht had heard every little thing. Yesterday, Amy had discovered her file was missing and had been searching for it ever since, quizzing everyone if they'd seen the file for Patient 1432.

*My name is Courtney and I deserved to know the truth.*

She'd been practising that speech in case she was busted, but Amy hadn't suspected her of taking it—so far.

She'd also been thinking about how to escape, but so far everything she thought of involved using her powers.

*I don't want to tear the building in half and I don't know if the training I've been given will be enough to escape. Especially when they seem to have all these extra military types stationed here recently.*

She shifted on her bed.

*Plus, I don't know if I've fully flushed the drugs from my system. I want to be one hundred percent before I go anywhere.* She briefly wondered if she was scared to leave.

Thankfully she was spared having to face that possibility by the strange vibrations that suddenly flowed from the floor, through the bed and into her.

*What the hell was that? Someone just appeared in this building from out of nowhere—down in the sewer system on the opposite side of the building.*

Courtney could tell the person was short, yet surprisingly heavy, and was most likely a man. He started moving towards the basement floor.

*He doesn't seem to have set off any alarms, so either their security is not as good as I thought, or this guy's got some kind of stealth ability.* As the minutes went by and the mysterious intruder made it into the main building, Courtney was convinced it was the latter. She turned it over in her mind.

*So, I could expose this guy and inadvertently reveal I can still hear them from in here, or I could use it as the opportunity I've been looking for.*

A small part of her said it was too early, that she hadn't worked out the details, but it was only a small part.

\* \* \*

### The Skull of Ra: 13 December 34 BZ

Anu Hopet watched the live feed from Disk's cybernetic eye on the ship's viewscreen. He had infiltrated the underground base as planned and had begun his sensor sweep. Unfortunately, the portable sensor was not as powerful as the ship's, so Disk had to scan the base in sections, which involved a lot of moving about.

*It was fortunate he has a personal cloaking device or he would surely have been discovered by now. His blundering is making this mission take too long.*

Field trips were not Disk's speciality.

Anu Hopet stood in his usual posture: chest out, arms behind his back, impassive to the telemetry he was watching.

*It was foolish of me to indulge him in this pointless exercise. We will not find who took the talisman there, or any trace of a Celestial One, I would wager.*

Suddenly, a shrill beeping rang out from the viewscreen.

'Great Armageddon, my presence has been detected. I believe it was the telemetry feed—so I will upload my scans now.' Disk's voice sounded even more robotic over the viewscreen. 'I beg your forgiveness for failing you, my liege.'

'Fool!' Anu Hopet boomed, his stony voice sounding even more terrifying when relayed to Disk. 'Forgiveness be damned—just tell me, did you learn anything important?'

'Yes, my lord. There is a Manifest here, the one responsible for the tremors I detected. She is extremely powerful, maybe more powerful than your quarry. She's connected…Earth…dormant Celestial One… vital…jamming me…' Disk's transmission flickered on the screen.

The last thing he saw before the screen went black was a blurry soldier and a rifle butt slamming into what would have been Disk's artificial eye.

'Unacceptable!' He smashed his fist into the console and destroyed it. It was fortunate that *The Skull of Ra* repaired itself, otherwise it would have been rent into scrap centuries ago. Anu Hopet cared not for consoles.

*That fool has been captured and his data burst corrupted! But more importantly, his brain's hard drive contains too much important information. Information I need before I can afford to destroy the planet.*

He returned to staring at the blank viewscreen and brooded on his next course of action. His remaining minions knew not to disturb him.

* * *

**Barton Correctional Facility: 14 December 34 BZ**

Chief Warden Walter Screw sat in the interrogation room and asked Studebaker to bring in the next interviewee. He'd taken her under his wing of late and she frequently assisted him with important tasks, such as the one they were currently undertaking. The task force he'd put together for the impending doomsday had been finalised, but he'd insisted on doing a final interview with them personally. With so much at stake by using criminals as a military strike team, it had to be perfect.

Studebaker slid open the large door and two guards steered a fluorescent yellow cylinder into the room, its flashing orange lights filling the room with colour. One guard controlled the cylinder's treads, while the other was there mainly as back up if anything went wrong.

'Thanks, guys,' Studebaker said and slid the door closed behind them when they left. Two other guards were already in the room as a precaution. She powered up the speaker that allowed communication with the prisoner in the cylinder and flicked on the mute button. 'Ready, when you are, sir,' she said to Walter.

'Who've we got now?' he asked, fidgeting in his seat. This had already taken two hours—longer than he'd planned for—and he was craving a cigar. He never smoked in the main prison.

'This one's called Tronk, Class C; it's a sentient machine that can explode things by pointing its remote detonator at them,' Studebaker answered, reading from her clipboard. 'Hard to believe, really.'

*It doesn't get any easier to believe, either.*

'How many more to go?' he enquired. *Surely there can't be many left.*

Walter had already interviewed Tanglor, Deathspawn, and the yellow and orange robotic killing machine, Avenatraitor, who'd allegedly been constructed by the Energy Lord.

Grasshopper and Rattlesnake were humanoid Manifest animals, while Asp was intelligent but trapped in its original body and unable to speak, so he didn't need to see them. He also hadn't bothered with Mind Syphon or Ooze—a regular guy who'd had the bad luck to

Manifest into an acidic puddle of goop—as they were beings that were unleashed, rather than talked to.

'Just one more after this, sir: team leader Joseph Starlen,' Studebaker announced.

'Excellent. Well, let's get this over with then,' Walter said.

Studebaker unmuted the speaker and the interview began.

It took less than ten minutes in the end, as Tronk wasn't programmed to respond with much more than 'don't sue me' when asked a question.

*It appeared to understand its mission, which is something at least. I have to just assume with the humanoid animals—who can know if they truly understand?* Walter couldn't believe things were so desperate that they were recruiting scum to defend them.

The final containment cylinder was ushered in and Walter began the interview.

'Joseph,' he began, as if chewing the name. 'I hope you will excuse the containment cylinder, we must think of safety first.'

'Didn't seem to bother you when you were beating on me in the past,' Starlen shot back, his breath misting the viewport in the cylinder.

Studebaker shot Walter a quick glance and then looked at her feet. He took it in his stride.

'Then let's just say the cylinder is for your own protection.' He smirked at the prisoner.

'How bromidic,' Starlen said sardonically. 'So, what did you want to "chat" about? I've already gone through countless evaluations just to get here, so it must be to reminisce. Did you want to talk about Jen?'

Jennifer White had been Walter's high school sweetheart before she left him for Joseph. It was something that Walter hadn't disclosed to anyone, even his son.

'Best you don't mention her name again if you want to continue to lead this mission—at least with a full set of teeth. I've been interviewing everyone on the team as a final evaluation before we consider letting you loose.' He felt another tobacco craving but suppressed it.

'Liar. You already know there's no one else that could keep the rabble you've assembled in line on the missions you're proposing,' Starlen said with a sly smile, the long scar running down his cheek tightening as he did so. 'No, you still blame me for her death, and can't live with the fact that your superiors chose me to lead this team. The full pardon they offered me must have really stung.'

*Not as much as my fists will if you keep that up.* He said nothing.

'Your silence just confirms my suspicions.'

'You killed her. There's nothing else to say about it.'

'It wasn't my fault, it was an accident,' Starlen said coldly. 'Destructo was a big robot and she got underfoot. She shouldn't have been there.'

'On that you and I both agree,' Walter replied, trying to maintain his calm. 'This interview is over.'

Studebaker muted the speaker and sent for the guards to take Starlen away. Although he couldn't hear, he could see through the viewport that Starlen was laughing.

'Wait a minute. Studebaker, I want him to hear this,' Walter said before the guards arrived. She flicked a switch and gave him the thumbs up.

'Oh, one last thing,' he whispered into the speaker. 'My superiors didn't pick you for this team, I did.'

'And why would you do that?' Starlen mocked.

'Because we're sending you to Hell.'

* * *

### Fatmandu's Safe House, Banksmeadow: 15 December 34 BZ

Naomi Bloodlust sat in the cramped tunnel as the stench of things best unknown assailed her nostrils. 'Do we have to hide out here?' she complained. 'Couldn't we have gone to Spindler's hideout instead?'

Spindler owned a small flat in Bronte, which was a dump, but it was lightyears ahead of the decommissioned stormwater drain that Fatmandu called home. Molecule lived here too, being mentally unfit to get a place of its own. In truth, the same could be said of Fatmandu, attested to by the piles of half-eaten, rotten food that littered the floor.

'Because it's too exposed,' Liu replied, 'and there's no way Gorg would think to look for you here—*you* didn't even know it existed a few days ago.'

*I wish I didn't know it existed now.*

'We can only hope what you say is true,' Naomi allowed. 'I'd hate to think we just ended up trapping ourselves in this filthy tunnel.'

'I'm sure it'll be fine,' Liu said, shifting on the dirty mattress he was sitting on. 'Besides, we only have to stay here as long as it takes us to strike at Scar.'

'How long will that be?' whined Fatmandu in his childlike voice. 'You guys are cramping my style, and the sooner this is done and you're gone, the better.'

Liu rolled his eyes at the comment. 'We're not ready yet.'

'Yeah…well, I've been thinking about that,' Naomi said, ignoring the irony of her comrade's statement and extending her right leg to ease her cramp. 'If Bojangles is to be believed, there's going to be some sort of extinction level event right here in Sydney on Christmas Day.'

'Not sure I buy that…' Liu began.

'Let me finish,' she said, cutting him off. 'If the world's ending in ten days, I say we get our kicks in before then.'

'Makes sense…' Fatmandu agreed.

'What are you proposing?' Liu asked.

'I say we hit him on Christmas Eve.'

\* \* \*

## Mullberry Residence, Canberra: 16 December 34 BZ

Dread Sedgewick stalked up to the front door of the unassuming house on the quiet street and rang the doorbell like a Jehovah's Witness. It was well past dinnertime. He stood back and started picking his teeth with his finger blade—he found cat to be a little stringy.

The wooden door opened to reveal a youthful woman with a bob of ginger hair, dressed in a purple summer dress. Even though there was a security mesh screen door between them, the recognition in the woman's eyes was instantaneous.

'Kids, run!' she screamed behind her.

*My reputation precedes me.*

'Looks like I'm at the right place,' Dread said jovially, kicking through the security door as if it were tissue paper, 'but is that any way to greet your stepson?'

If the woman heard him she didn't let on; she was too busy diving for cover.

Dread strode into the entranceway like he owned the place and sparked up a cigarette. A teenage boy and his young sister stood gaping from the hallway.

Their mother turned to them: 'Peach, Yam, didn't you hear me? Run!' This time they obeyed.

'Yes, run little piggies,' Dread called after them. 'The fun is in the chase.'

'You stay away from them, you monster,' she yelled. 'What do you want with us?'

'You must be Nikki,' he replied, flicking his lit cigarette into the lounge room. It landed on a cushion. 'You're the slut who stole my father from me.'

'What? You're mistaken…' Nikki Mullberry climbed to her feet. 'You've got us confused with someone else.' A couch in the lounge started smoking.

'Looks like "Daddy" lied to you as well,' he allowed. 'Not that it makes any difference. I'm still going to kill you all and eat your corpses.' He kicked her in the stomach, causing her to fly through the plaster wall that separated the entranceway from the kitchen. She smashed through the kitchen table and finally came to an abrupt stop next to the back door.

'Wait… Hunter never said…' she gasped weakly, before coughing up blood.

'Yeah, yeah, you're like a broken record,' Dread accused, walking through the hole he'd made in the wall. 'Weren't you listening when I politely told you that it doesn't matter whether Dad told you or not? I'm still going to slay you.'

'When Bentaz gets home, you'll be sorry,' Nikki spat. She could see it now; he looked like her son.

'Bentaz? Yam? Peach? What are you, a hippy? They're stupid names for children,' he said incredulously, while reaching into his coat and producing a long, slender knife. 'Although, I should thank you for letting me know Ballistic's real name—I'd never have guessed "Bentaz" in a million years!'

'And I suppose "Vicious Man" is so much better?' she retorted. She noticed the plumes of smoke billowing from the lounge.

'The media came up with that inspiring name,' he admitted. 'But where are my manners? My name's Dread, Dread Sedgewick. I named myself when I was born.'

*Somehow that seems to horrify her even more. Perfectamundo.*

By now most of the house was on fire and the kitchen was filled with toxic black smoke. Dread loved the smell of burning plastics. He raised the dagger. Nikki closed her eyes and drifted into the black.

Suddenly a brick smashed into his face, shattering into pieces when it struck. 'Get away from my mum!' a girl's voice screamed.

'Peach, get back here!' a man's voice said almost immediately.

Dread was confronted by a girl with pigtails standing defiantly before him. She held another brick in her hand. A man with long brown hair, close to Dread's own age, followed her into the kitchen from the backyard.

'How cute.' Dread smiled as he dropkicked the girl through the open door. She landed in a crumpled heap and lay still.

'Peach!' Yam cried, dragging his unconscious mother into the backyard. Dread sauntered out after them. The burning house lit up the night sky behind him like an enormous bonfire.

'This is getting old,' he said, closing the gap between them and grabbing the teen by the throat. Dread lifted him over his head and threw him hard at the ground, but to his surprise, Yam phased into the earth like it was water. 'Okay, that's new,' he marvelled.

Yam leapt up behind Dread and grasped him, pulling him down into the ground.

'Nice try.' Dread flexed his mighty thews and the entire lawn erupted in a shower of dirt. Yam went flying into the brick wall of the house and lost consciousness. 'All right, enough of this crap. I knew Dad wasn't home, as I wanted him to witness his dirty secret expunged, but I was hoping that—Bentaz, was it?—would be here. Oh well, I'm sure he'll come after me once I'm done. It's almost midnight, do you know where your son is?' He laughed at his obscure joke and twirled his knife. He looked at his three unconscious victims. 'So, who's first?'

Unexpectedly, a dimensional portal opened to his left and a dark blur slammed into his right side, knocking him through the portal and away from the suburban home. He found himself skimming through knee-deep water in a vast open plain. The Milky Way shone brightly in the night sky.

*Where the fuck am I?*

He turned back the way he'd come and saw the Mullberry family home through a window in reality—a window that five obvious superheroes were currently passing through.

*Those cock suckers! Taking my hard-earned justice away from me! Who the fuck do they think they are?*

'We are with the Heroes Squadron of Australia,' announced a winged demonic goat-man, as if in answer to Dread's thoughts.

'Yeah, and your ass is grass, and I'm a lawnmower,' said the blue blur as he came to a sudden stop. His eyes were covered by a strange mask that covered half his face in a similar pattern to Dread's facial birthmarks. Unlike Dread, he had an aquamarine cape that rippled dramatically in the nocturnal breeze.

'Did you have to use that cliché?' complained a pigman with metallic tusks and crest.

'Ignore Razorback,' said another hero, this one adorned in green armour with red spikes and a glowing rock in his chest. His legs turned into a beam of light when he flew around the plain. 'I'm called the Mauler, the pig's Razorback, portal-guy is Gate Crasher...' he said, referencing the weedy teen in the rainbow-coloured suit who brought them there, '... the demon is Hellgoat, and the wanker is Powerhouse.'

'Hey!' Powerhouse objected. 'I'm the toughest one here...'

Dread couldn't believe the audacity, *nor* the temerity, as he struggled to choose a noun. 'You cunts are gunna get fucked up, real bad,' he promised in unintentional Aussie drawl.

'Maybe we should contact HQ, let Ballistic know we found him,' Gate Crasher squeaked uncertainly.

'No need, I can handle this without *him*,' Powerhouse exaggerated.

'SHUT THE FUCK UP!' Dread bellowed with the power of a gale-force wind.

The HSA members all stopped to stare at the incarnation of destruction. The dark patch that spread across Gate Crasher's crotch thankfully went unnoticed. Dread took him down first with a surprise blade to the knee. He screamed as his leg fell out from under him and he plunged into the shallow water.

'Squeal, piggy!' Dread laughed, drawing another knife from his belt. 'You won't be 'portin' outta here anytime soon.'

'I'm the only pigman here,' Razorback yelled, launching his rocket-tusks at Dread's face.

'So you are,' Dread agreed, catching the tusks mid-flight and returning them to their owner's shoulders. Razorback squealed like a pigman. Dread tossed his other blade through Hellgoat's wing and kicked Razorback across the snout in one smooth motion.

Powerhouse appeared paralysed, so Mauler fired his rocket-propelled fists at the back of Dread's head, hoping to take him out with a sucker punch. Dread turned and sliced the hands to pieces with his finger blades. Mauler screamed.

'I can't believe you did that after you just saw what I did to your piggy friend. What kind of fool shoots a body part at their foe anyway?' Dread leapt into the air and elbowed Mauler across the face, sending him careening into the water, extinguishing his light beam and replacing it with his legs. 'However, I do like that sparkly rock poking out of your chest—reminds me of a stone some alien was carrying when I disarmed him at Fatty's. Do you think you can bequeath it to me in your will?'

A blur of fists rained down upon Dread with the force of a hurricane. He felt the pleasant sensation of his face burning and a moment later he was on his back and under the shallow water of the lake.

*I don't have time for this shit.*

He sprang to his feet and caught Powerhouse by surprise, slicing him from stomach to chest. The angle of the slice, coupled with Powerhouse's invulnerability, meant the wound wasn't fatal, yet it caused a serious gash. Powerhouse shrieked.

Before he could finish him off, Dread was engulfed in a ball of flames. The water boiled around him and a great pillar of steam erupted into the night.

Hellgoat circled above him, seemingly unaffected by the hole in his wing. 'My hellfire will roast your soul!' he roared demonically.

Dread was unimpressed.

'Who says I even have a soul?' he jibed, his trench coat falling in ashes from his body. 'That coat, on the other hand, was very dear to me, so prepare to snort your testicles.'

Predictably, Hellgoat instinctively guarded his groin, allowing Dread to jump at breakneck speed and knee him in the jaw. He followed through with a withering punch to the stomach, sending Hellgoat crashing into the lakebed.

He was having a good time despite his plans being changed unexpectedly.

*Yet something's missing. Maybe it'll come to me when I flay them?*

'Hello? HQ?' the strained voice came from behind him. 'It's Gate Crasher. I'm at Lake George, New South Wales. We've engaged Vicious Man and he's taking us apart. We need help. We need Ballistic.'

*Eureka! Turns out there's a silver lining after all.*

Dread smiled and looked south to the horizon.

\* \* \*

### Mullberry Residence, Canberra: 17 December 34 BZ

Bentaz Mullberry didn't get home until after midnight, only to find his house a blazing inferno. He'd heard sirens wailing in the distance on his way home but had been disregarding them. He couldn't get to every emergency in the world.

*If only I'd gotten here sooner, maybe they would still be okay. Dad hasn't yet returned from his work trip, which is no surprise.*

'Ballistic?' one of the firemen called out as he approached. 'Thank god you're here. We could really use your help getting this fire contained. The whole house has been gutted...'

Bentaz ignored him and flew straight up to the paramedics who were trying to resuscitate his mother in the driveway. His stomach dropped.

'Is there anything I can do?' he asked feebly. He'd never felt so helpless before.

'Stand back. This is no place for superheroes. Let real professionals work,' one of the paramedics snapped.

'She's stabilising,' the other paramedic said, 'but it's touch-and-go.'

*Where's Yam and Peach?*

He looked around frantically, finally going around to the backyard. More paramedics were working on his little sister in the far corner of the yard. His brother was nowhere to be seen. He floated over to his sister. 'Peach?'

These paramedics simply paid no attention to him as they slowly transferred her to the gurney.

'B-Ben-Ba-Ballistic,' she whimpered. Even now she remembered his secret identity even if he'd forgotten he was still in his 'work' outfit. 'He hurt them, he hurt Mum and Yam.'

'Who did? Where's Yam?' He didn't want to tell her about their mother.

'The ambulance men took him,' Peach answered as she was gently placed on the gurney.

'Are you in pain? Who did this to you?' Bentaz was getting more worked up with every second. He hated feeling powerless while his family suffered.

'It was Vicious Man…'

*Vicious Man! That monster was here? Why?*

'I overheard him…he told Mum he was her stepson…I was so scared…'

*Stepson? Does that make him my half-brother?* He roiled with anger and disgust.

'Peach, you're going to be okay. I'm going to make things right.' It was all he knew to say.

'I…I can't feel my legs,' she sobbed.

The revelation stung like a knife.

'I thought I'd Manifest like you and Yam, but instead…' She broke down into tears.

'We'll do everything we can for her, but it looks serious,' the paramedic said, wheeling her towards the ambulance.

*She's only twelve…*

Bentaz's hands glowed as the rage inside him approached breaking point.

Right then the communicator in his helmet squawked and he received an audio message forwarded from HSA headquarters.

'It's Gate Crasher. I'm at Lake George, New South Wales. We've engaged Vicious Man...'

Within a fraction of a second, Bentaz was flying north at supersonic speed, the shockwave flattening trees and houses alike as he pushed himself to go faster. All thoughts of collateral damage were forgotten as he rocketed towards Lake George.

*He should have run further. I'm going to make him pay for what he did to my family.*

For the first time in his life, his eyes started to glow. They were the same colour as the energy that crackled from his hands, a deep golden yellow.

As he approached, he picked up the local chatter coming from Gate Crasher's communicator. Tactician had insisted they all start using them as part of the preparations for the supposed apocalypse.

'He's coming, can't you feel it?' a voice said. 'At that speed...the impact...we've got to get out of here...'

Bentaz had every confidence they would get clear, but he wasn't going to slow down just the same. Instead he pushed himself harder, going faster than ever before, faster even than Powerhouse. The scenery flashed by as the very air began to burn, leaving a fiery streak across the night sky.

The lake was in an open plain, and Bentaz had an unspoiled view of the entire vista. He was distantly aware of Powerhouse and Hellgoat carrying some team members as they fled the area, but the focus of his attention was the psychotic looking man standing knee-deep in water with his hands on his hips. The man was grinning.

Bentaz hit Vicious Man with the force of a small atomic bomb, evaporating the entire lake and unleashing a massive blast wave that obliterated the nearby highway and was felt kilometres away.

At the centre of the newly formed crater, Bentaz slowly rose to his feet, his cape gone and most of his outfit in tatters.

On the other side of the crater, Vicious Man sat with a stunned look on his face. He, too, was in tattered clothes. 'Wow, what a rush,' he said with a smile. 'Can you do it again?'

Bentaz rammed his fist into Vicious Man's cheek, the impact sounding like cannon fire. He followed it up with another dozen blows, each one harder than the last.

The punches would have shattered a mountain, but Vicious Man shrugged them off and kicked Bentaz in the stomach, causing him to double over in pain. He then slashed Bentaz across the chest with his deadly finger blades, and for the first time since he Manifested, Bentaz saw his own blood. He looked at the wound in shock.

*How do I stop this monster?*

'I know what you're thinking,' Vicious Man taunted. 'You're thinking that you're supposed to be invulnerable. Well, let me tell you, invulnerable is just a word—as you're about to discover.' He pounced at Bentaz with feral agility.

Bentaz met him halfway and they clashed like titans.

Vicious Man tried to slice Bentaz's throat, but Bentaz blocked the blow with his right arm. Too late he realised it was a feint, as he felt a cold sensation in his side where Vicious Man's other hand was buried finger-deep.

Without thinking, he struck with all his strength channelled into a single blow to Vicious Man's right elbow, shattering the joint and severing the forearm. Before Vicious Man could react, Bentaz grabbed the severed arm by the stump and swung it at the arm still buried in his side. Vicious Man's finger blades sliced his own left arm clean off at the elbow. It slid from Bentaz's side.

'Hey! I need those!' Vicious Man complained, waving his bleeding stumps around.

'Not where we're going,' Bentaz replied, grabbing his opponent by the armpits and lifting him into the sky, leaving the severed arms behind.

*Only one place I know to take him where he won't be a problem.*

Vicious Man bit into Bentaz's helmet, tearing off chunks of metal in an effort to get to his face.

Bentaz continued skyward, soon reaching escape velocity and entering the cold of space. Without air resistance, his speed increased and he used every iota of stamina to fly even faster than he had earlier. It seemed like an eternity, but *this* trip to the moon had smashed his previous speed record.

Vicious Man appeared to be talking to him, but the words were lost in the airless void between worlds. He spat a frozen wad that bounced off Bentaz's chin. The moon loomed colossal above them.

Bentaz headed for the frozen crater he frequented, as it was the most familiar landmark to him. Vicious Man kneed him in the balls, but it was too late and they slammed into the crater with the force of a meteor strike.

The impact caused an enormous explosion that massively increased the crater's size and sent thousands of tonnes of dust and debris in all directions. The crater smouldered but was cooling rapidly in the airless dark. Dust was everywhere.

Suddenly a fist broke through the smooth bottom of the crater and Bentaz gradually crawled up from the molten depths. He staggered to his feet but could barely see through the dust cloud.

*The rock is molten at the moment, but soon it'll turn hard and entomb that monster forever. A fitting end for such an arsehole.*

Miraculously, two burned and broken timber planks remained of Bentaz's deckchair and were conveniently at hand. He fashioned them into a crude cross and shoved it into the ground.

*Here lies Vicious Man, world's biggest cunt.*

Bentaz staggered again, the exertion starting to take its toll.

*Have to get back to Earth. I don't think it's wise to pass out here.*

It took tremendous effort, yet he summoned reserves of strength he didn't know he had and began the journey back home. This time he wasn't going to break any speed records.

Finally, he reached atmosphere and took a deep breath.

*I should go back to Lake George and see if the others got away from the battle okay. Then the hospital to check on my family, but I can barely keep my eyes open and my side's bleeding everywhere. My team might have to end up saving me.* He smiled at the irony. *I don't know if I can make it. I don't even have the energy to slow down…*

He lost consciousness on his approach to the lake and overshot it by several kilometres before ploughing into the Earth with another explosion.

If he'd only remained conscious, he may have seen the green-skinned demon as it arrived in the predawn gloom. 'This is the last one my master wants for his experiment,' the demon said, picking up Bentaz and carrying him to the west.

# Week One

## Hyde Park, Sydney: 18 December 34 BZ

Seth Zaraxom stood in the warm summer night and stared at the new crater on the face of the moon. It was huge, and all anyone had been talking about since it happened. It scared a lot of people.

*If they only knew what was coming in only a week's time, then they'd really be scared.*

He finished his smoke and butted it out with his heel.

*Still, that crater is pretty fucking impressive. The media says it was some fight between Dread and Ballistic from the HSA. Both are presumed dead, along with five other HSA members and a dozen civilians who happened to be close to Lake George.*

He shook his head as he thought of his nephew.

*He just couldn't listen to his mother and me and leave his father's family alone.*

Seth wandered aimlessly around the park, not really sure what he was looking for.

*A clue, perhaps? I don't think Dread's dead and neither does Lilith, but that doesn't mean he's in good shape. And the other one? I saw him leaving old Arthur Mullberry's house. Maybe he's the one I've been searching for all these years?*

The more he thought about it, the more it seemed right.

*He'd be a major asset against the High Mage if it's true and I wouldn't even have to offer him money. This might just be our way out.*

Then it dawned on him.

*I hope Dread didn't kill him.*

* * *

### The Territories of Xph'Ish'Matarg, Hell: Circa 19 December 34 BZ

Mark Adams hung from one leg like a slab of beef. He'd been partially skinned, but only after his entire body was subjected to thousands of papercuts—even his eyes. In Hell, even your smallest dislikes were turned against you. A swarm of ravenous hellsquitos currently sapped his blood.

*They still can't trigger my Manifest seed despite putting me through tortures I didn't know existed. I wish it would, so this can end one way or another.*

He managed to force his left eye open and stare at his cacodemon tormentor's grotesque head atop a rusty pike. His eye was sore from the papercuts, but he at least could see, and it was worth the pain.

*I'm glad the demon lord punished it for failing to trigger my seed. I only wish I could've been the one to do it.*

He'd been strung up with a view of the great plain that represented the majority of Xph'Ish'Matarg's territories, from a giant tree-like sculpture made from grafted human souls. It put him at perfect face-height with the albino, goat-headed demon lord.

'We see Hell is rubbing off on you, in the form of your newfound aggression,' boomed the Lord of Hell. 'But your hope is offensive and must be extinguished. We may even revive the cacodemon to mock you. But first...'

The demon reached out with a furry paw, plucked Mark from the 'tree' and held him close to its dirty snout. It sniffed him and then held him at arm's length towards the plain.

*What new nightmare is this?*

He was too weary to care but knew he would the moment the torture started.

'The nightmare you refer to is truth, Mark Adams,' Xph'Ish'Matarg thundered, reading his mind. 'See this plain? It was not large enough to hold the legions of the Archdemon, which have already left Hell in accordance with the High Mage's plan. They are in the Mystical Realm, awaiting the appointed time to assault the Gates of Heaven itself. That will leave us to rule Hell in their absence. We will use your Manifest to consolidate our hold on this realm, should the High Mage's plan fail.'

*Is that even possible? Is this another trick?*

'No, not a trick,' Xph'Ish'Matarg answered. 'Sometimes the truth causes the most pain. Like the truth about your dead wife.'

The words stabbed into Mark's stomach and he felt their sting despite the physical trauma he'd suffered.

*Someone will stop you.* It was a feeble answer, and he knew it. So did the demon lord.

'Who? Lucifer is bound, and the Archdemon departed with the other major lords set to invade Earth. Those that remain have not the power to oppose me.' Xph'Ish'Matarg laughed, a sound not unlike a herd of goats bleating in agony.

*Someone will—that being the High Mage warned you of.*

'The Wraith is unaware of these machinations, and even if it were, we will destroy it. Can you feel it in the air? The tension? Reality itself groans in protest of what is to come.'

Mark could feel it and despaired.

\* \* \*

### Centrepoint Tower, Sydney: 20 December 34 BZ

The High Mage of Hell affixed the Soul Gem to a metal spike and attached it to the top of the tower.

*I'm surprised a building this tall didn't have a lightning rod already,* he thought, levitating back to the landing. *Good thing I brought my own.*

He looked up at the crystal, admiring the blue patterns it cast when struck by a light from the city below. He smiled and turned to face his maleficent companion. 'I have put a glamour spell on the Gem, so most people who see it will think it's part of the upcoming New Year's Eve celebrations, but you will ensure it's not disturbed, won't you?'

'Your will is law,' the Dark Destroyer replied emotionlessly.

*And soon it will be the law of reality itself.*

\* \* \*

## Dungeon Cell 9: 21 December 34 BZ

Andy Trailer was ushered out of his filthy cell, down the dank corridor and into a brightly lit chamber off the main command room. The fluorescent light hurt his eyes after hours alone in the dark, but he soon grew accustomed to the glare and noticed his master standing before him.

'M-Master, why have you brought me here? I hope I haven't offended you.' He was worried; he'd never been in this room before, and new usually meant something bad when Pulse Pounder was involved.

*Stop grovelling and reclaim your Night Demon identity,* Wisp commanded within Andy's mind. *You are pathetic.*

Andy ignored the voice, too concerned with the rows of metal cylinders connected to each other with tubes and wires. He knew those cylinders were designed to hold test subjects, and he had an unshakable feeling he was next.

'Fear not, slave,' Pulse Pounder replied in his melodious voice. 'I merely wanted to thank you for acquiring those Heroes Squadron Manifests for my experiments. For once you didn't fail me—like you did with Lorraine Freeman.'

'I-I'm sorry about that, I...'

'Silence! Your whining will soon erode all the goodwill I currently have for you,' his master snapped.

*Pathetic,* Wisp repeated.

'No, you have done well this time. After the failure of Project Substance and...*lack* of other test subjects—aside from you, that is—I had one final chance to get the results I was after. Now, with the addition of these Manifests, I am hopeful that will be the case. I won't know until I have finished setting up my equipment, however, which won't be for another three days or more.'

*Now, that is interesting,* Wisp intoned. Andy kept ignoring it, but it was getting harder. Instead, he asked Pulse Pounder a question: 'Who are they, Master? What do you plan to do with them?'

'That's two questions, but I'll allow it, despite your impudence to ask about my plans. I'm feeling generous, after all.' Pulse Pounder strolled between the cylinders. He'd got the idea for them from time spent in the Powder Keg and modified them for suspended animation. 'I don't yet know their real names, but I am familiar with their silly superhero names.'

*As opposed to the sensible name of Pulse Pounder? Do not truckle with this fool,* Wisp advised. *Bask in the glory of Gledandron and become the Night Demon again.*

Andy found Wisp easier to ignore this time as he didn't know what 'truckle' meant.

'This is Gate Crasher, a Manifest who can make wormholes,' Pulse Pounder continued, wiping the condensation from the cylinder to look at his captive's face. 'And this is Razorback, some sort of pigman, like that Vong character no doubt. This here is Mauler, who has an interesting piece of meteorite stuck in his chest. The rock gives off strange energy readings, which I have yet to identify. It even appears to have helped him regrow his hands.'

He walked from cylinder to cylinder as he talked. Andy thought these heroes sounded familiar, but his memory was so fractured it was hard to tell. Pulse Pounder stopped at the next cylinder.

'This here's Powerhouse,' he said. 'Class B Manifest, but lower on the scale than our next prize, Ballistic. As you would know, he put a great big bloody hole in the moon and made all the world leaders piss themselves. The power potential with this one is astronomical.'

Andy felt a sense of pride at having captured someone that powerful.

*You weak insect,* Wisp hissed. *You would not have been so successful had he not already been unconscious from a fight.*

*Stop always trying to bring me down! Can't you be happy for me for once?* Andy was so distracted he let slip a murmur.

'What was that?' Pulse Pounder had good hearing, despite not having ears.

*Think fast.* 'Ah, I was just wondering who the last one is, my master,' he lied.

'Yes, I thought you'd ask about this one,' Pulse Pounder said. 'He is perhaps the most valuable of the haul, regardless of Ballistic's raw power. This one is called Hellgoat and he's a lot like you, except talented. I believe he holds the key to the transmogrification process, but first I intend to clone them all in order to have a continuous supply of test subjects.'

'Won't it take years for them to grow to the originals' ages?' Andy was finding this fascinating.

'That's what this machine is for; it will allow me to instantly create perfect replicas with the flick of a switch, except genetically loyal to me alone,' Pulse Pounder gloated. 'At least it will when I have completed it.'

'And then what? What will my part in all this be?' Andy hoped it was freedom.

'And then I will transmogrify the originals and set them loose upon mankind,' Pulse Pounder replied, avoiding the second question. He smiled a wicked smile. 'Consider it my Christmas gift to the world.'

* * *

### South Western Sydney: 22 December 34 BZ

Desci Adams stood on the small balcony and timidly lit the cigarette with a thread of green fire from her finger. She wasn't a smoker but didn't want to risk setting anything else on fire while she learned to control her newfound powers.

Suddenly she felt a presence behind her and turned around to see her son.

'Obie! You startled me,' she said, dropping the cigarette over the balcony. 'I didn't know you were home.'

'I didn't know you smoked either,' Obie replied in a judgemental tone. 'How long have you been doing this filthy habit?'

'It's just a packet I found in your father's bedside table,' she lied. 'It's not like I've taken it up or anything.'

'Okay, Mum, if you say so. I was just popping in to grab some clothes and maybe have a shower before I go out again.'

The kids had been spending less time at home lately; Desci never really knew where or with whom. *Probably that fucking Blandley kid.*

'I was wondering if you'd like to help me set up the Christmas decorations?' she asked hopefully.

'Sorry, Mum, I've got to get back to Nathan's. Sebastian and Samara are already there waiting.' He headed for his bedroom.

*I knew it. It's always that fucking kid.*

'Well, will you be home for Christmas Eve dinner at least? You know it's a tradition in this house.' She felt she was pleading with her son and she didn't like it. She followed him to his room.

'*Dad's* tradition,' Obie called over his shoulder as he rummaged through his chest of drawers for t-shirts. 'I'm happy to skip it.'

Desci felt a sinking in her stomach.

'But Mark's not here to…'

'No, he isn't here and he's been gone almost a year now,' Obie snapped.

*Seven months and twenty-three days.*

'Besides, Sebastian, Samara and I are already going into the city that night. Thought we'd check out a church service,' Obie explained, before choosing a black shirt.

*Church service? When did my kids become so religious?*

'How are you getting there?' she asked. *Dragon Kong said there was danger approaching. Could he have meant the big hole in the moon?*

'Nathan's driving.'

'In his Datsun? That thing's a death-trap.' Desci knew it was hopeless as soon as she said it.

'Well, we're going,' he stated irritably, 'and unless you want to drive, then Nathan's taking us.'

*But he also said the children of Manifests become Manifests themselves.*

Inspiration struck. 'Maybe I *will* drive then. This family should be together on Christmas Eve.'

'But you haven't driven in ages,' Obie argued. 'Is your licence still current?'

'Yeah, I renewed it recently with that lotto money I won,' she lied again.

*I can't tell him about 'Dad', not yet at least.*

'Ha! Now you can't say no,' she teased.

'I…guess not,' Obie reluctantly agreed. 'I'll let the others know when I see them tonight.'

*'Dad' also proved that danger can be a trigger for a Manifest seed. So, if there really is danger coming, at least I'll be there.*

'I'm looking forward to it,' she said as Obie walked into the bathroom and forcefully closed the door behind him.

* * *

### Grand Satanic Headquarters, Kings Cross: 23 December 34 BZ

Marek Mahoney was so excited he'd peed himself twice already. As Satanists laughed in the face of clean underwear, he didn't let it faze him—hell, he wasn't even wearing any.

*Only two days to go. I can hardly wait! The new crater on the moon is a sign that nothing can stop us now.*

All the preparations for the High Mage's plans had been made, so Marek arranged to meet up with the other members of the inner circle for celebratory drinks to toast the impending apocalypse. He stroked his freshly lacquered moustache and reached for a beer.

They were squeezed into the dank meeting room and everyone was ignoring the cloying, fetid air that became the norm once Tom Higginbottom's flayed corpse had been hung up on display. Marek found it comforting.

He was standing between Floyd and Lancefield while the two of them were engaged in an animated discussion about the merits of shaving the scrotum. He looked over to Matt, hoping to grab his attention, except the big man was having his own conversation with creepy Navid—about what, Marek could only speculate.

Karen had taken up both seats of the couch and lay back on a mound of frilled pillows, beer in hand. She was due to give birth in a couple of days and her large belly poked through her flimsy gown.

*I'm still not game to talk to her since I convinced them Melissa was lying about me failing to heed my fellow team members. Although I have to admit I lack judgement—hiring Melissa is proof of that.*

'Then I guess you have no choice but to talk to me!' Blotch McMahn called from Marek's hand.

'I'm not going to talk to you,' he whispered, completely aware of the irony, 'so just be quiet.' He was reminded of a line from *Macbeth*.

'My apologies,' Lancefield said, believing Marek was talking to him.

'I realise the power of the scrotum can be intimidating—especially when shorn.'

The image of Lancefield's shaven nuts bored into Marek's mind like untreated syphilis. 'Uh, yeah, well Satanists laugh in the face of bald testicles,' he recovered with a smile.

'Nice save,' admitted Blotch McMahn. 'But how long can you keep it up while trying to IGNORE MEEEEE.' It sang the last part in baritone. Marek felt the now all-too familiar migraine coming on.

Satan must have been smiling, for a second later Matt started tapping on his beer bottle with the teaspoon he kept in the bottle's neck whenever he put it down. 'Can I have everyone's attention?' he called to the room. 'As you all know, the recent moon incident was augured to be an omen that we are on the unstoppable path to glory...'

Lancefield cheered prematurely.

'...and as proof of that I have an important announcement to make,' Matt continued, grabbing another beer from the table. 'Thanks to the money we collected with our door-knock drive, we saved enough to buy a communication system so we can all watch each other live during the event on big video screens!'

Now everyone else cheered, but Lancefield had just stuffed his face full of stale muesli bar and missed his opportunity.

'Excellent news,' Karen said from the couch, her eyes seemingly pulsing in the gloom. 'Now we just need to ensure they're working.'

'I helped set them up, so we know they're good to go,' Floyd bragged.

'You better let *me* have a look at them,' said a sulky voice from beneath the table. 'I am a savant, after all.' Melissa emerged from behind the long red tablecloth dressed in an ill-fitting cocktail dress, his man-boobs jiggling without a bra.

*Oh no!*

'What's *he* doing here?' Karen yelled, looking directly at Marek. 'This celebration is for the inner circle only!'

He started nervously stroking the thick black hair that sprouted from his forehead as he tried to come up with an explanation.

'Marek invited me along,' Melissa lied before Marek could answer. 'He said you asked for me especially.'

'Wait, that's not true!' Marek protested. Navid glared at him creepily.

'That Melissa guy's a real piece of work, isn't he?' Blotch McMahn observed.

*For once I agree with you.*

'Silence!' Karen wailed, her voice a shrill knife that cut through the small room. 'You're lucky it's too late to replace you, otherwise…well, otherwise, we would!' She seemed happy with her redundant statement.

'But, I…' Marek tried again.

'It's okay, we forgive you,' Melissa cut in. 'We all know how confused you get with simple instructions.' He helped himself to a beer and began to skol. 'Do you have any mead?' he asked, oblivious to the looks he was getting. 'I still don't think you should be going on daylight saving time, as an authority on celestial movements…'

Marek stopped listening.

*Satan help me, I'm going to kill him!*

But he couldn't; they needed six hundred and sixty-six members to invoke the Lords of Hell and he don't want to risk being one short. He guessed it was the same reason Karen kept him on.

*No, I've decided; I'm not going to let him spoil the apocalypse for me!*

'You're a dick,' Blotch McMahn commented.

* * *

### The Skull of Ra: 24 December 34 BZ 6:00 PM AEDT

Anu Hopet checked the display for the third time.

*It says there is a build-up of energy, but the ship cannot identify what it is. It also appears to be coming from this city, but I cannot pinpoint the exact location.*

'Bah! I need Disk back,' he boomed to the empty bridge. The remaining members of the Skull Band had been avoiding him of late.

*Is the knowledge in his head worth it? Or should I just cut my losses and destroy this world before this mysterious energy peaks?*

Anu Hopet paced back and forth, his arms tucked behind his back.

*The alarms have only just begun, so based on these readings I have at least six hours before that happens.*

He knew what he must do.

* * *

### South Western Sydney: 7:14 PM AEDT

Desci Adams sat behind the wheel of her rundown Ford Laser in the gridlocked traffic. 'There's an awful lot of police and military vehicles around,' she said to her children. 'I wonder what's going on?'

*Maybe this is what I was warned about?*

'I bet they're the reason for all this traffic,' Obie agreed. He sat in the front while his cousins sat in the back. 'Good thing we're not meeting up with Nathan until eleven.'

'Plenty of time,' Desci responded, moving the car forward several metres before stopping again. She secretly hoped they'd be late.

* * *

### The Moon: 8:37 PM AEDT

Dread Sedgewick used his freshly grown arms to dig himself free of his airless, frozen tomb.

*Time for round three.*

He smiled and got to work on carving a dimensional gateway.

* * *

### Saint Mary's Cathedral, Sydney: 9:06 PM AEDT

Lorraine Freeman handed over the last Christmas hamper to a dishevelled homeless man and looked at her expensive watch. 'I think it's time we headed down to Darling Harbour for the carols—we don't want to be late.'

She turned to her companion, Beat Master, who was talking to the priest about something wholly unrelated to their volunteer work providing Christmas relief to the poor. '...and I want to get into techno, as I have a feeling it's going to be pretty popular soon enough,' he said to the indifferent pastor.

'Samuel?' Lorraine prodded. 'Stop bothering the Father, we have to go.'

'Okay, okay, I'm coming.' Beat Master shook the priest's hand and turned to leave.

'Thank you once again for your help tonight,' the priest said amiably. 'Any friend of the Holy See is welcome here anytime. God be with you.'

*Obviously, he doesn't know of the little 'incident' that happened at the Vatican with Cardinal Ejigu,* Lorraine thought, remembering her attacker. 'Thank you, Father. I'm glad we could help.'

She took Beat Master by the hand and started walking towards their next appointment.

'There sure are a lot of police around,' he observed as they strolled along the footpath. 'And military too—is this common in Australia?'

*I wonder if Mum's caught up in all of this?*

'No, not usually,' she replied. 'Must be something important going on.'

'Good thing we don't have far to go then,' Beat Master declared, hitting the play button on his metallic suit.

They walked off to the sound of 'Jingle Bell Rock', followed by a horde of adoring fans.

* * *

## Undisclosed location: 9:23 PM AEDT

Courtney Yeht felt the explosion as it travelled through the hair she used to connect her sealed room to the rest of the complex.

*Holy crap, what was that?*

Whatever it was, it was big and the floor told her that chaos reigned outside the confines of her room.

*Maybe this is my chance.*

She'd been disappointed when the previous intruder had been captured by the guards, but at least she'd finally been able to flush the last of the drugs from her system. She was at full strength.

*And they never did discover it was me who took the file.*

Another explosion rocked the base and her room shook despite the magnets levitating it in place.

*Whoever that is causing the explosions, he's big. I can feel the fear he's spreading by the way the guards are hesitant to confront him. Who is he?*

Yet another explosion rocked the compound and this time Courtney could feel one of the guard's body fly into pieces and bounce off the walls.

*One thing's for certain—he's a lot more powerful than the other intruder. This is it—I don't think I'll get another opportunity.*

As if in answer to her thoughts, another explosion tore through the base, shaking its very foundations. The magnets holding her room aloft failed and it crashed into the outer walls and split open.

*I'm free!*

\* \* \*

**Barton Correctional Facility: 9:31 PM AEDT**

Walter Screw was enjoying a rare quiet moment when the phone on his desk started to ring.

*Goddamn it!*

He butted out his cigar and picked up the handset.

'Chief Warden Screw here,' he answered, rubbing his forehead with his other hand. The sound of his son's concerned voice was on the line.

'Tactician, what's going on?' He was aware that others may overhear the conversation and therefore remained professional.

'I just received word that Project Typhon is under attack by an unknown Manifest,' Tactician announced. His voice sounded tinny. 'This may be the start of the event we've been preparing for.'

*Let the games begin.*

'Where are you now?' Walter asked.

'Our outpost at Pheasants Nest,' Tactician replied. 'I'm going to go to Project Typhon personally, but it'll take time to get to Banksmeadow—even by helicopter.'

'Do it, but make sure you take some men with you.' Though their relationship was frosty at times, Walter still cared for his son's welfare.

'I will. I have a few MIBs with me at the moment. They're the ones who told me of the attack.'

'Okay, be careful and let me know how it goes.' Walter hung up the phone.

He lit up another cigar and tapped the intercom.

'Gordon, it's time to activate the Government Villains.'

* * *

### Scar's Warehouse, Ashfield, Sydney: 9:55 PM AEDT

Naomi Bloodlust crept into the darkened warehouse with the rest of the Blood Brigade bringing up the rear. They were all dressed in their work outfits. 'I don't like this, it's too quiet,' she whispered to Liu.

'Yeah, it feels like a trap,' he whispered back, his face obscured by his visored helmet.

Spindler and Fatmandu nodded in agreement. Molecule seemed oblivious.

'That's because it is,' said a familiar voice from the other side of the room.

Suddenly the lights came on and the Blood Brigade was confronted by the familiar (and ugsome) sight of Scar smiling a wicked smile. He was joined by his Seven Servants, who stood behind him like a motley crew—minus the big hair and play on words.

'Did you really think you could sneak in here without me knowing?' he asked with pompous hubris. 'I've been monitoring you ever since your pitiful stakeout attempt.'

*Bojangles was right; we were being obvious. Can't believe I made such a rookie mistake.*

'Well, that just makes our job easier then,' boasted Spindler, drawing an LSD arrow on the energy-bow that formed in his hand.

'Big words for a dead man,' Scar replied casually. His minions spread out at his words.

'Don't let them flank us,' Naomi advised, drawing her poisoned blades in a defensive posture. 'Remember, most of his goons are just Manifested objects and lack true intelligence.'

'They still outnumber us,' Liu cautioned.

'More for me to eat!' Fatmandu growled, his stomach rumbling.

Suddenly, the skylight above them shattered and Naomi found herself caught in a noose made of metal cables before she was hauled upward towards the roof. Thanks to her quick reflexes, she managed to slip a hand under the noose before it tightened, preventing her neck from being broken. It still hurt though.

*Fool, letting yourself be caught like that!*

Moments later she found herself lying on her back on the warehouse roof, face to face with a man in sleek grey and black armour and adorned with a silver facemask. Only his hateful hazel eyes were visible through the metallic helmet.

'At last we meet in person,' the man said. 'My name is Gorg, and it's a pleasure to finally make your acquaintance.'

* * *

### The Abyss: Circa 10:19 PM AEDT

Seth Zaraxom finished his beer and butted out his cigarette in the overflowing ashtray.

*The hour is late and Judgement Day is almost upon us.*

Despite the ominous overtones, Seth was feeling serene, which may or may not have been related to the joint he was currently sharing with Bojangles.

'Wow, these Binah Buds are great—good idea to toke up before we head out to our possible deaths and soul-destroying oblivion,' Bojangles japed as he took another drag and passed the dutchie back to Seth. 'Might not get another chance to smoke this sweet, sweet cheeba.'

'I just hope we can thwart our apparent destiny and overthrow the High Mage before he reshapes reality,' Seth agreed, taking the spliff from Bojangles.

'Whatever happens is meant to happen,' Mosh Lightley butted in from the other side of the bar as he puffed away on his own stash. 'Everything is predestined from the moment of the Big Bang—trust me, I know.'

'I'm not really sure if that's reassuring or not,' Seth sighed, a long trail of smoke streaming from his mouth. 'I thought my grandparents created the universe just to fuck with everyone, and now I know.'

'So, what you're saying is the universe is like some massive computer program turned on at the beginning of time, only the pattern is way too large for anyone to see?' Bojangles sounded spaced out. 'Wow, that's so deep, man.'

'What I'm saying is you better lay off the ganja before you battle the forces of darkness,' Mosh quipped, passing his joint to White Lion—who was really sick of not being worth mentioning until now.

'I think we should get going,' the albino man-beast suggested, 'right after I finish this.'

'Well, you guys have fun playing with Merlin,' Mosh enthused. 'I'll be there with you as you know.'

'Yeah, because you're everything that exists,' Seth groaned, getting up from the bar stool. 'We've all heard that one before. What I want to know is: where's my sister?'

'Lilith's decided to sit this scene out,' Mosh answered. 'She feels it prudent to prepare a backup plan should you fail.'

'Can't argue with that,' Bojangles chimed in, hopping off his stool. 'Let's scoot.'

*So this is it; all my planning has boiled down to this moment. Let's hope it's enough.*

'Okay, you both know what to do,' he said to Bojangles and White Lion as he walked over to one of the many doors lining the wall and stepped through to Earth.

* * *

### The Mystical Realm: Circa 10:42 PM AEDT

The High Mage of Hell stood on a golden sand dune and addressed the demonic legions. The False Archdemon towered beside him, a titanic abomination of teeth, bone and weeping sores.

'Fallen angels, finally, after six thousand years your moment of retribution is at hand!' The High Mage held his arms up to the broken yellow sky and the satanic host roared their approval. Somewhere, a puppy died.

The shrieking cacophony lulled, and the High Mage continued:

'Our enemies have only just become aware of our plans, but it is too late to stop us! They will search for us in Hell and the mortal realm, but none will think to look for us here!'

The infernal armada roared again. Somewhere, a woman died in labour.

'Ready yourselves, it is time to tear down the Gates of Heaven and feast on the bones of the False Creator himself!'

The High Mage smiled as the demonic army raised their weapons and shook the entire Mystical Realm with their war cries. Somewhere, a leader of men committed suicide.

* * *

### The Territories of Xph'Ish'Matarg, Hell: Circa 11:08 PM AEDT

Mark Adams still hung upside down from the 'soul tree' and suddenly shivered like he was buried in ice.

*What was that? It sounded like nothing I've ever heard before, like someone was torturing a thousand cats at once.*

'That was the sound of your doom, mortal,' Xph'Ish'Matarg answered, its enormous head level with the tree. 'You and all your kind.'

*No, it's not true…it can't be! Yet it is…there really is no hope.*

'In that you are correct, Mark Adams,' the demon lord bellowed. 'Nothing can stop us.'

'That is where you err, hell spawn,' boomed a sudden voice that seemed to come from everywhere at once. It was both harmonic and discordant and Mark's head swam at its sound.

*What's going on? Is this what the end of reality feels like?*

A grey spectre wearing plate armour and cloaked in a ragged cape slowly coalesced before them, its transparent form of a similar size to the Lord of Hell.

'Wraith!' Xph'Ish'Matarg spat. 'Hell is no place for you! Return to Heaven, begone!'

'We walk where we choose,' the Wraith responded in its paradox-ical voice, 'and it is not your place to deny us. The mortal has been brought here against Heaven's will and we have come to collect him. The Creator sees all.'

*I wonder if he's seen this demonic army massing at his door?*

'What was that, mortal?' the Wraith asked, suddenly turning to Mark.

*It can hear my thoughts too! This is a trap. They're planning on attacking Heaven!*

'Silence!' Xph'Ish'Matarg thundered, snatching Mark from the tree and holding him above its head. 'Your Manifest seed be damned. You have outgrown your usefulness. If the Wraith wants you so badly, then it will have to come through me.'

*This is it. This is the end of my mortal body. But what of my soul?*

He didn't have long to ponder, as Xph'Ish'Matarg opened its cavernous goat maw and dropped him into the mucous-lined depths of its throat.

\* \* \*

### Grand Satanic Clubhouse, Ashfield: 11:30 PM AEDT

Marek Mahoney had a raging hard-on as he chanted diabolic incantations and shuffled around the large pentacle painted into the floor of the community hall. Satanists laugh in the face of vandalism.

He glanced at the clock on the wall. Soon they would be humbled by the presence of Rancid, Dark Lord of Decay.

*We've been doing this for five and a half hours now—only thirty minutes to go.*

He had no doubt it would work, and neither did the other one hundred and ten fellow members of Lucifer's Coven crammed into the sweltering community hall like sardines. Not even Melissa, who'd been complaining nonstop prior to the ceremony beginning.

Projected onto a big screen at the end of the hall were the live video feeds from the other five locations the invocations were happening. There was Matt in Manly, summoning Leviathan, Dark Serpent of

Bindings and Restrictions; Navid in Bondi, calling Ishlarr, Dark Lord of the Frozen Mind; Lancefield in Banksmeadow, calling Zoolith, Dark Lord of Brimstone and Persecution; and in North Ryde, Floyd invoked Bahlor, Dark Lord of Despair and Failure.

Their images were displayed in the corners of the screen, and in the centre was the bigger image of the High Priestess, Karen. She was at Grand Satanic Headquarters in King's Cross, well into labour with the Antichrist, while her chapter summoned Ooblog, the Dark Lord of Perverse Molestation, around her.

*It's all happening according to the prophecies of the Satanic Scriptures, as foretold by the High Mage of Hell! The end of the world is nigh. What a great time to be alive!*

His erection twitched at the thought.

*What do you think about that, you annoying spot? Got nothing funny to say? No comments or songs to mark the occasion?*

There was no reply.

Marek rolled up the long sleeves of his brown cloak and looked at his hand. He saw nothing but the dead skin that had started appearing on his flesh since they began. Blotch McMahn was gone.

*Well, that's some good news—looks like Satan is looking out for me after all.*

\* \* \*

### Dungeon Cell 9: 11:58 PM AEDT

Andy Trailer paced anxiously around his dismal abode. He was full of nervous energy and felt like something big was about to erupt like a super volcano upon the world.

*The time is upon us,* Wisp declared from within his mind. *It is as we said it would be, is it not? While Pulse Pounder is distracted with his little experiment, he will not expect you to rise against him.*

*But he's my master,* Andy argued. *How can I stand against him after all he's done?*

*What has he done except confine you once more to this dungeon?* Wisp admonished. *Soon you will be his superior.*

*I wish I could believe you,* Andy admitted, stopping and dropping to his knees in the centre of the room.

*You will see,* Wisp promised. *In just a minute.*

\* \* \*

### Pulse Pounder's Secret Base, Simpson Desert: 11:59 PM AEDT

Bentaz Mullberry awoke in the confines of a metal cylinder and found himself immobilised.

*What's going on? Last thing I remember I was fighting Vicious Man on the moon.*

'Ah, you're awake,' said a voice through a crackling speaker inside the cylinder. A strange cyclops with no nose and a malicious grin loomed through the viewport. His single eye spiralled and pulsed. 'You're just in time to witness my little experiment.'

'W-who?' Bentaz forced himself to say. It was hard to speak, let alone move. He could see the cyclops was holding a control pad with a big red button on it.

'Prepare to evolve,' the cyclops replied. His finger hovered over the button.

The clock struck midnight.

# PART THREE:

# KNOTS

# 25 December 34 BZ

**Grand Satanic Clubhouse, Ashfield: 12:00 AM AEDT**

'…Incarnate…become flesh: Rancid, Dark Lord of Decay!' Marek Mahoney cried before uttering the final secret word of summoning under his breath and exulted as he felt the ground rumble. The other one hundred and ten members of his chapter of Lucifer's Coven stopped circling the cramped community hall and stopped to stare at the giant pentagram in the centre of the room. Looming large over the proceedings was the giant screen that streamed images from the other five locations where the coven was practising its dark arts. Matt had excellent contacts in the home entertainment industry, apparently.

The screen was ringed with the images of the inner circle, and the centre image—live from the Grand Satanic Headquarters at King's Cross—showed the High Priestess, Karen, who was in the throes of labour. The other clubhouses had finished their invocations at the same moment Marek's had, and each location was now rumbling along to the rhythm of the apocalypse.

*Finally, the time is here! The Antichrist is born! A new world awakens!*

'All hail the High Mage!' Marek cried.

'All hail the High Mage!' the group intoned.

The ground continued to rumble, growing evermore violent in its tremors. Marek started biting his nails in anticipation. He glanced at the skin on his fingers.

*That's funny; I don't recall ever getting eczema before.* He looked at his arm and discovered the rash covered more than just his hands. *It seems to be getting worse.*

Before he could give it any more thought, a shrill scream stole his attention. He looked at the giant screen and discovered Karen giving birth. Except instead of a baby, a slimy red tendril pulsed out of her vagina and wrapped around her leg.

*Well, that image is going to be burned into my mind forever,* he thought, trying not to be sick. *That doesn't look like the Antichrist to me; more like Ooblog, the Dark Lord of Perverse Molestation, whom Karen's group was summoning.*

He scratched absentmindedly at the back of his hand as other horrors started erupting across the screen like overripe pimples. Karen continued to scream in the centre image feed as more tentacles slithered out of her and snaked all over her body.

*It's like those Japanese cartoons I saw once.*

He also saw Lancefield's bushy ginger beard unexpectedly combust, consuming his face and melting his monocle while he screamed. The rest of his chapter in Banksmeadow burned behind him in the name of Zoolith, Dark Lord of Brimstone and Persecution.

Meanwhile, the Bondi chapter had all been frozen solid, with Navid's frosty visage looking even creepier as it stared blankly from the screen. Their silent, icy clubhouse was the perfect environment for Ishlarr, Dark Lord of the Frozen Mind.

*Should this… is this meant to be happening?*

Marek stood mesmerised by the images flooding in from the other five clubhouses and failed to notice his own chapter as they started calling out in distress. He started scratching furiously at his arm, oblivious to the flakes of skin falling from him and dusting the ground.

Floyd was next to cry out from North Ryde. Marek was shocked by the sight of Floyd's boiling flesh falling from his skull in clumps. The unholy dirge of Bahlor, Dark Lord of Despair and Failure, emanated from the bleeding walls as his chapter died.

*This…it wasn't meant to be like this…*

He looked at Matt's feed from Manly, and for a moment it was like their eyes met before a giant mouth burst from the floor and their chapter was devoured by Leviathan, Dark Serpent of Bindings and Restrictions.

*Have we been deceived?*

His eyes returned to the centre image of the Grand Satanic Head-quarters, but all that remained of Karen the High Priestess were her legs as they dissolved into a purple blob that filled the screen.

*We were meant to live forever as the High Mage's earthy agents...*

Marek's attention was suddenly caught by Melissa, who grabbed him by the shoulders and started shaking him. He locked eyes with the cross-dressing oaf.

*Geez, he's got a rash too! I hope mine's not that bad.*

Melissa tried to talk, but the words were lost in his throat. Moments later, his shrivelled tongue fell from his mouth, followed by what remained of his broken teeth. Marek recoiled in disgust and Melissa stepped back, clawing at his ugly face while his skin rotted from his bones.

'Fuck me!' Marek cried, backing away. He looked from side to side to see the other chapter members likewise decomposing alive.

*I should have listened to that annoying inkblot...*

And with perhaps the strangest final thought of the entire human race, Marek rotted to death and Lucifer's Coven passed into history.

\* \* \*

### Outside the Gates of Heaven: Circa 12:00 AM AEDT

And lo, the High Mage of Hell stood defiant on the titanic red dragon, named the Great Beast, and flew it towards the Host of Seraphim gathered to defend Heaven's Gates. A legion of demons led by the vile Archdemon trailed in the dragon's wake, and reality shook to the sound of their fury.

*My destiny awaits! I shall smash the armies of Heaven and tear the False Creator from his throne,* he thought as the two sides approached each other in formation beneath the radiant pearl of the celestial gates. *I can feel the power coursing through me, fuelled by the souls channelled by the Soul Gem from my agents on Earth. They successfully summoned the Lords of Hell to the mortal realm—something I seriously doubted they were capable of.*

He cast the thought from his mind as the Great Beast smashed through the first line of angels like they were as dense as the white clouds that encircled the battlefield. Hellfire billowed from the Great Beast's jaws and the High Mage cast destructive bolts of energy while the forces of Heaven and Hell clashed all around them.

And lo, Gledandron the World Eater lay hidden and watched. Watched… and hungered.

\* \* \*

### Dungeon Cell 9: 12:01 AM AEDT

Andy Trailer stood erect in the cramped cell and stretched his wings in ecstasy.

*Can you feel it? Do you see now?* Wisp cried within his mind, blocking out all other thoughts. *The truth of Gledandron flows through you now! We told you this would happen.*

*Wisp's right, I can feel it now.* Andy flexed his muscles and looked at the metal door. *It looks so fragile now, like I could just walk right through it.*

*You are much more powerful now that the hour of Gledandron has arrived,* Wisp promised. *It is time for you to finally have your revenge against all who have wronged you.*

*I couldn't agree more,* Andy thought, ripping the door from its hinges and striding into the hallway.

\* \* \*

### Pulse Pounder's Secret Base, Simpson Desert: 12:01 AM AEDT

Bentaz Mullberry lay in the metal cylinder and stared through the viewport at the menacing cyclops who stood above him, finger poised over a big red button on a handheld control pad. The cyclops had said something moments earlier, but Bentaz couldn't hear what it was from within the cylinder.

*I really need to work on reading lips,* he thought as he tried to move. *Limbs feel so weak; more than from my battle with Vicious Man. It must be this coffin I'm in. Whoever this guy is, he's obviously another deranged supervillain, so whatever that button does won't be pleasant. Last thing I remember was heading back to Lake George. I have to get out of here, find my team... and see how my family's going.*

He thought of Peach and his stomach dropped. *God, I really hope she's okay.*

Suddenly the whole room shook and the cyclops dropped his control pad and took a defensive posture.

*Something's happening. What the fuck is going on in this place?*

He caught a glimpse of a grey shape as it darted past the viewport, followed by a burst of flame that engulfed the room.

*That almost looks like... Could it be?*

His container was rocked by a violent impact and the image through the viewport spun. Moments later, the cylinder tore open, and Bentaz found himself face down on a cold, concrete floor.

The relief was instant.

*I can move again!*

He slowly stood up. He was still sore from his fight with Vicious Man, his injuries not yet fully healed. He may have healed fast, but the wounds had been severe. He looked around the room to see the cyclops retreating from a familiar grey, goat-horned demon with giant bat wings in a room full of metal cylinders and flashing computer panels.

*I was right, it is Hellgoat. And the rest of the team must be in those other cylinders.*

'Thanks for the assist,' Bentaz said to his friend. 'Keep him busy while I free the others.' Hellgoat didn't seem to hear and busied himself with his opponent.

Bentaz moved to the closest cylinder and looked through the viewport.

*Had to be Powerhouse, didn't it? Still, we could do with his raw power and speed—even if he is a complete arse.*

Before he could free his frenemy, the door to the room smashed open and *another* demon prowled into the room. The second demon also had bat-wings, except was a sickly green and wearing a stained heavy metal shirt.

*Who's this, Hellgoat's brother?*

'Die in Gledandron's name!' the green demon bellowed to the heavens. 'Perish at the hands of Night Demon!'

*And just when I thought this day couldn't get any worse.*

* * *

### Pulse Pounder's Secret Base, Simpson Desert: 12:05 AM AEDT

Andy Trailer had never felt so alive. He flew into the room and immediately joined the fight against Pulse Pounder alongside his grey counterpart. He ignored the other being in the room—a teenager dressed in shredded black and red clothing with a dented red helmet.

*This is amazing!*

*We told you,* Wisp replied, louder than ever in Andy's mind. *We told you to believe in Gledandron. The glorious hour has come!*

He recognised the other demon from Pulse Pounder's experimentation cylinders and remembered they were HSA.

*Fear not,* Wisp declared. *Can you not feel the connection with kin?* Andy wasn't sure exactly what he meant.

The commotion brought Pulse Pounder's lieutenant, Guillotine, and with him the terrible Trio: Hood, the android; Repulsive, the ten-drilled murder-machine; and Malice, the robotic dog, which Andy was all-too familiar with.

*Pulse Pounder will keep. Dispatch his flunkies first,* Wisp cautioned.

Andy leapt at Guillotine, raking him deep across his chest before he could bring his guillotine 'arms' to bear, and sent him flying back through the corridor he emerged from.

The Hood moved at him with breathtaking speed, its six weaponised arms moving with lightning precision and striking his vital parts with blades, saws and lasers.

Andy moved without thinking and used his wing to slice the Hood in twain from groin to head. He followed this by dive-bombing Repulsive and rending it apart before it could react. He turned to face Malice, but the metallic canine had already bolted away down the corridor.

'You think you can escape?' Andy roared, now fully immersed in his Night Demon persona. Malice kept running.

*Let it go,* Wisp advised. *Have your vengeance on Pulse Pounder. No longer will you call him Master. For you have a new master now—the almighty Gledandron!*

*Yes...* Andy could feel the truth of it. He turned to Pulse Pounder, who looked on the verge of defeat—his skin was charred and his clothing ashes, yet he fought on with grim tenacity.

'Sorry, brother, but I will not allow you to rob me of my revenge,' Andy said to the other demon as he stepped between them and hammered Pulse Pounder to the ground with brutal efficiency. The cyclops lay unconscious. 'I am the Night Demon, emissary of Gledandron.' Wisp had told him what to say.

'I...' the grey demon paused, '...am finally awake. Gledandron is irrefragable.'

Andy had no idea what that meant, but it seemed right to him.

'Hellgoat? What's going on?' It was the teenage superhero. He'd also managed to free the rest of his group from the experimentation tubes—all of whom were now recovering from paralysis. 'What's this demon talking about?'

'Hellgoat, is it?' Andy asked, already knowing the answer. 'See how he mistrusts us from appearance alone? Like all of his kind, he fears us. Destroy this sidekick and join me in Gledandron's will.'

*I'd never have thought to say that on my own. Why didn't I use your advice earlier?*

*The time was not ripe,* Wisp responded sagely. *Now it is; so let us into your core to help guide you. Gledandron will show the way.*

Andy could see no alternative.

'Don't listen to him,' the teenager said to Hellgoat. 'You and I, we've been friends for ages. I know you won't betray me for this satanic nonsense.'

'Then you thought wrong,' Hellgoat said to the teenager before shooting torrents of hellfire from his hand to consume him. The teenager screamed.

Hellgoat turned to Andy. 'We must leave before they recover.'

'I've not finished with Pulse Pounder,' he snapped. 'We leave when I say.'

'Ballistic will recover quickly, as will the others,' Hellgoat warned, continuing to pour flames from his hands at his former HSA team-mates. 'If you want to die here, then stay, but I'd rather be free.'

*Listen to him,* Wisp advised. *Pulse Pounder is not the one you really want vengeance upon, is he? No, it is…*

*Energy Lord,* Andy agreed. 'Very well, we leave now,' he said to Hell-goat.

They tore through the interior doors to the exit and found them-selves outside shortly thereafter. The desert air was cool and the stars lit up the sky.

'Now we're free to wreak revenge,' he said to Hellgoat as they took flight and glided into the night. 'Join me in my quest for justice.'

'I have justice of my own to dish,' Hellgoat answered, picking up speed. 'Gledandron wills the end of the HSA—I'm going to slaughter the rest of my teammates. I sense you, too, wish to journey to Syd-ney—the source of this newfound clarity. We will meet there after we each have our revenge.'

'So be it,' he replied, matching Hellgoat's speed. 'I'll kill the Energy Lord myself.'

*Before you get your vengeance, you will first have to do something for Gledandron,* Wisp revealed.

*That's okay,* Andy thought. *Whatever it takes.*

* * *

### South Western Sydney: 12:15 AM AEDT

Desci Adams was glad they'd decided to give up on the whole venture and turn back for home—especially now that the city appeared to be having a blackout. The strange thing was the moon was still bright in the sky, and combined with the other ambient light, the outlines of the skyscrapers should have been visible in the rear-view mirror.

*Except it's like there's a giant dome over the CBD. Must be an optical illusion.*

She slowed the car and stopped behind a taxi, keeping the engine idling. The drive back from the city had gone at glacial speed thanks to the detours the local government had set up. The traffic was gridlocked up ahead and a woman in a military uniform appeared to be redirecting cars.

*It must have to do with what my father, Dragon Kong, warned me about. Why else would there be many military and police vehicles around at Christmas?*

'Why are there so many cops around?' Obie enquired from the passenger seat, as if reading her mind.

'Can't you see something's happened to the city?' Samara asked sarcastically from the back. 'Sebastian can't stop staring at it.'

Sebastian didn't reply and continued to look through the back window.

'I wonder if Nathan knows what's going on?' Obie asked. 'He's right in the centre of it.'

'I'm sorry you didn't get to meet up with your friend and instead got to spend Christmas Eve in the car with your mum,' Desci said quietly to Obie, 'but I think it's probably for the best. We can go home and watch it on the news.'

'If we ever get home,' Obie sulked. 'This trip has taken hours already.'

'Yeah, the traffic's bad because of all these roadblocks,' she agreed as they slowly approached the head of the line. 'I've never seen it like this before—must be serious.'

She kept remembering her father's warning about something bad happening to Sydney, and her stomach twisted as she ran through options in her head. The taxi in front was currently being redirected by the female soldier.

They finally made it to the head of the queue and Desci wound the window down to speak to the soldier. 'What's going on?' she asked.

'Nothing to worry about, ma'am,' the soldier replied with a look of mild irritation on her face. 'Just a blackout is all. It's not safe to have civilians in the city without lights, so we're directing traffic to unaffected areas.'

'This area seems to be fine,' Desci observed. 'We're trying to get to Macquarie Fields, but the detours keep taking us in the wrong direction.'

'That's something you'll have to take up with your local member,' the soldier shot back. 'Now move along, you're holding up traffic.'

Desci wound up the window and drove towards the detour. There it split into two lanes: one that snaked back west and the other that took a more south-eastern route. She chose the latter.

*This is a sign I should get as far away from here as possible.*

'Hey, Mum, aren't we in the wrong lane?' Obie asked, looking back at the other route.

'It would be. If we were going home,' she answered. 'But I've decided we're going to Canberra.'

Her statement was met with chaotic protest from the three teenagers.

'Trust me, this is the right move. I'll explain on the way.'

She put her foot to the accelerator and they began the trip to the nation's capital.

* * *

### The roof of Scar's Warehouse, Ashfield, Sydney: 12:18 AM AEDT

Naomi Bloodlust drove her knee into Gorg's nuts and followed through with a left hook to his jaw. She then slashed at his belly with the bladed gauntlet she wore when in full costume, but Gorg twisted sideways, avoiding disembowelment. The whole building shook beneath their feet.

Gorg retaliated by raising his arms and firing from the rounded guns strapped to his wrists. She dived for cover as large chunks of the roof began imploding around her.

*What the fuck is he shooting? Objects just seem to pop out of existence whenever he points those guns around—it's like they just disappear.*

She leapt up from behind the air-conditioning unit and threw a slender knife at Gorg's head before springing to a new position behind a large skylight. He battered the knife away and pointed his gun at the unit, causing it to suddenly implode into nothingness. The ground continued to shake.

*Those guns explain all those 'vanished' mercenaries in Johannesburg. I just wish I knew how to stop them. Why didn't just shoot me through the skylight? Maybe he really does like toying with his targets, because it was only luck that I freed myself from his noose.*

Naomi again leapt out of the way as Gorg pointed his guns at her, causing sections of the skylight to vanish before her. The shaking intensified.

'This is pointless,' he called to her. 'Your fate was sealed the moment I took the contract on you.' He fired again.

She dodged the silent barrage and sprinted in a wide arc around Gorg, looking for an opportunity to strike.

'You've proven to be great sport,' Gorg announced, continuing to fire, 'but my black hole guns can't be avoided forever. So stop with your futile tremors and come face me.'

*That's interesting; he thinks I'm responsible for these mini earthquakes.*

She threw her last stiletto, but Gorg pointed his gun at it and it vanished from existence.

*Fuck it.*

She sprinted faster, then suddenly changed direction and leapt at Gorg, sliding low against the rooftop and knocking his legs out from under him. She made eye contact through his faceless helmet and his expression was one of shock. The temperature was rapidly rising.

'Your eyes...they're flames,' he muttered, '...but the tremors, I thought *that* was you...'

Naomi could feel the power roiling inside her and was about to cut loose when the tremors combined with the sound of buildings crumbling caused her to pause. She turned to look, allowing her power to remain a secret. Her jaw dropped at the sight.

*Holy shit...I mean...fuck...What is that?*

Gorg saw it too and immediately stopped struggling to ogle at the sight before them. '...the fuck?' he said.

Standing two blocks away, but at least twenty storeys high, was an enormous demon covered in protrusions of jagged bone and brown, decaying flesh. It had black pits for eyes and a salivating maw of razor-sharp teeth jutting from its horned skull. Its spiked tail lashed back and forth, demolishing the adjacent infrastructure.

Naomi and Gorg stood and gaped at the monstrous colossus as a foul stench hit them like an abusive husband.

'Puny flesh mortals,' the demon boomed across the night air, its voice the sound of a thousand mummies rising in darkened crypts.

'We are Rancid, Dark Lord of Decay, and this is your final hour, your final suffering. Rejoice, for the Age of Rot is upon you!'

*I think I'd like to pass on that.*

Naomi looked at Gorg, who was sitting on the ground beside her. He turned to meet her gaze. 'Truce?' he asked.

'Fuckin' oath!' she replied, still mesmerised by the Lord of Hell towering above the streets of Ashfield.

*This must be what Seth was talking about. The goddamn fucking apocalypse. Fan-fucking-tastic. Looks like my revenge on Scar might have to wait…for now.*

* * *

### Darling Harbour, Sydney: 12:28 AM AEDT

Lorraine Freeman shivered as the icy breeze blew in from the harbour. Like everyone else that had come for the carols, she stood and gaped at the bright pink beam of light that shot straight up into the black sky from Centrepoint Tower.

*I wonder what's going on?*

The carols she and Beat Master had come to perform were cut short at midnight when the lightshow began, accompanied by a deep rumbling that caused the nearby water to turn choppy. That was when most of the city lights had gone out and almost everyone decided to leave, despite it being a clear night. Those who remained stood around watching and shivering, as the warm summer air suddenly turned frosty.

*I'm invulnerable to knives, yet I can still feel the cold, it seems. Unless something else is going on—Samuel looks like he's positively freezing, and he's in an insulated metal suit!*

As if on cue, Beat Master turned to her and remarked about his nipples high-beaming through his armour.

Lorraine blushed when she realised his comment applied to her too. 'We should find out what that is,' she said to change the subject.

'You've been saying that since it started,' Beat Master replied with a grin, 'yet here we stand, freezing our tits off. Why's it so cold anyway? It's meant to be summer Down Under.'

*Down Under? Really?*

'Let's do something about it then. These people appear to be safe.' She stepped down from the stage and began walking towards the city. 'Well, come on then,' she called to her companion. 'Maybe we can also find out what's causing those rumbling sounds. Sounds like fireworks or something.'

Suddenly a bloodcurdling screech pierced the air and sent a different kind of chill down her spine and made goose bumps rise on her skin. 'What the fuck was that?'

'I don't know.' Beat Master pointed at the harbour. 'But whatever it was, I bet it has something to do with *that.*'

Lorraine shifted her gaze and was surprised to see the water freezing solid as if by magic. What was even more disturbing was that everything touching the water began to freeze too—a seagull snap-froze when it failed to fly clear in time. 'Oh my god,' she gasped.

Beat Master's usual cheerfulness looked strained to Lorraine, but it wasn't until a bystander who was leaning over the railing to get a closer look froze as well, that the urgency of the situation sank in and he was all business.

'You people, get back, get away from there!' he called to another group of onlookers close to the water's edge. One of them screamed when they saw the frozen man. 'Lorraine, honey, we need to get these people out of here!'

Lorraine never heard him, as she was too busy staring up into the sky. She wasn't looking at the beam coming from Centrepoint Tower, rather the frozen helicopter falling straight towards them. 'Duck!' she cried, diving for cover.

The helicopter overshot them and slammed down into the frozen harbour before erupting in a huge fireball.

*That ice must be thick; the chopper only impacted on the surface. What's going on around here?*

As if in answer to her idle thought, the ice grew into dozens of humanoid shaped monoliths, cracking and splintering until they took the form of what could only be described as ice demons. Their eyes took on an unnatural blue and their breath was hoarfrost.

'Warm…warm meat,' they hissed in unison as they climbed over the railing and onto the footpath. 'You will join us in the cold dark; your souls will feed Ishlarr, Dark Lord of the Frozen Mind.'

'I think I'll pass on that, if it's all the same to you,' Beat Master quipped, but his voice lacked conviction.

There was a sudden scream from behind and Lorraine turned quickly to see ice demons rise up from all over the harbour and begin bludgeoning civilians with glacial clubs. The scarlet blood stood in stark contrast to the white demons as it sprayed all over them and froze into their icy bodies.

*Holy shit! These creatures are dangerous!*

'We've got to do something,' she said to Beat Master as the demons lurched forward, closing in around them. 'Mum's with the rest of the X-Droids in Circular Quay, which isn't far away. She's got to know what's going on, so I'm sure they'll be able to help. We just have to get to her.'

*At least I hope so, otherwise we're fucked.*

'Okay, that's a better plan than I had,' Beat Master said, hitting the rewind button on his suit's inbuilt cassette-deck. 'I'm not sure what we can do to help these people anyway; we're going to have enough trouble helping ourselves. I need to draw on as much inspiration from my music as I can if I'm to get enough power to face these things. We're not dealing with the Hat Trick now. 'Eye of the Tiger' just won't cut it—it's time to get serious.'

He hit the play button and 'Flashdance—What a Feeling' blared from his shoulder mounted speakers.

Lorraine gave him a look.

'What?' he replied, doing his pre-battle warm up stretches. 'Can't a gay man like *Flashdance* without it being some kind of joke?'

* * *

### Project Typhon, Banksmeadow: 1:47 AM AEDT

Anu Hopet incinerated the man's flesh from his face and punched his charred skull through the concrete wall. 'Where is he?' he thundered, energy crackling from his clenched fists and illuminating his armour in a sinister light. 'WHERE?'

He'd been tearing up the place for several hours now and hadn't found his quarry. Each time he thought he'd searched the place, some other sub-level would be revealed and he'd have to go through the whole process again.

*It is already past the deadline for the energy build-up and I still haven't found Disk! At least whatever the build-up was, it does not appear to have affected this place, but that is beside the point. These fools have something of mine and I want it back!*

'Where is Disk?' he boomed again, his voice echoing off the concrete walls. 'I will find him!'

'Who are you talking to?' said a voice behind him, the speaker's identity masked by the respirator. 'You've already killed everyone down here.'

'You, if you are listening,' Anu Hopet replied before turning around to face the voice. There stood a man in a sleek armoured suit, with metal wings tucked behind and a visored helmet blocking his face. Every part of him, from the angles of his armour, to the turbines on his forearms, advertised speed.

Yet it wasn't the newcomer that Anu Hopet stared at, but rather the cybernetic midget who accompanied him. 'Oh, Great Armageddon, forgive your humble servant,' the midget said.

*Disk!*

'Give him to me and you may yet live,' he threatened, the energy from his hands arcing in anticipation.

'He's all yours,' the other man said, gently pushing Disk forwards. 'Believe it or not, there are other things going on around here that need my attention. I'm not really powerful enough to stop you…'

*The fool knows that much, at least.*

'… and you were just going to kill more people until you found him, so I thought I'd spare you the trouble. Now take him and go.' He gestured towards the way out. 'I'll follow you to make sure you leave.'

'Is this some sort of trick?' Anu Hopet asked as he grabbed Disk by the collar and held him securely.

'No trick,' the armoured man answered. 'Like I said: there's other shit going down and there's just no time to deal with you. I have to get topside anyway and this seemed like the best option. You can call me Concord, by the way. I'm with the Battle Suits.'

'I will call you dust if you lie to me,' Anu Hopet promised. 'Your "battle suit" is obviously built for aerial combat, which could be the real reason you need to get outside, and Disk is the bait...'

'I wouldn't...'

'... but then again, you already know you cannot hope to defeat me in any kind of combat, so lead the way.' He turned towards the fire stairs Concord had pointed to.

Despite the suit covering his entire body, Concord looked noticeably relieved.

A short time later they emerged from a secret exit disguised as a stormwater manhole. Anu Hopet carried Disk the whole way.

'Well, this is where we part company,' Concord announced, placing a noticeable distance between them. 'I've no idea where you came from, so I don't know where you should go, as long as it isn't here.'

Anu Hopet stared at him and considered annihilating him with a blast of antimatter, but reconsidered and stayed his hand. *I have what I came for; there is no need to sully myself in any more personal combat with mortals.*

Once Concord was certain he didn't have to fight, he turned his attention to a communication device in his helmet. 'Yeah, I'm outside...it worked, he's leaving...I can't see anything out here...no I don't know why communication with HQ is down...'

*Interesting. Perhaps it is the energy surge?*

'...yeah, I'll fly up and take a look, see if I can get above the city. Over and out.' Concord turned back to Anu Hopet, his metallic wings unfolding to reveal hidden jet engines that sprang to life. 'Sayonara, arsehole,' he said before shooting up into the sky with breakneck speed.

*Insolence! I should have killed him anyway.*

Before Anu Hopet could do exactly that, Concord exploded, his suit's reserves of jet fuel lighting up the night sky in a fiery epitaph.

*What happened? Nothing struck him that I could see. Could his suit have malfunctioned?*

'Disk, can you explain that?' he asked his lackey. 'Did his suit malfunction? What readings do you have?'

'It wasn't his suit, Great Armageddon,' Disk said, cowering. 'It's the same reason that he couldn't get a signal out—we appear to be caught within an enormous bubble.'

'A what?' Anu Hopet spat. 'Explain yourself!'

'I'll need the ship's sensors to be sure, but my hypothesis is that something happened to create an energy "bubble" that appears to have shunted a large part of this city into another dimensional plane,' Disk theorised, desperately trying not to be vaporised by his master's displeasure. 'It's what the energy build-up was for; it takes a great deal of energy to do something like that and a great deal more to sustain it. So, my guess is that it will use the energy within the bubble—which is why nothing can get out—but will fuel itself by allowing things *into* the bubble. That explains why we can still see the stars and are not suffocating.'

'So, the bubble is invisible from our side of the dimensional rift, but people outside will see a black dome, as a sphere would pass underground,' Anu Hopet answered for him, piecing it all together in his mind. 'Anything that passes through the sphere is trapped here; therefore, the pressure will continually increase until everything is crushed into energy. This is something that only a Celestial One could conceive of.'

*It all makes sense now.*

'We have to get to *The Skull of Ra* while we still can,' he said.

\* \* \*

### Project Typhon, Banksmeadow: 2:32 AM AEDT

Courtney Yeht sat motionless on the cold tiled floor and stared silently at the group of orderlies clustered around the only doorway that led through to the rest of the facility. Akash and Vernon, the orderlies she was most familiar with, stood at the front of group and tried to soothe her with platitudes.

'It's okay, Courtney,' Akash said in his accented voice. 'There's nothing to worry about, merely an earthquake that's the cause of all the commotion. Phil will be here soon, he'll tell you, you'll see.' He was sweating profusely.

*Most likely he can focus his attention on me now that the intruder has left.*

It had taken her a couple of hours to get completely free of her magnetic cell—mostly due to a fear of being caught—but she had stalled in her escape from the facility itself when confronted by actual people blocking her way. She'd sat here ever since, rejoicing in the vibrations the intruder caused as he demolished the other wing of the facility.

*I really don't want to hurt anyone, but there's no way I'm going back. I was hoping they'd all eventually leave to go after the intruder.*

She extended her senses through the floor until she located Phil to see whether Akash was lying or not. She soon discovered his unique vibrations running down a corridor towards her location. There were at least five others with him.

*At least Akash was telling the truth about Phil being here soon. It feels like he's got that bitch, Amy, with him, as well as that guy in the metallic suit. I'd recognise that whirring anywhere. I don't know who the other three guys are, but I can tell they're armed from the weight of their impacts as they run. They think they'll surprise me.*

She smiled and tied her dirty blonde hair into a ponytail.

*Don't they realise the floor hears every little thing?*

Courtney stood up and stretched in anticipation, her sudden movements causing the orderlies to all take a step back. Phil arrived and pushed his way past them, along with Amy and the armoured man. The three armed men who were with them stayed at the rear, trying to remain out of sight.

*I feel naked in this stupid hospital gown. The first thing I'm going to do when I get out of here is get some nice clothes, like that undeserving flake, Lorraine Freeman.*

'Courtney, it's me, Phil,' he said obviously. 'It's okay, it's all over now. It was just an earthquake, nothing more. I'm sure you can even feel the aftershocks.'

*Well, I have been able to feel <u>something</u> since I escaped, but it doesn't feel like an earthquake—more like a giant striding across the land. But that's unrelated to the intruder who tore up the place, that much I'm certain of.*

'You're lying,' she said at last, her voice taking on a menacing edge it had always lacked before. 'You've been lying to me since I got here and I've had enough.'

Phil started shaking but pressed on regardless. 'Please, Courtney, let me explain...'

'Patient 1432, you will go to your room,' the mechanised man commanded, his metallic suit whirring as he signalled to his men at the back of the crowd of orderlies. Phil shot him a look and shook his head. Amy looked at Courtney and smiled sardonically.

'I *hate* that name! My name is Courtney!' she spat, her repressed anger starting to boil over.

The guards moved to the front of the crowd and aimed their rifles at her.

'Tactician, no!' Phil said to the man in the mechanised suit.

*They don't look like any guns I've ever seen, more like ray guns from the old movies they sometimes let me watch if I behave.*

The memory made her angrier.

'Please, Courtney, they won't hurt you,' Phil pleaded, sweat pouring down his face and fogging his glasses. 'Here's the truth: they're just here to protect you from a very dangerous intruder. You must go with them to your room, for your own safety.'

'You're still lying! You're just going to drug me and make me do what you tell me!' She stood defiantly and glared at them like an indignant teenager.

'Fuck you, 1432!' Amy shot back, her eyepatch moving as she sneered. 'You're only a child; you'll do as you're told! We taught you better than this.'

It was a bold move.

'You taught me to be a killer,' she whispered. 'And my name is Courtney!'

The ground started to rumble.

The crowd of orderlies all tried to leave at once, creating a bottleneck at the exit.

Tactician signalled to his men.

The soldiers went to fire their rifles.

'Courtney, please! I love you like a daughter!' Phil lied, desperately trying to stop the inevitable.

'STOP LYING TO ME!'

Suddenly the ground parted before her and the two sides lifted up, crushing the entire group against the collapsing roof and forming an enormous sandstone canyon. It was a move worthy of Moses, complete with the silenced screams of enemies.

Courtney stood at the bottom of the newly formed chasm and smiled.

*Wow. I didn't know I could do that!*

She looked up at the night sky for the first time in years and it was the most beautiful sight she'd ever seen.

A fleeting pang of guilt twinged, and she reached out her senses for any vibrations that indicated someone survived her geological land-scaping. Or perhaps it was merely curiosity.

*That Tactician guy miraculously still lives, and I can hear that other guy they had locked up here muttering 'Antithesis' trapped further down, but otherwise everyone else is dead. At least in this part of the complex.*

She used her powers to raise the ground beneath her bare feet and lift her to the top of the chasm as it closed behind her. She stepped off her rocky platform just as the chasm closed, leaving only a crack as evidence it was ever there.

*All those who lied to me are buried beneath my feet. No more Phil, no more Amy, and no more Patient 1432. Now I can start my life afresh... whatever that's supposed to mean.*

She breathed deeply and stared at her surroundings. There was a smell in the air like sulphur and she could see large fires burning in the distance. There was also a deep thundering, like something massive moving around.

*There's something really big going on and that's why everyone was so distracted when I escaped. Maybe I should check it out and vent a little frustration.*

The air was humid, yet there was an unnatural chill in the air and it cut right through Courtney's thin hospital shift. She needed some proper clothes.

*Something like the nice outfits that spoiled slut, Lorraine Freeman, prances around in. The ground will guide me; the ground hears every little thing.*

She headed towards the glow of distant fires, almost dancing as her mind tuned into the vibrations of the Earth.

\* \* \*

**Outside The Skull of Ra, Banksmeadow: 2:49 AM AEDT**

Anu Hopet had never seen anything like it in his four thousand years of life. The demon lord stood at least twenty storeys high, its blackened bones illuminated by the hellfire billowing from its body. Its charred skull was horned, but it was the demon's eyes that burned with a furious judgement Anu Hopet found most unsettling.

*I do not think it is even really looking at me, but nevertheless, the creature's gaze is mesmerising. Who knows how long I have been standing here? I have to get Disk back to the ship and then we can finally leave this place.*

'We are Zoolith, Dark Lord of Brimstone and Persecution,' the demon boomed in the distance, the fire in its eyes burning an intense white. 'Your hour of judgement is at hand. Come forth and purge your sins.'

*Summoning a horror like that does not really seem like the Celestial Ones' usual tactics, but who else has the power to create this reality bubble I am trapped in?*

He looked down at Disk, who was standing a metre away staring at Zoolith, his cybernetic eye scanning and uploading data to his brain.

*The best course of action is to get Disk back to the ship unseen, so he can analyse his data and calculate a way to escape, before we are noticed by that thing.*

Kismet smiled at the naivety.

'YOU!' Zoolith thundered, pointing its skeletal, taloned finger accusingly at him. It started moving towards them, closing the gap quickly with giant strides.

*Now I cannot go to the ship or I will lead it straight there. I should have known the Celestial Ones would try to prevent me leaving.*

He was so busy watching Zoolith that he didn't see the flaming, bat-like demon dive-bomb them until too late. It snatched Disk, biting into his throat and ripping out his jugular in one swift motion before taking to the air a split second later, still carrying its victim.

'No! After all I went through to retrieve him.' Anu Hopet cried. He turned to fire bolts of antimatter at the demon, but it was already circling back towards Zoolith, who was almost upon him.

*Time to go. I will retrieve Disk's body later—after I lead this monster away from the ship.*

Reluctantly, he turned from the enemy and fled into the night.

\* \* \*

### Barton Correctional Facility: 7:24 AM AEDT

Walter Screw slowly placed the phone receiver down in its cradle and sighed. He gave himself a moment of reflection before opening the top drawer of his desk, removing a fresh Cuban cigar and lighting it. He leant back in his seat and savoured the moment, then turned his attention to his subordinates who stood patiently on the other side of his desk.

'Bad news?' Rick Gordon asked tentatively. Like Walter, he'd been up all night in meetings and looked tired.

'You mean *more* bad news,' Walter corrected wearily between puffs of acrid smoke. 'I just got word that the Defence Base up in Cameron Corner was destroyed sometime in the night by an unknown assailant. There were no survivors.'

'Well, there goes this country's main deterrent against foreign invasion,' Leslie Studebaker observed, still growing accustomed to being invited to these high-level meetings.

'Luckily Australia's defence doesn't rely solely on an armoured battle station staffed by robots and guys in giant robo-suits,' Walter said sardonically. 'Besides, invasion is an unlikely scenario—at least from another country.'

*Unfortunately, that's about as good as it gets.*

'Any idea who hit us?' Gordon enquired. 'Do we need to schedule another meeting?' His tone suggested that was the last thing he wanted.

'Satellite imagery showed a figure that looked…like a demon,' Walter replied, tapping ash into his pristine glass ashtray.

*I can't believe I just said that.*

'Could it be that guy from the HSA? Hellsheep, or something?' Gordon had a hard time remembering names.

'Hellgoat, sir,' Studebaker gently corrected. 'Wasn't he killed in the Lake George incident?'

*The same incident that started with a nuclear explosion then led to a giant crater in the moon, and made the governments of the world shit themselves in the process.*

'We believe so, yes.' Walter gestured to the chairs in front of his desk. 'If the intel is correct and Vicious Man really did die up there, then it's bloody well worth it,' he added.

'Ballistic's body was never found, even though he was tracked back to Earth,' Studebaker said, sitting down. 'So maybe Hellgoat survived as well.'

'We don't even know for certain that Ballistic survived, or even if Vicious Man is truly dead, for that matter,' Gordon chided as he took the other seat. 'So there's no point in wild speculation.'

'Although, having said that...' Walter let the words hang.

'You think it has something to do with this whole apocalypse thing?' Gordon asked.

'Are you kidding? Someone that looked like a demon and single-handedly destroyed one of the most impregnable places on the planet connected with this whole apocalypse thing? On the same day that a large chunk of Sydney vanishes within a black dome? No, not connected at all,' Walter said sarcastically, butting out his unfinished stogie. The lack of sleep was making him more irritable than usual. The fact that his son was in Sydney didn't help either.

*Stanley said he was going to Project Typhon to repel some kind of attack, and that place is within the black dome. I hope he's all right.*

Walter pushed the brief twinge of guilt over his relationship with his son out of his mind and focused on what he could control. 'Any word from Sydney?'

Gordon nodded to Studebaker.

'No sir,' she responded, picking up on the cue. 'As you know, contact was lost with Sydney at midnight when that dome—or whatever it is—appeared over the CBD and inner suburbs. We have no idea what caused it.'

*But I have a gut feeling it was this so-called Merlin character.*

'Yes, yes, I know all that,' Walter said wearily. 'Nothing new from the base at Pheasant's Nest?'

'No, sir,' Studebaker continued nervously, still unaccustomed to the pressure of these meetings. 'We contacted Field Marshall Hobbs about an hour ago; he hasn't received any contact from the...uh...Government Villains, since you ordered them sent into the dome.'

*They were ordered to report in every hour and that was just over four hours ago. Did they die the moment they entered? Were they transported somewhere? Dammit, I need to know!*

'Okay, so we don't know what happened to the team. They could very well have betrayed us—they were villains after all,' Walter posited, as he thought about whether or not to have another cigar, despite not finishing the first one. 'What *do* we know?'

It was all they'd talked about for the last seven hours, but going over the details repeatedly helped him take his mind off his son. Besides, his usual schedule was on hold until this current crisis was over, so it wasn't like he was wasting time.

'We assume the dome is actually more like a sphere, as drilling has discovered,' Gordon answered, taking over the briefing. 'It encompasses a large part of inner Sydney—the exact dimensions escape me at the moment—but at least from Manly to Bondi and west to Ashfield and North Ryde. We believe over a million people are trapped inside.'

*Including Project Typhon at Banksmeadow, where Stanley said he was going.*

'Yes, yes,' Walter said irritably, frustrated by the situation. 'But what about the sphere itself?'

'We know that things can pass into it, but nothing seems to come out, which is why it appears black—there's no light reflecting back,' Studebaker explained.

'Like a black hole,' Gordon added.

'Um... with all due respect, sir, it doesn't have the massive gravity of a black hole. In fact, its mass doesn't seem to have changed.' Studebaker waited for the reprimand that never came.

'So what *is* it?' Walter asked instead.

'We still don't know,' she confessed.

Walter shifted in his seat, resisting the temptation of another cigar. He needed coffee instead. Touching the intercom, he said, 'Three coffees, please, Roger.'

'Good idea, sir,' Gordon said, sitting up straighter in anticipation. The endless briefings had a somniferous effect on him.

'Did David or Neal say anything about any demons?' Walter enquired as they waited for their coffees.

'No sir, the Field Marshall and the Commissioner only reported their progress in evacuating the surrounding areas,' Studebaker replied, secretly wishing she could have a cup of tea instead. 'They said nothing about any demons, or hostile forces of any kind.'

'We need to find out everything we can about this being who attacked the Defence Base,' Walter said with a sudden burst of energy. 'Maybe we should start by asking our friends over at Heroes Squadron Headquarters to look into it. I hear they were looking for Satanists earlier in the year—we can link it to that. In fact, it probably *is* linked to that, come to think of it.'

'Their capacity has been severely limited since they lost Ballistic and the others,' Gordon reminded them.

'Yeah, but there are heaps of them,' Walter shot back. 'They do call themselves a squadron for a reason. I think…'

He never got to finish the sentence as a sudden boom shook the building, causing the lights to flicker before turning red and the alarm to wail.

Walter pressed another button on his intercom. 'Singh: report.'

'Prison is under attack,' came Singh's tinny voice from the intercom speaker.

'Who's attacking us?' Gordon asked.

'Hold on, visual feed coming in now,' Singh announced. 'It appears to be some kind of bat creature, or maybe a demon.'

Walter felt a sudden chill.

'This can't be a coincidence,' Studebaker said.

The prison shook again and again. The emergency lights flickered.

'Get prison defences scrambled now!' Walter screamed into the intercom. 'We've got to repel the attack before the prisoners escape.'

It was over as suddenly as it had begun.

'Defence team six reports the attacker has fled,' Singh reported. 'It flew off to the east. Team six pursuing.'

'Negative, we may need them here for urgent repairs,' Walter ordered.

'We've lost containment in sector four! Suppression field is intermittent!' Singh suddenly cried.

'Who's in that area?' Gordon queried with dread.

'Unfortunately, the only one I can think of offhand is that Nazi prick, Baron Von Ritzer,' Walter said, rising from his seat. 'Merry Christmas, folks.'

\* \* \*

### Pulse Pounder's ruined base, Simpson Desert: 10:36 AM AEDT

Bentaz Mullberry closed the lid on the metal cylinder, encasing Pulse Pounder in his own containment cell. His skin was stained black with soot and his shredded costume was charred, with some areas turned to ash. Aside from a haunting memory, he'd completely recovered from Hellgoat's treacherous attack.

*At least that ugly cyclops is now in the very same cylinder he'd held us in before we were freed by that other demon—Night Demon—who he'd apparently had imprisoned here.*

He turned and looked at his fellow team members, who'd stayed to mop up after Hellgoat had betrayed them and left them with their kidnapper.

Razorback was busy hauling various items of technology and machinery into the room, including the androids the Night Demon had deactivated. Mauler was occupied preparing Pulse Pounder's lieutenant, Guillotine, for his own containment pod.

Gate Crasher nursed his injured leg while he gathered his strength in anticipation of opening a portal large enough to transport Pulse Pounder and his minions, along with the technology they were confiscating, back to headquarters. Nevertheless, he was busy piling Razorback's haulage into organised groups.

That left Powerhouse, who had taken it upon himself to 'supervise' the clean-up, claiming only he had the leadership skills to oversee the job properly.

*Meaning he needed an excuse to do nothing but bark orders. Fuck this, I'm out of here. I have to see how my family are doing. I hope…I hope they're okay.*

'Hurry up with that, scum,' Powerhouse was saying to Mauler when Bentaz walked up alongside him.

Mauler rolled his eyes, but lifted Guillotine nonetheless and placed him into the cylinder he had reserved for him.

'Antithesis,' Guillotine mumbled repeatedly as he drifted in and out of consciousness.

*Where've I heard that before?*

'Powerhouse,' Bentaz said, interrupting his rival's tirade. 'You seem to have everything under control here, so I'm going to go and check on my family.'

'Well, if you want to let your teammates down again for personal issues, I'm not going to stop you,' Powerhouse said, as if he actually could.

Bentaz didn't have the energy to mince words with fools. 'Cool, well, I'll see you 'round then. Take care, everyone,' he said to the others before flying out through the hole Hellgoat and Night Demon had made when they escaped.

He'd not been long in flight when a message came through the radio inside his helmet, which miraculously still worked. 'Ballistic here,' he said, tapping the button inside the rim. A familiar cartoonish voice filled his ears.

'Ballistic? Is that you?' Chuck Cheese said through the earpiece, its voice a mixture of surprise and relief. 'We all thought you were dead! I was sending out a message on all channels as an emergency. I had no idea you would answer! Oh my, what a happy day! Oh no, wait, that's not quite true.'

'Chuck, just tell me what's going on,' Bentaz said firmly, accustomed to talking to the team's mascot.

'Headquarters is under attack,' Chuck Cheese replied. 'It's Hellgoat, he's gone mad. He's already killed Savage Scavenger and now he's turned on the rest of us!'

Bentaz sighed, knowing his family would have to wait.

'I'm on my way,' he said.

\* \* \*

### Manly, Sydney: 12:43 PM AEDT

Seth Zaraxom waded through the murky knee-deep water on his way to the forsaken beach. The whole area had started to flood on account of the seawater having nowhere else to go when the ocean waves passed into the bubble that surrounded Sydney. It was a dirty reddish-brown and reeked of dead fish and things that should not be.

*At least I'm heading in the right direction.*

Lilith had told him the False Leviathan turns water into blood as it moves, poisoning everything it touches. He hoped the real Leviathan would be up to the task of stopping the demon lord before it killed everything along the coast.

*I guess we're about to see if Sprite's little spell was worth all the trouble of acquiring it.*

Seth's mind moved from the mermaid's spell to Bojangles and White Lion. They'd each taken a door from the Abyss to different locations within the bubble, although the plan was for the other two to meet up later. He hoped they were both okay.

*This place is worse than I thought. I was expecting the High Mage to have an army, but I wasn't expecting him to have arranged to have six Lords of Hell roaming around Sydney. I suppose it really is the apocalypse.*

He looked around at the panorama of devastation surrounding him. The immediate area was flooded, with clusters of bloated corpses floating through the flotsam of the once-popular locale like islands of human chum. Lovecraftian horrors of various sizes patrolled the inundated suburb, feeding on the bodies as they passed by, and disturbing the soggy abominations that schooled underneath them.

All of this was framed by a backdrop of burning buildings, and set to a harrowing dissonance of demonic keening, punctuated with the occasional scream. The sky was dark with smoke.

*It's like a Hieronymus Bosch painting. I always told him he was talented. Still, I don't really want to meet any of these monsters up close—especially if there's as many as I think there are.*

It was apparent to Seth that if the Lords of Hell were here, then they would have taken at least half of their personal armadas with them, leaving the other half behind to guard their respective territories.

The water got deeper and he looked around for an appropriate area to cast the summoning spell. He looked back out to sea, and that's when he noticed the False Leviathan for the first time. It was coiled around the wreck of the Manly ferry: a dark red serpent with a spiky, dragon-like head, its rough scales slick with crimson ooze.

*It doesn't appear to have noticed me, but I won't tempt aunty Kismet by pushing my luck.*

He turned to his left and headed toward a partially submerged building, hoping it would obscure the demon lord's view while he cast the spell. As he ducked into the shadows of the flooded café, a deep voice challenged him. 'Freeze,' it said.

Seth came to a halt under the coffee-coloured eave. From the shadows of the entranceway stepped a tall, muscular man dressed in military fatigues with helmet and armed with a prototype Q6 anti-Manifest assault rifle. He appeared to have two surface-to-air missiles strapped to his back and was inexplicably painted in jungle camouflage. In comparison to the black leathers Seth was wearing, it was an ineffective choice.

'Who are you?' the soldier asked, his gun pointed at Seth's chest. 'I'm guessing you're not with those four Manifests who just left here, given they called themselves the Quartet.'

'Who are they, some kind of barber-shop losers?' Seth mocked, his tone scarcely belying his annoyance at this delay. 'Long story short: I'm Seth Zaraxom, world's oldest Manifest, and I have a weapon I can use against that glorified eel out there. The problem is I have to do it at midday—real midday that is, not this daylight savings bullshit—and I'm being stymied by some army reject who's dressed like he thinks that the swamped suburb of Manly resembles a tropical jungle. Now, does that answer all your fucking questions?'

The soldier looked nonplussed but lowered his rifle just the same. 'Okay, if you're telling the truth, then I'll follow your lead. How can I help?'

Seth looked around the corner of the building and saw the Quartet the soldier had mentioned engage some of the random demons patrolling the area.

*I remember those guys now, from that meeting with the so-called supervillains. Perfect distraction.*

Seth turned back to the soldier. 'All right then, you keep those creatures off my back while I perform the summoning ritual.'

'Did you just say what I thought you said?'

'Yes, yes,' Seth interrupted before the soldier could further delay him. He looked over to see how the Quartet were doing just in time to see the one called Armed Gunman get ripped apart by a giant crab monster.

'What did you say your name was, again?' he asked, turning back to the soldier.

'My codename is Super Trooper,' the soldier replied with a straight face.

'Sure, why not?' Seth said to himself, shaking his head in disbelief.

He began the ritual without saying anything more. It was quite simple, just stand knee-deep in water, face the sea, and say the words while thinking of whom you wish to summon.

'Klaatu barada nikto—Leviathan,' Seth chanted, right on midday.

Meanwhile, the commotion caused by the trio formerly known as the Quartet caught the attention of the False Leviathan itself.

'We are Leviathan, Dark Serpent of Bindings and Restrictions,' it hissed before slithering rapidly out of the surf, right past the ruined café Seth was in, and swallowed the Manifest known as Eye.

*Will they be known as the Duet now?* Seth thought idly, having finished the spell and turning to look at the battle. *Now I just have to get out of here and down to Bondi without being eaten like that poor sap. I suppose I should take soldier boy with me—it's not going to be pretty when the real Leviathan gets here.*

'Hey Zooper Dooper,' Seth called out to the soldier, who was still nearby and shooting at what looked like a mutated frogman. 'I've finished the spell, it's time to go.'

Super Trooper fired another burst into the frogman's misshapen head and turned around to look at Seth. 'You go on, I'll stay here and help Horsepower and High Flyer,' he said, referring to the remaining members of the Quartet.

'Forget about them, they're just supervillains,' Seth urged, trying one last time. 'That spell summons Leviathan, who, if you don't know, is an enormous sea monster. It could arrive anytime now—don't be a fool.'

'Don't worry about me,' the soldier said, reloading his gun. 'Besides, I don't believe in spells.'

*I suppose these demons got their invite to Sydney in the mail then? Oh well, I tried.*

Seth turned to leave when suddenly a horse-sized creature resembling a mantis shrimp leapt from the café's roof onto Super Trooper. Miraculously, he got to his feet and tried to bring his assault rifle to bear but the shrimp struck with its serrated forelimb and sliced him from his left shoulder to his right ribs.

The shrimp flicked the severed torso into the air and it landed with a splash at Seth's feet. Its eyestalks twitched at the Immortal.

*I guess that settles that debate. I'm leaving—I really don't have time to die.*

* * *

### The Territories of Xph'Ish'Matarg, Hell: Circa 4:00 PM AEDT

Mark Adams slowly dissolved in the demon lord's transparent stomach. As an added torture, his eyesight had remained intact to witness the other Lords of Hell when they entered the portal to Earth.

Xph'Ish'Matarg had ensured he'd seen it despite being engaged in combat with the Angel of Deicide, the Wraith. The demon lord fed on Mark's misery and so every little bit of despair made it stronger, like a bespoke battery to fight the angel.

Mark watched helplessly as Xph'Ish'Matarg slashed the Wraith with its sacrificial dagger, while the spectral adversary struck back with blasts of burning light. The demon lord transferred all of the pain from the blasts to Mark, who writhed in agony while his flesh melted.

*Please, stop. Please.*

*Silence, you pusillanimous slug!* The demon's voice boomed within Mark's mind.

His suffering reached new heights and he felt his final reserves start to crumble. He started to lose focus and a sound like a freight train grew louder in his ears. He made one last effort to assert control at the very same moment the Wraith deflected Xph'Ish'Matarg's blow and drove its armoured gauntlet into the demon's chest.

The Wraith emitted a wave of energy from its fist, vaporising

Xph'Ish'Matarg's torso…and then it happened.

*Oh my…*

It was like an explosion of orgasms within his mind; a perfect synergy of clarity, confidence, pleasure, and power. Flames emanated from his Manifest seed, consuming the rest of his goat-faced tormentor and engulfing the Wraith in a ball of fire.

The angel screamed and fled from the scene, leaving him alone and floating above the charred demon corpse, still racked in ecstasy. His new status of master was symbolised by the addition of the Dark Lord of Sacrifice and Penance's cloak upon his shoulders.

Mark's eyes burned red.

*Time to get the fuck out of here. Time to find my family.*

\* \* \*

### Pheasants Nest, New South Wales: 5:24 PM AEDT

Desci Adams pulled into the last free space in the makeshift dirt carpark after waiting for hours in line for petrol. An early Christmas dinner consisted of miscellaneous meat pies from the service station's warmer and a cup of Frozen Panta each. It was still a step up as breakfast had been a bar of chocolate, and lunch a packet of barley sugars.

She'd stocked up as much as she could; most of the good stuff had long gone. They weren't the only ones who'd decided to head for Canberra—especially after the news reported that Sydney had disappeared behind some kind of bubble.

*Looks like my gut instinct was right after all.*

At least the kids had stopped complaining and instead become fixated on the current crisis. They talked about possible explanations, ironically making her feel closer to them for the first time since her husband vanished.

*The kids reckon it all started when Ballistic and Vicious Man spoiled the moon, but I know that Mark's disappearance is somehow related. I just know it.*

Desci looked through the windscreen at all the activity around them while she chewed on a tasteless pie. There were military and police personnel everywhere, mostly coordinating the constant stream of civilians pouring south. They'd set up a temporary base with helicopters coming and going at regular intervals.

*There must be something important going on. I see Field Marshall Hobbs and Commissioner Jacobs.*

While most public officials are not known by the general public, cyborg ones were the exception. The thought sent fresh waves of uneasiness through her.

*I hope it's safe here.*

The radio had talked about demons attacking government facilities. The Defence Base up north, the supervillain prison in the south, and HSA Headquarters in Canberra.

She needed to rest after driving for hours as it was well known that driver fatigue caused more accidents than demonic attack. Her thoughts turned to what she would do if this place was attacked; Obie, Samara and Sebastian were completely oblivious to the frown on their mother's face as they joked around in the backseat.

She wondered if the government had brought along any of their pet superheroes. Sebastian didn't think so; he'd only spotted a bunch of Manifest teams uninspiringly called the No-Hopers and the Crappy Superheroes, and of course, everyone had spotted **Obvious Man** walking along with his flashing neon sign and personalised trumpet soundtrack.

*Sebastian so rarely says anything, I'd no idea he was into Manifest spotting. He keeps track of all their movements and sends them to his friends with something called email.*

It was amazing what you learned cooped up in a car for hours and forced to actually talk to one another. But there was one secret she chose not to reveal during the trip: what would they think if they knew she was a Manifest?

'How was dinner?' Desci asked over her shoulder, eager to escape her musings.

'About as good as yours,' Obie quipped, but his tone was light-hearted.

'I was so hungry, it tasted like the best damn pie in the world to me,' Samara added.

'Mmmph,' Sebastian grunted between mouthfuls. He was a slow eater.

'I'm sorry you had to spend Christmas like this,' Desci said, turning around in her seat to face them.

'Don't apologise, it wasn't your fault…Mum,' Samara said with a smile that said all was well between them again.

'Yeah, it could've been a lot worse,' Obie offered, before taking a sip of Panta from his straw.

'Mm hmm,' Sebastian agreed before chewing the last bite of his pie.

Desci's eyes welled up and she let her tears come without shame. She felt as if she loved them more than ever before. 'Merry Christmas,' she said, wiping her cheeks.

'Merry Christmas,' the kids echoed.

'Now, we have to get moving. It's going to take longer to get to Canberra than usual because of the alternate route they put around Lake George after that explosion,' she said before turning around and starting the engine. Movement through the windscreen made her glance up.

The sight of the grey, horned demon descending from the afternoon sky on bat-like wings sent a chill down Desci's spine. He was carrying the limp body of some superhero in his left hand and the dismembered chassis of what looked like a machine with a human head in his right.

'Oh my god, it's one of those demons they were talking about on the radio!' Desci cried, putting the car into reverse and backing out of the space to join the queue to Canberra.

'Don't panic, Mum,' Sebastian said soothingly. 'That's Hellgoat, one of the Heroes Squadron. He's on our side. Looks like he's carrying a couple of his teammates; the cyborg is Metallic Man and the guy with the radar in his chest is Tracker. Hellgoat's been missing, presumed dead. They must've been attacked and now he's bringing them in for medical attention.'

'No, something's wrong,' Desci replied quietly. 'Look how he's carrying them, like a bird of prey. No, they're dead, and I believe that demon killed them.'

A moment later she was proven right. Hellgoat dropped the bodies he was carrying and launched a stream of hellfire down into the military base.

'Holy shit!' Samara gasped.

Chaos erupted. Klaxons began to wail and panicked people tried to cut the queue, resulting in a fender-bender gridlock. This was exacerbated by mobs of civilian foot traffic who started fleeing the area, causing several people to be hit by cars.

'Looks like I was wrong,' Sebastian admitted.

'Um, maybe we should get out of here,' Obie suggested.

'I'd love to, but thanks to all these dickheads, there's nowhere to go,' Desci lamented, referring to the other drivers.

She desperately looked through the windows and tried to formulate an escape plan, but couldn't come up with anything other than running away on foot. Another burst of flame caught her eye and she watched as Hellgoat swooped down into the base and came back up carrying the smouldering body of Field Marshall Hobbs in one hand, before tearing off his head with the other.

The Field Marshall's armoured head was fused with titanium and made the perfect projectile to destroy **Obvious Man's** flashing sign. Hellgoat followed this up by roasting a morbidly obese Manifest whom Sebastian identified as Many Rolls Man, and then torching his companions, Vague Man, Stress Man and Sad Man, allowing the No-Hopers to ironically live up to their name by dying.

The Crappy Superheroes fared no better and Sebastian gave a running commentary as Decrepit Man, Prance Man, and Doink Man were likewise incinerated. He even told them it was Heroic Pose Man they were watching being dramatically torn to pieces a hundred metres away. He never bothered mentioning Irrelevant Man.

Desci decided she'd seen enough. 'Grab your things,' she told the kids. 'We're leaving the car.'

Moments later they were opening the doors and preparing to follow Desci's hastily constructed escape plan when Hellgoat noticed their movement.

*Oh no, please no.*

Before they could act, the demon was upon them, his red eyes radiating menace as he glared at them through the windows. They shut the doors and locked them, as if that would help in any way.

'No! Get away from my family!' Desci screamed, her eyes glowing a dazzling green.

Hellgoat merely grabbed their car and threw it over his head, before dousing the vehicle in a torrent of hellfire as it spun through the air. The kids screamed, but Desci felt oddly serene.

*Oh Mark, I'll see you soon.*

It was her last thought before the car landed on its roof in a gulley and exploded into an inferno of green fire.

* * *

### Heroes Squadron Headquarters, Canberra: 7:36 PM AEDT

Bentaz Mullberry walked slowly around the piles of rubble that was once the command centre of HSA Headquarters. Three bodies covered in stained sheets lay over to one side, close to the wall of broken monitors. Bentaz stopped to look at them one last time.

*So Hellgoat did truly betray us. Savage Scavenger, Grug and Gridlock had to pay with their lives because Powerhouse was right and I hated him too much to see it.*

'You know, I never even knew their real names,' he said to Chuck Cheese, who was standing behind him on his stumpy little legs.

'I'll see what I can find out,' Chuck Cheese responded in his comical voice. 'I'm sure there's a file somewhere.'

'No, that's okay,' Bentaz said. Sometimes the walking cheddar pyramid was too eager to help out. 'How's Tower Man?'

'Well, the hospital said he was stable,' Chuck Cheese answered with no pun intended, 'but given that nasty Hellgoat incinerated his hands, I'm sure he's in a sad place right now.'

*That's an understatement, I bet.*

The cheese's mention of the hospital took his mind back to his family.

*At least I got to call the hospital and established that Hellgoat had already left for Sydney. I'm glad that Yam seems to be recovering, but Mum's still in a coma and Peach...*

Bentaz tried to focus on the moment instead of his little sister's paralysis, knowing he would get to see them eventually but there was nothing he could do about it at the moment. If ever there was a time his powers were truly needed, it was here and now.

He adjusted his helmet and then his scarlet pauldrons. He'd also had time to change into the spare suit in his locker—a wise move—given his original outfit was mostly rags. This outfit was still being worn in and he kept adjusting it.

'Okay, so tell me what happened in Sydney again,' Bentaz said, now fiddling with his leather gloves.

'No one knows for sure,' Chuck Cheese explained. 'It just kind of went dark—like it was under some sort of dome. Then the Defence Base and Powder Keg were hit, and then us.'

'Hellgoat wouldn't have had time to attack all those places in that timeframe, but there was another demon with him when he left Pulse Pounder's base,' Bentaz mused, tugging on his red cape. 'It's conceivable they could've pulled it off between them. You said Hellgoat was going to Sydney, didn't you?'

'That's right,' Chuck Cheese agreed in his squeaky voice. 'At least that's what Tracker said when he and Metallic Man took off after him. I lost contact with them too.'

'How on Earth did you survive when the others were so brutally murdered?' Bentaz asked, finally content with his costume.

'I managed to activate the self-defence system,' Chuck Cheese beamed, the pride in his voice extremely noticeable.

'Good on you,' Bentaz replied, meaning it. 'Gate Crasher should be just about recovered enough to start moving all that stuff from Pulse Pounder's base, but the problem now is where to take it, as both here and the prison are no longer options.'

'Don't you worry about that; you *have* to go after Hellgoat.' Chuck Cheese had been briefed on the stakes when Bentaz first arrived. 'I'd be happy to go with you, though, should you need me.' The offer was genuine.

'I'm touched, really,' Bentaz said as he adjusted his belt again. 'But I think it's too dangerous for you there.'

Suddenly there was a swooshing sound and Powerhouse entered the room at super speed. 'I see you've had time to play dress-up when the rest of us were doing all the hard work at Pulse Pounder's base,' was the first thing he said.

Bentaz ignored the slight. 'So why are you here? Where's everyone else?'

'I took charge of field operations and assigned Mauler the task of guarding Gate Crasher until he recovers, while I came back here to stop Hellgoat,' Powerhouse exaggerated. 'Who, need I remind you, has murdered our teammates because you fucked up. Their blood is on your hands.'

'I'll accept responsibility for that,' Bentaz allowed, 'which is why I'm just about to follow Hellgoat to Sydney. Why don't you join me? I could really use your help with this crisis.'

'I bet you could,' Powerhouse gloated, a grin from ear to ear. 'But I'm afraid as the new leader of the Heroes Squadron, I'll be too busy coordinating events from here. Someone has to clean up the mess the old leader created.'

'Whatever. I don't have time to argue with self-righteous cunts,' Bentaz retorted. He turned to the team's mascot. 'I trust you'll keep me informed of what's going on from here, won't you?'

'I sure will, Ballistic, you can count on me!' Chuck Cheese enthused.

He patted the cheese on the head, gave Powerhouse the finger, and took off for Sydney.

After about thirty minutes, he arrived at Pheasants Nest. Even from above, the destruction was vast. The petrol station burned like a pillar of flame and it was surrounded by the smouldering shells of hundreds of cars and army vehicles. Scores of bodies lay in heaps strewn about the area and piles of charred bones glowed with dying embers in the twilight.

Bentaz flew down to the remains of what appeared to be the military's command base. Everything was in ruin. A burnt body caught his eye and Bentaz recognised it as Commissioner Jacobs.

*I'd recognise that chainsaw arm anywhere.*

He walked around a gutted building and was actually startled when he found a survivor. The man was wearing a homemade superhero costume with a broken sign strapped to his back. Bentaz could no longer read the sign, but the writing on the man's chest announced him to be **Obvious Man**. He was playing 'Adagio for Strings' from some hidden device.

'Hello, I'm **Obvious Man**,' he said. 'I survived.'

*Obviously.*

'Did anyone else survive?' Bentaz didn't have time for fools. 'Was it Hellgoat? Is he still here?'

'You're asking me?' **Obvious Man** asked, turning his head as if to see if someone was behind him. 'You *are* asking me!'

*I don't have time for this. It looks like Hellgoat's gone and no one else around here needs help. I need to press on to Sydney—I have to assume that's where Hellgoat's headed.*

He flew off without further comment and arrived at his destination a short time later. The black dome around the city was positively enormous. He felt dwarfed by its sheer size as he approached the cordoned off area where the dome met the earth. Familiar scenes of carnage told Bentaz that this was the way Hellgoat had come.

*I'm in the right place then, but why's there a Powder Keg bus backed into the dome like that? The prison's literally miles away.*

He walked up to the very edge of the anomaly and looked at the wall of blackness before him. It was so dark that it played tricks on his eyes, as not a single photon of light was reflected off its surface.

*Well, here goes nothing.*

Bentaz took a deep breath and stepped through the magical barrier without fuss.

* * *

### The Abyss: Circa 11:00 PM AEDT

Dread Sedgewick took a large gulp from his stein and braced himself for a lecture as he watched his mother come down the stairs to the bar. He didn't have long to wait.

'You selfish, nasty little bastard!' Lilith spat before slapping her son across the stylised birthmark on his cheek.

'Hi Mum,' he replied, weathering the assault. 'So nice to see you.'

'Don't give me any of your shit,' Lilith raged. 'Not after you went out and attacked your father's family after I expressly told you not to!' She slapped him again.

'We're his family in case you've forgotten!' Dread snapped back. 'I went through a lot too! It took ages for my arms to grow back so I could dig my way out of that moon grave and create a doorway back here.'

'I don't want to hear it! What kind of man are you, to beat up a little girl like that?' Lilith fumed, completely disregarding her son's protestations.

'The kind that beats up little girls, obviously,' Dread quipped before taking another sip. 'But I also beat up their big, tough daddies—well, I would have, if the prick had actually been there. Destruction doesn't discriminate and neither do I.'

'Who do you think you are, the reaper in that AIDS commercial?' Lilith mocked.

*Since when does Mum watch TV?*

'Well, if you ever want my respect again, you'll start trying to make amends to me,' she continued.

*Here we go.*

'Oh yeah? What?' he asked, sparking up a cigarette with his finger blades.

'You can go and help your uncle and half-brother fight the Lords of Hell in Sydney,' Lilith suggested. 'For a start.'

Dread knew his mother's anger was just an act—she'd been trying to get him involved in the whole apocalypse thing for ages and was now using guilt as her latest strategy.

*Yet I'd do just about anything to get away from this.*

'Okay, yeah, sure, as long as you shut up about it,' he agreed, before taking another drag of his cigarette. 'You know what? It could be a bit of fun, brawling with demon lords.'

'Good, then get going,' Lilith hissed, but Dread caught a smile on her face.

He butted out his smoke, downed the last of his beer, and headed for the door to Earth.

# 26 December 34 BZ

Naomi Bloodlust crouched in the dark warehouse wishing she was in a bar with a cigarette and a beer. Anything to take her mind off the current situation.

After her uneasy truce with Gorg, they had re-entered the warehouse and set about trying to convince everyone else. It hadn't been easy—especially as Liu had already killed two of Scar's Seven Servants.

*Yeah, the Five Servants of Scar just doesn't have the same ring to it.*

Naomi smiled and leant back against Liu, who accepted her without comment. He was lost in his thoughts like most everyone else as they listened to the apocalypse outside.

She looked over at Gorg, who was sitting on the floor with Scar and his remaining servants on the opposite side of Scar's office to the Blood Brigade. He glanced back and she felt a mutual respect pass between them. Not like Scar, however, who sat glaring at her malevolently, an expression of hatred chiselled into his scar-seamed face.

It had been an arduous twenty-four hours: beginning with breaking up the fight, followed by locking all the doors and hiding out in the office listening to the sounds of buildings being demolished and people screaming. Not long after, the eerie moaning began, which Spindler declared sounded like zombies from some old movie called *Dawn of the Dead*. No one had dared confirm this in case they were discovered, so they'd sat and frowned at each other instead.

*Worst Christmas ever.*

So far, Scar's warehouse had been left alone and Naomi had managed to get a couple hours of sleep. She pulled a chocolate bar from her work belt and unwrapped it before taking a generous bite. At her insistence, the Blood Brigade carried enough food and water for two days, except Molecule, who didn't need to eat, and Fatmandu, who could eat anything anyway and therefore didn't need to carry food.

*I can stretch my rations to maybe four days if I'm not too energetic, but damned if I'm going to sit here eyeballing Scar for that long.*

Naomi quietly rose to her feet with catlike prowess and softly padded towards the office door.

'What are you doing?' Scar hissed, flecks of spittle visible in the candlelight.

'Someone has to see what's going on,' she whispered before slowly opening the office door and slipping out into the dark warehouse. Filtered moonlight shone through the row of windows lining one side of the building.

It was mostly empty, but there were still several large shelves of boxes lining the walls, most likely filled with Scar's ill-gotten gains. It wasn't the boxes, but rather the two corpses lying in the centre of the room that caught her attention.

One was Jake, the cyborg from New Guinea, and the other was the creature, Pad, who according to rumour and hearsay, was a Manifest sanitary pad. Liu had obviously killed Jake by using his magnetic powers to rip the cybernetic components out of his body and using them to take out Pad. Naomi was used to the sight of death; what was disturbing about this scene was the blood that pooled out of Jake being soaked up by Pad.

*I could have lived my whole life without seeing that.*

She tried to ignore the gag reflex as she headed across the room. One of the few shelves stood directly under the row of windows and she lithely climbed to the top and peered out into the night.

*Much better than when Gorg took me up through the skylight.*

The enormous demon lord was nowhere to be seen, yet she could still hear it in the distance. It had cleaved a path of destruction through the neighbourhood, but there were fewer bodies around than expected. She could also still hear the moaning and wondered if Spindler was right.

A sound behind her caused her to turn around, but there was nothing there save for the bodies.

*Were they in a different position before?*

She heard a noise outside and glanced back to see what looked like two superheroes descending on rocket-boots—one was a being of crystal and the other appeared to be a zombie. They pointed towards where the sounds of the demon lord were coming from and disappeared from view.

*This could be the distraction we're looking for.*

She jumped from the shelf and landed with a roll before returning to her feet in one graceful motion. Moments later she was back in the office.

'We're leaving,' she said to Liu. He looked up at her from his seat in the corner. 'Couple superheroes are going to take on Rancid from the looks of it, so this is our perfect opportunity to leave.'

'And go where?' Spindler butted in.

'Anywhere has got to be better than here,' Liu decided, rising to his feet.

Molecule and Fatmandu also stood up and Spindler kept quiet as he joined them.

'Are you just going to let them leave after they come here and attack me in my own place of business?' Scar suddenly yelled at Gorg, who may have been dozing or just resting his eyes.

'We have a truce,' he replied calmly without opening his eyes. 'If they want to leave, that's fine with me.'

'This is outrageous!' Scar bellowed as he started to stand. 'I didn't pay you to pick and choose when to kill her. Do it now!' His five minions began to rise at his cue.

'No,' Gorg said simply. 'Besides, I pick the terms of my business deals.'

'I will not be humiliated like this! I'm one hundred and six years old and didn't become the man I am now by letting two-bit shysters tell me how to run my business!' Scar raged at the top of his lungs.

'Will you shut up?' Naomi hushed, using her hand to indicate that he should lower his voice. 'I thought I heard something.'

She looked back into the warehouse, but there was nothing there except the bodies.

*They were definitely in another position earlier. We have to go now.*

'How dare you hush me!' Scar continued.

'Do you want to bring that fucking monster down upon us?' Liu said, coming to Naomi's defence.

Both teams were now standing and faced off in the cramped office. All except Gorg, who still looked like he was napping. Naomi quickly assessed the situation.

*Okay, so if Gorg's sitting this one out, then Scar is the dangerous one, what with his ability to drain life force through his many scars. Next up is probably that walking cerebral parasite, Brainwave, or Scream with his sonic attack, followed by Tube and his organic guns.*

She wasn't worried about Grid or Box, who were as lame as they sounded and not worthy of a description.

Suddenly a pair of bloodcurdling screams pierced the air and Naomi assumed it was the superheroes. The moaning noticeably increased in volume and moments later a rhythmic banging began on the warehouse doors. The backdoor was next.

She turned at the sound and a chill ran the length of her spine.

Jake and Pad stood silently, their heads lulled at unnatural angles and their hands twitching with murderous anticipation. Cold, dead eyes stared at Naomi and she noticed how Jake's jaw opened and closed repeatedly, as if he was already devouring her flesh in his undead mind. They lurched towards her like marionettes on invisible strings.

'Guys, we've got a problem,' she said, drawing a knife and taking a defensive posture.

Suddenly the front roller doors were torn away and a red, four-armed, horned demon led a horde of zombies into the warehouse. 'Hee hee hee, that is an understatement, mortal,' the demon cackled as it stalked towards her. 'We are Ress'urekt, demon of the animated corpse, Scout of Gledandron, and ally of Rancid, Dark Lord of Decay.'

'Sounds like you're the demon of longwinded titles,' Naomi replied with false bravado. This was her first time exchanging barbs with a supernatural being. She noticed Liu and Gorg join her, the bounty hunter now wide awake with his guns aimed at Ress'urekt. Jake and Pad still lumbered at them.

The backdoor was next to break, and even more undead shambled into the warehouse.

'We've got to find a way out!' Naomi cried. 'Maybe the roof?'

'We can't get everyone up there in time,' Liu answered. 'Fatmandu alone will take three people to lift.'

'Forget them,' Gorg rasped through his faceplate. 'If they can't keep up, they're zombie chow.'

'I don't leave my teammates,' Naomi countered. 'We find another way.'

'There's another way out of here,' Tube interjected from behind them. 'Scar has a secret escape passage over on the north wall.'

'Silence, you fool!' Scar yelled, slapping his minion on the side of the head. 'I don't want them knowing about that!'

'It's a bit late for secrets, you shrivelled cunt,' Naomi spat as she extended the blades on her gauntlet and sliced Jake and Pad to ribbons. 'Magnet, get that guy to show us where the exit is.'

'Come on, show us the way out,' Liu said to Tube, both of them ignoring Scar's protestations. 'I'll keep the zombies off your back.'

'It's not the zombies I'm worried about,' Tube admitted, glancing between Scar and Ress'urekt. 'It's this way.'

He led Liu to a pile of boxes that hid a small button. He pressed it and a hidden door opened with a click.

'Stand back,' Liu warned. 'My team first. Miss Bloodlust, over here!'

*I haven't heard him call me that in a long time.*

The rest of the Blood Brigade, along with Scar and his men, moved towards the escape tunnel. The zombies staggered after them while Ress'urekt simply stood and watched; its cackling, jawless head encircled with a mop of stringy black hair that writhed like a nest of worms.

'You first,' Liu said to Fatmandu as he arrived at the escape hatch.

'Uh-uh, no way. I ain't getting stuck behind that fat fuck if he gets stuck,' Spindler said when he arrived a moment later. '*I'll* go first.'

'Suit yourself, just get your arse down there,' Liu snapped, ushering him through.

Spindler ducked through the hatch, followed by Fatmandu, who fit with space to spare. Molecule paused to disintegrate a zombie that got too close, before joining its teammates in the escape tunnel.

Liu turned to look for Naomi, and found her with Gorg, fighting to hold off the hungry undead mob. Scar's group rapidly approached the tunnel.

Box and Grid were too slow and the ghouls tore into them as they closed in on the rest of the group. Scar looked nervously over his shoulder at their demise, as he headed for the escape tunnel, now resigned to having his secret exposed.

The zombies ambled closer, and all the while the demon did nothing but watch like a nightmarish voyeur. Its sunken eyes bored into Scar while he fled and it was enough to unnerve the centenarian crime boss.

'You two, hold them off,' he said to Brainwave and Scream, who obeyed without hesitation. He arrived at the passageway a moment later. Liu was guarding the exit.

'Not before her,' Liu said and gestured at Naomi.

'Let me pass!' Scar commanded. 'Or I'll have your essence!'

'Give it a rest,' Gorg said as he joined them.

Meanwhile, Brainwave and Scream were dutifully attempting to hold back the tide of reanimated flesh. Scream's sonic attack proved ineffective against the dead, but Brainwave was able to render them inert with its mental commands. Ress'urekt had seen enough.

It pounced with pantherine agility, tearing through Brainwave's head before ripping Scream in half with its other two arms. It paused again to mock them. 'Give yourselves to me, flesh husks, and become one with Gledandron. There is no other choice. Hee hee hee.'

'Tube, stop that demon,' Scar commanded his final servant, who was leaning over a box shooting acidic chunks of bone from his organic tube guns.

'I'm not fighting that thing!' Tube protested.

Naomi stabbed a zombie priest in the eye and turned to Liu. 'You and Gorg go; I'll be right behind you.'

'But...' Liu began.

'Go!' Naomi shouted and Liu reluctantly followed Gorg into the tunnel. She turned back to Scar, who was still arguing with Tube while the demon watched only twenty metres away.

In one fluidic motion, she cartwheeled over the boxes that surrounded the escape tunnel, sliced through Tube's head with her gauntlet, and landed between Scar and the exit. He looked at her, dumbfounded.

'You know, I have a secret I've just been dying to show someone,' she purred, flicking her eyes between Scar and Ress'urekt. The demon was once again standing motionless and laughing.

Scar, on the other hand, attempted to push past Naomi to the tunnel beyond. She grabbed him and held his face close to hers. 'Not so fast,' she said. 'I haven't shown you my secret.'

A flame flickered in her eye and Scar suddenly felt unnaturally hot. He started coughing and his eyes grew wide with horror when he saw the puffs of smoke escape his throat. Within seconds he'd burst into flames, which Naomi flared into a wall of fire with her mind. Ress'urekt screeched and backed away.

*Not laughing now, motherfucker.*

She'd known she was a pyrokinetic ever since she'd made her father pay for his years of drunken abuse shortly after she'd Manifested. The only people who'd known her secret were those she'd used it on.

*I'm just lucky the Field Marshall and the Commissioner never realised I used my power to torch them, forcing Doctor Q to make them cyborgs to save their lives.*

The wall of fire shielded her escape into the tunnel.

'Sorry for the delay, oh, and I'm afraid Scar's not going to make it,' she said before turning around—to Gorg's black hole gun pointed at her face. He kept Liu covered with the other gun and the rest of her team had already fled down the tunnel.

'I'm sorry, baby. His armour seems to be made from some sort of plastic,' Liu apologised. 'I couldn't stop him.'

'We had a truce,' she said calmly to Gorg.

'*Had* being the operative term,' he replied. 'The truce was only good until we escaped.'

Naomi extended the blades on her gauntlet and in the blink of an eye she used it to slice through the black hole guns on both his gauntlets and bring her dagger up under his throat before he could recover.

'Do it,' he croaked.

'Listen here,' she snarled. 'Scar's dead, it's over. I *could* kill you now, but I won't—as a sign of good faith. You just need to leave me the fuck alone. *Capiche?*'

She smashed him in the temple with the handle of her knife before he could respond, knocking him out.

'Just in case he was going to say no,' she said in answer to Liu's questioning look. 'Come on, we've got to go. I don't think that demon will be far behind.'

* * *

**Outside Xenotech Inc Head Office, Circular Quay: 5:13 AM AEDT**

Lorraine Freeman had been fighting demonic forces for hours and really wanted to sleep. Instead, she drove her fist through the frosted features of yet another ice demon as it tried to pulverise her with the unwieldly club it was carrying. Its head shattered into a thousand pieces.

Her powers of suggestion had failed to influence the frozen demons so she'd resorted to brute strength in order to stem their tide. It was a losing battle.

*They seem to just grow out of the frozen harbour like a never-ending plague. This is futile; we need to stop that Ishlarr giant if we've got any hope of ending this.*

Lorraine ran over to Beat Master, who was performing what could only be described as a lethal brawl ballet to the tune of 'Total Eclipse of the Heart'. She called to him and he turned around with bright eyes.

'Lorraine! Isn't this a rush?' he yelled over the din of cracking ice. 'Well, apart from all the death, I guess. What's the plan?'

*It's funny how he keeps turning to me for the answers. He's older than me; he should be giving me advice.*

Yet she was a born leader and found the words came easily to her.

'We've got to coordinate with the survivors of T-Squad and the X-Droids,' she said, too exhausted to care about how silly that sounded. 'We have to target Ishlarr; it's the key to everything.'

'I'm surprised you can remember its name,' Beat Master observed, grabbing another demon and hurling it into the harbour.

'It keeps repeating it over and over, so it's hard to forget,' she replied as she prepared to fight yet another demon. 'Besides, can't you hear it in your mind? Like a great weight slowing down your thoughts?'

'I can't hear anything over Bonnie Tyler,' he joked, blocking a massive ice club with his forearm, before following through with a left hook that shattered his opponent's gruesome face.

Lorraine thought that maybe Samuel had unwittingly provided a clue to the demon lord's power. She didn't have long to ponder it, as her latest adversary moved in close with malice frozen on its jagged features.

'Feel the hoarfrost, mortal,' the demon croaked.

'Who are you calling a whore?' she cried, driving her fist through its head. 'Enough distractions. Samuel, follow me.'

Lorraine led Beat Master over to where her mother was coordinating the defence of the building's perimeter, her powers also ineffective against the monsters.

It had taken Lorraine and Beat Master several hours to walk the relatively short distance from Darling Harbour due to everything being frozen over and the relentless waves of ice demons. The trip had been a carnival of horror, with butchered civilians frozen in their tracks against the white landscape like some kind of sickly frieze…or terrible pun. In the distance, the pink beam continued to shoot into the sky from the top of Centrepoint Tower.

They'd arrived at Xenotech Head Office to find it under assault by the omnipresent demons and defended by the X-Droids and a government team calling themselves T-Squad—most of whom had been slaughtered during the night. Only their leader, T-Man; the plumber-turned-barbarian, Fire Axe; and the man with potato flesh, Spud, remained alive.

The X-Droids had fared much better, with two missing (but presumed dead) and another two having left on a mission to discover just how far west the demon lord's influence went. Lorraine's mother had been among the remaining eight X-Droids keeping the ice demons from entering the building to slay the civilians inside. They hadn't been entirely successful and Lorraine would never forget the sight of Toby Kim, the manager she'd met once before, lying with his head split in half and his brains leaking out his mouth.

Her reunion with her mother had been tearful, yet brief, as they'd had little time to spare while under demonic onslaught.

*I'll have to make time if we've got any hope of surviving.*

'Mum! We have to take the fight to Ishlarr,' Lorraine called, running closer. 'It's the one controlling these things!'

Lucy Freeman looked over to her daughter and then back towards the harbour, where the gigantic Lord of Hell towered above them.

'We are Ishlarr, Dark Lord of the Frozen Mind,' it boomed for the hundredth time, the very air freezing around its tusked snout and falling to the ground as needle-sharp hail.

'I agree, honey,' Lucy said, turning to her daughter. 'But how?'

'By hitting it with everything we have at once,' Lorraine declared, throwing a brick into another demon that got too close.

'We can try, I suppose, but I'm not sure we have enough raw power,' Lucy cautioned. 'If we only had more people…'

'Have you heard from those two guys you sent out?' Lorraine asked. Radio contact outside Sydney was down, but it seemed to work fine within the city itself.

'Crystal and Decompose reported engaging another demon lord in Ashfield…before contact was lost,' Lucy added grimly.

Lorraine paused before asking what was really on her mind. 'Mum…do you think Heather and Samantha are okay?'

Lucy paused before answering as well, and in that moment, Lorraine saw a look of worry flash across her face. 'Shara's with them, so I'm sure they'll be okay,' she said unconvincingly. 'Anyway, we have enough to worry about here. Put the word out; we attack Ishlarr on my signal.'

Lorraine and Beat Master did just that, fending off more ice demons in the process. They finished up with T-Man, Fire Axe and Spud, and soon after the sky exploded with a lightshow featuring all the colours in the spectrum.

The ragtag group of Manifests turned their attack on the colossal demon and the dawn came alive with laser beams and lightning bolts.

*Mum's right, it's not enough. I'll have to get right in close.*

Without warning, a large ice beast charged at them from the side, trampling T-Man and Fire Axe and splattering Spud all over Lorraine with a slash of its frozen paw. Chunks of the human potato landed in Lorraine's mouth and it tasted like blood and raw French fries.

*Gross!* She retched and spat but couldn't get the taste from her mouth. Luckily, Neutron, one of the X-Droids, had shattered the ice beast while she was distracted.

Overall it made no difference, as moments later Ishlarr loomed over the group and a frozen cloud fell over their minds. 'Foolish mortals, your souls are ours,' it bellowed, air freezing into spikes above them. Death seemed inevitable.

'Look at that!' Beat Master suddenly cried, pointing up at the sky. 'So bright…'

The ice knives evaporated in a radiant blast of heat and light and a flaming being descended from above to hover before them. He was naked and glowed white-hot, and Lorraine felt the cold fog lift from her mind in his presence.

'How may I be of asssissstansssse?' he asked in a strange voice that sounded like his saliva was sizzling.

*Oh, thank god! This may turn the tide.*

'Stop that giant demon!' Lorraine called out to him, not caring where he came from, only glad he was here.

Ishlarr took a step back at the suggestion. 'There is something about this mortal…' it said to itself. 'Something hidden and ancient.'

'I know not of what you ssspeak,' White Hot asserted as he floated slowly towards the Lord of Hell. 'I only know you are an abomination that mussst be ssstopped.'

*Come on! Flame that monster!*

Before White Hot could unleash upon Ishlarr he was caught up in a blast of frigid air that snuffed out his flame and sent him tumbling back to ground encased in ice. His blank eyes stared at Lorraine through the transparent block and once again she felt her mind begin to cloud.

\* \* \*

### Arthur Mullberry Residence, North Ryde: 7:11 AM AEDT

Bentaz Mullberry walked up to the front door of the quiet cottage-style house on the abandoned suburban street. The oak door was hanging off one hinge and had obviously been kicked in. He ignored the sinking feeling in his guts and cautiously entered his grandfather's house.

*You saw the devastation on the way here. You know what to expect.*

The inside of the house looked like it had been ransacked, but Bentaz recognised the signs of a struggle. The dried blood that had soaked into everything was the dead giveaway—and another terrible pun.

The house was so Spartan that it didn't take long for Bentaz to find his grandfather—well, at least he *assumed* it was him. The body was on the floor, skinned, and the top of its head removed, as if scalped. Piles of human viscera were lumped in the corner of the room along with shredded rags of clothing. A bloodstained khaki helmet similar to his own was lying discarded on the bed. He recognised it as part of his grandfather's Ally costume.

*I guess the reaper finally came after all,* Bentaz thought, and was immediately ashamed of himself. *I'm not sure why I came here. We didn't really part on the best of terms. Still, he's family.*

He picked up the helmet and placed it gently on the bedside table before removing the bedsheet and draping it over Arthur Mullberry's ruined body. He wondered whether he should say some sort of eulogy.

*Despite being an unlikeable arsehole most of the time, Grandfather lived such an incredible life that I wouldn't know where to begin. All anyone ever talks about is his rivalry with Axis, but he did so much more than that.*

Arthur Mullberry exploits were impressive. He took down the Red Baron—held his biplane by the tail and incinerated him with laser vision, as he told it. He battled the Super Six in World War Two and discovered Hitler in the bunker. He carried 'Little Boy' to Hiroshima. Later on, he fought the communists and helped form the new, more aggressive United Nations after they failed in Korea.

*But he wasn't just about war either. There was that controversy when Cecil B. DeMille made that movie about him and claimed he was an American. At least the remake he made of his own movie featured the American Way, who wasn't around in the thirties.*

Bentaz shook his head in wonderment. His grandfather had even channelled massive rivers and brought water to the interior of the country, allowing Australia to have a much larger population than it would have normally.

*Nothing I could say could do justice to any of that. Grandfather always assumed I knew nothing about him. He didn't know I used to idolise him—not even when he saw my original costume, which I based on his.*

He looked at his grandfather's body, the bedsheet now scarlet from his blood. This wasn't what he thought his Boxing Day would be like.

He grabbed his grandfather's helmet again and turned it over in his hands, lost in thought.

*Grandfather was a powerful Manifest—what could've done this to him? What could've done this to Sydney?*

Bentaz hadn't seen any sign of life since entering the bubble, although he had *heard* it.

*At least I know that jerk, Tactician, is alive. I can still hear him calling for help over the HSA emergency signal—he says he's buried under some government facility and can't get out.*

He placed his grandfather's helmet back on the bedside table and considered going to rescue Tactician.

*Fuck him. I'm done with the Heroes Squadron and being his flunky. All it has ever gotten me is grief—every time I'm away something bad happens—and my family is too important.*

His mind turned once more to his mother and sister and with it came the twinge of guilt that he wasn't with them. He suppressed the feeling, turned to leave the small cruor-drenched bedroom, and immediately moved into a defensive posture.

'You! Are you responsible for this?' he screamed at the intruder.

'Whoa, don't stain your panties, I had nothing to do with this!' Vicious Man replied, his hands in the air in a non-threatening gesture. 'I saw you walk in here and I thought I'd follow you. I really like what you've done with the place.'

Bentaz punched Vicious Man in the chest, causing him to smash through the front wall and into the street. Bentaz was on him in seconds. 'I should have known you wouldn't be so easy to kill,' he said as he whaled into his half-brother. 'This time, I'll make sure!'

Vicious Man retaliated with an elbow to Bentaz's chin, followed by a knee to the balls—one of his favourite moves, in fact. He rolled over and threw Bentaz off him and into the wilted lawn of a house across the street. They were both on their feet in moments and sized each other up from opposing footpaths.

'Will you chill for a second, Rambo II?' Vicious Man quipped. 'Amazingly, I'm not here to fight you. In fact, I've come to help you fight the Lords of Hell.'

Bentaz wasn't sure he heard correctly. 'What did you say?' he asked incredulously. 'Did you say the Lords of Hell?'

'Congratulations, your ears work,' Vicious Man said sarcastically. 'Yes, the Lords of Hell have invaded Sydney at the behest of some ancient fucker pretentiously named the High Mage of Hell. Personally, I think he should have stuck with Merlin.'

*So that's what's been going on! It certainly would explain the destruction and it fits with what White Lion warned us about.*

'Even if I believe all that, how do I know you're telling the truth about my grandfather back in the house? You did try and kill my family earlier—something that you and I are not finished with, by the way,' Bentaz promised.

'Oh, was that your grandpappy back there under the sheet?' Vicious Man queried, seemingly unfazed by the threat. 'I couldn't make out the family resemblance.'

Bentaz believed him in spite of himself.

'He was your grandfather too,' he said, finding it hard to admit the truth. 'But if what you say is true, then we don't have time to stand around and go over the family tree.'

*And the stakes are too high for me to get revenge right now, but when this crisis is over...*

'Meh, whatever.' Vicious Man shrugged. 'I'm not the one who's delaying us.'

'Well then, what's the plan?'

'To die in the name of Gledandron the World Eater, mortal,' said a sudden voice from the sky, the sound causing images of babies being skinned to flash through Bentaz's mind. It was followed by an unnerving nattering sound.

Bentaz and Vicious Man both turned and looked up to see three demons floating menacingly above them. One was orange with bat-like wings and long, bloodstained talons; one was a dirty brown with ram horns and a necklace of scalps; while the third was hidden beneath a cocoon of human skins and was the one who was nattering.

'We are Styryk, the Disemboweller,' the orange one rasped. 'These units are Racuse, the Scalper, and Saracuth, the Keeper of Skins.'

That's when Bentaz noticed his grandfather's skin staring at him with eyeless sockets from Saracuth's flesh-shell.

*It was them!*

'Am I supposed to be impressed by you *Hellraiser* rejects?' Vicious Man mocked, drawing twin blades from the inside pockets of his trench coat. 'I've taken dumps scarier than you lot.'

Bentaz imagined that was probably true, but the thought was soon forgotten as he looked back at his grandfather's skin and saw red.

'You might not know this, but I'm much more powerful than my grandfather was,' he said to no demon in particular. 'Let me show you.' His fists glowed with golden energy.

'You are nothing but a fearful little boy, still suckling on your mummy's teat,' Racuse taunted, pointing its long claw accusingly at Bentaz. It turned to Vicious Man. 'While you, Dread Sedgewick, also seek your mum…Aieeeeeee!'

Vicious Man tore Racuse in half midsentence, before driving one of his serrated knives through the demon's festering skull. 'How about a nice big cup of shut the fuck up?'

Meanwhile, Bentaz attacked Saracuth and ripped his grandfather's skin from the demon's repulsive cloak. He cremated it on the spot before it could be further desecrated.

Saracuth nattered again and horrific images once more flashed in Bentaz's mind.

'How dare you?' was all he managed to say before unleashing the full force of the energy beams from his hands, incinerating Saracuth in a puff of crimson. The demon had no time to scream before it was smoke.

Only Styryk the Disemboweller remained, and for the first time in its existence, it felt utterly alone.

'This is not possible,' it shrieked. 'No mortal has ever been a threat to us before.'

'Well, no mortal has ever had a dick with teeth before either,' Vicious Man retorted. 'I guess you're about to experience two new things today—this one, I call the cock chomp.' He started to unzip his fly.

'I've got this one,' Bentaz said urgently, desperately trying prevent what he thought was about to happen. He'd had enough images burned into his mind for one day.

Styryk hastily flew off during the distraction.

Bentaz turned to Vicious Man. 'Thanks for your help, but I think you should leave before I'm reminded of what you really are. I can handle a single demon.'

'Suit yourself. I hear there's plenty to go around anyway,' Vicious Man replied indifferently. He lifted his leg and farted. 'And on that note, I'm outta here.'

Bentaz let him go and pursued Styryk across the suburban waste-land. It didn't take long to catch up. 'There's no escape for you,' he said a little too dramatically.

'Foolish mortal,' the demon lilted, suddenly taking on a confidence that Bentaz found disturbing. 'You are in the glorious presence of one of the Lords of Hell.'

As if on cue, the ground started shaking and a huge crater opened up below them. An enormous horned demon rose from the earth, its hateful eyes glaring at Bentaz through a haze of dirt and dust. Its vile, malevolent face drew level with him. It opened its terrible, frothing maw and bellowed, 'We are Bahlor, Dark Lord of Despair and Failure.'

Bentaz immediately felt weak and afraid, buckling under the grav-ity of the situation and how he was powerless to stop it.

*I failed to protect my family and I've failed again here. It's hopeless, there's no way I can resist something as powerful as that.*

'Your heart knows the truth,' Bahlor thundered, toxic steam rising from the boiling acid in its gullet.

Bentaz floated into the foetal position as Styryk the Disemboweller moved closer.

* * *

### Mountains of rubble, Banksmeadow: 9:58 AM AEDT

Dread Sedgewick had never had so much fun in his entire life. He shredded the last demon in the horde and paused to spark up a cigarette.

*Turns out Mum was right after all, who would have thought? I guess it was mother's intuition that I would get a kick out of demon hunting.*

He took a long drag from his smoke and strolled aimlessly down the once busy street. He could see the fiery demon lord in the distance, sitting upon a throne that was once an office block and dispensing judgement on the hapless mortals trapped in its 'court'. The verdict was always guilty and the sentence was always death.

*Looks like my kind of place!*

He leapt the distance in a single bound and landed about a hundred metres behind the demon lord. His arrival was apparently unnoticed. From his position behind the demon's makeshift office-throne, he could hear all the courtroom drama as it played out like a nightmarish episode of *L.A. Law*.

'You, mortal, have been found guilty of resisting us,' the demon lord roared, its voice like an erupting volcano. 'We, Zoolith, Dark Lord of Brimstone and Persecution, sentence you to death.' There was a scream, followed by a hissing sound, as if something was rapidly evaporated.

Dread casually strolled closer to get a better look and discovered a makeshift metal cage, which contained three unusual characters. *Don't tell me this is all just another loser supervillain convention. Let's find out, shall we?*

He noticed a ruined couch jutting from a pile of rubble and sat down to watch. He could see the proceedings clearly from the sofa, including the demon lord itself. It was enormous and lanky, with jet black bony limbs, slavering face, and a body made of fire.

Zoolith reached over and removed the sheet metal roof of the cage, grabbed one of the captives—a human-sized locust—and turned to face the gathering of minor demons that cloistered around the giant's clawed feet. The locust squirmed in its grasp.

Dread sat back to enjoy the show when he was rudely interrupted.

'That's the end for Grasshopper,' one of the two remaining captives said when he noticed Dread watching. He was dressed in a military uniform, with a long scar that curved down from his left eye to the corner of his scowling mouth. 'The rest of my team suffered the same fate.'

'Shush, I'm trying to watch here,' Dread snapped, waving his hand in annoyance. 'Unless you have some popcorn, I'm not interested.'

'I still have a muesli bar on me, but no popcorn, I'm afraid,' the man said with equal annoyance. 'Look, the demons haven't seen you yet. There's time to free us and get out of here.'

'And ruin the rest of the show?' Dread reclined further into the couch and turned back to the trial, which seemed to consist of the demons hurling abuse at the humanoid grasshopper still in Zoolith's hand. 'Not bloody likely.'

The man in the cage grew more agitated. 'Please, I know who you are; you have the power to save us. I can make it worth your while.'

Dread turned back to the captive. 'If you don't be quiet, I'll judge you myself,' he growled. 'Even if I don't know who you are.'

'I'm Starlen and this is Mind Syphon,' the man said, referring to the other captive—a purple cyclops with no mouth or nose and a head like a pulsing brain. It looked wounded. 'We're all that's left of the Government Villains.'

'Well, that's a redundant name,' Dread scoffed, flicking his cigarette butt at the cage. 'You sound like a bunch of losers to me. But I'm a man of my word, and I warned you about blabbering while I was trying to watch.'

There was a sudden high-pitch scream from the 'courtroom' followed by the popping sound of roasting chitin. Dread looked back to see Zoolith removing its hand from its flaming torso, the burnt remains of Grasshopper crumbling to dust between its fingers.

'Aw, I missed it! That does it!' Dread leapt from the couch and slashed through the metal bars of the cage, ready to keep his word. 'I hope you like eviscerations,' he said to the captives.

*Maybe it's not a total loss after all.*

Yet, Kismet had other ideas and suddenly a giant hand reached down and plucked Dread from the cage, and he found himself staring into an enormous malevolent face full of fangs.

*And I thought my uncle was ugly...*

'Looks like a new trial is about to begin,' Zoolith boomed, holding Dread tight in its charred, bony hand.

* * *

## Barton Correctional Facility: 12:36 PM AEDT

Walter Screw dived for cover as the energy swastika passed over his head and exploded into the concrete wall behind him, covering him in grit and white dust.

*Shit! That one was close! I can't keep dodging these forever—have to think of a better plan. Unfortunately, that's easier said than done.*

He'd been dead on his feet *before* the prison had come under attack by an unknown demon over twenty-four hours ago, resulting in a loss of containment in sector four. Now he was trying to outwit one of the world's deadliest Manifests without having slept in over forty-eight hours. It wasn't going well.

Walter dived again to avoid another glowing swastika and rolled into a corridor that ran perpendicular to the one he was in.

'Ha-ha, not so cocky now, are you?' Baron Von Ritzer gloated in his heavily accented voice. He was dressed in his grey costume, which resembled a military uniform, complete with Iron Cross insignia over his heart. His helmet was still dented from when Ballistic had crushed it earlier in the year, but he'd done a reasonable job of fixing it while incarcerated. The swastika-emblazoned faceplate still muffled his voice, however.

*I can't understand a damn thing that kraut is saying with that stupid helmet on his head. Probably not worth listening to anyhow—I doubt he's telling me he's surrendering.*

Walter looked again at the charge on his wrist-mounted energy batons as he ran down the access tunnel.

*Hmmm, just under half-charge. What I really need is a Q5 carbine, but Gordon had the only one and it was shattered when the Baron first attacked us.* He felt a pang of sadness followed by anger when he thought of his friend and colleague, and how the gun wasn't the only thing shattered by the attack.

Things had seemed under control at first, despite the loss of power due to the unforeseen attack.

*We were lucky the demon fled straight after and there was a full complement of guards stationed, even though it was Christmas. At least I was right in insisting on that over the groans of protest from the staff and their militant union.*

He took another tunnel in the hope of being able to outflank the Nazi supervillain, all the while replaying the events in his mind. Hardly any of the prisoners were freed when the power died and the standard containment protocol kicked in, putting sector four into lockdown. Tungsten doors were designed to drop and keep prisoners trapped in the cells in a blackout.

*I never expected anyone to break through the back wall and into the access tunnels, let alone take out the power in the adjacent system while they were at it. Most escapees simply try to run away, not lay in ambush for me.*

Walter turned down yet another corridor, still running as fast as he could. He could hear the Baron thundering after him and feel the dull thud of his energy swastikas hitting the walls.

*No doubt he's shouting muffled clichés and throwing a tantrum. I wish I realised earlier just how personal he'd taken his imprisonment. He should be honoured I found him relevant enough to be a part of my new recruit training program.*

He started to tire and stopped to catch his breath.

*I can't believe all the wiring for the backup generators had been chewed through by cockroaches. It seems too extraordinary to be mere coincidence.*

Walter had spent most of the last day rounding up the few other escapees from the blackout and had gone with Gordon and Studebaker to the tunnels to inspect the damage to the cell walls when they were attacked by the Baron. Studebaker had managed to escape back into the main prison, but Gordon had been killed and Walter trapped when the Nazi used his powers to collapse the ceiling above the exit.

*At least the emergency lighting is still on in these corridors, which is precisely why I insisted on battery-powered backups. It's just a shame that batteries aren't powerful enough to run the prison's Manifest suppressors.*

He turned down another tunnel, now certain that he'd managed to circle around behind his adversary. He crept stealthily, listening out for the sounds of his prey.

*I can hear him trashing the corridor; he's just up ahead.*

He extended his energy batons in anticipation as he approached Baron Von Ritzer. He padded along silently, mustering all his hours of training and experience as the Nazi supervillain came into view, his back turned to Walter.

*He's more dangerous than that Great White alien, and I'm not even sure if these batons will have any effect.*

Walter charged when he was within striking distance, thrusting first into the base of the Baron's spine and then following through with a vicious swipe to the back of his knee.

The Baron crumpled. '*Schweinhund!*'

'You really are a living cliché, aren't you?' Walter mocked, smashing the Baron across the face with his right baton, before jabbing him in the throat with his left one. The German's skin crackled where the energy struck and the smell of ozone filled the dimly lit tunnel. The Baron merely laughed.

*Oh no.*

'Stupid colonial,' the Baron enunciated slowly as he regained his composure. 'I have suffered the blows of the mighty Ally himself. What did you think you could accomplish with your matchsticks, even if they do light up like a Christmas tree?'

'Well, I was hoping you'd die, if you must know,' Walter replied, backing away down the corridor.

'Wretched mortal,' Baron Von Ritzer said contemptuously. 'I would be as old as your grandfather, and yet retain my youth. I will still be alive when your bones are dust.'

'That may be so, but you'll still be a cocksucker,' Walter impugned. 'I bet you're not even a real baron, are you? What are you really, a homosexual African Jew? Is that why you cover every inch of your skin, out of shame?'

'Why you…I will…' the Baron stammered, too insulted to think clearly.

*That's it. Distract him enough and you may survive this yet.*

Walter swiped again at the Baron's knees with his batons and once more knocked his foe to the ground. It was for nought.

Baron Von Ritzer sprang to his feet and grabbed Walter by the throat, choking him as he slammed him against the concrete wall. 'Now you die,' came his muffled voice from behind the swastika faceplate. He raised his right fist and yellow energy crackled from it, coalescing into a golden swastika.

Walter squirmed futilely, trying to free himself from the Baron's iron grip. He never used to be scared of death, but recent near-death experiences had changed that. Suddenly the lights came on with a deep hum and the swastika fizzled into nothingness.

'What? Not when I was so close! Nooooo!' Baron Von Ritzer cried, a little too dramatically. He could no longer hold Walter up against the wall and within moments the Warden was free.

*I guess there is a God after all.*

Walter wasted no time in raising his energy batons and beating the Baron relentlessly into the cold concrete floor, the satisfying sound of bones breaking filling his ears with joy. He was still pummelling him when Studebaker arrived with a backup contingent.

'Sir! Once Singh got the power back on, the emergency doors opened and we were able to get around the collapsed tunnel...' she began, but paused when Walter didn't stop. 'Uh, sir? You can stop, he's unconscious...'

He didn't stop.

Studebaker signalled to two of the other wardens and they dragged Walter off the limp Nazi.

'Take your hands off me! This fuck killed Rick!' Walter protested, but calmed down once the wardens had let him go. 'Take him back to his cell.'

He leaned up against the wall and removed his helmet, dropping it to the floor. He wiped the sweat from his brow and rubbed his moustache before finally looking at Studebaker.

'Sir?'

'I'm okay now, thank you, Leslie,' he said, addressing her informally for the first time. 'Make sure Rick's body is properly cared for—it's back there near junction V, where we were ambushed. I'm going to get some sleep.'

\* \* \*

### Mascot, Sydney: 6:17 PM AEDT

Anu Hopet strode fearlessly down the devastated street, ignoring the piles of mutilated bodies that littered the area. The burnt-out wrecks of dozens of cars stood like silent sentinels for the ruined buildings that surrounded them. The silence was occasionally interrupted by a disturbing scream, but otherwise he could only hear his breathing through his battle armour.

*Looks like the carnage that happened here is long finished. I wonder if that Zoolith demon was responsible or whether some other demon lord has dominion here? At least it looks like it is no longer following me—it is too big to hide.*

He was thinking about heading back to *The Skull of Ra* when some hushed voices drew his attention and he turned down a side street to investigate. One of the voices seemed oddly familiar and stirred old memories.

*It cannot be him, not after all these years.*

Anu Hopet followed the voices to the back of a deserted house and confronted a group of odd-looking Manifests clustered around the back door. None of them looked familiar.

'Identify yourselves,' Anu Hopet boomed, his deep voice making the group literally jump. 'You are not demons; what purpose brings you here?'

'Uh, hi,' replied a thuggish-looking bald man. 'I'm Biff Man, and these are my companions: Queegul and Zeegul, Gwunk, and the Flaming Toilet Seat.' He indicated to the group, ignoring Irrelevant Man. 'We're the Newest Heroes.'

*Why would I think these fools were familiar?*

He was about to vaporise them with an antimatter blast when two more beings stepped out from inside the house. One was a white lion man and the other was an Aboriginal man with grey hair, dressed in all black. He was wearing sunglasses, but his golden eyes still shone through and Anu Hopet recognised him immediately.

'Bojangles! I thought I heard your whimpering voice,' he said coldly. 'How many thousands of years has it been?'

'Not nearly enough,' Bojangles countered, moving into a defensive posture. 'Everyone, this here is Anu Hopet, better known as Armageddon.'

*That is Great Armageddon to you.*

'Oh, so that's the guy you've told me all those horror stories about,' White Lion growled. 'I pictured him differently.'

'That is not something that will trouble you for long,' Anu Hopet spat, his hands beginning to glow. 'It is time for your friend to pay for his part in my enslavement.'

'Wait! We don't have time for this!' Bojangles pleaded, waving his open hands about. 'We've found something here that's more important than ancient feuds.'

'And what is that?' Anu Hopet asked, his hands still glowing.

'We've found the Tomb of Power—the same tomb that the Scouts of the World Eater use to instantly move across the globe,' Bojangles responded, desperately trying not to enrage the former Egyptian slave.

'Where? In that dwelling?' Anu Hopet scoffed. 'How could a tomb fit in there? Do not take me for one of these fools you ally yourself with.'

'Hey, I graduated from high school!' Biff Man protested, but was ignored.

'The tomb is trans-dimensional and can insinuate itself into the very foundations of reality,' Bojangles said, realising how ridiculous that sounded. 'See for yourself, if you don't believe me.'

'More likely this is some ploy to escape my wrath,' Anu Hopet rebuffed. 'Even if that were true, why should I care?'

'Oh, didn't you know? The Tomb of Power isn't just a fancy name, it's an actual tomb,' Bojangles replied with a cunning smile on his lips. 'It's the resting place of Prince Kiol Zol—remember him?'

*The whelp who enslaved me! I have waited centuries for my revenge on him and his bitch mother! I never thought I would get the chance since I lost that talisman.*

'Very well, I will see this tomb,' Anu Hopet declared.

'I thought you might.' Bojangles gestured towards the back door and ignored the stare White Lion was giving him.

Anu Hopet accepted the invitation and slowly walked towards the house. He ducked as he entered and found himself standing in a rather bland kitchen. He turned to say something, but Bojangles pointed at the doorway to the next room and said, 'Through there.'

Anu Hopet dubiously stepped into the next room and inexplicably found himself walking on a stone floor inside a spacious room lit only by the blue arcane energy that crackled between the twin shining pillars dominating the centre of the room. In the centre of the pillars shone a large golden sarcophagus inlaid with precious stones.

*So, Bojangles spoke the truth. I may even consider sparing him if I can have my revenge against the prince.*

Suddenly the background lighting grew brighter and he turned to see Bojangles and White Lion lead the Newest Heroes into the tomb behind him. The Flaming Toilet Seat brought the light.

'Wow, it's hard to imagine this place is unguarded,' Biff Man said, jinxing them by taunting Kismet.

'Foolish mortal, the Tomb of Power is never unguarded,' said a voice from the darkness, sounding like a mockery of Biff Man.

'That's Im'shtar!' Bojangles called to the others. 'Be careful, it can hide in any reflection!'

*It seems he has encountered this 'Im'shtar' before. That is why he told me about the Tomb; he needs my help and is using me to get it. Has he learned nothing in all these years?*

Anu Hopet silently took in his surroundings and calculated his next move. Bojangles was watching him, but everyone else was looking in all directions, trying to find Im'shtar. Experience had taught him it was better to allow an adversary to expose themselves first and so he waited.

He watched as Biff Man walked closer to one of the pillars and was the first to notice when the thug's reflection on the sarcophagus took on a life of its own. He remained silent.

'Maybe it fled,' Biff Man said hopefully as he looked around the pillar, oblivious to the danger hiding in shimmering gold.

'Maybe not,' the reflection said, growing out of the sarcophagus. The cloaked demon's grey bat-wings extended to frame it as it stepped in front of Biff Man. The leader of the Newest Heroes stared dumbstruck into Im'shtar's darkened hood.

'Th-that…that's me…' Biff Man whimpered before he started to age rapidly, turning to dust in the demon's talons.

Im'shtar turned towards Anu Hopet, its cowl once more a black void.

'Don't look at it!' Bojangles called to him from what seemed like an expanse of white noise. 'Destroy the pillars!'

The voice was faint, but it was enough.

Anu Hopet unleashed an onslaught of antimatter at Im'shtar, who vanished as the beam struck, allowing it to pass through it, annihilating the pillar and causing it to fall into the wall. The energy cascade between the pillars abruptly ceased, causing feedback and sending a burst of energy back into the sarcophagus. The effect was instantaneous.

Suddenly the sarcophagus erupted from within in a fiery blaze that sent chunks of gold flying in all directions and shattered the remaining pillar. Anu Hopet caught a glimpse of the pallid prince before he took off in a ball of light, smashing through the ceiling and out into the night beyond.

Anu Hopet experienced a strange shifting sensation and the tomb fell silent.

'He did it, he earthed the tomb!' Bojangles yelled triumphantly. 'They're not going anywhere in this anymore.'

'My vengeance…' Anu Hopet began.

'Will have to wait,' Bojangles answered as he gathered the remaining heroes around him. 'Everyone grab hold of me. We have to go find Prince Kiol Zol.'

'Stop!' Anu Hopet commanded in vain.

'Ciao ciao,' Bojangles teased, right before he teleported everyone away from Anu Hopet's tantrum.

When he finished smashing up what was left of the Tomb of Power, Anu Hopet decided to head back to his ship. The grey swirl in the shine of his armour went unnoticed.

* * *

### Circular Quay, Sydney: 10:34 PM AEDT

Seth Zaraxom used the severed mantis shrimp leg he'd been carrying to sever the head of the fishwife mutant who'd been following him for hours.

*I'm glad I took the time to split that creature's head open—thing's been after me ever since I killed that mantis shrimp monster. Strangest day ever.*

It had taken Seth almost a day and a half to make his way south from Manly, mostly due to the hordes of demons that slowly changed from Lovecraftian abominations to ice monsters, as he crossed from one demon lord's territory into another's.

He'd also paused to climb to the roof of an abandoned building to watch the elemental he'd summoned, Leviathan, arrive to confront the *False* Leviathan. Leviathan was an enormous, blue, four-armed sea monster with a fish's tail, and it had easily grappled with its serpentine namesake.

Seth had felt a deep sense of satisfaction watching the elemental tear off the demon lord's head in the bloody brine, despite the False Leviathan coiling its snakelike body around its attacker.

The demon lord's death sent a wave of confusion through its soldiers' ranks and seemed to drive the mutant fishwife to pursue Seth on an almost personal level. It had even followed him over the Sydney Harbour Bridge, now a frozen graveyard where each car had become its own icy hearse.

*Well, that thing's dead now and I can focus on the reason I came here.*

He paused behind a frosty police car and pulled his rucksack off his shoulder. He opened the flap and was instantly bathed in a golden light.

*I just need to find who I'm supposed to give this to.*

He looked around for signs of life. Despite it being night-time, the whole area was bathed in the pink glow radiating from the energy beam atop Centrepoint Tower.

*The energy's growing brighter, as if gaining power. It must be from all the victims flowing to the Soul Gem—thousands of them most likely. Dealing with that is a task for later—right now I have to work out how to remain unnoticed by that giant demon looming over there.*

'We are Ishlarr, Dark Lord of the Frozen Mind,' the demon boomed for the thousandth time. 'You cannot hide from us.'

*It seems interested in that building—looks like Xenotech Headquarters, so maybe there's someone still alive inside. Hopefully it's the person I'm looking for.*

Seth put his rucksack back over his shoulder and sprinted down the frosted footpath, making the distance to the Xenotech building in under a minute. Ishlarr noticed him. Suddenly Seth felt a heavy cloud fall over his mind and for a moment he forgot what he was doing. Luckily, someone else had spotted him and he found himself being hurriedly ushered into the building's foyer.

'Mister, are you okay?' said the voice of a teenage girl. 'How did you get past all those ice demons?'

Seth turned and instantly felt the cloud lift from his mind as he stared into the eyes of who might have been the most beautiful person he'd ever seen.

*Is this who I'm looking for?*

'My name's Lorraine,' the girl said. She indicated to her companions. 'This is Beat Master and Spectrum, leader of the X-Droids. The rest of her team are patrolling the building.'

'Well the surviving ones, anyway,' Spectrum said bitterly, before extending her hand to Seth. 'Hi, I'm Lucy. What's your story?'

*I'll give them the condensed version—it worked before.*

'My name's Seth,' he answered. 'I'm the world's oldest Manifest and I'm here on an important errand to save the world.'

'My god, the Immortal!' Lucy gasped before Seth could finish.

'Wow,' Beat Master added.

'I've always found that moniker a bit redundant, as all Manifests are immortal,' he replied, deliberately playing down his regenerative abilities on account of lessons learned from his nephew. 'I prefer Seth, but call me whatever you want. I'm really only interested in finding someone. I have a crown to give them.'

'A crown?' Lorraine asked. 'What good will that do?'

'It's called the Crown of Knowledge, and it's a very special artefact,' Seth explained, pulling his rucksack off his shoulder once more. 'It's actually a piece of the God of Sentience and bestows omniscience upon its wearer. Then they'll know how to resolve this mess.'

'That sounds like a bunch of hooey,' Beat Master declared from his position as lookout over by the door.

'Look, I've already taken down one Lord of Hell today, not to mention my thousands of years' worth of experience,' Seth snapped. 'I know what I'm doing.'

The sound of Ishlarr stomping around outside punctuated his statement.

'Please forgive us, we've been trapped in here for days under constant assault, so we're a little on edge,' Lorraine apologised, giving Beat Master a stern look as she did it. 'Do you know who you need to give the Crown to?'

'It will show me,' he announced confidently, reaching into his bag and producing a large golden crown that shone with preternatural brilliance. His three companions all gaped at its glory. 'At least it's meant to.'

'Why don't you use the Crown to find out?' Lucy asked.

'It's a little overwhelming, even for me,' Seth understated. 'Most people who wear it die of aneurysms and I don't have the time to go through all of that.'

He held the Crown in front of each of others but nothing appeared to happen.

*So, it wasn't for the girl after all.*

The Crown pulsed and sent a beam of light towards the foyer doors. It was a definite sign.

'Well, it wasn't me, you already checked,' Beat Master said. 'It must be someone out there.'

'I have to look, the stakes are too high,' Seth told them and turned to leave, before pausing. 'My only concern is I can't think if I go out there, and that's a problem.'

'It's that demon, Ishlarr,' Lorraine observed. 'It clouds your thinking—it basically advertises it in its demonic title. But I think Samuel has the solution.'

'I do?' Beat Master seemed dubious.

'Yeah, I thought about it earlier, and it all makes sense,' Lorraine revealed. 'You were the only one who wasn't affected by this mind-grip and I think it's because you listen to your music so loud.'

*I think she might be onto something.*

'Can you make the music loud enough with those speakers in your shoulders to drown out this demon's power?' Seth asked Beat Master.

'I don't know about that, but they do get pretty loud,' Beat Master boasted. 'I guess we'll see, won't we?'

'I guess we will,' Seth agreed, wasting no more time. 'Crank it. I'm opening the door.'

Moments later, the sound of Queen's 'Don't Stop Me Now' blared at ear-splitting decibels and Seth shoved through the frozen door faster than expected as if to escape the noise.

He held the heavy crown out in front of him and another beam of light shot out and struck a large lump of ice that lay nearby. The ice steamed where the light struck.

*Now why'd it do that?*

Seth's thoughts were interrupted by the demon lord towering above them, despite still standing in the harbour. 'Foolish mortal, you cannot defy our will.'

*Mortal? It obviously doesn't know me very well.*

'That's what you think,' Seth said under his breath as he dashed over to the lump of ice. Only then did he notice a frozen figure encased like a bug in amber.

*I've seen this guy before somewhere. Isn't he a supervillain or something?*

'That guy tried to help us earlier,' said Lorraine from behind him. She'd decided to tag along. 'I'm not sure what his name was, but he was white-hot and as bright as the sun. A bit like that crown...'

'Indeed. But how to put the Crown on his head?'

'I would've thought it would be too late, seeing as he's dead,' Lorraine stated.

'If he's the true heir to the Crown of Knowledge, then that won't be a problem,' Seth answered sagely.

'Then allow me,' Lorraine offered, before chopping the ice with her hand and breaking it away from White Hot's extinguished head.

Seth raised the Crown of Knowledge. 'Be whole once again,' he said before placing it upon White Hot's lifeless head.

'No!' Ishlarr thundered from above. 'Kill them, our children!'

Scores of ice demons suddenly grew out of the frozen harbour and moved towards them like an avalanche.

White Hot's eyes blinked opened and blazed with the light of million suns.

'Too late, you frigid motherfucker!' Seth called to Ishlarr as he shielded his eyes from the glare.

'I awaken,' White Hot said in an indescribable voice, glowing brighter every second and melting the ice he was imprisoned in.

Before Seth could ask how to stop Ishlarr and the High Mage afterwards, White Hot exploded with a brilliant shockwave that evaporated all the ice in the vicinity—demons included—but miraculously left everything else unharmed.

The reborn god hovered above Seth and Lorraine, still radiating blinding light so they couldn't get a good look at him. It also hurt Ishlarr and kept the demon lord at bay.

'No longer am I the one others knew as White Hot,' the being formerly known as White Hot said. 'Nor am I the Celestial One known as Sentience, as I was before my fall to Antimatter, now called Antithesis. No, I am Flame. Flame Lightley.'

*Did he just say what I think he said? Mosh does claim to have a lot of bastard children, but I always assumed he was only talking about Zoth and Orgamulva.*

Again, Seth was too slow to ask, for in that moment, Flame Lightley moved at light speed straight into Ishlarr's glassy eye before exploding its gigantic head into a cloud of vapour. He then flew off into the night, even as the demon lord's body fell on the harbour and smashed into pieces.

'That was so amazing!' Lorraine cried out in jubilation.

'Perhaps, but I'm afraid the main battle hasn't even started,' Seth replied ominously. 'See that beam of light coming from Sydney Tower? That's people's souls being used to power an ancient lunatic's quest to become God. The plan was to ask "Flame" the best way to stop this guy, as he had access to the Crown of Knowledge, but as you can see it didn't pan out that way.'

'Still, we stopped Ishlarr,' Lorraine said optimistically. 'I'll see what I can do later on, but for now I have to check on my family.'

'But I could use your help now,' Seth said a little too aggressively. 'The stakes are much higher than one person's family. We're all trapped in here together.'

'Not to me,' she said forcefully. 'Now listen here: I said maybe later, but for now I'm going home to check on my two little sisters. Is that clear?'

'Uh yeah, sure,' he said, almost sullenly.

*Why did I just agree to that?*

'Maybe Beat Master can help you,' Lorraine said cheerfully before walking back to the building to tell the others.

*Something tells me I'll need to keep an eye on that one, provided I can make it to the city in time to stop the High Mage's nefarious plan.*

\* \* \*

### The Former Territories of Xph'Ish'Matarg, Hell: Circa 11:53 PM AEDT

Mark Adams floated above the panicked demons in the same pose that comes naturally to those with the power to do such things. The demons had good reason to panic—he'd destroyed every one of them he'd encountered since the Wraith's attack had triggered his Manifest and destroyed Xph'Ish'Matarg in the process—but this time he was hunting one in particular.

*It's here, I can sense it. The goat was telling the truth about reviving it.*

He'd taken to learning his new powers with a natural zeal he'd never experienced before. After the initial elation of Manifesting, he'd soon discovered he could drain the last remnants of power from Xph'Ish'Matarg's husk and then expel it again as torrents of destructive hellfire that disintegrated demons as easily as cheap toilet paper.

*But this one won't get off so lightly.*

Mark paused as he located his quarry.

The cacodemon cowered against a bloodstained boulder, shielding its face from Mark's gaze.

'I'm not sure why Xph'Ish'Matarg put you back together again, but I'm glad he did,' Mark said menacingly.

'Please, please,' the cacodemon begged. 'We were just following orders from our lord. We would never have hurt you otherwise. You must believe us!'

Mark floated down to the ground and slowly walked towards the whimpering creature. 'This *won't* be quick,' he promised, licks of flame forming in his red eyes.

He was still dressed in his jeans and boots, except now he was adorned with Xph'Ish'Matarg's crimson cloak, which covered his shoulders and crossed his bare chest.

Therefore, there was no protection when the cacodemon suddenly sprang from its position under the boulder and dived at his stomach with fangs and claws extended.

To their mutual surprise, the cacodemon passed through Mark as if he were intangible and then burst into flames moments later. It screamed as it was consumed.

*What the fuck? Is that one of my powers too?*

He noticed another demon watching him and hovered over to it.

'I know that there's an invasion of Earth underway and I want to know where they're invading from,' he demanded. 'You witnessed what happened here, didn't you? Tell me what I want to know or you're next.'

'No...' the demon pleaded. It looked like a malevolent hare. It pointed towards what looked like a huge pink tornado that could be seen on the horizon. 'There, over there. The closest gateway is in Ooblog's territory. It was imprisoned there, over there.'

Mark Adams looked towards the tornado.

*It sure looks like it could be a portal.*

'Thanks,' he said to the demon before shooting a stream of hellfire into the hapless creature's face. It shrieked as it burnt to ash. 'In case you were lying,' he said to its glowing embers.

Mark turned and floated towards the horizon.

*I'm finally going home.*

# 27 December 34 BZ

**North Ryde, Sydney: 12:41 AM AEDT**

Bentaz Mullberry was alone in the darkness of his own soul when something inside him suddenly realised what was happening and his eyes instantly focused on his surroundings.

*What? Where am I?*

'The mortal awakes, sire,' said an orange bat-winged demon with syringe-like teeth, its lilting voice incongruous to its features.

*Styryk the Disemboweller.*

They were in some sort of cave that dripped with moisture and throbbed as if alive. His limbs were held fast and embedded in the slimy wall. Styryk stood in front of him and stared with empty sockets as black as pitch.

Bentaz could see the dun light of the cavern's exit but was powerless to free himself. *So close... It's like a form of torture.*

'Shall we spill his guts, Master?' Styryk asked, turning its head all around as if talking to the cave itself. 'Shall we allow his soul to witness the glory of Gledandron?'

The entire cave shuddered and Bentaz suddenly realised where he was.

*I'm inside the demon lord! Before I blacked out I noticed how it seemed to have deep chasms in its flesh—if that's what you call it.*

In truth, he didn't know what had happened. One minute he was confronting the demon lord and the next he was crippled by despair and trapped in a dreamlike depression—aware only that he was miserable and had himself to blame.

*It's the demon, it has to be. It must have some kind of emotional power or something. Somehow, it's convinced me this is all my fault and has kept me here to torment me.*

He tried to move, but the cave wall refused to budge.

'Prepare to join your grandfather,' Styryk threatened as it drew within disembowelling distance. 'You should have remained in the succour of Bahlor's mental embrace.'

*Ah yes, Bahlor, the Dark Lord of Despair and Failure, I remember now. It's so simple, I can't believe I missed it.*

'You know what I've just realised?' Bentaz asked rhetorically, full of a sudden confidence that confused the demon. 'You can't keep me trapped here unless I believe I deserve it. I've spent my whole life trying to do the right thing, always trying to be the hero, and what happens? Life goes and takes a great big dump on everything I've been trying to protect. Well guess what? I don't think that's fair and I don't deserve to be here!'

He effortlessly walked free of the cave wall and raised his fists. They crackled with power.

'Wait!' Styryk piped, taking a step back. 'You *do* belong here! It is *your* fault your family…'

'DO NOT SPEAK OF MY FAMILY!'

Bentaz grabbed Styryk by the chest, sinking his fingers into the demon's flesh, while punching into its stomach with his other arm. He then spread his arms wide, tearing the demon in half and showering the cave with thick, black blood.

The cavern shook and the cave mouth began to close. The demon lord's laughter rumbled through the floor like the sound of hunger pangs as Bentaz was plunged into abysmal darkness.

*Uh-uh, I've seen this movie.*

Bahlor ran a long talon down its chest where the chasm holding Bentaz used to be. It bellowed a gurgled laugh, spraying the area with the boiling acid in its throat.

'Foolish mortal,' Bahlor thundered as it stood astride two blocks lined with partially demolished buildings. 'You are no threat to Bahlor, Dark…'

The Lord of Hell's chest exploded in a wave of sizzling meat chunks the size of cars.

'It cannot be,' Bahlor stammered, staring at the smouldering hole in its chest. A red and black streak shot out like a bullet and flew off into the distance. The demon watched as it curved upwards and turned back.

Bentaz flew high and began his descent approach. The giant demon lord stood hunched over a broken building clutching at its chest, still in disbelief. It looked up at him and opened its gaping oral fissure, spewing a torrent of boiling acid which narrowly missed him as he flew in closer.

*Missed me, turd features.*

Bahlor roared its displeasure. Its hideous face with shrivelled, yet pitted skin and jaundiced eyes was the very image of demonic malevolence.

Bentaz was unimpressed. He'd spent a large part of his childhood watching reruns of *Astro Boy* and knew how to take out a giant with horns. He flew up once more and arced around for a dive-bomb manoeuvre.

He smashed into the top of Bahlor's emaciated head, splitting its skull right down the middle. The demon screamed and swatted at Bentaz with one clawed hand, while it clutched at the bloody crack on its ghastly face with the other. Bentaz zipped through its fingers at supersonic speed and grabbed one of its ebony horns, wrenching it downwards as hard as he could.

'By the power of Grayskull!' Bentaz yelled, mixing his pop culture references.

Bahlor's head ripped in half and its neck collapsed into the cavity in its chest with a spray of boiling acid. The demon lord's body staggered before toppling over and crashing through an abandoned building, reducing it to rubble. A cloud of grey dust billowed out from the impact.

*I guess it earned its title as the lord of failure.*

Exhausted, he floated down to the street and away from the putrid demon carcass, hoping to find another deckchair. Instead, he came across a strange green plant guy crying over the crushed remains of a giant Panta can with cartoonish arms and legs. He recognised them immediately as Asparagus Man and Panta Boy.

*I wasn't expecting to find them—I guess Grandfather wasn't the only Manifest to die today.*

Asparagus Man didn't appear to notice him—which suited him just fine—and he stopped to catch his breath atop a mound of shattered concrete.

From where he stood he could see the beam of pink light that shot from the top of Centrepoint Tower into the smoky sky—shining brighter than the fires that raged through the fallen city.

*That's where I have to go if I have any hope of stopping this, I can feel it.*

He started walking towards the CBD in an effort to conserve his strength.

* * *

## Outside the Gates of Heaven: Circa 1:00 AM AEDT

So it was that the High Mage of Hell unleashed spells most foul and rent asunder the Heavenly Host. Burning angels fell into oblivion like the tears of a dying god. A small detachment of minor angels tried to outflank him, but they were soon cast aside. Evidentially, scourging spells worked just as well on seraphim.

*I can feel my power rise as each one of the Lords of Hell I summoned falls to Earth's defenders. I wonder if they would have followed me had they known their essences would add to the souls of the mortals I promised them and used to power my assault on Heaven?*

The thought was rhetorical; he already knew the answer. He cast another spell and an angel exploded in a fiery ball.

*Soon only Ooblog will remain—to be my spawning matrix on Earth. After all, Ooblog is an elemental, not a demon, and therefore naturally acclimatised to the mortal plane. That must be why the False Lucifer captured it in the first place.*

The High Mage rode the Great Beast through yet another line of defence until only Life, and the archangels Michael and Gabriel remained. They floated defiantly, their shimmering glory only diminished by the Gates of Heaven themselves.

He looked around him and was empowered to see most of his army and the ferocious Archdemon arrayed behind him. Their numbers were legion.

*There is no way that the False Archangels can stop me. Creation is mine!*

The High Mage charged towards the shining gates, his demonic armada in tow.

* * *

### Freeman Residence, Neutral Bay: 2:56 AM AEDT

Lorraine Freeman crept through the broken front door, her stomach doing backflips as she did so. 'Mum? Heather? Samantha?' she called to the dark and seemingly empty house. 'Anybody?'

Silence.

When she'd left with Beat Master to attend the carols, her mother had told her that the staff were going to help look after the girls, as their other mother, Shara, was going to be busy wrapping presents and keeping them a surprise.

They'd never meant to be gone so long, but no one had really expected an invasion from Hell either. Anything could have happened in the three days they were away.

*That's why Mum looked so relieved when I said I was coming here to look for the girls.*

She thought of the anguish her mother must be going through, being forced to stay with the remaining X-Droids and coordinate an attack on the CBD for that weird ancient Manifest, Seth.

Lorraine looked around at the signs of a struggle and fought to contain the emotions that threatened to overwhelm her. The entranceway was dusted with frost, much like the rest of what was formerly Ishlarr's territory. It crunched under her knee-high boots.

*I wish I'd come sooner...and brought a torch.*

Guilt and fear gnawed at her mind.

*They needed everyone they could get, which is why I insisted Samuel stay with them, despite Mum having a cow over it. Now that I'm here alone in the dark, I wish I'd let him come. A bit of music might have taken the edge off.*

She called out again while she climbed the stairs in the entrance towards the bedrooms, but only the roaring quiet filled her ears. The silence, combined with her diminished sight, caused her to nearly jump out of her skin when she heard a scratching from the kitchen.

She went back down the stairs without looking in the bedrooms and crept through the entranceway, her heart thumping in her chest.

*Come on, Lorraine, you can do this. You're a Manifest, remember, and you've just spent the last three days fighting ice demons—pretty convincingly too. Whatever's in there, you can take it.*

As she walked towards the kitchen, she remembered the emergency kit they kept near the front door. Conveniently it had a torch in case of blackout.

Freshly illuminated, she opened the sliding door and entered the oversized kitchen. The scratching sound immediately stopped and she was relieved to see a rat scurry for cover at her intrusion.

*Who'd have thought I'd ever be glad to see a rat in my kitchen!*

Then she saw what the rat had been eating and screamed.

The body of the babysitter had been twisted into a knot, her splintered bones ruptured through flesh in a nightmarish sculpture of misery. Only her head remained untouched—apart from the look of terror frozen upon her face.

*Calm down, Lorraine, it's just a body, it can't hurt you. It's just the shock is all.*

Yet it wasn't just the shock, and suddenly Lorraine couldn't think of anything except getting to her sisters' bedrooms as fast as she could.

*Please...*

'Heather? Samantha?'

The girls' rooms were empty and looked unmolested. She checked her room next.

*Oh no!*

She pushed past the broken door and the furniture that had been pushed up against it from the other side. She wasn't the first to do so. Her flashlight shone on the bed and she immediately burst into tears.

'N-no, please no,' she sobbed as she dropped the torch, climbed onto the bed, and cradled her sisters' lifeless bodies in her arms.

* * *

**Pitt Street, Sydney: 7:03 AM AEDT**

Seth Zaraxom made his way down the devastated street towards Centrepoint Tower and the beam of pink light that still blazed from its top into the swirling vortex in the sky.

*So far, so good. Just because their lord is dead doesn't mean there aren't still a heap of ice demons running around, but I guess this must be another demon's territory, as I haven't seen any of those frosty bastards in a while.*

He climbed over the gridlocked cars that packed the abandoned street from one side to the other. The X-Droids who had joined him simply jumped over the roadblock with their corporate jet boots, whereas Beat Master deftly bounced everywhere to the tune of some 80s song best forgotten.

*I hope Bojangles and White Lion had success with their mission to free Prince Kiol Zol and gather other Manifests for the fight. Despite the crudeness of some of their abilities, we really need all the help we can get if we hope to stop the High Mage.*

Seth continued cautiously down the street towards the tower, the lack of civilian bodies coming more as a worry than a relief.

*Ishlarr and the False Leviathan left their human victims where they fell, but this part of the city appears to be empty. It can only mean we've passed into Ooblog's territory—it simply devours everything to spawn its 'family' instead of trying to horrify its victims. Devours… or inseminates.*

He suppressed a shudder at the thought of falling victim to the Dark Lord of Perverse Molestation. The other Manifests failed to notice.

*Yeah, just because it comes from Earth, rather than Gledandron, doesn't mean it's any less horrible… or deadly. I'll have to be really careful, as being taken by Ooblog when I can't die would be like going to Hell.*

Movement up ahead caught his eye.

'Be still!' he whispered harshly to his companions. To their credit, they obeyed without hesitation or complaint. Beat Master even turned his music off.

A black blob with writhing tentacles slowly flagellated across the street and oozed into a drain in the curb on the other side.

*An Ooblack! I was right about this being Ooblog's territory.*

'Remain motionless for another minute or so,' he said to the group. 'Those things hunt by vibrations.'

'What is it?' asked the female leader of the X-Droids, who was going by the name of Spectrum. Seth remembered her real name was Lucy.

'It's part of the Ooblog Family.' Seth used the pause as an excuse to light up a cigarette. 'It's an Ooblack.'

'Excuse me?' the X-Droid known as Doctor X-ray scoffed incredulously. 'What kind of absurd name is that?'

*Says the guy with a name from 1950s schlock sci-fi.*

'It is what it is,' Seth stated between puffs, largely ignoring the asinine remark. 'We've passed into Ooblog's territory now and we have to be really careful or end up like the rest of its victims.'

'What victims? I didn't see anyone,' said Reflex, another of the X-Droids, who had checked most of the area already with bionic speed.

'Unlike the other demon lords who brought their personal armies with them, Ooblog creates its offspring by converting organic matter into similar creatures called Ooblacks. They in turn create Oobrowns, who will then spawn a creature called an Oobeige, and so on, until there's a whole plague of the things,' Seth replied, neglecting to even talk of the other side of the Ooblog Family—the horrors spawned through the whole insemination thing.

*Some things are best not knowing about.*

'That's disgusting,' said the X-Droid, Mudman—a guy made of living mud.

'I think we should take a detour, just to be safe,' Seth suggested, without really caring if they were convinced. He was taking the detour anyway.

'Why can't we just fly over to Centrepoint and smash the tower down at its base?' asked Neutron, yet another X-Droid. 'I have the power to bring down the whole CBD like an earthquake.'

'That's a terrible idea! Look, if this whole thing collapses, then there's a risk it will keep collapsing in on itself, accelerating the process the High Mage put in place and crushing Sydney into raw energy with us inside,' Seth explained, turning to take his detour. 'No, a massive earthquake is the very last thing we need if the world has any chance of surviving this.'

\* \* \*

### Newtown, Sydney: 2:32 PM AEDT

Courtney Yeht had been walking for hours, mostly in a state of delirium. She'd had hardly anything to eat or drink since her escape, but scavenged from ruined houses and even untouched garbage bins when she was really desperate.

She'd also had little sleep, catching a few hours here or there holed up in some temporary refuge she occasionally found when hiding from the fiery, winged demons that had pursued her on her way to the pretty pink light that called to her like a beacon.

Every so often a demon would find her and she'd be forced to bury them like she did with everyone at the facility where they'd kept her prisoner.

She'd managed to find a change of outfit in her travels and felt more comfortable in jeans and a white t-shirt. Her feet were still bare, but she found it preferable to shoes, as this way she heard everything the ground had to tell her.

*Oh, and what an orchestra! Giants roam the land and the ground weeps from their poisonous infection. That's why the pressure keeps rising like a storm. It wants to be burst open like a boil, so it can scar over and heal, and it's calling for me to do it. But first I need to gather my strength.*

She meandered into a burnt-out newsagency and looked for a place to rest. A few minutes later, she was sitting in the back office chewing on a chocolate bar she'd found protected in the bar fridge under a charcoal desk. The fridge also held a can of Panta—a rare treat—and strangely, the latest issue of *Stylish Girlfriend* magazine. Lorraine Freeman smiled radiantly from the cover and was offering advice on boys.

*I hate that stuck-up bitch! So perfect in every way—what a crock. Like she knows pain or anguish in her perfect little world with her perfect superhero mum.*

She took another bite, tearing into the gooey chocolate with caramel centre and imagining it was Lorraine's face.

*Everyone seems to love her and I don't know why. Well, I hope she's suf-*

*fering right now and I hope I get to see that smug look wiped off her face.*

Courtney decided to get a little sleep while she was there, and in her dreams, the next issue of *Stylish Girlfriend* featured Lorraine Freeman's obituary.

\* \* \*

### Larger mountains of rubble, Banksmeadow: 5:48 PM AEDT

Dread Sedgewick inflicted a little move he liked to call a 'back of the knee' upon Zoolith, Dark Lord of Brimstone and Persecution. The demon lord's knee shattered into jagged cinders of bone and it crashed to the ground, adding to the piles of rubble that made up the landscape.

It tried to sit up, but was also missing a hand on account of grabbing Dread when they first met, and collapsed into a pile of concrete and steel girders.

'Come on, you can do better than that,' Dread mocked, lighting his cigarette from the inferno that comprised Zoolith's torso. 'Aren't you meant to be some kind of Lord of Hell or something? We've been at this for over a day now, and the only reason it's taken this long is because I've been holding back, hoping you'd do something interesting. I even took time out to kill that Starlen guy like I promised, and still the same tired old moves from you. I mean, you're twenty times my size or something—you must have some moderately entertaining attacks.'

'Foolish mortal! You dare defy the will of Zoolith?' the demon lord boomed, its voice ringing with judgement and fire.

'Well, duh,' Dread responded, his voice ringing with boredom and scorn. 'And by the way, can't you say anything else except "foolish mortal"? You demons all sound the same.'

'Insolence! Destroy him, our minions!' Zoolith cried, desperately trying to regain its integrity.

'You said that yesterday,' Dread yawned, before taking another puff of his ciggie. 'Those demons I didn't turn into kebabs fled off towards that lightshow you've got going on downtown. I'm afraid it's just us... oh and those guys over there I've just noticed.'

The group of odd-looking characters heard their cue, but in reality, had just stumbled on the scene by accident and in no way wished to be noticed by either Dread or Zoolith. Especially Dread.

'Don't be rude, introduce yourselves,' Dread commanded. 'I'm Dread Sedgewick, but I'm sure you three would probably know me better as Vicious Man. I prefer being called Dread. Just putting that out there.'

'My name is, uh, Nathan Blandley,' said an ugly teenager in baggy clothes, who was wetting himself as he spoke.

'Well, Uh Nathan Blandley, you're pissing your pants like some kind of Afflicted Existence,' Dread observed while flicking his cigarette butt into Zoolith's eye. 'In fact, that's what I'll call you, because your real name offends me. Now, who are you two?'

'I'm Homester,' said a try-hard homeboy in baggy clothes. 'From the Laa-De-Daa Gang.'

'From the what now?' Dread enquired politely. 'I should kill you for even saying those words in a sentence.'

*Why does every member of the human race appear to be some kind of fuckwit?*

'Can you believe this guy, Zoolie?' Dread said, nudging the giant demon with his elbow, causing it to fall over again.

'Foolish mortal...'

'Shush now. And you are?' Dread asked, turning to the last of the three arrivals. 'You seem familiar.'

The man was wearing some kind of powered armour, which was silver and covered his entire body, save for his roguish head. Suddenly, long silver tendrils shot out from his gauntlets, wrapped around Homester and Afflicted Existence, and choked the life out of them. 'I'm not with them—I'm Homey Killer.'

'That's a pretty narrow field of supervillainy,' Dread interjected, only slightly annoyed that Homey Killer killed those homeys before he could.

'That's what all those guys said to me in Terror Australis,' Homey Killer replied good-naturedly.

'*That's* where I know you from,' Dread declared, now moderately annoyed at being forced to recall the team of loser supervillains who'd tried to recruit him.

'Yeah, that's right,' Homey Killer agreed with a sense of nostalgia, which was entirely the wrong emotion to the one he should have been feeling. 'What would they say now if they could see me hanging out with Vicious Man?'

'They'd probably say you should have been listening when I said I preferred Dread. Hey, Zoolie, you might just get one more sinner after all,' he called to the demon lord, who had managed to roll over onto its side when no one was looking.

'Foolish mort...'

CRUNCH!

Dread threw Homey Killer into Zoolith's mouth midsentence and laughed at the irony of being killed by the word 'mortal'. He leapt into the air and landed hard on the top of the demon's head, slamming it down into the ground with enough force to shatter its skull and cause the few remaining buildings to collapse.

'Looks like you finally did something interesting after all,' he joked.

Zoolith's glowing red eyes turned black and its flaming body dimmed into smouldering embers. Dread farted in remembrance. He gazed out towards the smoky city.

*Looks like the real party's over there. And we all know there's no show without Punch.*

Dread sparked another cigarette and headed for the pink light in the sky.

\* \* \*

### Blue Mountains, New South Wales: 9:13 PM AEDT

Andy Trailer sat on the craggy hill and stared into the dark bush. He'd been sitting here for a couple of days now and could have been mistaken for a gargoyle or grotesque if anyone had been around to look.

*What are you waiting for?* Wisp asked again inside Andy's mind. *Gledandron has not blessed you to sit around, too scared to confront the Energy Lord.*

*I'm not scared, I'm meditating,* Andy replied. *Just like Achilles did at Troy.*

He was proud that he'd remembered that from an episode of *Sale of the Century.*

*You cannot lie to us; we are part of you and have been since birth,* Wisp intoned. *You proved your cowardice when you fled from the prison, rather than freeing all the prisoners as we bade.*

*But I used a better way to free the prisoners,* Andy thought, reaching into the festering wound at the base of his rib that still jutted from his chest, retrieving the fat female cockroach that lived there. *If it wasn't for her children's sacrifice—chewing those wires—then the prison's backup power would've come on and no one would have been freed. At least I freed that Nazi you wanted me to.*

*We have already told you Gledandron forgives you for your transgressions,* Wisp reminded him. *But not a second time. Attack the Energy Lord.*

*Not now, but soon,* Andy compromised as he stared lovingly at the cockroach in his hand.

* * *

### Grey: Circa 11:11 PM AEDT

Mark Adams climbed up through the quagmire of wounded realities, fighting against the sucking bog of Hell from whence he'd come.

*I assumed it would be easier than this after watching all those demons using it. Maybe it's harder because I have a physical body. It's like digging up out of a grave or being born again or something.*

He thought of his family: Desci, Obie, Sebastian and Samara, and pushed harder.

*Just keep going, for them. Upwards, ever upwards.*

# 28 December 34 BZ

Lorraine Freeman sat in the darkness of the silent house and wept. She hadn't stopped crying since discovering the bodies of her younger sisters and it was all she could do to cover them with the sheets where their bodies lay on her bed.

She didn't remember moving to the rocking chair in the lounge room, or how long she'd been there, only that she needed to get away from the grisly scene upstairs. Nor did she remember grabbing her sentient bong, Obtuse, off the shelf but she was glad *he* was untouched at least. Obtuse was in shock himself, and they sat in silence while she slowly rocked back and forth in the dark.

*I can't believe they're gone—Heather and Samantha, so full of life and potential—and Mum, who I wish I could've spent more time with.*

Her thoughts were interrupted by the sound of the front door quietly squeaking on its hinges, and a cold chill ran through her body. She heard footsteps approaching and tensed up, holding Obtuse even tighter than before. He remained silent.

*I guess those demons have finally tracked me down. Well, let them come, I'm tired of fighting.*

She trained her torch on the door and heard the footsteps stop right outside. It began to open… and the face of Shara Tiyarn peered into the room.

'Mum? Mum!' Lorraine cried, placing Obtuse on the floor and leaping up to hug her mother. 'I thought you were dead!'

She felt a twang of both guilt and stupidity that she hadn't checked the rest of the bedrooms after finding her sisters and just assumed her mother was dead in one of them.

'Lorraine? Oh, thank the gods, you're alive!' Shara replied, returning the hug in earnest. 'I was so worried about you and Lucy!'

'Mum's okay, at least she was when I last saw her,' Lorraine said, now worrying about her other mother. 'Where have you been?'

'The house was attacked by some kind of ice creatures early Christmas morning,' Shara recounted, grimacing as she recalled the events of the last few days. 'I managed to hold them off for a day, but then one grabbed me and dragged me next door. I eventually killed it, but not before it froze me in the neighbour's basement—I've only just managed to dig my way out of the ice. Heather, Samantha, are they all right?'

Lorraine simply burst into tears. She clung to Shara and released her grief in wracking sobs.

'Oh no...' Shara whispered, stroking Lorraine's head. 'Where are they?'

'In my room,' Lorraine mumbled between sobs. 'I put a sheet over them.'

'Take me to them,' Shara said sympathetically, taking her daughter by the hand.

'I don't know if I can.' Lorraine wiped away her tears and sniffed to stop her nose from running. 'There's also the body of the babysitter in the kitchen,' she added.

'We'll get to her after I see to Heather and Samantha,' Shara said compassionately, leading her daughter out of the lounge and into the entranceway.

'You don't need to see that...' Lorraine began as they ascended the stairs to the bedrooms.

'I don't think Lucy or I have ever told you what my Manifest ability is,' Shara gently interrupted when they arrived at Lorraine's bedroom. The door was closed.

'I... I always assumed it was your... um... gender,' Lorraine said, feeling slightly embarrassed. 'There aren't many hermaphrodites around...'

'Ha-ha. No, I was born this way, sweetie,' Shara laughed kindly. 'Let me show you what my power is. I'm sure it's not too late.' She opened the door and they walked into the bedroom.

The girls' bodies lay where Lorraine had left them, beneath a sheet now turned crimson. The torchlight wavered under her shaky control. 'I don't understand. They're dead. What can you do?' she asked her mother, not daring to hope.

Shara walked over to the bed and removed the sheet in one swift movement. Lorraine recoiled a little at the sight, but vowed to herself that she'd be strong.

'I can do *this*,' Shara answered, sitting on the bed and placing her hands on Samantha, who was closest. Suddenly the body began to glow, in such intensity that the torch became unnecessary. 'Oh, my poor sweet darling,' she said softly.

*Is Mum...?*

Moments later the glowing faded and Shara looked exhausted.

'What just happened?' Lorraine asked, her hopes teetering on the brink of collapse.

'L-Lorraine? When did you get here?'

Lorraine almost dropped the torch in shock.

'Samantha? Oh my god, you're okay!' She ran over and hugged her little sister, this time actually dropping the torch on the bed.

'Of course, I'm okay,' Samantha replied, sounding confused.

'Mum, thank you,' Lorraine cried, tears of joy now cascading down her cheeks.

'Just let me get my strength back and then I'll see to Heather.' Shara smiled wearily. 'Why don't you take Samantha downstairs until I'm done.'

Sometime later, Lorraine was once again leaving her sisters in her mother's care as she set out into the predawn with fresh determination.

*It's a miracle, is what it is. Mum even resurrected the babysitter since she stuck around when the other staff fled.*

But Lorraine did notice the toll it took on her—Shara never had grey hairs before. She walked up into the air above her street and looked towards the city and the beam of pink light shining in the dark.

*I'm glad Mum understood why I had to leave them again after such a shock. It's time I stepped up and became a superhero.*

Lorraine was so lost in her fantasy that she failed to notice the flaming demon as it flew up and struck her from behind.

\* \* \*

### The Energy Lord's Secret Base, Blue Mountains: 3:19 AM AEDT

Andy Trailer smashed through the armoured vault door as if it was tissue paper and flew into the base like he owned it.

'Energy Lord!' he bellowed into the brightly lit corridor beyond. 'The Night Demon has come for you at last!'

*Excellent,* Wisp said encouragingly, goading Andy on with its whispered mutterings. *Let Gledandron guide you to your revenge.*

*Yes,* Andy agreed. He issued a mental command and a score of flamboyantly dressed soldiers stormed through the doorway and began fighting with the base's defenders.

*Did we not tell you it would be an easy matter to take the minds of the Energy Lord's own soldiers like you have done with others in the past?* Wisp asked as Andy strode down the corridor, shredding Energy Lord's private army with talon and wing.

*True, but it was my idea to send my children in first to disable the alarms,* Andy thought defensively as he tore the throat from another defender—this one dressed like a futuristic cowboy.

*All your ideas stem from Gledandron,* Wisp reminded him. *Your family of cockroaches serve our god as well.*

Andy paused at the tunnel intersection, unsure which way would take him to his target. Suddenly he felt an intense burning in his back and was knocked facedown into the adjoining corridor.

'I am designation DYDX,' said a mechanised voice from behind him. 'I calculate your death is the only derivative of this encounter—like a downward slope on a graph.'

*What the hell does that mean?* Andy wondered, shrugging off the blast and turning around.

He faced a tall, silver robot with red photoelectric eyes and arms brandishing a variety of weaponry. It looked more menacing than anything he'd encountered in the base so far.

*It has no soul, it is an abomination,* Wisp warned. *Kill it now!*

Andy moved without hesitation, swiping at the robot's face with his clawed hands.

*It's surprisingly durable,* Andy thought, a tiny sliver of fear shooting through him.

'I am made of a titanium alloy,' DYDX boasted, as if reading Andy with some kind of sci-fi mind probe. 'My function is assassination and your function is corpse.'

*Go for its joints,* Wisp advised.

'Enough!' Andy screamed at the emotionless android, grabbing it under the chin and around the collar, and wrenching its head off.

The severed head fell to the concrete floor and came to a rest against the wall, its once glowing eyes now as dark as Andy's soul.

*Good, good, that was the Energy Lord's personal assassin automaton,* Wisp advised. *This means we have been noticed.*

*What's so good about that?*

*It means you will soon have your vengeance,* Wisp promised. *Now, find some more minions to possess and trust in Gledandron.*

Andy did just that.

\* \* \*

### Grand Satanic Headquarters, Kings Cross: 5:30 AM AEDT

Mark Adams pushed through the final labia of reality into the physical plane and cried as if born again. He climbed through the portal in the floor and collapsed in a heap in what looked like a ruined meeting room turned birthing chamber.

'Free at last!' he rasped, before falling into a deep, dreamless sleep.

\* \* \*

### The Skull of Ra, Banksmeadow: 8:44 AM AEDT

Anu Hopet opened the internal hatch with a verbal command and returned to pacing the bridge of his ship. It did not take long to notice his two remaining Skull Band looking at him anxiously from the back of the room. Their presence immediately irritated him.

'What do you two want?' he boomed without stopping his pacing. His crimson cloak was now tattered, but intact enough to flow behind him dramatically.

'Great Armageddon, nothing has happened in your absence. Bodyguard is still in stasis, but me and Backstabber were really wondering what happened when you were gone,' Battletank said nervously, despite wearing a massive suit of armour.

Anu Hopet no longer had the energy to berate his minions and answered the question instead.

'I will tell you what happened,' he thundered, pausing to stare at them angrily through the visor of his helmet. He still had the energy for that. 'That fool, Disk, has gone and gotten himself killed by these strange demons. On top of that, his body is missing and it contains data I need before I can leave this miserable world forever.'

His minions knew better than to interrupt mid-rant.

'These demons must have been brought here by a Celestial One,' Anu Hopet continued. 'How else could we be trapped in a reality bubble? Wait…'

*Maybe it is related to that giant tick I saw suckling on the planet when I first arrived? The ship's computer said there was nothing there, but Anu Hopet does not make mistakes. And it appeared to be feeding on this very landmass.*

'That would explain why there are so many strange Manifests and absurd cheeses here as well,' he thought aloud, still staring at his henchmen. 'They are like some sort of antibodies for the Earth.'

'Antibodies, sire?' asked Backstabber in its grating alien accent. It subconsciously touched the hilt of its dagger as if expecting an attack.

'Cheeses, my lord?' Battletank queried, always thinking of food. Plus, he and Backstabber had made a deal to take it in turns speaking—akin to a game of Russian roulette.

'Yes, cheeses,' Anu Hopet replied in disgust. 'There are many Manifests caught in this bubble too, and it appears they have all joined forces to attempt resistance. I must admit, I admire their tenacity. But I digress—one of these Manifests called himself Zambini and he had a whole group of strange talking cheese pyramids with him. They looked like they could have been an alien species at first, but then I realised they were like that horrendous creature that got inside the ship when we first arrived.'

'The one that, uh… FDAMed you?' Backstabber asked, remembering the ship's internal footage of the event that had been watched by the crew many times.

'What did you say? Is that what you call it?' Anu Hopet shouted at the impish cloaked alien, his hands beginning to glow with antimatter. Backstabber shrank back in fear, its green hand now grasping the dagger's hilt.

'Great Armageddon,' Battletank interrupted in an attempt to deescalate the situation. 'What is our plan now? The ship's scanners show the pressure is still increasing within the bubble and those demons can still detect the ship despite it being cloaked. A few tried to get in, but the ship's defences destroyed them. I predict more will come.'

'I will tell you what my plan is,' Anu Hopet answered, all hostilities temporarily forgotten. He did enjoy talking about his plans. 'We will remain on board the ship until this crisis is abated. It does not matter if the bubble collapses, I have faith the shields will hold.'

'Even against the collapse of reality inside the bubble?' Battletank enquired, trying to divert attention from Backstabber.

'This is an Evolver ship. They came here from another universe, and brought their reality with them,' Anu Hopet said confidently. 'The shields will hold.'

The demon hidden within a reflection in his armour was counting on it.

* * *

### Sydney CBD: 11:39 AM AEDT

Naomi Bloodlust and the rest of the Blood Brigade reached the central business district well before the herd of zombies that followed them. After leaving Gorg, she and Liu had caught up with the rest of the team before they'd exited Scar's escape tunnel.

They'd emerged in a deserted backstreet, but it didn't take long for a stray ghoul to notice them and begin the chase. Other zombies followed and soon there were hundreds on their trail.

The undead horde had forced them east towards the inner city and the mysterious beam of pink light that pierced the skyline from the top of Sydney's tallest building. The Blood Brigade had even managed to get some sleep (well, those who needed it) along the way, when they got far enough ahead of the zombies to lose them momentarily.

*Yet they always manage to find us again.*

She took a bite from her chocolate bar and placed it back in the pouch on her belt with the last of her rations. She unfastened her water bottle from its clip, took a swig, and looked around.

*The street looks abandoned, but that could just be because no zombies have noticed us yet. Though instinct tells me there's something else going on here.*

'Fan out, look for any threats,' she said to the group. 'I can't believe we'd be so close to that pink lightshow without finding something.'

Spindler, Molecule and Fatmandu spread out and began searching the street. Liu lingered behind to talk privately with Naomi. 'We have to press on. That demon lord, Rancid, seems to be coming this way too. I could hear him last night,' he said, using the opportunity to remove his helmet and clean its visor with his leather sleeve.

'I also caught a glimpse earlier of that other demon—Resurrect or something—I think it's the reason the zombies keep finding us,' Naomi added, wondering if Gorg made it out of the tunnels alive. She suddenly had the urge to have one of her few cigarettes while she could. 'Want a drag?'

'Sure,' Liu replied, reaching over to take the cigarette from her outstretched fingers. Suddenly he froze and cocked his head.

'What is it?' she asked.

'I thought I heard voices over in the next block,' he said, putting his helmet back on and heading off up the street.

Naomi softly whistled to the rest of her crew and soon they were following Liu's lead. It wasn't long before everyone could hear the panicked voices as well. Naomi also picked up the familiar sensation of Manifests approaching.

Within moments two men ran into view, both looking over their shoulders and failing to notice Naomi's team bearing down on them. One had long brown hair and was dressed in light blue spandex, while the other looked like some sort of rabbit, and bounded like one too. Naomi recognised them instantly.

*Jackrabbit and River Man—wannabe superheroes rejected by the HSA, who then turned to crime. I'm surprised they're still alive.*

They eventually noticed the Blood Brigade and were evidently pleased to see them as they ran over and stopped to catch their breath. 'We've...got...to...get...out of here,' Jackrabbit blurted between pants. 'Ooblog is coming!'

'I don't know what that is, but it sounds bad,' Naomi confessed, looking to see what they were running from.

'It is!' River Man declared as he used his powers to drip water over his face from his hands to cool down. 'The Immortal told us it was the Dark Lord of Perverse Molestation!'

*Yep, I was right, it's bad.*

'Is it worse than the demon lord, Rancid?' Spindler asked, putting on his tough guy routine.

'I'm not sure who that is,' Jackrabbit answered, having now caught his breath. 'But Ooblog is a giant puce blob that's covered in eyes, poison tentacles, and sphincter mouths, and it's right behind us.'

'I don't see anything,' Liu said. 'Surely something like that would make a racket.'

Molecule nodded its agreement with Liu's statement.

'That's the worst part,' River Man complained, looking around nervously. 'It's quiet, you can't tell...'

The ground rumbled. Fatmandu looked at its stomach.

Suddenly the street exploded under them and the entire group was flung in all directions. Naomi slammed into the base of a skyscraper, knocking the wind out of her and Liu landed on the curb nearby. She saw Fatmandu career off down a side street like a runaway bowling ball but didn't see what happened to Spindler or Molecule.

Dazedly, she got to her knees and looked back towards the bomb site.

*Except that's no bomb I ever saw.*

A giant amorphous blob undulated its way out from the sewer and oozed into the street. Crimson tendrils lashed the area, leaving trails of poison slime on everything they touched. Bloodshot eyes peppered the mounds of purple cytoplasm and puckered sphincters clustered around them, leaking rivulets of foul-smelling oil.

*If anything, it's even more disgusting than Jackrabbit described. He never mentioned it was covered with dicks for starters.*

Movement on the opposite side of the crater caught her eye and she noticed River Man attempting to get to his feet. Ooblog noticed too and in seconds had him ensnared in its writhing tendrils.

'Noooooooarrrrrrgggghhh!' River Man screamed as he was dragged into the sticky folds and thrust headfirst into a sphincter mouth. Then the horror truly began.

Naomi had a strong stomach, but even she couldn't watch as Ooblog earned its title.

*We are leaving now.*

Evidently, Jackrabbit had the same idea and attempted to bound over a pile of wrecked cars to freedom. Ooblog whipped out a tentacle, catching him by the ankle and severing it as it flicked him back towards the street.

Jackrabbit slammed into the wall next to Naomi and cried out in agony. His stump had been chemically cauterised by Ooblog's tendril, but dark purple lines were spreading rapidly up his leg.

*Didn't he say those tentacles were poisoned?*

'Antithesis,' Jackrabbit whimpered. 'It calls to me…'

*He's delirious; there's no point wasting any more time with him. I have to get Liu and get out of here.*

She hobbled over to where Liu was slowly rising to his feet, still recovering himself. Ooblog immediately turned an eye to the movement.

*I might be forced to use my pyrokinesis again if that thing gets too close.*

The ground started shuddering and suddenly a voice that could curdle milk echoed like thunder through the city streets. 'We are Rancid, Dark Lord of Decay, and this territory is now ours. We have grown in power with the demise of the other Lords of Hell who accompanied us to this realm and we have come to claim Ooblog as our spawning matrix. The High Mage promised us this realm and we shall have it.'

Ooblog's 'skin' rippled in response to Rancid's challenge and it disappeared back into the sewer. Naomi was relieved, but discombobulated.

*What the fuck was that all about?*

\* \* \*

## Pyrmont, Sydney: 1:25 PM AEDT

Courtney Yeht smiled as she wandered through the deserted streets and let the vibrations of the Earth wash over her. She was slowly heading for the pretty pink light that shot up from the centre of town, but didn't feel hurried and therefore wasn't making a beeline straight for it. The other factor was the pain she could feel from the vibrations it was emanating—it was worse the closer she got—making her want to tear it down and allow the ground to swallow it.

*Whatever that thing is, the Earth is screaming out in agony from its touch. It's like a festering boil that needs to be lanced and I'm the one to do it. Once I recover from what they did to me in that facility, that is.*

It was like on some level she was aware that while the drugs she'd been given had worn off, they had affected certain chemicals in her brain that would take months to recover. She was also scared and was avoiding thinking about the whole thing but refused to admit it to herself. She felt liberated and empowered since escaping and didn't want to jeopardise that.

Courtney did what she always did when faced with a hard truth about herself: she thought about something else.

*I haven't seen any of those fire demons for a while. I also haven't seen any bodies either, which means they probably got evacuated. Maybe that Rancid thing I can feel moving around is responsible for what's going on.*

She may not have seen Rancid with her eyes, but she could make out its outline from its vibrations. Not to mention she could hear its suffocating voice with supernatural clarity.

She stopped on the cracked footpath and ran her fingers through her matted, flaxen hair. She looked around at the abandoned buildings and empty cars frozen in an eternal gridlock, when suddenly she felt an epiphany.

*What are you doing? Are you going to be a sook like that spoiled bitch Lorraine Freeman, or are you going to take control of your life? If healing the Earth requires you to face that pink light head-on, then you need to step up and do it.*

She reached out with her mind and felt the reliable sturdiness of the earth beneath her feet waiting to obey her command. The ground she was standing on rose like a monolith until it was higher than the deserted buildings along the street. She stood atop the gigantic pillar and took in the panoramic view.

*This puts it all in perspective.*

Though it was close to midday, the sky was dark from all the smoke that had built up inside the bubble. Fires still burned in many parts of the city and every structure seemed to be damaged in some way.

She could see Centrepoint Tower and the pink beacon shining from its top, waves of nausea building whenever she focused on it. She also got to finally see Rancid with her own eyes as it fought with some hidden adversary in the next suburb.

*Wait…what's that?*

There was something flying towards her, but she was having trouble making it out as she couldn't use her powers to feel its vibrations.

*I think it's two things fighting…a fire demon and…a girl?*

Suddenly it erupted into a fireball and the girl crashed through Courtney's pillar of rock, causing it to crumble.

*Someone's attacking me!*

With her powers, she moulded the crumbling pillar into a spiral slide and used it to return to the ground unharmed.

*Why would that girl attack me? I wasn't doing anything!*

Courtney walked over to where her attacker was trying to free herself from a pile of rubble. The woman had brown hair, was wearing a leather jacket and covered in white dust. She looked up at Courtney's approach.

*I don't believe it.*

* * *

### Pyrmont, Sydney: 1:38 PM AEDT

Lorraine Freeman groaned as she extricated herself from the broken concrete and steel before slowly dusting herself off. Her black dress was ruined and her leather jacket had seen better days, but she was otherwise unhurt.

*I'm glad I finally managed to stop that demon; it's been hours since it grabbed me outside my house. That landing really hurt, but at least nothing seems to be broken.*

It was then she noticed a girl around her own age with dirty blonde hair staring at her with sunken eyes.

'Oh my god, are you okay?' Lorraine asked, concerned. She finished dusting herself and ran over to the other girl. 'I was fighting some demon and it suddenly exploded, which sent me crashing down here. You weren't hurt, were you?'

'No,' was all the other girl said, still staring with her haunting brown eyes.

'Well, my outfit's ruined, but I'm not hurt either,' Lorraine said light-heartedly.

'That's all you care about, your clothing?' the other girl spat, suddenly turning hostile.

'Well, no, I was just making a joke,' Lorraine replied, trying to diffuse the situation. 'My name's Lorraine, Lorraine Freeman.' She extended her hand.

'I know who you are,' the other girl hissed, a look of abject hatred on her face. 'You think you're so perfect with all your modelling when you're really just some stupid slut.'

*Wow. Tell me what you really think.*

'Look, I don't know who you are or what I've done to instil such loathing in you, but I've just been through a lot and don't really have time for this,' Lorraine snapped, losing her cool. 'I suggest you get to safety—I have to get to that pink light over there.'

'You…you're responsible for the Earth's pain…of course,' the other girl muttered. She locked eyes with Lorraine. 'You think you've been through a lot? You? What a joke! You wouldn't know the first thing about hardship with all your privilege!'

'You'd be surprised,' Lorraine shot back, thinking of all she'd been through since Manifesting. 'Now if you don't mind, I have to go now. Nice to meet you, uh…whatever your name is.'

'MY NAME IS COURTNEY!' the girl screamed, and the whole city block shook violently.

*Uh oh. That will teach you to be bitchy, Lorraine.*

The entire area was now shaking as if caught in the throes of an earthquake.

'I'm sorry...' Lorraine pleaded, attempting once more to dissipate the situation.

'You will be!' Courtney promised, raising her arms to the sky.

The ground gave way beneath Lorraine's feet and she fell into a large chasm that ripped the street asunder.

*Oh shit!*

Lorraine ran as fast as she could and found herself climbing out of the pit as if on an invisible staircase as her power kicked in. She leaped free of the danger and dropped down next to Courtney, following through with a jab to the stomach—a move she'd picked up fighting ice demons. The other girl doubled over and Lorraine drove her knee into her face with more force than she'd intended.

'Bitch!' Courtney snarled and gestured at Lorraine menacingly.

All of a sudden, the buildings on either side of the street twisted violently and toppled onto Lorraine, slamming into her and burying her in their crushing embrace.

*I didn't do anything wrong to this psycho, I don't deserve this!*

She cried out in defiance and began punching at the mounds of concrete that rained down upon her, shattering them to dust with newfound determination. Then the ground opened up beneath her feet again and she began to fall.

'You will be swallowed by the Earth and your cancerous influence after you,' Courtney yelled above the din, spittle frothing in the corners of her mouth.

Lorraine was pushed back by the onslaught and the black earth threatened to pull her down into its molten depths.

*Noooo!*

She summoned her last reserves of willpower and suddenly shot up through the air, knocking aside the chunks of concrete that continued to pour down at Courtney's command.

*I'm flying!*

Lorraine's jubilation was cut short when a chunk of a building's foundation struck her hard in the temple, causing her to slam into the ground at Courtney's feet.

She was dazed and could barely hold herself up on all fours.

Courtney stood over her and laughed, raising her hands above her head and tearing an entire city block from the earth with her mind. She levitated it up and let it hover above them.

Lorraine started to crawl away, trying to gather enough strength to fly again.

*It can't end like this. Do something, dammit!*

'I'm going to drop this on you and bury you so deep that everyone will forget you,' Courtney raged, sounding even more irrational than when they first met.

Lorraine looked up at the enormous mass of concrete above them and then down until her eyes made contact with Courtney's.

'DROP IT ON YOURSELF AND LEAVE ME ALONE!' Lorraine commanded, before using her remaining stamina to fly away as fast as she could.

'Okay,' Courtney said as if in a daze, but Lorraine didn't hear it.

The impact of the city block as it dropped onto the street was profound.

Lorraine was knocked out of the air and into the middle of another street, causing abandoned cars to fly out in all directions. The shockwave from the impact then rammed into her and sent her tumbling in a storm of dust and debris.

*That was close! I can't believe she actually obeyed me!*

She clambered to her feet and looked back at the devastation. She was so fatigued she could barely stand.

*At least she's buried under all that, so I won't be seeing that psycho again.*

She was so engrossed in the scene that she didn't think that this level of destruction would bring unwanted attention. She'd even dismissed the tell-tale thud of the approaching demon lord as nothing more than the rubble settling after the impact. It wasn't until it spoke that she realised the danger she was in.

'We are Rancid, Dark Lord of Decay,' the demon roared, towering over her with outstretched claws, 'and you, mortal, are mine.' Its decaying hands reached for Lorraine.

She had no strength left to flee and could only watch in horror as the gnarled and decayed fingers closed around her.

\* \* \*

### Pyrmont, Sydney: 1:50 PM AEDT

Bentaz Mullberry swooped in from the sky and grabbed the girl moments before the monstrous demon could snatch her with its taloned claws. He took her up and away from the devastation and the Lord of Hell, who bellowed like a petulant child at its loss.

Once he was safely clear, he dared look down at the girl he'd rescued. Her brown hair whipped across her face in streamers, but eventually he got a good look at the person he was carrying and gulped.

*Holy shit, it's Lorraine Freeman!*

'I…uh…I'm called Ballistic,' he said lamely. 'What are you doing in a place like this?'

*Oh brother! Could I be any cheesier?*

Lorraine smiled before answering. 'I'm Lorraine, and I've been caught up in this thing since the start. Thank you for saving me from that monster. I never believed in guardian angels until now.'

Bentaz blushed beneath his half-helm. 'Uh, no worries,' he said while they arced around and headed for the CBD. 'I saw that city block floating in the air and decided to check it out. It crashed before I could make it. Did you do that?'

'No, that was someone else,' she revealed with a shudder, but didn't elaborate. 'Where are you taking me?'

'Well, I was on my way to check out that pink light coming from Centrepoint Tower when I stopped to help you,' he replied as they drew closer to the centre of Sydney. 'How about we check it out together… unless there's somewhere I can drop you off?'

He hoped there wasn't.

'I'm supposed to meet my mother somewhere in town,' she said with a twinge of embarrassment in her voice. 'She's the leader of a superhero team,' she added quickly, in a teenage attempt to sound cooler.

'Okay, we can do that,' he agreed a little reluctantly. 'What team's your mum with?'

'She's leader of the X-Droids,' Lorraine answered. 'She left to stop this thing with a strange ancient Manifest, and my friend, Beat Master. But that was almost two days ago. I hope she's all right.'

Bentaz wasn't hopeful but didn't show it.

'Tell you what. I'll scout around the area a few times to see if we can find them,' he said kindly. 'Who knows? They might be waiting for you.'

He glided into a search pattern and they began searching for her mother.

\* \* \*

### Sydney CBD: 2:03 PM AEDT

Seth Zaraxom waved to the Manifest as he flew past overhead carrying a girl in his arms.

*That looks like Ballistic, Kismet be praised, but who was that with him? Was that Lorraine Freeman, Spectrum's kid?*

Moments later he was proven correct when they flew back and landed on the rooftop where his group had constructed a temporary bivouac. It was only chance that they'd stopped here—he'd insisted on getting a bird's-eye view of the city before getting any closer to Centrepoint—and they'd only just finished climbing the hundreds of fire stairs to get here.

'You must be the Immortal,' the teenage superhero said in greeting as he gently placed the girl on her feet. 'I'm Ballistic. Lorraine here told me you're marshalling a resistance movement.'

'Please, call me Seth,' he replied amiably, pleased that he was right about the girl, who ran over to greet her mother as he shook Ballistic's hand. 'I've seen you a lot on TV and I know your grandfather.'

*In fact, I was there all those years ago when he killed Axis.*

'I'm afraid Grandfather has passed away,' Ballistic said ruefully, looking at Seth through the eyeholes in his battered red helmet. 'It was these demons, or whatever they are.'

'I'm sorry to hear that, he was a great man,' Seth responded kindly as he tied his stygian hair back in a ponytail. He also thought Ally was a belligerent old bastard, but he wasn't going to tell the guy's grandson that. 'We're lucky you could pick up the mantle.'

'Uh, yeah,' Ballistic muttered awkwardly. 'So, to matters at hand; what's the plan to stop this...uh, apocalypse?'

'Maybe you should tell *all* of us just what's going on,' Lorraine interjected, wiping a tear from her eye and putting on a brave face. Her mother seemed to be in the same state, as if they'd just been sharing something deeply personal. 'I want you to tell us everything.'

Seth really didn't want to but felt compelled to nonetheless.

'Okay,' Seth agreed before realising it. 'For those who came in late, Satanists summoned some of the Lords of Hell to Sydney at the behest of the megalomaniacal High Mage of Hell—who wants nothing less than to tear down the Gates of Heaven and usurp God.'

*No point in telling them about the whole World Eater angle as that will only confuse matters.*

'Who's this guy?' asked Beat Master, who was standing among the numerous X-Droids. 'How come no one's ever heard of him before?'

'You would know him better as Merlin,' Seth answered, looking at the group one by one. 'The most powerful magician ever to live.'

'Great,' Ballistic said sarcastically. 'How are we meant to stop magic, especially magic so powerful it can kill God?'

'Well, for a start, technically there's no such thing as magic...' Seth began.

'But you just said...' Lorraine blurted.

'...the High Mage is just another Manifest like all of us,' he continued over the top of her. 'It's just his abilities take the form of what most people would think of as magic. Plus, he's ancient himself, so his mind is framed in that way too. He believes his abilities are spells—that's how he controls them.'

'But the question remains of how we stop him,' Ballistic said, turning to point at the beam of pink light that lit up the smoky air. 'And how do we stop *that*?'

'I'm getting to that,' Seth replied irritably. 'What happened was the High Mage promised the Lords of Hell the souls of their victims, but betrayed them, as all the souls get absorbed by the Soul Gem, which he then draws power from—hence the pink light.'

'So everyone who's died here...their souls were used to make this

High Mage guy stronger because of his god complex?' Spectrum said from behind her daughter. 'That's monstrous.'

'That's not the worst of it,' Seth proclaimed. 'It's the Soul Gem that's projecting this invisible sphere that's trapped us all in here. As things can pass into the sphere, but not out again, eventually the pressure will build up and convert everything within it to energy.'

'So that explains why half the city is flooded,' Ballistic observed. 'The seawater can't escape once it comes in with the tide.'

'That's right,' Seth agreed. 'But the upside is that because the Lords of Hell can't eat any souls, they grow weaker from exposure to this reality. That's why I was able to take out two of them earlier.'

'I took one out too,' Bentaz added without sounding boastful.

*Did you now?*

'But I saw one earlier, and it seemed pretty powerful,' Lorraine said. 'Ballistic had to save me.' She smiled at him demurely and he flashed her a cheeky grin.

*Teen love. Is there anything more sickening?*

'That was probably Rancid, the Dark Lord of Decay,' Seth explained. 'It gets its power from decay in all forms, so it doesn't need souls alone. Good thing it appears to be distracted by Ooblog for now, otherwise our job would be a lot harder.'

'And an Ooblog is?' Lorraine enquired.

'Basically, a horrifying purple blob with tentacles, apparently,' Beat Master answered for Seth. 'Well, that's what I hear, anyway.'

'So what *is* our job?' Ballistic asked, the conversation coming full circle back to a variant of his original question.

'We need to get over to the top of Centrepoint Tower, grab the Soul Gem, and kill everything that tries to stop us, of course...' Seth began.

'That's it? Really?' Ballistic scoffed. 'That sounds like a Vicious Man plan.'

'...Although I don't think it'll be that easy,' Seth cautioned, ignoring the reference to his nephew. 'It's bound to be guarded by a powerful demon or something of a similar ilk.'

'What happened to that Flame guy you gave the Crown to?' Spectrum asked hopefully. 'Can't he help?'

'Unfortunately not—he could be anywhere by now,' Seth said. 'I have a friend trying to free a powerful prince, but that's just a gamble. No, I'm afraid it's just us.'

'Do you want me to fly over and grab it now?' Ballistic queried, obviously itching to do something.

'Not yet, we'll give my friend a little more time. We'll need all the help we can get,' Seth instructed. 'But if he doesn't arrive soon, a group of us will go while the rest cause a diversion for all those members of the Ooblog Family that are lurking about in the water down on the street.'

'I can't believe it's got a family,' Ballistic said incredulously. 'I saw what it looked like earlier when I did a pass over the city.'

'You don't want to know how it reproduces either,' Seth warned, fast running out of verbs. 'Now I suggest we go over this all again and refine it while we wait for my friend.'

*Come on, Bojangles, hurry up. We need to stop the High Mage before he gains too much power.*

* * *

### Outside the Gates of Heaven: Circa 7:00 PM AEDT

The High Mage of Hell unleashed tendrils of hot flame that slithered from his fingertips and bound the archangel, Life, in a web of burning eels that leeched its vigour and fed it back to him.

*Now that there's only the False Archangels standing between me and ultimate victory, everything seems different, like I'm fighting on a higher level than ever before—even the sentences are longer.*

The High Mage knew not where that last thought came from and it didn't matter as he turned to the next archangel in his way. His legions of demons swarmed to his aid, spewing torrents of hellfire at the powerful seraphim.

The False Archdemon grappled with Gabriel, who was trying in vain to blow its horn.

*Perfect. Hold him still.*

The High Mage cast another draining spell from the back of the Great Beast, which struck Gabriel in the chest and transformed into a fiery net. Immediately the archangel collapsed in agony as its life force was syphoned away.

Only Michael the Archangel was left to defend the pearly gates from the hundreds of demons that still remained.

*With the power of Life and Gabriel, I should be able to do what the False Lucifer could not: slay the guardian of Heaven's Gates.*

'Attack my satanic soldiers—destroy the False Archangel!' the High Mage thundered. The demons obeyed.

'Foolish hellspawn,' Michael said, its voice incinerating the hordes of demons with its glory. 'We are the Will of God. We are the unyielding force. We are the banisher of Satan.'

'You are a pompous braggart,' the High Mage projected. 'I conquered the False Lucifer and stormed the False Creator's own home. You are nothing.'

Michael's eyes glowed in righteous indignation but the False Archdemon pounced upon its back and bit deep into its exposed flesh. Michael cried out in glorious anguish. It smashed its metallic Shield of Faith into the False Archdemon's spiked head, causing the monster to lose its grip.

The Archangel of Conformity and Obedience followed through with a slash of its Sword of Fire, cleaving the False Archdemon in blazing halves.

The High Mage only smiled as the demon's power flowed into him, courtesy of the subtle syphon spell he'd attached to each of his followers.

*With the death of each minion, I grow stronger. Combined with the powers of the angels I've slain and the archangels I've parasitised, not to mention the constant flow of energy from the Soul Gem, I've the power to take my rightful place as God.*

With that in mind, the High Mage prematurely drained the essence of the Great Beast and used the added power to bind Michael in the same trap as the other archangels.

'No, it cannot be,' Michael whimpered as the net drew tighter and its power waned.

'Finally!' the High Mage screamed to Heaven. 'Nothing stands within my way! Your moments are numbered, False Creator, for soon

I shall take your place as god of all reality!'

The High Mage cast his first spell against the unguarded gates of paradise. Reality wept.

\* \* \*

### Sydney CBD: 9:45 PM AEDT

Dread Sedgewick sloshed through the knee-deep water on his way to the annoying pink light in the sky. He paused to extricate a cigarette from the packet in his trench coat pocket and light it with a spark from his finger blades.

*Well, here I am in the heart of the city.*

He scratched his arse and puffed hard on his smoke.

*I guess it's time to do what I do best—I've always been a bit of a heart-breaker.*

He tossed his cigarette into the dirty water and continued walking.

# 29 December 34 BZ

**The Energy Lord's Secret Base: 12:21 AM AEDT**

Andy Trailer relaxed his taloned fingers and let the body fall from his grasp.

*You did it; I told you Gledandron rewards loyalty,* said Wisp's ubiquitous voice inside Andy's mind.

*It seemed too easy,* Andy replied, folding his wings behind him. *After all Doctor Frank put me through, I thought his death would be more satisfying.*

Doctor Frank was a nondescript man with short black hair, thick glasses and dressed in his stained lab coat. His blank eyes stared at the ceiling and his throat was a mass of bloodied, shredded flesh where the Night Demon had squeezed.

In truth, Andy could barely remember the role the doctor had played in his transformation, but Wisp had goaded him on with promises of vengeance and Old Testament-style justice.

It had taken him almost twenty-four hours to fight his way to this sub-level, despite the assistance he'd received from the guards he'd possessed, and he still had several levels to go until he reached the basement. Energy Lord had a lot of defences too, and not even his family of cockroaches could eat through enough wires to disable all of them.

'They're all dead now, except for you,' he said to the fat mother roach as she crawled out of her home at the base of his protruding rib and into the palm of his green hand. 'Only you, my oldest friend, still serve me.'

The cockroach began feeding on Doctor Frank's congealed blood that coated Andy's fingers.

*Are we not your oldest friend?* Wisp asked. *We were here long before the arthropod made a nest inside you.*

*Except I can't tell if you're separate or a part of me,* Andy thought, looking around the large concrete room that was home to Doctor Frank's laboratory.

The scientific equipment had been smashed in the fracas and the room was littered with the flamboyantly dressed corpses of Energy Lord's Elite—mostly the creations of Doctor Frank—who'd been stationed here to protect their progenitor. Andy absentmindedly looped his dirty brown hair behind his pointed ear and looked back towards the doorway.

There was a man standing there.

*Shit!* Andy jumped back a step and stretched his bat-like wings. *How'd he sneak up on me?*

The man was two metres tall and dressed in a navy-blue Kevlar uniform and jackboots. His head was covered by a silver helmet with yellow visored slits for eyes and another for a respirator. A vermillion cape flowed from his massive frame, which matched the glove of his right hand—currently gripping a very large axe. His other hand appeared to have been replaced with a robotic pincer.

'I am Hunter, and the axe is called *Hopebreaker*,' he said through the voice modulator in his helmet. 'Energy Lord is no longer amused by your antics and has sent me here to show you some manners. Plus he pays well.'

*Strike now! Quickly!* Wisp commanded urgently. *We have heard of this one. Kill him!*

*Why do I feel so heavy?* Andy wondered, as he found himself rooted to the spot.

'What's the matter? Starting to feel the gravity of the situation, eh?' Hunter laughed at his dad joke. He swung his axe suddenly and without warning.

Andy barely lifted up his arms in a defensive posture before the blade struck and a spray of blood spattered his face. Searing pain ripped through him and it took a moment to realise he was staring at Hunter through the space where his right arm should have been. He screamed, more in shock than pain.

*Control yourself!* Wisp boomed inside his head. *An individual limb means nothing compared to the glory of Gledandron.*

*I-I can't…my arm…*

'It's not fair,' Andy whimpered, falling to his knees, Hunter's gravity field suddenly too much to bear.

'What did you just say?' Hunter asked disgustedly as he approached. He looked down at Andy's twitching hand just as the mother cockroach emerged from the palm unscathed.

He stomped it to paste. 'Gross.'

'No!' Andy sobbed, still clutching his bloody stump with his left hand. 'She was like family to me.'

'You're a real freak, with horns and everything,' Hunter sneered, raising *Hopebreaker* above his head.

*Fight back! Gravity is all in the mind for you,* Wisp declared. *You are the Night Demon!*

'I *am* the Night Demon!' Andy said defiantly, forcing himself to his feet.

'I don't care,' Hunter replied dispassionately as he brought the axe down hard.

Andy drew on reservoirs of strength he never realised he had and caught the axe by the shaft before Hunter could finish swinging it.

'Now *that's* not fair,' Hunter complained to mask his surprise. He counteracted quickly, going for Andy's throat with his mechanised claw.

Andy was faster and smashed Hunter with both his wings, ripping *Hopebreaker* from the mercenary's hand and sending him flying into the corridor beyond.

*Yes! Now it's on,* Andy thought when the gravity around him returned to normal.

Hunter rose to his feet.

*For the glory of Gledandron,* Wisp intoned.

'For the glory of Gledandron,' Andy agreed as he stalked out of the laboratory, the skin on his stump having already grown over the wound.

* * *

## Sydney CBD: 5:17 AM AEDT

Mark Adams floated reluctantly towards the brilliant pink light coming from Centrepoint Tower. He'd slept for hours after returning from Hell utterly spent, but the rest gave his body time to heal. His first thoughts upon awakening were of his family: Desci, Obie, Samara and Sebastian, but then he saw the beam of light and knew what he had to do.

*If what I heard in Hell is true, then I have to stop that High Mage creep from destroying Heaven—and everything else along with it.* He looked around the flooded city.

*I could be the only one who knows what he's up to, and from the looks of it, the only one alive left to stop it.*

A bloated corpse drifted past, its tattered clothing indicating it was probably a teenager. Immediately, his mind turned once more to his family.

*I hope Desci and the kids aren't caught up in this. Xph'Ish'Matarg tried convincing me they were dead, but I don't believe it. They can't be. I didn't fight my way out of Hell just to lose them.*

He was so lost in his musings that he didn't notice the demonic centipede scuttle around the wall of a nearby building and launch itself at his back.

It passed through his chest and burst into flames before plummeting into the drowned street. Surprisingly, the water failed to extinguish the fire and it boiled until the demon's body had been consumed by the flames. Mark was unharmed.

*What the fuck was that? Shit, I better be more careful. It's lucky this power seems to protect me when I need it to—even if I don't realise I need protecting.*

He looked at his clothes: jeans, boots, and the scarlet cape he claimed from Xph'Ish'Matarg, which crossed his bare chest with crimson sashes.

*And look how I'm dressed. This cape makes me look like one of those Heroes Squadron guys. What will Sebastian say if I become one of those superheroes he's always looking out for?*

He ran his fingers through his ebony locks, refusing to believe his family was gone.

*At least I still have my hair and don't seem to have any lasting physical effects from my time in Hell,* he thought gratefully, not realising his eyes glowed red. The only mirrors in Hell reflected into your soul.

*But what about my powers? How can I embrace my wife if there's a risk she'll pass right through me before combusting?*

Mark let the thought go unanswered and looked back towards Centrepoint Tower.

*I'm getting ahead of myself; there's a real chance I'm not going to survive whatever's sending that pink light into the sky—especially if it's the High Mage.*

His hands silently burst into flames as he floated on towards the light.

* * *

### Sydney CBD: 11:54 AM AEDT

Naomi Bloodlust waded through the thigh-deep water and climbed onto the roof of the waterlogged taxi to get a better view. Her black leather work outfit wasn't as waterproof as she'd hoped, but at least the rest of her was dry.

*Where did all this water come from anyway? Maybe that Ooblog nightmare caused it when it smashed up from the sewer—there was no water around until it showed up. Then again, it smells like seawater mixed with piss, so it could be from the harbour.*

She signalled to the rest of her team and they cautiously moved out of the alley and into the main street. Liu used his mastery of magnetism to hover above the water, while Spindler and Molecule simply waded through it. Fatmandu had the worst time of it; being so short, the water was up to his neck.

Naomi had managed to find all her teammates after Ooblog left to answer the challenge that Rancid had issued.

*Thankfully, no one was seriously hurt, although Fatmandu has been pretty beat up.*

They were only a couple of blocks away from Centrepoint Tower, but the area was surprisingly deserted.

*Everything was probably eaten by the Ooblog creature.*

Suddenly she heard a strange whirring sound and something dropped from the window of the building above and behind her and landed in the street with a splash.

*What the fuck?*

The Blood Brigade were seasoned professionals and immediately moved into a defensive posture. They would attack on her signal.

'Don't shoot! Or laser-vision me, or whatever it is you do!' the new-comer called out in a deep male voice as he stood upright. He was wearing dented green power armour and his eyes were obscured by the visor of his helmet. 'My name's Tactician. I mean you no harm.'

'There's a first,' Naomi scoffed. 'I know who you are. You're that prick that's been locking my kind away for years.'

'If by "my kind" you mean criminal Manifests, then that's me,' he replied with hardness in his voice. 'But all that's unimportant now. We have to stop these demons from destroying the world.'

'We were heading to Centrepoint Tower to investigate that light,' Liu admitted, still levitating.

'How about I join you?' Tactician offered. 'Strength in numbers and all that.'

'Wait a minute,' Naomi protested, pinching the bridge of her nose to try to alleviate her migraine. 'How come you're still alive? Where did you come from?'

'Yeah, all the normals are dead,' Spindler added, drawing his LSD bow in suspicion. 'Only Manifests live now.'

'I'm proof that your assumption is bullshit,' Tactician shot back with rehearsed arrogance. 'But if you must know, I was buried alive under a mountain of concrete and it's taken me this long to dig myself out and get to this location. Now, I've had a bad last few days and I'd like to go stop this thing so I can go home and get some rest.'

'We were attacked by a giant decaying demon and are fleeing its zombie minions, so you decide who needs the rest,' Naomi quipped, retracting the blades on her gauntlet. 'But I'm willing to agree to a truce.'

*Yeah, because my last one worked so well.*

'Good,' Tactician said curtly, looking at a screen on the back of his hand. 'By all accounts we don't have much time. The barometric pressure is increasing rapidly and I can't tell how long it'll take to become a problem because there's something wrong with my suit's chronometer.'

*Maybe that's why I have such a bad headache.*

'Well, the light from Centrepoint just got brighter, so maybe that's it?' Liu suggested.

Tactician turned to look, almost panicked. 'We can't waste any more time, let's go.'

'Hee hee hee,' cackled a hostile voice from above them. 'The only place you are going is Hell!'

The group turned and saw the four-armed demon, Ress'urekt, drop into the street behind them, followed by a large group of soggy zombies, who moaned when they saw living flesh.

*They've caught up with us at last.*

Naomi backed away from the monsters, steeling herself for combat. She was even prepared to reveal her hidden power to everyone.

*No point keeping a secret at the expense of the world.*

'Forget about that thing; we've got to get to Centrepoint,' Tactician called, turning to make a dash for the tower. He stopped dead in his tracks.

At the other end of the street, a diaspora of demons assembled to block their way. There were ice demons, fire demons, Lovecraftian abominations, and creatures that resembled perverted versions of the natural world.

Naomi saw them too. *Mother of God…*

'Those units are the leaderless armies of the fallen Lords of Hell, still united for the glory of Gledandron,' Ress'urekt shrieked from the festering hole where its jaw and throat should have been. 'You have been chosen to die to further that glory.'

'Fuck you,' Naomi snapped, before flicking her wrist and sending a stiletto flying into Ress'urekt's skull. The demon squealed.

'Bitch! Whore!' it raged, grabbing the knife and pulling it from its forehead.

'Mind your language, that's my girl you're insulting,' Liu warned, using his powers to levitate the abandoned cars and sending them hurtling at the demon and its zombies.

The demons at the other end of the street charged.

'Blood Brigade!' Naomi shouted. 'Extreme prejudice!'

The battle for reality began.

\* \* \*

### Sydney CBD: 12:39 PM AEDT

Dread Sedgewick ignited his fart and incinerated the Ooblack before it could entangle him with its obsidian tendrils. 'Take that, you living constipation!' he said politely. 'Seeing you has been a gas.'

*Or should I have said blast? Would that have been funnier?*

He used the dying flames from his flatulence to light up a cigarette.

'This is bullshit,' he thought aloud, before taking his first drag. 'I was promised a battle for all existence, not a bunch of animated turds.'

As if on cue, the light from Centrepoint Tower thrummed louder.

*Something's happening with that tower.*

Dread thought that's where he should be, but couldn't see properly thanks to the inconsiderate building blocking his view.

*Luckily there's an easy fix for that.*

He kicked the building as hard as he could, which shattered its base and sent it crashing into the next skyscraper like a domino. A massive dust cloud billowed out to replace it and continued to obscure his view.

*Oh, for fuck's sake.*

Then the wave of displaced seawater slammed into him and extinguished his smoke.

*Motherfucker!*

'That's it, no more mister nice guy,' he said, spitting out a mouthful of brine.

Before he could make good on his threat, several sticky red tendrils lashed him from behind and dragged him backwards towards rows of puckered sphincter mouths.

'A guy just can't catch a break, can he?' he asked rhetorically, before he was swallowed by the purple goo of Ooblog's body.

\* \* \*

## Sydney CBD: 1:01 PM AEDT

Lorraine Freeman coughed and tried to blow away the concrete dust that drifted through the air after several neighbouring buildings collapsed.

*I guess we're lucky this building didn't go down with the rest of them.*

'I'm not so sure we're safe up here anymore,' Lucy Freeman said to the group.

They were still waiting on the roof for Seth's friend to show up, and had just finished going over the plan for what seemed to Lorraine to be the millionth time.

*Mum, Samuel, and the remaining X-Droids, go and create a diversion. While me, Ballistic, Seth, and his mysterious friend—if he ever shows up—go over to Centrepoint and grab the Soul Gem before the High Mage can become God.*

It didn't seem any less ridiculous the more she thought about it either.

'This could be the diversion we've been waiting for,' Seth suddenly announced. 'Get ready, this is it.'

'I thought we were waiting for your friend,' Lorraine complained, walking away from the edge and back to the group. 'We've been waiting for what, four hours? Now suddenly we have to go right this minute?'

'Actually, it's been closer to a day,' Seth revealed. 'We can't afford to wait any longer; not since that pink light got brighter—it means the High Mage is drawing on more power.'

'Wait, what did you say about it being a day?' Lorraine asked incredulously. 'That can't be right; it didn't even get dark, did it? With all the smoke in the air it's hard to tell.'

'Remember when I said that the pressure is building up inside the bubble around Sydney because things can get in but can't get out?' Seth reminded her.

'No, but go on,' she urged.

'Well, it's not just physical things that are trapped here,' Seth continued. 'Time is too, at least to an extent. Don't forget that this bubble is now its own piece of reality and so time is running at a different speed here. Essentially there are several different time zones radiating from the epicentre over there.'

'That can't be right,' Ballistic interjected. 'It's definitely been several days since this event started.'

*I wonder what he looks like under his helmet? I bet he's cute.*

'The time dilation gets worse the closer we get to that pink light and each time it gets brighter,' Seth responded, pointing at the light for added effect. 'It was only subtle at first, but it builds up like the pressure.'

'How does *that* work?' Lucy asked. 'And how do you know what the real time is?'

'I don't know the physics of it, I confess,' Seth replied defensively. 'Just trust me when I say we better get moving as time's running out.'

'That's for sure, I can see that Rancid demon heading this way,' Ballistic warned, pointing at the decaying giant.

'All right, then let's do it,' Lorraine said, tired of standing around talking about it. She turned to her mother. 'Mum, I want you to be safe out there.'

'That's what I'm supposed to say to you.' Lucy had tears in her eye. 'You make me so proud.'

Lorraine blushed from the rare compliment.

'You be careful yourself,' Lucy added. 'Shara might not be able to get to you in time, like she did with your sisters.'

A shudder passed through her as she remembered her ordeal back at the house. 'I will,' she said.

'Don't worry, sweetie, I'll look after your mom,' Samuel said, walking over to join them.

'You better,' Lorraine said, giving him a hug. 'So what song will Beat Master play to get his groove on?'

'Why only the best, of course.' He smiled and pressed the play button on his suit. The Bee Gees blasted from the speakers in his shoulders.

*Ha! Too bad he's gay.*

Lorraine waved them off as they headed for the internal stairs, taking the seven remaining X-Droids with them. She turned back to Seth and Ballistic. 'I'm ready.'

Suddenly an Aboriginal man with silver hair, sunglasses, and dressed all in black appeared from out of nowhere between Lorraine and the others.

'Whoa. Sorry I'm late, that time dilation is pretty bad, huh?'

* * *

**Sydney CBD: 2:12 PM AEDT**

Seth Zaraxom greeted his oldest friend warmly and gestured for him to meet the others. 'Lorraine, Ballistic, this is who we've been waiting for,' he said. 'This is Bojangles. Bojangles, this is Lorraine and Ballistic.'

'G'day,' Bojangles said with a grin.

'So, where's Prince Kiol Zol?' Seth enquired. 'The plan was to free him and bring him with you. We could use his shapeshifting powers right now.'

'Hold your horses,' Bojangles replied as he pulled a packet of cigarettes from his pocket and searched for a lighter. 'Geez, for the world's oldest guy, you sure are impatient. Let me explain. Yes, I managed to free the prince and earth the Tomb of Power—it won't be going anywhere again, now it's grounded. Kiol Zol is now back at the Abyss resting up with White Lion and Mosh.'

*That doesn't sound like a restful scenario.*

'What you have to understand is he's been trapped in a sarcophagus for the last couple thousand years and is in no condition to fight fucking Merlin,' Bojangles explained. 'He needs to recover somewhere safe, and where's safer than Mosh's place, right?'

*Nope, not a restful scenario at all.*

'Hey, did you say White Lion?' Ballistic asked, suddenly interested. 'As in a big, white lion man with an attitude, who's also a member of the Heroes Squadron? He was here too?'

'Yeah, kid, we're the friends he hangs out with at work,' Seth answered.

'He has a *job*?' Ballistic sounded like he thought a white lion man having a job was the strangest thing he'd ever heard.

'This is all well and good, but are we going to get on with it?' Lorraine asked. 'My mother's out there risking her life with a diversion, and we're standing around talking about jobs for lions. *Boys*, sheesh.'

'She's right,' Ballistic acknowledged. 'We were about to leave anyway, so we should consider Bojangles' arrival a bonus, rather than fret over someone who's not here.'

*They've got a point.*

'Okay, now that Bojangles is here, I suggest altering the plan slightly,' Seth said, making eye contact with them each in turn. 'The time dilation will be even worse over there, so instead of flying, we get Bojangles to teleport us all there together. That way we'll arrive at the same time, instead of potentially arrive hours apart.'

'Sounds like a plan,' Bojangles agreed.

'I'm in,' Ballistic said.

'Me too,' Lorraine added.

'Okay, let's do this,' Seth declared.

'Everyone, grab on to me,' Bojangles said, stretching his arms wide. 'The first time can be a little disorientating.'

Moments later they disappeared with a pop.

\* \* \*

## Centrepoint Tower, Sydney: 5:46 PM AEDT

Bentaz Mullberry suddenly found himself on the roof of the tower that he'd been staring at only moments before. The whole area was bathed in the blinding pink light that erupted from the Soul Gem he saw was attached to the top of the tower's spire.

He looked around to see that the group was still with him.

*Yep, that Seth guy made it and Lorraine's here, looking as beautiful as ever. Bojangles looks a bit off though.*

'That…hurt,' Bojangles said, as if reading Bentaz's mind. 'That's never happened before.'

'It must be from the close proximity to the Soul Gem,' Seth reasoned. 'Especially now that it's been corrupted by the High Mage's evil.'

'Or maybe it's the time dilation,' Lorraine suggested. 'You did say it would be worse over here.'

'While you figure it out, I'll go collect the Soul Gem,' Bentaz decreed and took off.

'Wait!' Seth cried. 'It will be protected!'

'You should listen to your elders, mortal,' came the sudden whisper in Bentaz's ear.

*Huh? What was that?*

Bentaz felt a cold hand grasp his ankle and screamed when its taloned fingers dug deep into his flesh. Before he could react, he was thrown forcibly into the group below, scattering them like tenpins.

He looked up and saw a being hanging on to the spire with its right hand. At first, he thought it was a man, but upon closer inspection he realised it was just man-shaped. It was wearing a dirty grey trench coat and hat that obscured its features, but its skin was stygian black and only its red eyes and gleaming white fangs could be seen with any clarity.

'You look like the private eye from Hell,' Bentaz mocked in a failed attempt to mask the pain in his ankle.

'We are the Dark Destroyer, mortal,' the demon barked. 'We are Satan's Assassin.'

Suddenly Bojangles teleported beside the demon and smashed it in the face with a left hook, sending it crashing down onto the roof. The others piled on.

Yet the Dark Destroyer was fast, quickly escaping their attack and regaining its feet—without even losing its hat. Bojangles appeared behind the demon again, but this time it was ready and brutally elbowed him in the face, sending him sprawling.

*Come on, you're meant to be the tough guy. Don't let a sprained ankle stop you.*

Bentaz flew at the demon at super speed and smashed it in the face with an energised fist. This time it did lose its hat and Bentaz was horrified to discover it looked more shadow than man.

The hesitation was enough for the Dark Destroyer to slash Bentaz across the exposed lower half of his face, drawing blood. It followed up with a kick to the stomach, which sent Bentaz flying into Bojangles and knocking him unconscious.

Lorraine was next to feel the demon's fury as it ripped at her with its claws.

'Pick on someone your own size!' Bentaz screamed, desperately trying to get to his feet.

Seth tackled the demon from behind and slammed it to the ground. It resisted fiercely, resembling a bucking bronco.

'Get the Soul Gem, I'll handle this thing,' Seth commanded as he wrestled the monster. 'That's the most important thing! Go now!'

Bentaz flew over to where Lorraine was struggling to her feet and offered her his hand. She took it and they floated up towards the Soul Gem. Seth returned to fighting the demon.

The dimensional distortions intensified the closer they got to the artefact until eventually they had to grab hold of the spire and try to climb up.

*I know Seth said there's no magic and it's just Manifest abilities, but what's this gem's story? I'm not sure I have the strength to climb up there and tear it loose.*

Just then a scream caught his attention and he looked down to see Seth torn in half and tossed aside like garbage. Dark Destroyer roared malevolently and started climbing the spire.

*At least we have a head start on that thing, but not for long.*

'I can't climb anymore, you go on,' Lorraine said weakly. 'I'll stay here and hold it off while you grab the Soul Gem.'

'I can't leave you…I,' he began.

'GO!'

Bentaz obeyed and returned to his gruelling climb. It seemed to take forever, but finally he was within reach of the radiant blue crystal that crackled with pink energy.

He placed his hands on either side of the Soul Gem…and suddenly he saw it.

His vision was hijacked with a scene of splendour that defied description and in the centre was the Gates of Heaven, shining with a pearly brilliance that made everything else pale into insignificance.

*It's so beautiful, so grand. How can I possibly hope to affect anything here?*

Then he noticed the archangels bound in fiery chains and the tiny man between them dressed in brown robes. Barbed chains of arcane energy burst from his hands and writhed across the gates, probing for weaknesses.

*It's too much. I can't stop this.*

From across the gulf of dimensions he heard a girl's voice.

'Ballistic, do you hear me? Ballistic! Pull the Soul Gem free!'

*That's Lorraine's voice. She who must be obeyed.*

Bentaz found himself back in Sydney with his hands still on either side of the Soul Gem. He yanked with all his might.

* * *

**Outside the Gates of Heaven: Circa 11:00 PM AEDT**

The High Mage of Hell drew on all the power at his command to cast the binding spells that tore into the gates of paradise.

'Open, I command thee!' he shouted, his long beard now rippling like a tide of worms. His baleful red eyes flashed with ancient hatred. 'I have defeated the Mystical Realm, I have defeated Hell, and I have defeated Earth. Now I bring my vengeance here to defeat Heaven as well!'

He could feel the energy flowing into him from the archangels and the Soul Gem and it was good. 'Open! Show yourself, False Creator!'

The Gates of Heaven cracked.

*Upwards, ever upwards.*

# 30 DECEMBER 34 BZ

**Outside the Gates of Heaven: Circa 12:00 AM AEDT**

The High Mage of Hell tore asunder the Gates of Heaven and basked in the full glory of paradise.

*Finally, it's all mine!*

'Show yourself, False Creator!' he thundered into Heaven's sterile whiteness. 'Face your successor, coward!'

He was so busy blustering that he failed to notice when the energy he was syphoning from the Soul Gem was abruptly cut off.

'Show yourself!' he repeated.

Kismet granted him his wish.

The False Creator appeared as a colossus in a shimmering grey suit of armour. Its eyes flashed white from the dark recesses of its horned helmet and it carried an immense lance that throbbed with the energy of creation.

It was also hundreds of times larger than the High Mage.

*Wait…where has my power gone?*

'I…' the High Mage began.

The False Creator struck the High Mage with the very tip of its lance and the wizard formerly known as Merlin was unceremoniously erased from existence.

'**It is undone**,' the False Creator commanded, and it was so.

\* \* \*

**Centrepoint Tower, Sydney: 2:07 AM AEDT**

Lorraine Freeman watched helplessly as Ballistic lost consciousness and toppled off the spire, still clutching the Soul Gem in a death-like grip. The arc of his fall was set to take him over the edge of the tower itself.

*Catch him, Lorraine, don't let him fall!*

Without thinking, she leapt from the spire and caught him as he fell. Next thing she knew, she was gently gliding down to the rooftop with the unconscious teenager in her arms.

*I'm doing it! I'm flying again and not just walking on air!*

She touched down on the roof and tenderly placed Ballistic—along with the Soul Gem he was still holding—at the base of the spire, before going over to check on Bojangles. He had regained consciousness but was groggy from the fight with Dark Destroyer.

*Dark Destroyer! I'd forgotten about that demon!*

Lorraine turned cold and spun around to find the demonic shadow creeping up behind her, illuminated by the pink glow of the Soul Gem.

'We will slay you and then reclaim the Soul Gem for the High Mage,' it threatened, its sinister red eyes glowing with malefic intent. 'We will—no…it cannot be!'

The light from the Soul Gem switched from pink to purple.

There was a sudden intense shuddering and a wave passed through her, leaving a feeling she could only describe as reality shifting phases, before the atmospheric pressure noticeably dropped.

The demon was screaming.

*Could we have won? Have we actually stopped the apocalypse?*

Dark Destroyer's shadow form lost its substance and began to drift away, as if caught in some intangible wind. A moment later its empty trench coat and hat followed it from the roof.

*What just happened? It was like it was sucked away.*

'Thank fuck for that,' Bojangles said hoarsely, still trying to regain his composure. 'I suppose we better help Seth.'

Lorraine's memory flashed with the image of Seth being torn in half by the demon and she grappled for the right words to tell his friend.

'He's…uh…he didn't make it,' was all she said.

'That's a matter of opinion, I reckon,' said a voice from behind her.

She turned around and saw Seth crawling towards them dragging his entrails, the bottom half of his body lying on the opposite side of the roof.

'Well, don't just stand there gaping,' he said amiably. 'Can you grab my legs for me please?'

* * *

### Centrepoint Tower, Sydney: 7:25 AM AEDT

Seth Zaraxom thanked Lorraine as she awkwardly handed him the bottom half of his body.

*Poor girl looks like she's going to spew.*

'Don't worry, it'll reattach itself in a moment.' He laughed in an effort to keep her calm. 'Much easier than growing replacements, I can tell you.'

'I thought you were dead. How can you still be alive?' She was in shock.

'Well, they don't call me the Immortal just because I'm really old,' he explained. 'As far as I can tell, I can't be killed. My time in Hiroshima taught me that.'

'It's true,' Bojangles confirmed, helping Seth tuck his intestines back in. 'Sorry, I thought you knew.'

'That's okay, there was a lot going on,' Lorraine admitted, facing away from the grisly scene. 'But I think we won in the end.'

'We sure did,' Seth agreed happily. His wounds were rapidly healing but his clothes were ruined. 'That pressure wave we felt earlier was the reality bubble realigning with normal space. It caused another time dilation, but the effect should start winding down now. You can already feel the pressure returning as the bubble starts to fade. Pretty soon it will be gone altogether and we'll be free.'

'But what about all the demons? Won't they be free too?' Lorraine enquired. 'Dark Destroyer may have vanished like smoke, but what about all the others? Or those giant Lords of Hell?'

'See the Soul Gem over there?' Seth asked, pointing to the large blue crystal that was still cradled in Ballistic's unconscious form. 'The energy around it has returned to purple, indicating it's free from the High Mage's influence. The spell that allowed the demons to escape Hell will now go into reverse, sending them all back again—demon lords included.'

*Hopefully Leviathan really will leave on his own, as I never learned from the mermaid how to banish him.*

'And now that the Tomb of Power has been earthed, maybe those fucking Scouts of the World Eater too,' Bojangles added optimistically.

'That would be nice,' Seth opined, his two halves now fully reconnected. 'It should work on anything that came up from Hell, which luckily takes care of Ooblog.'

'I still don't know how we did it,' Lorraine confessed. 'If all we needed to do was knock the Soul Gem loose from the spire, then why didn't we just get Ballistic to knock the tower down? He could have brought the whole city down; maybe then he wouldn't have been hurt.'

'It was the only way,' Seth replied. 'Grabbing the Soul Gem broke the circuit, robbing the High Mage of power, whereas collapsing the building may have accelerated the process. We were lucky it didn't happen when all those buildings came down yesterday.'

'Will he be okay?' she asked, referring to Ballistic. 'Should he even still be holding that crystal?'

Seth looked over at the unconscious Manifest. 'Yeah, he'll be fine. I'll take the Soul Gem off his hands as soon as my insides have finished untwisting. In the meantime, there'll most likely be reality "aftershocks", so we should probably just wait here until this all blows over.'

\* \* \*

### Sydney CBD: 10:02 AM AEDT

Dread Sedgewick rammed his fist out of Ooblog's sphincter mouth, grabbed one of the blob's flailing red tendrils and pulled himself free from its sucking foulness.

*And I thought being born was gross!*

Ooblog appeared shocked at this development—seeing as it was the first time it had ever happened—and attempted to pull him back in.

'Nuh-uh, I'm nobody's butt-plug!' Dread cried, slicing through the tendrils that tried to grab him. 'How about I trim your pubes instead?'

The tendrils fell to the flooded street with a splash, but then began a horrible transformation.

*What the fuck?*

The tendrils continued to morph until they became man-sized purple lumps with bulging eyes, gaping mouths, and red tentacles for arms. They burbled loudly at Dread and oozed towards him with unnerving speed. Ooblog silently watched from behind them with its many eyes that glinted with a perverse intelligence.

'You two look like my last dump,' he said before retrieving a pair of knives from their pocket dimensions and flicking them into the middle of their ugsome heads. 'Smell like it too.'

The creatures slumped into the brackish water as the knives returned to Dread's awaiting hands. He wiped their clear blood on his black trousers and raised his knives at Ooblog, who now seemed enraged by this development.

They sized each other up from a distance of only a few metres, each waiting for the other to make the first move.

The stalemate ended unexpectedly when an otherworldly 'ripple' passed through everything, leaving Dread unscathed, but dragging Ooblog and its fallen brethren away with it. The monstrous blob stretched and spiralled around as it was washed away.

*Just like flushing a turd. It's really been a day of metaphors, hasn't it?*

He looked around for whatever caused the ripple and noticed for the first time that the strange pink light had gone and the smoke was rapidly clearing from the sky. Sunlight shone through the clouds in shafts like some sort of religious scene.

'Well, bugger me, it looks like the party ended before I could even attend,' he said to himself. He paused to light up a smoke with his finger blades. 'I guess I should probably check, just to make sure.'

He waded through the receding water until he reached the base of Centrepoint Tower. 'I should have just done this earlier,' he said, before kicking it and demolishing its foundations. 'Tiiiiiiimberrrrrrrr!'

There was a sound of straining metal before the tallest building in

Sydney came crashing down, taking out several others on its way to the ground.

Dread laughed so hard he accidentally swallowed his smoke.

* * *

### Sydney CBD: 11:14 AM AEDT

Mark Adams looked calmly at the demon and contemplated his revenge.

*There are just too many choices.*

He never made it to Centrepoint Tower. He'd gotten within several blocks when he stumbled across a group of survivors in mid-battle with a pandemonium of demons.

At first, he thought the woman with the dark bob of hair was Desci; so keen was he to see her again, but it turned out she was a Manifest named Bloodlust. The rest of her companions were Manifests as well, except for one man who was wearing some kind of powered armour.

His arrival had been greatly appreciated as the tide soon turned in their favour—at least until a horde of zombies had attacked them from behind. That was when he noticed the demon who commanded the undead was one of the five demons who had abducted him and dragged him to Hell. Then it was personal.

His mind flashed back to what seemed like an eternity ago when he innocently found that bouquet of flowers, along with its cursed poem:

Thanks for the kiss.
You will see yourself soon.

*I think it's time I reciprocated.*

'Where are the rest of your friends?' Mark asked casually, his fear of demons long gone. 'You know, the ones who helped you drag me to Hell in that cheap Egyptian tomb knock-off.'

'Hee hee hee, they are busy torturing your family, Mark Adams,' the four-armed demon taunted. 'You will have to settle for Ress'urekt.'

'I thought my family was meant to be dead?' Mark quipped. 'You are full of lies and it's time I turned you to ash.'

His fists burst into flame in anticipation.

'Wait! We speak the truth when we say there is no escaping Hell for you, mortal,' Ress'urekt stalled, creeping closer to Mark as he hovered above the flooded street. 'A balance must be struck! For you to leave Hell now, another innocent must take your place. Are you prepared to sacrifice another just to save yourself from the perdition you deserve?'

Mark didn't even have to think about it. 'Absolutely.'

'Hee hee hee, and said in the presence of Rancid too,' the demon cackled, referring to the enormous demon lord towering over the street on the next block. 'Your selfishness is the very reason you were chosen in the first place.'

'But it won't come to that, as you're lying as usual,' he replied, remaining perfectly still, despite noticing what Ress'urekt was doing as it edged closer.

'Foolish mortal,' the demon hissed. 'We do not need to lie when the truth cuts as deep.'

Suddenly the pink light from atop Centrepoint went out and Ress'urekt screeched. 'No! It cannot be!'

Mark watched impassively as a strange pulse rippled towards them from the tower. The pulse slammed into Ress'urekt and the demon was abruptly caught in its pull.

'Noooo, we do not belong in Hell!' it screamed before it was swept off its feet.

It was flung straight at Mark and tried to dodge mid-air, resulting in only half its body passing through him before bursting into fire.

Ress'urekt shrieked as it was sucked away, the right side of its body now a blistering inferno. 'A balance must be struck for you to escape, mortal, we will see you soon,' the demon called before its jarring voice was finally silenced.

Mark wasn't really sure exactly what was happening, but it looked like whatever spell had allowed the demons to escape Hell had been reversed. This was confirmed a moment later when he felt himself being slowly pulled back the way he came.

*Oh no!*

He struggled vainly against the invisible force but was soon flying headlong towards the portal back to Hell—which he guessed was back in Kings Cross.

'No, please,' he begged to the heavens. 'Please, I don't deserve to go back!'

*A balance must be struck.*

'Take someone else, anyone else,' he yelled, hoping some divine force was listening. 'I don't care who it is; just not me!'

Kismet heard and a moment later Mark found himself free of the invisible grip. It took him a moment to realise his prayers had actually been answered.

'Oh, thank god,' he whispered before a feeling of profound guilt descended over him. *I wonder who they took instead?*

He pushed the thought aside and looked at the clearing blue sky, thinking of his family.

*Whoever it was, it was worth it to see them again.*

* * *

### Sydney CBD: 11:49 AM AEDT

Naomi Bloodlust sliced through one zombie's head with the blades on her gauntlet and threw a stiletto with her other hand into the eye socket of another. Next to her, Liu used his magnetic powers to take control of her stiletto and send it flying through the heads of eight more undead. It looked like they might actually win this one.

*If it wasn't for that strange Mark character showing up and taking out all those demons and then drawing Ress'urekt away, we'd all be zombies by now. I didn't even have to use my secret pyrokinesis.*

'Pour it on! We can do this!' yelled Tactician, who was still fighting alongside them.

'Shut up, wanker,' Spindler shouted back. 'You're not even a part of this team; Miss Bloodlust gives the inspirational talks around here.'

Molecule and Fatmandu both indicated their agreement before disintegrating and eating a zombie respectively.

'Ha! How about that, baby?' Liu said to her with a cheeky smile showing from under his helmet. 'Looks like even Spindler finds you a muse for his inspiration.'

'Very funny.' Naomi turned around to steal a kiss. 'Oh fuck!'

The charred corpse ambling towards her through the flooded street startled her.

*Scar!*

'I thought I killed you before; a mistake I won't be making again,' she said, before slamming her gauntlet into its face and extending the blades through its head. 'Okay everyone, listen up. All we have to do is keep this up a little bit longer. Give the superheroes time to do their shit.'

*Not that I've seen many, but I'm sure they're saving the day—that's what they do.*

Suddenly the whole street shook and within moments a gigantic demon with rotten flesh hanging from its spiky skeleton strode across the street: Rancid, the Dark Lord of Decay. It swished its serrated tail back and forth like a stalking cat.

'Good lord,' Tactician exclaimed.

'Foolish mortals, thinking you can defy a Lord of Hell,' Rancid boomed, its voice akin to a xyster across bone. 'The other lords were weak, but their death only fuels our power. Along with this dead city, we have enough strength to escape this bubble and bring the ecstasy of living decay to your world.'

'Let's not and say we did,' Naomi quipped with false bravado. The demon was still far enough away for her to steal the kiss from Liu she'd been denied earlier. She looked him deep in the eyes. 'I love you.'

The look of shock could be seen despite his helmet. 'Wow…I…er… love you too, babe.'

'I just wanted to say it before we fight that giant demon, in case… you know,' she replied, blushing slightly. 'Don't feel obligated to reciprocate.'

'It's not that, it's just I never expected to hear you say it,' Liu said defensively. 'But hearing you say that is the best thing that's ever happened to me. Heh-heh, and I thought your other speeches were inspirational!'

He gave her a sly smile and moved between her and the towering demon lord.

'Everyone, get away from the buildings,' he shouted to the group. 'I'm going to throw everything I have at that thing.'

There was a deep rumbling and soon pieces of metal were rising up from the flooded street or being torn from the surrounding buildings. Everything from cars and girders to street signs and garbage hoppers floated menacingly in the air before Liu sent them hurtling into Rancid.

*That's my guy.*

Naomi sliced another zombie as it went for Liu.

'Okay, everybody, keep those zombies off Magnet while he takes on the big guy,' she called to the others. 'Cut loose, honey,' she said to Liu.

Suddenly the pink light shining from Centrepoint Tower abruptly vanished and a blast wave that distorted like a mirage rushed towards them from the tower's peak.

'No, it cannot be!' Rancid thundered, unwittingly using the same phrase as the other demons when they witnessed their defeat.

The wave hit Naomi and her group from behind and it felt to her like reality changing octave. *That was intense!*

The wave neutralised the zombies—turning them back to regular corpses—but collected the bodies of the fallen demons in its passage. The wave slammed into Rancid and the giant demon fell to its knees and was dragged backwards by the invisible force.

'You were right! Those goddam fucking superheroes did it!' Liu shouted in jubilation. He turned back to Naomi, blocking her view of the struggling demon lord. 'We did it! We won!'

*I don't believe it. Maybe now I can have that life with Liu I dared not hope for.*

Liu removed his helmet as he sloshed through the receding water towards Naomi. He was smiling when their eyes locked. She grinned back, her heart bursting with joy for the first time since she could remember.

It was right at the moment their eyes were locked in mutual adoration that Liu did the strangest thing. He stopped smiling and looked down. Naomi's eyes followed and she gasped.

*No...*

A large spike protruded from the middle of Liu's chest and he looked at it in disbelief. 'What the fuck?'

It was the very tip of Rancid's long tail. His flesh began to rapidly decay around it. He screamed.

'Liu!' she cried, running towards him.

'A balance must be struck!' Rancid bellowed enigmatically, before finally allowing itself to be dragged back to Hell—with Liu still impaled helplessly on its tail.

That was the last time she'd see the one man she'd ever loved, and somehow she knew it.

Naomi fell to her knees in shock and stared numbly into space.

\* \* \*

### Sydney CBD: 12:35 PM AEDT

Bentaz Mullberry awoke to see Lorraine Freeman staring back at him.

'Am I in Heaven?' he asked groggily, attempting to sit up. He noticed he was in the street and that, surprisingly, he was still wearing his helmet.

'Not yet, I'm afraid,' Lorraine replied, blushing. She was sitting next to him.

'What happened? The last thing I remember was trying to grab the Soul Gem at the top of Centrepoint.' He looked down to discover he was still holding it.

'We won!' Lorraine beamed. 'You did it, when you grabbed the crystal!'

'I did?' Bentaz couldn't remember any of that. He looked around and noticed for the first time that they were with company. The surviving X-Droids milled about or tended to their wounds. Lorraine's mother, Spectrum, and the mysterious Immortal, Seth, walked over.

'You sure did,' Seth announced amiably, as he reached down and took the Soul Gem from Bentaz before secreting it away in his knapsack. 'I'll just take this and ensure it's given a safe home.'

'Sure,' he agreed, too tired to squabble over an artefact he knew nothing about. 'But how did I get down here?'

'I carried you down, after you passed out grabbing the gem,' Lorraine revealed. 'It's a good thing we left when we did, as Centrepoint collapsed soon after we'd come here.'

'That's lucky, I guess,' he said lamely, still reeling from recent events.

Something he couldn't put his finger on was bothering him. 'So that's it then?'

'Yeah, for now, sure,' Seth replied, slinging his knapsack over his shoulder. 'The bubble surrounding Sydney is gone along with all the demons, and the time distortions have probably all run their course now. Looks like things are back to normal. Well, normal, considering we have a world filled with Manifests. Ha, gives new meaning to the term Manifest Destiny, doesn't it?'

The words struck a chord with Bentaz and he filed them away in his mind for later.

'Anyway, it was nice meeting all of you and congratulations once again on saving the world,' Seth said to the group. 'I'm afraid I must be going. Lorraine, Ballistic; until next time.'

'There's one more thing—and please, call me Bentaz,' he said before Seth could leave. 'There's a word stuck in my head and I don't know what it means. It's only been there since I came to. I was hoping you could help.'

'It's not "Antithesis" is it?' Spectrum interrupted. 'A couple of our injured team members apparently said it repeatedly.'

'No, it wasn't that.' Bentaz finally managed to stand up. 'The word was "Gledandron". At least I think it was. Do you know what that means?'

He looked Seth in the eyes.

'That…that's a story for another day,' Seth finally answered. 'For now, I need to get some rest and I suggest you do too. Enjoy your victory now because inevitably fortunes always change.' He turned and left before Bentaz could ask him anything else.

Bentaz went to follow but was struck by a wave of vertigo and nausea and decided to sit back down on the curb.

*He's right, I need to rest up.*

He looked over at Lorraine, who noticed him staring and smiled back.

*On the plus side, at least I'm in good company.*

Bentaz may have been resting, but his teenage hormones knew no such thing.

\* \* \*

**Energy Lord's Secret Base: 1:15 PM AEDT**

Andy Trailer threw Hunter's unconscious body against the end of the corridor and smashed through the bunker door. Hydraulics screamed in protest before breaking under the strain, allowing him to stride into the inner sanctum. His severed arm didn't even slow him down.

*It's a shame Hunter's helmet prevented me from taking his mind,* Andy thought, waving the smoke from the door aside with his wings. *It would've been much easier if he'd been able to punch in the code on the keypad.*

*But also a lot less dramatic,* Wisp replied. *The Night Demon needs to make an entrance when he finally confronts the one who took his life away.*

*Even still, I've been fighting nonstop for days now and I could have conserved my strength,* Andy countered. The smoke finally cleared and he found himself in a gloomy concrete chamber. *This is the deepest room in the whole complex, it must be here.*

*And it is,* Wisp observed through Andy's eyes.

At the centre of the small bunker was a metallic throne, and seated upon it was a being of crackling yellow energy. It appeared to be robotic from the waist down, with a mechanised chest plate and gloved left hand—as if they were generating the rest of its form. Its body was the only light in the room. Dark patches in its glowing face hinted at malevolent eyes and a cruel mouth. It sat unmoving as Andy approached.

'Energy Lord!' Andy roared, spreading his bat-wings for added effect. 'The Night Demon is here to repay you for what you did to us!'

Andy never even noticed he referred to himself in plural. He was also too busy staring at Energy Lord to notice the ghoul shamble up behind him. A bolt of yellow lightning shot from its undead hand and struck him in the back.

'Argh!' he cried from between clenched teeth, the electric shock forcing his mouth shut. His back smouldered from the strike. He managed to turn on his attacker and saw a severely decayed zombie that twitched with electrical currents. It raised its arms at him again and they glowed with energy.

Andy was struck again, but as Kismet would have it, the resulting shock caused his wing to stretch out uncontrollably and slice off the top of the undead creature's head.

'So much for your Electro Zombie,' he scoffed as he rose unsteadily to his feet. 'Maybe now you're ready to face me alone. Or are you afraid?'

*Excellent,* Wisp advised.

Energy Lord radiated brighter, stood up from its throne, and turned to face Andy. The awkwardness of its jerky movements only enhanced its aura of evil. It laughed and Andy thought it was the most terrible thing he'd ever heard.

'You have been a most amusing distraction, but now it is time to stop playing games,' Energy Lord said, its voice akin to an old recording that crackled with static. 'Do you really think you are here for petty revenge and not because it is our will?'

'I'm here to kill you for what you turned me into,' Andy declared, but his voice lacked conviction.

'You are here because we called you home after a successful mission infiltrating the base of my rival, Pulse Pounder, and then destroying it,' Energy Lord continued as it spasmodically lurched towards him. 'Why do you think your Wisp encouraged you to come here?'

It laughed again as the words sunk in.

'No, you're lying,' Andy said weakly.

*It is true; you have been our puppet all along,* Wisp divulged coldly. *Energy Lord has always served Gledandron. Just like you now do.*

Andy felt crushed by the weight of it yet tried one last time to assert himself.

'There's a hole in your plan,' he said defiantly. 'You forgot Gledandron gave me the power to stop you.' He leapt at Energy Lord with animalistic ferocity.

Energy Lord merely gestured and a cage of pure electricity sprang up around Andy. He tried to force his way through it until the searing pain forced his compliance.

*What happened to all my power? I should easily be able to free myself from this,* he thought in a panic. His stump began to throb.

*Your additional power abandoned you when our pawn, the High Mage, failed in his quest,* Wisp intoned.

'Yes, the High Mage was supposed to defeat the False Creator and usher in the dawn of Gledandron,' Energy Lord said, as if reading Andy's mind. In truth, it was the hive mind that all Gledandron's spawn shared that connected it to Wisp. 'We even tried to use a young girl to assist him by razing Sydney, but alas, she was defeated along with the wizard.'

'Then I'm glad your plan was stopped,' Andy said spitefully. 'That's what you get for betraying me.'

Energy Lord laughed again and his blood ran cold.

'The High Mage did succeed in destroying the Mystical Realm and weakening the membranes between dimensions,' Energy Lord boasted, staring hatefully at him through the arcing bars of the energy cage. 'The Age of Gledandron will soon be here and this world will be consumed like Geburah and Harmen before it.'

Andy didn't know what even half of all that meant and had no time to ponder it before the voltage in his cage increased, causing him to black out.

He regained consciousness an unknown time later and found himself in a pitch-black stone cell. At first, he thought he was still in Energy Lord's bunker, but when he discovered it was too small for him to stand or sit comfortably he realised he was somewhere worse. The temperature was stifling and the air was thick and oppressive.

He felt alone and in hell.

*Except you are not alone,* Wisp mocked from within in his mind. *You have us to keep you company.*

'It's not fair,' Andy sobbed, as he suffered miserably in the scalding darkness.

# 31 December 34 BZ

Bentaz Mullberry stood solemnly and watched the dawn break over the devastated city. He'd slept through the rest of the previous day and had still awoken tired and sore.

*That Soul Gem sure does pack a wallop. I don't think even Vicious Man hit me so hard.*

He sensed someone behind him and turned to see Lorraine.

'Only one more day until the New Year. It feels like a new beginning,' she said softly as if afraid to scare off the light. A crisp breeze broke the still morning.

'The city took a hit, but we can rebuild,' he said, turning back to look at the broken skyline. 'No doubt this place will soon be crawling with AMPs and other government military types come to "restore order" or some other excuse. I wonder if they'll even let the public know what really happened here. Aside from a few Manifests, I don't think anyone survived, and they can easily dismiss us as troublemakers if we told anyone.'

'At least we'll know the truth,' she replied, taking his hand and placing her business card in it. 'I have to go and check on my family, but I just happened to have this on me and thought you might like to call me sometime. That's my personal mobile number.'

'Wow, you have a mobile phone,' Bentaz said, impressed. 'Thanks.'

'Okay, well, maybe I'll see you around,' she said, drawing out her goodbye like she was waiting for something.

Bentaz guessed what it was and his heart thumped even harder than when he confronted the demon lord, Bahlor. He removed his helmet and she smiled and came over to him. He realised it was the first time she'd seen his face. 'My real name is Bentaz.' He gulped.

'Bentaz is an unusual name...I think it's cute.'

He leaned in close and each experienced their first kiss. It was as magical as every teen movie would have them believe.

Kismet must have decided there had been enough magic for one day, as an abrasive voice suddenly interrupted them. 'Typical. Here I am putting my life at risk coming to Sydney, but when I do I find you here lounging around fraternising.'

It was the sanctimonious super-jerk, Powerhouse. He floated above them with a smarmy look on his face.

*Really? After all of this, he has to show up?*

'Do you know this guy?' Lorraine asked, decoupling quickly, as if embarrassed.

That's when Powerhouse saw who his HSA teammate was snogging. 'Lorraine Freeman? What are you doing with this loser? If you want a real man, my name's Powerhouse and I'm the real hero here.'

'Ugh, please,' she said distastefully. She turned back to Bentaz and kissed him on the cheek. 'Better put your helmet back on and don't forget to call me.'

She waved him goodbye and left, ignoring Powerhouse when he wolf-whistled after her.

'Man, she is *so* fine,' he said to Bentaz while ogling her arse as she walked away. 'Did you see how she checked out my package before she left?'

'Probably thought it was lost in the mail,' Bentaz said under his breath.

'What did you say?' Powerhouse asked indignantly.

'What do you want, Jean-Pierre?' Bentaz derided, knowing it irked him to be addressed by his civilian name. 'I can't believe you overcame your inherent cowardice and came all the way here from under your bed just to ruin my love life.'

'That's no way to speak to the leader of the HSA,' he blustered, still floating above Bentaz. 'You will address me as Powerhouse at all times. Don't forget, I can have you excommunicated for this!'

'It's not the fucking church, *Jean-Pierre*,' Bentaz retorted, wondering how long this would take before he could leave to check on his family. 'Now, if you have nothing important to say, I'm leaving. I have personal matters to attend to.'

'You'll leave when I say you can leave,' Powerhouse decreed, descending to block Bentaz's path. The water in the street was now only ankle deep. 'You have work to do rebuilding the city under my directions. Things will start to happen now that I'm here.'

*This is unbelievable.*

'You conveniently show up when all the demons are banished and start barking orders? You have more Gaul than the French,' Bentaz said incredulously, his terrible pun lost on the dolt. 'Now get out of my face.'

'Now you insult my heritage? There's no end to your depravity! It's lucky I took over as leader of the HSA, because you are unworthy,' Powerhouse ranted, still in Bentaz's face. 'Plus, you were too lazy to follow Hellgoat like you said you were going to, and I had to chase him around the countryside while you allowed Sydney to be trashed.'

*So Hellgoat never passed through into the bubble. Son of a bitch tricked me, knowing I'd be trapped in here.*

'I thought Hellgoat came here—there were certainly enough demons around. Congratulations on bringing him in,' Bentaz conceded. 'Now kindly get the fuck out of my face.'

'Hellgoat gave me the slip actually, thanks to me having to come here to rescue you,' Powerhouse relentlessly continued, *still* in Bentaz's face. 'Yet here you stand, getting all up in my face about how you saved Sydney from all these demons. What demons? I don't see any demons. No, all I see is some retarded, lying piece of shit who was too busy molesting some cheap slut to…'

Bentaz smashed Powerhouse in his smug, self-righteous face before he could use his super speed to dodge the blow. He skimmed down the street and crashed into a ruined building.

Bentaz prepared himself in case Powerhouse came at him, but when nothing happened he turned to leave.

Only to come face to face with Tactician, who suddenly appeared with a swarm of MIBs.

*Oh, for fuck's sake.*

'Fan out everyone. No one leaves here without being debriefed by me personally,' Tactician commanded his creepy agents. 'You, Ballistic. A word.'

'What?' Bentaz asked, his patience rapidly evaporating.

'I just want to let you know that your family is okay, your mother awoke from her coma and is doing well,' Tactician said quietly. 'Your sister is also doing okay, all things considered, and should be out of hospital soon.'

'How do you…?' Bentaz began.

'Please, did you really think the government would allow the identity of the world's most powerful Manifest to remain a secret?' Tactician chided. 'I'll debrief you later, but for now you can go. Oh, and thank you; I know what you did for all of us.'

*If only Dad shared the same opinion. I haven't heard from him since before Vicious Man attacked our home.*

Suddenly Powerhouse appeared at Tactician's side and pointed at Bentaz before pointing at the giant purple bruise that covered half his face. 'You need to arrest him for assault!' he whined. 'Look what he did to me for no reason at all!'

Bentaz was having trouble computing the sheer nerve of this guy, but this time Kismet was on his side.

'Shut the fuck up!' Tactician said to Powerhouse. 'Have you been crying? Is that why you're behaving like a child? Thank you, Ballistic, you may go.'

Bentaz wasted no time in flying away, the sounds of Tactician scolding Powerhouse drifting away on the wind.

*I guess Tactician's not a total jerk after all.*

He started to fly back to Canberra, but then remembered his grandfather's body and decided to collect it for a proper burial. A short time later he arrived in North Ryde and descended into the backyard.

Bentaz braced himself for the gruesome scene he knew he'd see, but he was unprepared for what he did find.

Nothing. His grandfather's body was gone.

* * *

## Sydney CBD: 6:08 AM AEDT

Naomi Bloodlust sat in a catatonic state on the car bonnet and stared at nothing. She was in shock from not only losing Liu, but also at how he died. She could still see him with the spike through his chest, desperately reaching for her as he decayed before her eyes while being dragged off to Hell. It was an image that would be with her for life.

*I can't believe he's gone. After all we went through together...*

Her emotions threatened to overwhelm her, so she shut her mind down again and replaced her thoughts with static. It was a technique she'd picked up to avoid torture—she never imagined she'd use it to avoid thinking about Liu.

She'd been sitting for hours as she couldn't see any point in going anywhere. Even when she'd spent months travelling the world taking contracts from the Kaiser, she always knew that he would be back home waiting for her.

*He was always so patient with me.*

Not even her teammates could convince her to leave, so they stuck around out of a mixture of guilt and loyalty—even Spindler. 'Hey, that government douche is back and he's got people with him,' he said, turning around to talk to the group. 'It looks like one of them is a fucking superhero.'

Naomi dimly remembered Tactician leaving them a while back, claiming he'd return with help.

'Hey, he never mentioned no goddamn Heroes Squadron guy,' Spindler persisted, his voice rising in alarm. 'I don't trust him. I say we get out of here before it's too late.'

Molecule and Fatmandu indicated their agreement, but Naomi just didn't have the energy to care.

'Naomi, are you listening to me?' Spindler yelled, grabbing her head and turning her face to his. 'Liu's dead and you can't change that, but we're not and we have to go.'

Something almost stirred in her but died before it was born. 'You go if you need to, I'll be fine,' she said.

'Goddamn it!' Spindler cried in frustration as he turned to the others. 'Fatmandu, prepare to carry her out of here after I hit her with one

Cameron Trindall

of my sedative trips…ah shit.'

'Everyone, stop what you're doing and stand with your hands on your heads,' Tactician commanded when he finally arrived. He had a squad of anti-Manifest police with him pushing large, yellow cylinders, as well as a flying superhero in blue spandex who looked like he'd been punched in the face. 'You're all under arrest by order of the United Nations' Convention on the Treatment of Hostile Manifests. Put the cuffs on them if you will, Powerhouse.'

The superhero moved as a blur and had the Blood Brigade cuffed in seconds.

'You fucking arsehole!' Spindler spat at Tactician. 'We should have let those demons kill you, rather than fight alongside you!'

'Yep, you should have,' Tactician agreed before signalling to Powerhouse. 'Prepare them for transport to the Powder Keg.'

Naomi didn't even resist when Powerhouse picked her up and shoved her into the cylindrical containment unit with 'Barton Correctional Facility' stencilled on the side.

\* \* \*

### Ashfield: 7:56 AM AEDT

Mark Adams wrapped his cape around him like a blanket and hobbled up to the soldiers patrolling the street who he'd spied earlier. He wanted nothing more than to get home to his family but didn't want to draw unwanted attention to the fact he was now a Manifest.

*I hope they buy my cover story.*

'Hey, you!' one of the soldiers called, drawing a bead on Mark. 'Identify yourself!'

*Here goes.*

'Oh, thank god! I thought I was the only survivor!' he said, using his best acting skills. 'My name is Mark Adams. I was kidnapped by some cult and then these things started killing everyone…and…oh thank god you're here.'

One of the soldiers checked something on a hi-tech device that looked like a satellite phone. 'Says here you went missing months ago,' he stated.

'That's when they abducted me; took me straight from my own house,' Mark replied, somewhat truthfully. 'I escaped them and discovered they'd taken me to Kings Cross. I've been walking ever since, trying to get home to Macquarie Fields.'

'Checks out,' the soldier with the device said to his CO. 'Matches the reported abduction and his address is correct. Plus, he looks like his missing persons photo.'

'Very well,' the commanding soldier allowed, lowering his weapon. 'You're a lucky man, Mister Adams. We'll escort you back to the safety zone.'

The patrol called for a helicopter and soon he was on board and being flown to safety. He was relieved to discover he was tangible again, and didn't pass through the helicopter when it took off. He soon drifted off to sleep to the rhythmic thud of the rotor blades.

*Desci, my love, I'm on my way home. See you soon.*

\* \* \*

### Freeman Residence, Neutral Bay: 11:30 AM AEDT

Lorraine Freeman stood on her sodden lawn and looked out at the shattered city. She'd made it home with her mother and Beat Master about an hour ago after parting ways with the rest of the X-Droids and was relieved to find everyone just as healthy as when she'd left them. All the ice had melted and everything was wet as if it had just rained.

She felt a mixture of excitement and sadness over what had happened and what would happen as a result.

'It's not really something you can put into words, is it?' Beat Master observed, walking up alongside her.

'No, not really,' she agreed, staring straight ahead.

'How about some music then?' he asked, hitting a button on his suit. 'Don't Fear the Reaper' played from his shoulder-mounted speakers.

She shot him a look.

'Too soon?' He stopped Blue Oyster Cult. 'Well how about this little Aussie number I picked up?' He ejected the cassette and turned it over, hit rewind for a bit and then finally the play button again. Crowded

House's 'Don't Dream it's Over' carried across the still morning air.

'Perfect,' Lorraine said, closing her eyes and drifting off with the music. She felt at peace for the first time since Manifesting and she allowed her mind to turn to normal teenage thoughts.

*I really hope Bentaz calls me.*

\* \* \*

### Australian Reptile Park, Wyoming, New South Wales: 1:37 PM AEDT

Dread Sedgewick sat on the yellow model sauropod and calmly lit a cigarette amongst the surrounding devastation. While 'The Event' as people were calling it, didn't reach this far north, the event known as Vicious Man wasn't limited by geological location.

*Well, slaying all these people turned out to be a lousy way to start my New Year's. It just seems like I've already had the party and all of this is me trying to chase the dragon.*

Fighting demon lords with reality at stake had set the doomsday clock in Dread's mind ticking over and now he was hungering for excitement like never before. He took a drag on his cigarette and contemplated his next move.

*I wonder where that old larrikin Captain Povo ended up. Maybe I should go look for him.*

\* \* \*

### The Ruins of Project Typhon, Banksmeadow: 2:23 PM AEDT

Anu Hopet stormed through the wall of soldiers that had formed a temporary blockade to keep people out of the base while it was being rebuilt. He was angry that he had to come back here again, but the tracking device implanted in his minion, Disk, had clearly shown his body was somewhere on the grounds.

*Someone did a number on this place after I left*, he thought, observing the giant crater where most of the base had been. It looked like it had been pushed out from within and then folded back over—like a collapsed bubble. *They must have had someone of great power imprisoned here. I wonder what happened to them?*

He had spared the lives of the soldiers in his mission to find Disk's body, and now they were busy calling up reinforcements with their radios. He ignored them and descended into the crater, his scarlet cape billowing out behind him.

Something grey stirred in the reflection of his metal armour.

'You should have killed them for standing in your way,' the reflection whispered, so softly it could have been his thoughts.

'I should have,' he murmured, believing it *was* actually in his head. Thousands of years of solitary brooding could do strange things to the mind. 'Perhaps I will remedy that when I leave. After I find Disk, that is. Now…they had him down here last time.'

His mind turned to the rest of his Skull Band as he looked around the rubble.

*I would not be here if they weren't all so useless.*

He grew more frustrated when he couldn't find Disk and decided to interrogate one of the soldiers for information.

*I could not even rely on Battletank or Backstabber to monitor events back on the ship while I was busy evading demon lords.*

They said there was nothing to report, but he later discovered the ship had detected a signal close to the harbour from what could only have been a Celestial One.

*I knew the Celestial Ones were involved.*

As he reached the top of a stone ramp that looked like it had been hewn out of the crater wall, he was greeted by a man in green mechanised armour and eight others in suits and dark sunglasses, who could have been octuplets.

Behind them was a giant armoured truck with more of the guys in suits unloading a refrigerated cylinder out of the back.

'They try and thwart you,' the grey reflection whispered again.

'I am warning you,' he boomed at the group. 'Do not try to stop me reclaiming the body of my servant. I know it is here—do not insult me by trying to deny it.'

'I wouldn't dream of it,' the man in green armour answered. 'In fact, we're unloading him from the truck as we speak. Why, you didn't think we had him back down there, did you? It's only been a day; we rebuild fast, but not that fast.' He laughed mirthlessly.

'I warned you people what would happen if you crossed me again,' Anu Hopet threatened, his fists beginning to glow with antimatter. 'Yet here you are, stealing my property.'

The men in black suits suddenly whipped out futuristic rifles and zeroed in on his head.

'Hold on a minute,' the armoured man said, raising his arms in a 'stop' gesture. His mechanised suit whirred with his movements. 'We found this guy dead in the ruins after we returned him to you alive and figured you mustn't have wanted him anymore. We had no way of finding you to let you know either.'

'He lies; kill him,' the reflection urged, except this time a little too loudly.

*What was that? That was not just in my head. There is something close by trying to influence me.*

Anu Hopet didn't have time to investigate, as a Manifest in a red and black costume suddenly descended from the sky. Despite the half-helm obscuring his features, Anu Hopet recognised him instantly.

*The God who Walks Like a Man! Here before me!*

'Is there a problem here?' the Manifest asked, staring at Anu Hopet. When he got no response, he turned to the man in green armour. 'Tactician, I want to talk to you.'

'Can't you see I'm busy with something?' Tactician snapped, waving over the two other MIBs who were pushing the refrigerated cylinder. 'Wheel it up next to him,' he said to them, referring to Anu Hopet.

'My grandfather's body is missing and I want to know if you're responsible,' the Manifest said, taking in everything happening around him. 'What's in those containers you have in that truck? Tell me.'

*This should prove interesting. Watching one's foes destroy each other is the highest form of entertainment.*

'What, you think just because the mighty Ballistic says something, then it makes it so? You're just a spoiled teenager,' Tactician scoffed, now fully engrossed in the argument. 'I thought I was doing you a favour, letting you off a debrief earlier, but I can see that was a mistake.'

The two MIBs placed the cylinder next to Anu Hopet and returned to their side of the standoff. He wiped away the condensation on the porthole and looked inside. Satisfied, he addressed Ballistic: 'Look at me, boy, and despair. For I am the Great Armageddon and I will overcome the prophecy by destroying you and everything you hold dear.'

Ballistic turned and looked at him with a confused expression on his face. 'Do I know you?'

'Not yet, but soon,' Anu Hopet promised, placing a smooth disc on top of the cylinder. It immediately shimmered and vanished from sight. 'I have to return to *The Skull of Ra* now but will see you again when you are ready—to prove I am your better and defy the Celestial Ones.'

'You know, I've had a really shit day,' Ballistic replied, his fists glowing with energy. 'I've had to deal with all sorts of crap and now this? Some nutjob in fancy armour and a cape rocks up out of nowhere and says he's going to destroy me on some unspecified future date without any fucking provocation whatsoever. So, fuck the future, I say why wait?'

Ballistic flew headlong at him at breathtaking speed. His red helmet shone brightly as it reflected the afternoon sun.

Anu Hopet swatted him aside as if he was a gnat. Ballistic bounced hard off the ground and careened into the back of the truck, causing more refrigerated cylinders to fall out the back.

'Fool,' he said, producing another smooth disc and holding it in his gloved palm. 'This just proves what I was saying about you not yet being worthy of challenging me. I do not know what the Celestial Ones see in you.'

*Hmmm, looks like I have decided to confront this prophecy head-on after all.*

He closed his hand into a fist around the disc and shimmered like the cylinder before him. 'Until my return,' he announced before vanishing, all memory of the mysterious voice gone along with reflection that made it.

\* \* \*

### The Ruins of Project Typhon, Banksmeadow: 2:46 PM AEDT

Bentaz Mullberry slammed into the refrigerated cylinders and went sprawling into the hard earth. Only his pride was injured, so he got back on his feet and dusted himself off like nothing had happened. He adjusted his helmet, failing to notice the grey reflection glimmer where it caught the sun.

*Fuck that guy hits hard! Who the fuck is he and what's his beef with me?*

He looked back, but Armageddon was gone, along with the refrigerated cylinder Tactician had given him. The realisation reminded him he'd actually come here for a reason.

*Grandfather's body! If it's here, I bet it's in one of these canisters.*

He began to check each of the cylinders that had fallen out of the truck, but he didn't recognise any of the bodies. He climbed into the back of the truck.

'Stop what you're doing!' Tactician yelled at him, striding over to intervene. 'That's United Nations property!'

'Try and stop me,' he dared, not caring if he'd been heard or not.

Bentaz checked several cylinders until he found the one containing the mutilated body of Arthur Mullberry.

*I can't believe I'm going to so much trouble over you, you crotchety old bastard.*

'Still, family's family,' he said to himself, lifting his grandfather's canister out of the truck to crack it open.

And of course, Powerhouse floated in on the scene and landed next to Tactician. 'You needed my help?' he asked, his face was still bruised.

*Of all the fucking people who could've shown up.*

Bentaz opened the canister and removed his grandfather's body, trying to ignore Powerhouse.

'I said stop,' Tactician repeated, his suit whirring as he pointed an accusing finger. 'Your grandfather's body belongs to the government.'

'He deserves a decent burial,' Bentaz stated, removing his cape and wrapping it around the body. 'He doesn't deserve to be in some Frankenstein laboratory being experimented on for who knows what.'

'That's not for you to decide,' Tactician said coldly. 'It's the law.'

'Like you can stop me.'

'Powerhouse, control your subordinate,' Tactician ordered.

'Stand down, little man,' Bentaz said authoritatively to Powerhouse, locking eyes with him.

'Maybe we should let him go,' Powerhouse said meekly to Tactician, remembering how he'd got his bruised face. 'It *is* his grandfather...'

Tactician's look of disgust was apparent even through his helmet. He turned back to Bentaz. 'I'll have you removed from the Heroes Squadron if you do this!'

'Bite me,' Bentaz replied in the parlance of the times. 'I quit.'

'You'll regret this, you'll see! You...'

Tactician's voice faded from earshot as Bentaz soared high into the sky, heading for the moon with his grandfather's body still wrapped in his cape.

*After I bury Grandfather where those creeps can't get him, I'll finally be able to see how Mum, Peach and Yam are doing. Hopefully even find the time to call Lorraine.*

His thoughts flowed to the events of the last few days. His mind kept returning to what Seth had said to him about Manifest Destiny, but in context of his experience with Tactician in general.

*Manifest Destiny is a mortal term and seeing how it's used, I think the world needs something better. It needs a Manifest...Empire.*

The Earth was bright from space, and the light reflected in his helmet briefly flashed grey before it was gone.

\* \* \*

### Barton Correctional Facility: 9:50 PM AEDT

Chief Warden Walter Screw reclined behind his desk and watched the news on the new television he'd had installed in his office.

'...the newly elected member for Warringah is among those confirmed dead on this sombre day. Also among the fallen was prominent Sydney businessman, Alfonso "Scar" Barbaro, who...'

There was a knock on the door and Walter turned off the TV with the remote. 'Come.'

The door opened and Tactician walked in, still wearing his battered green power armour. It whirred when he closed the door and crossed the room to the desk. 'Hello, Father.'

'Son! You got here fast,' Walter said jovially, getting up to shake his hand. 'When you called to say you were coming here, I didn't expect you until after midnight. I thought I'd have to celebrate New Year's alone.'

'I'm afraid you'll probably still have to,' Tactician replied, sitting down in the chair opposite his father. 'I'm stuffed and will probably sleep for a week.'

*Typical. Throws out my perfectly timed schedule.*

'Then there's no point saving this,' Walter said curtly, opening his desk drawer and producing a Cuban cigar, which he promptly lit. 'I'm glad you're okay though. You had me worried for a while there, but then I remembered whose son you are. But how did you get here so quickly?'

A cloud of smoke puffed across the desk as he talked.

'I've been using that dickhead Powerhouse as my personal taxi. He dropped me off,' Tactician answered, waving the smoke away. 'I'm glad he took over as leader—he's more easily manipulated—but I told Ballistic I appointed him. He's quit the HSA too, by the way—Ballistic that is, not Powerhouse.'

'I never liked that little shit anyway,' Walter confessed between puffs. 'Always so full of self-righteousness and egomania, you'd think he was some sort of god walking around as a man or something.'

'What happened here?' Tactician asked. 'Seems like there was a lot of construction work going on. And I see you've got a new TV.'

'Yeah, I had them install it while they're fixing up the joint. For research purposes, of course.' Walter laughed before ashing his cigar. 'The construction work is to repair the damage caused by some sort of demon who freed a bunch of cunts downstairs—including that prick Baron Von Ritzer. He killed Rick Gordon.'

His voice almost caught in his throat, but he subdued it.

Tactician noticed nonetheless but said nothing. He knew his father and Gordon went way back.

'I'm sorry to hear that,' his son said, meaning it. 'But a demon, you say? That's basically what happened in Sydney—demonic invasion. I was with the Blood Brigade of all people…'

'Oh, they arrived earlier, for your information,' Walter interrupted.

'…and we managed to hold back the demons, while Ballistic and—you're not going to believe this—Lorraine Freeman, somehow managed to reverse the whole thing and send them back.'

'Really? That little girl held off Judgement Day? The initial briefing we got when the bubble came down never said anything about that.' Walter couldn't believe it. 'That just goes to show that, at the end of the day, life is bloody unpredictable.'

'Amen to that,' Tactician agreed.

'How's Project Typhon? Is there anything left?'

'Some things are…salvageable,' Tactician admitted bitterly. 'Years of work down the drain for the most part, though. The apocalypse turned out to be a real inconvenience.'

'I'd say that was a win.'

'True. Ironically, most of the damage was caused by Patient 1432 and not the demons,' Tactician said, before noticing that Walter wasn't following. 'You know, the girl with the power over rocks. She escaped and is now missing, presumed dead. Anyway, she destroyed most of the base, but thankfully the assembly plant for the War Droids was untouched. They should be ready for field testing sometime late next year. Looks like we'll have to rush production due to recent events.'

'That's good news at least,' Walter said, butting out his cigar in his pristine ashtray. 'My New Year's resolution is to finally capture Vicious Man. The cell in the basement is ready; I just need to figure out how to bring him here.'

It was the very definition of being careful of what one wishes for.

'Well, that's a problem for another day.' Tactician yawned. 'I'm going to have to say goodnight. Powerhouse is waiting downstairs to fly me home.'

'Wait, before you go, how did the Government Villains work out?'

'Total failure. All dead and accounted for, except for that freak, Mind Syphon,' Tactician admitted. 'But we assume he was killed too.'

'Probably for the best—that creature was an abomination.' Walter still remembered the first time he saw the supervillain. 'Okay, I won't keep you any longer.'

'Bye, Father.'

'Ciao,' Walter said, not getting up. His son left and closed the door behind him.

He looked at the clock on the wall.

*At least his visit wasn't a total waste of time.*

* * *

### The Abyss: Circa 11:58 PM AEDT

Seth Zaraxom sat on his regular barstool, chain smoking and downing shot after shot. Strangely enough, surviving celestial obliteration only made him want to obliterate himself with drugs and alcohol.

*I can't fucking believe we pulled that off. I'd say it was a miracle if I didn't know they only happen when Mosh grows a hair on his head—and he looks pretty fucking bald to me.*

'And you look like a cat's arse to me, but I don't go around pointing it out,' Mosh Lightley pointed out from behind the bar. He poured Seth another shot and one each for Bojangles and Lilith, who were seated on either side of the Immortal. He then took a generous swig for himself.

'It's worth mentioning that I'm here too,' White Lion growled from his usual spot, cleaning glasses. 'So pour me a shot before you finish that bottle.'

'I might pour you down the chute to hang out with Jypx if you give me any more lip,' Mosh said half-jokingly, referring to the legendary ancient monster that lived under the Abyss.

'How's Prince Kiol Zol doing?' Seth asked, rolling a joint from the bowl of Binah Buds. 'I haven't had a chance to see him yet.'

'Yeah he's good, all things considered,' Bojangles said between drags of his Smex cigarette. 'Like I told you, I brought him back here after freeing him from that creepy tomb before I returned to help you fight that Dark Dickhead demon. Yeah, Triple D, we'll call it.'

'Actually, I was asking Lilith,' Seth said awkwardly before lighting his joint. 'Like you said, you told me all of that already.'

'Well, maybe you should have been clear on who you were addressing,' Bojangles said with mock indignation. 'Pass me that joint, would you?'

'He's resting upstairs in the brothel,' Lilith responded, before downing her shot like a pro. 'Recovering.'

'I bet,' Seth replied, taking a final toke on the joint and passing it to Bojangles. 'I don't know where Mosh even finds people to work upstairs, but there's always someone up there.'

'You'd be surprised,' Mosh said, giving Seth a conspiratorial wink and pouring them all another round—even White Lion.

'Horrified, more likely,' Bojangles suggested between puffs. He had the joint in one hand and the cigarette in the other and was taking turns smoking them. 'Say, Seth, did you end up having to pay anyone that million bucks a piece you were offering?'

'No, because they're all dead, I presume,' he answered. 'But then I never had any intention of it either.'

'You cunning bastard. You get the supervillains to fight for you by setting their greed ablaze, and now you don't have to pay. Good one.' Bojangles laughed, butting out his smoke. 'So, what are you going to do with that Soul Gem you snatched?'

*Good question.*

'I haven't really decided yet,' Seth admitted, holding the shot glass in his hand. It had a picture of a bullet on it. 'I guess I could trade it back to Summon, or give it back to its rightful owner, or maybe I'll just keep it. Dunno.'

'How enlightening,' White Lion grumbled as he cleaned yet another glass.

Seth ignored him.

'Hey Mosh, there's something I've been meaning to ask you,' he said after he'd downed his shot. He was starting to feel lightheaded.

*Whatever this booze is, it's fucking strong.*

'It's actually a home brew,' Mosh beamed proudly. 'It's been fermenting for about as long as the human race has walked the Earth. The barrel's even made from some extinct tree.'

'Tastes like it too,' Lilith said under her breath.

Mosh grinned at her, then turned back to Seth. 'So, what did you want to ask, as if I didn't already know?'

'If you already know, why make him ask?' White Lion complained.

'I like to hear people talk,' Mosh said defensively. 'Why are you so grumpy anyway?'

'I've got a blasted thorn in my paw, and Aesop died millennia ago,' White Lion rumbled.

'See?' Mosh said enthusiastically. 'I like to hear people talk—just like I got you to do.'

White Lion bristled at the ignominy of being tricked.

'Guys, we're getting side-tracked,' Seth pointed out.

'Then ask your question already!' Bojangles said exasperatedly as he passed the joint to Lilith, bypassing White Lion who was next in line. The beast man was too busy looking sullen to even notice.

'Okay, Mosh, so when I was out fighting evil, I gave the Crown of Knowledge to some guy who was frozen in a big lump of ice,' Seth began, recounting the last few days.

'Ooh, kingmaker,' Mosh interjected, but was ignored.

'Anyway, when I put the Crown on this guy, he said his name was Flame Lightley,' Seth continued, reaching over and grabbing the packet of Smex off the beermat. 'It's too much of a coincidence for him not to have been one of your children, so I was wondering why I've never heard of him before. I've known you for close to thirty thousand years now.'

'I don't see why that's so much of a surprise—you also know bugger-all about Krondonites too,' Mosh teased jovially, the metal bolts holding the top of his head closed glinting in the subdued light. 'Sure, he's one of mine, but I can't recall who his mother is. It may even be your grandmother.'

That was an image Seth would rather not think about.

*Except for Lilith, all my relatives who are older than me are deities, and we all know there weren't enough beings around to shag at the dawn of time.*

'How can you even have children if you're everything, anyway?' White Lion asked as he finally finished cleaning glasses and lit up a smoke he'd rolled earlier.

'That's a dumb question,' Mosh replied with a laugh. 'Think about it: if I'm everything, then I'm also my own children and therefore I can have children with myself, who are also myself.'

'Wait...' Lilith paused and passed the joint back to Seth. 'What?'

'Sounded wrong to me,' Bojangles quipped. 'That shit should be illegal.'

'No, what he said made perfect sense,' White Lion argued. 'Now if we analyse this...'

'It doesn't matter,' Seth intervened before the conversation got out of control again. 'It was just that I know Zoth, and I know Orgamulva is your daughter with Shara Tiyarn. I was just surprised you had another child I wasn't aware of, is all—and a godform, no less.'

'Seth, you're a great kid,' Mosh said to the man who once famously crossed the Alps with elephants. 'But what you're not aware of is about as large as the gape of my anus—how did you think the bar got its name anyway?'

*That's...something I can't and don't want to imagine.*

'My point exactly,' Mosh agreed with a smile. 'How many children I have should be the least of your concerns; especially when you'll soon have to deal with the Terminal virus, the menace of Mould Babian, the rise of Gledandron, and the invasion of the Zugnauts—or does that come later? Not to mention the horror in the next scene,' he added, almost as an afterthought.

*I wish he'd stop talking like we're characters in a book or movie or something.*

'But that would be lying.' Mosh winked at You the Viewer, while pouring another round of shots. 'I suggest we stop talking about the unholy nightmares yet to come and drink a toast to a sequel instead.'

*You've got to be kidding me.*

'Oh well, what the hell,' Seth resigned, grabbing his drink and throwing his head back. 'Happy New Year.'

\* \* \*

### The Skull of Ra, Saturn's Orbit: 11:59 PM AEDT

Anu Hopet hibernated through the entire trip back to his base on Titan, entrusting control of the flight to the advanced autopilot rather than his fellow Skull Band. Something about their behaviour in recent times had disturbed him—it was almost as if they were *too* incompetent. He had ensured they were all in their accelerated sleep capsules before programming the ship and joining them in dreamless slumber.

That is why he did not notice when Backstabber's capsule hissed open and the dwarfish alien clambered out, drew its knife, and scampered up to the navigational control on the bridge.

'Antithesis,' it said, before driving its dagger into the control panel, causing the ship to jarringly spiral out of control towards the moon of Saturn, klaxons blaring.

# Epilogue

## Banana, Queensland: 19 January 33 BZ

Courtney Yeht walked barefoot down the worn bitumen highway under the nocturnal light of the moon and stars.

*Oh, what a night to be alive!*

'Good thing I found you in that rubble and convinced you to dig yourself free,' said the black spot from the back of her hand.

'Yes, good thing, Blotch…ah…' she replied, her long blonde hair blowing in the balmy breeze.

'McMahn, Blotch McMahn,' the inkblot answered with a slight Spanish accent. 'That's McMahn spelled without the "O", if you were wondering.'

She wasn't wondering but agreed just the same. Instead, she was gazing at the moon.

*I can hear it calling; it wants to come to me.*

'Yes, I hear, I do,' Courtney called to the night sky. 'I can hear your orchestra, feel your symphony, know that you want to touch me. The Earth told me, the ground knows!'

*The ground hears every little thing.*

# Appendixitis

## Abyss, the

**Mosh Lightley**—Proprietor of the Abyss and all that exists
**Zoth Lightley**—Son of Mosh and aspiring band manager
**White Lion**—Humanoid lion, bouncer and part-time member of the HSA
**Jypx**—Ancient horror that lives down the chute in the Abyss (referenced only)

## Adams Family

**Mark**—Struggling labourer married to Desci, father of Obie, Samara and Sebastian
**Desci**—Ex-model, mother of Obie, adopted mother to her niece and nephew
**Obie**—Son of Mark and Desci and cousin/sibling of Samara and Sebastian
**Samara**—Sister of Sebastian, adopted by Mark and Desci
**Sebastian**—Brother of Samara, adopted by Mark and Desci
**Debbie**—Biological mother of Samara and Sebastian, sister to Desci (referenced only)
**Nathan Blandley**—Afflicted Existence, and friend of Obie, Samara, and Sebastian

## Alien Races

**E'hobans**—Lanky, purple-skinned inhabitants of Harmen (referenced only)

**Evolvers**—Almond-eyed grey aliens from popular culture (referenced only)
**Geburans**—Four-armed, chalk-white inhabitants of Geburah (referenced only)

## Blood Brigade

**Naomi Bloodlust**—Femme fatale, assassin and leader of the group
**Fatmandu**—Malformed maw of madness
**Magnet (Feng Liu)**—Master of magnetism and the obvious
**Molecule**—Giant caffeine molecule with destructive touch
**Spindler**—Stuck-up jerk with hallucinogenic powers

## Celestial Ones

**Flame**—God of Awareness and Epiphany
**Kismet**—Fickle Goddess of Understanding and Limitation (referenced only)
**Manifest**—Mysterious shadow believed responsible for Manifest seeds (referenced only)

## Deathly Duo

**Jackrabbit**—Agile wannabe
**River Man**—Unwelcome at parties

## Demons

**Dark Destroyer**—Satan's Assassin
**Im'shtar**—Demon of the Reflection
**Racuse**—The Scalper
**Ress'urekt**—Demon of the Animated Corpse
**Saracuth**—The Keeper of Skins
**Styryk**—The Disemboweller

## Dungeon Cell 9

**Andy Trailer (Night Demon)**—Unluckiest man alive
**Pulse Pounder**—Andy's captor and superhuman psycho
**Guillotine**—Pulse Pounder's apprentice

**Malice**—Robotic canine and part of Pulse Pounder's Trio
**Hood**—Android member of the Trio
**Repulsive**—Robotic abomination and part of the Trio
**Wisp**—???

## Energy Lord's Base

**Energy Lord**—Evil supervillain
**Doctor Frank**—One of Energy Lord's Elite

## Extras

**Chunky**—Belligerent university student
**David Leno**—Talk show host
**Ejigu**—Cardinal of the Roman Catholic Church
**Pepe Larouche**—Sleazy fashion designer
**Pimples**—Chunky's spotty friend
**Sam Shanks**—Jerk detective
**Toby Kim**—Senior operations manager of the X-Droids and consultant for Project Typhon
**Vsevolod Rasskazov**—Deviant businessman

## Freeman Family

**Lorraine**—Teenage supermodel
**Lucy (Spectrum)**—Mother of Lorraine, Heather and Samantha, member of the X-Droids
**Heather**—Daughter of Lucy and Shara, sister of Lorraine and Samantha
**Samantha**—Daughter of Lucy and Shara, sister of Lorraine and Heather
**Shara Tiyarn**—Hermaphrodite 'father' of Lorraine, Heather and Samantha
**Obtuse**—Manifest sentient water pipe

## Gangsters

**Scar (Alfonso Barbaro)**—Small-time hoodlum and grudge-holder
**Seven Servants of Scar**—Scar's gang

## Government Stooges

**Tactician (Stanley Screw)**—Commander of the United Nations task force on Manifests
**Akash**—Orderly at Project Typhon
**Amy**—Officious doctor at Project Typhon and assistant to Phil
**David Hobbs**—Field Marshall, Australian Defence Force
**Lex**—World-class stenographer
**MIB**—Classified
**Neal Jacobs**—Police Commissioner, Australian Federal Police
**Phil**—Efficacious doctor at Project Typhon
**Super Trooper**—Manifest soldier
**Vernon**—Orderly at Project Typhon
**War Droid 25Z (Braided Disposer)**—Under construction

## Government Villains

**Starlen**—Disgraced coup leader and team commander
**Asp**—Manifest snake and companion of Rattlesnake
**Avenatraitor**—Android monster
**Deathspawn**—Mutant war master
**Grasshopper**—Gigantic Manifest locust
**Mind Syphon**—Cyclopean horror to be avoided at all costs
**Ooze**—Not to be stepped in
**Rattlesnake**—Venomous snake-man
**Tanglor**—Summoner of tendrils
**Tronk**—Evil robot with a big red button

## Heavenly Host

**False Creator**—Creator god
**Michael**—False Archangel of Conformity and Obedience
**Gabriel**—False Archangel of Gullibility and Conversion
**Life**—Seraphim of life energy
**Mister Invincible**—Agent of Life
**Wraith**—Angel of Deicide

## Heroes Squadron of Australia (HSA)

**Chuck Cheese**—Living cheddar Class E Entity and team mascot

**Cloth**—The Flannelled Wonder
**Faceplate**—Non-powered adult member and all-around tool
**Flannelled Avenger**—Non-powered master of flannel
**Gate Crasher**—Opener of portals and old wounds
**Gridlock**—The guy that can shoot domes from his hands
**Grug**—The fat guy that can shoot streams of hair from his wrists
**Hellgoat**—Demon seeking redemption
**Hologram**—Master of illusion
**Killer Comedian**—Low-powered clown and douchebag extraordinaire
**Mauler**—Fast-talking, reckless superhero
**Medicine Man**—Incomprehensible healer
**Mercury**—The liquid liberator
**Metallic Man (Anthony Coulson)**—Misunderstood giant cyborg
**Pike**—Guy that has pikes burst from his wrists and knees
**Powerhouse (Jean-Pierre)**—Second most powerful member of the team
**Razorback**—Porcine protector
**Revenger**—Leader of black-ops subunit
**Savage Scavenger**—Bad-tempered lycanthrope
**Temple Man**—Sandstone behemoth
**Tower Man**—Hero who can grow to Brobdingnagian proportions
**Tracker**—Guy with a radar in his chest

## Historical Characters*
(*any resemblance to persons, living or dead is merely coincidence of course!)

**Edward J Perkins**—United States Ambassador to Australia
**Robert Ray**—Defence Minister of Australia

## Lords of Hell

**False Lucifer**—Ruler of Hell
**Bahlor**—Dark Lord of Despair and Failure
**False Archdemon**—Dark Lord of the Wounds that Never Heal
**False Leviathan**—Dark Serpent of Bindings and Restrictions
**Ishlarr**—Dark Lord of the Frozen Mind
**Ooblog**—Dark Lord of Perverse Molestation

Rancid—Dark Lord of Decay
Xph'Ish'Matarg—Dark Lord of Sacrifice and Penance
Zoolith—Dark Lord of Brimstone and Persecution

## Lucifer's Coven

Gavin—Youthful underachiever and welfare recipient
Karen—High Priestess of the coven
Floyd—Founding member of the coven
Matt—Junior accountant and sports fan
Navid—Creepy Persian guy
Tom Higginbottom—Always says his full name in the third person
Lancefield—Locum Satanist
Marek Mahoney—Eager new guy
Melissa Rupert Lump—Another locum Satanist
Anton—Founder and former member of the coven (referenced only)

## Miasma Creatures (Class E Entities)

Blotch McMahn—Out damn spot!
FDAM!—Disturbed conjoined heads that share a mouth and jump
around on stumpy legs
Roaring Twenties—Giant roaring numerals (referenced only)

## Miscellaneous

Courtney Yeht (Patient 1432)—Psychiatric patient (at least on paper)
High Mage of Hell (Merlin)—The arrogant antagonist
American Way—Leader of the World's Defence
Asparagus Man—Plant man from another world
Beat Master (Samuel Beatrix)—Rock star and walking stereo
Boganator & Boonatron—Champions of the Aussie Battler
Bojangles—Ancient Kurdaitcha man
Concord—Guy in a fast flying power suit, member of the Battle Suits
Failures—Loser superhero team
Gledandron—???
Gorg—Secretive assassin
Hat Trick—Team of supervillains who commit hat-themed crime
Heist (Fabian Swartzendruber)—Hi-tech thief

**Hell Hog**—Human/demon hybrid
**Kiol Zol**—Ancient Egyptian prince
**Laa-De-Daa Gang**—Collection of losers
**Leviathan**—Mighty sea-beast and Elemental
**Obvious Man**—**Obvious Man**
**Panta Boy**—Manifest soft drink can
**Quartet**—Supervillain team
**Sprite Superna**—Mermaid
**Summon**—Conjuror and trader
**Supernaut**—Racist juggernaut
**Tenebrous**—Ancient juju man
**T-Squad**—Government black-ops squad
**X-Droids**—Failed corporate superhero team
**Axis (Herman Himmler)**—First public Manifest and WWI hero (referenced only)
**Baba Yaga**—Witch from Russian folklore (referenced only)
**Destructo the Destroyer**—Monstrous machine of annihilation (referenced only)
**Kaiser Enigma**—Mysterious puppet master (referenced only)
**Kyra Zol**—Ancient Egyptian queen (referenced only)
**Outcasts**—Team of supervillains for hire (referenced only)
**Soul Master**—Medieval conqueror (referenced only)
**Thaddeus Q**—Doctor of everything and super-genius (referenced only)
**Vong**—Undead Pigman (referenced only)
**Zambini Surrealay**—Zany and oddly connected to the Miasma (referenced only)

## Mullberry Family

**Bentaz (Ballistic)**—Teenage protagonist and leader of the Heroes Squadron of Australia
**Arthur (Ally)**—WWI war hero and father of Hunter
**Hunter**—Superhuman mercenary married to Nikki and father of Yam, Bentaz and Peach
**Nikki**—Housewife and mother of Yam, Bentaz and Peach
**Peach**—Younger sister of Yam and Bentaz
**Yam**—Older brother of Bentaz and Peach

## Mystical Realm (Afterlife)

**Antithesis (Antimatter)**—Not to be freed
**Death**—Spawn of the Four Horsemen
**Element (Hieronymus Rhydderch)**—Unwilling inhabitant
**Flame of Eternity**—Core of the Realm
**Moros**—Unwilling Nazi inhabitant

## Powder Keg

**Walter Screw**—Chief Warden of the Barton Correctional Facility
**Rick Gordon**—Second in charge of the Barton Correctional Facility
**Singh**—Third in charge of the Barton Correctional Facility
**Leslie Studebaker**—Promising recruit

## Skull Band

**Anu Hopet (Armageddon)**—Ancient Manifest and prophesised usurper
**Backstabber**—Untrustworthy impish alien
**Battle Tank**—Frontline assault
**Bodyguard**—Self-explanatory
**Disk**—Cybernetic midget and techno-wizard
**Gurk (Great White)**—Alien shark-man

## Super Sechs (Super Six)

**Baron Von Ritzer**—Nazi supervillain and team leader
**Laser Mensch**—Nazi supervillain with laser powers
**Lichtschein Geschwind**—Flaming Nazi with super speed
**Squido**—Stretchy alien squid-man and Nazi thrall
**Stärke Mensch**—Enormous Nazi dreadnaught
**Unterbewusst Botschaft**—Limbless, floating Nazi mindbender

## Terror Australis

**Manipulator (Hilda)**—Megalomaniacal witch
**Beam**—Savvy armoured mercenary
**Brund**—Stupid armoured mercenary
**Segment**—Undead alien worm

**Bee**—Grown man in a bee costume
**Captain Povo**—Can make paint dry
**Crusher**—Angry Tiki-like guy
**Dinoman**—Ferocious dinosaur man
**Dogman**—Canine supervillain
**Dragon Kong (Zhang Po)**—Chinese dragon guy
**Dragonski**—Russian dragon guy
**Flybye**—North Korean cyborg
**Homey Killer (HK)**—Loser supervillain
**Iron**—Armoured deriver
**Mole**—Ridiculous Frenchman
**Multiman**—Segmented monster
**Rabboon**—Russian beast
**Short Fuse**—D-list supervillain with delusions of grandeur
**Unknown**—Mysterious alien with a glowing rock
**Vaccumax**—Loser with a vacuum cleaner strapped to his back
**Velocity**—Jamaican lightning man
**Vortex**—Creature with a vortex in its chest
**White Hot**—Aloof, radiant super being

## Zaraxom Family

**Seth Zaraxom**—Immortal from the dawn of time
**Lilith Zaraxom**—Immortal sister of Seth and mother of Dread
**Dread Sedgewick (Vicious Man)**—One-man extinction level event

# About the Author

Cameron Trindall lives a dramatic life of bureaucratic splendour in the nation's capital. He has a passion for writing, comics, and pop culture references. He is a family man and knows what is best in life.

www.ingramcontent.com/pod-product-compliance
Lightning Source LLC
Chambersburg PA
CBHW021929110726
47901CB00003B/772